THE WILDSIDHE CHRONICLES • VOL. 1-6

Created by
Diane Raetz & Patrick Thomas

PATRICK THOMAS • JUDITH TRACY
TONY DIGEROLAMO • MYKE COLE

With

DEB WUNDER and *DIANE RAETZ*

TALEHAVEN BOOKS

TALEHAVEN BOOKS
an imprint of Padwolf Publishing Inc.
www.talehaven.com

BOOK 1: WELCOME TO THE WILDSIDHE   by Patrick Thomas
 -*Dedication: To Diane*

BOOK 2: DOUBLE CROSS   by Patrick Thomas
 -*Dedication: For Christine, My sister the Sister*

BOOK 3: DARK PROPOSAL   by Judith Tracy
  -*Dedication: I dedicate this book to my youngest daughter, Stephanie Tracy. Her innocence and belief in all things whimsical and curious made writing this fantasy fun.*

BOOK 4: LEGACY   by Judith Tracy
 -*Dedication: I dedicate this book to my eldest daughter, Jessica Tracy. Her insight and comments made writing these novels a labor of love.*

BOOK 5: THE UNDERCOVER DRAGON   by Tony DiGerolamo
 -*Dedication: For my nephews Nicky and Paulie, from their favorite uncle.*

A DAY ON THE WILDSIDHE   by Deb Wunder, Diane Raetz, & Patrick Thomas

BOOK 6: CAR TROUBLE   by Myke Cole
 -*Dedication: For giving me a chance to believe.*

The short story A Day On The Wildsidhe originally appeared in Padwolf Presents #1

Omnibus edited by John L. French

Cover Art for all covers by Jeff Doten

Cover Design Roy Mauritsen

Created by Diane Raetz & Patrick Thomas

ISBN 10 digit 1-890096-86-5 and 13 digit 978-1-890096-86-1
First printing. Printed in the USA

BOOK 1: WELCOME TO THE WILDSIDHE   by Patrick Thomas

In an instant, a spell by the Fortesans Asgar rages out of control. Three hundred kids from Sparta, Pennsylvania pay the price. They quickly become pawns in a dark game between the Fortesanss Asgar and Queen Morna, neither of whom care if the kids get hurt. Cindy realizes she has powers she can't control. Terri's wheelchair gains the ability to fly. Justin must learn if he has what it takes to lead his classmates, while Wayne, Carmen, Ron, Miko, and the Bearclaw brothers must protect the rest form darkcat attack. Some days it just doesn't pay to go to school.

BOOK 2: DOUBLE CROSS   by Patrick Thomas

Back home, people are frightened. In order to prevent panic, the FBI has blocked off the town from the rest of the world and denied the existence of any spell. The FBI refuses to let anyone in or out of what remains of Sparta, even Tina and Bobby. Knowing Asgar's curse will bring over those kids left behind on their 11th birthday, Tina & Bobby try to run. The Wildsidhe claims the twins anyway. Rejected as a changeling spy by his friends and classmates, Bobby is taken in by Morna, unaware that he is even in danger. The Queen plans to trick him into volunteering to sacrifice himself to the Shadows. Now only Tina can save him.

BOOK 3: DARK PROPOSAL   by Judith Tracy

Centuries ago, the Treaty of Shadows granted the Wildsidhers a new home, but it was not without price. Even the Fortesanss who ruled the Wildsidhe were bound by rules laid down by the Shadows. One of these dictated that to become king, a Fortesans must marry into the royal bloodline. Asgar has learned that Cindy is of royal blood and has come up with a way to grab the throne for himself-he proposes. Cindy will be his no matter what he has to do. Justin says it will happen over his dead body. Asgar has no objections.

BOOK 4: LEGACY   by Judith Tracy

The kids are gone, but not forgotten. Back home, there is one person who knows what happened to them better than anyone-Alana, Cindy's grandmother. She ran away from the Wildsidhe and her fellow Fortesanss to live life on Earth as a human. She realizes Justin, Cindy, Wayne, Terri and the rest of the kids are in danger. To help them she has to escape from the FBI lock up of Sparta and return to the Wildsidhe. Alana is going to help the kids teach Asgar a lesson—You don't mess with family.

BOOK 5: THE UNDERCOVER DRAGON   by Tony DiGerolamo

Back on Earth, the FBI finds out that they can send 17-year-old Jamal over to the Wildsidhe. Getting himself and the missing kids back is up to him. Asgar can send him home, for a price: find the Grimstone. Now he has to go deep undercover in caverns filled with dragons & dwarves. The FBI never said there'd be days like this.

BOOK 6: CAR TROUBLE   by Myke Cole

One of the kids best defenses against the mystic dangers of the Wildsidhe has been their cars, helping them hold off even attacking Fortesanss. A dwarf clan decides they want a car for themselves and they try to bully one out of the kids. Miko says no, so the dwarves decide their best option is to steal one. Of course, Wayne Is not about to let anyone get through his security, especially thieves. The situation escalates. The kids are about to learn the difference between a single battle and all-out war.

Table of Contents

WELCOME TO THE WILDSIDHE

Book 1

Patrick Thomas

CHAPTER 1

Asgar watched and waited. She was here, somewhere. She had to be. When she had fled the Wildsidhe, she disappeared. Asgar had spent years looking for her, but she had been careful and used no magic, so he couldn't locate her. Recently that had changed.

The trail had gotten so cold that Asgar had not bothered to search for her in ages. Then about a year ago he sensed her. It wasn't much, just a twinkle of a spell that lasted only a few seconds, but it was enough for him to realize that she was still alive.

Periodically, he would sense her when she used magic, but she was smart. The amount of power she used was so small that only one of the Fortesan High Council would have been able to sense it.

Traveling to Earth had weakened the Fortesan Asgar greatly, but if he could find her it would be worth everything. Using his powers to track her infrequent use of magic, he was able to determine that she was in the town of Sparta, Pennsylvania. He just couldn't tell where. He had enlisted the help of others in power on Earth, none of whom knew his true purpose, but they were not able to help him.

Asgar would watch and wait until he found her, no matter how long it took.

CHAPTER 2

"How'd you do on that test, cuz?" asked Wayne Burns, as he and Justin filed out of their last period math class.

"Not bad, I probably passed. How about you?" asked Justin Burns.

"I did pretty good," Wayne said modestly.

"Pretty good? You haven't gotten less than a ninety-five on any of Ms. Haymaker's tests. You should probably be teaching instead of her, so what's with the modesty? Don't wanna ruin that jock image? Afraid of what all the guys on the football team would say if they found out you were acing her class?" asked Justin.

"No," Wayne said, looking away. Justin was hitting too close to home. Wayne was big and looked like a born jock. Problem was he was also a born brain, definitely not something he wanted the other jocks to know about. Even though both cousins were fifteen, Wayne was big for his age. Justin's brown hair tended to be on the longer side, while Wayne kept his in a buzz cut. It made him look older, which helped him fit in better with the jocks.

"So you trying to make your dumb cousin feel bad?" asked Justin smiling.

"You're not dumb. You just don't like studying. I've offered to help tutor you," Wayne said.

"I appreciate it and at some point I may even take you up on it. I'm just thrilled that I'm doing better in everything than I was in my old school in Boston," Justin said.

"Don't see how you can do worse. You failed everything including gym. How the heck do you fail gym?" asked Wayne the super jock.

"Simple, you don't go. In my old school, gym classes had no real supervision. The teachers were scared of the students, so they told the class what to do and then locked themselves in their offices. Too many fights broke out and too many people got hurt. It was safer just not to go."

"That's one thing Sparta's got going for it over the big city. The schools are definitely safer," Wayne said.

"That's for sure. You guys don't even have metal detectors here or any security guards. That's why Mom and Dad sent me out here in the boonies to live with Grandma," Justin said.

"They're worried about you falling in with the wrong crowd."

"I was doing fine."

"You were in a gang."

"So?" asked Justin.

"You stole a car. You're lucky your dad caught you instead of the police,"

Wayne said.

"Didn't feel so lucky when it happened, but after three months here, it ain't so bad," Justin said, jumping out of the way just in time as a barreling wheelchair almost ran him down.

"Incoming!" screamed Terri, her long brown hair flapping behind her as she raced her wheelchair.

"That is except for dangerous traffic in the hallways or lunatic drivers," Justin said, with a smile. His younger cousin had so much energy, it was practically contagious.

"Just trying to keep you on your toes, cuz. Don't want a big city boy like you to get bored," said Terry, opening up her locker and throwing her books from her last class in.

"My parents wanted me to get away from the wrong crowd. I don't think they factored in your little sister, Wayne," Justin said sarcastically. Justin's fourteen-year-old cousin responded in typical Terri fashion. She put her thumb on her nose, wiggled her fingers and gave Justin a raspberry.

"You guys ready to go?" asked Terri, shutting her locker and throwing her knapsack on the back of her wheelchair.

"Just waiting on you, oh speed demon," Justin said. The trio headed for the front door of school. Terri, in her wheel chair, got to the door first and held it open for the two gentlemen waving them through gallantly.

Justin smiled to himself. He didn't even feel the urge to open the door or otherwise go out of his way for Terri anymore. It had taken him a couple of weeks, but Wayne had broken him out of that habit. Wheelchair bound or not, Terri was as independent as any other teenager and wanted to be treated as such. She found people who offered to do everything for her insulting and demeaning.

Despite the boys' head start, Terri sped down the ramp and beat them to the curb. Terri had no trouble keeping up with the other two as they walked home.

"So is it true?" asked Terri.

"What?" replied Justin.

"That Cindy's staying over Grandma's house for the next few days while her parents are away on a business trip?" asked Terri.

"It's true," Justin said.

"You lucky dog," Wayne said.

Justin looked at his cousin with a look of worry in his eyes.

"Why do you say that? You don't like Cindy, do you?" asked Justin.

"Nah, not like that anyway. I've known Cindy since we were in kindergarten together. It'd be like dating my sister," Wayne said.

"Well, we certainly don't want that to happen," Terri said. Wayne laughed.

"So you don't have to worry about competition," Wayne said.

"Competition?" Justin said, uncomfortable with the course the conversation was taking.

"It's obvious you like her, man," Wayne said.

"What gives you that idea?" asked Justin innocently, but his blushing gave his real feelings away.

"Oh come off it. You got it bad for her. Whenever you're in the same room, it's all you can do not to drool," Terri said.

"Is it that obvious?" asked Justin.

"Yes," Wayne said and Terri in unison.

"So, does she like me?" asked Justin.

"I don't know," Wayne said.

"She does," Terri said confidently.

"How do you know? Did she say something?" asked Justin.

"Naw, a woman can tell," Terri said.

"So what women told you?" Wayne said, chuckling.

"Hardy har, har," Terri said.

"How'd ya know about that anyway?" asked Justin.

"I talked to Grandma last night. She told me and invited us over for dinner," Terri said.

"When were you gonna tell me?" asked Wayne indignantly.

"When I got back from Grandma's. Don't worry, I was gonna bring you a doggy bag," Terri said.

"Jerk," Wayne said grabbing his sister in a headlock giving her a noogie. To a casual observer, it would look like an unfair match up. Wayne was a jumbo sized kind of guy, big enough to play first string on the high school football team even though he was only a freshman. As almost anyone knows, looks can be deceiving. Terri held her own. Her arms were huge and strong from having to push her wheelchair around everywhere.

They got to the corner of Grand and Maple and split up with Wayne and Terri going home and Justin to his grandmother's house.

"Later, guys," Justin said.

"Later," said his cousins.

The rest of the way home Justin hummed happily to himself, thinking that just in a few short hours he was gonna see Cindy again.

CHAPTER 3

"Be good for Mrs. Burns. Okay, Cindy?" said Mrs. Hartman, kissing Cindy on the cheek and giving her a quick hug.

"I will, Mom," promised Cindy.

"We'll only be gone four days; we'll be back Sunday. You have the number of the hotel if you need to reach us for anything," said her father, being overprotective as usual.

"I know, Dad. Don't worry, I'll be fine," Cindy said.

"I know you will, but just in case," said her father.

"Go on or you're going to miss your plane," Cindy said.

"Well, Carol, I'd really like to thank you for looking after Cindy," said her mother.

"It's my pleasure, but before you go I have a surprise for both you and Cindy," said Grandma Burns, a woman in her seventies. With a flourish of her hand, she pointed toward the kitchen and out walked a woman with long gray hair who looked like she was in her eighties. Despite her age, she seemed in good shape, at least physically.

"Grandma!" exclaimed Cindy, moving to give her grandmother a hug.

"Mom," said Cindy's mother, also moving in for a hug.

"I went by the Sunny View Nursing Home earlier today and picked Alana up. I thought she'd like a night out and some home cooked food, not to mention a chance to visit with her granddaughter," said Grandma Burns.

"What a wonderful idea," said Cindy's mom, her words tinged with genuine happiness and guilt. She'd never gotten over the fact that she had to put her mother into a nursing home. Soon after Cindy's grandfather died, Alana's mind had begun to wander and she had delusions that she lived in a magic land. There was quite a bit of worry that if left living on her own, Alana might have hurt herself. A nursing home seemed the safest way to go.

"You two better say good bye to Cindy before she goes on her trip, she's going to be gone a very long time you know," said Alana.

"Mom, Richard and I are going on the trip, not Cindy," said Cindy's mother.

"Really? Are you sure? I really thought I was right this time," said Alana more than slightly confused. "You know, I think Nurse Mingold at the nursing home switched pills on me today. She said they were new arthritis pills, but my head feels all funny. You know anything about this, Rowan?"

Her daughter looked away guiltily. "No," Cindy's mother lied.

"I'll bet. I ain't taking them anymore and you can tell that to Doctor Kinkaid too. I'll spit 'em out," said Alana.

Cindy smiled and put her arm around Alana.

"I'm sure everything will be okay, Grandma," Cindy said, brushing her long white hair out of her eyes.

Justin walked into the room. He had known that Cindy had arrived, even before her parents had rung the bell, but he didn't want to appear too anxious. He waited before he made his entrance.

"Hey, Cindy. Hi, Mrs. Hartman," Justin said.

"Hi, Justin," Cindy said with a smile. Terri had been right about Cindy's feelings. Cindy had been looking forward to seeing Justin almost as much as he had been looking forward to seeing her.

"Can I get either of you something to drink?" asked Justin. Playing the host was something he never would have done at home with his parents. The combination of his grandmother's influence and Cindy's presence had inspired him to be a gentleman.

"Got any orange soda?" asked Cindy.

"Yup. How about you, Mrs. Freeman?" Justin asked Alana.

"I'd like a daisy nectar. The Pixies always use to make it and it was always delicious. They always served it in the tiniest glasses, mainly because that was the only kind they had. Do you have any of that, Justin?" Alana asked.

Justin had known about Alana's condition and had met her before. Still, he was not sure quite how to take those comments, but his Grandma said it was always best to just go along.

"No, I think we're all fresh out. Sorry," Justin said.

"Drat, I'll have an orange soda too, then," said Alana. Justin went into the kitchen to pour the sodas as Grandma Burns was sending off Cindy's parents. It was at the same time Terri and Wayne arrived. When Justin brought the two sodas into the living room, his cousins were already there. He gave drinks first to Alana, then to Cindy.

"Thank you, Justin, you're such a sweet boy," said Alana.

"Thank you, Mrs. Freeman," Justin said.

"Thanks, Justin. You're such a sweet boy," teased Terri. Justin shot her a dirty look.

"It's such a good thing that you know how to hot wire cars. It'll be useful when you go on the trip with Cindy," said Alana.

Justin cringed. His grandmother, his cousins, and their parents knew about his checkered past before he came into Sparta, but no one else did. Justin wanted to keep it that way. He especially didn't want Cindy to know. Justin decided it would be best to ignore that comment. So he turned to his cousins and asked, "You guys want anything to drink?"

"I'll get it myself," Terri said, as Grandma Burns came back in the house.

"Grandma, can I see you in the kitchen, please?" Justin said.

"Sure," said Grandma Burns. Terri and Wayne followed to get their own refreshments, leaving Alana and Cindy alone in the living room.

"Grandma, I told you I'm not the one going on the trip," Cindy said.

"I know you said that dear, but I just don't think I'm wrong on this one. If I'm right, I won't be able to see you on your birthday. I didn't have time to get you a gift," said Alana sadly. "Wait, I don't have to buy something. I can make something!"

Cindy looked at her grandmother and smiled as best she could. She had seen some of the arts and crafts they did at the nursing home. It was nothing to get excited about, by any means, but she would never hurt her grandmother by telling her that.

Alana clapped her hands together and closed her eyes in concentration. Watching, Cindy could have sworn there was a small glow coming from between her fingers and decided it must have been a trick of the light. When Alana opened her hands there was a tiny silver necklace, with a silver unicorn charm on it. Both Cindy and her grandmother loved unicorns and collections of statues and other trinkets covered both of their bedrooms. Alana reached over and fastened the necklace around her granddaughter's neck.

"Happy birthday, dear," said Alana.

"Thanks," Cindy said looking at the necklace and wondered how her grandmother could have made this. She'd tried to figure out how she had gotten it in her hands.

"Grandma, how'd you do that trick? Have you been practicing magic?" asked Cindy.

Alana's attention had already wandered to some pictures hanging over the mantel place. She turned back to Cindy confused.

"Do what?"

"Make the necklace appear. Have you been practicing magic?"

"Practicing magic, oh no dear I haven't done that since I moved to Earth. Be far too dangerous for me to do magic," said Alana, still giddy from the medicine. Motioning her granddaughter closer, she whispered in her ear, "They might find me you know, and that would be very bad."

Cindy nodded, humoring Alana, then changed the subject.

Meanwhile, in the kitchen, Justin was confronting his grandmother.

"Grandma, did you tell Mrs. Freeman about Dad catching me stealing that car back in Boston?" demanded Justin.

"No, I just told her you had some trouble and your parents wanted you to come stay with me for a while. I didn't give her any details. That's nobody's business outside of the family. Why do you ask?" said Grandma Burns.

"Because she just told Cindy my ability to hot wire cars would be good on the trip she was going on," Justin said.

Turning to her other two grandchildren, Grandma Burns said, "I didn't tell her. Did either of you?"

"No," Terri said and Wayne in unison.

Grandma Burns nodded. "I wouldn't worry too much about it Justin. Ever since her husband Howard died, she hasn't been with it as much as she used to be. She's still sharper than most people give her credit for, mind you. On the other hand, she's always said strange things and the even stranger part is a lot of the things she said were really true even though she had no way of knowing. I wouldn't worry too much about it. I'm sure Cindy still likes you," Grandma Burns said, putting her hand on her grandson's shoulder and smiling.

Justin thought about denying but saw the look in his grandmother's eyes.

"Does everyone know I like her?" asked Justin.

"Anyone who knows how to look," said Grandma Burns with a smile. "Don't worry about it. We won't say anything, will we, kids?"

"No," Wayne said.

"Well, maybe..." Terri said, a gleam in her eye.

Justin threw a dish towel at Terri's head as Terri laughed the entire time.

CHAPTER 4

Asgar felt it and then it was gone. Still, he knew it was her spell. It made no sense. It was not a spell he recognized. It was chaotic, as if it were cast by a novice, and that was one thing Alana was not. In her day, her power and skill rivaled his.

Luckily, this time he was close enough to pinpoint the exact location. It took a while. Asgar chose to walk, rather than feel imprisoned and powerless in a car made of steel and iron, which would weaken and dull his magic.

By the time he got to the block, it was more than two hours after he had first sensed the magic.As Asgar turned the corner, two old human women passed him in a car. Asgar paid them no mind. The woman he was looking for was neither old nor human. If he had, Asgar would have seen Alana hit the release lever on her bucket seat, collapsing the whole thing flat, giggling all the while. With the seat flat, she could not be seen from outside the car, as Grandma Burns drove her back to the Sunny View Nursing Home.

The magic was gone, but Asgar knew he had the right place. The source of the spell was inside one of the houses. Asgar approached the door and rang the bell.

Justin was so used to Sparta life, he had lost his city habit of checking before opening a door. In Sparta, it hardly seemed worth the effort.

"Can I help you?" Justin said.

"Possibly. I'm looking for someone," said Asgar, opening the screen door and pushing Justin aside with one outstretched hand. Asgar was tall, 6' 4", although he was very slender. He wore gloves to cover his unusual hands, which would instantly mark him as not human. He had an extra joint in his fingers, making them long and thin, like the rest of him.

"You can't come in here," Justin said.

"I can go anywhere I wish," said Asgar, ignoring Justin.

"Cindy, call 911," shouted Justin, as Cindy rushed to the phone. He then grabbed Asgar's arm in an attempt to restrain him. Asgar laughed.

With barely any effort, Asgar lifted his arm and snapped it like a whip, throwing Justin off the ground and smashing him into a wall. Wayne saw what happened to his cousin and reacted without thinking, charging at Asgar as if he were an opponent on the football field. Wayne had tackled players bigger and heavier looking than the intruder, but Asgar brushed off the attack without breaking stride, knocking Wayne to the ground. He stepped further into the living room.

Asgar stopped short as a sharp long piece of metal prodded him in the stomach. He looked down to see Terri holding an iron poker she had grabbed from the fireplace. This was a weapon that could hurt the intruder.

"You don't want to do that, little girl," threatened Asgar.

"I'll do what I want and I'm not a little girl," countered Terri.

"Really? How old are you?" said Asgar hoping to distract her.

"Old enough," Terri said.

"You are just children," said Asgar, backing away from the poker.

"We are old enough to act and think for ourselves," Terri said, pushing her wheelchair forward with her free hand.

"And how old are you when you become that mature," said Asgar, trying to distract her as he slid sideways.

"About eleven or so. And my age is none of your business," said the fourteen-year-old Terri.

"But your people don't consider you an adult until you are eighteen," said Asgar.

Wayne and Justin had managed to get themselves back up and, realizing they would need weapons against the intruder, grabbed two other pokers.

"We don't have to be adults to deal with you," Justin said, as he and Wayne helped Terri block in the intruder.

Asgar was surrounded.

"Now get out of my grandmother's house," Terri said.

"The cops are on their way," Cindy said holding the phone.

Asgar reached down and tried to pull the poker away from Terri. As soon as his fingers touched the iron, his flesh began to smoke, as if the poker had been just taken out of the fire. He was burned, even through his gloves.

Wayne and Justin lifted up their pokers as if they were baseball bats and Asgar's head was a ball. He was weak here, especially in the presence of so much iron. Any magic he could do would border on pathetic. Besides, he could only sense four people in the house and none of them was Alana. The girl using the phone resembled her slightly, but Asgar brushed that off as coincidence.

"Fine. I'll be leaving, but I won't forget this," said Asgar as he walked out the front door. He could hear sirens in the distance and already a plan was forming in his mind. Alana obviously had some bond with these children. She had always been a sucker for young ones. Asgar now had a plan. He would make Alana come to him.

Asgar was long gone before the police were even within three blocks of the house.

Inside the kids watched him go and seemingly vanish into the night.

"Who the heck was that and what was that all about?" Terri said.

"I wish I knew," Justin said.

CHAPTER 5

The next day in school Justin and Wayne had quite a story to tell. The story was so fantastic the listeners wanted a little verification.

"Cindy, is what these guys telling us true?" asked Carmen Perez, a pretty fourteen-year-old tom boy who was more at home under the hood of a car than in a dress. She lived just outside of town on her parents' farm and supplemented her meager allowance fixing heavy equipment for all the neighboring farmers.

"Yeah. Did Justin and Wayne really scare off a burglar last night?" asked fourteen-year-old John Bearclaw, as the group of them walked down the school halls.

"Yeah, seems a little hard to believe that these two took on some guy who was six and a half feet tall," said Chuck, John's fifteen-year-old brother. The Bearclaw brothers and Carmen were like the three musketeers, always hanging around together. The Bearclaws were a wild pair, but Carmen could keep them in line. Cindy looked at Justin and Wayne and smiled.

"Someone did try to break into their grandmother's house last night, but I'd say he was only about 6'4". They did try and take him out, but he threw them around like they were rag dolls. The real hero is Terri," Cindy said just as Terri rolled up alongside of everyone.

"Did I hear my name?" asked Terri.

"Cindy here was telling us you're a hero," Carmen said.

"Well I don't know about that," Terri said, in a rare display of personal modesty.

"These guys," said John pointing to Wayne and Justin, "were trying to take all the credit."

"They tried, but this guy was stronger. Terri grabbed a poker from the fireplace and puts it up to the guy's chest like he's a vampire and she's gonna stake him. Then he took off running," Cindy said.

"Way to go, Wheels," said Chuck. He was the only one who called Terri "Wheels," but it didn't bother Terri. Chuck had been calling her that since they were kids and Chuck had stepped in to stop some bullies from picking on her and Wayne. Wayne hadn't always been so big. Chuck had told the bullies to "Leave Wheels alone" and then he chased them off. The name had stuck ever since.

"Did the cops catch the guy?" Carmen said.

"Nah, the guy was long gone by the time they got there," Cindy said.

"Anyone know what the stupid assembly is for?" asked Justin. He had started out looking like a hero and wanted to change the subject before he was looking like a total zero.

"Some crime prevention thing," said John.

"In Sparta, you guys don't have any crime," Justin said sarcastically.

"Except for the thing last night," corrected Wayne.

"I think I'm gonna cut out of this thing," Justin said.

"Why waste a cut on something this stupid? Save it for when you really need it," Carmen said, wrapping her arm around Justin's shoulder. "Besides we could sit in the back and make fun of Randolph's toupee."

Mr. Randolph was the assistant principal and he did have a bad toupee. He wasn't well liked among the students in comparison to Principal Green, who was loved. Randolph was in charge of discipline and assumed everyone would listen to him just because of his position and if he yelled loud enough. He never bothered to try and gain the respect of his students or to be fair and it showed.

"Speak of the devil," said John as they turned the hallway corner and saw Randolph finish chewing out three students.

"Hey, that's Todd, Ken, and Marianne. I thought they were going on the senior trip today. They shouldn't be back till Monday," Wayne said.

"Heard they got kicked off the trip for trying to sneak beer on the bus," Carmen said. Randolph dismissed the three seniors, telling them to go into the auditorium. To say they were angry was an understatement.

"Those three look like they're on the war path," Terri said.

"Hey, Wheels, show a little ethnic sensitivity," joked Chuck. The Bearclaws were full-blooded Native Americans.

"Should we scalp her?" said John with a devilish smile.

"Nah, her hair's not long enough to make it worth our while," said Chuck with a wink.

Rather than go around the group the three seniors decided they would plow through it. Everyone moved slightly so they could get through. Everyone except Justin.

"Out of the way, Burns," ordered Todd.

"Not a chance, band boy," Justin said. Todd was the head of the school's marching band and also the school's biggest bully. Even Ken, the captain of the football team, followed behind Todd and did what he said. A band leader as a bully was so anti-stereotypical that Justin had trouble accepting it.

"Either you move, Burns or I'm gonna move you," said Todd, looking for a fight. Problem was Justin couldn't move aside, at least in his mind.

It was more than just that Cindy was watching. In the world of gangs where he had lived prior to coming to Sparta, getting out of his way would be viewed as a sign of weakness. It would have been viewed the same as putting a "kick me" sign on his own back. Justin still hadn't found a way to reconcile his old world and his new world, but he'd been lucky to keep out of major trouble, so far.

It looked like that was about to change.

Pride was not about to let him step aside, despite the fact that Todd had four inches and thirty pounds on him.

"Make your move," challenged Justin.

Before Todd could rise to the challenge, Wayne stepped in between the pair.

"Maybe you just better back off, Todd," Wayne said. Todd wasn't quite so anxious to start trouble than he had been a moment ago. While Wayne may have been an inch or two shorter than Todd, Wayne outweighed and out muscled Todd. Plus, he had seen Wayne on the football field. That didn't mean he was going to back off, just be a little more cautious.

"Wayne, what are you doing hanging with a freshman?" said Ken.

"I am a freshman," Wayne said.

"Oh yeah. I keep forgetting because you actually made the football team," said Ken.

"So why doesn't everyone just walk away and we'll all just forget about this," suggested Wayne.

"Fine," Justin said. Since someone else had made the suggestion, it wasn't a sign of weakness to do it.

"Whatever," said Todd. As he walked past Justin, he reached back and smacked him on the side of the head. Justin turned and was in the process of jumping Todd when Wayne reached down and grabbed him. Wayne then pointed to Randolph, who was suddenly interested in them.

Marianne walked by and mocked Justin by saying "Ha, ha."

As Todd walked passed Terri, she kicked out her leg, tripping him. Spinal bifida had made her legs so weak that she needed braces and a wheeled walker to even take a few steps, which was why she was in the wheel chair. Still, she was strong enough to stick one leg out at the right time.

Todd fell forward, landing face first on the floor. Growling he jumped up and turned toward Terri.

"Oops," Terri said innocently. "Sorry," she added insincerely.

"You think that's funny? I'll show you funny," said Todd moving as if he was about to hit Terri.

"You touch my sister and I'll break your arm," promised Wayne, rushing to his sister's side. He meant it too.

"Fine, I'll take you first," said Todd.

"You touch my brother and I'll break your other arm," Terri said. Having spent years in a wheelchair using her arms as her only means of propulsion, Terri's arms had gotten quite strong. She held the school chin up and push up record, to her brother's dismay and embarrassment.

"Then it'll be my turn and what I do won't be quite so nice," added Justin, smashing his fist into his other palm.

"And we got their back," said Chuck as he, John, Carmen and a nervous looking Cindy moved behind Justin.

"We'd better end this soon. Randolph is looking this way and he's got detention in his eyes," Carmen said.

Outnumbered, Todd chose the better part of valor and decided to walk away, but he had to get the last word in first.

"This isn't over," promised Todd.

Marianne walked by and whispered to Terri, "That was so dumb." She followed behind Todd and Ken like a lost puppy dog.

"What's her problem?" asked Justin.

"Marianne wants to be popular and joining the cheerleading squad didn't work for her. She started following the two of them around, hoping it would do the trick," said Chuck.

"Did it work?" asked Justin.

"What do you think?" said Chuck. They laughed, then followed everyone into the auditorium.

Justin whispered to Wayne and Terri, "I could have handled that, but thanks, guys."

"You're welcome," Wayne said.

"No problem, cuz," Terri said. The group of them had gotten the back row of the auditorium. Carmen filed in first, followed by the Bearclaws, then Cindy. Wayne went to move in next until Terri caught the back of his shirt and nodded towards Justin. Wayne smiled and waved his cousin in next then went in himself. Terri parked her chair in the aisle.

"Looks like they got the whole school here, except the seniors on the trip," Cindy said. Sparta High School and Sparta Middle School were in the same building. Grades six through eight were in the east wing and grades nine through twelve were in the west wing. The elementary school across town housed grades K through five.

Up on the stage, Mr. Randolph was trying to quiet everyone down so the presentation could begin. The Sparta chief of police and the mayor were on the stage. Both were giving part of the presentation.

"Okay everyone, listen up. We're going to get started here," said Mr. Randolph.

"Yes, please listen to the man," said a voice from the back of the auditorium. It was Asgar. He started walking down the aisle toward the stage.

"Hey, that's the guy who tried to break into Grandma's house last night!" Justin exclaimed.

"You got the chief of police on stage. Tell him," Carmen said.

Justin stood up and shouted, "Hey..."

"Mr. Burns, do not interrupt," Randolph said.

"But..." Justin said.

"No buts. If you don't sit down and be quiet, you'll get a week's worth of detention. You, sir, will have to leave," said Randolph to Asgar.

"Leave? Goodness no, I just got here. You should have let the little boy talk. He was trying to warn you about me, not that it would have done you any good. Hello, chief. Hello, mayor," said Asgar. The chief and the mayor seemed to recognize the Asgar and began to look very nervous.

By this time Asgar had reached the stage and leapt upon it as easily as a normal person would have stepped up a single stair. He almost appeared to float up.

"I've asked you for your help, but you just weren't able to give me what I wanted. So I'm afraid it's come to this. You will tell the Fortesan that hides so cowardly among you, that I have the town's children and the only way she could guarantee their safety is to turn herself over to me," said Asgar.

The chief of police stood up. "You aren't going anywhere with these kids."

"Aren't I?" said Asgar. He took out a spellstone, a crystal-like gem that could store magic. The spell he was about to cast would use up all the magic in the grapefruit-sized gem. It had taken him the better part of a century to save that much energy, but Asgar didn't care. He lifted up his arms and light began to spill out of the spell gem and float out over all the children in the auditorium.

In the back row without knowing exactly how, Cindy realized what Asgar was doing and shouted "No!" Asgar turned and looked at her with a condescending smile. His smile soon faded. Asgar was trying to take the students away and Cindy knew she couldn't let that happen. The use of so much magic so close had awakened something inside of Cindy. Using an instinct and a power she hadn't even realized she had, Cindy reached out to try and stop the spell, but it was too powerful and too far along. Still, Cindy tried picturing in her mind that she was anchoring the kids to the town. It didn't have quite the effect she was hoping for.

Asgar realized what she was doing, as sweat began to pour down his face. It was too late for him to stop as well. The backlash could well destroy him.

It became a battle of wills and a battle of skills. Cindy won the battle of wills, but Asgar was more skilled. In a blinding flash, most of the children from the auditorium disappeared, along with the auditorium, school, and part of the town itself. The adults and young children who still remained found themselves dropped onto a barren Earth that once was a large part of the town of Sparta.

Asgar was as stunned by this turn of events, as were the town's people. His spell was just supposed to take the children, not the town. That was at least until Cindy had interfered. Still, he was not about to let anyone know that.

"I've taken all your town's children from eleven to seventeen years of age." Asgar chuckled. His argument with the girl in the wheelchair had helped him decide on the ages. "Any child who enters your town and treads on this ground will be treated the same. On noon of your children's eleventh birthdays, they will be taken from you, over to my world and there is nothing you can do about it," said Asgar.

Still, magic had rules that bound even a Fortesan like Asgar. He had to leave them a way to get back to Earth. He was determined to keep as much control over that as possible.

"When your children reach 18, they can earn their way back at my discretion. Now you will find my errant Fortesan and bring her to me," said Asgar.

There were still many children who were ten and younger, a large number of whom were crying. Even the mayor had broken into tears. There was nothing left for blocks but the barren earth. With a flourish of his hands Asgar vanished, already thinking that if that girl who had interfered with his spell was what he thought she was, he might not need Alana anymore after all.

CHAPTER 6

From where the kids caught in the spell were sitting, it looked like the adults and younger kids had disappeared, when quite the opposite was true. No one knew what was happening and at first, there was silence, a kind of quiet rarely ever heard in a school. The only sound was that of people breathing.

Cindy had passed out briefly from the strain of interfering in Asgar's spell, but in all the confusion it went unnoticed.

Slowly at first, groups of students got up from the auditorium to explore the rest of the school. They quickly found out that the halls were just as devoid of adults and young kids as the assembly had been.

It didn't take long for the significance of what happened to start to sink in. Cell phones were useless, unable to get a signal but lots of children kept trying. Some were running around holding the phones up in hopes of getting some bars to show up on the screen. While many kids began to panic, the three seniors had a much different reaction.

"This is great, there are no teachers anywhere," said Ken.

"Teachers? There's no adults. You know what this means?" said Todd cheerfully.

"What?" asked Marianne.

"We're in charge," said Ken.

"As if," Terri said who was close enough to their conversation to hear, but far enough away that her comments went unnoticed.

The rest of Terri's group shared her sentiments, but that didn't go for everyone. Many of the other kids, especially the younger ones, were frightened and needed reassurance. There was confusion and fear. What had happened to the missing people? Were they okay? The seniors assuming the mantle of leadership helped to quiet some of that fear. It wasn't long before the three seniors had a large following.

It certainly didn't include everyone. Others ran yelling and screaming out of the schools as if they were inmates escaping from a prison riot. To them, a lack of adult supervision meant only one thing—there was fun to be had.

Still, others hadn't left the auditorium but were huddled together. Some were confused, some crying and others in denial as if the whole thing was one big April Fool's joke. Others were screaming for missing friends and siblings.

Justin and his group had a different take on what was happening. They wanted to know what was going on and why. Cindy longed to help them out on that matter. She knew that she had done something to account for what had happened, she wasn't exactly sure what. On top of that, she felt very ill, as if she had suddenly gotten a bad case of the flu. She decided it would be best for the moment to keep quiet until she knew more.

Dozens of kids had already run out of school, without worrying about getting into trouble because there was no one to ask for permission, let alone anyone to give out punishments.

Justin and his friends decided to see what was happening outside of the school. Maybe they could find some help or somebody to answer their questions. Walking past the teachers' parking lot, onto the street outside, they headed for the strip mall figuring they may find somebody there. There was not a soul to be found.

The street itself was a mess. The spell had been cast when there had been people driving. Even when the drivers weren't in them, the cars still kept moving. Autos were everywhere. Some had gone up on the sidewalk, while others crashed into trees and walls. Most of the engines were still running and the keys were in the ignition.

Ray Wallins and two other boys Justin recognized as sophomores, opened the doors of a red sports car while the engine was still going and jumped in. They quickly sped off down the street, their tires peeling rubber.

"This could get dangerous," Terri said, as she watched the boys drive down the sidewalk. Next, they went over a curb to disappear around the corner after going across somebody's lawn on the next block. Joanna Wilkins, her boyfriend Robert, and his buddy Mike got in a 4-wheel-drive and headed the opposite way through someone's backyard.

"You're right. Someone is going to get hurt or run over. We should turn off all the cars and take the keys out," Justin said.

Everyone agreed and quickly ran to all the surrounding cars. Wayne had an almost empty knapsack with him and opened it up for everyone to dump the keys in there. There were dozens.

"How are we going to figure out what keys go to what car?" asked Wayne.

"Don't worry about it. If it comes to that, we'll get in. Not all of us need keys to start a car," Justin said, with a wink.

"I thought you wanted to keep that a secret," Wayne said casting a sideways glance at Cindy.

"That was then, this is now. Hot wiring may become a useful talent in the situation we're in," Justin said.

"And what the heck exactly is that? That weird guy who tried to break into your grandmother's house goes up on stage and next thing we know all the grown ups and little kids are gone. What's with that?" said John. He tried to be flippant, but his voice cracked. He was as scared as the rest of them.

"I don't know, but we're going to have to find out," Justin said.

"What we need to do is check out the rest of the town and see if this effect is localized just by the school or if it's everywhere," Wayne said.

"Good idea. We'll head down Grand Avenue and we'll see what we see," Justin said.

"Sounds like a plan," Terri said.

It didn't take them long. About three blocks later, the streets of Sparta ended. It was as if something had sliced through the town. At one point, there were pavement, lawns, and houses. The next, open fields filled with flowers of almost every color imaginable, leading into distant woods. The fields ran right up into living rooms of several houses that had been cut in half.

All of them stood there looking up into the sky and they realized it wasn't so much blue but rather a light purple. They heard a screech of tires and watched Ray and the other two boys in the red sports car speed off the paved street one block down from them and ride off into a field, disappearing over a hill in the distance. They could see Joanna and her crew in the 4-wheel-drive going off in a different direction.

"I don't think everyone else disappeared. I think we're the ones that vanished," Carmen said.

"How very perceptive," said a voice. Asgar had suddenly appeared behind them.

"You," Justin said. All of them recognized him now.

"Who are you? What do you want?" demanded Wayne.

"My name is Asgar." Cindy's eyes opened wide and Asgar noticed. "You know my name? I thought you might. You look a little like Alana, but you're not her. After what you did back there, I knew there had to be some connection."

"Alana? You mean her grandmothe..." Cindy's hand lashed out to cover Justin's mouth, in an attempt to shut him up. The attempt failed.

"Grandmother? That explains it. I never realized a Fortesan would grow old on Earth. It is good information to know," said Asgar. "Although the thought of her mating with that human Howard sickens me to my core."

"I asked you what you wanted with us. And where is everyone else? Are they okay?" growled Wayne.

Asgar chuckled. "You think to order me? I am a Fortesan, boy. Do not seek to make demands of your betters. You had no luck trying to make me do what you wanted back at the house. What makes you think you'll have any more luck now?" asked Asgar, taking a step forward.

"You're wrong. Terri was able to make you go away," Cindy said. She ran over to where a chain link fence had been cut in half by the spell. The bars that held it had come loose. Cindy picked it up and stepped between her friends and Asgar. Her flu symptoms suddenly got much worse, but she wasn't about to show weakness in front of Asgar.

"She used iron on you and you were afraid of it. Here's a steel bar. Steel has iron in it. You take a step closer and I'm gonna knock your head off," Cindy said. "The rest of you grab some."

Everyone quickly did as they were told.

"You think a little iron is going to stop me?" said Asgar, taking another step forward. Cindy swung the steel bar. Asgar ducked and took a step back.

"That's exactly what I think. Casting that spell took everything out of you, so you're weak. You have no magic to use until you rest. Iron will hurt you even more when you're weak. You know the seven of us could beat you to a pulp, so I suggest you leave," Cindy said, hoping the stories her grandmother Alana told her were true. If not, they were all in even bigger trouble.

Asgar was indeed weak and realized it wasn't worth a fight right now.

"Well, if I'm to leave, you'll all have to step aside," said Asgar. The kids were standing between him and the field beyond the town.

"Wait, first answer Wayne's questions," Justin said. The tall Fortesan laughed looking down on Justin.

"All of you do amuse me so. Very well, I'll answer your questions. I thought you were the bait in a trap, but it looks like a trap I may not need any longer," said Asgar, looking at Cindy. "The rest of your pathetic town and people are still on Earth. That's all you are going to get out of me."

"Okay, you can leave," Justin said stepping aside to open a path.

"Oh, I may, may I?" said Asgar sarcastically. Still, he left through the opening. Asgar walked into the field and several yards out stopped and turned back. "I'll be back children, count on it," said Asgar before he disappeared, looking like he vanished into thin air.

"What was that about?" said Chuck. Everyone turned towards Cindy. She had an answer.

"I think I know where we are," Cindy said, dropping the iron pipe. The moment she did, Cindy felt much better, except the pipe had somehow burned her hands.

"Where?" Terri said.

"On the Wildsidhe."

CHAPTER 7

The kids sat down in a circle in the middle of this empty street, all except Terri of course, who had brought her own seat with her.

"Ever since I was a little girl, my Grandma told me stories about the Wildsidhe. One of the characters in her stories was a Fortesan named Asgar. Fortesans were a race of people who had magic powers. They looked like tall humans, except for an extra joint on their fingers. A long time ago, the magic on Earth was dying and there were people and creatures that needed magic to survive the same way we need oxygen. The Fortesans managed to find a safe haven and there was a mass exodus from Earth to the Wildsidhe. The Fortesans chose a high council and a king and queen to rule over the new land. According to Grandma's stories, Asgar was a nasty Fortesan from the High Council who wanted to be king," Cindy said. Now that she was sitting, she was feeling much better. Her hands weren't so much burned as red.

"We've all heard those stories too. At bedtime when we were 5. So you really think that's where we are? In a land of fairies and dragons?" asked Justin sarcastically.

"Yes," Cindy said.

"Come on," Justin said.

"Why don't you believe it? You can see the evidence with your eyes. His name, those fingers, that he says he's a Fortesan," Cindy said, obviously hurt.

"Sure, I'll agree we're someplace besides Sparta, but in a fairy land? I don't think so," Justin said.

"Well, where do you think we are then?" asked Cindy.

"On another planet. Asgar probably has a spaceship that kidnapped us. There was a blinding flash of light back in the auditorium. He's probably an alien. The guy's so tall and thin and he's got those freaky looking fingers," Justin said. Today Asgar had not worn his gloves.

"Aliens? You've got to be kidding," Cindy said. "Why is Asgar afraid of iron? Remember his hands smoking when he tried to grab the poker from Terri? And why did he turn tail now?"

"We outnumbered him. He was afraid of getting his head bashed in," Justin said.

"Why would an alien with a spaceship powerful enough to take half a town to another planet be afraid of a bunch of kids waving metal clubs?" countered Cindy.

"I don't know, but it still makes more sense than your explanation," Justin said.

"Why are you having so much trouble accepting that this is the Wildsidhe?" Cindy said.

"No offense, Cindy, but your grandmother is a little bit flaky," Wayne said.

"She's not flaky. She's just a little... different. She only got that way after grandpa died a couple years back. And she was medicated last night. She'd been telling me those stories since a long time before that," Cindy said.

"Look, I'd like to know exactly what happened as much as the next person, but I think we have a higher priority here—survival," Carmen said.

"What do you mean?" asked John.

"Look around. A little part of town was sliced out and came with us," Carmen said. "I doubt we have any electricity or running water. That means we're back in the Stone Age. Without indoor plumbing, there's no showers, baths, or even toilets."

"Yuk," Terri said.

"Exactly," Carmen said.

"What are we gonna do?" asked Cindy.

"Well, there's a limited amount of supplies in this town, and now we're in competition with our fellow classmates to get them. There are about 300 of us. How long do you think the food around here is going to last? Not too long. It's best we get to the supplies before anyone else does. I think we've got the advantage because no one else realizes exactly what's happened yet," Wayne said.

"Good thinking, Wayne. If there's this much town in the other direction, our Grandma's house should be here," Justin said.

"Then where's Grandma gonna live?" Terri said, worried.

"I don't know. There's nothing we can do to help her right now. We have to watch out for ourselves. We could use her house as a place to live for now. No electricity means no refrigeration, so we can forget about raiding any frozen food. We should get all the canned goods we can find or anything else that won't spoil. Cereal, cookies and stuff," Justin said.

"That sounds good, but I have to go find my brother Carlos first. I don't think my sister Ana came over. Hopefully, she's safe back at home," Carmen said.

"We'll help find Carlos," Justin said.

"How are we gonna move all the canned goods?" asked Wayne. Justin smiled and looked at a pickup truck. It wasn't one they had keys for. "Watch the master at work," Justin said.

CHAPTER 8

They found Carlos easily. He was standing out in front of the school when they pulled up in the blue pickup truck. In addition to Carmen's brother, they picked up Yeshika and Renee Desilver as well as Miko and Ron Wang. They brought them up to speed.

From the looks of things, the three seniors had many of the other kids following them and they seemed to have taken over the school, or at least a good part of it. Justin and the rest figured it was best to avoid them.

"Let's go grocery shopping," Justin said, speeding off.

The first stop was the supermarket. Carlos had pointed out that the school had a room sized freezer plus a huge storage room full of canned goods.

"Going there would tip off our hand. We're better off at the Tarman's Supermarket," Justin said. They had the place pretty much to themselves. In a town without adults, groceries were the last things on most kids' minds.

Everyone grabbed a shopping cart. Some did more than grab. The Bearclaw brothers decided to have some fun by racing the shopping carts. John climbed in, then Chuck got behind the cart and pushed it down the bread aisle.

Carmen, not wanting to be left out, managed to convince her younger brother Carlos to get in another cart. This feat was impressive because Carlos continued to protest and ask questions about whether or not they should be racing shopping carts. In the end, his sister's enthusiasm won out over Carlos' nervous insecurity.

"Guys..." started Wayne, feeling the need to impose a little order. He was cut off by his cousin.

"Let them be, cuz," Justin said.

"But they might get hurt," countered Wayne, watching as the Bearclaws turned a corner on two wheels, almost spilling John onto the floor. The pair did manage to knock down an end case display of cereal.

"They'll be fine. They just need to blow off a little steam. None of us have let it show yet, but this is a very bad thing. I think all of us are freaking out inside," Justin said.

"You too?" asked Wayne.

"Me too, but like everyone else, I'm trying to put on a good show. I'm scared spitless. What's going to happen to us? Was Asgar telling the truth about our families being okay? Will we ever them again?" Justin said.

"I wish I knew. You think all of us can handle it?" asked Wayne.

"For now, yes. I just think that when night comes and everything gets dark, things are going to change. Besides, there might be wild animals out there. I want to have everything that needs doing finished and be back at Grandma's house long before the sun sets," Justin said.

"Sounds like a plan," Wayne said.

Meanwhile, the cart races continued. Miko and Terri had rigged up their cart like a horse and buggy. Miko knelt in the cart and held onto the back of Terri's wheelchair, while she did her best to pull.

"Out of the way, Wheels, or pick up some speed, slowpoke," teased Chuck.

"Slowpoke? That's gonna cost you," promised Terri. Chuck sprinted ahead and around an outside aisle. Terri wasn't able to match him on pure speed, so she took a shortcut up one of the middle aisles. She got to the end before the Bearclaws did and cut them off.

"Hey, you cheated," yelled John from inside his cart.

"Take it up with the judges," yelled Miko, sticking out her tongue at John.

The usually reserved Cindy was feeling left out, so she grabbed a shopping cart and pushed it over to Justin.

"Want to race?" Cindy asked Justin, who suddenly became tongue tied.

"Um... You want me to get in?" he asked.

"Yes," she replied.

"I don't know," Justin said, blushing at how close Cindy was standing to him.

Wayne stepped over.

"Get in," Wayne said.

"What?" asked Justin.

"I said get in. Here, I'll even help you," Wayne said, as he wrapped his huge arms around his cousin's chest and lifted him into the cart.

"Thanks, Wayne," Cindy said.

"No problem. My cousin can be a little dense sometimes," Wayne replied.

"I am not," countered Justin.

"You have to ignore him when he's like this," joked Wayne, giving Cindy a wink. "Give him a good ride."

"I thought you were worried about people getting hurt," Justin joked back.

"You talked me out of that remember?" Wayne said.

"Hurt?" asked Cindy.

"You don't have to worry about hurting Justin, even if you drop him on his head. My aunt and uncle used to do that to him all the time when he was a baby," Wayne said.

"That explains a lot," joked Cindy.

"It does, doesn't it?" Wayne said, with a chuckle.

"Hey!" Justin said, lacking a better comeback.

"Hey, Cindy. Move it or you'll lose, especially with a handicap like my cousin on your team," Terri said as she went by.

"I'm getting it from all sides today," Justin said.

"Deal with it, cuz," Terri said. Behind her, Miko was plucking rolls of toilet paper off the shelves and tossing them at the Bearclaws, who were again in the lead. Carmen and Carlos passed Terri and Miko. Cindy got into the running and Miko threw another roll, hitting Justin on the head.

"Miko, careful with that. That may be some of the only toilet paper we have left," Justin said.

"What's the big deal? When we run out, we'll just have to use leaves," said John.

"Yeck," said Miko.

"Just be careful you don't use poison oak like John did when we were on a camping trip with our grandfather," said Chuck.

"Hey, I was only six. You knew and could have told me," said John.

"You dived on the ground and grabbed all the leaves, then told me I couldn't have any because they were all yours. I only listened to you and let you have them," replied Chuck.

Wayne had grabbed a cart and convinced Ron to get in. Not wanting to be left out, the Desilver sisters got a cart of their own, with Yeshika driving.

As Cindy rounded a corner, she lost her balance and felt light headed. She had to grab on to the cart to keep from falling over.

"Are you okay?" asked Justin, concerned.

"I'm fine," Cindy fibbed. "I haven't felt well since what happened in the auditorium."

"Want me to push for a while?" asked Justin.

"Sure," Cindy said, smiling as Justin climbed out, then helped her into the cart. She could have done it herself, but having her hand touching his gave her a warm, happy feeling.

CHAPTER 9

The cart races lasted only another couple of minutes. There were no clear winners or losers, but it wasn't as if anyone cared. Just as Justin had predicted, it was a good way to let off steam.

More relaxed, the kids turned their attentions to clearing out the aisles and storerooms.

They went to the cash registers and grabbed piles of paper and plastic bags.

John stopped to hit one of the cash registers and its tray popped open. He reached in and pulled out a handful of bills.

"Guys, we're rich," John said, waving the money in the air.

"So what? Money seems pretty useless now," Terri said, putting bags into the cart that Miko was pushing. Everyone else had a cart of his own.

"Wheels has a point. Where are you going to spend it? Everything's free for the taking," said Chuck.

"At least on a first come, first served basis," added Miko.

"True," said Chuck.

John pushed a wad of money into his pocket.

"I like the idea of having money anyway. If worse, comes to worst, it'll be good for tinder to start fires. I kind of like the idea of starting a fire with a hundred dollar bill," said John.

"What should we be getting?" asked Carlos.

"Anything that doesn't need to be refrigerated such as canned food, cereal, soda, water, juice, powdered milk, hot chocolate, and drink mixes," Justin said.

"I hate powdered milk," said Ron.

"Me too, but unless we find a cow, we don't have any other choice," Justin said. "They seem to be out of the kind in the boxes that doesn't need to be refrigerated."

"Candy won't go bad," said Chuck.

"Chocolate!" said John, ripping open a handful of candy bars. He managed to shove five into to his mouth and took a bite, chewing with his mouth open on purpose.

"Lovely," Terri said.

"Great, you hyper on chocolate. Just what I need," Carmen said, shaking her head.

"What about all the frozen food?" asked Carlos.

"Everyone pick out something to eat for dinner. My grandmother has a gas grill we can use to cook stuff, but after that, everything is probably going to waste," Justin said.

"Actually, we know how to smoke meat," said Chuck.

"Smoke meat?" asked Cindy.

"Didn't the surgeon general say that stuff is bad for you," Terri said.

"Ha, ha, Wheels. It's a way to make jerky and stuff. We could probably save most of it. We can grab some spices to give it flavor," said Chuck.

"I could probably rig up a generator to keep a couple of freezers going. My Dad has one on the farm," Carmen said.

"But we can't get to the farm," said Carlos sadly.

"I bet Z-mart has one," Carmen said, referring to the department store in the strip mall. "They have everything there."

"That'll be our next stop. I see one problem with the generator. Generators run on gas, right?" asked Justin.

"Yes," Carmen said.

"The only gas we have is in cars. I don't think there's any gas stations in the part of town that came with us. If we can't find one, we are going to have to ration gas big time," Justin said.

"Grandma had a freezer in the basement. Z-mart sells them too. What if we get another one and put it in Grandma's basement? Then Carmen rigs up a generator for them, just for a couple of days until John and Chuck can get all the meat smoked. There's got to be hundreds of pounds, if not thousands, to get to," Wayne said.

"Good idea," Justin said.

"Thousands of pounds? That's a lot of work," complained John.

"You'd rather not have any meat?" asked Chuck.

"Fine," sighed John, taking more bites, this time of only one candy bar at a time.

They packed the food right into the bags in the carts and the contents of the carts into vehicles. The pickup truck that Justin had hot-wired was quickly filled. Justin offered to hot wire more.

Wayne picked up his knapsack and jingled it.

"I think we'll just use the keys," Wayne said.

They filled up 11 cars, minivans, and trucks. Carlos didn't want to drive because he didn't have a license, but Carmen convinced him to give it a go. He had grown up driving tractors and backhoes. A car was easier than that, especially one with an automatic transmission.

Everyone except Terri got something to drive to Grandma Burns's house. Terri, over her brother Wayne's objections, held onto the back of the minivan Chuck was driving. It was something she never would have done normally, but Chuck didn't drive any faster than a bicycle so there was little danger.

They just piled everything into the house. It took them almost an hour. Justin decided it would be better to hit Z-mart, so they would unpack later.

Everyone got back in their vehicles and they convoyed it back to Z-mart. The streets were not deserted. Kids were out exploring on their own. Many of them had hit Z-mart themselves. Parts of the store had been picked clean and the kids were running past with their plunder.

"Why the heck are they taking that stuff?" asked Carmen.

"The toys and sports stuff?" asked John.

"No, the video games. The power lines were cut off when Asgar kidnapped the town. We have no electricity. With no electricity, the games are useless," Carmen said.

"Well, let's make sure our choices are more practical," Justin said.

"Let's hit the camping department first," Wayne said, as they passed the sporting goods section. Chuck stopped short in front of the archery set-up. The compound bows that were on display were locked up behind glass.

"I've wanted one of those for years, but I could never afford it," said Chuck.

"They're locked up. How are you going to get it?" asked Renee. Chuck smiled walked over and picked up a baseball bat, then proceeded to smash the glass. Chuck took out his new bow and kissed it

"You're scaring me, big brother," said John.

"You can have one too," said Chuck.

"Okay," said John, as he pulled one out. Renee watched in amazement.

"We can do that?" said Renee.

"Why not?" asked Chuck. Renee picked up a bat and motioned to her sister Yeshika.

"C'mon," said Renee.

"Where?" asked Yeshika.

"The jewelry counter. I've always wanted diamond earrings," said Renee.

"But you don't even have pierced ears. Mom wouldn't let you because she thought you were too young," said Yeshika.

"Well, Mom's not here and I'm going to pierce my ears tonight," said Renee. She got to the jewelry counter and lifted up the bat to smash the glass.

"Wait," said Yeshika, walking behind the counter.

"Why?" asked Renee.

"The keys are right here," she said and opened up the display door. "You know, Mom would never let me get hair extensions. I think I'm going to go get some."

Across the way in the toy department, four seventh graders were laughing and throwing around what looked like a Barbie-style doll wrapped in a net.

Cindy watched and shook her head. The things some people did for fun. Then Cindy head the doll yell for help. She looked closer and saw that the doll was moving. It was alive and the boys were torturing it.

Without thinking, Cindy ran in the middle of the toss and grabbed the net.

"Hey, give it back," demanded one of the boys.

"No, you're hurting her," Cindy said.

"I said give it back," he said.

"No," Cindy said. He tried to take it from her, so Cindy ran. The four boys chased her. Cindy headed toward the camping section, where Justin and Wayne were, and hid behind the pair. The four boys stopped short.

"What's going on?" asked Justin. The boys became suddenly quiet.

"Is there a problem, guys?" asked Wayne, whose sheer size was enough to intimidate the younger boys.

"No. We were just leaving," said the seventh grader, as he and his three friends ran off as fast as they had come.

"What was that about?" asked Justin.

"This," Cindy said, holding out the net with the tiny woman in it.

"Holy..." Wayne said. "Is she alive?"

"Yes, but I think they hurt her," Cindy said, unwrapping the net.

"Look, she's got pointy ears and wings. What is she?" asked Wayne.

"I think she's a pixie," Cindy said.

"Pixie? Cindy, we're not on the Wildsidhe," Justin said.

"Then explain her," Cindy said.

"A tiny alien," Justin said.

"You're hopeless," Cindy said. The pixie was trembling in her hands, trying to get away. "Don't worry. We won't hurt you. Oh no, look at you. They tore your wing and it looks like your leg is broken. Those guys make me so angry. I wish I could undo what they did."

Cindy's anger fueled her desire and there was a tiny flash of light and power. A second later, the pixie's wounds were healed and Cindy felt weak again, like she was going to pass out.

The pixie fluttered her wings and danced in the air. "Pretty lady fix Lissy's wing. Thank you, pretty lady," said the pixie.

"How you'd fix her?" asked Justin. Cindy kept her mouth shut.

"Maybe it's a genie and gave Cindy three wishes for saving her," Wayne said. "Wish us back home."

The pixie darted back and forth like a nervous dragonfly. It giggled at

Wayne's words.

"Lissy can't grant wishes. What is pretty lady's name?" asked the pixie.

"I'm Cindy. This is Justin and Wayne. Your name is Lissy?" asked Cindy.

"Yes, Lissy is my name. My name is Lissy. Thank you for saving me from those mean boys. I think maybe I go drop big rocks on their heads," said Lissy.

"Don't do that Lissy. They might catch you again," Cindy said.

"Cindy is right. I better go hide and warn my siblings about mean biggies. But not all biggies mean. Cindy, Wayne, and Justin nice biggies. Help Lissy. Someday maybe Lissy help them. Bye, must hide," said Lissy, fluttering away and out the door.

"This place just gets weirder and weirder," Wayne said.

Chuck ran over.

"We found maybe a hundred bows and tons of arrows in the storage room," said Chuck. He noticed that Cindy, Justin, and Wayne were staring out the door. "What's going on guys?"

"Long story," Justin said.

CHAPTER 10

Night seemed to come quicker than usual. Not earlier, just quicker. Usually, the sun set gradually. Tonight it seemed to drop out of the sky.

Justin and his crew set up shop at his grandmother's house, except for Renee and Yeshika Desilver. Their house was right around the corner and they decided to stay there.

Most of the rest of the kids had made themselves at home at the school. As there were no beds, it was not very comfortable and most of the kids would have sore backs and necks in the morning from sleeping on the floor.

Out of all those who could not sleep, two girls were being watched. The first was Marianne. She had found her younger sister Jane and the two of them had originally moved into the teachers' lounge. Once he had found out it had a couch, Todd had kicked them out and claimed the room as his own. They found an English classroom that was not nearly as comfortable.

Amazingly, Jane fell right to sleep. Marianne had no such luck. After an hour of staring at a wall filled with student essays, she was about ready to go stir crazy. It was so bad, she may have actually read some of them if there had been enough light. The school had an emergency generator that kicked in once the power went out and it was hooked up to flood lamps. They weren't bright enough to completely light up the school. Apparently, they had been designed to light up the halls in case of a fire. They cast an eerie glow, making the halls look creepy. Worse, the generator seemed to be losing power because the lights were getting dimmer as the night went on. Marianne pointed this out to Todd, but he didn't seem too concerned. He said he'd look into it in the morning. Judging from the way the lights were flickering, Marianne knew morning would be too late.

If only Todd would listen to her, but he didn't. Nobody did. It was a sore spot with Marianne. After all, she knew better than anyone, or at least she thought she did. Everyone else had a different opinion. Marianne believed her problems in obtaining popularity were because others couldn't appreciate her greatness. She never considered it might be because she put herself before everyone else and only cared about people in terms of what they could do for her.

The only exception was Jane, who was so deep in sleep that she was drooling out of the corner of her mouth. In one respect, Marianne was jealous of Jane. The younger of the two sisters was a natural beauty. Marianne spent hours trying to make herself look beautiful, but the best she could achieve was the high end of average.

Amazingly, Jane not only loved her big sister but thought she was the coolest and most beautiful girl she knew. Jane was the only one that thought that highly of Marianne, so jealousy never became a problem. Marianne looked at her sister and smiled, but a moment later the boredom was back.

Marianne decided to go for a walk. Each classroom had a fire escape window, even the ones on the second floor. Marianne had never understood that. When she was a freshman, a junior had jumped out of one of the second-floor science labs on a dare. He broke his leg and got suspended. Being on the first floor, exiting through the window was no problem.

The night air was crisp and cool. Marianne headed for the front gate to take a walk around the streets.

Meanwhile, across town, Terri was having a similar problem sleeping. The front and back doors of her grandmother's house had ramps, but after what she had seen today, Terri didn't want to be wandering around at night. Instead, she had rolled out on the back porch and was relaxing as she looked out at the night.

The presence that was watching from the darkness chose to approach her first.

"Greetings, child of Earth," said a voice from out of the darkness.

"Who's there?" demanded Terri of the night. The night answered back.

"There is no need to fear, child. I come as a friend."

"Where I come from, friends don't hide in the dark. Show yourself," Terri said.

"Very well," said a woman, as she stepped out of the darkness. The first thing Terri noticed was that the woman was tall, tall enough that for a brief second she thought Asgar had come back. A black cloak with a hood hid most of her features.

"What do you want?" demanded Terri, debating about whether or not to shout for the others. The woman seemed to sense her thoughts.

"Let your companions sleep. My business is with you."

"And what business is that?" asked Terri

"I wish to be your friend," said the woman.

"That's the second time you've said that. Who are you? Why single me out?"

"There is something different about you. Unlike your companions, you sit in that contraption."

"It's called a wheelchair," Terri said.

"I suppose it is. You cannot walk, can you?"

"Other than a few steps with a walker and leg braces, no. Not that it's any of your business," Terri said, annoyed.

"But if I choose to make it my business, this curse would no longer plague you."

"What are you talking about?"

"I can make you walk again," said the woman.

"Yeah, right," Terri said.

"You doubt me? Let me show you a small taste of my power," said the woman, throwing her cloak back over her shoulders. With a flourish of her hands, she began to glow, then rose up off the ground.

Terri's jaw dropped. "You're flying."

"Mere child's play. There is little that I cannot do. Take my hand and you will walk, that I promise you," she said. Terri had always fantasized about being about to walk the way most kids imagined being able to fly. It was just as unrealistic a dream. Yet here was a woman who could fly and was offering her the power to walk. It was a dream come true. Terri started to reach for the outstretched hand, then noticed something. The woman had long, slender fingers with an extra joint. Terri had seen hands like that before on Asgar. Alarm bells went off inside her head and Terri pulled back as she realized her dream come true might be more of a nightmare.

"What do you want from me in exchange for this gift?" Terri asked.

"We can talk about that later," said the woman.

"Sorry, but I want to know first," Terri said.

The woman frowned. It was obvious that she was not happy.

"You Earth children are new here."

"And where exactly is here?" asked Terri. The woman smiled and ignored the question.

"You need someone to lead and guide you."

"And you want it to be you?" asked Terri.

"Yes. The other Earth children in this house will follow your male relations."

"You mean Wayne and Justin?"

The woman nodded and floated down to the ground.

"They, in turn, will listen to you. I will ask you to be my advocate," said the woman.

"In what way?" asked Terri.

"That I will tell you only after you agree," said the woman.

She wanted what the woman was offering, but Terri had a bad feeling in her gut. The decision was tearing her up inside like a blender on puree.

"Why can't you tell me now?" asked Terri.

"I do as I choose. I do not answer to children," said the woman.

"Then I can't make a deal," Terri said.

"Do you realize what you are giving up?"

"Do I ever," Terri said. She wanted to walk more than anything, but she didn't trust this woman. Terri didn't realize how right she was to go with her instincts.

The woman was furious.

"You ungrateful whelp!" she screamed, rising back up in the air. The glow around her became more like fire. "I'll teach you to spurn my gift."

Terri rang an old fashioned school house style bell that her grandmother had put on the back porch to call Terri's father and his siblings in for dinner years ago. It still worked and it was loud.

"Your friends won't help you now, girl," said the woman.

"And here I thought you wanted to be my friend," Terri said, pulling out the iron poker she had stuck in the backpack on the back of her wheelchair. "Asgar was afraid of iron and I'm willing to bet you are too."

"I'm nothing like Asgar. Nothing can hurt me."

"I think you're bluffing," Terri said, remembering her weird fingers. It couldn't be coincidence that she and Asgar had the same kind of hands. What hurt him had to hurt her. Footsteps inside were running toward the back door. "And my friends will have more iron."

What Terri didn't realize was that with all the iron that came over with the town, it was difficult and painful for the woman to do magic here. Unlike Asgar, she had not brought a spell stone and had no outside power to draw on.

Defeat at the hands of children was a more horrifying thought than retreat.

Wayne was the first one out the back door.

"Terri, what's wrong?" asked her concerned brother.

Terri started to tell him, but the woman had vanished back into the darkness.

CHAPTER 11

Marianne had already walked a few blocks and had decided to head back to the school. The deserted streets and houses were creeping her out, making her even less tired.

That's when the woman dropped down out of the sky. Flying took up much energy, but it had impressed Terri so much that the woman decided to use it to win over Marianne.

It worked. Marianne was dumbfounded.

"Greetings," said the woman.

"Hi," said Marianne, watching the woman float down to the street. She had misjudged how badly Terri had wanted to walk. Terri cared more for her family and friends than she did for herself. That wouldn't be a problem with this one. She decided to get down to business.

"I come to offer you a gift," she said.

"Really?" said Marianne. The woman nodded.

"I have been watching you." That was true. "No one appreciates you or your talents." That may not have been true, but Marianne believed it. "I offer you the one thing guaranteed to make you as popular as you deserve."

"What?" asked Marianne, seemingly determined to not answer in any sentence longer than one word.

"Beauty," said the woman, playing the one word sentence game, then handing Marianne a silver mirror. Marianne held it up and looked. The face staring back was hers, but changed. It was gorgeous. She turned the mirror so she could see the rest of her body. She had always had an average figure, but the Marianne in the mirror had the body of a runway model.

"Wow," said Marianne.

"You like?"

"Yes," whispered Marianne.

"With looks like that, how can you not be the most popular girl anywhere?"

Marianne looked up with a smile.

"All you have to do is take my hand," said the woman.

Without hesitation, Marianne reached out and took the hand.

"Don't you want to know what I want in exchange?" asked the woman. She had to ask. Magic had rules which even a Fortesan like her had to follow. She did not have to tell all, but she had to tell some if Marianne demanded it.

"Not really. When do I become beautiful?" asked Marianne. Her benefactor smiled. If Marianne didn't want to know the price, then she did not have to tell. It made things much simpler.

The woman put a ring with a red stone on Marianne's finger. An instant later, Marianne became identical to her beautiful image from the mirror.

Marianne looked down, saw that she had changed and grinned from ear to ear.

"How does this work?" Marianne.

"The ring gives you a glamour."

"A glamour?" asked Marianne, spinning around and trying to watch herself at the same time. She almost fell over.

"It's a spell that makes you look beautiful."

Marianne stopped short.

"A spell? As in magic?" asked Marianne. The woman nodded. "So it's not real?"

"As far as anyone, including yourself, can tell, it is real. And it will last as long as you wear the ring."

"I'll never take it off," said Marianne. The woman smiled. Marianne smiled back. "I just realized. You just dropped out of the sky, made me drop dead gorgeous and I don't even know your name."

"My name is Morna. You can call me Queen Morna or Your Majesty," she said.

"What do you want me to do?" asked Marianne.

"I will let you know soon," said Morna. Marianne looked again at her reflection. When she looked up, Morna had disappeared back into the darkness.

Marianne didn't care. She shrugged her shoulders and practically skipped her way back to the school. Morna may have been gone, but two other pairs of eyes followed her. One set sat above a tiger-like body that was covered in black fur with even blacker stripes. It was a predator known as a darkcat and it served Morna. It was larger than a tiger and then some. Its jaws had enough razor sharp teeth to make a shark envious.

The other pair of eyes was attached to a Changeling Lord, who was in his natural form. It was a gray hairless human-like shape. The Changeling, for fun, changed his form briefly. If Marianne had chosen that moment to turn around, she wouldn't need a mirror to see an exact replica of herself. The Changeling would have taken care of that for her.

CHAPTER 12

The morning came and chased away the night. Most of the kids woke up with the hope that what had happened was all but a dream. Those hopes were smashed as soon as their eyes opened. The only one who woke happy was Marianne. Her dream had not faded with the morning light. Marianne was still beautiful.

The first to notice was Jane.

"Wow, you look great," said Jane.

"Is it that surprising?" asked Marianne.

"Kinda. You never looked your best in the morning. Today your hair's not even messed. Have you been working out or something?" asked Jane.

"Something," said Marianne, debating on whether or not to tell her sister the truth. The decision was sidetracked by Todd and Ken throwing open the classroom door, without even bothering to knock.

"Wake up. It's time the ruling class, the senior class that is, got to work," said Todd.

"Yeah, c'mon, Marianne," echoed Ken, as he got his first look at the new and improved Marianne. Ken did a double take. "Whoa."

Marianne smiled. Ken had reacted that way to other beautiful girls, but never to her before. The glamour ring was working.

"Yes? You see something you like?" asked Marianne teasingly.

"Yes. No, I mean..." stammered Ken. Marianne had never been dateable material. He and Todd had let her hang around because she helped feed their egos. Everything had suddenly changed. Now she was gorgeous and definitely dateable. Marianne the puppy dog was gone, replaced by Marianne the beautiful. "Did you do something with your hair?"

"I slept on it," said Marianne, batting her eyelashes. Jane gave her sister a funny look. She had never seen Marianne act like this, flirting so blatantly. Of course, had she done something as silly as bat her lashes before, the guys would have asked her if she had something in her eye. Now they were entranced.

Todd was just as impressed as Ken, but he was higher on the pecking order.

"Marianne, there is something different about you and I definitely like it. You look fantastic," said Todd, stepping forward, pushing Ken out of his way. Ken made a face but said nothing. Todd put his arm around Marianne's waist. It sent shivers up and down Marianne's spine.

"Thank you for noticing," she said.

"I'm just surprised I never noticed before," said Todd.

"Better late than never, I suppose," said Marianne, putting her arm around his shoulders. She was in heaven. The most popular boy in school, at least in her mind, finally liked her. It was wonderful.

"Care to join us as we inspect our new kingdom?" said Todd, half seriously. The mention of a kingdom brought thoughts of Queen Morna to mind. For an instant, Marianne wondered about something she hadn't cared about last night. What price would Queen Morna ask in exchange for the beauty she had given Marianne? Then she blinked back to reality and saw Todd's eyes looking into hers and all other thoughts fled from her mind.

"I'd love to," she said. "Jane, you wanna come with us?"

Jane didn't know what to make of what was happening. At eleven, guys had not become anywhere near as important to her as they were to her sister. She didn't see the big deal.

"Naw. I'm going to go find some of my friends and maybe go outside and check out the town," said Jane.

"Hey, you need to ask my permission to leave," said Todd, taking his arm away from Marianne. She wasn't happy about it. Ken looked on, hoping he might still have a chance with Marianne.

"Says who?" said Jane, annoyed. While many of the kids had fallen in line behind Todd, they wanted someone to help out, not to order them around. Todd was headed for more trouble than he realized. "You ain't the boss of me."

"Want to bet? I'm in charge here," said Todd.

"Says who?" asked Jane.

"Says me," shot back Todd.

"Ha. No one voted for you," said Jane.

"This ain't no democracy," said Todd.

"It ain't the Kingdom of Todd either," said Jane.

"It will be."

"In your dreams," said Jane.

"Keep this up and you're gonna be in major trouble," threatened Todd.

"Right. What are you going to do? Throw me in jail?" asked Marianne. Todd got a dangerous gleam in his eyes.

"Maybe I will. Maybe I will right now," said Todd. Jane failed to be impressed, but Todd was serious. He was already making plans to convert one of the janitor's closets into a single cell.

That's when Marianne stepped in.

"Hey. Don't you dare threaten my sister," said Marianne.

Todd would have ignored or laughed at the old Marianne if she had spoken that way to him. Now he listened, afraid of getting her mad.

"But..." stammered Todd.

"No buts. You apologize to my sister right now," ordered Marianne. There was no threat, but Todd listened just the same. He had plans for changing the relationship between him and Marianne drastically and he did not want to mess that up.

The funny part is yesterday Marianne would probably have asked Jane to apologize. Her new beauty had increased her confidence a hundredfold.

"Sorry," muttered Todd. Jane smiled.

"I think maybe Marianne should be in charge," said Jane.

Marianne raised her eyebrows in alarm. From what she thought she knew of men, they wouldn't like her if she was in charge. While that may have been true of Todd and Ken, it wasn't true of all guys. Marianne just wasn't willing to take that chance.

"Oh, I don't want to run stuff," Marianne said, brushing off the comment and put her arm around Todd. He returned the favor. Looking up at Todd, she added, "Maybe we should get going now."

"Yeah," said Todd, trying to save face by ignoring Jane as they walked out into the hallway.

The lights in the hallway had gone out. The generator that Marianne had been so worried about finding just the night before had run out of power. Today, Marianne couldn't have cared less. The life she had always deserved was finally beginning.

CHAPTER 13

Terri's midnight visitor had freaked her out, not to mention that her story did the same to the rest of her friends. Justin tried to explain it away as a dream, but even he didn't buy it. Terri was too reliable and level-headed to confuse a dream for reality.

That left him with too many unanswered questions. Wayne, on the other hand, was worrying about how they could defend themselves against someone who could move half a town across time and space. Asgar may have been scared off a couple of times by iron pokers, but he had seemed weak and tired. What happened after he rested? Would he be back? Would they be able to scare him off again?

Wayne also worried about this new woman. Terri had said she resembled Asgar, down to the weird hands. Was she as powerful as Asgar? Were they friends? Enemies? Wayne preferred enemies in his mind. Maybe he could figure out a way to turn them against each other.

Wayne's mind was working overtime. As good as he was in sports, he was even better at strategy games, although he was embarrassed to admit it in public. One of his favorite games was chess, although he mostly played against the computer or on the Internet. The main reason was he didn't know anyone who could give him a challenge. Walt Smythe, the captain of their school's chess team, had taken second place in the statewide high school chess tournament. Once Walt had made the mistake of insulting the intelligence of jocks in front of Wayne.

Wayne challenged him to a chess match, best two of three. Wayne won all three. He had even tried to make the last game more interesting by purposely sacrificing half of his pieces, including his queen. Wayne still won, much to Walt's embarrassment. Then Walt, whose ego did not stop his head from knowing a good thing when he saw it, tried to convince Wayne to join the chess team. Walt had visions of the national championship dancing in his head. Wayne was tempted but ultimately turned him down, not wanting to endure the teasing of his football teammates.

Right now he was taking stock of the situation and trying to figure out a strategy. Problem was, in chess and the other games, he knew the rules and had a basic idea of the enemy's abilities. Where Asgar and the woman were concerned, he was clueless other than the fact that both of them were for some reason afraid of iron. That made him more inclined to believe Cindy's theory of this being the Wildsidhe, rather than Justin's alien world idea.

"What are we going to do today?" Terri asked, at breakfast. Carlos was making omelets on the gas grill using up the eggs and milk before they went bad. He was a great cook. The Bearclaws had gotten up at the crack of dawn to dig a half dozen pits in the backyard and made a sort of tent over each one. They lit fires in the pits and started smoking the meat. They had gotten Ron to help then. Everyone else was sitting around enjoying Carlos' cooking.

"Good question," Justin said.

"I'd love a shower," Cindy said.

"You and me both," said Miko. "Any chance of getting the plumbing working?"

"Not in the near future, although I might be able to rig up a way to heat some water up and get it into a tub," Carmen said.

"That sounds great," Wayne said, as the Bearclaws and Ron came in to get another batch of meat for smoking.

"What does?" asked Chuck.

"Carmen thinks she can figure out a way to get hot water into a bathtub," Wayne said.

"All right, Carmen," said John.

"Don't get towels ready yet. There may be a few problems. One, we'll need to use a fire of some sort, so it'll have to be outside. Which means we'll have to make sure there is some sort of wall," Carmen said.

"Why?" said John, trying for innocent and falling short.

"To keep peeping Johns and Chucks away," Carmen said.

"Are you implying that we would spy on you ladies?" asked Chuck.

"Do I need to remind you about last summer down at King Lake?" Carmen said.

"What happened?" asked Terri.

"Some college girls had rented one of the cabins for a couple of weeks. It was one of the ones with a semi-private cove. John and Chuck had been walking through the woods and noticed them skinny dipping. They hid and watched for an hour," Carmen said.

"That's normal. Are you telling me you wouldn't have done the same if it had been a college football team swimming in the buff?" asked Justin.

"I would," Terri said.

"So would I. What I wouldn't do is buy a snorkel and mask, then spend half the next morning camouflaging the snorkel as a reed. I also wouldn't have gone back there the next morning and hid under water waiting for them to do it again."

"Did they do it again?" asked Ron.

"Every day that week at seven in the morning," said John with a smile.

The guys smiled. The girls looked worried.

"It's not like we'd be looking at you, Carmen," teased John. "I mean, get real."

"Besides, I think you girls would be smart enough to notice if we were in the bathtub before you got in," said Chuck.

"We girls will just have to stand guard for each other," Terri said.

"Wheels, I'm hurt," said Chuck.

"You will be if you try anything like that," Terri said.

"There is a couple of other problems. I have an idea on how to circulate the water back through the heater for more baths, but we'll have to use the same water," Carmen said.

"Gross," said Miko.

"I can use some drinking water filters to help clean it up a little," suggested Carmen.

"Do whatever you can. I think our first order of business is finding a port-a-potty or two," Justin said.

"It keeps getting grosser," said Miko.

"We can't use the toilets. Each has only enough water for one flush and who knows if they will flush or back up. We can't keep using the neighbor's back yard. It is going to start stinking pretty soon. Plus, if Carmen gets a bathtub working, we'll need soap and shampoo. None of us thought to take any yesterday when we cleaned out the stores," Justin said.

"We should also map out how much of the town came with us and make sure we got everything we could," Wayne said.

"Sounds good," Justin said.

"Is it right to get everything for ourselves? What about the other kids?" asked Carlos, finally sitting down to eat some of his own cooking.

"We have to look out for ourselves first. Besides, they have everything in the school. Don't worry, we won't let anyone starve, but we won't go without either. You think Todd or Ken would share with us?" asked Justin.

"Not really," said Carlos.

"Let's go exploring. Chuck, John, and Ron, are you guys okay with staying here and finishing up?" asked Justin.

"We got a lot of meat left. We aren't going to be finished for days, so you might as well go. Just come back in a couple of hours to give us a chance to go off and play," said Chuck.

"Fair enough. Everyone find something with iron or steel in it, just in case," Justin said.

"So you're ready to admit we're on the Wildsidhe? You saw a pixie," Cindy said.

"I saw a tiny woman with wings fly away," Justin said. "A tiny alien woman."

"For the last time, she wasn't an alien. Why are you telling everyone to bring iron then?" asked Cindy.

"Iron worked before, so why take any chances?" Justin said.

"I still say you're hopeless," Cindy said.

"But he's cute," Terri said, butting in.

"That's debatable, but he is ticking me off," Cindy said, but Justin was happy when he noticed that she half smiled as she said it.

CHAPTER 14

Exploring what they had of Sparta didn't take long. The town went for about two and a half blocks out from the center of the school in all directions, making a circular cut through everything from pavement to houses.

Justin swore under his breath. He had been right. If the street had gone another half block, they would have two gas stations. The way it worked, they had none. That meant the only gas they had was what was in the tanks. It was going to have to be used sparingly.

As they made their way around town, they ran into other kids who were also exploring. Everyone was trying to figure out what had happened. They also picked up grumblings and complaints that Todd was trying to boss everyone around and it wasn't going over well.

As they walked around the town border, the ground shook once and then again.

"Earthquake?" asked Wayne. The ground kept shaking at regular, rhythmic intervals. Cindy was the first to realize what was happening.

"I don't think so," Cindy said, pointing toward the distant forest. Trees were crumbling. The first thing to come out was an orange winged reptile soaring through the sky.

"A dragon!" exclaimed Terri.

"But that wouldn't make the earth shake," Wayne said, confused. The trees continued to fall.

"No, but that would," Cindy said. In hot pursuit of the dragon was a giant, easily 20 feet high. The dragon looked down, saw the town in a field that should have been empty and paused in mid-flight, seemingly confused. The chasing giant roared and the dragon pumped its wings to pick up speed and soar over the town, hoping to slow the giant down.

The dragon's plan worked. The giant was so intent on watching the dragon that he wasn't watching where he was going. He tripped over one of the half houses at the border, reducing what little was standing to so much rubble.

The giant quickly got up, brushed himself off and resumed the chase. In order not to trip again, he ran straight down Vine Street, making potholes as his huge feet pounded the pavement. In moments, he had gone out the other side of the town and both giant and dragon disappeared over a distant hill.

"What was he yelling at the dragon?" asked Carmen.

"It sounded like 'You're going to be my dinner,'" said Carlos.

The idea of coming up with a defense against what he had just seen blew Wayne's mind. He stood still, staring into the distance where the two titans had disappeared.

"Oh boy," Wayne said.

The least freaked out of the bunch was Cindy. In fact, she found a certain smug satisfaction in the sight and turned to Justin.

"You believe me now?" Cindy asked, barely able not to add, "I told you so."

"Yeah. We are on the Wildsidhe," Justin said.

CHAPTER 15

Almost everyone had seen the dragon and the giant and felt the ground quake as the giant raced by. Very few took it as calmly as Cindy.

All the kids who had been out exploring were running as fast as they could back toward the school. They all converged on Todd, demanding answers. He had been inside the whole time, sitting in the principal's office with his feet up on the desk and enjoying his supposed power. Todd was about to learn that with great power comes great responsibility.

Todd, Marianne, and Ken had felt the giant's footsteps but hadn't seen anything. In groups, frightened kids poured into the principal's office, demanding answers and reassurance.

"There was a dragon," said Gary, Ken's 12-year-old brother. Ken was snickering and shaking his head.

"Listen, chubby, get a grip," said Ken. Gary was overweight and sensitive about it. Ken knew and never hesitated to take advantage of it.

"Don't call me chubby, jerk," said Gary.

"There was a giant chasing a dragon. He fell on a house," said Brina, Todd's 11-year-old sister.

"Brina, what are you talking about? There are no such things as dragons and giants," said Todd, dismissing his younger sister.

"She's telling the truth," said Jane, who had been with Brina and Gary.

"Yeah, right," said Ken, making circular motions with his finger by the side of his head, the international sign for crazy. Other kids yelled that they had seen it too.

"If don't believe us, come see for yourself," said Jane.

"What do you mean?" asked Marianne.

"The giant left footprints," said Jane.

CHAPTER 16

"Smells like a barbeque," said Ron. All the smoking pits had all the meat they could hold, so the three guys had found three reclining lawn chairs and popped open some cans of soda and sat around relaxing.

"Yep, only I don't think I'm going to want to see meat for a week when we're done with this," said Chuck.

"How'd you guys get all the fires started so fast? Your grandfather teach you how to start a fire by rubbing two sticks together?" asked Ron.

"He did, but that's not what we used," said John.

"How then?" asked Ron.

"Promise not to tell the others?" asked Chuck.

"Sure," said Ron. Chuck looked at John, then walked over to a wood pile with a tarp pulled over it. Lifting up one corner, Chuck revealed dozens of plastic containers of charcoal lighter fluid. He pulled one out and held it up to show Ron.

"A lot faster with this stuff," said Chuck. "And this," he added, holding up a lighter.

"So much for your nature skills," said Ron.

"Do I constantly have to strive to fight against stereotyping? We live in the burbs. We only spend a month or so during the summer on the reservation with our grandfather," said Chuck jokingly.

"How much longer until the meat's smoked?" asked Ron.

"A few hours. We can relax until then. As far as everyone else is concerned, we spent hours slaving away," said John.

"Works for me," said Ron. That's when the ground started shaking. They watched the dragon soar overhead and saw the top third of the giant as he raced through the far end of the town.

"There's something you don't see every day," said Chuck.

"We just saw giant monsters. How can you joke?" asked Ron.

"It's a gift," said Chuck.

Even Chuck was silent when he heard the deep growl from the next yard. The trio turned slowly to see a huge darkcat glaring and barring his teeth at them. Its light black fur had deep black stripes and was the size of a mule.

"This isn't good," said Ron.

"Let's try to move slowly into the house. No sudden moves," said Chuck. The back door was 30 feet away. The darkcat was a hundred feet away. It was no contest. The darkcat covered the distance between it and the back door before the boys moved ten feet.

"This isn't good," repeated Ron.

"You already mentioned that," said John. "Any ideas, big brother?"

"Working on it. What do you think are the chances that it's looking for a squeaky toy or a ball of yarn?" asked Chuck.

"Not good," said Ron, who had an idea. He lifted up the flap of a smoking pit and pulled out a hunk of pork. "Maybe it's hungry and smelt the meat."

Ron tossed the meat toward the darkcat. It sniffed the pork, then ignored it and took a step toward the teens.

"Maybe not," said Ron.

"Or maybe it's kosher," said John.

The darkcat took another step. Chuck was still holding the plastic container of lighter fluid.

"I got it. John, toss Ron a lighter fluid container and grab one for yourself. Ron, you grab a couple of logs from the fire."

They understood immediately. Luckily the darkcat didn't. It seemed to have more intelligence than a mere beast. The teens were unknowns to the darkcat and potentially dangerous. It was sizing them up, careful not to attack too quickly.

It could smell their fear and saw no weapons. The time for hesitation had ended. The darkcat decided that they could not hurt him and attacked, leaping into the air, straight at Chuck.

The darkcat was wrong.

Chuck dropped the lighter fluid, grabbed a log from the wood pile and smashed the darkcat on the side of its skull. Stunned, the huge cat fell to the ground. John and Ron were already squirting the lighter fluid from jaw to tail. Chuck picked up his bottle and added a third stream, aiming for the feline's eyes.

The fluid burned the creature's eyes, blurring its vision. The darkcat didn't need eyes to hunt. As long as it could smell, it knew exactly where the three teens were.

Ron threw a flaming log, but it bounced off the darkcat harmlessly. He threw a second, which ignited the fluid, turning the beast into a fireball.

The darkcat smelt the burning flesh and in the spilt second before the pain hit its brain, it was confused. It knew the difference between the smell of live and dead meat burning, and this was that of a live animal. A moment later, it realized that it was the one on fire.

The darkcat's roar of pain was deafening. The trio chose the better part of valor and ran for the back door of the house. They were safely inside before the beast could attack again.

It turns out safety wasn't everything it was cracked up to be. The darkcat dropped to the ground and rolled, putting the fire out. It then leapt through a plate glass window into the dining room. It cornered John.

"Good kitty," John said.

The darkcat narrowed its eyes and opened its jaws. John was looking at more pointy teeth than he could count. John closed his eyes and said a prayer, expecting to be able to deliver it in person in a few seconds.

Then his prayer was answered.

"Yo, cat. Over here," said Ron. Justin's grandfather had collected military swords before he died and several of them hung decoratively on the wall of the house. Ron had taken one down and pulled it out of the sheath. The point of the steel blade was pointed at the darkcat.

It turned and snarled at Ron. Without hesitation, Ron stepped forward and thrust the point into the cat's throat. It gasped in surprise and pain. The iron in the steel burned.

"Want some more?" said Ron. It would have been a great tough guy line if his voice hadn't cracked as he said it. The darkcat growled, but it sounded like a gurgle because of the blood coming out of the hole in its throat.

Ron lashed out again at the cat's face. It pulled back, but not fast enough. Ron sliced off its left ear, which only made it madder.

"Hey, pussycat. Smile for the birdie," shouted Chuck, from across the dining room. The darkcat turned. Chuck was holding one of the compound bows they had gotten from Z-mart, with an arrow cocked. The hand that held the bow also held a flash that had been taken off the top of a camera. A second before Chuck let the arrow fly, he pressed the flash button. The flash blinded the darkcat for a second. It couldn't see the arrow, so it couldn't dodge it. The arrow lodged in the darkcat's left eye. It howled in agony.

John, having nothing else at hand, lifted up a wooden chair and smashed it over the beast's head.

The darkcat was wounded, in pain, and half blind. It had sorely underestimated the humans and had paid the price. It made the decision to flee the way it had come, through the smashed window.

John stared out the window and shook his head.

"Thanks, guys," said John.

"No prob, little bro," said Chuck.

Ron just collapsed into a chair.

"Pretty impressive stuff there, Ron," said Chuck.

"I've never been so scared in my life," said Ron.

"Me either," said John.

"Make it three. What was that thing?" asked Chuck.

"I have no idea," said Ron, letting the end of his blade touch the floor.

"You handle that sword like a pro. You come from a long line of samurais or something?" asked Chuck.

"You'd think with all your speeches about stereotyping, you wouldn't do it yourself. I'm not Japanese. My great-great-grandparents came here from China. My Dad was on the fencing and saber teams in college, and he started teaching Miko and me as soon as we could walk. You're pretty handy with that bow. Your grandfather teach you that, too?" asked Ron.

"Yep," said Chuck.

"At least you were a better shot now than you usually are," said John.

"What's that? You aren't normally a good shot?" asked Ron.

"I'm okay. I can hit a target pretty consistently, but I usually miss the bullseye. Or in this case, cat's eye," said Chuck.

"That was a great shot," said John.

"I was aiming for the middle of his head," confessed Chuck. "I just realized something. Wheels and the rest of the guys are out there. There may be more of those things. We better go find them."

"If there's more of those things out there, we are going to need all the weapons we can find," said Ron, moving to pull more swords down from the walls. "I'll run around the corner to get the Desilver sisters."

"It's too bad we haven't been able to find a single gun," said John.

"Maybe, for some reason, they didn't come over. We'll just have to make do with what we have," said Chuck.

"Those guys are on foot. We should be able to find them faster if we take a car. Which one?" asked John.

Chuck walked to the front of the house and across the street at a black convertible he had his eyes on.

"That one," Chuck said, pointing at his dream car.

"Okay, but I'm driving," said John.

CHAPTER 17

Chuck had been right. Darkcats were attacking throughout the town. A pair had come across Justin and the rest near the town border. The group was spread out, exploring the rubble on the edge of town.

Without knowing why, Wayne turned to the fields outside the town and was the first to see the predators moving slowly toward them.

"What are those things?" shouted Wayne, looking down at the iron poker he was holding and wishing he had a more substantial weapon.

"Darkcats," screamed back Cindy from half a block away, remembering her grandmother's stories.

"What do we do?" yelled Justin, who was near Wayne. The two darkcats had spread out across the field.

"I don't know. They shouldn't like iron, but if we are close enough to use it, they're close enough to tear us apart with their teeth and claws," Cindy said.

"We better run for it," Justin said.

"You know a predator's instinctual reaction is to chase something that is running away from it, right?" Wayne said.

"It's either run or stay and fight, unless you have a better idea?" Justin said.

"No," Wayne said.

"Then let's move before they get any closer. Head for the blue house," screamed Justin.

All the nearby homes were missing important protective features like four walls and ceilings.

From all along the block, everyone took off running, except for Terri. Even pushing her wheelchair at top speed, she couldn't keep up with the runners unless she was going downhill. She made a good effort, despite that.

Seeing their prey fleeing, the pair of darkcats gave chase.

Terri looked back, instead of keeping her eyes on the pavement and her right wheel fell in a sewer grate and got caught.

"Help! I'm stuck!" screamed Terri, as she frantically tried to free her wheel.

"Terri!" screamed Wayne, as he made a desperate U-turn to reach his sister. Justin followed, a close second, but they were almost a block away. Cindy was closer and got there first. She added her efforts to Terri's, but they still couldn't get the wheelchair loose. The darkcats were closing in fast.

"Undo your seat belt. I'll carry you," Cindy said.

"You're not strong enough and I'd only slow you down. They'd get us both. Get out of here," ordered Terri.

"I'm not leaving you," Cindy said.

"No sense in both of us getting killed. Besides they won't get me without a fight," Terri said, waving the same iron poker she had used to scare off Asgar.

"Give me that. Maybe I can use it as a lever to get you out of there," Cindy said, wedging the poker under the wheel. It didn't do any good.

"Get lost. The only way I'm getting out of here is if I suddenly learned to fly," Terri said.

Cindy's back was to the field, but she could hear the darkcats growling as they charged and the sound filled her with fear. The fear of dying and of Terri being killed mixed together and something happened deep inside her. It was the same thing that had happened in the auditorium and again in the Z-mart. Magic, wild and untamed, surged within her. Terri's words about the only way out being if she learned to fly, combined with Cindy's desire to save her friend in an unexpected way. An unseen surge of power exploded outward from Cindy and focused on Terri's aluminum wheelchair. An instant later, the wheelchair rose up, pulling the struck wheel free of the grate.

"Wha...?" Terri said, as her own desire to be away from the darkcats took over. The wheelchair flew up and away.

Cindy looked on in awe, knowing without a doubt that this time she had been the cause. Then she screamed and threw down the iron poker she had been holding. Her hand had been burnt raw where she was holding it. Then she felt ill and starting vomiting.

Wayne, seeing Cindy was helping his sister, told Justin to help the two ladies. Justin did as he was told. One darkcat had been bearing down on his sister and Wayne cut a path to intercept it.

The darkcat saw the charging human and turned toward him. Wayne ran at him like he would an opponent on the football field, only swinging his iron poker at the darkcat's face an instant before he made contact. The shock disoriented the beast, but didn't do much more than stun it. Wayne didn't stop there and leapt on its back. He wrapped his legs on the darkcat's side and put the iron poker in front of its throat, holding one end with each hand. Wayne pulled back for all he was worth, hoping to strangle the cat.

Meanwhile, Justin had reached Cindy and watched as his cousin took to the skies. Terri wove through the air erratically.

He put a comforting hand on Cindy's back. She seemed to have stopped vomiting but was still dry heaving.

"Are you okay?" asked Justin.

"I will be," Cindy said, but she wasn't sure if she was trying to convince Justin or herself.

"We've got to move," Justin said, as he watched the second darkcat turn toward them. He helped Cindy to her feet and moved toward a car. He planned to get Cindy safely inside the car, then go to help Wayne.

"How'd she start flying?" Justin asked, pulling the door handle, which thankfully was unlocked.

"I did it," Cindy said, weakly climbing in the driver's side door.

"How?" asked Justin.

"I don't know," Cindy said. The darkcat had moved faster than they expected and was almost on top of Justin. "Look out!" screamed Cindy. She pulled Justin in and across her lap and shut the door just as the darkcat slammed into it.

"Hot-wire the car!" Cindy said. Justin turned himself around and reached under the dash board to pull out the wires.

The darkcat swiped at the driver's window with one paw, shattering it. Cindy hit the horn, which had the desired effect of startling the big cat. It took a couple of steps back.

"Start it," screamed Cindy.

"I'm trying," Justin said, barely able to think. He pulled, but there wasn't enough exposed wire to get a spark. "I need a pocket knife."

The darkcat was over the surprise and was hunting again.

"It's coming back," Cindy said.

"Make the car fly then like you did Terri's wheelchair," Justin said.

"I told you, I don't know how I did it the first time," Cindy said. The darkcat was almost at the door again. Cindy screamed. So did Justin. Suddenly, another horn honked and the darkcat turned its head to watch.

A speeding black convertible plowed into the darkcat, smashing it into the air. It landed and bounced twice. The convertible drove right over it, smashing it beneath its wheels.

John, who was behind the wheel, let loose a rebel yell. "Yeehaa!"

Cindy and Justin rushed out of the car.

"Is it dead?" asked Cindy.

"Don't know. Better make sure," said John as he spun the car around and ran over the darkcat again. The Desilver sisters were noticeably uneasy, holding onto the backseat.

"Maybe we should put a stake in its heart," suggested Ron from the backseat.

"That's for a vampire, not a darkcat," Cindy said.

"Is that what those things are called?" said Chuck. "We just had a run-in with one. Unfortunately, it's still breathing. Get in and let's go help the others."

Down the block, Wayne was still on the other darkcat's back, holding onto its neck like a cowboy at a rodeo, but just barely. Miko, Carmen, and Carlos had caught up and were trying to help him by rushing in, smashing the big cat with their iron bars, and rushing out before it could get them. It was a dangerous version of keep away.

Miko and Carmen had managed to damage a front and back leg respectively. Carlos did his best, but he couldn't keep up with the two girls. Wayne kept hoping the beast would pass out, but that didn't seem to be happening anytime soon.

The convertible pulled up. Everyone now had compound bows drawn and pointed at the darkcat. Problem was, they couldn't shoot without a good chance of hitting Wayne.

Ron grabbed one of the swords, still in its sheath.

"Miko, catch," Ron yelled, and tossed his sister the sword. She caught it and unsheathed it. Ron jumped down, his sword in hand.

"Carmen, Carlos back off. Ron and I can hand this," said Miko. Carmen looked doubtful. Neither of the Wang siblings was very big. She was almost as tall as Ron.

"You sure?" asked Carmen.

"Yep. Wolf pack attack?" asked Miko.

"With swords? It might work," said Ron.

"It's been working with iron bars so far. Wayne, hold on. We're going to try to hurt it enough so that you can get away from it," said Miko.

"Hurry, my arms are going numb," Wayne said.

Miko stepped in first and lashed out at the right front leg, the same one she had wounded with the iron bar. The sword was sharp and bit into the flesh, cutting a tendon. The leg buckled but didn't collapse. The darkcat lunged toward her, but she was already out of the way. Ron moved in, slicing into its side and the left back leg with the same swing of the sword. The darkcat lunged toward him. Miko moved in, swinging the sword like an ax. She cut the rest of the tendons behind the knee, and the right front leg went down. The darkcat turned its head and snapped its jaws. It bit down on the upturned blade of Miko's sword and screamed in pain. Miko pulled her blade out and moved away. Ron used the opportunity to finish off the left rear leg. The darkcat couldn't run, but it was far from helpless.

"Wayne, come over toward me," said Ron. Wayne let go and rolled off. The darkcat snapped its jaws but missed. With its head turned away from her, Miko was able to swing her sword into the fleshy throat, again swinging like an ax.

The darkcat's eyes rolled back in its head and it collapsed.

"Is it dead?" asked Ron.

"I certainly hope so," said Miko, as she hugged her brother. Both Wangs were sweating and breathing heavy.

"Great job," said Chuck. "What's this wolf pack attack?"

"It's more of a strategy than anything else. When a wolf pack attacks a bigger animal, like an elk, they take turns attacking, moving in and out before the bigger animal can nail them," said Ron.

"Your Dad teach you that too?" asked John.

"Nope, my Mom," said Ron.

"Mom's got a second-degree black belt in three forms of Kung Fu. She taught us to fight individually and as a team, while Dad taught us how to use swords," said Miko.

"Remind me never to get you two mad at me," said Chuck. Miko and Ron smiled.

"I think you two better teach the rest of us," Wayne said. "And thanks for saving my butt back there."

"You were trying to help Terri," said Miko. Wayne looked, saw that Justin and Cindy were in the black convertible with the Bearclaws, but his sister was nowhere to be found. With all of his attention focused on the darkcat, he hadn't seen what had happened.

"Hey, Justin, where is Terri?" asked Wayne. "Is she okay?"

"I think so," Justin said.

"Wheels wasn't in the car with you two. I didn't see her anywhere," said Chuck.

"You weren't looking in the right direction," Cindy said.

"Huh?" said Chuck and Wayne in unison.

"Look to the skies," Justin said.

As if on cue, a voice from the sky yelled, "Wheee!" Terri was still airborne and making her way back toward the group.

"Hey guys!" she yelled as she passed them and kept going down toward Vine Street.

"She's flying! How?" asked Wayne, amazed and thrilled.

"Me. And before you ask, I don't know how," Cindy said.

"Is she safe up there?" asked Wayne.

"I think so. There is also something I need to let all of you know. I think I'm somehow responsible for bringing the town over," admitted Cindy.

"You brought us over? I thought Asgar did that," Justin said.

"Not us. The town. When Asgar started his spell, I knew what he was doing and somehow I reached into his spell and changed it. He was trying to bring us over. I tried to anchor us to the town. Asgar's pull was stronger than my anchor, but the anchor was strong enough that part of the town got yanked along with us," explained Cindy.

"How were you able to do that?" asked Wayne.

"Remember when he was looking for my grandmother? I think she must have lived on the Wildsidhe for a while. That's how Asgar knows her. She must have some magic talent, which I inherited somehow. I think I also healed that pixie," Cindy said.

"So how do we get back?" asked Carmen.

"I don't know. From what I remember, my grandmother said that whenever a major spell was forced on someone, they had to be given a way out," Cindy said.

"Like the lady who had to guess Rumpelstiltskin's name to keep her baby or the prince whose kiss woke up Sleeping Beauty or Snow White?" Wayne said.

"Pretty much. We just have to find out what that was. Asgar would have had to come up with it when he cast the spell. It's just a matter of us finding out what it is and doing it," Cindy said.

Terri had managed to circle back around and began circling the group.

"I think I'm getting the hang of this. I'm just not sure how to get down," Terri said.

"Any ideas?" Wayne said to Cindy.

"None," Cindy said.

"I have an idea," said Carlos shyly.

"I'm open to suggestions," Terri said, still going in circles in the sky.

"Pretend you're a plane and use the street as a runway. Your wheels should act like landing gear," said Carlos. "What do you think?"

"I like it. It makes sense. Good idea, Carlos," Terri said. Carlos beamed at the praise. "Clear the runway."

"Wheels, we'll have ambulances and trucks with anti-fire foam standing by," said Chuck.

"Thanks for the support," Terri said. "Out of the way everybody."

"Be careful," Wayne said.

"Ditto," Justin said.

"I will," Terri said. She made a wide circle and then straightened out, gradually getting lower until she touched down on pavement. There was a sudden bump or two, but the chair rolled to a halt without Terri falling over.

Everyone ran over to her.

"Are you okay?" Cindy said.

"I'm suddenly exhausted," Terri said.

"Me too. It happened to me the three times I did magic. Magic must take energy to use, which makes the user tired," surmised Cindy.

"Three times?" asked Terri.

"I'll explain later," Cindy said.

"What was it like to fly?" asked Renee Desilver.

"Amazing. Once I got over being scared and figured out that I could fly in any direction I wanted just by thinking, it became the most incredible experience of my life," Terri said.

"Can you take me for a ride?" asked Renee.

"Maybe later. There is a problem. When I flew over Vine, I saw the seniors and a bunch of other kids. I also saw a darkcat heading toward them," Terri said.

"Todd, Ken, and Marianne are jerks. They don't deserve our help. They wouldn't help us," said John.

"That's true, but if we don't help, people are going to die. I don't think I can live with that on my conscience, even if it was Todd. Besides, there are other kids with them. Todd will probably throw them to the darkcats in order to get enough time to get away," Justin said.

"You're right, unfortunately," said John.

"Besides we have all the weapons and we have cars," said Chuck.

"Speaking of which, how'd you get the convertible going?" asked Justin.

"We watched you do it the last time. It wasn't that hard," said John. Justin's face fell.

"We better get moving," Justin said, changing the subject.

"Justin, hot wire that station wagon and that mini-van. We are doing a rescue operation here. They both have back doors. We can pop them open and everyone can pile in, then we can speed off," Wayne said.

"I'll get the minivan, John you get the station wagon. Everyone else get some bows," Justin said.

"Let Chuck get it. I'm driving the convertible," said John.

"I don't think so. You already had your turn. Now it's my turn," said Chuck.

"I don't wanna drive a station wagon. It's a mom car," whined John.

"Move it or Justin will have his started before you," said Chuck. John sped off. "Renee, Yeshika, take these and ride with John." Chuck handed them compound bows and arrows.

"I don't know how to use these," said Yeshika.

"Me neither," said Renee.

"Ron, can you teach them?" asked Chuck.

"Sure," said Ron.

"Wheels, can you fly?" asked Chuck. "If not, there's enough room in the back seat for you and the chair."

"I'm beat, so I better ride," Terri said. Wayne and Chuck lifted up the chair and put it in the back.

"Wayne, wait until you see what we figured out how to do with lighter fluid," said Chuck.

"I can hardly wait," Wayne said.

Meanwhile, Justin had already broken into the mini-van. This time it took Justin less than a minute. Cindy was with him.

"That was quick. Why couldn't you do it that fast last time?" asked Cindy.

"I was under a little pressure at the time," snapped Justin.

"Easy. I was just kidding. I appreciate you coming to my rescue," Cindy said, leaning forward.

"It was no big deal," Justin said. "I was trying to help you unstick Terri."

"Still, I'd like to say thank you," Cindy said, looking into Justin's eyes.

"You would?"

"Uh-huh," Cindy said, leaning into Justin. Their lips met for a moment, when Miko, still holding her sword, climbed into the back seat.

"People to rescue, remember? There will be time for kissy-face later," said Miko. Justin looked up at Cindy and smiled.

"I guess there will be," Justin said. Miko meanwhile had opened the back door and was tossing the seats out.

"What are you doing?" asked Cindy.

"Making more room," said Miko.

"Makes sense," Cindy said. Ron climbed in and handed out compound bows and quivers of arrows. He had his sheathed sword tucked in his belt. Carlos followed behind him.

"One for everyone," said Ron.

"I don't know how to use this," Cindy said.

"Me neither," said Carlos.

"Neither did Renee or Yeshika. I gave them a quick lesson. I'll do the same for you, then Justin drives. I gotta get to the convertible. Put the arrow on here, pointy side in front," said Ron.

"That much I know. I'm not an idiot, you know," Cindy said.

"Just having some fun. Put the string in the notch of the arrow and pull it back. Aim it at something and let go. With any luck, you might hit something," said Ron.

CHAPTER 18

A while earlier and under protest, the seniors had left the school to inspect the supposed footprints on Vine Street.

Todd was speechless when one of the potholes looked just like a giant footprint.

"See. We told you," said Jane.

"It looks like a footprint," said Marianne. The shock of the crater was enough that Todd wasn't even looking at her when she said it.

"What is it?" asked Ken.

"I'm not sure," said Todd, his grasp on reality slipping away.

"We told you. It's a footprint," said Brina.

"But if that's a footprint..." said Todd, letting the sentence hang in the air.

"Wheee!" had come the voice from the air.

"What's that?" asked Brina.

"It looks like Terri and she's flying," said Brina.

"But that's impossible," said Ken.

"Apparently not," said Jane, in a tone of voice that made it clear she thought she was talking to an idiot.

"How is she doing that?" asked Ken, ignoring Jane.

"I don't know," admitted Todd, watching her disappear.

A moment later she was back.

"Everybody hide! There's a darkcat a few blocks over," shouted Terri.

"A what?" yelled Todd.

"You're all in danger," screamed Terri.

"Sure we are," screamed Ken.

"She sounds serious," said Brina. "Todd, maybe we better listen to her."

"Maybe. Everyone head back to the school," said Todd. Terri had already flown off again, not having control of her flying yet.

Unfortunately, it was too little too late. Their scents carried on the wind, allowing the darkcat to pinpoint where they were. It moved in front of them, cutting off their escape route to the school.

It stepped out from behind a house, right in their path. Before the darkcat could make a move, the black convertible came from behind them, speeding down Vine, swerving around the giant's potholes. At the wheel, Chuck tried to run it down. This darkcat was quicker than the other, and jumped out of the way. Wayne let loose an arrow, which stuck in its back. Chuck began circling it, hoping to get another chance to run it down. The station wagon and mini-van were following close behind. They moved in front of Todd and the rest in a V position, the point between them and the darkcat. They opened the back doors.

"Quick, everyone get in," said Renee from the back of the station wagon.

"What she said," said Carlos from the mini-van.

"But..." said Todd.

"Todd, shut up and do what they said," said Jane. Todd glared at her, so Marianne intervened.

"Todd, please," pleaded Marianne. Todd nodded and got in the mini-van. With everyone inside, Justin shouted to the convertible.

"We'll get these guys to safety first and come back and help you, okay?" Justin said.

Chuck was still circling.

"We got a plan. Go," Wayne said. Concentrating, Terri's wheelchair lifted up again and she was holding two flimsy plastic bags filled with fluid. She rose up and flew over the darkcat, dropping the bags as she passed over it. They hit the big cat and burst open, covering it in lighter fluid. Wayne took out a lighter and set fire to three arrows. He gave one each to Ron and Carmen, keeping the third for himself. The three of them fired. Ron missed, but Carmen and Wayne hit. The darkcat burst into fire. The flames distracted it long enough for Chuck to hit it with the corner of the front bumper. The darkcat ran to a nearby backyard, leapt a fence, and jumped in an above ground pool, putting the fire out. It then turned its head around and pulled out the two arrows with its teeth.

"Did you see that?" Carmen said.

"Yep. What are you waiting for? Go after it," Wayne said.

"But if I smash through the fence, I could damage the car," said Chuck.

"And if we don't kill it, it will come back and kill us," Carmen said. Chuck actually had to think about it.

"I finally get the car of my dreams and I have to wreck it the first day I have it," said Chuck, putting it in gear and going up on the lawn and through the wooden fence.

"If it makes you feel any better, it's technically not your car," Carmen said.

"Doesn't help," said Chuck. The darkcat jumped out of the pool and over another fence.

"It's getting away," said Ron. Terri had swooped down.

"No its not," said Chuck, plowing through the second fence, over another lawn, down a curb, then back onto the street.

"It's going that way," Terri said from the air. She chased after him.

"Stay away from it, Terri," shouted Wayne.

"I will, but the way Chuck's driving you're going to lose it," Terri said.

"We will not," said Chuck.

The darkcat was now running down Grand Avenue and it had a head start. Terri caught up to it fast enough, but the convertible lagged behind.

It got to the end of the town and kept going into the fields. Chuck screeched to a halt before he ran out of road. Terri circled back around.

"Should we keep after it?" asked Chuck.

"I can follow it," Terri said.

"No, let it go. There could be more of them out there," Wayne said. Terri landed. It was much easier this time.

"I feel like I could sleep for a week," Terri said.

Wayne hopped out and managed to lift his sister, wheelchair and all, into the back seat.

"Maybe when we get back," Wayne said.

"This is so bad," said Ron. Chuck got out of the car and walked around to the front.

"There's one good point," said Chuck.

"What's that?" asked Carmen.

"The fender's only scratched," said Chuck. Wayne, Terri, Carmen, and Ron looked at each other and shook their heads.

CHAPTER 19

By the time the black convertible and its passengers got back to the school parking lot, things were already hitting the fan. Almost all three hundred kids who had been transported to the Wildsidhe were standing around in the parking lot watching.

John had told Justin and the rest how the darkcat had leapt though the window into Grandma Burns' house. They quickly came to the conclusion that the houses were not safe, and the safest building to be in was the school. The brick walls were strong enough that the darkcats could not knock them down, and the outside windows were easy enough to board up. Plus, an iron chain link fence ran around almost the entire school grounds.

Todd was listening in on the entire conversation.

"Sure, you all can come live at the school, as long as you are willing to do what I say. I'm in charge here," said Todd.

"Says who?" yelled Jane, who had also been eavesdropping.

"Me," said Todd. "I'm the oldest and I'm best able to take care of everyone."

"Like you took care of us when that darkcat attacked? If it wasn't for Justin, Wayne and the rest of these guys, we'd all be dead. You didn't even believe us when we told you about the giant," said Jane.

"Well I believe you now and I'll start doing something about it," said Todd.

"What?" asked Carmen.

"We'll get guns and shoot any giants or darkcats that come back," said Todd.

"Bullets would be like a pea-shooter against that giant," said the weary but spunky Terri.

"They'll still hurt those darkcats. We'll search the town and get some," said Todd.

"Won't do you any good. We already searched the town and there isn't a gun, rifle or shotgun to be found. We've got no clue why," said John.

"So now what's your plan, big man?' asked Jane.

"I've had enough of your mouth. Shut it or I'll shut it for you," threatened Todd, raising his hand.

"Don't you touch my sister," said Marianne. Todd was so angry that he didn't care about ruining his chances with Marianne.

"Or what?" snapped Todd.

"Or we'll finish what we started the other day," Wayne said, stepping between Todd and Jane.

"Fine," said Todd, pulling out his pocket knife and pointing it at Wayne, who stepped back.

Chuck pulled out a compound bow, notched an arrow and aimed it at Todd's chest.

"Drop it or I'll drop you," said Chuck.

"No!" screamed Justin. "We are not going to use weapons on each other."

"But he pulled a knife on Wayne..." said Chuck.

"We can stop him without shooting an arrow into his chest. Chuck, put down the bow," Justin said softly. Chuck listened. "Wayne, step back." Wayne looked at his cousin hesitantly. "I'll handle this. Trust me." Wayne put one hand around Jane's shoulders and moved the young girl away.

"You'll handle me, Burns? I don't think so," laughed Todd.

"Believe it," Justin said, bending down on one knee and pulling up his pant leg. He removed a switch blade from his sock, then pushed the button. The blade snapped out. "Before I came here, I lived in a bad part of Boston. I joined a gang when I was eleven. My old school was so bad, I made sure I brought one of these every day or I wouldn't go. But then I came to Sparta and things changed for me. I didn't need to go armed anymore and I hadn't worn it again until today."

"So you have a switchblade. Big deal," said Todd.

"It's more than having one, it's knowing how to use it. Not to mention the one I have is meant for fighting. That toy you got there is for cutting rope on a camping trip. You ever been in a knife fight before, Todd? I have and I'm still breathing," Justin said.

"Bull," said Todd.

"You want proof? I'll give you proof," Justin said, pulling off his shirt. There were two scars horizontally across his chest. "These took thirty five stitches to close up."

"What happened to the other guy?" asked Todd, a little worried now. Justin pulled one finger across his throat. "You killed him?"

"No. Cut his throat. He lived, but never spoke again. I was twelve when that happened. He was sixteen. I'm older and faster now. You want to try me? Go for it, but it's your funeral," Justin said.

Todd looked at Justin, then down at his smaller knife. He made his decision and tossed his knife away.

"I'm still in charge here," said Todd, trying to save face.

"I know how to solve this. We'll vote," said Jane. "Everyone who wants Todd to be in charge, go stand behind him. Everyone who wants Justin, stand in back of him."

"Me?" Justin said, surprised. "Why not Wayne?"

"Because you're a natural. And because I don't want the headaches,"

Wayne said, stepping behind his cousin and putting his arm over his shoulder. One by one, the Spartan students followed Wayne's lead and stood behind Justin. The only ones behind Todd were his sister Brina, Ken and his brother Gary.

Marianne was the last student to decide. She looked at Todd, then at the crowd behind Justin. She would have preferred for Todd to win. Him she could control. She had learned that today, but her vote was not going to make it so. The masses had chosen Justin. Problem was, he had eyes only for that Cindy girl. Normally, even before she got the glamour ring, a freshman would be beneath her, even when she was a freshman. Under the circumstances, the status quo had changed. She might be able to get Wayne to do as she wanted, Marianne thought, as she stepped to Wayne's side.

"Marianne?" said Todd, sounding hurt.

"Sorry, Todd, I have to vote my conscience," lied Marianne.

"I guess that's that. Justin is our fearless leader," Wayne said. The kids cheered.

"I don't know what to say," replied Justin.

"Just don't start making long speeches or I may have to change my vote," joked Chuck, moving up to shake Justin's hand. "I just hope you don't forget all the little people."

"Munchkins? Cindy, are there munchkins on the Wildsidhe?" joked Justin.

"No, that's Oz. A balloon isn't going to get us out of here," Cindy said, hugging Justin in congratulations. She then pulled back and gave Justin a kiss on the lips. The crowd hollered and yelled.

"Is it later yet?" Justin asked with a smile.

"Not yet, but soon," Cindy said. Then Justin noticed the palms of her hands were hurt.

"What happened to your hands?" asked Justin.

"I was holding an iron poker when I used magic to make Terri's wheelchair fly. The iron burned my hand. I think that when I use magic, iron hurts me the same as it does anything else magical on the Wildsidhe," Cindy said.

"Does it hurt?" asked Justin.

"Not much," admitted Cindy. By this time, there was a line of people who were waiting to congratulate Justin.

In the commotion, Marianne pulled Wayne aside. Wayne saw her and did a double take.

"Marianne?!" Wayne said.

"Yes. Why do you sound so surprised?" she asked.

"Don't take this the wrong way, but you look great," Wayne said.

"Why would I take that the wrong way?" Marianne asked coyly.

"Well, some girls might take that it to mean that they didn't look so great before," Wayne said. Marianne was surprised by his honesty. She was used to guys who played games.

"I have gone through some changes lately," Marianne surprised herself by admitting.

"Well, they're for the better," Wayne said.

"Thank you. I just wanted to thank you for stepping in to protect my little sister Jane," said Marianne.

"It was no big deal," Wayne said modestly.

"It was. Let me show you my gratitude," said Marianne, wrapping her arms around Wayne and hugging him tightly. When the hug was over, Wayne was blushing.

"Wayne, c'mere please," Justin said from across the way.

"Be there in a sec," Wayne said, then turned back to Marianne. "I gotta go. Will I see you later?"

"Count on it," promised Marianne with a wink. Wayne blushed again, then went over where Justin and the rest were.

"If I'm going to be running things, I need to get started. One thing, and it may be the only good thing, I learned by being in a gang was that a good leader delegates authority. That's what I'm going to do. First off, if today was any example, we need security. Wayne, I want you to be in charge of that," Justin said.

Wayne thought about that a minute. The wheels in his head were turning, coming up with ways to make the school safer. "I can handle that," Wayne said.

"I know you can. I want Chuck, John, Ron, and Miko to be your officers. Your first order of business is to make the school a fortress," Justin said.

"Hey, what about me?" Carmen said, insulted at being left out.

"You can help them out, but I have an equally important job for you to head up. You did a great job coming up with the idea of using the generator to run the freezers. We have tons of machines here, but no way to run them, because we have limited electricity. I want you to get anything working that you can, and try to figure out how to get us more power. Also, we have cars, but limited gas. Maybe you can figure out a way to get more," Justin said.

"Is that all?" Carmen said sarcastically.

"For now. We also need to eat, which means we need someone to run the kitchens. Carlos, you up for it?" asked Justin.

"Me?" asked Carlos.

"You make a mean omelet. I bet you can do wonders in the kitchen," Justin said.

"Sure, but all by myself?" asked Carlos.

"No. All of you will have people helping you. You'll just be the ones in charge. Also, Chuck and John, you guys know how to hunt, right?" asked Justin.

"Sure," said Chuck.

"We are going to need more meat. What we have isn't going to last long. There must be something out there that's edible," Justin said.

"What about the dead darkcats?" asked John.

"If you think the meat is safe, go for it. Once Wayne feels the school is secure, you can start hunting. We'll have to figure out a safe way to do it. Terri, we have things in the town like clothes, beds, and shoes that we are going to need. I want you in charge of getting that stuff together and organizing it, then making sure it gets handed out fairly," Justin said.

"I have another idea, Justin," Cindy said. "There are fruit trees in the woods and berry bushes in the fields."

"Carlos, you're in charge of food. What do you think?" asked Justin. Carlos seemed a little startled by being consulted, but answered quickly.

"No animals came over with us, so the only way we have to see if it's safe is to actually have people try it. Start off with a mouth full and wait a day or two. Then eat a little more. If nobody gets sick it should be okay," said Carlos.

"All right, we can ask for volunteers. Just make sure the first few tastes are only a mouthful," Justin said.

"I have a question. I remember hearing stories of people who ate Wildsidhe food and were trapped here," Wayne said.

"We're already trapped here," said John.

"But we might figure out a way home. I don't want to stay if I have a choice," Wayne said.

"Good point. Cindy, did your grandmother tell you anything about Wildsidhe food?" asked Justin.

"Yes. Wild food is okay. It's food that is prepared by a Fortesan with Evals powder that shouldn't be eaten. Not only would it trap a person here, it would give the Fortesan power over them. They would have to do whatever the Fortesan told them," Cindy said.

"So far we can assume Asgar is a Fortesan. Plus, it's a good guess that the woman that visited Terri last night is one too. We'll just get the word out. Don't take food from strangers," Justin said.

"What about planting our own food? Z-mart has a huge section of seeds. We can start our own farm," said Miko.

"Great idea. You're in charge of it," Justin said.

"Me? I don't know anything about farming," said Miko.

"I don't know anything about leading a community of three hundred kids. We are all going to have to learn. Carmen and Carlos lived on a farm. You guys help her and find anyone else who knows anything about farms. Don't worry, everyone will help with the hard parts," Justin said.

"No offense, bossman, but everyone here is a teenager or pretty close. As a group, we're notoriously lazy," said Chuck.

"Chuck, you're stereotyping again," Terri said.

"Maybe I am, Wheels, but I think I have a good point. How are we going to make sure everyone does their fair share?" said Chuck.

"I thought about that and I think I got the answer from something we learned in history class," Justin said.

"And here I thought you just slept during class," Wayne said.

"Luckily I was awake that day," Justin said, with a wink. "I'm going to make a policy like we learned George Washington had in the Revolutionary War. If people want to eat, they have to work."

"Isn't that a little harsh?" asked Miko.

"Not really. Let's say for the sake of argument, we are the only ones who do any work. There is only a certain amount of food we can get together. Are you going to go hungry to give it to someone who goofed off?" asked Justin.

"Well, when you put it like that, it makes sense," admitted Miko.

"What am I going to be doing?" asked Cindy.

"One, I want you to work on figuring out how that magic stuff you do works. If you could make all of us fly, we wouldn't have to worry about darkcats. Two, I want you to help me with everything I have to do. I'll need a second in command. I want it to be you," Justin said.

"Justin's playing favorites with his girlfriend," teased Terri.

"Girlfriend?" Cindy said.

"That's another thing we'll take care of later," Justin said, but everyone else knew it was already a done deal. "Do you accept?"

"Hey, you didn't ask the rest of us," teased Terri. "And which one are you asking? The second in command or the girlfriend part?"

"Doesn't matter. The answer to both is yes," Cindy said, practically glowing. Justin had to catch himself before he jumped and screamed, "Yes!"

Just then, Jane came rushing over.

"Justin, Todd and Ken are leaving and they're taking Brina and Gary with them," said Jane. Justin and the rest of his advisors ran over.

"Todd, where are you guys going?" asked Justin.

"We're leaving. We'll find a house or something. I know when I'm not wanted. You losers are on your own," said Todd.

"Todd, the houses aren't safe. The darkcats can get in," explained Justin.

"Whatever," said Todd, but the other three looked worried.

"You guys are welcome to stay," Justin said.

"And listen to what you tell me? No way. We're outta here," said Todd. Justin turned to Ken, Gary, and Brina.

"You guys can stay, you know," Justin said.

"Naw. Friends gotta stay together," said Ken. "He ain't gonna make it on his own."

"What about you two?" asked Justin.

"Ken may be a jerk, but family has to stick together," said Gary. Jane came over.

"Brina, don't go. Please," begged Jane.

"I gotta. Gary's right. Todd's my brother and I should stay with him," said Brina.

"I'll miss you," said Jane, hugging her friend and crying.

"I'll miss you too," said Brina, tears streaming down her face.

"Let's get out of here," ordered Todd.

"If the darkcats return, you guys can come back," Justin said.

"Right," said Todd, turning his back and walking down the street.

"Thanks," said Ken, before he turned to follow. Gary and Brina trailed behind him.

"That didn't go well," Justin said.

"No one said being in charge would be easy, cuz," Wayne said. Justin nodded his head.

"We better get to work on everything we have to do. Spread the word and tell everyone we'll meet in the auditorium in an hour to go over everything," Justin said.

"A lot of these kids haven't had a real meal in a day. It might make a good impression if their fearless leader fed them tonight," said Miko.

"Good point. We'll put off the meeting for a couple of hours and eat right after it. Carlos, can you put something together?" asked Justin.

"For three hundred people in a couple of hours?" said Carlos worriedly.

"How about the meat you guys were smoking?" asked Carmen. "It's already cooked."

"There should be enough done," said Chuck.

"The cafeteria had industrial sized canned food. I guess between the two, I could get something ready, but I'll need help," said Carlos.

"We'll all help," Justin said.

Ron, Miko, Carmen, and the Bearclaws went back to get the meat, armed with swords and bows. Everyone else went inside to the kitchen. Carlos was already trying to figure out what he was going to cook on, if the stoves didn't work.

Wayne and Terri pulled Justin aside.

"Loved that story about the knife fight. Had a few problems with it,"

Wayne said. "You were nine when you got those stitches, not twelve."

"Yeah, and you weren't in a knife fight. You and Wayne were climbing the tree in our backyard and you fell out and cut your chest on a couple of branches," Terri said. "You made the whole thing up."

"Guilty as charged, but it worked. Todd gave up without anyone getting hurt," Justin said.

"Why all the concern for a jerk who's given you nothing but grief since you got to Sparta?" asked Wayne.

"Things have changed. Our differences don't matter so much anymore. There are things out there who want to kill us. We all have to stand together. It's us against them," Justin said.

"When you say it like that, it makes their leaving sound bad," Terri said.

"Opinions change. With any luck, they will all be back," Justin said.

"Speaking of changing opinions of people, what's the deal with you and Marianne," asked Terri.

"What do you mean?" asked Wayne.

"We saw you hugging her, man. You like her now?" asked Justin.

"I don't know," Wayne said, looking away, his cheeks turning red.

"He's blushing! You do like her," Terri said.

"I thought you said she was a jerk," teased Justin.

"People change," Wayne said.

Terri started singing. "Wayne and Marianne, sitting in a tree. K-I-S-S-I-N-G. First comes love. Then comes marriage. Then comes Wayne in a baby carriage."

"Shut up!" Wayne said.

"Make me," Terri said.

"Okay," Wayne said, moving to give her a nuggie. Terri concentrated and her wheelchair lifted off the ground, flying across the cafeteria.

"I thought you were tired," Wayne said. Terri landed after a short distance.

"I am, but that isn't going to help you catch me," Terri said. A bunch of the kids had gathered in the cafeteria and most of them hadn't seen her fly before. They rushed over to ask Terri how she did it. In a moment she was as mobbed as a rock star.

"Your sister's a hit," Justin said. "Maybe if you're nice to her, you can get her autograph."

"Very funny," Wayne said.

"Guys, we need help," said Carlos from inside the kitchen.

"We're coming," Justin said.

CHAPTER 20

The next few days went better than expected. Justin was meeting with his advisors once a day after lunch in the conference room in the main office. Everyone used the time to report on their progress.

"A lot of kids have been coming to me and asking what they should do about going to church or temple, or religious services in general. I realize that not everyone is religious, but lots of kids are and it's an important part of their lives. No churches of any sort were in the part of town that came over, not to mention none of the kids are ministers, priests or rabbis. We can't supply those things, but I figure we can set aside the auditorium for an hour or two on Saturday or Sunday for kids who want to get together to pray. We certainly could use the prayers, at any rate. Wayne, why don't you tell us how the security beef-up is coming," Justin said.

"As of last night, we have all of the first floor windows re-enforced," Wayne said proudly.

"That was a good idea to strip the legs off the steel student desks and use them to make metal armor for the windows," Justin said.

"Thanks, but it was Carmen who rigged up the pulley system, so we can raise, lower or lock them in place. We can even shoot arrows out of them if we need to," Wayne said.

"Good job to both of you. Where is Carmen? And Carlos, Terri, and Miko?" asked Justin.

"They were supposed to start plowing and planting in the field outside the town border that we picked this morning," Wayne said.

"I know. I wanted to hear how it went," Justin said.

"I guess they are just running late," Wayne said.

"Okay, we'll wait until they get here. What's your next step for security?" asked Justin.

"We're going to start on the second floor windows today. Then I'd like to reinforce the fence," Wayne said.

"Why?" asked Justin.

"If the darkcats, get up to the school, it's too late already. I'd like to stop them before they get that close. Since everything on the Wildsidhe seems to be hurt by iron, I say we use iron and steel parts to do it. Terri found some rolls of barbed wire. We can put that around the steel fence. We built a real gate at the front of the school, so there is only one way in and out. We make regular patrols of the school grounds and maybe even of the town border. We could use bikes, since we are trying to conserve gas for the cars," Wayne said.

"Don't you think you might be getting a little too paranoid?" said John.

"Maybe, but do you remember how you felt when the darkcat snuck up on you guys in my grandmother's backyard? You guys were almost kitty chow. It's my job to make sure that doesn't happen," Wayne said.

"The patrol of the school grounds is a good idea. Start that today. The town may be a little more than we can handle now. Plus more dangerous. I like the idea of a wall re-enforcing the fence. What would you use?" asked Justin.

"Anything we can find. I was thinking maybe take apart some backyard sheds. Or we can take the hoods and trunk lids off some cars," Wayne said.

"Take the cars apart as a last resort. Also, our plan to get all vehicles inside the school parking lot is going well. There have been plenty of volunteers to help. The Bearclaws and I have been hot-wiring the cars and the volunteers have been driving them to the parking lot. We also have a few motorcycles, dirt bikes, trucks, and RVs. Terri and Chuck made a great find yesterday. Since Terri's not here, why don't you tell everyone the good news, Chuck," Justin said.

"We have found twelve porta-potties total. Turns out, Mr. Monroe rented them out to fairs and stored them in a big garage. Now, once we add these to the outhouses we already built, we should see an end to bathroom lines. Plus, we can put a couple in the basement, where we hopefully won't notice the stink. That means we won't have to be going outside at night with an armed escort just to go to the bathroom," said Chuck.

"Who's cleaning them?" said John.

"Everyone will get a turn to make it fair," Justin said. Everyone shrugged their shoulders and didn't argue. Until they could get indoor plumbing to work again, this was the best available option.

"Justin, I'm getting a little worried about Terri, Miko, Carmen, and Carlos. They should have been here by now. I'd like to go check on them," Wayne said.

"Why don't we cut this meeting short and all of us go see what's going on out there?" suggested Justin.

CHAPTER 21

What was going on in the fields was chaos. Carmen had rigged up an old fashioned plow to a 4 x 4 and she drove it across the field, making a trench. Terri followed behind in the air, dropping seeds in to it.

The next step in the plan was for Carlos, Miko, and a dozen others to walk behind and put dirt over the seed, and pour water on top. There was a stream not too far away that they got the water from. Carmen had plans to build irrigation canals in the coming weeks so they didn't have to lug all the water themselves.

That was the plan, but it wasn't working out that way. As soon as Terri dropped the seeds onto the ground, nearby pixies flew out of the tall glass to snatch them up, eat them, then fly away.

At first, it looked cute as none of them had seen pixies before, but the novelty wore off quickly. The pixies picked up every seed Terri put down. Terri was upset to put it mildly. She used her chair to try to become an airborne scarecrow. So far it wasn't working well. The pixies were smaller and had more experience flying. They could make sharper turns, and were running circles around Terri, which was only making her angrier.

That was the scene when Justin and the rest arrived. All eyes were wide with wonder, watching the new creatures, but the situation was comical and Chuck couldn't resist putting in his two cents.

"She flies through the air with the greatest of ease, it's Terri doing her imitation of a flying trapeze," sang Chuck. The pixies taunting of Terri stopped short and they fluttered over to Chuck. It looked like a swarm of humming birds had surrounded him.

"Biggie man make nice music," said Lissy.

"Chuck's singing music? They obviously don't have any taste," Carmen said, who was sitting frustrated on the hood of the 4 x 4. Terri landed next to her.

"Biggie man sing more," said Lissy.

"Why not?" said Chuck, finishing the rest of the song. When he was done, the pixies all clapped.

"More! More!" they clamored.

Cindy walked over and looked carefully into the swarm.

"Lissy, is that you?" asked Cindy. Lissy broke away from the crowd, and hovered in front of Cindy.

"Pretty lady Cindy!" exclaimed Lissy. "This is the biggie lady who saved Lissy."

With that all the pixies mobbed Cindy, speaking quickly.

"She is pretty."

"Nice hair."

"Very big."

It looked like a hive's worth of giant bees were flying around her.

"Lissy, what are you doing?" asked Cindy.

"Pixies eating seed food," said Lissy.

"Why? It's not yours," Cindy said.

"Biggies no want food. Flying biggie throwing food away. Pixies just eating what biggies wasting," said Lissy.

"Wasting? We're not wasting it," screamed Terri, still aggravated.

"Terri, let me handle this. Lissy, we're not wasting it. We're planting it to grow more food," Cindy said.

"Plant? Why? Trees and berries grow on their own. No one planted them," said Lissy.

"We need to grow more food, so we have more to eat. That's why we are putting it in the ground," Cindy said.

"That's such a silly idea," said Lissy, giggling.

"Will you please stop eating the seeds so we can finish planting them?" asked Cindy.

The pixies went into a giant airborne huddle and tiny voices were heard discussing the question.

"If pixies not eat throw away seed food, what is in it for pixies?" asked Lissy.

"I don't know. What do you want?" asked Cindy. Again, the pixies went into huddle mode. Lissy came out.

"Pixies want two things. Biggies share biggie food with pixies when it's grown," said Lissy.

"Share?! It's our food. We'll be the ones doing all the work," Terri said.

"Pixies share work. We help plant. We chase away birds who would eat seeds," said Lissy.

"That does seem fair," Cindy said, looking over to Justin. He nodded. "We can agree to that. What's the second thing?"

"Biggies make music for pixies," said Lissy.

"Well, I guess we could do something a couple of times a week," Cindy said.

"No. Biggies make music every day," said Lissy.

"Chuck, you up for it?" asked Cindy.

"Sure. Plus any of the kids in band can come out here and practice their instruments," said Chuck.

"Biggies have musical instruments? Yippee!" said Lissy.

"Why not," Cindy said.

"Biggies and Pixies have treaty?" asked Lissy.

"Yes," Cindy said.

"Biggies no want pixies to sign paper in blood, like Fortesans?" asked Lissy.

"No. A handshake will be fine," Cindy said, extending her hand. Lissy used both her hands to shake one of one of Cindy's fingers.

"Time for pixies to work," shouted Lissy. The pixies flew at Terri and into her seed bag.

"Hey," Terri said.

The pixies came out with handfuls of seeds, which was about five seeds per hand. They flew along the dug rows and dropped in seeds. One of the male pixies, turned around and started to put a seed in his mouth. Lissy flew up behind him and slapped him on the back, causing him to spit out the seed.

"No eat. We have treaty. Plant," yelled Lissy. The male pixie obeyed.

Carmen started up the 4 x 4 and dug more rows. Some pixies flew behind the 4 x 4 with Terri and dropped seeds. Others helped fill the dirt back in and used tulip-like flowers to carry water to put on the planted seeds. The kids sang while they worked, which thrilled the pixies. Using teamwork, they cut the time by a good third. The pixies and kids worked together for the next few hours and got that field planted.

"Planting done?" asked Lissy.

"For today," said Miko. "They'll be more to do tomorrow."

"Good. Pixies come back and help," said Lissy.

"Lissy, we wanted to thank you and the others for your help," Cindy said.

"We happy to help. Biggie Cindy help Lissy, Lissy help Biggie Cindy," said Lissy.

"Great, but please don't call us biggies. Just use our names," Cindy said.

"Okay, Cindy," said Lissy. Suddenly, as one the pixies turned their heads. "Danger. Bad change-thing come. Biggies run."

The pixies fled, disappearing in an instant.

"Everyone, grab your bows. Carmen, get the plow off the 4 x 4. If it's a darkcat, everyone climb in it or on it and we'll turbo it back to the school," Wayne said.

From around the corner of one of the half building, stepped several figures, which the kids recognized.

"Oh, it's just Todd and Ken," Wayne said, putting down his bow. Gary and Brina were with them and so was someone else.

"Hey losers, look who I found," said Todd. It was someone who shouldn't have been on the kid infested Wildsidhe. It was a grownup and one that they all knew.

"Principal Green!" Justin said, recognizing the plump middle aged woman.

"Hello, Justin and everyone else. As for you, Todd, that is no way to speak to your fellow students," said Principal Green.

"Sorry," muttered Todd.

"How did you get here?" asked Justin.

"She found a way to get us home," said Ken.

"For real?" asked Chuck.

"For real," replied Principal Green. "There is a man in town who spent time here on the Wildsidhe and he escaped. He knew of a secret entrance and showed the adults back home. We took a vote on who to send for you. Everyone decided on me, because all the students would know who I was. Unfortunately, the doorway is small, just big enough to fit a person, not much more. I'm going to have to take you to it in small groups, so we can avoid Asgar and those black tigers."

"They're called darkcats," offered Brina.

"They are? Well, we have to avoid them," said Principal Green.

"Who're you going to bring back first?" asked Justin.

"I can take the first group back now. I'll take you by families. Todd and Brina Wilson. Ken and Gary Holt. Terri, Wayne, and Justin Burns. Cindy Hartman. That will probably be enough for the first trip," said Principal Green.

"I don't want to seem ungrateful, but everyone picked me to be the leader. I should be the last one to go," Justin said.

"That's very noble of you, but going first is actually more, not less dangerous. You will be the first one to face any danger," said Principal Green.

"I don't know," Justin said.

"Justin, man, go. I'll hold down the fort here," said Chuck.

"You'll hold down the fort?" Carmen said.

"We can discuss it later," said Chuck.

"I don't know if I want to go," Terri said.

"Why? Don't you want to see Mom, Dad, and Grandma?" asked Wayne.

"Sure I do, but if I go home, I'll just be a girl in a wheelchair again. If I stay here, I'm a girl in a wheelchair who can fly. Flying is the most amazing feeling. I'm not sure I want to give that up," Terri said.

"Dear, you may not be giving it up. You may still be able to fly. Magic must work back home or none of you would be here right now," said Principal

Green.

"She's got a point," Wayne said.

"I guess," Terri said.

"We have to move fast. The man who had escaped the Wildsidhe warned me about the darkcats. He told me that they can smell iron and would be able to find us easier. If we bring any, we increase our chances of being caught," said Principal Green.

"No weapons? That seems foolish. If we do get caught, we'll be defenseless," Wayne said.

"I can get us there safely. I got here all right, didn't I?" said Principal Green.

"Yes," Wayne said, still unsure.

"Wayne, you've known me since you were ten years old. I wouldn't harm any of you for the world. You have to trust me," said Principal Green.

"I do," Wayne said reluctantly.

Cindy pulled Justin aside and whispered in his ear.

"Something about this doesn't feel right. I just can't figure out why. Grandma told me about crossing over. From Earth to the Wildsidhe, there are doors, but they don't go both ways. Humans that go through them are trapped here. There are only two types of Wildsidhers that have the power to cross over to Earth without major magic. One was the Fortesans and I'm trying to remember the other. Principal Greene shouldn't be able to take us back unless she's one of those two," Cindy said.

"You think she's a Fortesan?" asked Justin.

"I don't know. Maybe she's the woman who talked to Terri the first night we were here in disguise," Cindy said.

"That woman was as afraid of iron as Asgar was. I have an idea," Justin said, walking over to Terri. She had kept the iron poker in the knapsack on the back of her chair just in case she needed it. "Terri, I need to borrow this for a minute."

"Sure, but why?" asked Terri.

"I have to give a test. Principal Green, catch," Justin said, tossing the iron poker. Principal Greene caught it without flinching and held it in both hands with no signs of burns or pain.

"What's this for?" she asked.

"Just checking your reflexes," Justin said, realizing it was a weak answer. He went back over to Cindy. "She's no Fortesan. Maybe she found something your Grandmother didn't know about. It is possible you know."

"I hope so or she may be stuck here with us," Cindy said, still not convinced, but like the others, she was willing to ignore her misgivings for a chance to get home.

"We have to leave now," said Principal Green. "Once I see how this trip goes, I should be able to take more of you with me at a time. To start with, I want to play it safe. I'll be back tonight to take the second group."

The chosen students said their good byes, knowing that even the one they were leaving behind would be home soon.

The journey wasn't a long one from the town border. The doorway was just over a nearby hill, the same one the giant had run over. Terri was able to maneuver over the uneven ground by flying her wheelchair low.

"Can't believe she picked you losers," whispered Todd to Justin, as they took up the rear.

"It seemed like she picked the kids who were standing closest to her," Justin said.

"That's probably it," said Todd. Cindy pulled Justin aside again.

"I'm still having a problem with this. Doesn't it seem weird to you that she picked the kids who were most likely to be in charge? You, Wayne, even Todd."

"That was a little odd," admitted Justin.

"Okay, we're here," said Principal Green. "The door to Earth is just around this hill. I'll take you around one at a time. Cindy, you first."

"No," Justin said. This last request was setting off alarms in his head he couldn't ignore.

"What?" asked Principal Green.

"We all go together. The rest of us can watch your back. Or is there some reason you want to separate us further?" asked Justin.

"My way is safest and I am the Principal. I'm in charge," said an annoyed Principal Green.

"Wrong. Once we get back home, you may be in charge, but here I'm still in charge. We aren't moving, unless you do what I say," Justin said.

"Burns, shut up and get over yourself," said Todd.

"Justin, I hate to agree with Todd, but what are you doing?" asked Terri.

"Something here doesn't feel right. We could have gotten here just as easily and faster in a car. We could have gotten more people and we should have weapons," Justin said. Wayne nodded, because he had been thinking the same thing, but the hope of getting home safe had made him over look his objections.

"I told you about the darkcats," said Principal Green.

"And right now, I'm having my doubts. I'm not letting you spilt us up," Justin said.

"Listen..." screamed Principal Green, her face turning red.

"I'm done listening. We go together or not at all," Justin said. Principal Greene walked up to Justin and stared him in the eye.

"Fine. It's not at all then. You were never going home anyway," said Principal Green, as her hands morphed into giant sledgehammers. She punched Justin in the head, knocking him unconscious with a single blow.

"You're a Changeling!" screamed Cindy at the shape shifter, as she rushed to Justin's side. "I remember now. Changelings are the other Wildsidher that can cross over to Earth and back."

"Too little, too late. And I'm a Changeling Lord. Comparing me to a Changeling is like comparing one of the High Council to an ordinary low Fortesan. I've been to your Sparta. Oh what beautiful chaos. While I visited, I saw who best to imitate to fool the lot of you," said the Changeling Lord.

"But I saw you hold iron," Cindy said.

"When a Changeling takes a form, it has the same strengths and weaknesses as that form. Iron doesn't bother a human, so it didn't bother me. If you had any iron now, it would burn my flesh and give me unbearable pain. Sadly, for you, you have no iron," said the Changeling Lord, laughing. "Queen Morna wants all of you dead. Without you to lead them, the other Earth children will follow her. Imagine, an entire army that can wield iron weapons. No one will ever threaten her again, least of all Asgar. As for you, my dear Cindy, Asgar has special plans for you, whatever they are. That makes you are the most dangerous one among them. Morna wants you eliminated most of all," said the Changeling Lord, which had morphed into a gray skinned, hairless humanoid. He took one of his sledgehammer hands and hit Cindy in the side of the head, knocking her out. The Changeling Lord turned toward Brina and Gary.

"Let's deal with the little ones next. You two weren't technically on the kill list, but never let it be said that Lord Troc shies away from dirty work," said Troc.

"No!" screamed Ken, using a football tackle to knock Troc down. Ken managed to get Torc's arms pinned. "Nobody hurts my brother!"

Wayne moved in to help him.

"Wayne, no. You and Terri get Gary and the others out of here. Todd and I will handle Troc," said Ken.

"Are you nuts?" said Todd. "Let them handle it and we'll get out of here."

The Changeling morphed, making his hands disappear so Ken had nothing to hold onto. Ken backed away from Troc, lifted up a basketball sized rock, and smashed it on Torc's head. With no hands, Troc couldn't block it and was stunned.

"Troc is going to kill Brina, too," said Ken. That caught Todd short. "We can hold this scumbag off long enough for the others to get away."

"I..." stuttered Todd.

"Todd, for once in our lives, let's do the right thing," said Ken. Todd stared into space for a second and reached deep inside to find a courage he didn't know he had. He picked up another rock and hit Troc in the head with it. The Changeling Lord fell to his knees.

"Okay. Let's take this sleeze out. Terri, can you fly out Burns and Cindy?" asked Todd, throwing another rock.

"No, they're too heavy," Terri said.

"How about Brina and Gary?" asked Todd, throwing two more. Ken hit Troc with another rock. Wayne got in a few shots of his own.

"I think I can," Terri said.

"Well, get them out of here," said Todd. He lifted Brina up, hugged her and kissed the top of her head. "Brina, I never say it enough, but I love you."

"I love you too," said Brina, crying.

"If I don't make it back, and you do, tell Mom and Dad I love them too," said Todd.

"Don't talk let that. You're going to be fine," said Brina, trying to convince herself as much as her brother.

"You're right. I'll see you back in town," said Todd.

At the same time, Ken was saying good bye to Gary.

"Gary, I'm sorry I always called you Chubby. I was just trying to toughen you up, because I cared," said Ken.

"I know," said Gary.

"Troc's up," shouted Wayne.

"Terri, get them out of here," ordered Todd. The pair climbed into Terri's lap and she took off. The weight was heavy and the strain was great, but Terri managed to get into the air, barely.

"Terri..." shouted Todd.

"Yeah?" Terri said, gritting her teeth with the strain.

"Thanks," said Todd, turning back to face Troc. The Changeling Lord was back on his feet, but still shaky and he hadn't made a move yet.

"You're welcome," Terri said as she and her passengers went over the other side of the hill.

"So, how are we gonna take him?" asked Wayne.

"We aren't. You are going to take Justin and Cindy and run back to the school," said Ken.

"But..." Wayne said.

"No buts. You're stronger than me and Todd. You are the only one who could carry them both back," said Ken.

"Okay, but I'll be back with help," Wayne said, throwing Cindy over one shoulder and Justin over the other.

"Do it fast," said Ken. "We'll hold him off until then."

Wayne took off running as fast as he could, carrying so much weight.

Troc was standing up straight now.

"Running away won't matter. I'll still get them, right after I take care of you two," said Troc. Ken threw another rock. Troc ducked out of the way with ease. "The first one caught me by surprise. It won't happen again," said Troc as he morphed his hands into long, sharp blades. "Time to say good bye."

CHAPTER 22

Terri got back long before Wayne and told what had happened. The Bearclaws, Carmen, and the Wangs grabbed bows, quivers, and swords. The Bearclaws lifted Terri into the backseat, because she was too exhausted to fly any longer. Then the rest of them hopped into the black convertible and sped away. They met Wayne when he was still crossing the field.

"We..." Huff. "Have to go..." Gasp. "Help Ken and Todd," Wayne said between heavy breaths.

"Don't worry, we're gonna kick some Changeling butt," said Chuck.

"It is too late for that," came a voice from around the hill.

"Asgar," said Chuck. Chuck saw that Asgar was carrying Todd's still body in his arms. Assuming Asgar had killed the senior, Chuck notched an arrow and aimed it at the Fortesan's heart.

"No, don't shoot!" shouted Ken, jumping in front of Asgar.

"What?!" said Chuck.

"Ken, you're alive," Wayne said.

"Thanks to Asgar," said Ken.

"You can't be serious," said Chuck.

"But he is," said Asgar, gently placing Todd's body on the ground.

"The Changeling Lord had morphed his arms into swords and as he was about to impale me, Todd threw himself on the blade. He saved my live, but that only slowed Troc down for a second. He was about to do the same to me, when Asgar showed up out of nowhere and hurled some sort of explosive laser beam at him," said Ken.

"A simple mystic power bolt," said Asgar.

"Troc got scared, turned into a bird and flew off," said Ken.

"Is Todd..." asked Miko.

"Yes, child. Todd is dead. I was too late to save him," said Asgar.

"Why save any of us in the first place? It's your fault we're even here," said Chuck.

"True, I did bring you here for my own purposes, but Troc was working for Morna, whose purposes are not mine," said Asgar.

"Who's Morna?" asked Carmen.

"None of your concern. However, for foiling Morna's plans, I do find myself indebted to three of you. This is not a favorable situation," Asgar said, looking at Terri, Wayne, and Ken. A side effect of his spell meant that he had to repay any favors done him by the spell's victims. "It is in fact intolerable.

Therefore, I will grant you each a gift."

"You mean we get a wish?" asked Wayne.

"No. It is my choice as to what the gifts are, but they must be helpful to you."

"Send us home," Wayne said.

"I think not."

"Give us weapons to defend ourselves," Wayne said.

"So you can use them against me? No," said Asgar.

"Then answer some questions," Terri said.

"Fair enough," agreed Asgar. "Choose them carefully, because my answers will free me from your debt," said Asgar.

"How do we get home?" asked Terri.

"Very good. By the nature of my spell, when each of you reaches eighteen, I must give you a task to complete for me. If you are successful, I must send you back to Earth," said Asgar. "You boy are next."

"Tell me how we can defend ourselves against these Changelings," Wayne said.

"A normal Changeling can hold one form at a time, but it must be a natural form. A Changeling Lord can become anything they wish or imagine. When either takes a form, they take on that form's strengths and weaknesses. If they become a dwarf, iron will not hurt them much. As you just learned, if they transform to a human, iron will not hurt them at all. The key to determining whether a creature is a Changeling is knowing that they can only hold an assumed form for about a day," said Asgar. "The last question."

Ken started to open his mouth, but Wayne cut him off. "Wait. Asgar just said that when we turned eighteen he had to give us a task to do and if we did it, he has to send us home."

"Yeah, so?" said Ken.

"Ken, you're eighteen and you did a task for Asgar. Ask him to send you home," Wayne said. Ken's face lit up.

"Send me home," said Ken. Then, meekly, he added, "Please."

"Bah. Very well. You have meet the conditions of the spell," said Asgar, begrudgingly.

"You mean I can go home?" said Ken. Asgar nodded yes. "What about Gary, too?"

Gary was still back at the school, where Terri had dropped him and Brina.

"Your brother will get his chance when he turns eighteen," said Asgar.

"Can I say good bye?"

"No."

"What about Todd? Can he go back too?" asked Ken. Asgar sighed.

"Yes. Lift up your friend," ordered Asgar. Ken did as he was told and Asgar waved his arms. Ken and Todd vanished.

"Our business is done for now. Tend to Cindy's wounds or else I will become very angry," said Asgar

"We take care of our own," Wayne said.

"I will be back," said Asgar, as he walked back around the hill and disappeared.

"What do we do now?" asked Ron.

"We get Justin and Cindy to the nurse's office and make sure they are okay. After that, I have no idea," Wayne said.

CHAPTER 23

It was the next morning before Justin opened his eyes. Wayne was sitting by his side, reading a sports magazine.

"Hey, cuz, you're awake," Wayne said, throwing down the magazine.

"Where am I?" asked Justin.

"In the nurse's office. You've been unconscious for almost a day," Wayne said.

"I feel like I got run over by a truck," Justin said, sitting up. The blood rushed to his head, making him dizzy.

"Pretty close," Wayne said. Justin looked over and saw Cindy with her eyes closed on the next bed.

"Is Cindy okay?" asked Justin, worry all over his face.

"She was hit right after you were, but she woke up last night. She's fine, just tired. None of us are doctors, so we figured the best thing to do was let you guys sleep it off," Wayne said. Justin looked at the bed on the other side of him, and saw Terri. She was snoring like a chainsaw.

"Did Terri get hit too?" asked Justin.

"Naw. She just knocked herself out flying. She's been sleeping almost as long as you. She may have been serious when she said she could sleep for a week," Wayne said.

"So we all got out okay?" asked Justin.

"Not exactly," Wayne said, telling Justin about Todd's death and Asgar sending Ken home with Todd's body. "I guess Ken and Todd turned out to be okay guys after all."

"Yeah, they did. Eighteen, huh? We're going to be here a long time. At least with Ken going back, people back home will know what's going on," Justin said.

"That's true," Wayne said.

"Man, I'm tired," Justin said, Justin said, lying back down.

"Go back to sleep. We'll all still be here when you get up," Wayne said.

CHAPTER 24

It was night when Ken reappeared back in Sparta holding Todd's body. He was on the edge of the barren earth left behind when the town was taken.

He was thankful to be home. He would have to find his mom and dad and let them know that Gary was all right. Then he was going to have to find Todd's folks and tell them about their son.

Ken walked to where the pavement started again. He was surprised at how deserted Grand Avenue was. There wasn't a soul in sight.

Five dark, black sedans suddenly sped around the corner, tires screeching. They stopped ten feet in front of Ken. Men and women in dark suits jumped out of the cars. Most of them were wearing black sunglasses, despite it being nighttime.

Ken was more curious than anything, until they pulled out their guns and pointed them at him.

"Freeze, FBI. Keep your hands where we can see them. Put the body down slowly," ordered one of the men in suits. Ken gently put him down. The man threw him against the car and handcuffed his hands behind his back.

"Who are you, mister?" asked Special Agent Ficarro.

"Ken Holt."

Agent Glass stepped closer. "Sir, he's one of the missing students."

"He is, is he? Well Mr. Holt, maybe you'd care to tell us where you've been all this time?"

DOUBLE CROSS
Book 2

Patrick Thomas

CHAPTER 1

"I can't believe we have to go to a stupid assembly. This stinks," muttered Bobby, as he and his classmates marched two by two to the auditorium. It was embarrassing. They were sixth graders in the middle school, but were in the same school building as the high schoolers. None of the older kids had to line up. They were allowed to come on their own. No wonder the older kids picked on them. Worse than that, Mrs. Popus, their teacher, insisted on lining him up next to his sister Tina. She thought it was cute because they were twins, but Bobby didn't. He had enough of her at home. He would much rather hang out with Ben Matzel.

"What was that, Mr. Shelly?" asked Mrs. Popus, using the same tone of voice she used in class when she asked him a question, knowing full well he had been daydreaming and not paying attention.

"Nothing," muttered Bobby.

"Then kindly keep your nothing quiet and to yourself," said Mrs. Popus.

"Whatever," muttered Bobby. Mrs. Popus glared at him, so Bobby made a motion as if he was zipping up his lips. Mrs. Popus frowned, but didn't say anything. Wisely, neither did Bobby, but Tina giggled. Bobby gave her a glare of his own, but his twin turned her head forward and refused to look at him.

Fine, if she was going to be that way, Bobby would take care of her. He slowed down so he was a couple of steps behind her, then reached over to the back of her left sneaker with the toe of his right high top, knocking the heel of her sneaker off. His mission to give her a "flat tire" was successful.

Tina wasn't about to give her brother the satisfaction of seeing her react. Instead, she bent her knee up backwards and over to the side, kicking her twin in the butt. There was only one problem, Tina hadn't stopped to fix her sneaker and it flew off her foot. Worse, it hit Mrs. Popus in the arm.

Now it was Bobby's turn to giggle.

Mrs. Popus bent down and picked up the sneaker. "Whose shoe is this?"

Tina rolled her eyes back in her head, resolved to her fate. "Mine."

"Why did it just hit me?" she asked.

"It's a pump sneaker and I overdid it when I inflated it this morning," Tina said hopefully. Mrs. Popus wasn't buying it. "I didn't tie it tight enough?"

"Give me one good reason not to give you detention," said Mrs. Popus.

Tina was stumped. She was more of a goodie-goodie, at least compared to her brother. She wasn't used to getting in trouble. Bobby was.

"Actually, Mrs. Popus, she tripped on a piece of paper and almost fell.

That's when her shoe flew off. The school's lucky she didn't fall and hurt herself. We'd have a lawsuit then," said Bobby. Bobby was quick to tell anyone who'd listen about how great a lawyer his Uncle Bill was and had threatened to sic his uncle on several people before. Mrs. Popus wasn't impressed or intimidated.

"Hey, Bobby, isn't your Dad the one who's supposed to clean up the floor? Wouldn't that be his fault then?" asked Arnold Dywer. Bobby and Tina's Dad worked at the school as one of the janitors. Tina was embarrassed by it, which Bobby thought was wrong, but sometimes he found himself being self-conscious when other kids said something. After all, janitor wasn't the most glamorous job, like being a doctor or a secret agent. His Dad had no problems or shame over what he did for a living. It was good, honest work and that's what he told his kids. Still, when Bobby saw him cleaning up some kid's puke on the floor, part of him cringed.

"Shut up, Dywer," growled Bobby.

"What are you going to do? Sue me?" asked Arnold.

"Maybe," said Bobby.

A look from Mrs. Popus shut both of them up.

"Somehow I doubt your explanation, Mr. Shelly, but one thing I'm sure of is that you were somehow involved. Both you and Ms. Shelly have detention. And if Mr. Dywer continues to talk, he can join you."

Arnold got very quiet.

"Detention? For a shoe?" said Bobby.

"I could easily make it two days if you like, Mr. Shelly," said Mrs. Popus, with what Bobby was convinced was an evil grin. She handed Tina back her sneaker and the class got moving again. When they got to the auditorium, the sixth graders had to sit up in front. The cool kids, like Justin Burns and his cousin Wayne, and the very pretty Cindy Hartman, not to mention the wild Bearclaw brothers, Chuck and John, sat in the back.

Bobby sat in the third row, with Ben on one side and Tina on the other. Ana Perez sat next to Tina on the opposite side.

"You could have kept your mouth shut and not got in trouble," whispered Tina.

"Now you tell me," said Bobby, sarcastically.

"What's the deal? You get frequent flyer miles for detention?" asked Tina.

"Yep. Three more and I get the trip to have my next detention in Hawaii," said Bobby.

Tina half laughed. "Thanks for trying to get me out of it."

"No problem. I can pick on you, but no one else better," said Bobby.

"Ditto," said Tina.

The assembly was some sort of "Say No to Crime" thing. The chief of police and the mayor were sitting on the stage. *Great,* thought Bobby, *an hour of boring speeches.* Still, it was better than Math.

"Hey, Bobby, there's your Dad," said Ben. Andrew Shelly, in his janitor's overalls was on the opposite side of the auditorium leaning against the wall.

Bobby turned and waved. Tina did the same, but kept it quick, hoping nobody noticed.

"Hey, where are all the seniors?" asked Ana.

"They went on their senior trip. They won't be back until Monday," said Ben.

"Then what are they doing here?" asked Tina, pointing to Ken Holt, Todd Wilson and Marianne Blossum; three seniors who had just walked into the auditorium.

"I heard they got kicked off the bus for trying to sneak on beer," said Ben.

Mr. Randolph, the assistant principal, was on stage trying to quiet everyone down so the speeches could begin. He wasn't having much luck. In the back of the room, a tall man started strolling down the aisle. None of the sixth graders recognized the man, whose name was Asgar. Soon they would never forget him.

Apparently Justin Burns, who was sitting in the back row, did recognized him. He stood up and yelled, "Hey . . ."

"Mr. Burns, do not interrupt," said Randolph, cutting Justin off.

"But..." Justin said.

"No buts. If you don't sit down and be quiet, you'll get a week's worth of detention. You sir, will have to leave," said Randolph to the tall man. Asgar laughed.

"Leave? Goodness no, I just got here. You should have let the little boy talk. He was trying to warn you about me, not that it would have done you any good. Hello, chief. Hello, mayor," said Asgar. The chief and the mayor seemed to know Asgar and they began to sweat.

Asgar reached the stage and seemed to leap, then float up.

"I've asked you for your help, but you just weren't able to give me what I wanted. So I'm afraid it's come to this. You will tell the Fortesan that hides so cowardly among you, that I have the town's children and the only way she could guarantee their safety is to turn herself over to me," said Asgar.

The chief of police stood up. "You aren't going anywhere with these kids."

"Aren't I?" said Asgar, taking out a glowing crystal, which looked magical. As Asgar waved his weird looking hands. They had an extra joint on the fingers. It looked to Bobby as if he was casting a spell.

Bobby had no way of knowing how right he was. The crystal, called a spellstone, began to explode with light. A glow flashed out over all the children in the auditorium.

In the back row, Cindy Hartman, somehow realized what Asgar was doing and shouted "No!" Asgar turned and looked at her with a condescending smile. He was confident there was nothing she or everyone else could do to stop him.

Asgar's smile soon faded. He was trying to take the students away using his magic and Cindy somehow was holding the spell back. Sweat began to pour down Asgar's face, but he couldn't stop. It was too late for that. The feedback from the spell could kill him.

The mystic match came down to a battle of wills and skills. Cindy won the battle of wills, but Asgar was more skilled.

In a blinding flash, Bobby watched as most of the older kids from the auditorium disappeared. Then he noticed that the school had disappeared with them.

Bobby knew trouble and this was it, in all capital letters.

"What happened?" said Tina.

"I don't know," said Bobby, and it was the truth. After the older kids disappeared, things got crazy. From the looks of things, the school wasn't the only building that was gone. As far around as Bobby could see, there was nothing for blocks, except for orange-brown barren ground.

Ana started screaming, then crying, and she wasn't the only one. Arnold Dywer was hysterical too, along with a dozen more kids.

All the people on the stage, including Principal Greene, had plummeted down to the ground when the stage vanished. Principal Greene was holding her ankle, and it had blown up like a balloon. The mayor and the police chief picked themselves up. The chief looked around and started to freak out. The mayor was crying almost as much as Ana was.

Asgar was just as stunned by this turn of events as the town's people were. His spell was supposed to take the children, not the town. That was at least until Cindy interfered. Asgar would lose one of his extra-long hands before he would admit that to anyone, let alone a bunch of humans.

"I've taken all your town's eleven to seventeen-year-old children," Asgar chuckled. He had based this part of his spell on a conversation with Terri Burns, a girl in a wheelchair who had managed to hold him at bay with an iron poker the night before. Terri had gotten lucky without realizing that Fortesans like Asgar had a weakness to iron. "On noon of your children's eleventh birthdays they will be taken from you, over to my world and there is nothing you can do about it," said Asgar. Magic had rules that bound even a Fortesan like Asgar. He had to leave the kids a way to get back to Earth. He was determined to keep as much control over that as possible.

"When your children reach eighteen, they can earn their way back at my discretion. Now you will find my errant Fortesan and bring her to me," said Asgar, staring at the mayor and police chief.

Asgar waved his hands and vanished, just like the missing kids.

Things went downhill from there. Most of the people who stayed behind, adults and kids alike, began to sob hysterically.

Andrew Shelly walked over to the two town officials, wanting answers.

"What in heaven's name is going on here? Why did that man act like he knew you?" asked Andrew Shelly.

The mayor didn't answer. When Andrew moved closer, the mayor turned and ran off across the barren earth, toward buildings in the distance.

The chief turned toward Andrew. "I don't answer to you, janitor."

"Wanna bet?" said Andrew. The chief moved as if he was going to push Andrew, but the police chief was overweight and out of shape. Andrew Shelly wasn't. When Andrew didn't back down, the chief spun around on his heels and ran after the mayor. Andrew started to chase him, but wasn't willing to abandon the other victims. "There are kids here that need help. Get back here!"

Neither the mayor nor police chief seemed to care. Neither turned back. Andrew Shelly had already seen that his kids had not vanished with the rest, before he had confronted the two men who were now fleeing.

His kids ran to him. Bobby and Tina were frightened and confused, but otherwise unhurt. They wanted comfort and answers. The first he provided, the second was beyond his abilities.

"Dad, what happened?" asked Tina.

"I don't know, but I think we better get everyone out of here before we try to figure things out," said Andrew, not adding that the barren ground looked like what he had heard about ground zero after a nuclear explosion. Andrew was worried about radiation and wanted everyone away quickly, especially his kids.

Mr. Randolph was trying unsuccessfully to restore order, but he was only making things worse. His solution was to yell at everyone, assuming they would listen to him because of his position as assistant principal. So far it wasn't working.

Ana Perez was hysterical, but her tears had slowed to a trickle. She ran to Mr. Randolph for comfort.

"Carmen and Carlos, my sister and brother, are gone. Where are they?" Ana asked.

"I don't know. Leave me alone," said Mr. Randolph. Ana started crying, louder than before. "Stop crying." Ana couldn't. "Oh, shut up, already!" Ana's cries turned into screams and sobs. "If you don't stop, you'll have detention for a week."

Ana screamed, "No. You leave me alone, you…"

Andrew Shelly put a hand on Ana's shoulder. She was a friend of his daughter's and had been a dinner guest at his home, not to mention a full-fledged giggling member of several of his daughter's slumber parties.

"Mr. Shelly, I'm so scared," said Ana. He knelt down and enveloped her with his arms.

"I know. I am too," admitted Andrew.

"What are we going to do?" asked Ana.

"We're going to get everyone out of here. I can see some buildings over there. Everyone line up and we'll go there," said Andrew. Now that someone rational sounding had taken charge, the students and teachers listened and fell into the two by two lines that Bobby had been complaining about earlier.

"Wait a minute, Shelly. I'm in charge here," said Mr. Randolph.

"That's funny. I thought I was," said Principal Greene, limping over, putting most of her weight on another teacher and hopping on her good foot.

"You're incapacitated. That means I'm in charge," said Mr. Randolph.

"I'm not the president and you're not the vice president. You work for me, not the other way around," said Principal Greene.

"I can handle this," said Randolph.

"Like you handled things with Ana here?" asked Andrew.

"Shelly, you're a janitor. Keep out of this," growled Mr. Randolph.

"I'm not a little girl. You aren't going to be able to make me cry," said Andrew.

"Assistant principals don't answer to janitors," said Mr. Randolph.

"But they do answer to parents. My two kids are here and if you had talked to either of them like that, job or no job, you'd be on the ground right now, minus a few teeth," said Andrew.

"All right, Dad!" said Bobby. More than a few other kids, who had been on the receiving end of one of Mr. Randolph's rants, cheered Andrew on.

"And you can rest assured, I'll be telling Mr. and Mrs. Perez how you treated their daughter. Have you ever met Mr. Perez?" asked Andrew Shelly.

"No."

"Juan's a big man. A farmer. Very protective father. I'm sure you'll be meeting him real soon. Right now, shut up and get in line."

"You can't threaten me, Shelly," said Mr. Randolph.

"But I can," said Principal Greene.

"Principal Greene, I can do this. The children respect me," said Mr. Randolph.

"I doubt respect is a word that very many people would use to describe you. You're a bully who got his job because your brother sits on the Board of Education. Right now, we have a bunch of scared kids on our hands. Andrew, you're in charge. Get us out of here and we'll figure out the rest later," said Principal Greene.

"But…" said Mr. Randolph.

"Shut up and get in line," said Principal Greene.

"Yes, ma'am," said Mr. Randolph, finally listening.

Andrew gave out instructions, including for Mr. Wilson, one of the gym teachers to help carry Principal Greene.

Andrew started calling out "Left, left, left, right, left," like he was an army drill instructor. The kids and some of the teachers chanted along. It got their minds off what had happened. It wasn't long before they passed people who had been driving, shopping, and one unfortunate man who had been on the toilet. Most of these people were in even more of a state of shock than those who had been in the school. The teachers and students at least knew who had caused the disappearance. The others were clueless and frightened, but at Andrew's instructions fell in line with the kids.

The marching chant changed, "left, right," becoming Andrew saying, "Sound off, one, two."

"Three, four," the crowd replied.

"Bring it on down," said Andrew.

"One, two, three, four. One… two… three, four," said everyone together. In between, Andrew Shelly spouted funny verses. One in particular had everyone laughing, except one certain assistant principal.

"Hold your nose and hold it high, Mr. Randolph's coming by. Sound off…"

"Tina, I just thought of something," whispered Bobby.

"I think I thought of the same thing," said Tina.

"Our birthdays are in a couple of weeks," said Bobby.

"And we turn eleven."

"Do you think we'll vanish and go where that Asgar guy took everyone else?" asked Bobby.

"Yes," said Tina softly. Sister and brother both reached out and held the other's hand.

"You think Dad realizes that?" asked Bobby. As they looked over at their father, he smiled, but it looked forced. He brought his hand up and wiped a tear from his eye so quickly that nobody besides his kids realized it.

"He knows," said Tina.

CHAPTER 2

Everyone left behind had gotten out of what was being called "ground zero" safely, but things had turned to chaos quickly.

School staff started calling parents whose numbers they could find, but word had traveled fast. A fight or a car accident brought a crowd. The disappearance at ground zero brought a mob.

Worried parents were frantically searching for their children and too many weren't there to be found. Other people's homes, cars and even businesses were gone. Several unfortunates had lost their homes, possessions and kids in the blink of an eye. One woman was so hysterical that a doctor had to sedate her.

The police were at a loss as for what to do. Without the guidance of the missing police chief, they made do on their own initiative. They tried to keep the crowd away from ground zero, but the area was blocks long.

Somewhere along the way, several people made calls to the FBI. These were decisions all of Sparta would soon regret.

It was less than two hours before the first FBI agents arrived in Sparta by helicopter. At first, they believed it to be a prank, but after several people made phone calls saying the same thing, they checked it out. When satellite surveillance revealed that part of an American town had indeed vanished from the face of the Earth, Sparta became the FBI's number one priority.

Sadly, the FBI's first order of business was not to mount a rescue, or even find out if such a thing was possible. No, the first thing was to put a lid on the entire situation in order to make sure the rest of the country and the world didn't find out what happened.

Within four hours, the president had declared martial law in Sparta, Pennsylvania.

The police chief had come out from the rock he had crawled under soon after the FBI first arrived. They had already made several preliminary interviews with the townspeople.

The chief approached the men in the dark suits.

"Are you Special Agent Robert Ficarro?" asked the chief. The man nodded. "I heard you were in charge of the investigation. Both my department and myself are at your disposal."

"That goes without saying. Agent Glass, take this man into custody," ordered Special Agent Ficarro.

"What? This is an outrage!" screamed the chief, as Agent Deborah Glass slipped handcuffs on his wrists.

"I agree. According to all the witnesses we've interviewed so far, this Asgar character claimed to have a deal with you and the mayor to hand over someone to him. You appear to be working in conjunction with the most powerful terrorist the United States has ever faced. That is an outrage. We're looking for the mayor now. Do you know where he is?" asked Ficarro.

"No."

"Is there anything you'd like to tell us now about this Asgar character now?"

"I want a lawyer," said the chief.

"Get used to wanting."

"I know my Miranda rights. You have to give me a lawyer if I ask for one."

"The president has declared martial law. All rights, Miranda or otherwise, are suspended until I say so. We've already set up road blocks. Nobody is leaving Sparta," said Ficarro.

"What about all the people who live here, but are outside of town?" asked the chief.

"They'll be taken into custody when they return and are being put into internment camps for the time being. We have already appropriated several motels for this purpose."

"You don't have the manpower to pull that off," said the chief.

"We will. Even as we speak, several army battalions are on their way here." Ficarro pointed to the sky as a pair of helicopters flew by. "Our airborne sentries are already on duty. There is now a 9 PM curfew in effect. Anyone caught on the streets after curfew will be subject to arrest. But enough about that. You were about to tell me everything you know about this Asgar."

"I was not," said the chief.

"That's your choice. However, remember we can use any interrogation techniques we like. You've already been asked nicely. Now I just have to decide do we go with beatings or truth serum drugs next," said Ficarro.

"You're joking, right?" asked the chief.

"Agent Glass, do I have a sense of humor?" asked Ficarro

"No, sir," replied Glass. Ficarro smiled, but there was no warmth in the expression.

"We've set up headquarters in the post office. Take him there for now," said Ficarro.

"Yes, sir," said Glass.

"But…" stammered the chief.

"If he speaks before I get there, shut him up. Hard," said Ficarro.

"Yes, sir."

CHAPTER 3

The people of Sparta were too upset to protest martial law too much. All of them were hoping the FBI would give them answers about what had happened and why. Answers would be worth the loss of some liberty, or so they thought.

Already the story of what had happened was changing and evolving from being told over and over. Many of those doing the telling were not even there when it happened, but were speaking as if what they were saying was gospel. Asgar was an alien in some versions and a mad scientist in others. Some said he was an evil wizard, which although not right, was closer to the truth. In several uglier versions, the children were already dead, killed by Asgar.

Days went by and there was no word. Phone lines were turned off. Jamming devices blocked everything from shortwave and CB radios to cellular phones, not to mention regular radio and TV broadcasts. Satellite dishes were only good as bird baths. Cable was shut down. There weren't any carrier pigeons, but if there were, they would probably have been confiscated. In short, Sparta had been cut off from the rest of the world.

The president used every government agency at his disposal to keep the situation in Sparta secret, not to mention the fact he had declared martial law, something not done since the Civil War. It was a constant battle, but so far nothing had leaked out.

From interviews with those that had been present at the event, the FBI believed the man witnesses identified as Asgar had somehow been responsible, but couldn't admit it publicly. If they did, parents nationwide would begin to worry about the safety of their children. With the government helpless to provide any guarantees, there could be riots and unrest. It would undermine confidence in the government of the United States, both at home and abroad. It was an unacceptable scenario.

However, now that the first step in the government's plan had been completed and the town and its people had been contained, it was time for stage two. Special Agent Ficarro's next job was to convince the people of Sparta that some natural disaster had befallen the town and the missing students. The plan was to blame a gas leak that incinerated the town so fast that very little was left behind. The fictional blast started at the school. Sadly, many of the students were incinerated along with the town. The blast spontaneously combusted everything that was non-animal in nature, sparingly what was alive. They had enough scientists who would give out enough techno babble to confuse anyone. The story should work, especially since all pets seem to have been left behind. Once the townspeople were convinced, the town would be opened up again and the cover story released to the press. There would be a period of national mourning for the allegedly deceased students.

Once the cover story was in force, the government could concentrate on tracking down and neutralizing the threat that Asgar posed to national security. Then, a rescue would be mounted for the missing children. If successful, a new cover story would have to be made, Special Agent Ficarro would worry about that when the time came.

Tonight he had agreed to meet with Andrew Shelly, who had been pestering and badgering for a chance to talk with him since the first day the FBI arrived. Another agent had interviewed Shelly about what he had seen. Ficarro had agreed to the meeting in order to test out the cover story. Shelly had been at ground zero and witnessed what Asgar had done first hand. It he could convince someone like Shelly, the cover story should work. If not, he would just change it until it did work.

Agent Deborah Glass led him into the FBI temporary headquarters.

"Mr. Shelly, I'm Special Agent Ficarro. What can I do for you?"

Andrew Shelly bit his tongue. He was not happy at being made to wait days for this appointment. He was not pleased with what the FBI and army troops had done to his town, but he had more important things on his mind. He shook Ficarro's hand.

"Thank you for seeing me. I was wondering what progress you had finding the missing children?" asked Andrew.

Ficarro paused, looked at Glass and sighed.

"I'm sorry, Mr. Shelly, but our investigation has lead us to believe that the missing children are… dead."

"You mean Asgar's killed them?"

"That's another thing. We found no evidence of some mythic Asgar. What we did fine was evidence of a gas main explosion."

"That's ridiculous."

"Why?" asked Ficarro.

"The school didn't use gas. It used oil," said Andrew, annoyed at either dealing with an incredibly stupid man or one who was lying to him. Ficarro did not seem to be stupid and the he wasn't. He was already altering the story so it worked.

"The gas pipes didn't go to the school itself, but they did pass underneath it."

"I saw what happened. It wasn't an explosion. It was some sort of light from a gem Asgar had," said Andrew.

"About this Asgar phenomenon. We've determined it was a mass hallucination brought on by the gas fumes."

"Are you trying to tell me that everyone in there had the same hallucination?"

"Yes. It's very common for people under stress to interpret something in the same way. The human brain is very funny that way," said Ficarro.

"Not half as funny as this story you're trying to sell me. If it was an explosion, why weren't we all killed?"

"Spontaneous human combustion. Where the survivors were positioned and what they were wearing may have protected them."

"What about the missing chuck of town?"

"The heat from the explosion vaporized it, but the moisture on the skin of the people and animals may have shielded them."

"So you are trying to tell me that the people who had the worst deodorants and were sweating survived?"

"Perhaps." Ficarro smiled enviously and wished he had thought of that idea. He would use it though.

"This is a load of crap. If this is just a gas explosion, why have you taken control of Sparta?"

"Simple. Because of the intensity and nature of the explosion, we have to determine if it was a terrorist attack. We also need to determine exactly how it happened, so we can make sure it doesn't happen again."

"Look, I'm not buying this, but I'll say I am if you want me to."

"Why would you do that?" asked Ficarro.

"I came here to ask for your help. I need to get my kids out of town."

"Why?"

"Asgar, my so-called hallucination, told us he would take all of our children at noon on their eleventh birthdays. My kids turn eleven next week. If I get them out of town, maybe Asgar won't be able to take them."

Ficarro sat and pondered for a moment. This was something he hadn't considered. If more kids started disappearing, the story would never hold. He would have to come up with a solution for that.

"Mr. Shelly, I doubt a hallucination is going to kidnap your children. I'm sorry, but I can't help you," said Ficarro.

"Thanks for nothing," said Andrew, storming out and slamming the door behind him.

"What do you want to do about Shelly?" asked Glass.

"Nothing right now. He said his kids' birthdays were next week. That morning, take him and the children into custody. That way if they do disappear, we'll be the only ones to see it. Also, draw up a list of the town children's birthdays and see how many are about to turn eleven. That way we'll have an idea of what we're dealing with."

"Yes, sir," said Glass.

CHAPTER 4

Andrew Shelly fumed as he walked home. Actually, it wasn't technically his home. His home was in the part of town that went over with the kids. So was his car and everything he owned. That was bad enough, but what was worse were the things he could not replace, especially the pictures of his late wife. She had been killed almost two years ago by a drunk driver. He still missed her.

Luckily, his brother, Bill, lived in the part of town that hadn't disappeared. Bill had taken him and the kids in. Bill was a bachelor and four people living in his two bedroom house was rather cramped, but it beat the tent city the army had erected in the town park for the other people who had been left homeless.

The curfew did not officially go into effect for half an hour, but the army patrols weren't taking any chances. Andrew Shelly was stopped and asked to state his business. Luckily, he still had the written appointment card from Special Agent Ficarro, so the patrol let him continue on.

When he got to his brother's house, he found three anxious faces awaiting him.

"Dad, how'd it go?" said Bobby.

"Are they going to let us out?" asked Tina.

"No," said their father simply.

"I wish there was something I could do, but the FBI has no use for lawyers in Sparta these days. Or for the law either," said Uncle Bill.

"Then we have no choice," said Andrew.

"What do you mean, Dad?" asked Bobby.

"We've got to escape from Sparta."

"Escape? How?" asked Tina.

"I have a plan. Bill, do you still have all that scuba gear?" asked Andrew.

"Yeah, but why?" asked Bill.

"The FBI and the army have the roads blocked and helicopters in the air to watch for people sneaking through the outlying farm fields, but they don't have submarines."

"You mean swim the Susquehanna River?" asked Tina.

"Exactly."

"Andrew, that's nuts. The river is too murky to see and the current is strong," said Bill.

"But they aren't expecting anyone to try it. They only have a couple of boats they commandeered from the locals and the helicopters only patrol it part of the time. We can do this."

"It's going to be dangerous," said Bill.

"More dangerous that letting Asgar take them away? It certainly isn't as dangerous as trying to run a roadblock. We'd be shot up before we even got close. But this isn't my decision alone. Tina, Bobby, what do you think?"

"I don't want to disappear," whispered Tina.

"Me neither," said Bobby. "And my birthday is first."

"I forget that even though you two are twins, you have different birthdays because Bobby was born before midnight and Tina after," said Bill.

"Right, so if we are going to disappear, I'm going to go first. I say we go for it," said Bobby.

"But you can only swim doing the doggie paddle," said Tina.

"So, I'll learn. Besides, we'll have air tanks so we won't be able to drown," said Bobby.

"Bobby, that's not true. Scuba diving is dangerous and you'll have to be very careful," said Bill. "I only have three oxygen tanks, so I won't be able to go with you. I'll have to start teaching all of you how to scuba right away. We'll have to train in the pool at night so the helicopter patrols don't see us practicing."

"We better start tonight. We only have four days left," said Andrew.

The time went fast. They spent most of the days sleeping and most of the nights learning how to handle themselves underwater. Bill insisted they use snorkels, because he had no way to refill the air tanks once they were empty.

Bobby was not quite as hopeless as Tina thought, but neither of them were experts. Andrew had scuba dived, but it had been years and he was rusty.

After the lessons, the two adults snuck out of the house, carrying one complete set of scuba gear. Under cover of darkness, the men snuck through back yards to avoid the army and police patrols, so they could stash the gear safely underneath a river dock that Bill owned. Then they would carefully make their way back and sleep until early afternoon.

It took three nights to get everything under the dock.

The easy part was done. The hard part would start soon.

CHAPTER 5

While the Shellys planned their escape, the kids who were taken to the Wildsidhe had to get used to living in a world much different than their own. For the children of Sparta, the Wildsidhe was no longer some imaginary place they had heard about in fairy tales and bedtime stories. For better or worse, it was now home. Each of them had to adjust to the fact that here magic worked and creatures out of myth and legends really existed. In just a short time, they had witnessed a giant chasing a dragon and befriended a tribe of pixies. The pixies were tiny winged people who lived near where the missing part of Sparta had appeared. They also learned that Asgar was not the only Fortesan. A Fortesan named Morna tried to kill them several times, including having the darkcats she controlled attack the kids. They had battled for their lives several times against the huge black tiger-like beasts. Justin Burns managed to rally the kids. Together they used their wits, along with whatever weapons they could find, and the cars that came over with them to drive off the darkcats.

Justin had come a long way from the ex-gang member whose parents had sent him to live with his grandmother in Sparta to keep him safe. Justin had smiled sadly several times at the irony of his situation. He would have been safer in the worst part of Boston than he was on the Wildsidhe, not to mention more comfortable. Because the part of Sparta that had come over had been mystically sliced out, they had no electricity or running water. They still had the pipes and wires, but were a long way from getting them back in working order. The kids still had a lot to learn.

One thing they had found out is that the people and creatures of the Wildsidhe had a weakness-iron. The more magic someone or something had, the more iron could hurt them. Cindy Hartman discovered that she had magic powers of her own when she messed up Asgar's spell and somehow caused part of the town to come along. Unfortunately, she couldn't control her magic and the only time she seemed able to use it was under times of stress. When Terri Burns, Justin's cousin and Cindy's friend, was about to be slashed by a darkcat, Cindy cast a spell that caused Terri's aluminum wheelchair to suddenly fly into the sky. Terri returned the favor by helping to rescue Cindy. Terri and her wheelchair have had the power to fly ever since, at least together. Terry had tried it by herself unsuccessfully and had let her friends try to fly her wheelchair but none of them got off the ground.

It wasn't all soaring over buildings in a single swoop. Flying exhausts Terri like running would most other people. Carrying weight or other people tires her even faster, but it was one of their biggest advantages.

For the next killing attempt, Morna used a Changeling Lord, a Wildsidher that had the power to change his shape, to lay a trap. The changeling took the shape of Principal Greene and told them she had found a way to get them back home. Justin saw through the trap, but it was too late. Two bullies, Todd Wilson and Ken Holt, were willing to sacrifice themselves to save the others, including their siblings.

The hero who saved the day was a real surprise. Asgar came to the rescue. Years of animosity between him and Morna were enough to have him fight the Changeling Lord. Asgar managed to save Ken, but it was too late for Todd. The bully had died a hero.

Asgar felt that Todd and Ken had performed a service for him, and the Fortesan granted Ken the right to go home. Ken tried to bring his brother, but Asgar would not allow it. He had just revealed that at eighteen they would all get a chance to go home. He failed to tell them that more kids would be coming.

The Fortesan ordered Ken to pick up Todd's still body and then waved his hand. Ken and Todd disappeared. Asgar told them the remaining kids he would be back and left.

It was night when Ken reappeared back in Sparta, holding Todd's body. He was on the edge of the barren earth left behind when the town was taken.

Ken was thankful to be home. He would have to find his mom and dad and let them know that his brother Gary was all right. Then he was going to have to find Todd's folks and tell them about their son.

Ken walked to where the pavement started again. He was surprised at how deserted Grand Avenue was. There wasn't a soul in sight.

Five dark black sedans suddenly sped around the corner, tires screeching. They stopped ten feet in front of Ken. Men in dark suits jumped out of the cars. Most of them were wearing black sunglasses, despite it being nighttime.

Ken was more curious than anything, until they pulled out their guns and pointed them at him.

"Freeze, FBI. Keep your hands where we can see them. Put the body down slowly," ordered one of the men in suits. Ken gently put him down. The man threw him against the car and handcuffed his hands behind his back.

"Who are you, mister?" asked Special Agent Ficarro.

"Ken Holt."

Agent Glass stepped closer. "Sir, he's one of the missing students."

"He is, is he? Well Mr. Holt, maybe you'd care to tell us where you've been all this time?"

Ken did. Ficarro rewarded him by placing him in "protective" custody, because Ken's tale would blow the FBI's cover story.

"What do we do with Todd Wilson's body?" asked Glass.

"We can say we found it in the ruins of the school and use it to back up the gas main explosion story. This proves that there is travel between this Wildsidhe place Holt was and here. Better bring the Shellys into protective custody a few hours early to be on the safe side," ordered Ficarro.

Glass took out a special FBI issue hand radio that was specially designed to work within the jamming field that engulfed Sparta and relayed the orders to agents in the field. A few minutes later they radioed back.

"Sir, agents at the home of Bill Shelly report that the house is empty," said Glass.

"Tomorrow is the boy's birthday. Blast, they must be trying to get out of the town. Alert the patrols. I want the Shelly's taken into custody immediately," said Ficarro.

"What if they resist?"

"I prefer they be taken into custody alive, but they cannot be allowed to leave this town under any circumstances."

"But, sir, these people aren't criminals. The father and uncle are just trying to save the kids. Perhaps we can issue the patrols TASERs. The electric shock would knock them out, without any permanent damage," said Glass.

"The TASER's are a good idea, but they must not be allowed to leave Sparta. That is our first priority. Have I made myself clear?"

"Yes, sir."

The Shellys were huddled behind some bushes as the helicopter and its searchlights passed overhead.

"That's the second one in fifteen minutes," said Andrew.

"Something's up. They must know we're gone," said Bill.

"How?" asked Bobby.

"I don't know," said his father.

"Dad, look," said Tina, pointing to an army jeep. It was about two blocks away, aiming a searchlight at houses as it drove by.

"If they stop by the docks, we're done for," said Andrew.

"My dock is less than a block away. I'm not going with you anyway, so you guys keep going. I'll distract the army guys," said Bill.

"Bill, are you nuts? They have guns. If they see you running, they'll shoot you," said Andrew.

"Then I'll just have to turn you guys in," said Bill.

"What?" said Bobby.

"Not for real. I'll say I was out here trying to stop you guys, but you wouldn't listen and kept going. I'll cut them a deal. If they promise not to hurt any of you, I'll tell them where you went on your bicycles," said Bill.

"But we're not on bicycles," said Tina.

"Exactly," said Bill, smiling.

"I get it," said Tina.

"Good thing it wasn't complicated," said Bobby. Tina elbowed him in his ribs.

"Stop it you two. Bill, are you sure about this?" said Andrew.

"Deals are a lawyer's life. I can handle these civil servants. Besides, the important part is to get my favorite niece and nephew to safety."

"We're your only niece and nephew," said Tina. Bill pulled her and Bobby close in a hug.

"Even if you guys weren't, you'd still be my favorites. Be careful and listen to your dad, okay?" They nodded. "I love you guys. Now get out of here."

"We love you too, Uncle Bill," said Tina.

"What she said," said Bobby.

"Thanks, little brother," said Andrew, as he hugged his brother for what might be the last time. "I love you, too."

"Ditto, big brother. Now, enough of the mushy stuff. Get going," said Uncle Bill. He waited until they had cut through the next backyard, before he stood and walked into the middle of the street.

Bill moved very slowly, with his hands over his head.

It did not take the army patrol more than two seconds to notice him.

"You there. Keep your hands over your head and don't move," shouted a sergeant, pointing a rifle with a laser sight aimed at him. The little red dot was in the middle of his forehead.

A couple of privates, side-arms drawn, approached him, put him in handcuffs, then brought him to the sergeant.

"You are in violation of curfew and are being taken into custody…"

"That's great, but we're wasting time. I think you better call Special Agent Ficarro and tell him Bill Shelly has a deal for him that he can't refuse."

CHAPTER 6

Tina, Bobby, and their dad got to the dock unnoticed. They immediately stripped off the sweat suits and sneakers they were wearing and stashed them in the small overnight bags each of them carried. The bags weren't waterproof, but they had packed clothes and other necessities in plastic zip lock bags, which hopefully were waterproof. They were already wearing their wetsuits. The three of them slipped quietly into the water and swam under the dock, so nobody on the streets or in the air would see them. Each of them pulled on the hood of their wetsuit, then their flippers. Andrew helped his kids get their tanks strapped on, before putting on his own. It was a challenge to get dressed in the water, but they had practiced enough in Bill's pool that they were able to do it. They then put the shoulder straps of their bags diagonally across their chests so the bags were snug against their chests. It made swimming a bit awkward, but not as much as trying to go on the lam in a wetsuit.

Andrew Shelly attached a piece of clothesline from him to each of his kids, so they would not get separated. Back at the house, he had fastened a pocket knife to each of their wrists so they could cut the rope if it got caught on anything, but that risk was less than the risk of them getting spilt up. The rope also gave them a way to communicate underwater. Two tugs meant dive, three meant surface.

"You guys ready?"

"Yes," said Tina.

"Yep," said Bobby.

"Remember, we have to be careful. We won't be able to see much, especially underwater, so we'll swim near the surface. If anyone sees a boat or a helicopter, give the signal and we dive. Once we start, we can't risk talking. At night, our voices will carry and could give us away," said Andrew.

"We know, Dad. We've been over this a thousand times," said Tina.

"Yeah, but this time's for real," said Andrew Shelly.

"Let's do it," said Bobby.

"Wait. Before Mom died, she'd always say a prayer before we were going to do something hard. Maybe we should say one," suggested Tina. Her father nodded.

"God, please protect all of us and lead us to safety," said Andrew.

"Amen," said the twins in unison. Andrew turned on the twins air tanks and Tina returned the favor to him. They put on their face masks.

"Let's go," said Andrew Shelly. The three of them slipped their mouthpieces in.

Andrew was the first to swim out from the safety of the underside of the dock. The twins followed. Only their heads, above the nose, stuck out of the water.

They swam the first hundred feet with all of them expecting a hidden soldier to jump out and scream "Halt!" It didn't happen and the first hundred feet became two, then three hundred feet. They reached the middle of the river and let the current carry them along, letting them conserve their energy.

The river carried them along swiftly and miles started passing by. It wasn't easy. They still had to swim enough to keep facing forward and occasionally fight to keep their eyes above water so they could see where they were going. There was real danger. Without the scuba gear, they would have probably drowned.

They traveled downstream past several towns. Tina was amazed that their luck was holding so well. They hadn't even seen anyone in a boat. The FBI quarantine had virtually eliminated all other river traffic. There weren't even many cars on the bridges they passed under.

Just then, something floated by her head. Nervous and paranoid about being found out, she thought an alligator had somehow snuck up behind them. It was purely a gut reaction, unaffected by the logic that there was probably not a wild alligator anywhere in the state of Pennsylvania. It only lasted a spilt second, but it was long enough for Tina let out a little scream. Her mouthpiece was still in place and that was underwater, so the noise was covered up by the sounds of the river. Too late, she realized it was a small log and it was headed for her father. She started to tug on the clothesline, but before the second pull could tell him to dive, the log hit her father in the back of the head.

The blow wasn't enough to render him unconscious, but it did knock him for a loop. It dazed him enough that he couldn't swim on his own. His body turned around and the current started to pull him under.

Tina could not tell if his mouthpiece was still in place. If it wasn't, her father would drown. Bobby had his eyes focused on his side of the river, on the lookout for trouble, so he hadn't realized what had happened yet, so it was up to her. Straining against the current, she sped to her father. By ducking her head under the water, she was able to see well enough to tell that the mouthpiece was still in place. She grabbed him under the shoulder and did her best to pull him along with the current, but it was much harder that swimming along. She needed her brother's help. She pulled on the rope that attached her father and brother. Bobby misunderstood and went under the water.

Tina pulled three times to make him surface. He did, and stared at her. She motioned for him to come closer, but he didn't understand. Tina switched to her father's other shoulder and reached out to grab her brother. She got the zipper of the clothes bag that was strapped around his front instead. Tina yanked and instead of pulling Bobby closer, she opened his bag. Clothes in plastic bags started floating with the current. Since they were smaller and lighter, they moved faster than Bobby. It took him a second to realize his wardrobe was floating away and by then it was too late for him to do anything, except make helpless grabs at empty water. He zippered the bag shut and turned his attention on his sister. It was only then that he noticed his father was hurt.

He looked at Tina, who gestured with her hand that something had hit their father in the back of the head. She motioned for Bobby to grab hold of their father's other shoulder and he understood.

He pointed downstream, then at the shore. It was a question. Even with two of them pulling, swimming while carrying their father along was hard work. Not to mention, they didn't know how badly he was hurt. They wanted to get further down river, but getting to shore seemed like the safer option.

Tina pointed to shore. Bobby nodded and they made their way to the bank on the opposite side of the river from where they started. It took a while and as they kept flowing with the current, Tina noticed several empty docks. It looked like a group of vacation cabins. Since it wasn't summer yet, or even spring break, there was a chance the cabins were deserted. It seemed as good a place as any to go ashore. She pointed to Bobby and they swam even harder. When they finally reached dry land, they were exhausted.

Ignoring the dock, they went straight to shore. They pulled their Dad onto land, but he was much heavier out of the water. They got the tank, mask, and mouthpiece off him as quickly as possible.

"Dad, are you all right?" said Bobby, much too loudly.

"Bobby, be quiet," scolded his sister, but in a whisper.

"Oops," said Bobby, embarrassed.

"Dad?" whispered Tina.

Their father slowly opened his eyes.

"What happened?" he asked, still groggy.

"A log hit you in the back of the head," said Tina. Her father rubbed the knot the driftwood had left and winced at the pain.

"Feels like it was a truck. How'd I get here?"

"We swam you," whispered Bobby.

"The two of you worked together, without killing each other? I'm impressed," joked Andrew.

"We don't always fight," said Tina.

"No, sometimes you sleep. Just kidding. You guys did great. Thanks."

"Our pleasure," said Bobby.

"Are you okay?" asked Tina.

"I'm no doctor, but other than a full sized headache, I think I'll be fine."

"You might have a concussion. You'll have to stay awake for twenty four hours just to be on the safe side," said Bobby.

"I wasn't planning to sleep anytime soon," said Andrew.

"Wait a second. How do you know anything about concussions?" asked Tina.

"I read it," said Bobby.

"Since when do you read anything you don't have to?" asked Tina.

"It was in a comic book. The Night Avenger got one after fighting the Jester and he had to stay awake. He also had hallucinations and flashbacks, but I think that was just a way for them to tell what had happened in previous issues," said Bobby.

"If I start having flashbacks, I'll let you know. I don't see any lights, so there probably isn't anyone around, but we need to be sure. We need to see if there's anyone in those cabins. Bobby, think you can handle it?"

"Sure. Just call me the Night Avenger."

"If anyone catches you, just tell them you're playing a game of hide and seek, okay?" said Andrew.

"Got it."

"You better change first. The wetsuit will make people suspicious," said Andrew.

Bobby opened his bag, then remembered what had happened in the river.

"Tina pulled open my bag and my clothes fell out. They floated away," said Bobby.

"I was trying to get your attention to help me with Dad," said Tina, defending herself.

"Do you have anything left?" asked Andrew.

"Just my sneakers," said Bobby.

"Tina, you packed sweatpants and t-shirts, right? Give one of each to your brother," said Andrew.

"I'm not going to dress in my sister's clothes," whined Bobby.

"My stuff is too big for you. You and your sister are about the same size. Her clothes will fit you," said Andrew.

"Fine. Give me your blue sweats," said Bobby.

"I didn't bring them," said Tina.

"The green ones?"

"Nope."

"Which ones do you have?"

"I only brought one. The Heart Throb Boys one," said Tina.

"Oh no. The pink ones with the hearts on the legs?"

"The hearts are only on one leg."

"I ain't wearing that."

"Bobby…" interjected Andrew.

"Dad, I'll look like a wuss."

"Put them on," said Andrew. His tome left no room for argument.

"Fine. Do you at least have a decent t-shirt?"

"I have the Heart Throb Boys Philadelphia concert t-shirt. Or the one from their *Heart Throb Street* album and their second album *The Boys are Back.*"

"Do you have anything without those wimps on it?"

"I have one from their greatest hits album."

"They only had two other albums. How could they have a greatest hits album?" asked Bobby.

"They had three other albums. You forgot *A Heart Throb Christmas,*" said Tina, holding up all four. They had been among her choices of what to bring. Bobby had offered his opinion-that it was a dumb choice because they hadn't brought a CD player. Tina hadn't cared.

"How could I forget? You played it every single day between Thanksgiving and Valentine's Day. Don't you have anything else?"

"Nope."

"I don't believe this. Give me the *Boys are Back* one. At least it's black," said Bobby. "Hey, what am I going to do about underwear?"

Tina pulled out a baggie with a handful of briefs in, with various heart shaped logos on them. "Take your pick."

"No way. I'll do without."

"Whatever," said Tina, smiling.

"Hey, turn around so I can get dressed," said Bobby.

"You don't have anything I haven't seen before," said Tina.

"Excuse me? You're not even allowed to date young lady," said Andrew, barely hiding a grin.

"Dad, please. I meant we used to take baths together," said Tina.

"When we were in diapers. We don't wear diapers anymore," said Bobby.

"Some of us apparently aren't wearing underwear anymore either," said Tina.

"Tina…" said Andrew.

"Dad, I'm only yanking his chain," said Tina.

"I know, but turn around and give your brother some privacy."

"Like I want to see Bobby naked. The thought makes me sick," said Tina.

"I thought just looking at your face in the mirror was enough to do that. Looking at your face sure makes me sick," said Bobby.

"Both of you stop it. Bobby, change, check, and get back," said Andrew.

Bobby did as he was told. He went and checked out all the cabins, then came back. His father and sister had already changed.

"Nobody's around," reported Bobby.

"Good. We need to hide the scuba gear. That looks like a shed. Let's see if we can find some shovels and we'll bury the stuff, then get moving."

Chapter 7

It was almost eleven thirty in the morning when they got to a motel. It was on the rundown side, but it did not seem like the kind of place where people asked a lot of questions. That was more of a priority than curtains made in the last decade. Andrew checked in, using a fake driver's license that his brother Bill had used in college for sneaking into bars. He paid in cash.

Bobby spent most of his time hiding under the staircase by the soda machines, so nobody would see his pink-and-black Heart Throb Boys ensemble. As soon as his father got back with a room key, Bobby was trying to get him to open the door. He was even aggravated that his father stopped to buy some soda. When the motel room door was finally opened, Bobby was the first one in.

"We'll rest here for a few hours," said Andrew.

"Dad, you're not supposed to sleep yet. Remember, you might have a concussion," said Bobby.

"I'm still not planning on sleeping anytime soon. I got the local paper from the front desk. I'm going to find a cheap used car so we can move faster."

"What are we going to do for license plates?" asked Bobby.

"Remember the convertible your Uncle's been working on for years?"

"The one he never got to run?" asked Tina.

"That's the one. It's in his garage on blocks, but he registered it in hopes he would someday get it to move without a tow truck. I got the plates here," said Andrew, reaching into his bag and pulling them out.

"Bobby, what time is it?" asked Andrew. Bobby was the only one who had brought a watch. His was waterproof.

"12:04. Why?" asked Bobby. His father smiled at him. "Holy…" Bobby finished the phrase, and his father glared at him. "Sorry, I didn't mean to curse, it's just that it's past noon and I'm still here."

"I think under the circumstances, we can overlook it this once," said Andrew, picking up his kids in his arms and swinging them around. "We did it! This deserves a toast."

"Beer?" said Bobby hopefully. After all, he had gotten away with cursing.

"Sure."

"Really?" asked Bobby, not believing his ears.

"Sure. What kind of beer—birch or root?" asked Andrew, snickering and holding up the soda cans.

"Real funny. Gimme the root beer," said Bobby.

"That leaves birch beer for my princess," said Andrew, giving Tina a can.

Everyone popped their tops and raised their cans.

"A toast to the safety of my two children and to my family's freedom," said Andrew. The three of them clinked cans and took sips.

A second later, a soft glow enveloped Bobby and he started to fade.

"Bobby!" screamed his father, rushing forward to try to grab his son. He was too late. The pop can fell, spilling soda onto the motel rug.

Bobby was gone.

"Dad, what happened? Where'd he go?" said a frantic Tina.

"I don't know. It was after twelve noon."

"Bobby always set his watch a few minutes fast because he was always late. How do we get him back?" asked Tina.

Her father looked at her, tears streaking down his face, unable to speak.

"You mean it doesn't matter if we're in town or not? Asgar can still get us?"

Her father nodded.

"But that means on my birthday tomorrow, I'll… disappear too."

"I'm sorry, baby. I don't know what to do…"

Andrew pulled his daughter into his arms. Together they cried, each trying to comfort each other, but their terror only grew.

CHAPTER 8

The light temporarily blinded Bobby, so when his sight returned he was shocked to see that the motel room with his father and sister had vanished. Instead, he was standing in the missing section of Sparta, in front of the clock tower that sat atop town hall. It was bonging the last of the twelve beats of the noon hour.

He looked at his wrist.

"Stupid watch! What am I going to do?" asked Bobby out loud. Nobody answered him, but he did hear voices on the next block, past the Flagship Diner. He went to investigate.

A group of kids were carrying mattresses and box springs out of a house and loading them on the back of a pickup truck.

Bobby recognized one of the kids, Ron Wang. He was standing on top of the cab of the truck, with a compound bow. He looked like he was watching for something. He was. Although Bobby had no way of knowing it, the kids who had vanished the first day had more to worry about than just Asgar. Darkcats and Morna, the queen of the Fortesans, for instance. Ron had fought them before and was in charge of getting this group of kids safely back to the school compound.

Bobby knew one of the others, Brina Wilson. The two of them hadn't exactly been friends, but they had been in the same class, before the older kids had vanished.

Ron noticed him before the others.

"Hey, you! What are you doing out here by yourself? You know Justin's rules—nobody leaves the school alone. You want to be darkcat chow?" asked Ron.

"I don't know what you're taking about. I just got here," said Bobby.

"What do you mean you just got here?" asked Ron.

"Part of Asgar's curse makes any kids born in Sparta vanish on noon of their eleventh birthday. Where is here, anyway?" said Bobby.

"You don't know that you're on the Wildsidhe? Where have you been?" asked Ron.

"I told you, I just got here. Wildsidhe? You mean the magic land with dwarves, elves, and dragons? You gotta be kidding me."

"What's your name?"

"I'm Bobby Shelly. My dad was the janitor at the school."

"How do I know you're who you're who you say you are?" asked Ron.

"Brina knows me. Hey, Brina," said Bobby.

"Hey, Bobby," said Brina, who had just laid her half of a mattress on the truck flatbed. He looked again and snickered. "Love the outfit."

"Brina, you know this guy?" asked Ron.

"Sure, I know Bobby. He's got a twin sister Tina. We all were in Mrs. Popus's class," said Brina. A second later, her eyes got real wide. "Bobby and Tina didn't come over with us."

"Everyone in the truck," screamed Ron.

"What's going on?" asked Bobby, as he took a step forward. Ron pointed the bow at his chest and pulled the arrow back. "Hey, watch it! You might shoot me."

"That's the idea, Changeling. The tip's steel and I'm pretty sure it'll kill you. If you want to find out for sure, take another step," said Ron. "Miko, move it!"

"What's the hurry?" said Miko, stepping out of the house. Bobby recognized her as Ron's sister.

"Changeling," said Ron, pointing at Bobby.

Miko pulled out a sword and pointed it at him.

"Be careful. That thing looks sharp," said Bobby.

"It is sharp, Changeling. Now back away slowly," said Miko.

"If you are trying to be a Samurai, it's working," said Bobby, putting his hands over his head.

"My great, great grandparents came from China, not Japan," said Miko.

"Whatever. Look, you guys know me. I'm not a Changeling, whatever that is," said Bobby.

"Nice try. The last one of your kind pretended to be Principal Greene," said Ron.

"And killed my brother!" screamed Brina.

"Todd's dead? I'm sorry."

"Save it, murderer," said Brina.

"Brina, you know me. We might not have always gotten along, but you know I never killed anyone. And I know Principal Greene is still back home. She broke her ankle when the school disappeared," said Bobby.

"No more talking. It's just trying to trick us. Hold on, I'll get us out of here," said Miko, opening up the pickup's cab. She hopped in, started the engine and sped off toward the school. Ron keep the bow trained on him until they were out of sight.

"What the heck is going on?" said Bobby. No one answered, so with no other options he turned and walked toward the school.

CHAPTER 9

The pickup truck sped up to the front gate of the school, honking the horn.

"Wayne, open the gate!" screamed Ron.

Early on, the kids had hot-wired and moved all the cars from their own little chunk of Sparta inside the school compound. Most were in what was the teachers' parking lot.

The front gate, and the fence surrounding the rest of the school, had been fortified under Wayne's supervision. Some of the older cars had been stripped down and the parts, as well as whole cars and other assorted iron and steel objects, were used to build up the fence. Small platforms and parts of the bleachers were put up to serve as watchtowers around the fence line. Wayne had organized security patrols to keep watch and Justin had instituted a policy to insure that everyone pitched in.

The speeding and honking truck had Wayne worried, as he stood in the watchtower at the front gate of the school. There didn't seem to be anything chasing them, but because of Changelings, he instituted a safety precaution before anyone was let in. Nobody got in without the password, which changed every day.

"Password," Wayne said.

"Quarterback," said Ron. Wayne, a super-jock, picked the passwords.

It was the right one, so Wayne yelled for the gate to be opened. With the fortifications, it was the only way in or out, but because of all the metal weighing it down, it took a while to open, even with the wheel rollers.

As soon as they were safely inside, Wayne ordered the gate closed, then climbed down from the tower.

"What's going on?" Wayne asked. "Darkcats?"

"Worse. A Changeling," said Ron.

"What? Are you sure?" Wayne said.

"I think so. You made a list of all the kids who crossed over, right?" said Ron.

"Yes. I think it has everyone, even the ones who left town and disappeared," Wayne said.

"Was Bobby Shelly on it?"

"I'll check, but I don't think so. Why would a Changeling impersonate one of us who isn't even here?" asked Wayne.

"Who knows? The last one pretended to be Principal Greene. Maybe they figured we'd be fooled easier by a kid disguise. He fed us some story about kids coming over on their eleventh birthday," said Ron.

"Besides, he screwed up. Bobby has a twin sister. If that was true, where's she?' asked Miko.

"Actually, they have different birthdays. I went to Tina's party last year, and I remember them saying that Bobby was born before midnight and she was born after," said Brina.

"So if his sister shows up tomorrow, he's telling the truth," said Miko.

"Unless it's another Changeling," suggested Ron.

"How are we going to know for sure?" asked Brina.

"I don't know," Wayne said.

"What don't you know, handsome?" asked Marianne Blossum, walking up to the crowd. Actually, she didn't so much walk as wiggle. Marianne had always looked kind of ordinary, until recently. Now every boy in the school was practically drooling over her. Nobody had figured out what exactly had changed, and with everything else that had happened, no one wasted much time trying to figure out the answer.

Of course, Marianne wasn't about to tell them about the magic ring that made her beautiful or that she had got it from Morna.

Wayne wondered about the sudden change, but was so thrilled that she seemed to like him that he didn't waste much time thinking about it. They had been paying a lot of attention to each other lately and he was very happy about it.

"We may have a Changeling in town," Wayne said.

"How horrible," said Marianne, putting a hand over her mouth to help make her point. Then she switched gears. "Does this mean I… I mean we, won't be getting our beds by tonight?"

They had steadily been raiding the town for things they needed and the latest item on the list was beds. Sleeping on the floors of classrooms had gotten very uncomfortable and raiding houses for beds seemed the best solution.

"If there is a chance there *is* a Changeling out there, I'm not sending anyone back into town. It's too dangerous. Luckily, the other teams already came back for lunch, so there isn't anyone else in town. Right now, everyone is confined to the school," Wayne said.

"Speaking of lunch, I brought this out for you," said Marianne, handing him a plastic grocery bag, filled with food. The plastic bags were constantly being recycled and reused. After all, they weren't going to be getting any more any time soon.

They were using the food sparingly. Without freezers, all the bread had gone stale and so had much of the frozen food. The school had a large stock of gallon-sized canned goods and they had cleaned out the supermarket that had come over with them. As they raided the houses for bedding, they were also piling up canned goods inside the front doors, for pick up later.

"Thanks," Wayne said, opening the bag and looking in. It had fruits and berries, which grew in abundance in the fields and woods just outside the town. They had made friends with a gaggle of pixies, who had shown them what was edible and what wasn't. One of them, named Lissy, had been especially helpful.

Some of the pixies had taken up residence in one of the houses near where the town ended. They had gathered brightly colored objects and decorated the place like a neon nightmare, but they liked it. The pixies were also helping to guard their crops by scaring away birds, insects, and other scavengers. Originally the pixies had almost wiped out their crops before the seeds were even covered over in the ground. Pixies have to eat several times their own body weight each day, and figured the seeds were fair game. The kids made a treaty with the pixies. In exchange for their help, the pixies would get two things. A share of the harvested crops and music. The pixies were music junkies and enough of the kids played instruments, or sang, to keep them very happy.

Lissy was the only pixie who spent any length of time inside the school compound. The rest of the pixies were too afraid of all the iron and steel to stay long.

Wayne's lunch also included some jerky the Bearclaw brothers had made from the meat from the local freezers before it went bad. The jerky was filling, but everyone was getting sick of it. Wayne hadn't felt comfortable to let a hunting party go out yet, although Lissy had offered to be their guide and the Bearclaws had hunted with bows back home on their grandfather's reservation. The Bearclaws were looking forward to getting the okay.

Fortunately, there was enough variety among the native and canned foods to kept menus interesting. Plus Carmen's brother Carlos was a wiz in the kitchen, making dinner unusually enjoyable. It was amazing what he could cook, even with school food.

When Wayne looked up from his lunch, Marianne leaned over and whispered in his ear.

"Do you think you could get me one of the beds that were already brought in?" she asked.

Wayne's first reaction was to say they would have to be divided up fairly, but then Marianne smiled at him and suddenly he just couldn't say no to her.

"I'll see what I can do," Wayne said.

"Great. Thanks, sweetie. I'll see you later," said Marianne, leaning in to give him a slow kiss on the lips.

"Okay," Wayne said, a goofy smile on his face.

Marianne strolled away.

"Sweetie?" said Miko, in a teasing tone. "I take it things are going pretty well between you and Marianne."

"Oh yeah, you could say that," Wayne said, unable to stop grinning.

"You in love, man?" asked Ron.

"I'm in something," Wayne said.

"Good for you, but we still have this Changeling thing to worry about," said Ron.

"Wayne, someone's coming," shouted someone from the tower. Wayne motioned for Ron, Miko, and Brina to follow him up the tower ladder.

"Is that him?" asked Wayne.

"Yep," said Ron.

"Brina, you knew Bobby. Could this be him?" asked Wayne.

"Maybe. It looks and sounds like him, but I can't be sure," said Brina.

"Is there anything that only the two of you would know?" Wayne said.

"Not really. We weren't that close," said Brina.

Bobby walked up to the gate.

"Hello, up there. Are you going to let me in?" said Bobby.

"No," Wayne said.

"If you don't, I'll huff and I'll puff and blow your house in," said Bobby.

"It definitely sounds like Bobby," said Brina. "He was our class clown."

"What's with the armored fence? To keep people out of school? Maybe they should have tried that to keep us in school. Look, I'm a kid, not some shape changing monster. I got sent here the same as all of you, just a little later. How can I prove it to you?"

"The pixies could smell darkcats coming. And they warned us about the fake Principal Greene, although we didn't understand their warning in time. Maybe they could smell him?" suggested Miko.

"That might work. Somebody go get Lissy," Wayne said.

The pixie had been with Cindy. Cindy had saved Lissy's life and the pixie had adapted the girl as her friend, following her almost everywhere. The pair came running.

"What's up?" asked Cindy. Wayne explained.

"I thought maybe Lissy could be able to tell if this guy is really a kid or a Changeling. Unless you can come up with a way for you to tell," Wayne said.

"You know I have no idea how I managed to use magic," Cindy said. Wayne nodded.

"How about it, Lissy? Can you smell a Changeling?" asked Wayne.

"Lissy know Changeling smell. Changelings smell stinky, but when shifty shape, they mimic smell as well as form. Last time, Changeling Lord shifted nearby. Still, Lissy try for biggie friends Cindy and Wayne," said the pixie.

Her wings humming like a dragonfly, Lissy fluttered down to Bobby's head. She began sniffing at his hair.

"Hey! Watch it!" said Bobby, swatting at the pixie.

"You watch it, biggie. You almost hit me," said Lissy, then she flew back up to the tower, careful not to touch any iron or steel.

"Well?" asked Wayne.

"Can't tell. Smells human, but also smells like dirty river and rubber," said Lissy.

"I told you I had to use scuba gear to get out of town," screamed Bobby from below.

"He did," said Ron.

"Well? Am I coming in or not?" asked Bobby.

"I don't know who you are and until I do I can't let you in," Wayne said. He knew from earlier experience that iron wouldn't hurt a Changeling in human form. A moment later he got an idea. "Asgar told us Changelings can only hold their shape for about a day. How about you let us lock you in a steel locker for a day and a half? If you really are who you say you are, you'll still be human."

"Spend a day and a half stuffed in a locker? Are you nuts? After shoving me into a locker, are you going to steal my lunch money next? Listen, I had to sneak by the freaking FBI and the army and I still got sent here. I don't need this. I'm going to my house. Brina knows where it is if you people change your minds. I saw you stealing stuff from houses. You better not have taken anything from my house…"

"We didn't get to your block yet, Bobby," said Brina. Wayne turned and glared at her. "What? He sounds like Bobby. He might be Bobby."

"I know. Look, Bobby or whoever you are, stay at your house tonight. Lock the door, don't let anyone in. Tomorrow, we'll figure something out," Wayne said.

"Whatever. I'm outa here," said Bobby. Disgusted, he turned and walked away, alone and rejected.

"Wayne, I feel so bad. Did we do the right thing," said Brina.

"We did the only thing we could," Wayne said.

Bobby found the spare key to his house over the back door jam and went inside. Everything was as he remembered it, except the garbage stank and the food in the fridge had all gone bad. He threw out the garbage and decided not to bother opening the fridge again.

Bobby sat down in front of the TV and hit the remote's on button before he realized there was no power or TV signal to watch. Video games were out too. Wayne and Brina sounded serious when they said there was danger outside. He was too tired to deal with it, so he got up to go in his bedroom. He looked up on the living room mantle and stopped short. Staring him in the face was a picture of his parents, taken a couple of months before his mother had died.

He took the picture down and carried it with him into his room. Bobby curled up on his bed and held the picture close. There was nobody to show off to or be a clown for. Bobby was alone. Looking at the picture of his parents, whom he would never see again, his tears stained the glass and Bobby cried himself to sleep.

CHAPTER 10

Everyone worked. That was the rule. Survival didn't come easy. What one person did affected the other three hundred. Because of that, if somebody didn't work, they didn't eat. That was Justin's rule. At first, it seemed harsh, but not for long. The kids were in a hostile place and the only people they could count on were themselves. There was nobody else to do things for them, so there was little choice. There were none of the comforts of home—no electricity, no place to buy food or clothes, no indoor plumbing. That was the worst. None of them had really appreciated it until they didn't have it anymore. They had found porta-potties and installed most of them outside, but inside the fence line. There was one kept in the basement for the nighttime, when everyone came inside and the school locked down, to keep the things that went bump in the night outside.

Marianne Blossum was on guard duty. Since she was dating Wayne, who was in charge of security, she figured she would get out of doing her watch. Neither Wayne nor Justin played like that. Justin had made sure the unpleasant jobs, especially emptying the porta-potties, were rotated among everyone, himself included. Each of them pulled night watch, same as everyone else. The chore was rotated, so no one had to do it too often. Marianne was still upset she had to do it at all. Usually, a pout was all she needed to wrap Wayne around her finger, but on this he wouldn't budge.

Marianne would make him pay for it tomorrow. Tonight she was in charge of the side door. It seemed stupid. It was made of steel and it was locked. Nobody was coming in, whether or not she was here. Night watch was a waste of her time. She had complained to her sister Jane, but even she sided with Wayne.

Marianne, came a voice inside her head.

"Who said that?" she answered, looking around.

Have you forgotten already the one who gave you your heart's desire?

"Morna?" she said, talking to the air.

Excuse me?

"I'm sorry. Queen Morna. Of course I haven't forgotten you. Thanks to you, I'm beautiful."

The glamour was a simple spell, but one you promised me favors in exchange for. I have come for the first of these favors.

"Where are you?" asked Marianne, still looking around.

I'm outside.

"How can I hear you then?"

By accepting my gift, a bond was formed between us. I can now enter your mind.

"Oh," said Marianne, clearly not thrilled by the idea.

Come to me.

"But I'm not allowed to open to the door."

Rules are not for such as we. However, if you do not want to hold up your end of the bargain, I can take back my gift and you can go back to the sad little thing you were before.

"No!" shouted Marianne before she could stop herself. Marianne had not been beautiful before she came to the Wildsidhe, but she had not been ugly. She was average, which in Marianne's mind was the same as ugly. She tried to get in with the popular kids, but it hadn't made her popular. Morna's gift of the red ring had. Instantly. The boys looked at her differently now, like she was somebody.

On the Wildsidhe, Justin Burns had become their leader and therefore the most popular boy. He never gave her a second look. The poor child was in love with Cindy, but that was okay. She liked Wayne better. He was bigger, stronger, and as the head of security, probably the second most popular boy. Wayne not only gave her a second look, but a third and fourth.

She wasn't going to give up Wayne or her popularity.

"I'll be outside in a minute," she said, looking around. There was a flyer on the wall from before they crossed over. Marianne took the paper down and folded it several times. She opened the door and slowly shut it behind her, making sure the folded flyer kept the door from locking.

She saw two eyes in the darkness on the outside of the fence. Without a moment's hesitation or consideration for the danger she could be putting her friends in, she climbed over the fence to join Queen Morna in the shadows.

It took several minutes for the knocking to wake Bobby. It had never been his job to get up in the middle of the night to take care of things. He put the picture frame on his night stand and got up to investigate. The knocking was coming from the back door.

He pulled aside the curtain and looked out. A girl was standing outside.

"Who is it?" he asked.

"Marianne Blossum. Are you going to open up?"

"I don't know."

"Please?" Marianne said, turning on the charm. Even at eleven, Bobby was susceptible to her spell.

"I guess," he said, unlocking and opening the door. "What are you doing here?"

"I thought what happened between you and Wayne today was a little harsh, even if he is my boyfriend. I know you're not a changeling."

"Apparently, you're the only one."

"I have a better idea than staying by yourself in this house. I have a friend, her name is Morna…"

I will not be addressed so informally…

"She's a queen, but she's a little uptight about it. She offered to let you come stay with her in her castle."

"Why?"

A woman stepped out of the shadows. "A fine young man such as yourself shouldn't have to scrounge around in a town of ghosts."

"What's in it for you?" asked Bobby, suspiciously.

"I do you this favor now, you do me a favor later," said Morna.

"I don't know," said Bobby.

Marianne, he must come willingly. I cannot force him for what I need him to do. Make him come.

"Queen Morna, is a friend of mine. She wouldn't do anything to hurt you," said Marianne.

"You wouldn't?" asked Bobby.

Morna hesitated. Words and promises had to be phrased carefully. "I would not ask you to do anything you would not do willingly."

"Well, maybe. Do you have cable at the castle?" asked Bobby.

"We have many cables, holding many things up or in place," said Morna.

"I can see this is going to be fun. Tell me more," said Bobby.

Morna did and eventually Bobby left with her, riding off into the night on the back of a darkcat.

CHAPTER 11

As the clock tower rang out the twelfth bell of noon, Tina arrived on the Wildsidhe. Her face was still wet from her tearful good bye to her father. He had tried to get her even farther from Sparta, in hopes that more distance would save her. It hadn't.

Her father's desperate screams still echoed in her ears. It had all been for nothing. Well, like the Heart Throb Boys sang on their "Heart Attack" single, *"When you got no choice, make the best of a bad situation."*

It couldn't get much worse than this. She looked up to see a girl in a flying wheelchair.

"Terri?" Tina asked as her jaw dropped.

"Tina Shelly, I presume. How'd you do that?" asked the hovering girl.

"Asgar cursed the kids he left behind. On noon of our eleventh birthday, we get sent here, wherever here is," said Tina.

"You're on the Wildsidhe," Terri said.

"Fairyland? You're kidding me."

Terri shook her head no.

"I guess not. You are flying, after all. That's so wild. How'd you learn how to fly? Can you teach me?"

"It's a long story. The short version is that Cindy can work magic, but she can't control it very well. She somehow did this, so you'll have to ask her."

"Okay I will, but you should already know about me coming over? Didn't my brother Bobby already tell you about it? He came over yesterday. Didn't he?"

Terri looked guiltily away. "Yes, but we didn't believe him."

"Why not?"

"We've had bad experiences with changelings, creatures who can make themselves look like anybody they want. We thought he was one of them. Now he's missing."

"What do you mean missing?"

"He wouldn't submit to an anti-changeling test."

"Bobby hates tests. What did this one involve?"

"Changelings can only hold a shape for about a day. We were going to lock him in a big locker for about thirty hours to make sure he was who he said he was."

"Can you blame him for refusing?" asked Tina.

"No, but we couldn't let him in the school. We couldn't risk everyone else's life," Terri said.

"What do you mean?"

"The first changeling we met disguised itself as Principal Greene, then tried to kill some of us, including me. It did kill Todd Wilson."

"Oh no."

"Since I can fly, my brother Wayne decided I was the best candidate to wait here and see what happened at noon. Looks like Bobby was telling the truth," Terri said. It was only then that Tina noticed the older girl was carrying a bow and a quiver of arrows.

A tiny fluttering of wings dashed alongside the floating Terri.

"Terri, is new biggie friend or foe?" asked Lissy.

"Friend, I think," Terri said, annoyed at the little pixie, who had constantly been showing her up in the flying department. Terri found her irritating and annoying.

Lissy fluttered over to Tina and hovered a foot in front of Tina's face, her wings beating like a humming bird.

"Hello, biggie," said Lissy.

"Hello, yourself. You're a pixie! That's so cool."

"Lissy not cold. Biggies talk so strange."

"I could teach you how to talk like biggies… I mean kids, if you like," offered Tina.

"Lissy would like that very much."

"First off, instead of saying your name, say *I* would like that very much," said Tina.

"Lissy… oops, Lissy means I understand."

"We've got a lot of work ahead of us," said Tina.

"Perhaps, I could be of some assistance," said a man, who had suddenly appeared as if out of nowhere.

"Asgar! Biggie run!" screamed Lissy, pushing at Tina's head as if the little pixie would move her alone.

It was enough. Tina had recognized the Fortesan and started to sprint down Grand Avenue. A moment later it was as if someone had slammed a chair into the back of her legs. Tina fell back and suddenly she was airborne.

"I'm flying!" said Tina.

"Courtesy of Terri Burns Air. Keep your arms and legs inside the ride at all times and return your tray to the full and upright position. The ride could get bumpy."

The pixie fluttered and flew to hover near the girls' heads, then darted forward. "Terri, follow Lissy."

Terri didn't argue. The pixie had been flying a lot longer and would be able to figure out the quickest way back to the school. Besides, carrying Tina's extra weight at a high speed took enough of Terri's concentration.

She didn't waste any time thinking about what Asgar would do. There was no doubt he would follow.

Wayne was on duty in the watchtower near the front gate. He always was when he sent his sister out alone. In his head, he knew she could get out and back quicker and safer than anyone else, but he was still a protective big brother.

Plus, he was feeling guilty. He had taken a patrol to check on Bobby at his house to see if he was really there. He wasn't taking any chances. The patrol had consisted of Terri, Carmen Perez, John and Chuck Bearclaw, and Ron and Miko Wang.

Some idiot asked him why he was bringing three girls. Carmen was one of their best shots with a bow, Terri could fly, and Miko was amazing with a sword. Wayne's grandmother's house had been one of the ones to come over and inside it was his grandfather's collection of swords. He had had dozens of styles. Unfortunately, only Miko and Ron were any good with them, but they were teaching the rest of them. Their father had been on his college fencing team and had taught his kids how to use a sword since they could walk. Miko was even better than her brother Ron, and had fenced competitively at the national level. In a few years she may have made the Olympic team, if they hadn't ended up here.

They hadn't found Bobby, but the back door was left unlocked and it was obvious that he had been there. His bed was sleep in and a picture of his parents was next to it. Ron argued that he was probably a changeling that had taken off when he realized his plan wouldn't work. Wayne wasn't so sure. He figured it wouldn't hurt to check out his story, now that he could. Bobby had said that he had appeared in front of the clock tower at noon and that his twin Tina would do the same. It was easy enough to check out.

He was just worried about his sister. He had even sent Lissy along as lookout, as someone who could come back for help if Terri needed it. The fact that having the pixie along would annoy the heck out of his sister was an added bonus.

When he saw Lissy and Terri, with Tina on her lap coming in fast over the houses, his heart dropped. He had an air horn can and pushed the button. It blared.

"Battle stations! Lock the gate!" screamed Wayne. He had drilled everyone often enough, to make sure they weren't taken by surprise again. His patrol was still there and they took up positions in the various watchtowers and the bleacher planks along the wall. Each of his team had compound bows. Justin and Cindy had joined them, as had several others.

Terri came in quick and fast, using the wheels of her wheelchair as landing gears on the parking lot inside the fence line.

First thing was first.

"Darkcats? Changeling?" asked Wayne, remembering how a pack of the beasts have attacked all of them on more than one occasion.

"Worse. Asgar," Terri said, breathless.

"Crap. You okay, sis?"

"Yeah."

"Why are you all out of breath?" asked Tina.

"Flying takes effort. Imagine if you had to carry a person a couple of blocks. That's how I feel right now," Terri said. "I'll be okay once I rest. Right now we have to worry about Asgar."

"Are you sure she's not a changeling?" asked Wayne.

"Pretty much. I saw her appear out of nowhere," said Tina.

"We don't know that they can't do that, but we'll have to accept it for the moment," Wayne said.

"Cuz, Asgar's coming down the street," Justin said. "Get up here."

"Hello, children. Such a welcome. It might make me think you weren't happy to see me, if I didn't know better," said Asgar.

"You're not welcome here, Asgar. What do you want?" shouted Justin. The iron in the gate made him cautious.

"Maybe I just wanted to stop by and visit," said Asgar. "Especially to take in such visions of loveliness. Hello, Cindy."

Carmen and Cindy looked at each other.

"I think Asgar is hitting on you, Cindy," whispered Carmen.

"Leave us alone, Asgar," shouted Cindy.

"Certainly, if that is your wish, I will comply. At least for now," said Asgar, muttering under his breath something that sounded like, "At least until you are of age."

Asgar turned to walk away, then paused and turned back.

"I almost forgot why I had come. I see you have learned more about my gift to Sparta. What the girl and boy have told you is true. The leaders of your town did not give me what I wanted, so in retaliation I claimed every one of Sparta's children. On noon of their eleventh birthday, your fellow children will join you here."

"Asgar, send us back," begged Cindy.

"Say please."

"Please."

"No," said Asgar with a laugh. "When any of you turn eighteen, come talk to me and I'll offer you a deal. For you dear Cindy, maybe I can work out something special, a bit sooner. But you should be more worried about the boy."

Tina ran up on the tower.

"You know where Bobby is? Tell me!" she screamed.

"Ah yes, the twin. Legend has it that twins share a special bond. Some say even two parts of the same soul. If that is true, you should be very worried," said Asgar.

"Why?"

"Because your twin is with Morna, Queen of the Fortesans and High Lady of the Wildsidhe, and she means him ill," said Asgar. Marianne's face turned white. Asgar turned and smiled at her. She relaxed when he didn't give her away.

"It's your fault we're here. Why would you help us now?" asked Wayne.

"The same reason I helped you against Troc, the Changeling Lord. He was serving Morna and what serves Morna does not serve me. You might have been able to handle a typical changeling, but a Changeling Lord is another matter. Some of you here owe me your lives, including you. I am offering you the chance to save another," said Asgar.

"Why don't you save him yourself?" asked Chuck Bearclaw.

"You obviously know nothing of politics," said Asgar, with contempt.

"What's this Morna going to do with him?" pleaded Tina.

"She is going to hand him over to the Shadows," said Asgar.

"Why?" asked Tina.

"That is a Fortesan matter. It is not your concern," said Asgar.

"I'll tell you why later," Cindy said.

"And just how would you know?" asked Asgar.

"That is my business. It is not your concern," Cindy said, turning the Fortesan's words back against him.

At first, Asgar's face turned a dark and angry red, but then he caught himself and smiled. "Whatever you desire, dear Cindy. Let me just add that not being able to deliver the boy to the Shadows would be very bad for Morna, therefore very good for me. Now, I must be on my way, but I leave a parting gift."

There was a burst of light and an object about the size of a deck of cards appeared at his feet.

"The inside of this finder is hollow. Put a piece of something that belonged to the boy and the arrow will point the way to him. You must hurry. You only have until midnight tomorrow."

With that, Asgar took his leave, casually walking down the street and out of the town. The kids waited until he was out of sight before they went outside the gate to get the finder.

CHAPTER 12

"It's got to be a trap," said Chuck Bearclaw.

"Of course it's a trap. What else could it be?" asked Ron. "Besides, we don't even know that this girl's not a changeling."

"My name is Tina. Don't talk about me like I'm not here."

"I think Asgar was telling the truth or at least his version of it," Cindy said.

"I think Asgar has the hots for Cindy," Carmen said.

"Say what?" Justin said.

"Don't worry, Justin. I only have eyes for you," Cindy said, leaning over to kiss him.

"Cindy, you said you'd tell me why this Morna chick would give my brother to a bunch of shadows," said Tina.

"My grandmother used to tell me stories about the Wildsidhe. I think she spent some time here when she was younger," Cindy said.

"We're not going to go through this nonsense again, are we?" asked Justin.

"Justin, shut up. I was right about this being the Wildsidhe. You thought we were on an alien planet," Cindy said.

"And you haven't let me forget it," Justin said.

"You should have believed me," Cindy said, still annoyed. "One of my grandmother's stories was about a tithe…"

"A what?" asked Chuck.

"It's like a rent payment. The Wildsidhe used to belong to a race of Shadows. A long time ago, the magic races had to leave Earth in a hurry, but there wasn't a safe place for them to go. Somehow the Fortesans made a deal with these Shadows, and got the Wildsidhe. All the magical creatures fled Earth for the Wildsidhe. Since the Fortesans arranged for everything, they became the rulers of the Wildsidhe. They were the ones who also had to pay the price," Cindy said.

"What price?" asked Tina.

"Every few years or so, I don't remember the exact number, the tithe comes due. The price is a living being. At first, the Fortesans, paid it from their number, taking only volunteers. There came a day when there were no volunteers. There were different solutions. Volunteers from other races, oath breakers. Apparently, according to the rules the Shadows set down, the person had to go willingly or have broken a deal with a Fortesan. Morna must be planning to trick Bobby into being the volunteer."

"We have to go get him," said Tina.

"Yes, we do," Wayne said, feeling like the entire situation was his screw-up. "I'll go and get him back."

"Wait a second, Wayne. You are in charge of security here. Nobody else can handle things here as well as you. If you leave, it puts everyone else at risk," Justin said.

"But it's my fault. I wouldn't let him in," Wayne said.

"Wayne, you did the right thing," Justin said.

"I don't know," replied Wayne, still blaming himself for Todd's death.

"Justin's right. Terri told me what happened with you guys and the changeling. If Bobby had been a changeling and you let him in, people would have died. Bobby shouldn't have been so pig headed and let you guys test him in the locker," said Tina.

"Thanks. I'll tell you one thing. I'm going to make sure somebody is at that clock tower every day at noon to make sure this never happens again," Wayne said. "We still need to figure out who's going after Bobby."

"I'll go," Justin said.

"Justin, the same thing that you told Wayne applies to you. You're in charge here. You're needed here," Cindy said.

"But..."

"No buts. Cindy's right," Wayne said.

"I'll go," said Chuck.

"I'm in," said John.

"I'll go too. Someone's got to keep an eye on these two jokers," Carmen said, pointing at the Bearclaw brothers.

"Count me in," Terri said.

"Me too," said Miko.

"You guys aren't going anywhere without me," said Ron.

"Or me," Cindy said. Justin started to open his mouth, but Cindy cut him off. "I'm only your second. Things here will go on fine without me."

"I'm going," said Tina.

"No, you're too young," Wayne said.

"I am not! I got past an FBI blockade. Can any of you say the same?" asked Tina.

"There's only enough room in a car for six," offered John, trying to help out.

"Then take two cars," said Tina. "Besides, if only six fit, where are you going to put Bobby on the way back? Besides, he's my brother. Would any of you stay behind if it was your brother? Or sister?"

"She's got a point," Terri said.

"So does John. We only have so much room," said Chuck.

"I could fly," Terri said.

"Right, Wheels. You'll fly for hours without a rest. You'll be totally wasted when we find the kid. We'll have to carry you back or tie you on the hood like a deer," said Chuck.

Terri conceded Chuck's point.

"I have a solution. Convince somebody to stay and you can have their spot," Justin said.

Tina looked over the group and decided that Cindy would be the easier mind to change and started pleading.

"Please Cindy, can I have your spot. Pretty please?"

"I guess," Cindy said. Tina jumped up and hugged her.

"Thankyouthankyouthankyou!"

"You're welcome," Cindy said.

"Can you make me fly like Terri?" asked Tina. "Or maybe shoot lightning bolts. That would be cool."

"That was a fluke. I still don't know how I did it and I've tried to work magic since. I only seem to be able to do it under times of stress," Cindy said.

"Darn. Thanks anyway," said Tina. Everyone said their good byes. Both Justin and Wayne told everybody to be careful. Tina took a deep breath and kept talking. "Let's stop by my house first so we can get something of my brother's, then we can put it in the finder thingee. Then we can get moving, but we have to hurry, cause that Asgar guy said we only have till midnight tomorrow and..." said Tina, barely stopping to take a breath. She walked out, expecting everyone to follow her. The funny part is, they did.

"Who put her in charge?" asked Chuck.

"Beats me. I'm just hoping she'll shut up soon. I don't want to listen to her flapping her gums the whole way," said John, as they left to follow.

Cindy turned to Justin.

"You did that on purpose," Cindy said.

"Did what?" asked Justin, innocently.

"Told her she could go if she got one of us to stay."

Justin smiled. "Prove it."

"You can't protect me just because I'm your girlfriend," Cindy said.

"Can you think of a better reason?"

"I insist on being treated the same as everyone else. Even with dangerous stuff," Cindy said.

"Absolutely," Justin said, as he put his right arm around Cindy's shoulders. With his left hand, he crossed his fingers behind his back.

CHAPTER 13

"Wow, this is amazing," said Bobby, checking out the castle. "You live here all the time?"

"This is just a vacation spot, for when the pressures of ruling get too harsh," said Morna.

"A vacation spot? This place is huge," said Bobby.

"I use this villa mainly as a retreat. Consider it your new home."

"Why are you being so nice to me?" asked Bobby. He was watching servants running around, taking care of things. One brought him a blue pastry that melted in his mouth. He could never remember tasting anything that good. He had three more.

"Can't someone do something for another without an ulterior motive?" asked Morna, taking the pastry tray from the servant and handing the entire thing to Bobby.

"Well…" Bobby started to say, but was soon too busy shoving pastries in his mouth to care.

"If it will make you feel better, you can do me a favor at another time to repay me."

"I suppose," said Bobby. The tray was empty.

"Excellent," said Morna, snapping her fingers. Another servant rushed over to take the tray. Another brought him a mug of some brown liquid.

"What is it?"

"Moonflower nectar. It took a clan of pixies two weeks to gather enough to make that much. It can only be harvested at night when a moon is in the sky. Luckily, the Wildsidhe has two moons, unlike your Earth, which makes the job easier," said Morna.

Bobby took a sip and his eyes went wide. "Wow! This is amazing." Bobby started to gulp it.

"Slowly. Savor the taste," said Morna. "Now, as I was saying, if it will make you feel better, you can promise to do me a favor later in exchange for my hospitality…"

Morna was interrupted as the great hall's main doors opened. All the servants dropped to one knee and bowed their heads.

"What is it?" asked Bobby.

Morna had to change her facial expression to hide a scowl before she answered. "It is my husband, Penrod the King."

"Wow. I've never met a king before. Should I kneel too?" asked Bobby.

"The decision is yours," said Morna. Bobby was unaware that Morna would have punished anyone else for not kneeling instantly at the king's approach.

Bobby decided to stand and watch. Penrod was as different from Morna as night was from day. Where Morna was dark, in everything from her hair and eyes to her clothes, Penrod was bright. His robes were colorful. He smiled and laughed. He seemed to know the servants by name, insisting they all rise and not make such a fuss over him.

The king made his way to where Morna and Bobby stood. Bobby decided it might be best to do something at this point, so he bowed his head and shoulders.

"Please, Bobby Shelly, do not bow to me. It is I who should bow to you. To find one as young as you, who is both brave and willing to give up so much. I am honored to meet you," said Penrod, grasping Bobby's hand and shaking it vigorously.

"I'm not all that brave," said Bobby.

"I would differ with you on that. Even the bravest Fortesan warrior could take a lesson in courage from you. That none have shames me," said Penrod.

"I'm confused. What were you saying about me giving stuff up?" asked Bobby.

"Penrod, we should really let Bobby enjoy our hospitality, not bother him right now. Bobby, you need only snap your fingers as I did, and the servants nearest you will rush to do your bidding," said Morna.

"You're kidding, right?" asked Bobby.

"Try it," suggested Morna.

Bobby snapped his fingers and a lady Fortesan, as beautiful as any model or pop star, rushed up to him and bowed her head.

"How can I serve you, honored one?" she asked. She was many inches shorter than the others. Other than Bobby, she was the only person in the room under six feet tall. Bobby realized that she was a kid like him.

"You mean you'll do anything I ask?" said Bobby, shocked.

"Of course," she answered.

"This is too much. Do you have a boyfriend?" Bobby asked.

"A what?"

"Never mind," said Bobby, blushing. "Do you have any more of that Moonflower stuff?"

"We do. Shall I get you some?" she asked.

"That'd be great," said Bobby.

Morna chimed in. "Narel, why don't you take Bobby with you."

"Certainly, my queen," she said. "Bobby, please follow me."

"No problem. See you guys later," said Bobby, as he followed Narel off.

"Morna, why are you giving him all the Moonflower nectar? You know it's my favorite. It takes the pixies forever to make it," whined Penrod, like a big kid.

"Penrod, the boy is going to be sacrificed to the Shadows tomorrow night. Let him enjoy his last hours. We owe him that much at least," said Morna.

"Are you sure he knows what he has agreed to?" asked Penrod.

"Of course," lied Morna.

"You're not using Evals powder to control his mind are you?" asked Penrod, suspiciously.

"Penrod, you know as well as I do that the Shadows will not allow someone under the spell of Evals powder to be used as the sacrifice. The person must agree to do it willingly or must be bound by a promise or a deal," said Morna.

"And Bobby has agreed to save all of the Wildsidhe by sacrificing himself?"

"Of course," lied Morna. Bobby was clueless. She had been on the verge of getting Bobby to promise her an unnamed favor when Penrod ruined everything just by showing up. According to Morna, that would describe their entire marriage. By Fortesan law, the king ruled the Wildsidhe, but could only become king by marrying someone of Morna's bloodline. It was one of the rules set down by their pact with the Shadows. Morna chose to marry Penrod, because she knew he cared nothing for power. Morna could control him and rule the Wildsidhe herself. At least as long as Penrod was kept occupied, which was easy enough. The king loved games and toys, and Morna made sure he was supplied with both.

Penrod's appearance here was unexpected and annoyed Morna. She hated the knowledge that much of her own power was dependent upon keeping Penrod too busy to care.

"I have already sent for the royal sculptor to add a statue of him to the hall of heroes," said Penrod.

"Penrod, dear, that's really not necessary…"

"Oh, but it is. Ages ago, when Earth's magic began to fade away, those races that needed magic to survive were threatened. The Fortesans and the other races would have eventually died, if the first Fortesan High Council had not made the pact with the Shadows. The High Council was given part of the Shadowlands. They banished the darkness and gave it life, then allowed all who were in danger on Earth refuge here in this land which became the Wildsidhe," said Penrod.

"I know all this," said Morna, irritated.

"Of course you do dear. You also know the price the Shadows charged. Each generation, one person, willing or oath bound, must be delivered to where the Wildsidhe borders the Shadowlands, on midnight of the anniversary of the pact. It is a horrible price the Shadows demand, but without it thousands would die. This generation, not one Fortesan, elf, dwarf, giant, dragon or member of any other Wildsidhe race came forward to volunteer. I was understandably worried as my duty as king would demand that I be that sacrifice. This Bobby Shelly is not only saving the entire Wildsidhe, but my life as well. I had to come thank him in person," said Penrod.

"That is wonderful, Penrod, but we should really let him enjoy the little time he has left in peace," said Morna. She had to get rid of Penrod, before he ruined everything. If she didn't arrange for a sacrifice, Penrod would have to offer himself. By Fortesan law, Morna, as reigning monarch, would have only three days to remarry or give up her position as queen. Her new husband would be the new king. Asgar would make sure no one else would marry her but him. Asgar would not allow her to rule as Penrod had. Asgar would take all the power for himself, leaving Morna a mere figure-head. Morna would not allow that to happen. "Why don't you head home and we'll meet you at the border to the Shadowlands tomorrow night."

"If you think that would be best, dear," said Penrod.

"I do. Now, I think we should also call off the sculptor," said Morna.

"Absolutely not. This brave boy and his fellow humans are new to our kingdom, yet they shame us with their courage," said Penrod. Neither Morna nor Asgar had told the king the real reason the kids had arrived on the Wildsidhe and Penrod had not thought to ask. "His image will be added to the hall of heroes and songs will be sung of his courage."

"But dear…" started Morna, but Penrod was not backing down.

"This is a royal decree. It will be done," said Penrod.

"Yes, dear," said Morna, trying to come up with a way to explain it to Bobby that he wouldn't become suspicious.

CHAPTER 14

It didn't take long for Tina to find something of Bobby's. She went straight to his room, picked up a dirty sweat sock and cut a piece of it off with a scissors.

"Why'd you pick a sweat sock?" asked John.

"That's what I'd give a bloodhound," said Tina, who then went into her father's room and did the same with one of his dark socks.

"Why'd you get something of your Dad's?" asked Carmen.

"I figure that maybe after we free Bobby, we put my Dad's sock in the finder and maybe it will show us a way home," said Tina.

"Hey, that's pretty smart," said Chuck.

"Yeah. We should try that first," said John.

"Why?" asked Tina.

"If there's a way, Wayne, Cindy and Justin could look for it while we're gone. That way, when we get back, maybe we can go home," said Chuck.

Tina shrugged and put it in first. The finder did nothing.

"Maybe it's broken," said Miko.

"Try putting in the piece of your brother's sock," suggested Ron. Tina did and an arrow lit up above the box.

"It's working fine. Maybe it will only work for Bobby?" said Tina.

Carmen took off one of her rings and handed it to Tina. "Here, try this."

Tina put the ring in the finder. The arrow lit up again, bigger and brighter. It was pointing at Carmen and followed her as she walked around the living room.

"I guess it only works for people here on the Wildsidhe," said Tina, sadly.

"Hey, it was still a good idea," said Miko.

"Yeah, it was," agreed John.

"Thanks," said Tina, giving Carmen back her ring and putting the piece of her brother's sock back in the finder. "Let's go find Bobby."

"Why are they making this statue of me again, Narel?" asked Bobby.

"King Penrod's orders," said Narel. The young Fortesan was confused. Queen Morna had ordered her not to discuss the details of the sacrifice with Bobby, but that made no sense. Bobby was a hero to have agreed to give himself over to the Shadows. Whenever a Fortesan volunteered, they spent the entire year before being treated like royalty. The poor human would barely have two days. Why couldn't she tell him how wonderful she thought he was? It made no sense. Still, it made even less sense to question the queen. She would be punished severely for that.

"Please stand still," ordered the Fortesan sculptor. He didn't act like any sculptor Bobby had ever heard of. He had a huge hunk of marble, but no hammer or chisel. All he had was an "X" shaped handle, with different kinds of brushes on each of the four ends.

"Sorry," said Bobby, feeling foolish. He was standing with one foot up on a rock. He had his hands on his hips and he was looking off into the distance. He would have preferred to look at Narel. Although he enjoyed being waited on hand and foot, he had stopped asking Narel to do it. Instead, he simply asked her to hang out with him. Narel had been honored to do so.

"There—that's it! Whatever you do, don't move," shouted the sculptor. He started twirling the X-handle around like a baton. It started spinning like a buzz saw and glowing like a spotlight. As the sculptor touched it to the marble, chunks and pieces flew away. As he kept moving it, the hunk of marble started to resemble a person. Moments later, the sculptor collapsed to the floor, exhausted.

"It's done," he said, wiping the sweat from his brow. As he looked up, he added "I think this may be my greatest work ever."

"Can we see?" asked Bobby.

"Certainly, honored one," said the sculptor, bowing. Bobby and Narel walked to the front of the statue. "What do you think?"

The sculptor seemed nervous, waiting for Bobby's opinion. Nobody, let alone an adult, had ever been so interested in his opinion before. It felt good.

Bobby looked up and was speechless for a moment. The statue was over ten feet tall and made him look like a cross between a king and an movie star.

"It's beautiful. You made me look like some sort of hero," said Bobby.

"And why not? You are," said the sculptor.

"Why does everyone keep saying that?" asked Bobby. Narel was torn by what to do next. She was saved by another servant, entering with yet another Moonflower nectar for Bobby.

"Thanks," said Bobby.

"It was my pleasure, honored one," said the servant, who bowed and quickly left. The sculptor thanked him for his kind words on the statue and followed the servant out. Bobby lifted the mug to his lips and took a sip.

Narel looked at him with envy. "What does it taste like?"

"You mean you've never tried Moonflower nectar?" asked Bobby.

"Oh no. Just that glass that you're holding costs more than my entire family makes in a year," said Narel.

"You're kidding? Why are they letting me drink so much of it?"

Narel answered carefully. "Queen Morna has decided that you should be allowed to have whatever you want."

"Queen Morna is so cool. Narel, how would you like to have the rest of my nectar?" asked Bobby.

"Oh, I couldn't."

"Sure you could." Bobby handed her the mug. "Bottoms up."

Bobby had drank half of it, but Narel didn't mind. She was more than happy to get any Moonflower nectar. She drank it. The taste made her deliriously happy.

"Thank you so much," she said.

"My pleasure," said Bobby.

"I have to get this back to the kitchen," she said, turning to go. She spun back and impulsively kissed Bobby on his check. "Thanks again."

Narel ran off. Bobby was left standing there, rubbing his check and smiling.

"Wow," he said, then looked up at his statue. He puffed up his chest. If Tina was there, she would have said he was getting a swelled head. She would have been right. Bobby found himself missing his twin sister and wishing she was here. He wondered if she had made it over okay. He would have to ask Queen Morna if she would check on her, maybe even bring Tina to the castle. She would love this.

CHAPTER 15

"Can't you make this crate ride smoother?" asked Tina, as the car hit what felt like the zillionth bump and her head bumped into the roof again.

"The roads around here aren't exactly paved," replied Chuck, sarcastically.

"Couldn't you just put extra heavy shocks on this thing?" asked Tina.

"Sure. We'll just stop at the next auto supply store and make the switch," said John.

"Fine. It was just a suggestion. It's not my fault you can't drive very well," said Tina.

"Is that so?" said Chuck, who was behind the wheel. He looked over at John, who was next to him in the middle front seat and the brothers smiled. Carmen, who was riding shotgun in the passenger seat, caught the look, as did Ron and Miko who were in the backseat with Tina. They all knew the Bearclaw brothers well enough to grab onto something and hold on tight.

Chuck sped up and headed for a huge bump in the dirt road. Tina, the only one not holding on, was slammed hard into the ceiling again.

"Hey! You did that on purpose!" she yelled.

"I would never do something like that," said Chuck, innocently.

"Right," said Tina.

"Is that finder thing still working?" asked Miko, diplomatically changing the subject.

"Yep. Still pointing straight ahead. Hey, can you turn on the radio again?" asked Tina. It was the fifth time she had asked the same question.

"Tina, I keep telling you, there are no radio stations on the Wildsidhe, so there's nothing for the radio to pick up," explained Carmen. She was the resident whiz kid, an expert on things mechanical.

"Are you absolutely sure?" asked Tina.

"Pretty sure," Carmen said.

"One of these Wildsidhers stole half our town and all of us. If they could do that, how can you be sure they haven't invented radio stations yet?" asked Tina. Carmen let out a frustrated sigh and turned on the radio. She hit the scan button and it ran around the whole dial without picking up a single sound except static.

"Satisfied?" asked Carmen.

"I guess. I just hate car rides without any music. Of course, we would still have music if it wasn't for John," said Tina. Apparently, the former owner of the car had the same taste in music as Tina because they found the Heart

Throb Boys album "A Heart Throb Christmas." Tina had insisted on playing it again and again. By the third time, John had cracked from Heart Throb overload. He ejected the tape and "accidentally" threw it out the window. Tina hadn't forgiven him yet.

"If it wasn't for me we would still be listening to the lamest renditions of Christmas carols ever recorded," said John.

"The Heart Throb Boys aren't lame. They are the greatest group ever," defended Tina.

"Dogs barking Jingle Bells are more enjoyable than those guys," said John.

"I love that one," said Chuck.

Before Tina could comment again the glowing arrow changed direction.

"Turn right here," she shouted at a fork in the road. Chuck slammed on the brakes and turned sharply, kicking up a cloud of dust. As they rounded the next hill, they saw a castle in the distance.

"Do you think that's where Morna took Bobby?" asked Tina. Next to her, Ron looked over at the finder.

"I think so. The arrow's bigger and brighter," said Ron.

"How are we going to get in there?" asked Carmen, looking at the stone wall that surrounded the place.

"I'm clueless. Tina, you have a plan?" asked Chuck.

"I have no idea. Go up to the gate and knock?" suggested Tina.

"That'll work well. Should we suggest to them to put us in the same cell as Bobby?" asked John.

"I don't know. I've never rescued somebody before," said Tina.

"We need a plan," Carmen said.

A dark shape jumped on the hood of the car. Its paws sizzled from the contact with the iron in the steel hood, but this only seemed to make it angrier. Its growl drowned out the motor.

Inside, the kids' screams made the giant feline's growl seem like a whisper.

"Darkcat!"

Bobby and Narel were out for a walk, exploring the inside of the upper castle wall.

"This place is so beautiful," said Bobby, looking out over the rolling hills. "I'd rather be home, but this place isn't so bad in the meantime."

Narel looked at him, confused, knowing that he was going to be sacrificed in mere hours. How could he be thinking about going home? Before she can say anything, a noise blasts out.

"What is that sound?" asked Narel.

"It sounded like a car horn. C'mon," said Bobby, running around the catwalk to the front of the castle. "It is a car. Hey, that darkcat is chasing them."

Chuck had honked the horn, briefly startling the darkcat on the hood, then slammed down the gas pedal. The darkcat was thrown off the car, but it landed on its feet and gave chase.

The car sped along the road toward the castle.

"Why is it bothering them?" asked Bobby.

"Morna ordered the darkcats to protect the castle and you," said Narel.

"My sister might be in that car. We have to do something," said Bobby.

"But we couldn't stop a darkcat."

"Why don't the darkcats come in the castle?" asked Bobby.

"Morna doesn't allow them when she's not here," said Narel.

"Then we have to get the car in the castle," said Bobby.

"But…" started Narel, but Bobby was already moving. There were two guards by the gate.

"Open the gate," said Bobby.

The guards looked at Bobby, then at each other. The pair laughed.

"We don't take orders from you, child," said one of them.

"Do you know who I am?" asked Bobby.

It was obvious they didn't.

"This is one who will be the tithe," said Narel. Both guards snapped to attention.

"I apologize, honored one," said the guard.

"Open the gate, please. My sister might be in that car."

"We have orders not to let unauthorized visitors into the castle."

The darkcat was gaining on the car, and the road ended at the castle gate. There would be nowhere else to go. Bobby thought and came up with an answer.

"Didn't Morna leave orders to do anything I asked?" said Bobby.

"Yes."

"Then open the gate," said Bobby.

The guards looked at each other. The queen did leave those orders. Plus, Bobby was the honored one, who was going to save them all from the Shadows for another generation.

They opened the gate.

CHAPTER 16

"The castle gate is going up!" yelled Carmen.

"Do you think it's a trap?" asked Ron.

"Don't know and at this point I don't care. There are three more darkcats in the rearview mirror. We're going in," said Chuck, pushing the pedal to the floor.

The car sped through the gate and Chuck slammed on the brakes before they hit the wall on the far side of the courtyard. The darkcats stopped short of the gate, unwilling to violate their mistress' orders. They were not happy and growled their disapproval. The gate slowly closed, trapping the kids inside the castle courtyard.

From inside the car it looked like they had gone from the frying pan and straight into the fire. Guards had surrounded them and were pointing spears, swords as well as bows and arrows.

"What do we do?" asked Miko, frantically. She had pulled her sword out, but inside the car it was useless.

One of the Fortesan guards made the mistake of slamming on the roof of the car. He had never encountered steel or iron before. The contact burned his hand and he screamed.

"Iron hurts these scumbags. We're inside of the biggest weapon they've ever seen," said Chuck, spinning the car around. The guards moved to avoid it.

"Good thing I convinced you to not take the sports car with the fiberglass body," Carmen said, smiling. "That and the fact that this one has a 20 gallon gas tank and a trunk big enough to hold seven five gallon gas cans."

"You're brilliant. Now figure a way for us to get out of this," said Chuck, driving the car in a circle, then switching directions to keep the guards at bay.

"We could use the gas to make a flame thrower," suggested John, holding on to the dashboard as his brother spun the car again.

"Out of what?" Carmen said.

"Couldn't you use parts of the engine to make one?" asked John.

"I'm good, but not that good. Besides, if I take apart the engine, we're sitting ducks. You want to get out to get the parts? Or the gas?" asks Carmen, sarcastically.

"We could send Tina," said John, but he was not serious.

"Real funny. How are we going to find Bobby?" asked Tina.

"That may be easier than you think," said Ron, pointing in front of them, where Bobby had just jumped.

"Stop!" he screamed, holding up his hand. Chuck had to slam on the brakes to stop from hitting him.

"Bobby!" screamed Tina.

"Tina!" said Bobby. "You're here!"

Tina moved for the door handle, but Ron stopped her.

"What are you doing?" asked Ron.

"I'm going to get Bobby," said Tina.

"Nobody is getting out of this car," said Chuck.

"You ain't my Dad," said Tina.

"No, but I'm not about to let you outside until I know what's going on. Those guys are still pointing their weapons at us. I'm not going to let you get killed, understand?" said Chuck.

Tina looked at the weapon wielding Fortesans surrounding them. Every one of them was over six feet tall, with those weird long fingers with the extra joint. They were outnumbered badly.

"Okay, but we're not leaving without Bobby," said Tina. Chuck didn't say anything.

A Fortesan guard starting banging on the glass with his sword. Before Chuck can get the car moving again, Bobby started yelling.

"Move away from the car," said Bobby. The guard hesitated. "My sister is in there. Move away. Please."

The guard reluctantly listened.

"You can get out. These guys are okay," said Bobby.

Everyone inside the car looked at Chuck.

"He could be a Changeling," pointed out Ron.

"That's what got us in this mess in the first place," Carmen said.

"Tina, what's something that only your brother would know?" asked Chuck. Tina thought about it for a minute.

"Ask him what he did up until he was in second grade," said Tina. Chuck opened the window a crack and did.

"I'm not answering that question," said Bobby.

"Then we're not getting out," said Chuck.

"Ask her for another question," said Bobby.

"You don't know it?" asked Chuck.

"I know it. I don't want to say it," said Bobby.

"It's the only way to prove to us you're not a Changeling, which means we're going to have to fight our way out. That means all of us, including your sister, could get hurt. Or worse," said Chuck.

"Fine," said Bobby, then muttered under his breath.

"What? I couldn't hear you," said Chuck.

"I wet the bed," said Bobby, his face a bright pink. John and Ron started to laugh uproariously. "I haven't done it in years."

"The two of you shut up," ordered Chuck. The pair listened. "Tina, is that right?"

"Yeah," said Tina.

"Okay, we can get out, but if I say so, everyone gets back in on the double," said Chuck, opening up his door. The others followed suit and got out.

Tina rushed over to hug Bobby. He didn't hug back.

"What's the matter with you? I would've thought you'd be happy to see me," said Tina.

"I was until you told everyone about my… old problem. I can't believe you did that," whined Bobby.

"Chuck asked for something only you would know and I knew you would never have told anybody about that. Look, we're trying to rescue you from Morna," said Tina.

"Rescue me? Why would you rescue me? I'm having the time of my life here," said Bobby.

"But Morna kidnapped you," said Tina.

"Morna invited me here," said Bobby.

"That's because she's planning on sacrificing you to some creatures called the Shadows," said Chuck.

"Who told you this?" said Bobby.

"Asgar," said Chuck.

"The same guy who cursed us all? Why would you listen to him?" asked Bobby.

"He hates Morna. He took out the Changeling that killed Todd and almost killed a bunch of other kids," said Chuck.

"That explains why you guys are so paranoid about Changelings, but what does that have to do with Morna?" asked Bobby.

"Morna sent the Changeling," said Chuck.

"She wouldn't," said Bobby.

"She did. And she sent her darkcats after all of us," said Miko. "We barely survived."

"Tell me you're kidding," said Bobby. No one did. "But she's been so good to me."

"Fattening you up like a lamb to the slaughter," Carmen said.

"This can't be true. Narel, come here please," called Bobby. The pretty, young Fortesan walked over. All of the guys followed her appreciatively with their eyes.

"Yes, honored one?" asked Narel.

"Narel, is Morna planning on sacrificing me to some Shadows?" said Bobby.

"Bobby, you are the honored one. The choice to offer yourself to preserve the Treaty of Shadows is yours. But you have to know that. The tithe cannot be deceived into making the sacrifice. The queen had to tell you, didn't she?" said Narel.

"Morna never told me. She kept trying to get me to say I'd promise her something that she would name later, but I never did," said Bobby.

"Sounds like she was trying to get you to promise to be this tithe," Carmen said.

"The queen would never do that," said Narel.

"I think you may be wrong about that one," said Miko.

"But Marianne said Morna was okay. She said it was okay to go with her," said Bobby.

The kids from the car exchanged looks.

"Marianne knew about Morna. If she told you that, it means she's in league with Morna," said Chuck. Behind him, the gate had reopened and in rode the queen, on the back of a darkcat.

"Isn't everyone?" said Morna.

CHAPTER 17

Chuck said something that Tina would have never said in front of so many adults because she would have been afraid of getting yelled at. Then she realized that all the adults were Fortesans and yelling would be mild compared to what was coming.

"Everyone in the car!" ordered Chuck. Everyone that came with him obeyed. Bobby had other things on his mind. He was angry and wasn't thinking right. Worse, he was heading toward Morna and her darkcat.

"You lied to me! You were planning to kill me!" screamed Bobby. Chuck ran after him.

"I was doing what I had to in order to save every other living being on the Wildsidhe, including your human friends," said Morna.

"So killing one kid to save thousands is okay?" asked Bobby.

"Yes. If there is no tithe, the Shadowlands will reclaim the Wildsidhe. Nothing alive can survive in the Shadowlands," said Morna.

"That was where you were going to send me though," said Bobby.

"Where you are still going," said Morna.

"The tithe has to volunteer. I ain't volunteering," said Bobby.

Chuck grabbed Bobby's arm. "Bobby, get in the car."

"I'm not going anywhere," said Bobby.

"You are going to the border of the Shadowlands with me. If we leave now, we should be there before midnight," said Morna.

"You have a hearing problem? I ain't volunteering," said Bobby.

Morna smiled, but it was a cold, dark grin. "I think you will. Your sister is here." The queen snapped her fingers and the gate slammed closed. "She and the other human children are trapped here. If there is no volunteer, I cannot guarantee their safety."

"Are you threatening my sister?" said Bobby, as Chuck lifted him up, trying to drag him toward the car.

"The choice is yours," said Morna.

Bobby looked at his sister, then back at Morna. "You would promise your protection to Tina?"

Inside the car, Tina couldn't believe her ears. "Bobby, No!"

"Bobby, we can get out of here. Don't do this, man," said Chuck, still dragging Bobby, but he was fighting all the way.

"If you volunteer, nothing would happen to your sister that I had the power to prevent. I promise," said Morna.

"Bobby, you don't have to do this," said Chuck. The only reason Tina had not burst out of the car is Carmen and Miko wouldn't let go of her.

"She's gonna kill Tina. What am I supposed to do?" said Bobby.

"So, you agree?" asked Morna.

"I...I...I...," stammered Bobby. Suddenly, a bright light caused everyone to look up to the sky over the gate. King Penrod was using his power to levitate himself and the darkcat he was riding on over the gate.

"By Ankor, this stops now," said King Penrod.

"But Penrod..." said Morna.

"Morna, you may run the kingdom, but I still rule it. The Fortesan High Council once stood for honor and nobility. Have we fallen so far that you would threaten children?" said Penrod, landing his mount on the ground and stepping off.

"Penrod, if we do not have a tithe..."

"I know the consequences. If there is no volunteer, the Treaty of Shadows is clear. The duty of the king is to offer himself up to preserve life on the Wildsidhe. I will sooner sacrifice myself than an unwilling child," said Penrod.

"Penrod, I cannot bear the thought of life without you," said Morna.

Penrod laughed. He knew his wife better than she thought. Penrod knew she feared losing her grip on the reins of power. He did not care for the day to day aspects of ruling. Morna thrived on it. Penrod was much happier when left to his games, but he believed in honor and would not stand by idly while it was perverted. Morna did truly care about saving the kingdom, but her methods left much to be desired.

"The boy did not offer himself. Do you have a promise from him?"

"No," admitted Morna.

"Then Bobby, Shelly, and his companions shall be set free. Open the gates," said Penrod.

The guards obeyed. Penrod walked over to Bobby and Chuck. Extending his hand, he shook each of theirs. "I apologize for this incident. Please go and live long and happy lives."

"Does this mean you're going to die, your majesty?" asked Bobby.

Penrod chuckled. "I suppose in a way I will. The Shadows will claim me, so that which I am will no longer be. Still, I love games and life is the biggest game of all. I will play this out to the end."

"Thank you, your majesty," said Bobby.

"I only did what was right, Bobby," said Penrod.

"I'd still like to somehow thank you," said Bobby.

"If I manage to survive past midnight, perhaps you might teach me some games of Earth," said Penrod.

"It would be my pleasure," said Bobby.

"I'd love to teach you how to play basketball. With your height and those extra-long fingers, you'd be a natural," said Chuck.

"I'd be happy to learn. You had best leave. I have a long journey to make before midnight," said Penrod. He could see Chuck looking uneasily at the pack of darkcats outside the gates. "Don't worry. The darkcats will not harm you. They were mine, before I allowed the queen to command them after... the loss of her totem. You will get back safely to your school."

Penrod told the truth. They got into the car and nobody stopped them as they drove off.

The king went to his queen and kissed her softly on the lips. A tear came unbidden out of her eye. They walked inside to the king's private quarters, holding hands.

"You noble fool," she said, softly. Penrod smiled.

"I must be on my way," said Penrod.

"I won't let you do it," said Morna.

"You have no choice," said Penrod.

Morna opened her hand and blew dust into Penrod's face. "What!?" he said, then passed out onto his throne.

"I won't be bond to Asgar and I...care for you too much to let you die," said Morna. "Not when there is one who has promised me whatever I wished in exchange for a gift."

CHAPTER 18

It was dark by the time the kids got back to the school complex. Chuck waited outside the gate and honked on the horn. Terri flew out the door in her wheelchair and was the first one to the gate. Justin, Wayne, Cindy, and dozens of others weren't far behind.

"Password," Wayne said.

"Field goal," said Chuck. Wayne got about opening the gate and when it was high enough, they drove the car in.

"Did you get him?" asked Wayne.

"Yep," said Chuck.

"All right," shouted Wayne.

"Was there ever any doubt?" said Chuck.

"With you on the case? Never," Terri said, smiling.

"Thanks, Wheels," said Chuck, as everyone was piling out of the car.

Wayne walked up to Tina and her brother. "Bobby, I'm so glad you're okay."

"Wayne's been worried sick about you," Terri said. "He feels guilty about letting Morna get you."

Chuck and Carmen were standing nearby and exchanged worried looks.

"Um, bud, about that. It wasn't your fault. One of our own sold us out and told him to go with Morna and that she would take care of him," said Chuck.

"Who?" asked Wayne.

"You're not gonna want to hear this man. It was…"

Just then, Marianne rushed outside and into the crowd of well-wishers. "You're okay. Thank goodness," said Marianne, hugging Bobby and pulling him close.

"Get away from me," screamed Bobby, pushing Marianne away.

"Hey! That's my girlfriend you're pushing. I know you've been through a lot, but that's no reason to take it out on an innocent person," Wayne said.

"Wayne, Marianne isn't innocent," Carmen said.

"What are you talking about?" Wayne said.

"Marianne's the traitor," said John.

"She told me to go with Morna," said Bobby.

"There has to be some mistake. It was a Changeling disguised as Marianne," Wayne said.

"Morna admitted it in front of us," said Chuck.

"Marianne, is this true?" asked Wayne.

"Wayne, honey, you don't believe any of this, do you?" said Marianne.

"I asked you if it was true. Why don't you answer me?" asked Wayne.

Marianne's sister, Jane, pushed out of the crowd. "Marianne, you'd never hurt someone else, would you?"

Marianne started to cry.

"All right. I did it. I had to. Morna forced me to. I didn't have any choice," said Marianne.

"In the stories my grandmother told me about the Fortesans, they usually offered something in return for favors. What did Morna offer you?" asked Cindy. Marianne didn't answer. Cindy looked at her and squinted. "I never noticed it before—you have a glow about you. The same kind Terri has when I squint at her."

Justin looked at the two girls. "I don't see anything."

"But I do. Morna put some kind of spell on Marianne, but what?" Cindy said, then noticed the ring. "I got it! A glamour."

"A what?" asked Wayne.

"A spell that makes someone look different, usually beautiful. Grandma used to tell me stories about how the Fortesans would use them at balls," Cindy said. "Marianne suddenly became a sex symbol since we got here. It makes sense."

"It's true. Morna made me beautiful. If she took the spell back, I'd go back to the way I was before—a nobody. If I didn't tell Bobby what she wanted, she'd undo the spell and take back the ring. I had to," wept Marianne.

"How could you? I cared about you. I was falling in love with you," Wayne said.

"Right. Was it me or what Morna's spell made me? You never liked me when we were back home, did you?" asked Marianne.

"Well, no," admitted Wayne.

"So you see my point," said Marianne.

"You could have come to me. We could have figured something out," Wayne said.

"Yeah, we could have figured out the only reason you liked me was because I was suddenly beautiful," said Marianne.

"Maybe, but maybe not. We'll never know now, will we?" Wayne said.

"Guess you're breaking up with me, huh?" said Marianne, giggling now.

"After what you did? Can you think of a better reason?" Wayne said.

"Guess not," said Marianne, suddenly cold. "I knew the only reason any of you liked me was because I was beautiful."

"That's not true, Marianne. I love you, regardless of how you look," said

Jane.

Marianne's face softened for a moment. "Yeah, I guess you do, little sister, but you're the only one. What happens now?"

Everybody looked at Justin. As leader, this fell in his lap.

"We can't trust you. You turned one of us over to an enemy, who would have killed him. If she had, you'd be as guilty of murder the same as if you'd killed him," Justin said.

"So? What are you going to do? Put me in jail?" laughed Marianne.

"We don't have a jail and we don't have enough food to waste on someone who isn't working. Plus, you'd be a danger to us all," Justin said.

"So what are you going to do to me?"

Justin thought about it for a minute. "What they used to do in the old days. We're going to exile you from the town. You are no longer welcome here. You have to leave."

"You're kidding me?" said Marianne. One look at Justin told her he was very serious. "You can't do that. I'll die out there."

"Maybe, but if you stay, you may betray us again. Maybe next time, some or all of us may die. I can't allow that. You are the oldest one here. You knew what you were doing and you have to accept the consequences of your actions. Does anyone object or disagree?"

The only one who spoke up was her sister Jane. "Can't she just live in one of the houses in town?"

"No. She's too close and might still help Morna," Justin said.

"Wayne, you're not going to let him do this to me, are you?" pleaded Marianne.

"Marianne, he's right. If we let you stay, we risk everyone else's life. I'm in charge of keeping everyone here safe. No matter what I feel for you, I can't put you ahead of three hundred other people," Wayne said.

"So it's like that, huh?" said Marianne. Wayne simply nodded.

Jane spoke up again. "Justin, can I go with her?"

"You don't have to," Justin said.

"I know, but she needs someone, and she is my sister," said Jane.

"Okay, if that's how you want it. We'll put together some food, enough for a few days. After that, you're on your own," Justin said.

"I'll just run in and get some things," said Jane.

"Me too," said Marianne. Wayne stepped in front of her.

"I can't let you back in there. I don't know what you'd do," Wayne said.

"C'mon, Wayne. Let me get my stuff," said Marianne, turning on her charms. They weren't enough to change Wayne's mind.

"Jane can get anything you need," Wayne said.

"I'd prefer if you waited for her outside the gate," Justin said.

"You're joking," said Marianne.

"You were an accessory to an attempted murder. I just don't see anything in that to joke about," Justin said.

Reluctantly, Marianne walked out the gate and sat on the curb on the opposite side of the street as the school.

It took Jane awhile to get everything together and come back out. As Jane was saying her good-byes, Chuck saw something down the far end of Grand Avenue.

"Darkcats!" he screamed. "I think Morna's riding one."

"Close the gate!" yelled Justin.

"Marianne's out there," Wayne said. Justin looked at him. "We can't let her just get killed, can we?"

"No, I guess not. Get her in," Justin said. Wayne ran to the gate.

"Marianne, get in here quick. Darkcats are coming," Wayne said.

Marianne smiled. "I think I'll take my chances out here."

Bobby ran up to the gate. "Marianne, you can't trust her. She'll hurt you. Trust me, I know. Even after what you did to me, I don't want you dead." In his mind, he could see his father smiling at him for doing the right thing.

"I'm in no danger. Morna and I have an understanding. The rest of you, on the other hand are in deep trouble," said Marianne.

"Shut the gate," yelled Wayne. The gate was quickly closed, but Jane tried to run out. Wayne grabbed her with one arm. "You can't go out there."

"Don't worry, Sis, I'll make sure my buddy Morna doesn't hurt you. I can't promise that for the rest of you though," said Marianne, laughing.

Wayne ordered everyone who didn't have a bow and arrows back inside the school. Morna stopped on the opposite side of the street, by Marianne.

"Your majesty, I'm so glad to see you," said Marianne.

"As I am to see you out here alone. It makes what I have to do simpler," said Morna.

"Those losers in there kicked me out, just for following your orders. They don't seem to realize you are the queen and what you say goes, no matter what," said Marianne.

"I'm glad you feel that way. Remember your promise to do anything in exchange for becoming beautiful?" asked Morna.

"Of course," said Marianne.

"I've come to collect. We need a tithe for the Shadowlands and there is no way I am going to let Penrod sacrifice himself, when I have a much more suitable substitute," said Morna. Marianne started to back away, but another darkcat cut her off.

"You know, I don't want to be beautiful anymore. Take it back," said Marianne, throwing the red ring at Morna. The queen waved her hand and it flew back on Marianne's finger.

"It's too late for that, my dear. You are indebted to me. Your sacrifice to the Shadows will erase that debt," said Morna.

"You can't make me," said Marianne.

"But I can," said Morna, throwing three glowing, bronze shackles into the air. The first and second wrapped themselves around Marianne's hands and feet, while the third clamped over her mouth. Morna picked her up and put her belly down on the darkcat she was riding.

Justin saw all this from the watchtower. "Morna, let her go."

"Not a chance," said the queen.

"Morna, this isn't fair. Let Marianne go," Wayne said.

"Life isn't fair, boy. What I'm doing is saving your miserable lives too," said Morna, as she turned and rode away. They could hear Marianne's muffled screams even after they couldn't see her any longer.

CHAPTER 20

The journey to the Shadowlands border was long and dangerous, even for the Fortesan Queen. When Morna finally arrived, the other twelve members of the Fortesan High Council were waiting there, each with their own animal totems. Morna's birthright totem had been lost or stolen years ago when her sister fled the Wildsidhe because of the love of a mortal. Luckily, Penrod had been generous enough to grant his queen the use of his darkcats. Morna had not seen her sister Alana in over fifty years, and despite the theft of the totem, she missed her sister. This was not the time for sentimentality.

Asgar was the first of the High Council to greet her. He stepped forth from the shadows that hid the others.

"Where's Penrod?" he asked. Morna smiled. She suspected Asgar had been the one to alert the human children to where Bobby was and what she had planned for him. Fortesan law forbade the killing of another Fortesan, and it was a law that not even Asgar dared break. He would not be able to slither his way out of those consequences, so this was the only way for Asgar to get rid of Penrod and become king himself.

Morna had heard rumors and mumbling among her subjects that many brave souls had come forward to offer themselves as the tithe, but Asgar had managed to convince the Fortesans not to present themselves. The non-Fortesans were either similarly convinced or disappeared without a trace. Morna knew it was Asgar, but without proof she could do nothing. The only revenge she had available to her was to tell Asgar what she had done.

"The King has fallen ill and unconscious, unable to be woken. He is being cared for. Sadly, an unconscious king cannot offer himself as the tithe, at least not in accordance with the Treaty of Shadows," said Morna.

"We are doomed," cried one member of the High Council.

"No, one of us must offer ourselves up," said another.

There was silence for a moment, then two voices sang true the Darkness.

"I offer myself," said one of the Council, stepping forth from the shadows. He was a large, bearded man and he rode a Horsehound. The Horsehounds resembled horse-sized dog, and like darkcats, were one of the thirteen animal totems controlled by the High Council.

"No, let me," cried a woman council member. She carried a bow and stood beside a winged horse as the Pegasus was her totem.

Asgar began to tighten his face muscles. His eyes were furious. Penrod was safe and his plan had been foiled.

"Stop. None of you need sacrifice yourselves, although rumors abound that one of our number actively discouraged those who were willing to volunteer," said Morna, looking directly at Asgar. "If these rumors prove true, it means the one who did this, knew full well his actions would have meant genocide for all the races of the Wildsidhe, including our own."

"Who among us did this?" demanded the Fortesan who had been first to offer himself.

"I would not slander one of our own, without the proof, but I have spoken to many who swear to the truth of these rumors. Ask questions of your own subjects and listen to the answers you get," said Morna.

"Enough," spat Asgar, his anger unhidden. "Are you telling us the reason we need not sacrifice ourselves is you have chosen to offer yourself as the tithe in Penrod's place?"

"Asgar, I do not remember hearing you volunteer. If I was mistaken, I will step aside and keep silent on my plan. You need only speak up," said Morna. Asgar did not make a sound. "As I thought. Unlike Penrod, you do not have the mettle to offer yourself as the tithe. No, I have a human who has made an open-ended promise to me. In order to fulfill her obligation, she will be the tithe."

"But I heard the human boy never promised you anything," said Asgar.

"Very true, but the tithe is a human girl," said Morna, waving to a darkcat, who walked up carrying Marianne on its back. She was still bound and was crying hysterically.

"What!?" said Asgar.

"My queen, the stars are in alignment. The first stroke of midnight is striking. The tithe must be offered!" shouted the Fortesan who had offered himself.

Morna grabbed Marianne and carried her up to the ebony altar. Asgar stood in her path.

"Asgar, stand aside. We haven't the time for this," said Morna. Several heartbeats had passed. In just a few more, it would be too late.

"Morna, you may think you have won, but you haven't won. You aren't the only one of the royal bloodline," said Asgar.

"All the women of the bloodline are wed," said Morna.

"Are they?" said Asgar. Morna did not yet realize that Cindy Hartman was Alana's granddaughter and the queen's great niece.

"Asgar, midnight is almost passed. Stand aside or..."

The darkness around the altar grew thick and grew into the shape of a man.

"It is too late, Fortesan Queen. Midnight has gone and no tithe was made," said the shadow.

"The tithe was here on Shadowland ground," said Morna.

"But not on our altar. It is a violation of our treaty," said the shadow.

"Lurker, forgive me. I was delayed by this one," said Morna.

"Morna, do not try to blame this one on me, I…" said Asgar.

Morna turned toward him and snapped. "Asgar, shut up!" Her arm flew up and a bolt of energy blasted Asgar off his feet.

"I like your style, but that does not excuse the lateness of our tithe. I'm afraid we require something more to stop us from reclaiming what is now ours by right," said the shadow.

"Lurker, name what it is you desire and if it is within my power, it shall be yours," said Morna.

"Anything?"

"Yes," said Morna.

"Even offering yourself as the tithe?" asked the shadow.

Morna's eyes went wide in fear. The idea terrified her, but she was queen. She had a duty to protect the Wildsidhe at all costs, even her own life. "Yes."

The shadow laughed. It was a cold, dark sound that sent shivers down the spines of all present.

"Nobility from you. How novel. I think you would make a good shadow. Perhaps too good and too dangerous. No, I think I will accept the tithe you meant to offer, but know that because you have broken your covenant with us, light remains on your precious Wildsidhe at my whim. There may come a time that my whims may change," said the shadow.

"We could make a new treaty, Lurker," said Morna.

"No. The Treaty of Shadows shall remain in effect. For now. Bring our offering forward and place it on the altar."

Morna did as the shadow instructed, but Marianne was kicking and screaming the entire way.

The shadow stood over Marianne and she tried to turn away.

"Your terror is delicious, but not necessary. The tithe does not die. You shall become one with the darkness, a living shadow. You will be transformed and know power like you have never even imagined. It is a glorious fate which awaits you," said the shadow. "First, we must do away with this metal gag."

The shadow waved his hand over the bronze mouth shackle and it flew off of Marianne's face.

"You will need to scream. It will make the change easier to bear. It is quite painful, expelling all the light from a living being, but well worth it. Even the least of the Shadows is as powerful as the mightiest Fortesan. Do you accept your fate?"

Marianne looked up. There was hate and anger in her heart and it is from such things that shadows are made. The offer sounded too good to turn down, so she didn't.

"Yes," she said softly.

"Excellent. Then let the Shadowlands claim you as their own," said the shadow that talked as a man.

Tentacles of darkness snaked out from the darkness, enveloping Marianne. Her skin began to turn dark. As she opened her mouth to scream, a dark tentacle poured into her mouth and down her throat and the shadows began to claim her from the inside out.

Moments later, Marianne's humanity was gone and all that was left was a dark husk. The two remaining shackles fell off and clanked to the ground. Unlike the other shadow, features could still be made out on her face and Marianne was smiling.

"This is wonderful," said Marianne.

"Yes, it is, isn't it?" said the shadow. "Come with me and let me show you your new home."

"In a minute," said Marianne, walking to Morna. "I should thank you for this, Morna," said Marianne, daring to address the queen by her first name. "But I won't. I owe you for this and I will pay you back. You and my former friends. Think about that at night, when you look out and all you can see are shadows, because one of those shadows may be looking back."

Asgar looked on and smiled. Morna had made a powerful enemy and that would only help Asgar in the long run.

"I am not afraid of you, girl," said Morna.

"Your mistake, queenie. See you soon," said Marianne. She turned and followed the Lurker into and past the Shadowland border and was swallowed up by the darkness.

One by one, the Fortesans left, to return home. None would be able to sleep until the first rays of dawn chased away the darkness of night. The light would give them the illusion of safety, but they knew that was all it was. Someday the shadows would come for them and they knew in their hearts they could do nothing to stop it.

CHAPTER 21

At the school compound, things were going well. A party was thrown for Bobby and his rescuers. Tina was even allowed to go to her house to get her boom box and since it was hers, she was allowed to play her Heart Throb Boys CDs until the batteries ran dry. The music was such a pleasant reminder of home that nobody, except Bobby and John Bearclaw, complained that Tina played the same songs over and over again for hours.

Bobby thanked everyone for saving him from a danger he was oblivious to. Tina pointed out that he was oblivious to a lot of things. Bobby told his sister to shut up, but they were both smiling. Things were back to normal. At least as normal as they could be, considering the circumstances.

A lot of the kids had been churchgoers back on Earth, of various different faiths. No church or temple had come over with them, but many of the kids felt the need to pray. Justin had set aside one of the classrooms as a sort of chapel. On Sundays, many of the kids, regardless of religion, got together to pray, even the ones whose faiths worshiped daily or on Saturdays. It was by no means mandatory, but they found that kids who would never have set foot inside a house of worship back home were coming on a regular basis. Whether or not they admitted it, they were scared and praying to a higher power gave them hope and maybe made things a little less scary.

The Sunday after the rescue, they met in the chapel for a different reason. Marianne may have betrayed them, but she was still one of them. They didn't know if she was alive or dead. Jane was distraught over the loss of her sister and Cindy suggested a memorial service might help her. And Wayne for that matter, who was still blaming himself for everything bad that had happened.

Justin agreed.

It was a beautiful service. Everyone said nice things, even if nobody actually mentioned if she was alive or dead. Next, Brina Wilson got up and spoke about her brother Todd, who had lived as a bully, died as a hero, and who saved six other lives from the deadly Changeling Lord Troc. Everyone praised Todd and by the end, more than a few people were crying.

Afterward, Wayne gave Bobby and Tina a tour of the school complex.

"I can't believe everything you guys have done with the place," said Bobby.

"We did what we had to," Wayne said.

"So we really have to learn how to shoot bows and arrows?" asked Tina.

"We have to be prepared for anything this place throws at us," Wayne said.

"Now about this work part. I think I'm best suited for a supervisory position," said Bobby.

"Nice try, slick. Everyone works at everything. The jobs rotate, so nobody gets stuck with the nasty ones all the time," Wayne said.

"What happens if we don't work?" asked Bobby.

"Easy. You don't eat," Wayne said, smiling.

"I can work," said Bobby.

"With all the food you inhale, you are going to have to work two or three jobs," joked Tina.

"Be quiet," said Bobby.

"I'll show you where you'll start working tomorrow," Wayne said, stopping to get a compound bow for him and regular bows for the twins, plus enough arrows for all of them.

"Where?" asked Tina.

"Follow me," Wayne said. The twins did and they ended up at the farm fields.

"We're going to be farmers?" asked Bobby. "Do I need to find a pair of overalls?"

"We only have so much canned food. We're going to run out eventually. Lissy and the pixies are helping us gather fruits and berries, not to mention help keep scavengers away from our crops. Kind of pint-sized scarecrows. Speaking of which," Wayne said, as a gaggle of pixies fluttered their way.

"Hello, biggie friend Tina and Bobby," said Lissy.

"Hey Lissy," said Tina.

"You aren't going to start smelling me again are you?" asked Bobby.

"Are you going to try to hit Lissy again?"

"No," said Bobby.

"Then Lissy not smell biggie Bobby," giggled Lissy. "Lissy is happy Bobby is not nasty Changeling."

"Me too. You going to help us be farmers?" asked Bobby.

"Lissy be happy to. Tina friend is going to teach Lissy, now?"

"How about tomorrow?" said Tina.

"Tomorrow is good," said Lissy.

"You're teaching Lissy? What, about the Heart Throb Boys?" asked Bobby.

"No, for your information, Lissy asked me to help her speak like a biggie, I mean a kid," said Tina.

"Lissy want to learn," said the pixie.

"Good luck. With Tina, you'll need it," said Bobby.

"Thanks," said Lissy, not catching the sarcasm.

"Bobby, look up there," said Tina. Terri was flying by in her wheelchair and the pixies were crowding around her. Terri started to shout at them to get away, but it didn't last long. She started to dive and play in the air with the pixies. Ever since Lissy had helped Terri and Tina get away from Asgar, Terri had been warming up to the pixies.

"Ooo, Lissy go play tag with biggie friend Terri," said Lissy, fluttering off.

"Hey Lissy," Terri said.

"Hello, friend Terri," said Lissy, getting close enough to touch her arm. "Tag. Terri friend is it."

"Not for long," Terri said, diving for the pixie, but she missed.

"Friend Terri be chasing Lissy for days if she flies like that," said Lissy, gliding in a circle around Terri.

"We'll see about that," Terri said, as she managed to tag the pixie. Lissy got her back almost right away.

"Terri flying better," said Lissy.

"Thanks," Terri said, barely missing Lissy, but she managed to tag another pixie. Now they were both trying to keep away from someone else. That pixie tagged another one.

"Terri still needs to learn to fly better," said Lissy.

"Hey!" Terri said.

"Lissy mean no offense. Lissy offer to teach friend Terri how to fly better."

"Thanks. I'd like that," Terri said.

"Good. Then Terri friend will fly better than big rock," giggled Lissy. Terri laughed and chased after her. "Hey! No fair. Cheating. Biggie Terri not it."

Terri flew up to the pixie who was it and held out her hand. "Tag me."

The pixie did and Terri flew after Lissy.

"Now I'm going to get you," Terri said.

"Funny. Terri doesn't look like Terri is sleeping, but she must be," said Lissy, dodging Terri's dive.

"Why do you say that?"

"Because Terri friend is dreaming if she thinks she can catch Lissy," said the pixie, fluttering away. Terri gave chase.

"That is so cool, seeing Terri fly," said Bobby, looking on.

"It is. I'm still not used to it. She's going to be exhausted later. Flying takes a lot out of her. At least the pixies are around. They know a darkcat is coming long before we do," Wayne said.

"Terri flew me in her wheelchair the day I got here," said Tina, bragging to her brother.

"No way? She can do that?" said Bobby.

"Well, she was rescuing me at the time," confessed Tina.

"Terri has tried to give everyone a ride, even though it makes her even more tired," Wayne said.

"Do you think she'd give me a ride?" asked Bobby.

"Probably. You'll have to ask her," Wayne said.

"Is it safe?" asked Tina.

"The pixies will let us know if there is anything wrong. They fly away at the first sign of trouble. Go ahead. I'll stand watch," Wayne said.

"Great. I'm going to ask her to fly me again," said Tina.

"Not if I get there first," said Bobby, sprinting for the spot where Terri was flying. Tina ran to catch up.

Wayne smiled and thought happy thoughts for once. He even allowed himself the luxury of thinking that everything was going to work out just fine. That only lasted a minute before he started scanning the distance for trouble, just in case.

A DARK PROPOSAL
Book 3

Judith Tracy

CHAPTER 1

"**S**urprise! Happy Birthday!"

Cindy tried to look amazed as all her friends shouted their best wishes in unison. She had known they were planning something for days, but didn't want to spoil their fun by letting on that she knew.

The room was decorated with streamers and handmade signs. She could see that they had gone to a lot of trouble. Turning sixteen was a milestone and to be stuck here, without her family, had put a damper on things. This party was a perfect remedy for the blues.

Justin winked at her. Cindy finished hugging and thanking everyone. At least all her friends were here and the effort they had gone to make her feel special wasn't wasted. The smile she wore was genuine. Justin walked over and kissed her lightly on the cheek.

"Woo hoo," teased Wayne. He was really happy that Cindy and Justin were going together. Justin was his cousin as well as his best friend and he had known Cindy as far back as he could remember.

The kiss wasn't lost on the other kids either. They giggled until Justin gave them a dirty look. It didn't stop the snickering, but then it wasn't intended to. Today was going to be a day of celebration. He wanted everyone to relax and party. There were so few things to be grateful for since that fateful day when they transported to another dimension, another world where magic was real...the Wildsidhe.

Since they didn't have an oven, Terri had made her a no-bake cheesecake. Carmen, Bobby, and Brina huddled around the table while Cindy blew out the candles and everyone clapped.

"It's time to open the presents," Terri said, wheeling her chair to the corner where the stack of gifts was laid out.

"You shouldn't have," Cindy said. "But I'm glad you did. I don't know what to say."

"No need to say anything but thank you," replied Terri.

All of a sudden a tall figure appeared in the doorway. Everyone turned their heads when they heard the man speak. "Am I too late?"

A hush fell over the room. Cindy stopped unwrapping the gift and stared.

"What are you doing here, Asgar?" Justin said.

"I've come to wish the young lady a very happy birthday. May I come in? Ron has already given me consent. You do trust your guards, don't you?"

Justin was about to shout no, but Wayne pulled him over to the side, whispering in his ear. "Let him in. He probably cast some spell on Ron to get past him, and this way if he's up to something, we may find out."

"Come in, Asgar," Cindy said. Though she could have done without his presence, she felt they had no choice but to welcome him. There was no sense making him angry.

"I'm glad to see someone here has manners. Thank you." Asgar glared at Justin, making sure that Justin knew the insult was intended for him.

Asgar stepped in the room, tossing his cape over his left shoulder. He was very aware that all eyes that were glued on him. The very way he carried himself gave the aura of importance. Had he not been the reason they were separated from home, some may even have grown to like him.

In his hand was a package, bundled by gauze and tied with twine. Cindy couldn't help but notice the gold ring worn on his elongated, middle finger. The crystal that was imbedded in the middle of it was magnificent and it reflected a rainbow of colors. Cindy tingled inside as she accepted the gift.

"Happy Birthday. This is for you. I hope you like it."

Cindy kept her voice pleasant and answered, "I'm sure I will. Thank you."

She was about to set it aside, when Asgar protested. "Open it now, I mean, please open it first."

It was a command hidden in politeness. Cindy figured it was better to comply than to start an argument. She untied the fabric and lifted the silver bracelet in the air to show everyone. The links were delicate and dangling from the end was a tiny, silver unicorn.

"It's beautiful, Asgar. Thank you."

There was no denying that Cindy meant it. Unicorns were her passion. Back in Sparta, Pennsylvania, she had a vast collection of figurines and framed pictures. It was one of the many things she had in common with her grandmother Alana. Her grandmother. The thought made Cindy miss her even more.

"It belonged to her, you know?" Asgar said.

"Who?" asked Cindy.

"Why, Alana. Her mother had given it to her when she came of marrying age. It's fitting that it should be yours now."

Cindy fondled the charm as if it would bring her closer to her grandmother just by touching it. They both collected unicorns and it looked almost exactly like the one Alana had created for her. Though it had been a couple of months ago that Alana pulled the necklace out of thin air, it seemed like days ago. The memories of their last day together was still fresh in her mind.

Asgar smiled at Cindy. "You are very much like her, you know? I miss her as well."

Cindy nodded. "Justin, Wayne, why all of us who knew her, miss her. Thanks again."

Cindy set it down and began to open another present when Asgar interrupted again. "Please put it on now."

Before Cindy had a chance to obey, Justin shouted. "Who do you think you are? She'll put it on when she chooses. You are just a guest here, an uninvited one at that."

Wayne had to yank Justin aside to calm him down. "Don't make an issue of this. Cindy is being polite. The last thing we want to do is cause a fight in here."

Asgar sighed. "At least one of you boys has the good sense to know your place. You are a guest in my world. I allow you to live."

Wayne clamped his hand over Justin's mouth before he had a chance to reply. Chuck had to jump up to help Wayne keep hold of their struggling friend.

"But I know when I've overstayed my welcome. Miss Cindy, may this day be just the beginning of many happy moments to come. I was hoping you would be so kind to allow me to reciprocate and show you the hospitality of my realm."

"Thank you, Asgar. Perhaps, someday, that would be nice."

"Tomorrow then. I will be here at the same time. Good day to you all."

Asgar bowed and backed out of the room, his eyes never leaving Cindy. The room remained silent and no one spoke until they were sure that Asgar had disappeared.

Wayne and Chuck released their grip and Justin ran to the door, leaning on the doorpost as he looked down the hallway.

"Darn good thing he's gone, otherwise I'd have been forced to punch his lights out. Who does he think he is?"

No one answered. When Justin was like this it was best to humor him. When it came to Cindy, he was very protective.

The silence made Justin feel a bit uncomfortable. He lowered his voice and said to Cindy, "You're not really going to go, are you?"

"Of course not, but he didn't give me much time to refuse. When he arrives tomorrow, I'll politely take him aside and decline the invitation. I wish I knew what it was he wanted with me."

"He doesn't have to have a reason. He's Asgar," Justin said.

Cindy just kissed Justin on his cheek before returning to unwrap her presents. Soon everyone was lost in the thrill of seeing Cindy accept the many special gifts that they had chosen. It was obvious that Justin or Wayne had allowed them into town to pick out a few things from the shops.

After that, they played a few games and sang a few songs. Too stuffed from the cheesecake and the cookies they raided from the local grocery store that had been transported over with them, their school, and several blocks of Sparta, they all skipped supper. With a full day of catch up work, they eagerly went to bed early.

Cindy was fast asleep when Justin snuck into her room and woke her. "Shh, come here a minute."

Cindy slipped out of her bed. It was hard to see in the oil lit room, among all the beds raided from the empty houses that lay just outside the fortress that they had made out of their school. Without electricity, no street lamps illuminated the outside world. Even the two moons didn't shed enough light for her to see much more than a foot or two away. She waited until her eyes adjusted to the dimness and made her way to the door.

Justin was waiting for her there and he motioned for her to follow him. Cindy was too tired to ask why and did as she was asked. There, under the flickering flame of oil lamp, Justin kissed her.

"Happy Birthday. With all that went on this afternoon, I completely forgot to give you this. Well, not totally. This is sort of personal."

Cindy thanked him and opened the box that Justin handed to her. It wasn't wrapped or even taped, not that it mattered. As she peeled the tissue back, the light that seemed to be coming from within grew brighter.

"Justin, that's the biggest diamond I've ever seen."

"I'm sorry to disappointment you, but I don't think it's a diamond. It's too polished and it shines too much. Diamonds are rough before they are carved. I know because collecting rocks is my Dad's hobby. Besides, this one is much too big."

"You're not kidding," Cindy said. "It's pretty heavy too. It's beautiful though. I'll cherish it."

"I found it out digging in the garden. Even in the ground it sparkled. Perhaps it's just a gut feeling, but I think it's very valuable."

"Oh it is. It is because you gave it to me." Cindy kissed Justin. The two of them clung to each other, until Justin heard the rustling of blankets.

"You better hop back to bed or the others will razz us."

Cindy nodded, knowing how much Justin hated to be teased. As soon as she made it back to her sleeping bag the alarm clock went off. It was one of the noisy, wind up types, with a bell on either of side of the ringer. It could wake up the dead and often had to.

The celebration was over and it was back to work. After dressing and eating breakfast, the work group assigned for gardening headed out the door. The kids worked five days a week. If they finished their chores, they got the weekend off. Most of them anyway. Certain shifts like kitchen duty and security were 24-7, the schedule changed monthly and no one had to do more than their share.

Today, Cindy, Justin, Wayne, Carmen, Ron, Brina, Tina, and Bobby were on garden duty. It was more of a farm really. Only so much food had come over with them, so they decided to use the boxes of seeds they had found in town to grow more. Out of all the chores, this was the most pleasant. It gave everyone a chance to be outdoors.

When they arrived at the farm the pixies were already waiting. Lissy flitted over to greet them. Her gossamer wings were like rainbows in the sunlight.

In the beginning, the pixies were a nuisance. It didn't become a real problem until Carmen and Terri caught them eating the seeds.

Cindy discussed the situation with them and struck a deal that was beneficial to both. They would share their food. Since the pixies needed to eat more than their body weight every day, this would be a great supplement to the berries and apples they found in the forest. The kids made their first treaty. As part of the treaty, the pixies wanted music, so the kids would sing and the pixies would hover nearby listening.

Though the pixies were sociable and everyone got along, it was Lissy that developed into a friend. She was especially close to Cindy since Cindy had saved her life, and Lissy always went out of her way to greet her.

"Where's Terri?" asked Lissy.

Cindy laughed. Lissy loved to dart in and out with Terri's flying wheelchair. At first, Terri would get aggravated at the pixie fluttering about and getting in her way. She swatted at Lissy as if she was an insect and Lissy would taunt her. For a time it looked like the two of them were going to end up hurting each other.

Eventually, Terri realized that her flying skills improved with the game. She got so good at flying and handling the sharp stops that they ended up becoming good friends. Many times Lissy would hitch a ride on Terri's lap.

"Sorry little friend," Cindy answered. "Terri ran to town for us to get some supplies. She should be back later." Having a flying wheelchair, Terri was able to get to and from town quickly and, so far, safely.

Lissy pouted. "That makes two days in a row. I miss her."

"I promise you, she'll be here tomorrow."

Lissy nodded and flitted away. Cindy set the tools down and grabbed a hoe. Today they were transplanting some seedlings that Terri had found in one of the gardens at a nearby home. There were enough to keep them all busy.

Hours later, after a hard day's work, Cindy yelled for Brina and Tina to join her to finish some weeding. The two younger girls retrieved some tools and headed over to the newly toiled ground. All of a sudden, Brina shouted.

"What the heck is that?"

Off in the distance, above the treetops was a huge, flapping manifestation slicing through the horizon. Everyone stopped what they were doing to look where Brina was pointing.

"Is it a bird?" shouted Bobby.

"It sure ain't a plane," Carmen said.

"I don't know," Justin answered. "But I've never seen any bird that big and there's more than one. Whatever they are, I don't like it. They're moving too fast to outrun. Wayne, maybe it's time for battle stations."

Wayne, who was in charge of security, nodded and began to hand out bows, arrows, and slingshots. "This isn't a drill, folks," he commanded, as he handed out the weapons. "Everyone into position."

The formation was instantaneous. All those weeks of practice had paid off. With feet firmly planted and arrows pointed skyward, the kids awaited their next order.

The largest flying beast drew closer. Its wing span blotted out the light, casting an eerie darkness over the land. Everyone stood frozen, silent, and terrified.

Immediately the pixies scattered. Only Lissy remained and she shouted as she flew to Justin's side. "Run away. Hurry. Danger, danger."

CHAPTER 2

The eagle-like bird landed with a thud. Four others remained airborne and encircled the kids. Justin stood in place, his bow aimed at the man straddling the huge creature that had landed. He should have known it would be Asgar. Justin winked at Wayne twice. They had developed a non-verbal means of communication for just this type of emergency. This was the first that they had to put it to use.

"Hold off shooting until we see what is going on," Wayne shouted, turning his head to face the younger kids. They were the ones most likely to panic. He could see their hands shaking and looks of fear and awe on their faces, but they remained in formation.

A tall, muscular man dismounted, his long, shoulder length hair was tangled and fluttered in the wind.

"Asgar," mumbled Justin.

"None other." He bowed, a sly grin pasted on his face.

Cindy moved next to Justin. The huddle of boys and girls all whispered amongst each other.

"What is that?" they asked in hushed tones.

Asgar walked around the huge bird, patting it on the neck. The bird cried out, its piercing shriek was ear shattering. Its ruffled mane of brown, black, and white feathers framed its large, golden eyes.

"This is Maelstrom, my friend. He won't hurt you as long as you don't do anything rash. So lower your weapons."

"What do you want?" asked Wayne.

"What sort of welcome is this?"

"The only one you'll get from us," replied Justin.

"Boys, boys, boys. Quit trying to play tough. You're way out of your league. Now, I'm not here to cause trouble, but if you start something, I'm going to finish it. Please, don't make me."

It was Asgar's spell that had trapped them on the Wildsidhe in the first place. They feared the Fortesan, but they would not, could not bow down to him.

"Leave now," commanded Justin, "and there will be no trouble. Our arrows and spears may be crude, but they're made of iron."

The kids had learned early on that iron could hurt a Wildsidher, even a Fortesan.

"It will take more than mere children's toys to harm me. But this is silly, boys. I'm here to pick up Cindy. We have a date. As soon as she joins me, we'll be gone."

"Cindy isn't going anywhere. I don't know what you want with her, but she doesn't want any part of you."

"Jealous? Does Cindy feel this way? All I've heard is your opinion."

"She's quite happy where she is." Justin turned his bow, aiming his arrow straight for Asgar's heart. "Please leave."

Asgar took another step closer. The tip of the arrow was made of iron and he winced, but he didn't step back.

"I won't tell you again. Cindy, come with me."

Before Cindy had a chance to object, Asgar grabbed her by her arm and pulled her to him. Cindy cried out in surprise.

"I'm sorry. I didn't mean to alarm you or hurt you. These idiots you call your friends don't realize the depth of my power or the repercussions of my anger."

When he spoke to Cindy, his voice softened. He was still threatening though. Asgar was at least a head taller than the others. His arms were muscular even though he was slender; his fingers were long and gangly due to an extra joint. Standing beside the great bird, he struck a formidable position. As intimidating as he was, Asgar was also handsome and rugged.

Cindy looked at Justin and then at Asgar. "I know my friends are only trying to protect me, but to be really honest, I'm happy here. I mean no disrespect to you. Your offer is kind and I'm flattered, but I must decline. Thank you anyway."

"Do you know what you are giving up? Accompany me to my palace. You will find it much more comfortable and much more suitable for one of your station."

"Please don't take it personal, but I'd rather stay with my friends."

"You're a fool. They're doomed. Do you think for an instant I brought the lot of you here for fun and games? Do you wish to stay and die amongst them?"

"Then why did you bring us over?"

"You figure it out since you're so smart."

Asgar laughed. Ron and Wayne clicked their tongues and in unison they released the arrows from their bows. Instantaneously, Maelstrom's strong beak grabbed both arrows and with a crunch, it snapped the wooden sticks with its sharp beak.

"And what do you babies have planned for an encore? Cease and allow Cindy to come with me. Don't force my hand."

"Over my dead body," yelled Justin.

"That can be arranged." Asgar waved his hand and the lionhawks stopped hovering and took flight. Justin pushed Cindy behind him.

"Stay close," he shouted.

Ron and Wayne drew another arrow from their quivers and began to shoot at the birds. The younger boys used their slingshots, but none of the weapons did any damage. It was the strangest of things. The iron-tipped javelins rippled through his plastic-like chest plate, and came clear through his body. It was as if Asgar was made of liquid.

Hovering overhead, the other birds began to pick up rocks from a nearby rock pile left behind by the children after cultivating the field. The hawks released them and the group, no longer able to stand still, scattered. Loud piercing screams of fright and pain echoed through the fields. Wayne and Ron hoisted their bows over their shoulders and covered their heads as if there was a way to shield themselves.

Justin grabbed Cindy by the hand and the two of them dashed towards the school, following the trail of swirling sand left by those retreating before them.

The children ran; their terrifying screams muffled by the shrieking birds and the whooshing noise of flapping wings. It was like running in a tunnel of wind, two steps forward and one back. They were getting nowhere.

When Maelstrom landed, the earth trembled. Rocks and dust scattered everywhere, blinding them. At first Justin thought it was the weight of the hawk that caused the ground to explode. But when it cleared he could make out its sharp talons digging a trench. Before he could warn the others, the lionhawks began to pick up the runners. In seconds, all but Cindy and Justin were thrown in the pit.

Helplessly, Justin and Cindy watched. They had no way to escape. The lionhawks blocked them. There was no escape. Asgar stood motionless behind them just a few yards away.

The cries of their friends brought tears to their eyes. Cindy shielded her face in Justin's chest and he held onto her tightly. The last thing she saw was Maelstrom lowering himself over the hole.

"Will you come with me, now?" Asgar asked.

Justin looked at Asgar, his chest heaving as he held Cindy tight. "Let them go. What did they do to you?"

"Nothing. I'm not interested in them at all, which is to say, I couldn't care less whether they lived or died. But die they will unless Cindy comes with me. I'll even let you listen to their screams as they suffocate."

Cindy struggled free of Justin's grasp. She faked a smile, tears streaming down her cheeks. "I'm ready, Asgar. Set them free."

Justin grabbed for Cindy's hand. "No, Cindy. Don't go. We'll figure a way out of this."

"There's no time. Besides, what can you or I do against these lionhawks? I don't have a choice."

Asgar nodded. "None at all."

The great bird lowered its neck to the ground and Cindy climbed into the saddle. She could hear the sound of blood rushing in her ears as her heart pounded furiously against her ribcage. In order to ride the beast, she had to straddle it, knees bent, with her legs resting on the wings.

With nothing to hold onto, she grabbed a fistful of feathers. She knew Asgar was seated behind her, as she saw him mount the bird, but she couldn't feel his body heat or his presence. When she turned to see for herself, her face merged with his chest and the body rippled. She knew then, he was just an image.

With a snap of fingers, the lionhawk was aloft. The piercing cry of the bird and the flapping of its wings were deafening. Even if Asgar was to speak to her, she wouldn't have been able to hear him. Nor could she make out the words Justin was shouting as they flew farther and farther away.

In one way she was grateful. She would remember him the way he was. Holding her in his strong arms. The soft caresses as his fingers raked through her blonde tresses. Those were the memories she would cherish, for she doubted she would ever see him again.

Justin shouted for Terri and realized that she had never returned from her trip to town. Wayne, too, wondered where she was, but they had no time to worry. He had to get them out and back to safety. He knelt by the edge of the trench and lowered his hand. Wayne was the last to emerge as he helped the smaller ones out first.

Justin turned his head. The lionhawks were slowly disappearing from sight. "Let's get back to the school before Asgar changes his mind and re-attacks. Hopefully, Terri will be there. It's not like her to be gone this long."

"No, it's not. If she had been here, she could follow Asgar. Now, we have no clue where he's taken her," Wayne said.

"I can follow him," said Lissy emerging from the bushes.

"But, I can't even see the birds. It's too late."

"We Pixies have good eyesight. Besides, lionhawks leave a stinky trail I can follow."

"Thanks, Lissy. We owe you one," Justin said.

The pixie never answered. She disappeared before their eyes. All Justin and the others could see was a bright speck of light fluttering through the horizon as the sun's rays reflected radiantly off the shiny wings of their little friend.

Justin herded the children together and ordered the Bearclaws to lead the group back to the school. Wayne waved, running all the way to school. He was sick to his stomach about Terri and wanted to see if she had made it back safely.

The school was lit as the sun soon would be setting. Bobby stood quietly at the chain link gate entrance with an armful of flaming torches. As they entered, he handed one to Ron, Chuck, John, and Wayne. Wayne moved around the fence line, getting reports from the kids on guard duty and he didn't like what he heard.

"Terri isn't back, Justin. Do you think Asgar has her?"

"I doubt it. He's not into subtle. If he had her, he'd have let us know. He's after Cindy and I wish I knew why. I miss Cindy already. She's the one thing in my life that made this place bearable and now she's gone."

"Well, Terri's my sister. She could be dead and we not know it. I feel just as rotten as you do," Wayne said. "I'm going to go look for her."

"We can't go looking for her now, it's getting too dark and too dangerous. Asgar could have lionhawks waiting out there. Plus there's always the darkcats. I'm worried sick, but it's not going to do us any good to panic," Justin said, "but if you want to talk about it, I'm here for you."

"Not really. I can't think clearly and I'm exhausted. Why don't we drop it? I'm not in the mood to talk to you or anybody else. Okay?" Justin knew Wayne too well. He was going out, no matter what anybody told him.

All of a sudden, John interrupted. He was out of breath from running from the gate. "Wait. Someone's coming down the street. I can't make out who it is, but we aren't out of danger yet!"

CHAPTER 3

They sprinted toward the front gate. Wayne, worried about all the kids inside the school looked at his friend and froze. "Did you barricade the doors?"

"Yes, but I think we should prepare for another attack," answered John.

Wayne nodded. "I'll take the front tower." Justin motioned for him to get moving.

"Be careful. Don't do anything stupid."

"Ditto."

Justin ran to the gate to look out. Walking down the street, he could make out the silhouette of a woman. She was cloaked in black from head to toe, her face hidden in the shadows. Only the sparkling tiara woven through threads of raven braids could be seen under her hood.

It took a moment for his eyes to adjust to the darkness. As she neared the gate, the overpowering scent of gardenia's almost made him gag. His gut feeling told him to double check the lock on the gate.

Justin waited for the woman to make the first move, but she remained mostly hidden in the shadows of the night. Though the torches burned brightly, it was too far away to shed enough light for him to identify her. He made a mental note to add more lamps, especially at the front gate.

The flowery scent was familiar. Justin racked his brain. Where had he smelled this before? He shifted his stance to get a better view of the stranger, but she remained cloaked.

"Who are you? What do you want?" screamed Justin. The woman didn't answer. "Stop where you are or we'll open fire!"

"Is that what you wish?" said a sweet, feminine voice. "Then perhaps I'll return when it's more convenient. Terri can spend the night with me."

Justin and Wayne turned their heads to see the trail of a black cape disappearing down the street. Justin looked up at his cousin in the watch tower. Their eyes and mouths were wide open. In unison they yelled, "Wait! Who are you and what have you done with Terri?"

It was the sound of Terri's voice shouting that startled him. "Justin... Wayne....are you there?"

"If you want to find out about Terri, then come out here," said the woman.

Having no choice but to open the gate, he did so slowly. Justin stepped out, torch in hand, palming his switchblade and tucking it under his other sleeve. He trusted no one. He made out the shape of a girl in a wheelchair.

"Terri, are you all right?"

"She's perfectly fine, Justin. I've taken good care of her."

"Who are you?" Justin asked, stepping out into the open.

The woman moved closer to the flickering flame. Her shadow towered over her, reflecting an image of a giant on the street behind her.

"Don't you remember me?"

Morna moved closer to Justin, extending her arm. Justin hesitated. His eyes never left the woman. Close up, he recognized her.

"Queen Morna. Of course I haven't forgotten."

Justin shook her hand and shivered. It was an uncomfortable large hand, with long spindly fingers and pointy red nails filed dagger sharp. But it was Morna that winced and drew back. For a moment he thought it rude, but realized the knife hidden under his sleeve was made of iron.

It was then that he could make out the girl in the green wheelchair. He relaxed a bit when he identified her as truly being Terri.

Justin tried to hide the sarcasm in his voice. "Thank you for bringing Terri back. It was very kind of you."

"Oh, it was my pleasure. One of my kitties had her cornered. Lucky thing I came along when I did. I shudder to think what Shalimar would have done to her, hadn't I noticed her absence."

Justin looked at Terri. "You're okay then?"

"Just fine. Queen Morna arrived just in time. A second later and I would've been darkcat food. But, then again, if she hadn't placed me in that position in the first place, I wouldn't have needed her help."

"Why Terri, how could you say that? I came to you to offer you my hand in friendship. I'm terribly sorry Shalimar found you first."

Justin wondered just what Morna was up to and what she wanted with Terri. Had she tricked her as she did with Marianne? But now was not the time to question her or to rile Terri up either. The last thing they needed was to start something with Morna. He decided to play it diplomatically.

"Again, thank you."

Justin headed down the steps slowly. "You must be exhausted, Terri. Why don't you head inside?"

Terri caught the wink and maneuvered the wheelchair around Morna. She didn't stop to wave good bye and disappeared inside the fence line before Morna could object.

Morna tilted her head and grinned, but kept her distance. Justin knew it was the iron that protected him. For a minute he thought about capturing Morna, but even though Fortesan's magic was limited around the metal, he didn't know to what extent. He dismissed that idea. Asgar was afraid of her.

Why jeopardize everyone?

"I thank you for bringing her back. If there isn't anything else, it's been a long day and I'm very tired."

"Very well, then," said Morna waving good bye.

Justin turned to head back to the others when Morna spoke again. "I guess you don't want to know what's happened to your Cindy."

He stopped abruptly. His heart began to race and he shouted. "Wait a minute, please."

"She's with Asgar," Morna said sweetly.

"I know that; tell me something I don't."

"Do you know where Asgar is? Well, I do and I'll even take you there. We haven't much time. You do know he'll never let her leave?"

"I figured as much. You're not telling me anything I don't know already. What does Asgar want?"

"He wants my kingdom, but in order to gain it, he must first marry into royalty. Otherwise the land will reject him and he'll lose face and magic."

"Cindy isn't royalty."

"Obviously you don't know your girlfriend or the secrets she keeps. It's not up to me to tell you. Now, do you, or do you not, want me to take you to Asgar's castle?"

Justin nodded and said, "Yes."

Morna smiled a crooked smile. "Then I guess all we have left is to talk about is price. I've already done you one favor today by bringing your dear friend Terri back alive. This time, you owe me."

"Name it," Justin said.

"We can discuss the terms later. Right now, we've Cindy's welfare at stake. I'll take you at your word."

"No way, Morna, not without knowing the consequences. Not after what you tried to do to Bobby. And what happened to Marianne? Did you kill her?"

Justin had no way of knowing that Morna had sacrificed Marianne to the Shadows in Bobby's place. Now Marianne had become a living shadow, but even Morna did not know how powerful a shadow. The queen was not about to admit to ignorance.

"What I do doesn't concern you. Do we have a deal?" said Morna.

"What do you want? Tell me, or it's a no go."

"Every minute we stand here haggling puts Cindy in danger."

"I doubt if he'll harm her, if he needs her."

"Oh, I don't mean that he would harm her, but he has ways of getting what he wants. You have no idea what an enchanter Asgar is. He's quite a catch and handsome too. There was a time, not so long ago, that I fell victim to his charm. Wait too long and he will win her heart…and her soul as well."

"That's not going to happen. I'm not willing to give you an open-ended promise. You could end up owning my soul or trying to sacrifice me like Bobby. Tell me what you want and I'll do it."

"But you see, that's the problem. Right now, there's nothing I need. Just a simple promise for the future favor is all I ask. Who knows, I may never cash it in."

"No. Not on those terms. Besides, I don't think it's to your advantage that Asgar has Cindy in his power. If we work together as a team we can stop it. It'll serve both our purposes."

Morna turned and headed down the street. "Perhaps, but there's one difference. I don't care whether Cindy lives or dies. I just want her out of the way. I was just thinking of you. Poor, poor, Cindy," she whispered. "I guess human love has it limits."

Justin ran after her, trying to grab her tightly by the arm. His hand went through. Morna glared at him as the image of her shook free of his hold.

"Don't you ever touch me again or you will pay dearly."

Justin shivered. He knew enough about the queen to know she meant every word. Marianne's absence was proof enough of Morna's treachery. Not that Marianne was an innocent by any means. She had given Bobby over to Morna willingly. Though he knew he'd made the right decision, Justin still felt sick to his stomach.

Justin watched Morna go. Not once did she look back. The night wind made his torch flicker, and for a minute he thought it might blow it out.

Morna's image moved into the darkness. The real Morna stepped out of the shadows and the image merged with the real Fortesan Queen. The iron barricade around the school was enough to make her hesitate about coming inside herself. Immediately two, huge cats growled off in the distance. Even though the light was dim, Justin could see the beasts pacing. It took only a moment for Morna to reach the street and he watched as the great cats greeted her, both of them exposing a mouthful of huge, ivory fangs.

Justin got back inside the gate as quickly as he could.

Morna patted the pets, her long, tapered fingers vanish in the thick, luxurious fur of the cat's nape. Glancing back over her shoulder, she smiled once more.

"Call me if you change your mind," she shouted.

Justin closed the gate and barricaded it with the iron chains and combination locks.

Darn it, he said to himself. What is this place? Why were they here?

Lost in thought, he jerked when he felt a hand rest on his shoulder. It was Wayne.

"Look, I'm sorry man. She is one wicked woman. Terri told me what happened. Morna's cats had her cornered. She was totally surprised and outnumbered. She had to promise to take Morna here. She feels awful about that."

"No big deal. What's done is done."

"We'll get her back, I promise. Lissy will find her. Don't give up yet. What you need now, what we all need, is a good night's sleep. We can make plans tomorrow when we're all rested and clear headed. Let's say we call it a night."

Justin nodded and got up, too upset to talk. The two cousins made their way back to the classroom where they had set up sleeping quarters.

The room was dark when they opened the door. Sounds of snoring and coughing filled the stillness of the night. The lamp was out and though it would be dangerous not to keep it going, Justin left it alone. The darkness hid his watery eyes.

After taking a deep breath, Justin carefully maneuvered between the rows of mattresses. Without making a sound, he slipped under his blanket still wearing his clothes. He pulled the cover up to his chin and closed his eyes, but even though every fiber in his body ached and his eyes burned, he couldn't fall asleep.

For the first time in ages, maybe in forever, he started to pray. Over and over he kept mouthing, "Please keep Cindy safe. Please, dear God, please bring Lissy back."

CHAPTER 4

Winklo looked at Nash, the depth of his green color seemed to glow. He was staring through the lead-paned window and ignoring everything around him, including his beloved dwarf companion.

"Nash, what's going on?"

Winklo tried to push him away using her hip, but he refused to budge. "Cut that out. I want to see what's going on. The lionhawks have landed and it looks like there is a lady dismounting. Yep, it's a lady all right."

"Let me see. Let me see!" Winklo pushed Nash to the floor. "She's pretty, even for a Fortesan."

"I don't think she is one, Winky. Though I sense the aura of magic about her, it's raw."

"Well, what else would she be? Sometimes I wonder about you, Nash. If I didn't love you so much…"

"You'd do what?"

Nash smiled and rubbed his nose against her cheek. "You wouldn't hurt someone smaller than you, would you?"

Winklo rolled her eyes. "I sure would if you hadn't gotten out of the way. No…she's a Fortesan, and a high one at that. Asgar is coming out to meet her and bowing. He's not Mr. Courteous with anyone but his own."

"Unless he wants something, pet. I do remember when we thought him nice."

Winklo sighed. "That seems like ages ago."

"Two years is a long time, but I'd rather be a prisoner here with you, than free on the outside without." Nash nosed her again and took her hand. "We better go make some refreshments. I certainly don't want to make him mad again."

"Nor do I. Three days of separation is worse than the work. Beat you there."

It was three flights of winding steps to the kitchen. Nash had started down first, but Winklo, even though she was a head shorter, was quite a bit stronger. She pushed him out of the way. She was already setting out the trays when Nash caught up with her.

The two bustled about the room pouring Iceberry tea into porcelain cups and cutting the sugarcoated teacake into slices. Nash opened the heavy wooden door to the garden to fetch some flowers.

His beautiful babies. Thorn blossoms of all colors edged the path and he stopped to choose the most beautiful blooms. With his magical touch, the buds opened. He clipped two of the red and one each of the pink and white.

The vase was filled with water by the time he made it back in. Asgar stood at the doorway smiling.

"Excellent, my friends. The Lady Cindy should be very pleased."

Nash and Winklo bowed. They were curious as to the visitor, but knew better than to ask.

"Will there be anything else, milord," Winklo asked.

Asgar shook his head. "That will be all. You may return to your rooms. The lady and I will dine at sunup."

"As you wish," Nash said.

Asgar walked over the top cupboard, mumbled a few words and the doors sprung open. Nash looked at Winklo and she at him. Though that door remained magically locked, both knew it contained jars of potions and Evals dust.

"Out both of you. You've been dismissed. Take advantage of the night off or I'll take advantage of you."

Asgar began to rotate both his hands and silvery sparks crackled through the air. Simultaneously, they struck both the elf and the dwarf on their rears. Rubbing themselves, they scampered up the steps.

Asgar chuckled to himself and sprinkled some of the dust on both the cakes and the tea. Other than a slight shimmer, the food didn't look any different. After relocking the cabinet, Asgar grabbed the tray and left the room.

Cindy was sitting on the edge of the purple plush chair. She was tired from the long ride and felt dirty. Her lovely blonde hair was wind-blown and tangled and she tried to smooth it out with her fingers. Asgar stopped at the stone archway to watch her.

Cindy had heard the footsteps and stopped once she saw Asgar leaning against the wall. "I'm tired, so tell me what's going on. Am I a prisoner?"

"Not at all. You're my guest."

"Then I'd like to be shown to my room. I'm tired and want to get some sleep."

"Of course. Forgive me for not ushering you to your room first, but I thought you might be a bit hungry."

Asgar held out the ornate silver tray. "This is Iceberry tea, my favorite. The juice from these little, blue berries give the tea a natural sweetness. And these teacakes are wonderful. Just right for a snack. Please, try one."

Cindy was starving and the food looked delicious. It took all of her will power to keep from taking a bite, but she knew better. The Fortesans tainted their food with something that put a spell on whoever ate it. She remembered the stories her grandma used to tell her when she was little. Back then she thought them to be fairy tales. Now, here in this awful place, she knew them to be true.

"No thanks. I'm not hungry. I just want to go to bed."

Asgar took another sip from his teacup and uncrossed his legs. "I'll just take this tray with us in case you change your mind. Follow me."

He led her up the stairwell to the second floor. Many oil lamps lighted the hallways and in between each, were beautifully painted portraits. If she hadn't been so tired, she would have to stop to admire them, but more than anything she wanted to get away from Asgar.

The door to her room was open and candles were burning everywhere. In the center was a huge, intricately carved, four-poster bed. Heavy velvet curtains almost concealed the leaded window, which was ajar. The breeze was chilly and Cindy shivered. Asgar closed them and laid the tray down on the table. The drapes stopped fluttering and he loosened the drawstrings, blotting out the light from the two moons.

"I hope this meets with your approval. I chose this wing to allow you some privacy. Feel free to make this your home. If you find a different room you feel more comfortable in, just say the word. Your happiness here is the most important thing to me now. Off to the side there is a magical bell. Just ring it and one of my servants will be at your disposal."

Cindy nodded. "If my happiness is all that important, then take me home."

"That's the one wish I can't grant."

"Can't or won't?" asked Cindy glaring at him.

"You'll see things entirely different in the morning. Get some rest. Tomorrow we'll take a tour of the grounds. There's a lot to see. I think, if you give it a chance, you'll find it much more comfortable here."

Cindy was about to open her mouth to disagree but chose not to. She didn't want to prolong his company another minute "Good night, Asgar," she said lowering her head so he couldn't see that he had upset her.

"Good night, sweet princess. I'll see you in the morn."

Asgar shut the door softly behind him. Cindy ran to the door to see if it was locked. She really didn't believe him when he said she was a guest. When the door opened, she smiled, but only for a second. Asgar was waiting only inches away when she peered down the hallway.

"This is to be your home. I'll never lock you in it. When a Fortesan gives his word, it's binding. Don't ever doubt that."

"I don't remember any promises from you."

"Then I will give you one. You are free to roam the castle. There's a lot of my family history here and I think you'll enjoy exploring the many rooms here. The garden is lovely. All that is in within the fences, you have at your disposal. On that I give you my word. I wish you to be happy here and to make this your home."

"Never," shouted Cindy turning her back on Asgar.

"Never's a long time. Oh, I almost forgot again, good night."

This time instead of leaving, Asgar bent down and kissed Cindy lightly on her cheek. She stepped back, but it was too late. Asgar bowed, winked, and vanished.

After a few hours of slumber, Cindy awoke to voices in the hallway. At first she tried to drown them out, wanting so badly to get a few more hours of sleep, but her curiosity got the better of her.

There were two people outside the door. She suspected they were the servants that Asgar had spoken of earlier. If they thought her asleep, they'd be inclined to speak freely. Cindy kept her eyes closed and pretended.

"She's not a Fortesan, I tell you. You can be so frustrating. I'm not stupid," Nash said softly.

"I guess that means I am." Winklo shoved Nash gently.

"No love, but take a good look. Her fingers are shorter, and besides, why else would Asgar taint her food? He wouldn't have to do that if she were one of them."

Winklo nodded. "True, but it sure doesn't make any sense to me. I can't figure out why she is here."

"Neither can I. My magic isn't geared to reading minds. The way he spoke to her, milady this, princess that, mayhap she's his girlfriend."

"Oh just what we need. Some la-de-da mistress to curtsey too. As if we didn't have enough work waiting on our dear lord and benefactor."

"Why do you always look at the dark side of things, Winky dear?"

"Why? Because, when one expects the worst, one doesn't get disappointed. Our life is like a cow pasture. You know the pies are out there, it's just a matter of time before you step in it."

Nash laughed. "That's what I love about you. Your unique way of looking at life."

"Shhhh, you're going to wake her. And...I love you too, Nash."

The couple started to embrace, totally forgetting where they were and what they were supposed to be doing. Cindy slipped out of bed; the sudden silence made her think they had left. Quietly, she tiptoed to the door and peeked through the crack. They were snuggling. This was her chance.

As fast as she could move, she opened the door and snatched the two creatures by the backs of their collars, dragging them into her room. Using her foot, she shut the door and leaned against it.

Nash and Winklo gasped. Cindy released them and shoved them towards the bed.

"Okay. Who are you and what are you doing spying on me?"

CHAPTER 5

Cindy stood rigid, barring the door. Nash and Winklo dropped to the floor, prostrating themselves.

"We beg forgiveness, oh great one. We meant no harm. Please don't tell Asgar. We'd be forever in your debt."

Cindy looked at the green elf. For a male he was awfully small and soft-spoken. He was quite the contrast from the lady dwarf. She couldn't help but think what an odd couple they made.

"Get up. I'm not great and I certainly wouldn't hurt you. Why would you think I'd tell Asgar anything? What did he tell you? Did he tell you I was his guest?

The couple slowly stood up, eyeing Cindy very cautiously. Neither one spoke. They both just looked at each other.

"I heard you talking about me in the hallway. You know it's rude to spy on people."

Winklo began to whisper in Nash's ear, prompting him to do the speaking. "Again, we're sorry, ma'am. It's just that we've never seen the likes of you. I can tell you're not a Fortesan, your fingers are different, but we also saw you arrive on the back of a lionhawk. Only Fortesans can manage any of the twelve beasts. It's all so confusing. You even smell of magic. Just who and what are you?"

"I'll answer your questions if you answer mine," Cindy said.

"Okay," said Winklo, "You first."

Cindy paused and then decided to comply. "Okay. I'll start. My name is Cindy Hartman, I'm fifteen, no, oops, sixteen years old, and I'm from Sparta, Pennsylvania. My species are called human. I've no idea why I'm here. Now who are you?"

"Forgive me, miss, but we never get guests here. Well, almost never, and the few that do, well, they don't stay long. For our own protection we keep a watch out. Asgar isn't to be trusted. Honestly, we didn't mean any harm. We're just servants. Allow me the pleasure of introducing my lovely companion Winklo. My name is Nash."

"Nice to meet you. I'm sorry too. I didn't mean to scare you like that. I just figured that Asgar sent you to spy on me. He gives me the creeps and I don't trust him one bit. He brought me here against my will. I guess I'm just a bit jittery, not to mention tired and hungry."

Cindy turned to look at the tray of food on her nightstand. It had been hours since she'd eaten and her stomach was growling.

"Don't eat that. I probably shouldn't be warning you, but we think Asgar covered it with Evals."

"Evals?"

"Magic powder. Fortesans use it to turn others into their slaves. Asgar is a very powerful magic user. The longer you stay here, the more dangerous it will become. You better leave."

Cindy sighed. "I wish I could. My friends are somewhere far away from here. I couldn't find them even if I did have a way out. He calls me his guest, but honestly, I'm a prisoner. Though the doors aren't locked, I'm at his mercy. I've no way of finding my friends and I've been warned not to go past the fences. Why do you two stay?"

"Similar reasons. Our families and friends don't approve of Winky and me. They tossed us out like yesterday's trash. Perhaps it would have been better to die out there, but at the time Asgar seemed so nice. You see, I love Nash and he loves me. It was the only way we could be together. Elves and dwarves don't mix."

"Tell me more."

"I wish we could, but it's getting late. It's a lengthy story and I'm afraid we've been here too long already. Asgar expects his breakfast on time. We'd best be going," Nash said.

Winklo smiled and bent down to whisper in Nash's ear again. "You're right," Nash said. "I'll go fetch her something to eat while you see to Asgar's needs."

"What are the two of you up to?" she asked.

"Nash is going to get you some untainted food. That way you won't be hungry at the breakfast table. Asgar expects you to dine with him, but most likely the food will be poisoned."

"That's so sweet of you. How can I ever thank you? I'm starving."

"No need. It's just nice to make a new friend."

Winklo waved and scurried out of the room.

"I'd best be going too. Maybe this afternoon we can talk more. Asgar always seems to be busiest then."

Cindy waved and got up to shut the door. She figured she ought to get dressed before Nash returned. If this had been home, she would have taken a shower first, but here there was no plumbing. She would have to wait to bathe.

Across from her four-poster bed stood a huge wardrobe with intricately, carved doors, but no handles. Cindy tried to pry it open with her nails. After trying for what seemed like an eternity, she plopped down on the bed discouraged.

"Try using your magic. Concentrate."

Cindy looked around half-expecting Nash or Winklo to be at the door, but it was still closed.

"Or just knock, but you need to practice your skills." This time the voice was louder.

"Are you talking to me?" Cindy looked around the room, her eyes wide open and looking directly at the chest. "Is there anyone else here?" she said.

No answer. I must be hearing things, she said to herself. But this is a magical place. I guess it couldn't hurt to listen to the voice.

Cindy knocked on the door and the wardrobe jiggled. Instantly, both doors swung open. Inside, on a long wooden rod, were dresses of many colors and styles. Cindy started to look through them. Some of the gowns were very heavy and elaborate, studded with jewels and trimmed in gold. Much too fancy, she thought.

"The blue one is pretty."

Cindy looked around the room, but could see no one. The voice seemed to be coming from the corner, but all that was there was a massive Cheval mirror on a framed stand.

The gowns separated. Some moved to the right and the others to the left, leaving one in the middle. It was a simple dress of sapphire blue, long and silky. Cindy fondled the fabric.

"It's lovely. Thank you for your help."

"Don't mention it. My pleasure."

The voice was beginning to sound familiar. Cindy shivered. It was as if a frosty wind had iced her. She took the gown from the rack and tiny matching slippers materialized on the floor underneath it. The whole outfit was so medieval like, it made her think of fair ladies and knights on shining steeds of white. Cindy slipped the gown over her head and felt transformed.

Standing before the mirror, she admired her reflection. It had been a long time since she'd worn anything as lovely as this. Even the dances at school were casual. Most everyone wore pants. She had never realized how something this delicate and silky could make her feel all feminine and beautiful.

Holding the skirt in her hands she began to twirl. Around and around, the skirt swirling about her legs. Cindy laughed. She felt radiant.

"You look lovely, milady."

Cindy stopped, almost tumbling to the floor. There, in the mirror, staring back at her was a man dressed in an elaborate tunic made of purple and gold rope. He doffed his feathered cap and bowed low. No matter how handsome or princely looking he was, he was still Asgar.

"Spying on me? How dare you watch me dress? Is this how you treat your guests?"

The mirrored image disappeared. Cindy turned the mirror around so the glass would face the wall. Look at that next time, she thought.

Cindy was so busy moving the furniture around that she didn't notice Nash come in. He was holding a tray filled with fresh vegetables and fruit.

"Miss Cindy, should I set this on the table?"

Cindy screamed and Nash, startled, dropped the tray. Fruit and vegetables rolled everywhere. While they were picking them up they Cindy warned him about the mirror.

"Are there others?" she asked.

"Many, but it's not just mirrors that you should be aware of. The paintings in the hall…they talk to him. It's as if this whole castle is an extension of him. If he wishes to know something, there's no way to stop him."

"Then, he could've been listening earlier."

"Could have, but I've a bit of magic of my own. Not on his level, mind you, but enough to frustrate him. I can't stop him from listening, but I can make living things resonate. Those vibrations cause so much irritating static that he's unable to hear much. The problem is that I can't do that very often or for long. It can be very tiring. You should try it. I can teach you the spell."

"I don't know a thing about magic."

"You don't have too. You have the gift, I can tell. You are very powerful. The potential to perform magic is something you're born with it. It's just takes training to harness it. What you have is categorized as raw. It's very strong, but not very controllable."

"And…it's not reliable. It doesn't always do what you want it to do," added Cindy, thinking of the few times she had been able to use magic.

"I'll go into more details later, but now isn't the time," Nash said. "You're hungry and you need to eat before Asgar gets here. I'll be back."

The mention of food stopped her from questioning Nash further. She was starving and it all smelled wonderful.

"They're safe. Picked them myself early this morning. I'm sorry I can't do more."

"Please, don't feel that way. I'm so grateful. You've done more than you should. I'm sure if Asgar were to find out, you'd be in real trouble."

Nash looked down at feet and grinned. "It was worth the risk. Now, hurry. Asgar will be here soon to escort you to the dining room."

Cindy didn't wait for Nash to leave the room before picking up a long, red, tubular shaped item. The aroma reminded her of apples and bananas. She bit into it and the juice squirted all over her cheeks. Instead of being sweet it was tart and it made her lips pucker, but she was so hungry she ate all of it.

There were so many to choose from. The best tasting of all was the ones she saved for last. They were ugly, shriveled, yellow kernels and looked nasty. Though they looked like raisins, they were much larger. Cindy finished every last one and just in time. No sooner had she wiped her mouth, then there was a knock on the door.

"Breakfast is ready, my sweet," said Asgar.

Cindy shoved the empty tray under the four-poster bed. She opened the door and stepped out.

"You are even more beautiful than I remembered. You do know you resemble Alana?"

"How did you know my grandmother? You never explained."

"I know lots of things and with the proper training and education, you can too. Did your grandmother not tell you about me?"

"Not much I'm afraid, sir."

Asgar rubbed his nose and was silent. "What about the Wildsidhe? Did she ever talk about Morna?"

"Grandma talked about a lot of things, but we all thought she was getting senile. All I know about her past was that she was a Wildsidher and I only found out about that a few months ago. It was right after Grandpa Howard died."

"Howard. What a pitiful excuse for a life form."

"How dare you talk about my grandfather like that! He was a loving, warm, caring man, but I should have expected an attitude like this from you. You wouldn't know a single thing about respect and decency."

"Watch your step. You speak from ignorance so I'll excuse you. You know nothing about Howard in his younger days. He was a thief. Alana was blinded by his foolish promises and bewitched by his sweet talk."

"You're bitter. I had no idea you knew either one of them so well."

"Oh, I did. I was engaged to Alana. The necklace you're wearing, the silver unicorn, it was a wedding gift to her. There were only two of them ever made. One I gave to her and the other disappeared when she did."

"Do you want it back?"

"Of course not, it's fitting that it hangs around your neck. It was meant to be yours as much as you were meant to be mine."

Cindy wanted to rip the charm from her neck. She wanted no part of Asgar, but neither did she want to anger him. Besides, Alana had created the unicorn from magic. She saw her do it. Asgar had to be lying. Jealousy begets lies. Still, something inside her told her there was some truth to his words.

The rest of the walk they didn't talk. She was grateful for his silence, as she was lost in thought. Sometimes, like when he smiled, he really did seem to be charming.

Surprisingly, the dining room was bright and cheerful. All the drapes were fastened to the side by gold ropes and the bright rays of the sun filtered through the open windows. A large, oak table that could seat at least twenty people rested on an intricate carpet of many colors.

Asgar held the seat out and Cindy sat down. She could feel his presence behind her, the soft touch of his fingers as they entangled in her hair. His nose nestled by her ear. Cindy closed her eyes and shivered when he kissed her neck. *What is happening to me?* she asked herself.

Asgar sat down across from her and rang the bell. Immediately Winklo scurried in, followed by Nash holding a tray. Cindy held back a smile. Their friendship was to remain a secret for all their sakes.

An apron covered Winklo's dress. She looks kinda cute, Cindy thought. She was just a few inches shorter than Nash and he was shorter than Cindy. It felt awkward looking down on them, as they were much older than she was.

Winklo, from a distance, resembled a girlfriend of hers from school. Both had jet-black hair that contrasted their fair skin. The difference was that Winklo was a quite a bit heavier. From behind, she looked more like a man and her short, choppy hair looked like someone used a bowl to guide the scissors. Obviously, Nash was her beautician.

Asgar rubbed his nose and sniffled. "What are you thinking about? You look lost."

"I'm sorry. I was just watching your servants."

"Nash must look a bit strange to you, being green and all. No elves where you used to live, I bet."

"No, and no dwarves either. In fact, very little here resembles my home. Most of what appears to be normal here are just legends where I come from."

"All legends have a foot in reality. There was a time these creatures roamed your land. But your kind killed first and asked questions later. Dragons almost became extinct before finding a safe haven here on Wildsidhe. Such a pity too. They're such majestic creatures and very misunderstood."

Winklo set a plate in front of Cindy filled with sausage and eggs. The smell was delightful. It had been a long time since she had been offered a cooked meal. Even though she had eaten her fill earlier, her mouth watered just looking at all that food.

Asgar had already started to eat. He watched Cindy as she drank in the delicious aroma of the freshly baked bread spread thick with butter.

"Eat. You must be famished."

Winklo shook her head slightly, her eyes wide open. Asgar glared at her and the dwarf looked down. He lifted a platter stacked high with pancakes covered in some blue, goopy syrup. The steam swirled, filling the air with a delightful scent.

"Thanks, but no. It sure does look good, but I'm not all that hungry."

"I'm not all that surprised, with all the fruit you had to eat earlier."

"You were spying on me then. Is that how you expect to earn my trust?"

"Nothing goes on in my home that I don't know of. I want you to be well aware of that so you don't try anything foolish. Besides, you will soon understand why."

Cindy would have asked why, but she started to feel a bit queasy. Her stomach was churning and she felt nauseous. She looked at Nash and Winklo standing at the doorway shaking their heads. Something was wrong

Cindy tried to speak, but found it difficult. Her tongue felt thick.

Asgar leaned back in his plush chair, a sly grin on his face. "Are you okay, Cindy?"

Cindy couldn't respond. Her eyelids grew heavy. The room began to spin.

Winklo cried out when Cindy's head hit the table. Both flew to her side.

"What did you do to her? You poisoned her, didn't you?" said Winklo.

"No, not at all," said Asgar. "You did. I just paid your garden a visit early this morning."

CHAPTER 6

"How do you feel?" asked Winklo, fluffing Cindy's pillow. "A little woozy, but all right. What happened? All I can remember is that Asgar and I were talking and then, poof, I'm here."

Nash looked at Winklo and she at him. "I feel so horrible. I wouldn't blame you if you never trusted me again. I'm so sorry."

Cindy shifted positions, trying to get comfortable in her bed. "What are you talking about?"

"I poisoned you. Not on purpose, but I never thought Asgar would taint the food still growing in the garden with Evals powder. I should have known better."

"Oh no," gasped Cindy. "Does this mean I'm his slave? I don't feel any different and I certainly don't like him anymore than I did before."

Winklo and Nash hopped on the bed. Poking and prodding, they lifted Cindy's eyelid, stared into her ears, and even sniffed her. They hmmmm'd and hahhh'd, settling into a comfortable position next to her on the mattress.

"Something strange is going on. You don't look spellbound. What I mean is, you don't have that glazed look that creatures get when they become a Fortesan's slave."

Winklo nodded. "Nor does she smell any different. Do you think Asgar is bluffing? I wouldn't put it past him."

"Could be. If Cindy thought she was already a slave, she may feel it's useless to refrain from eating and then, voila, he's got a new servant."

"That must be it. You washed the fruit and vegetables off. I think it's all a clever ruse to get you to eat the real poisoned food."

Cindy smiled at Winklo. "I sure hope you're right. I'd rather die than be his slave."

"Just be careful, Missy. You need to get some rest. We can visit you later."

"Wait…" Cindy, said. "I'm not sleepy or tired and besides, you promised to tell me the story of how you and Nash met."

Nash nodded. "I suppose just laying here and listening won't affect your recovery and it's a good time, too, with Asgar out feeding the lionhawks and all."

Winklo agreed. Nash always looked to his beloved as if to ask permission. Cindy wondered if it was an elf thing or just something about the couple. She would ask them later. For now, she was curious about the two and really wanted to learn more.

"Dwarves and elves don't mix," began Nash. "Oh, we trade for things and occasionally work together on projects that'll benefit us both, but as a rule, we keep pretty much to our own kind.

"I know you've already noticed my green skin color…"

Cindy smiled. "Yes, it's a bit strange, but only because I'm not used to seeing it."

"Well," Nash continued, "All of us have different coloring, somewhat dependent on our magical capabilities. Not all elves have magic and some are better than others at casting spells. I'm green because my specialty is linked to vegetation. The stronger and more capable our magic is, the deeper the color of our skin and the more iron affects us. That is one way to differentiate between elves. I chose to enhance my magical capabilities even though there are some negatives to being trained in the sorcerer's ways. That's why some elves choose to remain magic free. My brother, for instance…"

"Cindy doesn't want to hear about your brother, or your mother, or even about elves in general. Just get on with the story, or do I need to tell it?"

"Will you stop interrupting me? I can take your pushiness just so far woman, and then…"

"Isn't he cute when he gets mad?" Winklo giggled.

Cindy chuckled softly. They were so different in both physical features and characteristics that she was becoming more curious by the minute wondering what led to their romantic relationship.

"What harm would it do to let him go off on tangents? I know so little about this world, that everything is interesting to me."

"So be it. I tried. Nash can go on for hours rambling about nothing. If you want to listen, I'll just sit here and close my lips. Far be it from me to interrupt again. Yes indeedy. Zipping my lips and shutting them tight."

Winklo pouted and crossed her arms. Nash bent over and kissed her on the cheek. "Thank you, dear. It's very gracious of you to let me tell this tale. After all, I was the one that was there."

"Now, I was telling you about my brother, Froth. He's blue and had a natural talent for handling flying creatures. He also is as timid as a country mouse. Because he feared iron, he never wanted to develop his magical talents. His magic is what we call raw. It's really a shame too, because he might be alive today had he some formal training." Nash sighed. "But that's neither here nor there and I'm getting well ahead of myself."

Winklo rolled her eyes and leaned into Cindy. "See, I told you so. He admits it himself. Ramblin' on to hear the sound of his voice and then forgetting."

Cindy raised her finger to her lips. "Shh. Let's give him the courtesy of listening."

Nash flashed his girlfriend a subtle grin and continued. "I, on the other hand spent three years developing my skills. I'm quite good. Those roses on your table were just buds when I picked them. I made them blossom."

"They really are beautiful. I should've thanked you earlier."

"I had a feeling they'd brighten your day. Always works for my Winky."

Winklo's eyes sparkled. "That's the truth. Nash is one of the most romantic suitors I ever had."

"You had others?" Nash remarked loudly.

"Does that shock you?"

"No, er not at all. You must have had dozens. Your beauty shames the thornbuds that grow in my garden."

Winklo blushed. "And he is the best gardener in the land."

This time it was Nash that blushed. "Well, I was the chief gardener of the Enchanted Gardens of Curn. Held that position through four elections, I might add, but the gardens have nothing to do with my story 'cept that there I was doing my job when my brother comes running down the path of my prized thornbuds. He was just a screaming and a hollering. Tearing up some of the new blossoms, not looking where he was going. He had this letter in his hand and it was flapping away in the morning breeze. It was, I think, two years ago. Let's see, Winklo and I met on Lumintosh, the holiday of the sun. The whole community picnics..."

"Nash. Please, get to the point."

"I thought your lips were zipped."

"How can they be? You go on and on about nothing. Asgar won't be tending to the lionhawks all day."

"You're right, precious one. I'll get to the point. Where was I? Oh, the letter. Can't remember it all, but the gist of it was there was a dragon attacking dwarves and they needed our help. Supposedly, it was a huge one, black with yellow tipped wings. It was blocking one of the older tunnels, scorching and killing all that came near. You do know dwarves are mostly miners? Always excavating. They are the best architects on the Wildsidhe. We trade favors with them for their expertise on tunneling and since we have the magic and they had a dragon, they wanted to barter. Have you ever seen a dragon?"

"Yes, one when we first arrived."

"Huge creatures when they reach maturity. Beautiful too and very intelligent. Also, quite shy and easily distractible. They tend to live underground in tunnels and caves. That's why they're often found in dwarven mines. In most cases, from what Winklo has told me, the miners make so much commotion, the creatures move on, but back to the letter.

"There was something in it about Froth and I attending the town meeting that night. I can tell you that he was not a happy elf at all. Dragon hunts are terribly dangerous, even for accomplished magic users.

"Of course we both attended, it was mandatory. There the mayor told us that this particular dragon had been burning many a dwarf and they needed our magical expertise to run it out. Though they didn't want to kill it, as that would anger other dragons, but they were left with no choice, as nothing would make this creature move. In return, they offered to do the work for these underground passageways we had planned to build. It was more than a fair exchange. At least the mayor thought so since he was too old and too scared to participate."

Winklo hawumphed, loudly, this time.

"I'll get to the point. After choosing a team of six, we all set off to this dwarven realm. Froth did everything he could to get out of going, and as I look back now, I suppose we should have left him home-side, but that's hindsight. He was needed cause of his raw magic over winged creatures.

"The dwarves were quite happy when we arrived. Banners welcoming us were everywhere. They even planned a party in our honor. Quite a lot of singing and dancing went on that night. Dwarves can be real party givers. After having my fill of food and drink, we left to sleep at our assigned hovels. The inn was full as every dwarf's aunt and uncle had been invited to see us off, so we had to make our beds with some of the kind villagers. I stayed with Winklo and her family as they were kind enough to offer their hospitality."

"I see," Cindy said. "It was love at first sight."

"Not at all," said Winklo. "At first I thought him ugly. All yichy and green. And his brother, he stayed with us too. He was rude and arrogant. It was the first time I had any contact with elves other than to say hi in passing.

"And, truth be known, we didn't offer our homes either. We drew lots and our family lost. There's no real love between our people. My father for days reminded me to stay away from them, so at first, I saw little of Nash and Froth."

"Do you want to finish? I thought I was telling the tale?" said Nash glaring at Winklo.

"My, we're testy. I'm just filling in the parts you might not have known."

Nash laughed. "You've only told me a hundred times how at first you didn't like me one little bit. My memory doesn't fail me. Now shush and let me get on with it.

"After days of planning, we entered the tunnels. Armed with spears and bows and arrows for backup, the dwarves led the way down the winding tunnels. They were dark and musty, lit every few feet by an oil lamp. We could barely see anything. On top of that it smelled awful. I had to hold my nose for the stench was unbearable. Even the dwarves, who were used to the foul odors, could hardly stand it. Though dragons normally don't stink, this one did. When we finally reached its alcove, all of us were puking and choking.

"The dragon knew we were coming. There was no way we could be quiet. Froth, Bobo, Mari, and myself entered first. Spells abounded. Crackles of light filled the room. The dragon reared and Froth was caught off guard. His magic in many ways was stronger than ours is because it's unrefined, but it's also untamed due to his lack of control. Though he was successful in crippling the beast, he died in the attempt. All of us were badly hurt. I was burned from the creature's last, fiery breath.

"Winklo and her family nursed me back to health. It was then that we fell in love with each other. Her loving, gentle hands tended to my singed flesh. She sat beside my bed, feeding me, bathing me, and even singing to me. Winky has a golden voice, enchanting to say the least. I would have died if not for her."

Nash held out his hand and grasped his beloved's tightly. They smiled at each other and for a minute, they were silent. Cindy could see the strong bonds of love that held them together.

"Oh, what a romantic story. I can see how much the two of you love each other, but why did your families kick you out?"

"They tried to break it up," said Winklo. "Mom and Dad forbade me to see him after he left. When Nash came to visit, they actually refused to let him in the house. They were so obnoxious. Called him the green menace. We had to meet in secret just to be together. I cried myself to sleep many a night."

"Dry those tears, my sweet. We're together now and nothing and no one will keep us apart again. Even living here with Asgar is better than a life apart."

"And your family, Nash, did they feel the same?" Cindy asked.

"My parents weren't happy about things either, but they at least wished us well and helped us out a bit by giving us some supplies to set up our own house. They refused to marry us, or let us live with them, but at least they didn't disown me as Winklo's parents did.

"Dwarves can be so stubborn and stupid. I'm sorry to speak ill of your kind, Winky, but it's the truth. I buried my brother because none of them bothered to find out why the dragon wouldn't budge."

"What are you saying?" Cindy asked.

"The dragon was a she. When they cleaned out the remains of the lair, they found her eggs. Most were destroyed in the fire, but a few remained. That's why she fought so fiercely. She was protecting her young. And that smell, there was rotting food all around. I guess she was so terrified of leaving her eggs, she hoarded her supplies. Those darn dwarves, not a one bothered to talk to her. Winklo is better off with me."

"Of course, darling. I love you, too."

The two hugged and Cindy smiled, basking in the warmth of the moment. Winklo and Nash were so caught up in each other that they didn't hear the knocking at the window pane.

Cindy slipped out of bed unnoticed to investigate. She moved the curtains apart just wide enough to look. There, fluttering outside the lead panes, was Lissy.

Caught off guard, Cindy opened the windows. Exhausted and breathing in shallow gasps, Lissy flew in. Winklo and Nash were also surprised and began to shout.

Cindy panicked. The last thing she needed was for Asgar to hear the couple's cries. Without knowing what to do, or even what she was doing. Her body started to glow, the light flowing from her head to her hands.

Lightning crackled from her fingertips. Sparks of blue and silver flashed through the room engulfing Winklo and Nash.

"Stop," cried Lissy. "You're killing them."

CHAPTER 7

Cindy collapsed on the bed in pain. Lissy fluttered about not knowing what to do.

"Cindy, wake up. Are you all right?"

Cindy closed her eyes and grabbed her stomach. The cramping was fierce and she felt sick. She barely managed to nod. The few times she had been able to use magic, it always made her sick. "I'll be okay," she said softly. "Are Winklo and Nash alive?"

"Who?" Lissy asked.

"My friends, the dwarf and elf on the floor. Did I kill them?"

Lissy knelt down beside them and tilted her head, laying her ear on their chests.

"They're alive. Just spellbound."

"How can you tell?" asked Cindy.

"Lissy a magic user. It's obvious to me."

Cindy felt a bit better just knowing they were still alive.

"Are you feeling all right, Lissy. You look pale."

"Lissy… I mean I need to eat. I flew here as fast as I could, only stopping to eat once."

"I have some fruit. Will that help?"

Lissy smiled. "Please. Lissy starving." Lissy had been around humans enough to better learn their speech patterns, but she still sometimes fell back to using pixiespeak and didn't use pronouns, but she continued to work on it.

Cindy handed the pixie a tray filled with washed fruit and watched as her friend gobbled it down. Every few seconds she looked towards the door, but thankfully, Asgar didn't appear.

After finishing the last bite, Lissy wiped her mouth her tiny hand and clapped.

Cindy looked down at the motionless couple on the floor. "Are you sure they'll be okay? They haven't moved."

"Yes, yes. They're just out 'cause Cindyfriend used raw magic. Don't worry. Dwarf and elf will wake up soon. Cindy needs to get training. Then you won't have these awful side effects. Cindy's magic won't be as powerful, but it's more important to have control."

"Lissy, I hate to change the subject, but how did you find me?"

"Justin had me follow Asgar. It wasn't easy either. Lionhawks fly fast and I couldn't get too close. Their wings are so strong and powerful, I might have been blown to bits. Or gobbled up.

"But finding you was easier than getting in here. A mighty barrier of sorcery encloses this castle. Good thing I'm tiny. There were holes, one just large enough for me to slip through."

"Well, I can't begin to tell you how happy I am to see you."

"And I'm delighted that you're still okay. I thought Asgar would never leave you alone. Now that I know you're safe, I can go fetch Justin and the others."

"Please hurry, Lissy. Asgar's talking marriage even though I'd never consent to it. I'm doing my best to discourage him, but I have this feeling it's not up to me. The best I think I can do is stall."

Lissy was about to reply, when a loud knock at the door drowned out her words.

"Are you all right, Cindy? I sensed the use of your magic. Since you aren't trained, its usage could be damaging. I need to check on you."

"Hide, Lissy, hurry." Cindy motioned for the pixie to leave the room. "I'm fine, Asgar."

"That may be so, but I want to see for myself. I'll honor your privacy to a point, but not when it can jeopardize your health."

The door opened and Asgar stepped inside. His boots were covered with mud and his hair was tousled. It was obvious he had rushed to her side. Cindy looked up as he entered and was overcome with a very warm feeling.

She watched as he bent down to check out Nash and Winklo. When he looked up, she smiled. He wasn't all that bad. In fact, she thought, he can be quite considerate.

Nash moaned and she hopped off the bed to examine him. Asgar was still stooping beside the couple and she watched as his fingers massaged their temples. A yellow light emanated from the tips and both Nash and Winklo glowed.

Every so often, while he was doing this, his arms would brush against her. The very closeness of him made her shiver. Though it was obvious he had been working, his scent was pleasurable. His eyes were closed and she guessed he was using magic.

She could feel the heat emanating from Asgar's body. It encompassed her also and the sensations made her stomach cramps disappear completely.

"They'll be just fine. The spell was weak and should wear off soon. They won't remember a thing. What surprises me is that you haven't a clue at all about using magic. It's almost random. Didn't Alana teach you anything? Not even the basics?"

"To be honest, I didn't believe her when she finally told me she was a

Wildsidher and I only learned that after grandpa died. All of us just thought she was getting old.

"As a child she used to tell me fantastic stories about Wildsidhe, but that's all I thought they were, made up fairytales."

"And she never used magic?"

"Not that I can remember...except for this unicorn which she created for me." Cindy tugged on the silver charm, as if to make sure it was still there.

"Hmmm," said Asgar standing up. "I was sure that was the one I gave her."

Cindy stood up, also. "No, she created this one from thin air. It was an early birthday present. Somehow she knew we'd be apart. It was if she could see into the future."

"That unicorn has brought us together. It was her spell of casting that alerted me to Alana's presence. Even though it was a simple one, it reached through the barriers of our worlds and I knew then that she was still alive. You know it was fate. Our destiny was written on that day..."

"Seems that way, doesn't it?"

Asgar looked down and gazed into Cindy's sparkling, blue eyes. His long, tapered fingers reached for her face and he tilted her chin upward. For a moment their lips met. The kiss was short and sweet.

Cindy's eyes were closed. She relished the feeling of his lips on hers and hungered for more, but Asgar stood up, leaving her curious and wanting more.

"Let me go clean up and I'll be back to show you around."

Without waiting for an answer he disappeared. Cindy kept her eyes tight. Though he had gone, she could still smell him and the kiss lingered in her heart and thoughts. It wasn't until she heard Nash rousing that she opened them.

Lissy flitted back in the room. "What's gotten into you?"

"I don't know," answered Cindy, as she jolted back to reality and began to cry. "Something came over me. I can't explain it, but when he kissed me, I found myself wanting him to kiss me again. Now, just the thought of him makes me ill."

"He wasn't lying then. He did cast a spell on you. Oh what is to become of all of this?" Winklo said, moaning dramatically.

"This is awful," said Lissy. "And it's all your fault. I'd better warn Justin. The sooner we get her out of here the safer we'll be. It's obvious the spell only works in his presence. Just keep him away from her."

"And how do you propose I do that?" asked Winklo. "Asgar's the Lord of this realm and I'm nothing but a mere dwarf. Why don't you perform some of your pixie magic?"

Cindy sat back on the bed, sobbing. "Can you do anything, Lissy? Cast a counter spell?"

"I can try," said Lissy as she fluttered about powdering pixie dust on Cindy.

Cindy sneezed. The sparkling sprinkles scattered everywhere and Lissy, caught by the force of the blow, was slammed against the wall.

Cindy ran and picked her up from the floor. "Are you all right?"

"I'm fine, but the dust didn't work, otherwise you wouldn't have sneezed. Asgar's magic is potent. The only thing you can do is to stay away from him. Maybe Mr. Elf and Miss Dwarf can keep Asgar entertained elsewhere."

"Worthless pixie dust. Just as useless as the pixie herself." Winklo scrunched her nose.

"Stop it both of you. This bickering isn't getting us anywhere."

Lissy stuck her tongue out at Winklo and fluttered over to Cindy. "Be careful. Don't trust anyone here. I promise to get you out of here. Justin will know how. CIndyfriend can count on Lissy."

"For a cold perhaps. She's got you sniffling and wheezing with her valueless, sneezing powder. If I were you, I wouldn't trust her," said Winklo. "Pixies are only beholden to themselves."

"And how would dwarf girl know that? You're nothing more than tunnel trash."

"Well, I'll be." Winklo folded her arms and gave Lissy a raspberry. "You going to let her call me names, Nash?"

Before Nash had a chance to step in, Cindy clenched her fists and shouted at them to stop.

"I've had enough of this. Put your differences aside right now. We have to work together. There's no way I want to spend the rest of my life with Asgar and live amongst the Fortesans. I give you my word that Lissy can be trusted and Lissy that was an awful thing to call Winklo. She's been a good friend to me."

Lissy pouted. "For your sake, Lissy calls a truce. Lissy sorry. Name calling isn't nice, but they weren't nice to me either."

"Your turn, Winklo," Cindy said, tapping her foot.

"Well, since she apologized first, far be it from me to hold a grudge. Truce, for the time being. I'm sorry."

"Thank you. If Asgar's going to be stopped, we're going to need every helping hand we can get. Cindyfriend will be depending on you. It's up to you two now. I can fly fast, but it's at least two suns there and two suns back."

"You keep up your bargain and Nash and I will do our best to keep her safe."

"Good. Can you keep Cindy and Asgar apart?" Lissy asked Winklo.

"We can try, but it's not going to be easy. The sooner you get back here, the better."

"Lissy will hurry. Lissy will save you."

Cindy watched the pixie zip out the window and went to watch. She stood there, waiting until she could no longer see any sign of her. Nash and Winklo huddled beside her and also waited until the pixie was out of sight.

"It's going to be all right, Cindy. No matter what happens, we won't let the wedding take place."

Cindy had heard Nash's words and was about to answer when she noticed Asgar's reflection in the window. He was standing in the doorway, holding a bouquet of white and blue petaled flowers. She turned to face him, her eyes sparkling with a strange glow.

From that point on, nothing mattered. She even began to question herself on why she had shed tears earlier. Asgar was a warm, caring man. She felt honored to be the recipient of his affections.

Nash and Winklo looked at each other and grabbed a hold of Cindy's skirt. It was a useless attempt. Cindy, eyes glazed and totally entranced, could not be held back. Without a word to either of her two friends, she flew into Asgar's open arms.

CHAPTER 8

They had party hats and streamers. Every one of his friends, all three of them, were sitting around the table fighting over who got the biggest piece of cake. Ben Mazel had made his wish, but he knew it wouldn't come true. At twelve o'clock noon, whether he wanted to or not, he was headed for the unknown.

Even though he had told his parents not to, they went ahead and bought him the new video game console he had his heart set on. Mom wanted him to open it, but why bother? This way they could take it back to the store in the original box. Same with his aunt and uncle's gift of video games. Ben and his parents had moved in with his aunt and uncle, since their house had been in the section of Sparta that disappeared with his sister and the other kids.

Ben tried to hold back the tears. Life was over for him. All those years of Hebrew school were for nothing as he would never have a bar mitzvah. His father was going to lend him his great grandfather's prayer shawl to wear on that day. It had been in their family for years, brought over from Russia when his ancestors immigrated to the United States. A lot of history was in that Tallis. As far back as his father could remember, all the men in their family wore it when they when they turned thirteen and became a son of the commandments. He was going to be the first to break tradition.

Harry and John were singing, "Happy birthday to you; you belong in a zoo." Ben rolled his eyes. That song had long since stopped being been funny, but he pretended to laugh anyway. He wondered why they were so happy. Didn't they realize their time was coming soon? Harry punched him in the arm and told him to get with it, but Ben only nodded and faked a smile.

Somehow, ice cream and chocolate cake at eight o'clock in the morning didn't seem like much of a birthday party. He opened his friends' gifts and went through the motions of thanking them. He looked at the pile of scrunched up wrapping paper and colorful ribbons piling up on the floor. His friends had obviously gone out of their way to make this special for him, even down to their computer generated cards which they created just for him.

It was a school day so they had to leave just an hour after arriving. Harry tried to say something, but he ended up stuttering.

"You know what I mean, bud," Harry said softly trying to hide his speech impediment.

"Yeah," Ben nodded, "I do. Go on to school. I'll be okay." When their school vanished with the missing kids, classes had been relocated to the elementary school. The FBI had insisted classes restart almost immediately for the remaining kids, to preserve a sense of normalcy under the circumstances.

The tears were welling in their eyes when they hugged good bye, but Ben waited until they were out of sight before actually crying. Even though the situation warranted it, he wasn't going to have their last memory of him crying like a baby.

Aida Mazel, Ben's mother held him tight, as they both watched the boys disappear down the street. Her shaking fingers ran through her son's thick, brown, curly hair. "Shah," she said over and over. "Things could be worse."

Ben laughed through his tears. "What, Ma? What could be worse?" But he didn't expect an answer.

"Things happen for a reason, son," Mark Mazel said. "Just keep your faith and don't give up. The FBI will find out what's going on and we'll find a way to get you back."

"Do you really believe that, Dad?"

"Hope has wings. From my mouth to God's ears. Now let's make the best of this birthday. Why don't you open that new game and we can play a round or two."

Ben knew better than to argue with his father and he pretended to delight in the silly little creatures running around some strange land, bumping and jumping and falling and dying. The music was catchy and had he more time he might have really enjoyed it. As it was, they were just wasting time. Neither one of them knew what to say to each other.

At 11:15, Aida came into the room and handed a small package to Ben. Ben unwrapped the present very carefully. Both his parents watched as he looked at the beautiful Star of David on a thick gold chain and the gold watch setting atop the thick wad of cotton.

"But this was Sadie's, I can't take her necklace."

"We want you to give it to Iris. If what rumors we've heard are true, the only thing you can take there is what you have on. Please wear it and give it to your sister if you should find her. And the watch, it was Grandpa Kahn's, my father. He survived the holocaust, you will survive this."

Ben hurried to hug his mother. He buried his head in her chest. Mark walked over and the three of them clung to each other, silently sobbing.

Aida stood at the door waving, watching as her baby got into the car. Ben had never seen his mother weep this much except for when Sadie died and Iris disappeared. He hoped she would be okay.

The ride to town was silent. Mark tried a few times to talk to his son, but he couldn't manage an entire sentence without crying. Ben reached over and took his father's hand in his. They rode the last mile with fingers entwined.

No one was there to see them go to the empty park. They had wanted to go to the border of the barren land left behind when part of the town disappeared, so people could see what happened. The FBI had the army troops section off that part of town. They never would have gotten close. If they hadn't lied to the FBI about Ben's birthday, the FBI would have "taken him into protective custody" to make sure nobody saw him disappear. They had done it to other kids whose parents hadn't had the foresight to fib.

In the long run, it didn't matter where they were. Ben would disappear. The FBI had been trying to tell everyone it was a gas pipe explosion, but the families who had children disappear knew better. Mark handed a letter to Ben; the envelope was crumbled from being folded in his pocket.

"I want you and Iris to read this when you get there. We've talked about this for the past few weeks, but just in case you forget, you will have this to remind you. Please tell her we love her and miss her. And Ben..."

Mark got down on one knee and pulled his son into his arms. "Don't ever forget that we love you. No matter what, we will never stop praying for your return."

"I love you too, Dad. I don't want to go. Please, don't let them take me. Please help me, Dad."

It was almost 12:00. Wayne stood in front of the clock, bow and arrows slung across his back. After his screw up with Bobby Shelly, Wayne made sure someone was at the clock tower every day at noon. Instead of going himself to meet and greet, he got into the habit of sending Carmen or Ron, but, today was different. He knew someone would be coming. Today was Ben Mazel's eleventh birthday.

Iris insisted on accompanying him and Wayne agreed. He felt she would be a great help acclimating her brother to his new surroundings. Most were in shock for days. Those that had older siblings adjusted quicker.

"What's going to happen?" Iris asked.

"Watch. You'll see for yourself in..." Wayne looked at his watch, "two minutes, give or take."

Iris took a deep breath and stood there fidgeting. It was a bit nippy out and the thin jacket she was wearing was more fashionable than practical. Old habits were hard to break. She was concerned with how she looked and hoped Wayne would notice. Wayne, however, was too hurt by Marianne's betrayal, not just of him, but of all the kids, to be looking for a new girlfriend any time soon.

The loud chime of the noon time bell heralded the appearance of a short, skinny boy with brown, curly hair. He looked like he was holding something in his hand, but there was nothing there. Other than adjusting his glasses, he stood there motionless, just staring through Wayne and Iris as if they weren't there.

"Ben," shouted Iris. "It's okay."

Ben snapped his head and looked behind him, then to the right and left.

"Over here. Come on. It's not safe standing out there in the open."

Ben started to walk the few feet to where his sister was standing. "Where's Dad?" he asked.

"Dad? He's still back home, I suppose. Why do you ask? Adults don't get transported, only kids are cursed."

Ben ran to Iris. "He was holding me tight. He thought he would cross over too. I guess it didn't work."

"There aren't any grownups here, but we're managing just fine. I want you to meet Wayne Burns. He's head of security here and a really nice guy."

Iris looked up at Wayne and smiled softly. When he returned the grin, her eyes lit up.

"Let's talk back at the school. Too many know that bell means a cross over."

"A cross over?" Ben asked trying to keep pace.

"Those that come here from Sparta. We'll exchange information in a few minutes. You go on, Iris, and take Ben. I think I hear something."

"You mean that buzzing sound. I hear it too."

Ben just looked at the two of them. "Are there monsters here?"

"Sorta. Here take this and do your best."

Wayne handed Ben a slingshot and then grabbed an arrow from his sheath. Startled, Ben looked at the wooden contraption, almost dropped it and started running in the opposite direction.

"Where are you going? Get back here, Ben," cried Iris.

"The letter. Dad gave me a letter to give to you, sis. I think I lost it."

Wayne started to go after Ben, yelling as he ran. "You can't take anything but the clothes on your back. If it wasn't in your pockets, the letter is still in Sparta. Now don't be stupid and stay close."

Before Ben could stop, Lissy dropped out of nowhere followed by a large, black bird. Wayne took aim and the arrow sped by the pixie and hit its target. The bird fell to the ground with a thud and feathers flew everywhere.

Ben screamed and ran to his sister. "What was that? A monster?"

Iris laughed. "That was Lissy, a pixie and a black bird, just a plain old black bird. Now let's get back to the school and we'll tell you everything. Good shot, Wayne. You're amazing."

Wayne beamed. "Thanks," he said. "No big deal."

"Wait 'til I tell the others. That bird was a blur. It was flying so fast I was sure Lissy was a goner. You're a hero. You saved Lissy's life."

Wayne blushed and continued to walk at a brisk pace, trying his best to keep one step ahead of the others. Iris skipped along, babbling on and on about Wayne's marksmanship. She did her best to keep up with Wayne without losing her brother.

Ben had to run to keep up with them. "Pixies?" he mumbled. "Next thing you'll be telling me is that there's trolls and dragons."

"No, now you're being silly. No trolls, just dragons. And this is the yellow brick road." Iris and Wayne laughed. "Lionhawks, dragons, and darkcats, oh my!"

After welcoming Ben into the fold, the group quit what they were doing to listen to Iris's account of Wayne's bravery. She looked at Ben for confirmation and then continued to exaggerate the size of the bird and the danger they were all involved in.

"My hero," Justin said in a high-pitched voice, hiding a wink. He patted Wayne on the back and added, "Just kidding. Good shooting."

Ben made himself comfortable on his sister's mattress and sat there quietly. He recognized few of the kids and felt very much an outcast. Terri was sitting in her wheelchair off to the side and he recognized her immediately. She was one of a kind and everyone knew her. There were a few others, like Tina, but he really couldn't call her a close friend, as he knew her from school but never hung out with her. He was friends with her twin brother Bobby, but Bobby had work detail helping out in the kitchen. He had learned everyone here worked. None of his other classmates were here and after studying the faces, realized he was the youngest and smallest.

He had a lot of questions to ask, but they were so busy talking to the pixie that none of them even bothered with him. When Justin called for everyone to come make a circle, Ben wasn't sure he was welcome. He stayed where he was and did his best to keep from crying.

Lissy had quit flitting around and sat on Wayne's shoulder. She very quickly recounted her tale.

"Cindy won't marry Asgar," Justin said.

"Justinfriend doesn't seem to understand," Lissy said. "She's bewitched.

Asgar has her spellbound."

Justin stood up, his fists clenched. "I can't believe he would do that. Love isn't something you can force."

"He doesn't love her, he needs her. Asgar will stop at nothing to get what he wants."

"Then there's no time to waste. We better head there now. Gather up what weapons we have and let's get going."

"Hold on," said John Bearclaw. "We've got to have a plan. No sense going out there half-cocked. It's going to take more than just iron tipped arrows to break into Asgar's castle. We barely survived Morna's villa and that wasn't even heavily guarded. I'm sure the place is guarded. Let's not forget those lionhawks."

"John's right," Wayne said. "We need to think this out. Chuck, gather some weapons and as much scrap iron as you can stuff in a backpack. Renee, Brina, Ron, give him a hand. Iris, would you get together as much food as you can and don't forget water? You can get some of the others to help. We need to think this through."

"We'll think of something on the way," Justin said. "It's going to take a couple of days to get there. I'm sure we can come up with something before then."

"I'm going with you," Wayne said.

"No. You're needed here. Someone has to watch over everyone and hold this fort down. If I'm successful, Asgar and his lionhawks are going to know we're headed back here. You'll have your hands full fighting them off."

"Well, no way you're going alone. It's going to take more than just you to free Cindy."

"I'll have Lissy with me," Justin said. "I don't want to endanger anyone else."

"I'm going with him," Terri said. "I can watch over things from above and don't forget, I'm a good shot."

"That's why you're staying here. You need to be a lookout for Asgar and possibly Morna. Wayne can't do this alone."

Wayne smiled at Terri. "I really can use your help, Terri. Why not take John and Chuck? They're both good shots, not to mention great trackers."

"I'm better than both of them," Carmen said, "So I'm going too."

"Fair enough," Justin said. "Carmen, you come with me in the convertible. John and Chuck, you take the white sedan. Lissy can ride up front with us. There's less iron and with the top down it shouldn't be too painful for her."

"Good, then it's all settled," Carmen said. "We can figure out something later. Until we get there, we can't do anything anyway. Now let's get out of here."

Ben sat there watching everyone rushing about. He would have offered to help, but he didn't know what to do. A couple of times, in their haste, they almost stumbled over him. Since now wasn't the time to ask questions, he got of their way.

Ben went to the window. From his vantage-point, he could see everyone below loading the cars with supplies. Someone he didn't recognize was siphoning gas from one of the many-parked cars in the lot. There were no gas stations on the Wildsidhe.

Terri was over by the fence, opening the gate. Suddenly she took off, wheelchair and all, straight up. Ben gasped as he watched her hover above the cars, shouting, "All's clear." He was at a loss for words.

"Cool, isn't it," Terri said, as she positioned the chair next to Ben's window. "It's magic. Sometime, when all this is settled, I'll take you for a ride."

"Thanks anyway," said Ben, "But I'm not much for flying. Aren't you scared?"

"Scared? Of what? Heights? No way. This is awesome."

Ben nodded. "What's going on?"

"Too much to go into now. I'm just making sure Asgar and his lionhawks aren't around, or Morna and her pet cats. Didn't think they would be, but one can't be too sure. I'll follow them a ways, just to make sure they don't run into any dragons either. As soon as I get back and things calm down, I'll fill you in."

"Thanks," Ben mumbled.

"You're welcome." Terri's voice trailed in the breeze as she zoomed away. Ben could hear her yell for them to get a move on. He watched mesmerized as the green wheelchair bobbed up and down and the cars drove out of sight.

Iris was standing next to Wayne. Ben, knowing his sister wouldn't see, stuck his tongue out at her. One thing was for sure, she wasn't any nicer to him here than she was at home. Oh, she put on a good show in front of Wayne, but he saw through that. She hadn't found even five minutes to talk to him.

When the town disappeared and Iris vanished, Ben found himself missing her. Now that he was here, he could see the feelings weren't returned. At least Terri and Wayne seemed nice. As soon as he had a chance, he would talk to them and tell them the news. It was a good thing he had read the letter.

CHAPTER 9

Ben waited for the commotion to die down and for everyone to filter back in. He didn't like being here already. Even though he was mostly a loner, here he felt alone and not by choice. Being the new guy made him feel lost. *Heck*, he thought, *I am lost.*

Iris made no attempt to talk to him. It was as if he wasn't here. He could see that things were going to be no different here, then they were at home.

"Wayne," Ben said in a weak voice. "Can I talk to you?"

"Sure, Ben. One minute. Didn't mean to ignore you, but there's a lot to do around here."

"It's important," Ben said.

"Just a minute. Okay?"

Ben nodded. Wayne was busy talking to Iris and waved him off. He wondered what could be so important about talking to her? She was a girl and not a very pretty one at that. Without her makeup or hair fixed, she was a fright.

Ben was glad his father made him memorize the letter. It was just a shame that it didn't make it over with him. Then again, maybe not. He knew all the information it contained and except for the mushy parts on how much his parents loved them, it wasn't really a loss. He decided not to tell Iris the part of the letter that was written just for her. That would teach her for ignoring him.

Tired of waiting for his sister to stop hitting on Wayne, Ben decided to check out things for himself. He still had his slingshot. He really didn't believe in dragons and such. Sure, there was this pixie, and it did make him wonder, but dragons were a different story altogether.

Without saying a word, he left the room and school, and headed outside. No one saw him leave. No one paid attention to him. He had something really important to say and not a soul even bothered to give him the time of day. That was typical though. No one paid any attention to a nerd in Sparta. Obviously it was going to be the same here.

His surroundings looked the same. It was all so confusing. The buildings were all in the same place, the sky was blue, and the sun was still in the heavens. It was just the odd silence in the background that made him conscious he was no longer home.

No cars moved, no sounds of music coming from portable CD players. The streets were empty, void of stray dogs and cats. It was like he was stuck in a dollhouse world.

Ben looked up at the window and saw no one looking out. The gate was still open from when the cars went through. Sighing, he went through and left the schoolyard, not bothering to latch it shut.

As soon as Wayne finished talking to Iris, he noticed Ben was gone. He knew the poor kid had to be scared and confused, but at the time he didn't think Ben's request was so urgent.

"Iris," Wayne asked. "Have you seen your brother?"

Iris looked around the room, noticing the empty chair by the window. "No…No I haven't."

"Anyone seen Ben, the new kid?" Wayne shouted.

No one answered with a yes. Iris ran to the window. "The gate's still open. Do you think…?"

She was afraid to finish the sentence. If he had gone off on his own it was her fault.

"I'll find him. He couldn't have gone far."

"I'll go with you," Ron said, popping into the room.

Wayne went to grab his bow and bumped into Iris. "Where do you think you're going? It's getting late."

"He's my brother. I'm going with you."

Wayne shook his head. "Stay here and help watch the others. We'll make better time."

Iris refused and rushed out the door and down the hallway, passing them. Wayne and Ron followed, yelling at her to slow down.

"Miko," Wayne yelled to Ron's sister. "Get up in the tower and yell if you see anything. Then find out who is supposed to be watching the gate. I want to see that person in my office as soon as his or her shift is over. We'll be back as soon as we can."

His voice echoed in the hallway as he ran down the steps, Ron trailing a few steps behind. In seconds they had caught up with Iris.

"We all stick together or I'm going to carry you back to the school. You hear me?"

Iris answered with a soft yes.

"Good. Any ideas where he might have gone?"

"Home?" Iris half answered, half asked. Their house, like many others, had come over.

"Then let's head there first."

The three of them set off down the street, Iris leading the way. The Mazels lived only a short distance from the school. Iris had hated it because it meant they had to walk. Since both their parents worked, both Ben and she had to tromp through the snow and all sorts of nasty weather conditions while others got to ride a warm bus.

It took only ten minutes to reach their house. The front door was closed, but not locked.

"He's here," Iris said. "Probably down in the basement. That's where dad keeps his computers and ham radio."

Iris made it down the steps first and that's exactly where she found her brother. He was hooking up the portable generator to the equipment.

"You idiot," Iris shouted. "What do you think you're doing? Don't you know it's dangerous to be out here all by yourself?"

"Who died and made you my boss?"

"Why you little…"

Wayne had to separate them. "Calm down. We've enough to deal with here without the two of you fighting. Iris, go sit down. I'll handle it. Ben, what are you up to?"

"What does it look like? This is a ham radio. I'm hoping to contact Dad."

"Ben, it's a good thought, but we've already tried everything. Nothing works. If you had asked, we would have saved you this trouble."

"I did try. You were too busy."

"I'm sorry. It's not an excuse, but it takes a lot of work just to survive in this place."

"It's not a big deal," Ben answered, never turning his head to look at Wayne. "So, you've already tried contacting people on the ham?"

"Well, maybe not a ham radio, but we've tried other ways."

"Then leave me alone and let me get on with this. I had the settings in the letter I was trying to bring over, but that vanished. Still, I think I remember the right frequency. It's worth a shot."

"No, it's not," shouted Iris. "We can use that generator for lots more important things."

"She's right, Ben. That generator can be a lot more useful back at the school."

"Well too bad. Iris knew it was here. You could have gotten it. It belongs to our family and I found it first."

"You said it. It belongs to our family, so I have as much right to it as you do. You're so selfish." Iris folded her arms and glared at her brother.

"Like you really care about anything but yourself. If you weren't so busy making goo-goo eyes at Wayne, you might have thought about this sooner. I can't believe you couldn't take one minute of your precious time to talk to me. You didn't even ask about Mom and Dad, or anyone. All you care about is yourself, and you have the nerve to call me selfish."

Iris blushed and stuck her tongue out at Ben. Ben returned fire with words that would have gotten him grounded for a month.

"Enough," Wayne said. "This isn't getting us anywhere. Ron, will you please take Iris back?"

Ron nodded. "Come on, let Wayne handle this."

"He can have him," replied Iris, standing up and walking up the stairs.

"Don't try to talk me out of this," Ben said, looking up at Wayne. "This belongs to me now. I can do what I want."

Wayne agreed. "No one can make you return with me, but do you really want to fend for yourself? At least we have an idea what we're up against."

"I'm not a kid. In one more year, I would have been Bar Mitzvahed and considered an adult."

"No one's calling you a kid. Even adults need others to survive."

"I'll be fine," said Ben.

"Okay, but if you change your mind, you know where to find us. Watch out for Queen Morna and her darkcats. And Asgar, you remember him? He has an army of lionhawks. They're huge birds with great big beaks, only about fifty times as big as bald eagles. Oh, and I almost forgot…there are changelings. They can take the form of anything and are really nasty creatures."

Wayne headed up the stairs. "Be very careful and trust no one. I'm telling you this for your own good. Take care. Bye."

Ben watched Wayne disappearing up the stairs and shouted, "Wait. Wait please."

Wayne peeked through the crack of the open cellar door, "Yes?"

"Can we talk? Seriously, I mean."

Wayne hopped back down the steps two at time.

"Can we make a deal?" asked Ben.

"What sort of a deal did you have in mine?"

"Can we take the generator, radio, and computer back to the school? I really don't mind sharing. Just let me use the radio once a day for five minutes at 4:00. That's when Dad and I agreed to try and contact each other. I know it's a longshot, but at least we can try."

"That sounds fair enough. I hate to tell you that it's not going to work, but who am I to take away hope. And who knows. You might get lucky."

"Thanks," said Ben. "I mean that, too. I really didn't mean to be so selfish. It's just that sometimes, Iris makes me so angry. I just say things without thinking."

Wayne patted Ben on the back. "Don't I know that? I have a sister too."

"Terri? But she seems so nice."

"She is. Most of the time. Now what do you say we get outta here and tomorrow we can pick up this equipment? I can fill you in on life here on Wildsidhe while we walk."

Ben agreed. He switched off the equipment and turned off the generator. "Just keep Iris away from this. And from me. Man to man, she's a real pain."

Wayne laughed. "Thanks for the warning. Now, let's scoot."

Wayne filled him in on what was going on and the trouble Cindy was in. He promised to introduce him to the pixies and wrote his name on the work roster. Without Carmen, the Bearclaw brothers and Justin to chip in, everyone would have to work a bit harder.

Ben found out that things weren't as bad as he first thought they would be. Wayne was good to his word and they set the generator and the other electrical equipment in the science room, which was just down the hall.

He even made friends with the pixies as he had a great voice and the pixies loved music. Singing made the work go faster and the other kids joined in. Wayne must have said something, because everyone seemed just a bit friendlier. But soon, very soon, if all things worked out, he would be liked for a different reason. Ben was going to save them all.

CHAPTER 10

Cindy felt like she was in paradise. There was no place in Sparta to compare with Asgar's land. The grass really was greener, the vibrancy of the wildflowers, awesome.

With her hand tightly clasped in Asgar's, they toured his realm. Animals of species she had never seen before seemed to lower their heads as he passed. It was as if all that surrounded him were at their best to please him.

He pointed his elongated finger, shouting out names of some of the beasts that she had only read about in mythology. Griffins, centaurs, and even winged horses all grazed peacefully in the distance. She was in an enchanted land and totally in awe of the man that was in command.

They walked for hours. Asgar led Cindy to a crystal pond. The mirrored reflection of the sun's golden rays rippled as Cindy skimmed stones across the water's surface. Ducks swam by, followed by a trail of yellow down, ducklings. It was so peaceful here, she felt so felt safe she found herself muttering out loud that she wished she never had to leave here.

Asgar smiled. "You don't. Stay here, with me, forever."

He knelt on one knee while reaching for her hand. "Will you marry me, Cindy?"

Something stirred in her. Thoughts of Justin rushed through her mind. It was all so long ago. Part of her wanted to say yes, but there was little voice that kept her from answering.

"I'm only sixteen."

"Wonderful. You're precisely the right age."

Cindy sighed. "But, we've really only known each other a short time. My heart wants to say yes, yet something keeps my lips from saying it."

"Come sit."

Cindy sat down on the bank and drew her legs underneath her. Asgar faced her, caressing her cheek with his hand.

"I don't know what customs you have back where you are from, since I wasn't there long enough to learn about them," Asgar lied, "but I can guess they're different. Here, we keep things simple. Some marry for alliances, other's for power. There are those that marry for love and some for revenge. It is forever here."

"Forever is a long time for a hasty choice. I have plenty of time to commit."

"Do you? As my wife, you will be accorded all the privileges and respect that my station demands. You will be safe, for those that would harm you wouldn't dare if you belonged to me. All that I have will be yours, Queen Cindy of Wildsidhe.

"May I have some time? I'm too overwhelmed by everything to think clearly."

"Of course. I'm rushing you." Asgar looked away.

"Don't take it so personal. I haven't said no."

Asgar feigned a smile and drew Cindy close. His arms enveloped her as he lowered his lips to hers. The kiss made her shiver. Cindy melted and returned the passion eagerly. Her arms slid around his neck as she pressed her body tightly against his.

Asgar gently broke the embrace. "Your lips says yes. Don't fight it. You were born to be mine. You feel it as much as I do."

Cindy could barely catch her breath before she found herself agreeing.

"You won't be sorry. I'll make you happy."

Asgar leaped to his feet, picked up Cindy and swirled her around. "We must hurry back. So much to do and so little time."

He kissed her once more, this time quickly, and before she had a chance to say anything else, he had her in tow. Cindy felt like she was flying. Her feet barely left an impression in the grass below. Everything whizzed by her. Though she remembered the forest and the grazing animals at pasture, they were a blur as they sped back to the castle. What had taken hours to reach, took only a few minutes in returning.

The castle bridge lowered at Asgar's nod. They scurried over and with another nod, it raised to close them in.

"Are you tired, my lovely?" Asgar asked.

"A bit winded. My you run fast."

Asgar left. "A simple spell of speed. I keep forgetting you've had no formal training. Tomorrow, after the wedding, I will begin your lessons. It won't take you long to learn."

"Tomorrow? So soon?" asked Cindy.

"Tomorrow you will start training. Tonight, in the veiled shadows of our Lady of the Moons, we will say our vows. I will contact Penrod now."

Cindy found herself backing away. "Can't we wait? Perhaps get married by the pond? Please, Asgar."

"If you wish it so, so then be it. Tomorrow then. Now go rest. The evening meal should be ready soon. I am looking forward to toasting our future."

Cindy scrambled up the steps. No sooner did she make it to the corridor adjoining her room, than she began to feel sick. The afternoon and the realization of what she had agreed to made her knees weak. She stumbled to her and collapsed upon her bed.

Burying her face in a pillow, she began to cry. She felt so helpless, so utterly without hope. Even if Lissy had made it back to Justin, she doubted they would make it back in time. And even on the remote chance that he did come to rescue her, what could he do? It was all so hopeless.

CHAPTER 11

It was aggravating following Lissy. Since she was so tiny, she had to stop every little bit to eat. Justin felt like it was taking forever, even though they had brought food for her.

At first, she started off sitting on the windshield. The whole purpose of taking the convertible was for Lissy's sake. There was less iron and he felt she could ride more comfortably, but that lasted only a short while.

"I just can't sit," she tried to explain to Justin. "It's just not natural, and by flying, I can see where I'm going."

There was no arguing. No sense in angering the pixie, so he turned up the sound of the CD player and kept the music going and Lissy happy.

Well into the drive Justin began to relax a little. Carmen had tossed a few ideas at him and he mulled them over, discarding them all.

They knew so little about the creatures they were dealing with and even less about the land. Asgar was powerful, but were his guards? Did he even have any and if so, how many? Were they armed? What about the lionhawks?

They stopped to make camp and eat. Lissy picked a concealed area not too far from the road. It was clear enough for them to lay a blanket down and dense enough that the tree branches provided cover.

It was getting dark and Chuck and John wanted to stop for the evening, but Justin objected.

"Let's eat and get a few more miles behind first," he said.

"We're tired and none of us know our way around. This place is perfect. Who knows what we'll find up ahead and I for one don't want to sleep in the car," Carmen said.

"This isn't a camping trip. Cindy is in danger and every second counts. If I had my way, we'd drive through the night."

"No, no, no," said Lissy. "The Shadows roam at dusk and we're too close to them as it is."

"Shadows? The ones Morna wanted to sacrifice Bobby to?"

Lissy put her tiny hands over her ears. "No, no, no. No more talk of the Shadows. Too dangerous. Carmen's right. It's safest here."

"Justin, hang in there. All of us care about Cindy. You're not the only one, but we won't do her any good if we arrive there exhausted. Let's use this time to make plans, eat, and rest. We've been driving now for over four hours without a break," said John.

"Okay. You guys are making sense. Let's get these cars off the path as much as possible. I don't want to sleep in them either, but next to them, well the iron can help keep us safe."

"Do you think that's a good idea? You know out here in the wild, if you stray you can get lost. Some sort of magic confusion spell," said John.

"That's right. I remember Cindy saying that," Carmen said. "What should we do?"

John looked at his brother. "Is there any rope in the trunk?"

"I think so," answered Chuck, shuffling the supplies around. "Yep, right here." He handed the bundle to his brother.

"How about we tether ourselves to the convertible?"

"And the other car?" asked Justin.

"We park it in the forest to be safe. I'm sure inanimate objects aren't in danger."

"I think it'd be a good idea if we took shifts. Each one of us can take a turn sleeping in the car until morning. I'd hate to lose our food supply," Justin said. "Lissy, where are you going to sleep?"

The pixie fluttered about. "In the treetops. I can keep a better watch from there."

John shut the trunk and attached the rope to the passenger side door handle. He walked to the clearing, gave himself a few extra feet, and notched the rope.

After that he measured the same length for the others. They ended up one length short.

"Whoever is taking the watch won't need to be tied. When it's time to change shifts, we can tug on the rope," Carmen said.

"Then we have a game plan, at least for tonight. Now all we have to do is think of a way to help Cindy. Let's eat here. We can divvy up the weapons later," Justin said.

They ate fast, barely tasting anything. It didn't matter that in their other life, vegetables were the one item the dog got. The mainstay of their diet here was vegetables and fruits. Hunger made them taste delicious.

There was a container of beef jerky. They were lucky that the Bearclaw brothers were good hunters. Though meat wasn't plentiful, they treasured catching the squirrel like rodents and small, feathered birds, which looked like ducks, but had snouts instead of bills. They were anxious to go off hunting for bigger game, but so far Justin had told them not to go too far away from the town.

By the time they finished it was twilight. A blanket of pitch darkness slowly replaced the red-ribboned streaked heavens. Few stars scattered the sky and the double moons, were both in different phases and shed very little light.

Carmen volunteered for the first watch and she propped herself inside the convertible. Even though the top was up, she didn't feel very safe. It wasn't the same as having a steel roof. Lionhawk claws could easily rip through the fabric, but then again, she thought, they could probably tear through anything.

Justin, John, and Chuck set up their blankets close together. Too proud to admit they were scared, they felt the closeness was justified both for safety and warmth.

Lissy had left to watch immediately after eating, with a promise to wake them early. The boys whispered, tossing out various plans and plots, but without knowing what they were up against, they could do very little. Tired mentally and physically, they drifted off to sleep.

Unfortunately, every noise, every rustle of the leaves, awoke them. Once some slithery snake-like creature crawled in between them. This one had two front legs and a double tail. Carmen grasped it by the tail and threw it near the car. Chuck jumped up and clubbed it to death with the blunt end of a spear.

Too jittery after that incident, they took turns watching. Justin had the last watch. When the first rays of light filtered through the branches, they were already up. "I'm going to get Justin," said Chuck. "We might as well grab a bite to eat and get on our way."

Chuck hollered for Lissy. He could hear her make her way through the leaves and smiled at her before heading back to the car. After reaching the edge of the woods, he sighed. The car was still there, but something was wrong. The headlights were on.

It was only a few steps to the convertible. From his vantage-point, Chuck couldn't see anyone sitting in the vehicle and his heart began to race. His gut told him something was wrong.

To his dismay, he was right. He opened the door on the passenger side and no one was inside. Justin had disappeared.

CHAPTER 12

Winklo grumbled. "What if I don't give her this dress? Do this; do that. That man orders us about as if we were his slaves."

"Now don't go making Asgar angry. The marriage will take place whether or not Miss Cindy wears that gown. I just wish there was something we could do to break this spell."

"Your powers are strong, but nothing compared to his. Even if they were, with all the other Fortesans there, you'd have no chance. I don't want you trying something stupid and ending up as a radish."

"A radish? Do you think he would?"

Nash opened the door so Winklo could pass. "I put nothing past him. You are too precious to me. No sense fighting when we've already lost the battle. Just behave for once."

"Now don't go worrying. I'll admit I can be headstrong, but I'm not stupid. I just feel so helpless. There's not a thing we can do. I just wish it was our wedding. You know, he did promise to marry us."

"Yes, but he never said when." Winklo sighed. "That's one lesson we learned. Be specific when making a deal with a Fortesan."

"No use shedding tears over the past. Learn and move on. I guess you'd better deliver that parcel."

"Wanna join me?"

Nash nodded. "Maybe we can talk some sense into her. When she's not near him, she thinks more clearly."

Very carefully, Winklo rested the red, satin gown across her arm. It was very heavy and she had Nash follow her up the stairway holding the train.

The door to Cindy's room was closed and Winklo knocked three times without getting a response. "Do you think she's okay?" she asked.

"Cindy," Nash hollered. "You there?"

They waited a minute, alternating knocking and shouting, but Cindy never responded.

"I'm going in," said Winklo turning the brass knob.

The door squeaked open and the couple slipped in. Cindy was sitting on a chair staring out the window. She didn't even turn her head to look at them when they spoke to her.

Winklo laid the gown on top of the bed. "We've brought you your wedding gown. It really is very lovely. There are more diamonds and spellstone crystals sewn on this gown than are locked away in the royal treasure chamber," Winklo exaggerated.

Cindy turned and glanced at the couple, eyeing the gown very carefully. "Spellstone? What's that?"

Winklo laid the gown on the bed and fluffed it up. "See these tiny crystals around the neck and sleeves, the ones that are multi-colored. They're called spellstones."

"That's a curious name for a crystal." Cindy thought about the one that Justin had given her on her birthday. It was in the pocket of her dress. The ones on the gown were just a smaller version of the one she had.

"Not really. They're called that because they enhance and store magic, when used properly of course. Very valuable jewels for magic users. We find them in the mines and use them to trade for things we need," said Winklo.

"How does it work?" asked Cindy.

"You'll have to ask Nash. I don't use magic, so for me, they're just pretty."

"Why do you want to know?" asked Nash. "Are you thinking of using your magic? If so, forget it. Those stones are small and even combined they won't help much. Besides, you've no training and wouldn't be a match for Asgar and all his Fortesan friends."

Cindy hopped off her chair and opened the wardrobe. She stuck her hand in her pant pocket and sighed happily. It was still there.

"What about this one?" Cindy pulled the gem out and opened her fist.

Nash and Winklo gasped in unison. "Where did you find that?"

"I've never seen one so big before," said Nash.

"It was a birthday gift from my…friend. He found it while gardening."

"May I see it?" asked Nash.

Cindy handed him the crystal. Nash held it up to the window and turned it from side to side. His tiny elfin hands made the jewel glimmer various shades of green, as if it reflected the color of his fingers.

Both Cindy and Winklo watched him intently, listening to his hmmmmm's and ahhhhhh's and wow's.

"Well?" said Winklo tapping her foot on the hardwood floor. "What do you see?"

"Patience, woman."

Winklo stuck her tongue at Nash. "I saw that," said Nash. "You can be the most infuriating person. It takes time to measure the magic level."

"Time is something we have little of. The wedding is supposed to take place in a couple of hours and we've a lot to do."

"The wedding isn't going to take place," Cindy said, "cause I won't be here. I will not marry that evil man, spell or no spell."

"Do you have an escape plan?" asked Winklo.

"You might say that."

"Well tell me," said the dwarf. "I, I mean we, might be able to help."

"There's nothing you can do," Cindy said with a sigh. "I wish there was."

"Then how do you figure you're going to get out of this mess?"

Cindy looked at Winklo with tears in her eyes. "It's a long way from this room to the ground. I doubt one will live if they jump from this window."

Nash almost dropped the jewel. They both cried out, "No."

"They say that suicides become shadows. That's even worse than being Asgar's bride."

Cindy looked at Nash curiously. "Why?"

"They are hideous creatures, evil to the core. The living are their prey. I've heard all sorts of terrible stories on how they devour flesh. In some ways they are more powerful than the Fortesans, but their magic, if you can call their powers magic, is dark. If you jump, you may willingly join them. Don't do it. Do you want to turn against all your friends and all that you hold dear?"

Cindy started to sob. "No, but…but…"

"There might be another way," said Nash, "but you're gonna have to work very hard at what I can teach you and most of all, you're gonna have to trust me. Are you willing?"

"Oh yes. Anything. I'm willing to do anything. The two of you have been so wonderful to me. I wish there was a way to repay you."

"We're friends. Friends help each other in need," said Winklo.

Nash kissed Winklo. "Indeed we do. Now listen carefully. While I'm explaining the plan, I want you to get dressed."

Winklo glared at Nash. "You expect her to take off her clothes while you are here? How rude."

Nash shrugged and rolled his eyes. "You never cease to surprise me, Winky. It's not what you think. I'll turn my back. If this is going to work, we need all the time that's left. I need to teach Cindy a little magic and that's not going to be easy. If she's dressed, that's one less thing she'll have to do."

"Magic?" Cindy began to undress as soon as Nash had turned his back.

"Yes. With this crystal and my help, I think we can pull this off. This will amplify your spell tremendously. I've honestly never seen one this huge. Even a simple spell using a spellstone this large could be devastating."

"You know, I think Asgar used a spellstone, even bigger than this, when he pulled the town over to the Wildsidhe and cursed us."

"That would explain where even he got that much power," said Nash. Fumbling with her fingers, Cindy almost lost the spellstone. "Whatever you do, don't drop it. If it shatters, it will be less powerful. It must be on your body for it to work."

"Asgar will see it then," Cindy said slipping the wedding gown over her head.

Winklo started to fasten the back, buttoning the row of tiny pearls. "Stay still," she shouted, "There's more buttons here than there are stars in the sky."

"Drop it down your neckline. You've enough bosom to hold it in."

"Nash! Men don't talk that way."

"Winky, be quiet. This isn't the time for etiquette. It's the only place I can think of that Asgar won't go looking for it and he's certainly going to sense it after a while. If it's around the neck, he can figure it's the spellstones on the gown that's giving off the aura. Obviously it isn't just Cindy that's gonna have to trust me."

Winklo nodded. "I'm sorry. You're right."

Nash just looked to the ceiling and shook his head vigorously. "Now sit, Cindy, and listen very carefully for I'm going to have to whisper this to you. Winklo, I'll tell you later when we're alone. I don't have enough time to explain it twice. For the time being, I want you to go and get everything ready. I need this time to prepare Cindy and I may not be able to help."

Begrudgingly, Winklo left, mumbling her complaints just loud enough for Nash to hear. Cindy waved and sat quietly on the bed as Nash began to whisper instructions in her ear. Periodically she would nod and when he finished, she smiled broadly.

"It could work."

"Yes," agreed Nash. "I think so. Now let's get to work. Put the spellstone down for the time being. No sense in tapping it now."

Nash began by teaching Cindy how to hold her hands. He taught her the proper position for beginning a magic spell and the gesture she would need to make this one spell she would cast work.

It amazed Cindy that there was so much to do and that different spells required different motions. She understood why training was necessary.

"I think we're ready to try now. Asgar is far enough away and my spell of silence may just hold. Wiggle your ears."

"Wiggle my ears?" asked Cindy.

"For luck. It's just a saying amongst us elves."

"We cross our fingers for luck."

"Don't do that. Otherwise, this spell will work differently. Everything from how high you hold your arms up and where each finger bends is important. If you cross your fingers, instead of a spell of breakage, you'll cause frogs to rain."

Cindy laughed. "That wouldn't help, but it sure would be funny to have a field full of croaking frogs."

"With the stone, we'd be knee deep in them. Now do what I've told you and concentrate on the vase over there."

Cindy faced the table where the vase that Nash had brought her the other day still stood. She raised her right hand just a bit higher than her left and whispered the magic words that Nash had taught her.

The vase began to vibrate. So did the oil lamp and the breakfast tray that was also on the table. The toast and silverware began to hop, bouncing up and down until they finally landed on the floor.

"Not bad for a first try," said Nash. "Raise your left arm to your waist and bend your elbow a bit more. Try it again."

This time the breakfast tray shattered and tiny shards of metal sprayed throughout the room. Nash pounced on Cindy sending her tumbling to the floor. He covered her body with his as the bits of metal ricocheted off the walls and furniture.

"Ouch," Cindy said as she fell.

"Cover your face and be quiet."

The door opened and Winklo shouted. "What is going on in here?"

"Shut the door woman and duck."

Winklo screamed as the shards whizzed past her. Nash and Cindy could hear the door slam shut and the plinks and plunks as the last few pieces of the tray dropped to the floor.

"Not bad," said Nash. "You broke the tray. You're getting the feel of it."

"I almost killed us all," Cindy said. "This isn't easy. I don't know if I can do this."

Winklo returned with a broom and began to sweep up the mess. "Everything is ready and you have about thirty ticks until Asgar will be back. You'd better hurry."

"Plenty of time. She's a fast learner."

Winklo smiled and swept the debris into a pan. "Don't feel bad, Cindy. I've seen Nash practice. Once he gave our fish wings. Never did figure out how to undo it."

Cindy chuckled, thinking about a flying fish.

"Out woman. She needs to practice," Nash said, closing the door with a gesture and making sure the door smacked Winklo on her rear as she left.

"Magic can be very useful," he said snickering.

"I see," Cindy said turning to the vase. "Shall I give it another try?"

"Go for it." Nash covered his eyes and peeked through his fingers.

Once again Cindy braced herself. With her hands in the same position, she began to say the magic words while twirling her wrists just a bit faster.

The spell ended with her pointing her index finger at the vase. This time the vase cracked and broke into little pieces. The water splashed on the table and the roses fell to the floor.

"You did it," shouted Nash, "And in your second attempt. You're a natural."

Cindy clenched her fists. "Yes. Yes!"

Her heart was racing and she could barely contain the excitement she felt. All of a sudden the mirror moved and turned itself around. Asgar's reflection rippled in the glass.

Cindy jumped back. How much had he seen or heard. Her heart fell to her stomach and the smile on her face disappeared.

"Practicing a bit of magic, my sweet?"

CHAPTER 13

Wayne was true to his promise. The computer and ham radio were functioning ten minutes after the boys had brought them in. Unfortunately, all Ben received on the transmitter was static. Once, he thought he heard voices and tried to amplify the station, but either it was hopeful thinking or he wasn't quick enough and lost the connection.

It was all so frustrating. His father and he had set up the channels ahead of time, as well as the hours to try and reach other. Though he had only tried twice, he had been unsuccessful in making contact.

Ben looked at his watch. He would give it five more minutes and then give up for the day. He wanted to work on his idea for a new weapon. His secret. An iron blaster.

Ben sat down at the desk and began to make a list of his ideas. What they needed was something that would hurt these creatures and not backfire on them. Something they could get their hands on easily and a means to propel it that didn't require electricity or batteries. They would need iron, but not in a solid shape. Shavings perhaps, but how were they going to chip enough to make it worthwhile. They could always make iron bullets, but no way did he want to handle a gun. Statistics showed that more often than not, guns were used on their owners. Besides, for some reason, they had found no guns on the Wildsidhe.

Then it struck him. Copiers. They used a form of iron powder to transfer the printed image to paper, before the toner made the copy. It was called the starter. Copiers were everywhere. They had a bunch in the school and almost every business used one.

Ben turned off the computer after researching the inner works of a copier and ran down to the principal's office. Sure enough he had his own personal machine. It was easy pulling off the panel and the starter was where the picture said it would be. What surprised him was how heavy it was.

This was going to be a draw back. He wanted something portable, but the weight was going to make it difficult to use in quantity. He carried the container upstairs and set it down on the desk at the opposite end of the room.

Wayne had mentioned to him that Carmen was a genius at coming up with ideas and fixing things. He wished she were here to bounce his thoughts off of. What kind of container could he use that was light? What could he use to propel it? He wondered if a squirt gun would work, or even a spray bottle.

The only way he would know was to experiment. Ben walked into the multi-purpose and found Wayne making arrows. Iris was beside him smiling and flirting, to little avail. He remembered the necklace around his neck and felt it through his shirt. Part of him felt guilty for not giving it to Iris. He did make that promise to his mother, but he never did say when he would, only that he would. Iris would have to wait.

"What's up Ben?" asked Wayne. "Everything okay?"

"Can I talk to you…alone?"

"Sure." Wayne excused himself and got out of the chair. "Wanna go out in the hall?"

"Come into the chemistry lab. I want to show you something."

Wayne followed Ben in the room. He saw the plastic container sitting on a cloth and picked it up. "Heavy. What's in it?"

"Iron powder. Copiers use it and there are plenty of machines in the school and all around town."

"Ben, you're a genius. We can use it against our enemies."

"Yes and no. You've seen for yourself how heavy it is. That's the drawback. We need something light, but strong, and a means to control the direction. I don't know if it'll work, but I thought we might try a water pistol or maybe even a squirt bottle."

"Have you tried it out yet?" asked Wayne.

"No. I need to go to town and get some different things to experiment with. I was hoping you might go with me to help."

"No problemo. We'll head out first thing in the morning. There's a hardware shop on the way and a toy outlet in the strip mall. In the meantime, let's not say anything to anybody. Until we get this figured out, there's no reason to get them excited."

Wayne was true to his word. The following day, the two of them went to town and picked up squirt guns, spray bottles and cans of compressed of air. In the back of the hardware store were leaf blowers and both Wayne and him grabbed a few of the powerful gas models that came on wheels and had to be pushed like a mini-lawn mower.

There were guards on duty to open the gate and let them back in, after the trouble with the kid who was supposed to be on watch when Ben slipped out the first time. As a punishment, his food supply was cut in half for three days.

No one paid any attention to them as they carried their packages up the steps. Most thought Ben a bit weird and left him to himself anyway and with Wayne accompanying him, they didn't ask any questions.

They worked on it until lunch. The squirt guns and the aerosol spray containers were a bust. There just wasn't enough air to force the heavy powder out, but they struck it lucky with the compressed air cans from air horns, the type annoying people used at pep rallies.

They devised an attachment using PVC pipes, the same piping that plumbers used. It was made of plastic and lighter than metals ones. They welded it to the opening of the can and when the nozzle was pushed, out sprayed the iron in a mist. They would need a lot of them, but it worked and that was the main thing.

What was more cumbersome was using the industrial leaf blowers. They were bigger than the kind you carried, but they came with wheels. It just make them difficult to maneuver. Epecially with a makeshift, screw on attachment. They were challenging to steer but were so powerful each covered a huge area.

It took two kids to safely lift it, but this weapon could be used from a window, the roof, or even in a car. They tested it first with talcum powder, not wanting to use up the precious iron powder. When it was successful, they called the group to come watch and carried the contraption into an unused classroom they had covered in plastic.

Everyone stood by eagerly as they attached the nozzle filled with the iron and propped it on the floor by the window.

"Ben this is your baby. You thought of it, you may have the honors."

Ben smiled while everyone watched intently. Using all the strength he could muster, Ben yanked on the string and the motor started. Iron powder sprayed all over. Later they would sweep up the iron from the plastic dropclothes to use it again. They had debated about using the talc again, but decided if they were betting their lives on these weapons, they needed to know if it would work with the heavier iron powder. Luckily it did.

"It works," the kids cried. "You're a genius, Ben."

Everyone clapped and cheered. The boys patted Ben on the back and the girls hugged him. Iris even kissed him on the cheek. For the first time in his life, Ben was the hero. He would remember this moment for the rest of his life.

CHAPTER 14

Chuck felt sick to his stomach. Where was Justin? He wasn't in the car. Where could he be?

Just as he stepped out of the car and was ready to call for help, he heard a voice in the distance. "Justin…is that you?" he shouted looking all around.

A voice in the distance yelled back. "Over here. Look at this."

Chuck ran across the road and was about to scold Justin for leaving the vehicle when his friend thrust a piece of parchment in his hand.

"Read this. It was tied to a rock. I saw it fall over there and ran to see what it was."

Before giving Chuck a chance to even unroll the paper, Justin went into a tirade. "It's an invitation to Asgar and Cindy's wedding. I don't believe it. I just don't believe it. I'm going to kill him. I'm going to tear him to shreds and toss the pieces to the wind. Better yet, I'm going to blind and cripple him. He's taunting us. He thinks he can keep us from getting there in time to spoil the wedding. He must be scared of us."

John and Chuck looked at each other. Carmen, who had heard the screams joined them and leaned against the car. Though none of them had ever seen Justin so angry, the three of them knew there was little they could do to change what had happened. As for Asgar being afraid, that was a joke, but to point that out to Justin at this moment would serve no purpose. He was beyond talking to.

Justin pounded on the hood of the car, but ended up hurting his hand. He shook his fist as if that would relieve the pain and bit his lip. As foolish as he had been acting, he wouldn't cry.

Carmen ignored the string of unmentionable, curse words. Justin had every right to be upset. Besides, she hung around boys and was used to their language. There were a few girls at the school whose language could put even this display to shame.

"C'mon," she said. "Knock off the Mr. Macho act and quit acting like a kid. We're just wasting time. Cindy wouldn't marry him out of choice. This is just an attempt on his part to try and get us to give up and go home."

"You may have something there," Justin said. "Cindy and I were pretty tight."

Carmen looked at the Bearclaw brothers and used her head to silently urge them to agree. Both of them, taking the cue, nodded their heads.

Lissy fluttered about. "No. Asgar doesn't play games like that. If he said there was going to be a wedding, there will be a wedding. I saw Cindyfriend.

She's bewitched. When she's with him, she acts all feminine and smiley."

Carmen lifted her finger to her lips and shook her head no. Justin gave Carmen a dirty look.

"Don't humor me. I know you mean well, but don't treat me like I'm an idiot. We've been through too much."

"Let's get going," said Chuck. "We're just guessing. We don't know anything for a fact. The sooner we get there, the sooner we'll have answers. Besides, now we don't have to sneak in. We have an invitation."

"You think we should just walk in?" Carmen said, not believing what she was hearing.

"Better plan than the five of us storming a castle," said John.

"He's got a point," said Chuck. The matter was put aside in favor of getting back on the road.

They were on their way in just seconds with Lissy sitting on the windshield pointing the way. At times the road got bumpy. It was obvious that carts and horses had used these paths as they could see hoof-marks and gouges. There were also impressions embedded in the dried earth of animal foot prints, some of which they had no clue as to what had left them.

"How much longer, Lissy?" asked Justin.

"We should make it there before it turns dark, if we hurry," the pixie answered.

Justin sighed. "Cindy will be married by then. Isn't there a shorter way?"

Lissy shook her head. "I'm sorry. This is the only way I know. If you could fly, it would be different."

Carmen put her hand around Justin's shoulder. "We're going to rescue her. Don't give up hope."

"I'd feel a whole lot better if we could get there sooner."

"It really won't be so bad, getting there at night. Might even make things easier for us. It's a lot harder to see at night."

"But that's assuming they're still there. What if they leave for a honeymoon?"

"Justin, there are too many what-ifs to worry about. Who even knows if there is such a thing as a honeymoon here? Maybe Cindy escaped and is heading down this very road even as we speak. She could even have killed Asgar all by herself."

"And pigs can fly," Justin said, laughing.

Carmen choked. Justin patted her on the back. "It wasn't that funny," he said.

"I know," replied Carmen, "But I was just thinking, here on the Wildsidhe, who knows? Maybe they can."

CHAPTER 15

"A sgar." Cindy smiled and tried to keep from looking shocked. "It was for a surprise, for you. I asked Nash to teach me. I'm afraid I've made a mess of things, though. I'm not too good at this. I never realized there was more to practicing magic than just thinking and wishing."

"It's an art, my dear. One must have the potential to begin with, but it takes years of hard work to master. I wish you hadn't asked Nash, though. It's best to learn from an accomplished sorcerer."

"I just wanted to do something special for you. Had I asked you to teach me, it wouldn't have been a surprise."

"You are forgiven, of course. Are you ready now? The guests have begun to arrive."

"Guests?"

"The Fortesan High Council of course. This momentous occasion should be witnessed…I mean shared with everyone. When we put the wedding off, I had time to invite them. Soon they will be your friends, also."

Cindy stared in the mirror. "Give me just a moment. Nash can escort me down. Now, be off. You do realize it's bad luck to see the bride before the ceremony? I hope this isn't a bad omen."

"Where did you hear that?" asked Asgar.

"It's custom, a tradition, from my world. I suppose it's just an old superstition, but we honor it."

"Then I shall too. In honoring that which you hold dear, I honor the lady herself."

The reflection of Asgar bowed. His image rippled like a pebble skipping over a silver sea and as he vanished, the mirror became solid.

"That was close," said Winklo.

"You can say that again," said Nash.

Cindy sat on the bed, fluffing the heavy gown around her dangling legs. "It's curious, but the charm spell doesn't have the same effect as when we're in person. I felt no love for him. Just antagonism and contempt."

"It wasn't him in the mirror, just a magical portrayal of his likeness. The incantation he has cast on you must be one of contact. It's effect works by touch or smell," Nash said.

"If that's the case, then this plan has a great chance of working," cried Winklo. "I was worried that once she was in his presence, Cindy might not want to go through with this. Now, we have the answer."

"What do you mean?" asked Nash.

"I don't know what you'd do without me, dear. You may have taught Cindy how to tear a hole in the force field, but did you stop to think that maybe, once she's with him, she wouldn't want to go through with it?" Winklo chuckled. "Sometimes you fail to give me credit for my acute sense of reasoning and keen eyes for observations."

"Never. How could I overlook them, or even forget them? You wouldn't let me."

"Was that meant as insult?" asked Winklo. "Sometimes I don't know whether or not you're teasing me."

"Winky, you know better. I'd never say anything to hurt you. My life without you would have no purpose."

Nash winked at Cindy and she returned it. Though she had known the couple only a short time, she had become very close to them and envied their loving relationship. No two people ever deserved themselves more than Winklo and Nash.

"Now, Cindy," continued Winklo, "This may be hard for you to force yourself to do, but you must hold your breath prior to performing your magic. Nash can make you sneeze just long enough for you not to inhale the substance that has you bewitched."

"Sneeze?"

"If you're sneezing you're exhaling. If you're not breathing in Asgar's charm you should be clear enough to cast the spell Nash taught you. If you're successful, there will be a rip in the force field. As soon as you see it, make a run for it. Simple."

"Winky, it's a good plan, but it's going to take split second timing. I can carry some kerchoosie flowers and hopefully no one will notice. I can blow on the tufts and that should make her wheeze at least."

"Why don't you just put it in my bouquet?"

"What do you mean?"

"The bride always carries a bouquet of flowers. It's tradition. Isn't it here?"

Nash shook his head. "That's a new one, but since you've requested it, I'll make one up, kerchoosie flowers and all."

"Wonderful. It's perfect. Cindy, you're saved."

Winklo jumped. Cindy just shook her head. "How will I know if I've succeeded? Where will I go? How will I get home? I don't know my way around. You both make it sound so easy. I'm so scared. There are so many ifs."

"There's no other choice. You don't really want to marry Asgar do you?"

Cindy shook her head.

"Then I'm afraid you're going to have to take some chances and go with it," continued Nash. "It will be very clear if the spell has worked. There will be a rainbow of light highlighting the tear. It won't last long. If Asgar asks what you are doing, just tell him it's your surprise. Just make sure you're quick 'cause as soon as Asgar discovers what you're really up to, he'll close it. As for finding your way, we can draw you a map," said Nash.

"This is all so complicated and it's all based on luck. I wish you would go with me."

Nash and Winklo looked at each other.

"Yes, that's the answer. I don't know why I didn't think of this before. Come with me. You're not happy here. Justin, Wayne, and the others would love to have you. We could all escape together."

Winklo nodded and clapped her tiny hands. "Oh Nash, let's. She's right. We've nothing to keep us here."

"Are you sure we'd be welcome? I really don't want to impose," Nash said.

"Positive. They will love you as much as I do." Cindy grabbed them both and hugged them. "I can't imagine why I didn't think of this before. I know I'd miss you terribly if I had escaped and left you here. You'll be so much happier with us. Things won't be as easy. We work mighty hard, but you'll be free to come and go as you wish."

"Then it's settled. Thanks, Cindy. We feel the same way about you. Anywhere is better than this place. The only thing that has made life bearable is having my sweet Winky here with me."

"Well, we better not keep Asgar waiting or he's going to get suspicious. We'll hold off for a minute to allow Nash to make your bouquet," said Winklo.

Nash scurried out of the room. Cindy sat on the bed, smiling and humming softly to herself. She closed her eyes, crossed her fingers and said a silent prayer. Soon she would be back home. Not Sparta, but with her friends. After all, home is where your heart is.

CHAPTER 16

Winky was spying on the guests through the half-opened door. "Morna and Penrod are here. The king is taking his place by the gazebo and Morna is strutting around like a kaleidoscopy bird. What a showoff. You should see the dress she is wearing. Doesn't she know it's impolite to out dress the bride?"

"Who cares what she is wearing? Get back here. I don't want Asgar to see you spying on him."

"It's too late for that," said Asgar pushing his way through the door. "Anxious are we, Winklo? Excited? All is forgiven. I'm too happy a man today for anything to trouble me. Are you ready, Cindy? Everyone's waiting."

Cindy smiled. He was so handsome. So charming. She felt warm all over whenever he was he near.

"I'm ready and quite nervous. Is there anything I should know? Your customs are quite different than ours."

"No reason to be jittery. I'm here. It will all be over in a matter of a few minutes. Just follow Penrod's lead. Repeat what he says when he asks. After he proclaims us legally wedded, look to the sky. There will be fireworks. My present to you, my love."

"Oh Asgar. You are wonderful. I guess I'm as a ready as I'll ever be."

Cindy held out her hand and Asgar grabbed it, pulling her to his side. He tucked her arm under his, and glanced once more into Cindy's sparkling eyes.

"Nash, would you mind opening the door?"

It wasn't a question. Nash scurried over to the door and opened it wide. He motioned for Winklo to stand beside him and followed the couple as they stepped into the fresh air. Quickly, he closed it behind him and then took his place behind Asgar.

They had made it to the stone fence that separated the castle proper from Asgar's acres. Asgar stood at the closed gate and waited for Nash to open it.

Cindy stood mesmerized by the amount of people that had gathered for their ceremony. Though they were all seated, she could see that in height they all were as tall as Asgar and Morna.

King Penrod stood in the gazebo. His crown glittered as it caught the sun's rays as it streamed through the enclosure. Morna was at his side. She looked gorgeous in her gown that seemed to change color in the sunlight. They looked very regal together.

"They've all come to pay you tribute, my dear," Asgar said. "Soon you shall be one of us. Soon you shall be queen. It was Alana's legacy and rightfully yours. That gown of Morna's, the one you are in awe of, is as old as Wildsidhe. It was worn by the mother and gifted to the first ruler. Since that day, each queen has the honor of wearing it at special occasions. It is made of layers and layers of wings that pixies have shed.

"With each succession, another layer is added. Soon, there will be one more…when Mora passes the gown to you. And now, I think we've made them wait long enough. Let's proclaim our love for each other publicly."

CHAPTER `17

All eyes were on the couple as they stood before King Penrod exchanging their vows. Cindy's smile was so broad it covered her entire face and even Asgar was beaming. Morna, however, remained solemn and motionless by her husband's side. If looks could kill, Asgar would have fallen victim to the queen's icy stare. She had just learned that Cindy was her sister's granddaughter and the marriage would give Asgar the right to challenge Penrod for the throne. Of course, Asgar didn't know that she knew yet. That could be helpful.

"Do thou, Asgar of Wildsidhe, take Cindy Hartman of Earth as your wife, to share in all of all life's treasures, be it good or bad, until thee no longer draw life-giving breath?"

Asgar looked at Cindy and proclaimed loudly, "I do."

Penrod smiled. "And do you, Cindy Hartman, take Asgar of Wildsidhe as your husband, to share in all of all life's treasures, be it good or bad, until thee no longer draw life-giving breath?"

Cindy's lips began to move, the word yes was at the tip of her tongue, when all chaos broke loose. It all happened so fast that not a person could remember the details of the fiasco in sequence. Nash blew on Cindy's bouquet scattering the wisps of Kerchoosie petals everywhere. Not only did they effect Cindy as planned, but Asgar, Penrod, and Morna started sneezing as well.

Winklo shouted, "Now!" and Cindy, sneezing uncontrollably, jerked to attention. Remembering everything the elf had taught her, she began to move her arms and wrists, chanting the few words necessary to complete the spell.

There was a loud tearing sound as the barrier began to rip. Contrary to what Nash had told her, there was no small hole. The power within the spellstone amplified the incantation. The tear was huge and the repercussions of it caused it to flicker and totally disappear.

Nash and Winklo grabbed Cindy, one hand each, and started running. It was quite a distance to the forest. If they could make it there before Asgar had a chance to reinstate the force field they would have a chance. But, Asgar regained his composure instantly. All around them they could see the sparks of lighting beginning to mend the barrier. It rippled and crackled as tiny fingers of sparkles wove the net that in another second would enclose them in once more.

"I don't think we're going to make it," cried Cindy. "What are we going to do?"

"Just run," shouted Nash, "we've got to try."

All of a sudden the bright flashes of light and the half-woven threads that were about to seal them in vanished. The three of them stopped to see what was happening.

"Run, you idiots," commanded Morna. "I can't hold Asgar off for long. Run as fast as you can. I'll do what I can."

They took off running once again. The screams of confusion coming from the guests added to the pandemonium. Luck was with them as they bounded into the woods, safe for the moment.

"Now where to?" asked Cindy breathing heavily as she leaned against a tree.

"I'm going to take the lead. You and Winky hold tight and run. Now's not the time to rest. Just follow me."

Nash took off, darting around trees and bushes. Cindy, holding tightly to Winklo's hand, made sure to keep the elf in sight. She had no idea where they were going, but totally trusted her friend. They ran for what seemed like hours. It was dark under the thick growth of the trees, but she could tell it was still daylight, as tiny beams of light filtered through the entwined branches.

Nash would stop intermittently, allowing them to regain their strength, but Cindy could see that he was very nervous. No one spoke about Morna's interference as if mentioning her name would change their luck. In fact, no one said much of anything, as they were so out of breath that speaking was an effort.

The scariest thing was they could hear a rustling coming from the uppermost tree branches. Though they couldn't rule out the wind, in their hearts they knew it was Asgar riding Maelstrom. He wasn't one to give up easily. The forest provided them a hiding place, but what would they do when they reached the edge? No one wanted to talk about it, so they kept on dodging low-lying bushes and gnarly roots that seemed to pop out of nowhere. They ran until they could no more. Their legs ached, but they continued onward, walking until finally they were at the border where the grass-laden pastures greeted the last few, scraggly trees.

It was getting dark. Nash felt it safer to sleep in the woodlands then somewhere out in the open. Winklo and Cindy agreed and they curled up by each other to keep warm. Nash nixed a fire as the smoke would certainly draw attention to them and give away their position.

The few stars that were out glittered like diamond dust in a velvet sky. Nash snored and Winklo blew little putt-putts of air as they slept. Cindy dozed a bit, but was too hyped to get any real sleep. Suddenly, from a distance she heard the sound of a motor.

"Nash," Cindy whispered, shaking him awake. "Listen."

"I hear it, but I don't know what it is. It doesn't sound like any animal I'm familiar with. If we were close to a mill, perhaps it might be the sound of a grinder."

"I think it's a car."

"A what?" asked Winklo who heard the voices and had awakened.

"A car, a motorized carriage."

They both looked at her quizzically.

"It doesn't matter what it is. My people use them for transportation. They're much faster than a horse. I'm hoping it might be Justin and Lissy."

"Faster than a lionhawk?"

"I don't know, but it's a whole lot faster than running. Can you see anything? Maybe I'd better run ahead and see."

"If you go, we all go," said Nash. "There's safety in numbers."

The three of them started to walk, but Cindy burst into a run and ran ahead. She was too excited at the prospect of it being Justin. Off in the distance she could make out the shape of an automobile and without thinking she started to yell.

It was too late for Nash to warn her. Out in the open, sounds carried and within seconds, the flapping of wings drowned out the sounds of the motor.

"I've got you now, Cindy. Give it up," yelled Asgar.

"Drop," ordered Nash. Winklo and Cindy plunged to the ground where hundreds of blades of grass grew tall and wrapped them in a cocoon. Above them they could hear Asgar screaming. They could feel the turbulence caused by Maelstrom flying low. A couple of times Cindy thought for sure Asgar would find them, but the longer they stayed concealed by the blanket of grass, the safer she felt. Unfortunately, Asgar's untimely appearance prevented her from knowing whether or not Justin heard her calling. All she could do was pray that he had.

It was Nash that tapped her and released the blades of bondage. She hugged him and thanked him for saving her life once again.

"I owe you so much," she said. "I fear I'll never be able to repay you. I hate to ask you this, but can you do me one more favor?"

"Sure," Nash answered. "Name it."

"Is there any way to cut these weeds down. They're taller than me and I can't see the road."

"I have a safer way. Follow me."

Nash began to walk and as he did, the grass separated allowing them to see straight ahead. It rippled like dominoes, until finally there was clearing all the way to the road. And on the road, she could see a car.

Cindy didn't know who saw whom first, but she started running and so did four other people. Within seconds she was in the arms of Justin, Carmen, John, and Chuck. She was so happy to see them she burst into tears.

"It's okay, Cindy. You're safe now," Justin said.

"Not really," said Winklo. "No one is ever safe from a Fortesan."

"Who're they?" asked Justin, staring at the pointy-eared little man and short, stout woman.

"That's Nash, and next to him is his girlfriend, Winklo. I'll introduce all of you, but right now, I want to go home. Can we?"

"They're coming?" asked Justin.

"Yes, they are. If it weren't for them I'd never have escaped. I owe them my life many times over."

"Thanks, you two," Justin said. "Any friend of Cindy's is a friend of ours."

The others nodded in agreement and Carmen opened the back door to the convertible. "Hop in. The sooner we get back, the better."

Winky hesitated. "It's made of iron. It will hurt my Nash," she said.

"It's a long way back," Justin said. "You'll never make it if you walk. I can put the top down. I just don't know what else we can do."

"I'll be okay," said Nash crawling inside and wincing from the iron reaction. "We need to hurry and I'll not be the reason we don't make it to Cindy's house safely."

Winklo crawled in beside Nash, followed by Carmen. Cindy hopped in the passenger seat next to Justin. John and Chuck climbed in the white sedan. As soon as everyone was in, the boys made a U-turn in the open field and headed back.

It was a nerve-wracking ride back. Everyone was on the lookout for signs of Asgar. At one point, the white sedan ran out of gas and with the convertible running low, they decided to cram into one car and save the emergency can of fuel for just that, an emergency. They'd come back and get it later.

The car was cramped, but it did give everyone a chance to get acquainted with each other. Nash was mostly silent, as the iron in the car had given him a ferocious headache and slight fever. Cindy was glad that Winklo was able to sing him to sleep and Lissy was delighted because Winklo had a beautiful voice.

Often, as they made a few stops to stretch and change drivers, both

Cindy and Justin got the feeling that they were being followed. Sometimes it was the huge shadow that seemed to come out of nowhere that made them shiver. Other times it was the cry of a bird that jolted them out of their conversation, but they never did see any physical signs of Asgar.

Even when they arrived back at school two days later, there were no signs of the huge lionhawk or its owner. Everyone but Cindy, Justin, Winklo, and Nash felt they had won. Since they didn't want to ruin the homecoming celebration, the four of them made a pact to be silent and on guard.

The party went on well into the night. Everyone was excited to meet the new members of their society and Winklo was in her glory with all the attention lavished on her. Nash slept peacefully. The swollen, blister-like rash brought on by the iron caused him to have a high fever. Somehow, he managed to sleep through the noise.

They talked until they couldn't keep their eyes open any longer. Those that hadn't already fallen asleep, had no problem doing so. All except Cindy, who kept having nightmares. She was positive she heard the loud shrills that the lionhawks made and at times could swear there was a rapping at the window. Too upset, she decided to vanquish her fears by going to take a look.

The two crescent moons shed light on the parking lot beneath them. It all looked quiet and peaceful. Cindy relaxed, sat on the chair and leaned back. She was about to doze off when she heard a clicking. Turning her head in the direction of the sounds, she looked out the window once more. This time, she saw something other than her own her reflection in the pane of glass.

"Asgar," she cried out, surprised.

It was too late for Asgar to quiet Cindy. Everyone in the room woke up. Justin ran to Cindy, shutting the window that Cindy had just opened.

"Leave me alone," she shouted, shoving Justin away. "I'm old enough to make my choice and I choose to be with Asgar.

Even through the closed window they could hear Asgar laugh. "You heard her, boy, get out of out of her way."

Lightening crackled from his fingers as Maelstrom's massive beak shattered the window that separated them. Asgar leaned over, extending his arm for Cindy to hold onto, but Justin blocked her.

"Help," he screamed. "Help me keep Cindy away."

Nash and Winklo held onto Cindy's ankles while Carmen and Chuck ran to fetch their bows and arrows. Cindy struggled to break free, trying vainly to get a grasp on Asgar's hand, but her friends had too tight a grip. It was push and pull. Finally, Brina and Bobby chipped in and the four of them managed to drag Cindy into the hallway.

Cindy came to her senses. "That was too close. Thanks, guys."

"You better stay here," said Bobby. "I'm going to help the others."

"We'll guard her. I'm afraid we'd be of little help fighting. I've never seen such weapons," said Winklo. "Good luck."

The two younger kids disappeared in the multi-purpose room. Cindy leaned on the wall and slipped to the floor. She had tears in eyes and covered her face with her hands. Winklo consoled her. It wasn't her fault she was bewitched.

Kids were rushing in and out. Ben zoomed by and ran down the hall. He was gone only a second and emerged from the science room pushing a cart and his weapon.

"What's that?" asked Nash.

Cindy looked up and watched as Ben wheeled the thing into the room. Wayne followed him. Though Cindy asked, the boys were too busy to answer.

"I don't know. It looks like a push leaf blower with a shower nozzle attached."

"A leaf blower? Why would you want to blow leaves?"

"I'll explain it to you later. Let's go watch," Cindy said.

"Oh no you don't," said Nash. "You're not going anywhere near that room."

"We can watch from the doorway."

"Only if we can hold onto you."

"Whatever," Cindy said, standing up and peeking around the doorframe.

Nash and Winklo held tight to Cindy's arms. She could feel their hands as they pinched her skin, but she didn't complain. They were only trying to protect her.

Asgar didn't notice her watching from the hallway. He was too busy maneuvering Maelstrom from window to window. As soon as the bird broke one window, Wayne, Carmen, John, Chuck, and Ron starting shooting through it. Arrows whizzed out the holes, but as huge as the bird was, he was also very agile and was able to dodge the iron tipped arrows or whisk them away with a flap of his wings.

It was a sight to behold. Asgar sat high on the back, straddling the lionhawk, his knees guiding it left and right. One hand held onto the long, ruff of neck feathers and he used his free hand to send swirling balls of fire. The younger kids starting rushing about, grabbing fire extinguishers. Small fires were burning everywhere. Cindy quickly organized them in a long line reaching from the multi-purpose room to the bathroom. Though the plumbing wasn't working, there was still water in the toilet bowls.

It was systematic chaos and it looked like Asgar was going to win. Ben tried valiantly to position the leaf-blower at the window but couldn't get close enough. The fireballs were hurdling to fast and too frequent. Wayne yelled for Carmen to help, but they couldn't get close to the window, either.

"There's only one way we can stop him and I'm the only one that can do it," Terri said. "I can fly. Give me the blower and I can attack from outside."

"No way," shouted Wayne. "You're no match for Asgar or that bird."

"Unless you have a better suggestion, I suggest you move. We're losing this battle. There's a lot more than Cindy's safety at stake. If he defeats us here, we will all end up his slaves. Or dead.

"I have to attack from behind and surprise him. So unless you can fly, strap that baby on this wheel chair and get out of my way."

Unfortunately, she made sense. Ben and Wayne laid the blower it on Terri's lap.

"It's heavy. Are you sure?" asked Ben.

"I can't feel a thing," Terri said, winking. "It's why I'm in a wheelchair in the first place. Don't worry and get going."

They laid the blower vertically on her lap so the nozzle leaned against the right armrest. The rope was woven through the openings in the back of the chair and then wound around Terri's waist twice before they knotted it. Once secured, they tilted the nozzle outward.

"The iron powder is heavy. Terri, are you sure you can manage?"

"I've flown this thing with you on my lap, Wayne. This should be a piece of cake. Now let me get up to the roof. Stay out of sight and keep your fingers crossed."

Terri's chair bobbled a bit as she took off, but it didn't take her long to get accustomed to the extra pounds. She was speeding down the hallway in no time, leaving Wayne and Ben far behind.

"Be careful, Terri," shouted Wayne.

"Start the engine first, before you go outside. You may have to pull the string a few times, it's not easy," yelled Ben. "Make sure you put on that face mask so you don't breathe any of it in. Stay out of the way of the bird's wings."

"Stop worrying, you two, it's a piece of cake. Who's able to leap tall buildings in a single bound? Terri the Terror to the rescue! Here I come to save the day..."

Cindy ran down the hall, a few feet behind Ben, who was trying hard to keep up with Wayne. Nash and Winklo followed Cindy, flailing their arms. "Stop. It's not safe for you to be outside where Asgar can get at you. Do you want to ruin Terri's chances?"

Cindy quit running. Her new friends were right. She was too easy of a target on the roof.

"Wait here," said Winklo. "I'll go."

"Oh no, you won't. If anyone goes, I will," said Nash.

"Get out of my way, green man. It was my idea first."

"And what help are you going to be? I at least can do magic."

"Unless there are plants growing on the roof, you're useless."

Cindy shook her head. "If the two of you don't stop arguing, the battle will be over before either one of you makes it up there."

Nash gave Winklo a dirty look. "I wear the pants in this family and unless you want to dispute that, sit woman and stay."

Winky answered with a "Yes, sir. Whatever you say oh high and mighty one," but the humor was lost on Nash. He dashed up the steps leading to the roof.

Cindy turned to see the kids still handing buckets and pots of water down the chain and took her place in the line to help. So did Winklo. They strained their ears to hear what was going on.

All they could make out were the cheers coming from the boys and girls inside. "Go, Terri, go!"

Cindy wanted to look in the doorway. Her curiosity was aroused, but she knew she was needed and safer where she was. She kept on passing the water-filled containers until finally, Carmen yelled, "Enough. Fire's out."

From the hallway, they could all hear the piercing shrills of Maelstrom. When it became silent, all the kids rushed to the multi-purpose room. Cindy tried to push her way forward, but Winklo made her wait until she was sure Asgar was gone. From all the applause and clapping, she knew the kids had won.

"We did it!" Justin said grabbing Cindy around the waist and twirling her around. "Asgar and Maelstrom left."

"What happened? I want to know everything."

Just then Terri zoomed by and landed. The kids all huddled around her hugging and congratulating her. The happiness was deafening. Justin smiled. "I think I'll let our heroine tell the story. Terri?"

Terri was in her glory. "It wasn't easy, but I did it. With all this iron, it was almost impossible to get off the ground. It affects whatever magic lets me fly. It took all the concentration I could muster, but as soon as I was airborne, the rest was a cinch. This weapon is awesome. As soon as I turned it on, the iron powder scattered. The lionhawk's wings made it even more devastating. It seemed to draw the powder to it like a magnet.

"Asgar started to shield his face. I moved in closer. The bird backed away. I flew my wheelchair in front of them both and blasted them in a full frontal attack. It was fantastic. Asgar howled and the bird screeched. The next thing I knew, they were flying away."

Everyone was so excited they didn't seem to mind the mess. Wayne hugged his sister tightly. "You're one heck of a warrior, sis."

Terri smiled. "I can't take all the credit. If it weren't for Ben's weapon, I don't think we'd have had a chance. Let's hear it for Ben!"

Ben could barely keep from blushing. This was the first time in his life he was the center of attention. Even Iris hugged him.

"That's my brother," she said, "The genius."

Winklo and Nash stayed next to Cindy, basking in the room filled with love.

"I think we've found a real home," said Winklo.

"You bet you have," Cindy said, pulling them close and kissing them both.

"Let's have a victory party," shouted Brina.

The other kids all cried out in agreement. "We want a party! We want a party."

"Don't you think we should clean this place up a bit? We're going to have to move to another room until we replace all this glass. There's enough work here to keep us all busy for quite a while," Cindy said grabbing a broom.

"And I need to fortify all the windows, not just the ones on the first floor. There are still plenty of metal desks left that we can use," added Wayne.

Justin took the broom from Cindy's hand and tossed it away. "The mess isn't going anywhere. We've all earned a day off. You're home safe. We have new friends. There's a lot to be grateful for. Let's just give thanks."

Cindy smiled at Justin. "Thank you, Winklo and Nash. And you too, Carmen, Chuck, and John. All of you saved my life. Heck, thank you everyone. Most of all, Justin, thank you."

Justin smiled. "As a team, we're the greatest. Let's grab what we need and head to the gym."

He didn't have to wait for an answer. Everyone grabbed their blankets, pillows, and meager belongings and rushed out of the room, leaving Cindy and Justin alone.

"He'll be back, you know," Justin said. "This was only round one."

"I know." Cindy nodded. "We need to make some changes. Perhaps set up some permanent weaponry on the roof. It also might not be a bad idea to stay in the gym. There are no windows there and..."

Justin kissed Cindy. His arms enveloped her holding her tight until he could feel her melt in his embrace. The kiss lingered. Cindy clung to him feeling safe and warm.

"You win. Enough talk about work. Shall we join them?"

Justin grinned. "You bet, in one minute."

And he kissed her again.

LEGACY
Book 4

Judith Tracy

CHAPTER 1

"**G**et out, Mrs. Freeman, Now. Immediately, if not sooner."
Alana was too busy laughing in the back of the room at Mrs. Prin attempting a series of toe touches. She was not only not in rhythm, but her futile attempts to reach past her ankles were hilarious. All that huffing and puffing and for what? Emily Prin hadn't seen her feet in years, unless it was in the mirror.

"Mrs. Freeman? Is anyone home?"

Alana pointed to herself. "Me?"

"Is there another Mrs. Freeman?"

"I don't know. You tell me."

"Get the..." the instructor stopped in mid-sentence and drew a deep breath. "Leave, and never come back," was all she could muster saying politely.

Everyone in the aerobics class stopped to stare. Alana tugged on her sweatpants, exposing the lily-white skin of her behind before heading to the door. Everyone chuckled and yelled.

Alana, seconds before the door closed behind her, added, "What makes you think I want to?" Though she wanted to see the woman's face, it would have ruined her dramatic exit had she allowed the instructor to get in the last word.

No one was in the hall to see her leave or get on the elevator, but she knew she would hear about this later. Nurse Mingold would go out of her way to tell the doctor. She made sure Doctor Kinkaid heard about Alana's every little infraction of the rules at Sunny Days Assisted Living Apartment Complex.

Assisted Living. A fancy name for a nursing home for disposable old people. Politically correct language. She wasn't sick. Rowan, her daughter, hadn't condemned her to this place for health reasons. Alana, except for a touch of arthritis and dimming sight, was quite healthy for a woman in her eighties. No, Rowan had committed her here because she didn't believe her own mother.

Was it so hard to accept that her mother wasn't human? That she too came from the same world that Asgar did? But then again, it was an awful lot to digest. Asgar did waltz into town and abscond with half the community and most of the children. Things like that didn't happen every day, especially in a small town such as Sparta.

With special effects being what they were today, people just didn't trust their own eyes and ears anymore. The FBI's latest report to the captive Spartans blamed some gas explosion. Pish, tosh. Anyone who bought that nonsense needed to have their head examined.

Alana locked the door to her living quarters and slipped out of the sweat suit. Even though she had lived amongst these people for fifty-plus years, old habits didn't die. She was royalty and royalty dressed appropriately. That meant a dress. The flowered one would do. The only thing she resigned herself to wear were the sneakers. They were so comfortable and with her varicose veins, a necessity. She looked funny, but who cared? Who would look at her and find her attractive? Wrinkles, silver gray hair, and a figure that had surrendered to the forces of gravity a long time ago.

That was what made the exercising classes a farce. Sure, it did build stamina and strengthened the heart, but Miss Bower kept yelling absurdities like, "Let's tighten those abdominal muscles, ladies. Let's firm those derrieres." Who were they kidding? At her age a firm rear-end wasn't an asset. Let her keep the little fat she had on her rump. It made sitting on those hard, wooden chairs a bit more bearable.

Alana looked at the clock on the little end table by her recliner. It was time for lunch and if she missed her one o'clock assigned time to eat, she would have nothing until dinner. The snacks here were horrible. Rowan used to bring her cupcakes and cookies, but Rowan was caught outside Sparta and the FBI wouldn't let her in. Not until they discovered what happened to the children, and that wasn't going to happen anytime soon. It was all so futile, like hiding an empty cookie jar after all the cookies were gone.

The cafeteria was filled. Alana helped herself to the slop they called food. Sliced mystery meat, lumpy potatoes, wilted, salad greens, and a slice of apple pie. She ate her dessert first, wondering if she would hit the jackpot and get an apple slice hidden in thick goo between the two layers of cardboard.

Old man Gander was crumbling some saltines in his bowl of tomato soup. Alana couldn't bear to watch. The man couldn't remember from one minute to another where he left his things. Once they found his dentures in the ladies bathroom in the lobby. What they were doing there, no one asked, but it did make quite a stir. It wasn't one of Alana's finer practical jokes, but it was one that caused Gander quite a bit of notoriety.

Alana's favorite prank was to sneak in the back of the building where the staff entered. In a little room off to the right, there was a rack of time cards and a clock. Alana loved to get a hold of Nurse Mingold's card, punching her out an hour or two after she arrived. One week she got paid for only ten hours. Revenge was sweet. Unfortunately, after that incident, they locked the room and only the employees could get in.

To her left, sat Myra Something-or-other. Most of these people weren't her friends so she didn't bother to remember their names. Myra was a busy body. Alana avoided any type of conversation with her when possible. She was eating a fruit salad and commenting on the evils of eating meat.

Alana was about to flick a spoonful of apple goop at Myra, when Dr. Kinkaid joined them.

"Good afternoon, all," said the doctor. "I hope you're enjoying your lunch. Please, don't let me stop you. Eat. I just stopped by to talk to Alana."

"In trouble again, Alana?" Myra smirked. "I bet it's about that fiasco in the gym this morning."

"What happened in the gym?" questioned the doctor. "Alana, did you start something again? No, forget I even asked. Don't tell me. I don't want to know."

"Doctor, could we take this conversation elsewhere?"

"No need. I was just going to set up an appointment for later this afternoon, though I don't know why I bother. You're not going to listen."

"Of course I'll listen. Whether or not I'll take your advice, well, that's a different story."

"Alana, I can only hope. So what time would be convenient for you?"

Alana rolled her eyes. "Well I don't know. I've such a busy schedule. I think I may have some time between changing the roll of toilet paper in the bathroom and dusting off the TV screen that hasn't worked in weeks."

"Always with a snappy comeback." Dr. Kinkaid stifled a smile.

"Alana's the home's court jester. I wouldn't take her seriously. I know I don't." Myra grinned.

"Like you know the difference between important matters and trivial ones. And this word of wisdom is brought to you by Myra, the columnist for the Sunny Days Newsletter. I just loved your article entitled, *I can see clearly now, or using ammonia to clean your bifocals.* I would've laughed for hours if I hadn't thought you were serious."

"There isn't a nice bone in your body, Alana Freeman. I'm leaving. I'm choosy about the company I keep."

"That's obvious, otherwise I'd be worried about you and Gander playing all those all night card games."

"That's enough, Alana. I'll see you in my office now."

Myra stuck her tongue out at Alana and snatched her tray from the table. She didn't get a foot from the table, when Alana set hers on top of Myra's.

"Since you're heading that way, I'm sure you won't mind dropping mine off. You know you're way better to the garbage cans. You socialize with trash more than I do."

Before Myra had a chance to protest, Alana was halfway across the room. The doctor held the door open and waited for Alana. "My office, pronto."

"Ruh-roh," said Alana. "I've really done it this time, eh?"

Dr. Kinkaid laughed. "You are too much. I'm so tired of unruffling feathers here. If I didn't like you so much…"

"But you do and you know why? Because I'm a rebel. Because I'm not here just passing time, waiting to die. Because I refuse to be considered disposable and mostly, because I boldly go where no one else dares."

The doctor's office, for a psychiatrist, was tastefully decorated and comfy. There was no leather couch and except for a few, framed diplomas hanging on the wall, it could have passed for a waiting room. There were serene pictures of jungles and forests and bright, cheery curtains. After the doctor made himself comfortable behind the oak desk, Alana sat on the cushioned leather chair across from him.

"What's up, Doc?" she asked.

Dr. Kinkaid was still smiling. "I like you, Alana, but you're the reason I have an ulcer. Still, you always make me laugh. You're so alive."

"Ahh, you noticed."

He shook his head. "Yes I have, but sadly, so has half of Sparta, especially the local police force. Unfortunately, they don't quite know you as well as I do. They didn't perceive your late night jaunt as a laughing matter. You stepped out of bounds on this one. I can't brush over this like it was another one of your pranks. Whatever possessed you to do that? The soldiers found you out on the corner of Mulberry and Knob Street wearing nothing but a nightgown. No socks, no shoes, and no panties."

"Pish Tosh," said Alana. "Don't believe everything you hear. I had a raincoat on."

"Alana, you're missing the point. First off, the FBI and the military have us under martial law because of the missing children and the vanished hunk of Sparta. They seem to be able to do whatever they want and nobody can stop them. We don't want to antagonize them. Nobody from outside the town seems to even know something's wrong. All that aside, you know you're not allowed to leave here unattended."

"No one stopped me."

"You sneaked out the employee's entrance. You stole a key. Now we have to install a security system on the door. That's going to cost them a lot more money they budgeted for. I don't know what I'm going to do with you. It's a darn good thing they found you. You could've been mugged."

"In Sparta? I doubt there's been two muggings in ten years. Besides, who's going to bother some daffy old lady? I didn't even have a purse to steal."

Dr. Kincaid groaned. "And what's this Myra was talking about? You might as well tell me now and save me from Mingold's endless bantering."

Alana told the doctor about the little incident in the gymnasium. She was detailed and left nothing out, including her obscene gesture.

Dr. Kinkaid shook his head. "You leave me no choice at this point. We're going to have your things moved to C wing."

"No," Alana shouted, standing up. "Please don't. Besides don't you need to get Rowan's permission?"

"Since the FBI has turned off the town's phones, I've written a letter to Mrs. Burns. She is listed as an emergency contact. It might take a few days, but I can't trust you anymore. It's for your own good."

"C wing is a prison. They medicate you there. You already tried to drug me up once. I was that way the last time I saw my daughter and granddaughter. That was one time too many. From now on, I just say no." Alana had been lucky. The doctor only had Rowan's permission for a one week trial of the medicine. After that, he had to stop it. Alana still held a grudge because Nurse Mingold had lied and told her it was a new arthritis medicine. She wouldn't fall for the same trick twice and spit the pills out for the rest of that week. "I'm not a threat to anyone. I've hurt no one."

"You are a threat to yourself. I really care about you, but you're exhibiting signs of senility."

"Cow chips. All the tests were negative. I don't have Alzheimer's or dementia. I'm in great health. The real problem is that I am alive. You said it. I still have a brain and I think. I'm not a child who should be forced to participate in activities I've no interest in. Aerobics... I have no aspirations to wear a bikini and my heart can't take all that strengthening. After years of eating fatty foods and clogging my arteries, my body finds healthy foods an absurdity. I'm alive, let me live. Let me live the way I want."

"Alana, it's not so easy. If I let you, I'll have to let others."

"And what's so wrong with that? Most of us are here because our families don't want to take us in and they feel guilty about us living alone. So they ship us off to these places to die and you guys fill up all our time with required activities. This isn't pre-school."

"You act like it is."

"If you treat me like a kid, I might as well act like one. Doctor, let me go home."

"Are you going to start talking this nonsense about this Wildsidhe world?"

"It's the truth. Have I ever lied to you?"

"No, but these delusions, well they are indicative of an active imagination."

"Is there any harm in humoring me? Take me to the site and if I don't disappear, then go ahead and lock me up. Put me in prison. But, please give me a chance to prove to you that I'm not making this up."

"Alana, if I agree to this, will you give me your word that you'll behave? Participate in the community activities without complaints or causing trouble? Get along with Nurse Mingold."

"Do I have to get along with her?"

"Yes. Those are the terms. Take it or leave it."

"Then I agree. Let's go."

Dr. Kinkaid laughed. "I can't today. How about Saturday?"

"But doc, that's five days away."

"You've waited this long, what's a few more days? I'm giving up my day off as it is."

Alana smiled. "No problem. I can be patient."

"Then it's settled. You're on good behavior as of now."

"Starting now? Today? This very minute?"

"Do you have a problem with this?"

Alana crossed her fingers and grinned. "Not at all, not at all. I promise."

CHAPTER 2

It was time for her afternoon pills. Alana hated taking medicine, but sometimes the arthritis in her hands was so painful that she welcomed the relief those little yellow pills offered. If only Nurse Mingold weren't on duty. That woman was insufferable. Even if she was first in line, she made Alana wait. It was her way of getting even with Alana for all those nasty, practical jokes that had been played on her.

Today, Alana was last in line. Every time a new patient stepped in place, she moved to the back. She was going to be last anyway, why give the woman the satisfaction of bypassing her? If she was going to be served last, why not be last? That way it was Alana's choice and she would have the satisfaction of getting the better of Nurse Mingold.

Alana was shocked when "Goldie" called her name first. Goldie was the nickname given to Nurse Mingold because of her white-platinum hair. Though it was obviously a beauty-parlor color, at least from what Alana could tell, it was well kept. There were never any black roots showing. The only thing black about Goldie was her heart.

"My, this is a surprise," said Alana holding her hand out.

"I just thought I'd be nice today since you'll be leaving us soon."

"Leaving? Where did you get that idea? I'm not going anywhere."

"Oh no?" smirked Goldie, handing the plastic cup of water to Alana, but dangling the little yellow pill just inches from her reach. "That's not what the orders on your chart say."

"What are you talking about, Goldie? What orders? Tell me, you know you're dying to."

"Well, it says right here that you are being moved to C wing on Saturday. It's signed and everything. I knew it was just a matter of time before they would you lock you up."

"Give me that chart," demanded Alana, grabbing the clip board out of Goldie's clutches.

Alana stepped back and flipped through the pages. Sure enough there was the medical order assigning Alana to the second floor of wing C. Dr. Kinkaid had already put his "X" on the requisition and dated it. The line for authorization was blank.

Alana was fuming, but she did her best to hide her anger. "I wouldn't be too smug if I were you. Rowan won't be able to sign this and if she could, she wouldn't."

Nurse Mingold laughed. "That's what you think. I happen to know that a

Mrs. Burns was contacted and is expected here later today. She'll sign it when Dr. Kinkaid gets done talking to her and if he can't manage to convince her, I will. Your days are numbered, crazy lady."

"Crazy lady?"

"Pixies, dragons, and dwarves. Some Queen Morna is your sister. Why you're as nutty as Lorna. You remember Lorna Munstan? She's in C wing too. She thinks she's the Queen of England. The two of you can rule together."

"You read my confidential files, you…you…ancient, lying, basket of barf. You defile the entire medical community with your angel of mercy act. The only reason you have a job here is 'cause you've been fired from every hospital in the city. You prey on the weak. Well, I may be old, but helpless, I'm not. You're just lucky that I can control my temper, otherwise I'd haul off and beat the daylights out of you."

"You and what army?" retorted nurse Mingold.

Alana couldn't believe they had tied her arms to the bed. She tugged at the restraints, but they were fastened too tight. What had started out as a petty disagreement between her and Nurse Mingold, had escalated to a fist fight.

Though Alana had no regrets, it was just plain stupid losing her self-control. Even if that woman did deserve it, she still shouldn't have hit her. That was all the proof they needed to lock Alana away. Still, if it just hadn't been so funny, she might have gotten away with it. For some reason doctors considered anger normal and laughter a form of insanity.

Nurse Mingold did look silly sprawled out on the floor. How could Alana have known she was wearing a wig? She snickered again just remembering the incident. Although everyone knew Goldie's hair color was fake, no one knew she wore a wig. Now they knew she was wearing one to cover up the tiny tufts of spiked, gray hair. Good, old Goldie was not only not a blonde, but she was almost totally bald.

Alana continued to giggle picturing the flying wig, balled up in a heap on the floor. It reminded her of those fuzzy, animal slippers. Even the janitor, who heard the cheering and had come running, stood off to the side snickering.

All might have died down if Alana had just bit her tongue and had let the woman leave with a shred of dignity. But no, Alana was having the most fun she had in months and her audience loved it.

The minute the word "Spikey" left her lips, Alana knew she had stepped out of bounds. Goldie muttered something, gathered her hairpiece, and left the nurses station in a huff. But, the damage had been done. It took seconds for the new nickname to replace the old. Seeking revenge, Spikey called Alana's doctor and threatened him with a lawsuit. He knew Alana was dangerous and she was going to hold him responsible if he didn't do something immediately.

"Don't worry, Mrs. Burns. She's just sedated. We had to restrain her to keep her from hurting herself."

Alana was too much in a haze to speak. The tranquilizer had made her sleepy, but she was conscious enough to hear her best friend and the doctor talking. Keep me from hurting myself? What liars. What they meant was to keep this little old lady, weighing in at a hundred and two pounds from knocking the teeth out of him. It was a good thing she had changed her Fortesan appearance before accompanying Howard here. She would really have been intimidating if she had remained six foot six, although the extra finger joints would have helped her case.

"Doctor, I do understand, but why is she laughing like that?"

"Sometimes sedative's react that way. There's nothing to worry about. Your friend, for the moment, is just fine, but we do have to discuss a serious matter.

"Alana has become a threat, not only to herself, but also to the staff. I'm afraid we're forced to move her to C wing and administer some mood-altering medication on an ongoing basis."

Carol Burns nodded. "You mean the loony bin?"

Dr. Kinkaid sighed. "It's called a mental health wing."

"I was afraid this was going to happen. All this talk about pixies and unicorns. She hasn't been the same since Howard died and it's gotten worse since half the town has disappeared."

"That's the shame in all of this. There's not a single person here who isn't upset about the circumstances surrounding the disappearance of the town and the children. My own grandchild is out there somewhere and there's nothing I can do to help her. But, most of us deal with this realistically. Alana can't cope with the loss of her granddaughter and it's manifesting in a dangerous psychosis that requires immediate attention."

Carol nodded. "I cry every day over the loss of my grandchildren Justin, Terri, and Wayne. My house... everything I owned vanished with my babies. I'm even scared to leave my son's house. Who knows what will happen next? And all those soldiers patrolling the streets with guns. The sirens are deafening. It's enough to drive anyone over the edge."

"Well," said the doctor, "That's exactly what happened to your friend. She's not handling this in a rational manner. I'm glad you understand. If you'll head over to the nurse's station, there are a few papers you'll need to sign. We'll move her to her new room tomorrow."

"Why do you need my signature?"

"We can't reach her daughter. I've tried contacting the FBI but they're not giving out names of the townspeople that are being detained. Since you're listed as an emergency contact, and considering the unusual circumstances, our lawyers got the FBI to give permission for you to stand in for the next of kin."

"Then you're absolutely sure there is no other way."

"I wouldn't have sent a messenger to your home if I didn't."

Carol sighed. "I hate doing this, but if I must...I must."

The doctor whispered a thank you and left the room shutting the door behind him. Carol looked down on the hospital bed, trying very hard to muster a smile. She stroked the silvery tendrils that had fallen in Alana's face and secured them behind her head.

"I'm so sorry," she whispered. "I'm at a loss for what to do. This is so unlike you."

Alana wanted to scream, don't do this, but all she could do was laugh. The entire situation was so helpless it was comical.

Carol picked up her purse and headed for the door. Alana, realizing this was her only chance, managed to stop chuckling long enough to shout, "Wait! Don't let them do this to me. I'm not a violent woman. You know that."

"Alana, I've know you for over fifty years. I really do want to believe you, but I'm at a loss for what to do. I wish we could get a hold of Rowan."

"I do too. We think the FBI has her, but none of us are sure. The phones still aren't working and it could be months, maybe longer before the FBI decides it's safe to let us have phones again. With the military signal blockers out there, cellular phones are useless and no radio transmissions can get outside Sparta. Just don't sign those papers. Tell them you feel it's up to Rowan to make that decision. Buy me some time."

"Time for what?"

"To get out of here. I have to get back to the Wildsidhe."

"Where? You're scaring me again. That's no way to convince me, talking utter nonsense."

"No, it isn't. Where are your grandchildren? Where did half the town disappear too? Have you an explanation? I know where they are and I can help them. Humor me. Just what if I'm right? Are your grandchildren worth the gamble? Help me... help them."

"I won't sign the papers, at least not today. Okay?"

"Thanks, Carol. Oh, and one more tiny favor?"

Carol had sucked in her top lip, a habit she had when she got nervous. Alana was going to ask for the impossible. She knew this the instant she asked in that squeaky voice.

"What are you up to ole girl? Don't go getting me in trouble like you used to. We... I'm too old now."

"Oh have some fun. You're old, not dead."

"Lord help me, what do you want?"

Alana snickered. "Nothing much. I just want you to sneak me out of here."

CHAPTER 3

Alana chuckled to herself. Carol refused to sign the papers and there was nothing the doctor or staff could do about that, but she wasn't safe at all. Spikey continued to threaten her, but Alana knew that it would take at least a week to get a court order from the town's only judge. Sometimes the political system here worked in the victim's favor. With chaos still presiding over the loss of the kids, signing a medical paper to have Alana committed wasn't a priority.

As long as she behaved and there were no more incidents, she had a reasonable chance they wouldn't do anything. The last thing she needed was to be put on mind-altering medications again. Cindy needed her.

She looked at the clock and sighed. There was nothing to do. The TV in her room was broken and though she had put in a request for it to be fixed, no one ever came in to repair it. Obviously, Nurse Mingold had seen to it that the form conveniently got lost. It wasn't a big deal. The FBI approved afternoon programming held nothing but soap operas and the evening line-up wasn't much better.

Alana sat down in her rocker and leaned back. It was dismal outside and the blinds were closed. Though she wasn't sleepy, the back and forth rhythm of the chair was making her drift off. She crossed her legs and caught sight of her reflection in the glass of her broken television screen.

She looked old. Her lovely, thick, strawberry-blonde hair was now silver; her deep turquoise eyes were faded and glazed. Spider veins laced her legs, but the heavy support stockings she wore hid them. Without the use of magic, she couldn't even deceive herself with a magical, youthful appearance. Some of the residents of Sunny Days dyed their hair, but they were fooling no more than the mirror. A dried-up raisin with blonde hair looked ridiculous.

The age old saying, "Vanity, thy name is woman," was still a priority for most of the women here. They held make-up sessions, had a beautician come in and do hair for those that made appointments, and of course there were those aerobic classes. Every Monday, Wednesday, and Friday. Alana figured it was a human thing. Everyone on Wildsidhe, or at least the Fortesans, used their magic to keep the illusion of youth and beauty. Though they weren't immortal, their lifespans were many times longer than the people here.

Power was what kept them going, at least for those on the High Council: Morna was captivated with it, Asgar was obsessed with acquiring it. Perhaps the people here were really no different. Both worlds had its own priorities.

It was just a matter of perception.

Alana couldn't help but laugh at all the old people. She didn't consider herself one of them. In her mind she was still that beautiful blonde whose hand was sought after by many suitors, even Asgar himself. She wondered what Asgar would think if he saw her now. In many ways her outward appearance was similar to all the other residents here.

Sunny Days was populated with clones, each with loose, flabby skin, double chins, droopy jowls, and bottomed-out fannies. Watching them do jumping jacks, push-ups, and tummy tucks were just a form of entertainment for her. No one here had a sense of humor.

Well, no one could take away her memories. In the recesses of her imagination, she still was that lovely young lady that escaped the Wildsidhe to be with Howard. Never once did she regret it. Her years with him were filled with joy and love. And then, there was Rowan, their daughter. She thought she knew everything about loving someone, but when she held her daughter in her arms for the first time, it was overwhelming.

Many years later Cindy was born. She saw in her granddaughter all that her own child didn't possess. There was an immediate bond between them, even at infancy. Alana knew that within Cindy was the innate ability for magic. It radiated from her eyes. Sometimes, it seemed so obvious, that Alana was surprised no one else noticed.

Well, no one but her daughter. Rowan sensed a closeness that their relationship lacked and at times Alana felt the backlash of jealousy. It took years for them to realize that Alana had enough room in her heart to love them both dearly and unconditionally.

When Cindy disappeared, it was Alana that bore the brunt of the loss. It was as if a part of her own body had been ripped away. No... there were no ifs. She was only half there. Without Cindy, she was missing pieces of herself that even her daughter couldn't replace or realize.

Out of boredom and to pass the time while she waited for Carol, Alana switched on the TV. Even though the picture was broken, she could still access the sound. All the TV's in the home were hooked up to cable and two channels carried the town's two radio stations. Because of the government's jamming devices, the only way to hear the radio was through the cable. The first was a popular music station that her granddaughter loved. Now that was noise. All that scritchin' and scratchin', booming and bopping, about nothing. She couldn't understand half of what they were singing about and when she did, she wished she hadn't. Such vulgarity, such violence. Rowan's music wasn't anything like that and she didn't really like that either. Alana refused to listen to any of it. It played on the channel that flashed things for sale, like cars or houses.

In lieu of music, she listened to the other station, which was all talk shows. It was on the channel that ran messages from the town hall. Even months after the town's disappearance, it was still a hot topic of discussion. The radio kept her company and made her feel less alone. Today they were interviewing an FBI agent. What a waste. Anything important that he might know would never be exposed to the public and the truth, the fact they knew nothing, they'd never admit to. In fact, since the FBI was controlling the shows allowed in through the cable, why wouldn't they do the same with the radio? There were mostly all new hosts and DJs on both stations, and Alana suspected the lot of them were really undercover FBI agents.

Once a few weeks ago, Alana called the station. She didn't know what possessed her to do such a thing, but at the time it seemed the right thing to do. It was just a week or two after it happened. Well, to say the least, they laughed at her.

Jimmy Joe Ray, was a radio host that swore there were alien corpses hidden away in a hanger in Wright Patterson Air Force Base, in Dayton, Ohio. He was one of the few hosts that kept his job, probably because his disappearance would only lend credibility to his government conspiracy theories. He alluded to the disappearance of the town being connected to aliens. The US government made a trade and allowed the aliens to take the town and the living specimens in exchange for… what? That he didn't know. How absurd. It angered her that Jimmy Joe had the audacity to snigger at her when she told them the city had been transported to a parallel dimension called the Wildsidhe.

When she asked him why they just took the kids, Jimmy Joe just hemmed and hawed and never really said anything that amounted to anything. Fifteen minutes of incoherent references about overseas governments and terrorists and another ten about nuclear bombs, and biological warfare. Nothing but rubbish, if you asked her opinion. But, no one asked her…

That was part of the reason she decided she would return. And if she was so crazy, why did the station go off the air for two hours right after her call?

Unfortunately, her constant comments about the Wildsidhe revoked her field trips. Her midnight excursion in her bed clothes and her little boxing match with Spikey almost had her permanently sedated. As much as she didn't want to rely on anyone else, she was forced to ask Carol for help.

Alana had it all figured out. Thursday was Spikey's day off. With her out of the way she had a much better chance of her plan working. As long as Carol did exactly as she was told to do, it would work. Two more days, well a day and half. All she had to do was be on her best behavior. Play the

Wednesday night bingo extravaganza, smile and be docile. In other words, act like the other senior citizens. She could do it. She had to do it. Cindy's life and the welfare of all the children depended on her.

"Bingo!" Alana waved her hand and stood up. Amidst the groans and protests of the losers, the recreation therapist read out the numbers.

"It's a good one," she said.

Alana walked up to the table to choose her prize. It was difficult picking a cheap trinket. There were brushes and combs, bottles of cheap perfume and after shave, even a few items of Paste-A-Dent denture cream. She wondered where they got all that junk. Alana was about to take a box of cookies when she saw a small, glass figurine of a unicorn. Surrounded by all the junk, it seemed to smile at her.

After winning, Alana wanted to leave, but she stayed another twenty minutes. She waited until they were busy checking a card and quietly slipped out of her seat. Proud of herself for behaving, she wished the attendant at the door a good night and retired to her room.

The crystal unicorn was an omen. Alana set it on her dresser, opened her closet, and pulled out a small overnight bag. She set the case on her bed and unzipped it. In the bottom of the leather satchel, still wrapped in tissue paper was her totem. Alana pulled it out and set it on her chest next to her Bingo prize.

Of anything she ever owned, either on Wildsidhe or in Sparta, this was her most coveted treasure. It was her birthright, well, hers and Morna's. Oh how mad Morna must have been when she discovered it was gone. They used to fight over it as children, neither one of them wanting to share it.

"I will marry first and then it will be mine," Morna used to say.

"Then I don't have a thing to worry about. Who in their right mind would want you for a wife?" Alana would tease back.

Their Grandmama would end up taking it away, swearing neither one would get it if they didn't stop arguing about it. They were so young then and just in training. It was only on a very special occasion when they would be allowed to command the graceful creatures that embodied the wooden totem. Holidays like their birthdays, Lumintosh, and the anniversary of their mother's death.

Alana's mother had died giving birth to Morna. Grandmama Eustacia would tell them stories about Rowena being the perfect lady, the perfect student, and of course, the perfect child. The girls grew up in their mother's shadow, never living up to Grandmama's expectations. Neither of them ever felt loved by Eustacia and it was the one thing in common that kept the two sisters together.

Rowena. She didn't have any real memories of her mother. All that she knew of her were from stories. There was a portrait of her on the great, stone wall of the castle. It was next to Grandmama Eustacia and all the other females from their bloodline. All the women were attractive, even Grandmama when she was a lady. She was different; she was the only one with amber tresses. Rowena's thick mass of wavy tendrils framed her delicate, ivory face just as the gold, gilded frame did the painting. She was a thornbud amongst the weeds.

Rowena was wearing the traditional gown of royalty. No artist could capture the opalescent glimmer of the skirt, which was made from shed pixie wings. Both Alana and Morna looked forward to their sixteenth birthday, when they would be of age to wear that gown and have their portrait added to wall. By now, she was sure Morna's picture hung on the wall. She wondered if there was an empty space where hers was to be added. Had they forgotten her?

Well, if they had, they would soon remember. Alana was going home. Perhaps they wouldn't recognize her. Eventually her magic would revitalize. When it did, she would be the Alana of old, for Alana had inherited her mother's turquoise eyes. It was an undeniable birthmark. Her daughter Rowan had the same deep, blue-green shade. Dear, sweet Rowan, whom she named after her mother; poor, innocent, Rowan who would never know her ancestry.

Alana's eyes filled with tears. She would miss her daughter, but Cindy needed her. It was going to be a bitter-sweet homecoming.

CHAPTER 4

Carol was late. Alana kept looking at her watch and strumming her fingers on the arm of the wooden chair. If she didn't get there soon, they would have to postpone the great escape for another week.

Had the phones been working, she would have called her friend, hoping she wouldn't be at home to answer. But, with the lines still down, she had no way to contact her and had to rely on her word. The most nerve-wracking thing of it all was that Carol was usually never late. Alana began to fidget, thinking of all the horrible things that could have happened to her friend in the past few days.

Seven-fifteen. At eight they locked the doors and visitors had to leave. Forty-five minutes would still be enough time, but that was if her friend got there soon. The FBI curfew for people to be off the streets started at nine.

Too antsy to sit any longer, Alana got out of her chair and shuffled to the window. Her legs ached. The arthritis always acted up on wet days.

Alana bent the slats of the blind and peered outside. It was drizzling, a light, steady mist of rain beat against the windowpane. The light reflecting off the tiny droplets made it almost impossible to see from a distance.

Perhaps, the weather situation was an advantage. Fewer people would be out on a cold, rainy night. She stared down at the building's entranceway and watched the bobbing umbrellas.

Her room was on the third floor, which afforded her a great view of the entrance. Many a day she would watch the comings and goings. Some were of course the workers and the staff, while others were family and friends coming to visit. She could tell the difference by the pace. Usually visitors were in a rush.

Tonight things were quiet except for an occasional umbrella, or a passing car. Alana sighed. It was too dark to see the make of the cars parked in the adjacent lot. Suddenly, there was a knock on the door. Alana jumped and turned, facing the door.

"Who is it?" she asked, crossing her fingers and hoping to hear the right answer.

"Just Carol. Sorry I'm late. Can I come in?"

"The door's open."

Carol shut the door behind her, leaning her taupe and burgundy, striped umbrella against the door. "It's nasty out there. The car wouldn't start. I think it's all this rain."

"I know your heart's not in this, but I really do appreciate it," said Alana.

Carol slipped the hood off her head and unbuttoned her raincoat. Folding it gingerly, she laid it over the back of the chair.

"I still don't think this is a good idea. You could get in trouble, I could get in trouble. There must be at least a hundred things that can go wrong. I can't even guarantee my car will start. Even if you do succeed in making it to the barren ground, there are FBI agents and armed soldiers you have to get past. Then, what will happen if you can't get back there? What are you going to do? Come back here? They'll lock you away for certain."

"My goodness girl, you sure do worry about everything. If I don't make it there, if I can't find Cindy and the others, I really don't care what happens to me. I'm an old lady with little to live for anymore. Howard's dead. Rowan has her own life.

"My granddaughter needs me. It's my fault she's in trouble in the first place. Whatever the danger, I'm willing to risk it all to save her.

"Now, did you bring the flashlight?"

The mid-stream topic change caught Carol off guard. "Yes," she answered. "I put fresh batteries in them this afternoon."

"Good. Thanks. I don't mean to be rude, but if I'm going to have any chance of making this plan work, I have to get a move on, so...can I have your clothes now?"

Carol just shook her head and mumbled to herself. Though the two women were of similar height, Carol was more than a few pounds heavier. She had spent hours going through her closet trying to decide what might fit Alana. Finally, she decided on a pair of drawstring sweatpants with a matching sweatshirt.

The two women exchanged clothes and Carol slipped on Alana's nightgown. It was a bit tight, but she would manage for the few hours she had to wear it.

"Your shoes. I need your shoes, Carol," Alana said pulling the rope and tightening the pants as much as she could.

"They aren't going to notice the name brand on the sneakers. Trust me, you don't want to switch my size nine for your size seven. They'd be enormous. You'd clomp out of here like a clown and give yourself away completely."

"I suppose you're right." Alana slipped on her old tennis shoes and tied them. "Well," she said turning around, "Do I look like you?"

"No, but once you put on the raincoat and cover your head with the hood, you'll pass. I coughed a few times as I passed the front desk, so just pretend you have a cold."

"Did you bring the duct tape?"

"It's all in my purse, or should I say your purse? Do you really need to bind my hands?"

"If this is going to look real, yes. I won't do it too tight, promise."

Alana had Carol lie in her bed and wrapped her wrists together with one thickness of the sticky tape. In the drawer of her nightstand was a bandana already neatly folded.

"You're going to gag me too?"

"If I don't they'll wonder why you didn't scream for help. For both our benefits, I want this to look as realistic as possible."

Carol bit down on the cotton and scrunched her nose. It tasted horrible and though Alana hadn't pulled it too tight, it still cut the corners of her lips.

Alana walked over to her dresser and grabbed the totem. She had taken it out of its locked trunk just a few hours ago. One of the nurses had asked her about it earlier in the day, remarking how realistic the unicorn looked. She had even asked Alana if she wanted to sell it. Of course, she refused. Here it was just an intricately carved figurine. On the Wildsidhe, it was power. Her ace.

Alana tucked it under her pants and pulled the sweatshirt over it before donning the raincoat. She made sure to button all the buttons and tied the belt tight to keep the totem in place.

Looking over at Carol, she said, "I'll never forget you my dear friend. You've been like a sister to me all these years. If there was a way I could take you with me, I would. Of all the people I'll miss, other than Rowan, I'll miss you most of all."

Carol nodded. Both women had tears in their eyes. "I'd turn on a TV show for you, but it's not working. Besides, all we can get now are FBI approved shows and they're pretty lame. I'll switch the radio station channel on for you, instead. It'll help pass the time until one of the nurses does a bed check. Hang in there girl. I love you."

Alana shook the umbrella before tucking it under her arm. Sighing, she kissed Carol on the forehead and turned the knob. First, she made sure the hall was empty. Satisfied that she was alone, she closed the door behind her and began her trek to the elevator.

Things were a bit quiet this time of night as most residents were in for the night. Though she wanted to run, the last thing she wanted to do was draw attention to herself. Some were still awake as she could hear the sounds of their working TV's blaring.

The elevator was just one floor away when she pressed the down button. It creaked to a stop and the sliding doors opened. Alana hesitated before entering, hoping it was empty. Once again, luck was with her and she smiled at her good fortune. She pressed the button marked "G" and the elevator groaned as it slowly made its way to the ground floor. Seconds later the doors opened again to an empty lobby.

The guard looked up and Alana immediately opened Carol's purse. She didn't want to be conspicuous; but she didn't want the guard to recognize her. As long as she was busy searching through the bag, she had a good excuse not to look up.

Fred, the guard, bade her a nice evening, and Alana coughed, then nodded. With keys in hand, she dangled them, the noise muffling the sound of her own voice as she returned his good byes with one of her own.

Through the corner of her eye she watched Fred. All he had to do now was press the button that would release the lock on the front doors. He didn't even have to get out of his seat. The buzzer was loud. The guard remained glued to the TV show he was watching. Alana pressed her hip against the metal bar and sighed when it opened easily. She had made it outside without a hitch.

It was drizzling ever so slightly. Alana opened her umbrella to use as a possible shield to keep from being recognized. Even though the chances were slim she would bump into someone she knew, she wasn't about to take any chances.

The parking lot was nearby and amazingly full. Carol drove a black car and in the darkness, it was impossible to tell the colors apart. Her heart skipped a beat when she realized she had forgotten to ask Carol where she was parked.

As quickly as she could, she began to walk down the first row. Though the rail had let up, it was still slick outside. At times she skidded. It was a good thing she was wearing sneakers.

So intent on finding the auto, she accidentally bumped into a body who was walking in the opposite direction. Alana, caught off guard, grabbled for something to hold on and fell backwards, dropping her purse and umbrella.

"Here, let me help you," said a man extending his hand.

Alana slipped hers into his and swaggered her way to her feet. "I'm sorry. It's dark and hard to see out here. I was looking for my car and wasn't watching where I was going."

"No harm done," said the man, his voice ringing a familiar chime. "What kind of car is it?"

Alana didn't know how to answer. She knew it was a black, four-door, sedan, but she didn't know the model or make. If she admitted as much to the man, he would wonder.

Alana looked down the aisle. "Oh, it's right over there," she said lying and pointing to a car far off in the corner. "Thanks anyway."

"Have we met?" asked the man. "Your voice sounds faintly familiar. I'm Dr. Kincaid."

Alana's heart was racing. She felt it pound against her ribcage and fear gripped her even more tightly than the wet, frozen, sweatpants that now clung to her thin legs.

"I don't think so," she answered coughing, and lowering her voice two octaves in an attempt to disguise her voice.

"No matter then. Sure you'll be okay?"

"Just dandy. Thanks."

Alana picked up her umbrella and scurried off in the direction she had pointed to a moment ago. She could feel the doctor's eyes boring holes into her back. With each step she prayed. Finally, in desperation, she cast the tiniest of where—spells and prayed that her magic would still work. She was in luck. Carol's car headlights blinked on and off, once, but it was all she needed. Alana was only five cars away and as fast as she could run, she headed for the car, all the time keeping her eye on the doctor as he entered the building.

Time was of the essence. She had to get out of the gate before she missed. It had been quite a few years since Alana had been behind the wheel. Her hand shook as she slipped the key into the ignition and turned it.

Nothing happened. She jiggled the gas pedal and tried again. Still nothing. Now she was not only nervous, but sick to her stomach. So close and yet so far. Carol had mentioned that she had trouble earlier. If she had only asked her what she did to get it to work.

"Come on. Start up. Please, please."

She must be going crazy talking to the car. In frustration she began to bang on the steering wheel with her fists. What was she going to do? Was her magic strong enough for another spell? She had to try.

Alana took a deep breath. Concentrate, she told herself. Relax and concentrate. Sparks flew from her fingertips, tiny little crackles that lit the interior for a second or two. The electric discharge surged through the key and the car stuttered, chugged, and then started. Luck was with her. The spark started the engine in spite of all the iron.

Alana shifted into first gear, screeched, and jerked the car. It lurched forward an inch, then one more. Finally, she got a hold of herself and pulled out of the parking space without hitting the car next to her.

Not bad, ole girl, she thought to herself. Now just go the speed limit, smile, and get the heck out of here. One hour until the government curfew. Following the exit signs, Alana made it to the guard. There was only one car ahead of her and she did her best to keep from looking scared. Her fingers were wrapped tight around the steering wheel to keep from shaking. The knuckles were white and her nails dug into the palms as she tapped the gas pedal and began to drive by the guard who had just finished talking on the intercom.

"Wait," the guard shouted.

Alana slammed on her brakes. The car skidded a bit and idled while the guard took a few steps to the car. The beam from the flashlight rocked, shedding light on the empty street just a few, safe feet from where she had stopped.

The night watchman shined his light through the window.

"Can you open it ma'am?" he asked. "I need to see your driver's license."

Alana rolled down the window and leaned to her right, fumbling in the purse for Carol's wallet. She let out a small stream of air, all the while praying her friend had left her identification in the purse.

This time she was lucky. She opened the wallet, turning it so the man could see it.

"Is everything all right, officer?" Alana asked.

"You'll have to get out of the car, ma'am." The guard stepped back and his right hand moved to his holster.

Alana stepped on the gas pedal. The car swerved and skidded as she made a right on Sunset Street. In her rear view mirror she could see the guard using the intercom. It wouldn't be long before police vehicles would surround her. Dr. Kinkaid must have discovered Carol. It was now or never.

Not caring that the road was slick, Alana pressed the gas pedal to the floor. There hadn't been time to roll up the window and the icy rain and cold wind whipped her face as the speedometer reached sixty.

The light was red, but there were no other cars in sight and Alana zipped right on through. The school used to be only a few more blocks away. It looked like she was going to make it. All she had to do was make a lefty and head straight down the road.

It wasn't that easy. The car spun out of control just as she turned the corner. Alana screamed as the rear end fishtailed and hit the parked car on the right side of the street. Before she could manage to regain control, she hit two garbage cans, flinging them into the air. Garbage flew everywhere, landing all around her and covering the windshield.

Alana was as good as blind. A newspaper got caught in the wiper blades and it swished back and forth totally blocking her view. She had to brake and brought the car to a halt, but not before knocking over a mail-box and hitting a tree.

The sounds of a siren blasting were getting closer. Alana opened the car door to see people rushing out of their houses. Along with the street lamps, every porch light was on.

"Are you okay, lady?" a man asked rushing to help out. He was wearing nothing more than pajamas and a robe.

Alana felt bad. She looked over all the damage and commotion she had caused.

"I'm fine," she said pushing him out of the way.

It took only a minute for her to notice the flashing red and blue lights. The squad car was getting close, but the garbage cans had kept it from pulling up behind her. Without thinking, she grabbed Carol's purse and took off running.

"Stop her...somebody stop her!"

Alana could hear the policeman's voice as he shouted over the screams of half the neighborhood.

"Run, lady, run!" cried one elderly man a few feet ahead of her. He was waving his fist wildly in the air, dressed in a tattered brown and red flannel robe. "I'll stop 'em. Show 'em what us old folks can do. Did you rob a bank?"

"Thanks," Alana huffed, as she galloped by the man, almost knocking him down. "I need all the help I can get."

"Right on, lady. Go."

For some reason, the neighborhood was cheering her on. Some people even blocked the policemen as they tried to catch up with her. The entire street had turned into an angry mob. The police were following FBI orders, as were the soldiers in the town. People were sick of being under martial law and this was a chance to fight back. Plus, it seemed no one liked the law chasing a little, old lady.

The barren ground, where the school had disappeared just a while ago, was in sight now. All Alana had to do was make it past the yellow, taped, police barrier and she would be home free.

She was out of breath and steam now. The only thing that kept her going was thoughts of her beloved granddaughter. Every muscle groaned in protest as she pushed her body harder. Limits were made to be broken.

The street lamp up ahead was broken in half, as was the tree that stood beside it. Long, branching limbs divided the living from the dead. Beyond and as far as she could see, there was nothing but dirt and unearthed pipes. Steam rose from the ground. The smell was acrid, as if the land had decayed. Alana, drenched from the rain, gasped and wheezed.

The branches were blocking her escape. She had to part the brittle branches, and as they snapped, they clawed at her, tearing her pants. Her legs ached as she tried to step between the limbs and it was too dark to see where she was going. The ground beneath her foot squished, the cold water splashed, as her foot made contact with the pasty ground. On top of everything else, she had just stepped into a puddle.

Before she could she take another step, a policeman's vice-like grip tugged her back onto the concrete. Alana screamed, more from being surprised than from pain. She had made it, well almost.

"And where do you think you're going, Grandma?" asked the officer as he slapped cuffs over Alana's wrists.

CHAPTER 5

The crowds continued to mull around. This was better than any cop show on TV. The policeman holding Alana in custody started shouting at them, all the while ducking from Alana's attempts to break free.

"The show's over, folks," yelled the cop. He motioned for the people to disperse and began to weave through the throng of bathrobes and slippers. "Everything's under control. Just head on home."

It was like talking to a bunch of zombies. Nobody moved; nobody even pretended to hear the officer. Alana felt like she was an exhibit at the zoo with everyone staring.

"Please, let me go. You don't understand. I have to help my granddaughter. She's in grave danger."

"It's going to be okay, Grandma. Dr. Kinkaid called us on the radio and we really do understand."

"I'm not your grandmother, and no you don't. I don't need some punk kid just out of diapers telling me it's all right when it isn't.

"Just look around you. Half the town's gone. I don't know what the good doc told you, but I've got all my faculties and they're working fine. Just because I've got a few gray hairs don't mean I've lost my ability to know when things aren't the way they're supposed to be."

The policeman tightened his grip as Alana continued struggling to break free. "No one's questioning anything, ma'am. We're only doing our job." The ma'am was emphasized.

"Police brutality," shouted a man in a blue, tattered robe. He raised his fists. "Let the lady go. If she wants to go tramping through the muck, it's her business."

A few other people shouted in agreement. The officer that was holding onto Alana whispered to his friend. "It figures we had to stop her in the middle of this grey rights convention. Now we're gonna be accused of mistreating the elderly. I should have called in sick."

"You are pathetic," said Alana. "There are real criminals roaming the streets and you're out arresting a little, old lady for trespassing."

Alana tried kicking the man in his shins, but the policeman held her at arm's length. Then an idea struck her, but she really hated to do it. Still, they were giving her no choice.

It was the different sounding siren of the military vehicle approaching that gave Alana her chance. Most of the people that were huddled about protesting turned and began walking back to their homes. Whoever was holding her stopped when he saw the flashing red and blue lights.

This was her chance. Her last chance. If they took her back to Sunny Days they would certainly get a court order. Drugged, she would be helpless. Carol, most likely, wouldn't even be allowed to visit her.

All she had to do was make it to the other side. Unlike all the rest of the adults, she could cross over. She belonged there. It was home. With the soldier re-enforcement's just a few feet away, the officer quit trying to move her forward. In fact, she could tell the difference in his grip as well.

With split second timing, Alana bit the policeman's hand. Hard. Her teeth sank into his flesh and drew blood. Instantly, he let go, screaming in pain and cursing Alana. The few stragglers who had remained to watch seized the opportunity and ran to block the policemen who were running to catch the escaping woman.

It was only a few feet to the barrier. Alana knew it would take too much time to step over the branches. Even though the neighborhood had stepped in to help her, they were no match for the four soldiers that were there to apprehend her.

Alana dived over the obstacle, tearing the tape and landed on her stomach. Pain shot through every fiber of her body as mud splattered everywhere. Her head felt liked it weighed a hundred pounds and she was unable to lift it. Both her arms were pinned beneath her and she was unable to move them. She could barely muster the strength to breathe. Too weak to move, too dizzy to see, she passed out.

CHAPTER 6

"Well, look here. Who do we see, Shalimar? It couldn't possibly be my long lost sister, Alana, no could it? She looks so… pitiful, I almost didn't recognize her. Too human for my tastes."

Alana awakened to the sound of the darkcat's growl. The huge black cat that was King Penrod's totem, bared its teeth. In spite of the threat, she pulled herself up to a kneeling position and looked straight into the face of the woman that towered over her.

"It's wonderful to see you, Morna. You haven't changed a bit, I see. Still sweet-tongued and hospitable, but I must admit, I'm glad to see you. It's good to be back. Would you mind helping me out? These handcuffs are burning my wrists and my magic isn't what it used to be."

Unable to work magic directly on the steel, Morna enchanted a stick into a key. With a wave of her wrists, the key levitated into the keyhole, the cuffs opened and dropped to the ground, out of harm's way. "You're a mess. I guess I'd better play the part of a good hostess and offer you a warm bath. Grab a hold of Shalimar's ruff and follow me."

Alana stood up, thanking Morna profusely. The pain had disappeared and though she had physically aged those fifty years with Howard, she no longer felt it. The power of magic flowed through her again. She could feel it returning, surging through her bloodstream and healing her ailments and broken bones.

The castle was up ahead. It looked no different than it did so long ago when she abandoned her life here. Over fifty years had passed. Morna hadn't aged at all. It was one of the things she had given up when she left this land. Eternal youth for the powerful. Magic had its benefits.

They walked silently back to the castle. Alana wondered about the huge cat and tried to remember to whom the cat totem originally belonged. She had stolen the unicorn totem and had left her sister with nothing. Obviously something had occurred as she commanded the beast with ease.

The sun felt good on her back and had dried the mud that caked her body. Perhaps there was a good reason she had found herself in the same spot she had vanished from years ago. She just wished she had given the cross over more thought and had been better prepared.

In some ways there were some advantages ending up at home. Morna would eventually catch her up to date and she might even know where Cindy was. One thing she had never forgotten was that knowledge is power, and power was the only thing a Fortesan respected.

Morna paced back and forth in the great room. The sound of her heels clicking on the stone floor echoed off the walls and grew louder with each passing minute.

"Must you make so much noise, dearest? Can't you see that I'm busy?"

"Penrod, you infuriate me sometimes. Put down that brock and help me out. Everything is falling apart and you sit here as if nothing has happened."

Penrod slammed the oddly shaped, granite brock on the floor and watched as it bounced around in a circular pattern around Morna. It picked up speed each time it hit stone and kept Morna stationary. Every time she tried to move, either backward or forward, the brock nipped at her.

"There," Penrod said. "That's better. No more clickety-clacks. A man can't think with all that racket."

Morna held her tongue. Though Penrod was little more than an overgrown boy, at times he exerted his power and it was best to humor him. He was the king, after all.

"I'm sorry for being so annoying. I realize now that something is bothering you, also. Please call off this pet toy of yours and let's talk. Tell Morna what's troubling you."

Penrod blinked twice and the brock bounced back to him and landed in his hand. He got off the floor, straightened his pantaloons, and stood up.

"This silly Asgar and Cindy wedding has you in a turmoil. It's all you talk about. One would think you're jealous."

"Jealous? Me?" shouted Morna. "Of Cindy? You are almost as stupid as you are simple. Why should I care about who Asgar marries, or if even if he does. What concerns me is the repercussions it will cause."

"You worry too much. Are you afraid he will challenge your authority to rule?"

"If only that were the case. He will take over. That is the only reason he wanted to marry me in the first place. He didn't love me. He is incapable of loving anyone, except for himself."

"You've gone over the deep end. I am the King. No one would dare challenge the crown. I'm only a couple hundred years old. Morna, Asgar can't hurt either of us."

"Go back to playing with your toys. You know nothing of politics. Alana is back. If she sides with Asgar we're doomed."

"Now why would she do that? She doesn't like him anymore than either of us do."

"Because after talking to my prodigal sister, I know why Asgar wants to marry the Earth girl. She is of the royal bloodline. Asgar is going to be Alana's grandson-in-law. Don't you hear a word I say?"

"It won't happen. Now let's be on our way. I've given my word to perform the rites and if I don't fulfill it, then there truly would be cause to question my ruling abilities. We are already late."

"Not late enough," retorted Morna.

"Woman, I grow weary of your sharp tongue. Be still. When I say it's time to go, then it's time to go."

"Let me fetch my things," grumbled Morna, turning and leaving the room.

The whole argument was another lesson in futility. She married Penrod because she usually was able to wrangle the upper hand. The same personality qualities that made him easy to control, were also the ones that made him a simpleton. It was so infuriating.

Morna slowly made her way up the steps. As she reached the top floor and turned the corner, Alana was waiting for her.

"You clean up nice," she said, "for a used up, dried up, ole prune. And a human-looking one at that. Your short hands look so hideous."

"Let's dispense with the compliments, sister," said Alana. "Tell me about Cindy's wedding. I can see I've arrived not a minute too soon."

"You've been spying on me. That's not very nice, you know."

"Since when have we ever been "nice" to each other? I want to know about Cindy and Asgar. NOW."

"Alana, Alana, Alana. Time certainly hasn't changed your disposition. Follow me into the bedchamber and I will fill you in while I gather up my things."

Alana shook her head and sighed. "At least I've arrived in time to stop this nonsense."

"Stop the ceremony? Hmmmm…."

Morna stopped to glance at herself in the mirror, fluffing the skirt of her long full gown. Though she normally dressed in black, today she was wearing a gown made of shed pixie wings. It was almost translucent, so sheer and delicate was the weaving of the fabric. In one light it reflected pink, in the other blue. The more she moved, the more it glistened. It was if the dress had captured a rainbow. And, thought Alana, *it was mine first.*

Alana had to admit that it looked a lot better on Morna than it would have had she worn it. Age had taken its toll, and on her it would drag on the floor. She was about eight inches shorter than she used to be. Morna was beauty and I'm the beast, she thought. But beauty is as beauty does, and in that case, Morna was still a witch.

"It is lovely, isn't it?" Morna said. "I'd let you borrow it sometime, but I think it would be a waste. You look more like a potato sack sort of person."

"Still as sweet as ever. Yes it's lovely, Morna. Stunning. Now tell me about Cindy."

"You heard. Penrod is performing the rites. We're on our way now."

"And Cindy is going along with this? She wants to?"

"I didn't say that." Morna picked up a golden brush and continued to admire herself in the mirror while she raked the bristles through her black tresses.

"He's cast a spell on her. Evals powder, probably. I knew it. My granddaughter isn't so shallow that she would fall for that inept, braggart."

"He is full of himself. When he couldn't marry me, he settled for her."

"I'm sure that was the case. He was so heartbroken over your loss, that he is marrying your grandniece for revenge. I don't think so. He wants to wear the crown. Your crown."

"The crown that rightfully belongs to our family. You passed your opportunity to rule by foolishly running away with that human, Herman."

"Howard," said Alana.

"Whatever. Now it's mine and it's going to stay that way. It would even behoove you to side with me this time. Would you like to help me spoil this little plot of his?"

"You bet your last spellstone I do, but not because I give a hoot about your queenliness. I love Cindy and I want her to be happy."

"Then go get dressed. Hurry. You can accompany us to the wedding in our carriage."

Alana didn't spare a second. She ran out of the room and into her old bed chambers. All of her things were still there. When she had first arrived back, before taking a bath, she had spent the good part of an hour touching and looking at all the things that were once part of her past.

The sad thing was, that even though all her old dresses were still there, none of them looked suitable for a woman that had aged. These had all been made for a maiden of sixteen. She couldn't make her entrance back into Fortesan society wearing any of those youthful gowns. Besides, she was a lot thinner and taller way back then.

Morna arrived at the doorway of Alana's room carrying a black wad of material. "Too bad you can't wear any of your beautiful dresses. Try this on," she said tossing the bundle at Alana. "It was Grandmama's."

Alana felt the teeth of sarcasm. The offer of the dress was as much an insult as the biting words of Morna's comments, but she didn't have the time for a rebuttal. Penrod would most likely lose patience and not be willing to wait for her, so she hurried.

Alana looked at herself in the mirror. The black, velvet frock was snug, but not as tight as her old dresses would have been. Its high neck choked her and she had to leave the top button open. It had been a short skirt, but it was long on her. Her ankles hung out and all she had to cover her feet were the white sneakers she was wearing when she arrived. She had to laugh at herself.

"You do look silly and I truly mean this, I'm sorry. I wish I had something better to offer."

Alana looked at Morna trying to stifle a giggle. Even throughout their adolescent years they had their moments of friendship and comradeship. At one time they were the best of friends, each united in making their Grandmama Eustacia's life miserable. How ironic that today, Alana was stuck wearing one of her old dresses.

"Did you keep her bonnet?" asked Alana. "The one with the dragon scaled brim and the Kaleidoscope bird feathers?"

Morna broke out in a full laugh. "Yes, I did. Why? Don't tell me you want to wear it."

"Go get it," Alana demanded.

Morna returned a second later with the monstrosity. It was as ugly as both women remembered.

"Oh, it's ever more awful than I recollect," said Alana posing in the mirror. "The feathers have wilted. I look like a half-eaten bird."

The plumes of the freshly plucked Kaleidoscopy bird normally stood straight and were about two feet long. After years of being in storage, most of the stalks were bent and the multi-colored feathers that once were bright and radiant had now faded. They drooped everywhere and hung in Alana's face, almost shielding it.

"No, you couldn't possibly consider wearing it. Not even you, Alana, would take a joke that far."

"It's perfect for this occasion. It was your suggestion I wear this dress anyway. You have the crown to wear. I have to wear something on my head. Besides, it goes so well with these high-fashioned slippers." Alana wiggled her left foot in the air, proudly displaying the mud-caked sneakers. "Now, shall we get going? Don't want to hold up this joyous occasion a minute longer, do we?"

The two sisters laughed all the way down the circular, stone steps. Penrod burst into hysterics after catching a glimpse of Alana. He was laughing way to hard to comment on her accompanying them.

"It's good to see you again, Alana. Welcome back," Penrod said through the chuckles. "Let me help you into the carriage. I certainly don't want you to mess up your finery."

Morna smiled at Penrod. At times she admired her husband for he had a wonderful sense of humor and was always gracious and well mannered.

Alana shuffled over to make room for Morna. Penrod was assisting Morna when all of a sudden the carriage began to rumble and shake. She reached for Morna's hand but it was too late. Morna tumbled backwards.

Before Alana could get out of the coach, she had to clamp her hands over her ears to drown out the loud, piercing squawks coming from above. When things quieted down, she managed to step out, just in time to see the carriage, with Morna and Penrod, lifted into the sky by the lionhawk.

"My king and queen, you should arrive at my wedding in style. Allow me to provide transportation," said Asgar. With a gesture, he mystically unharnessed the horses from the carriage.

"Asgar," Alana screamed, running toward them. "Take me too."

Asgar grinned. "Sorry. No room, no time. But don't worry. I'll bring Cindy by later, after the ceremony."

The big bird took off. Alana fell to her knees and covered her eyes as the gusts of wind stirred up the sandy soil made it difficult to see. When it was safe to look again, the lionhawk was only a spec in the sky.

Alana began to cry. "What am I going to do now?" she sobbed. "Oh, what am I going to do?"

CHAPTER 7

Alana was frustrated to say the least. She kicked the wooden wheel of another carriage, but only succeeded in hurting her foot. How could everything get so messed up? The timing was off. Had she returned a day or so earlier, she may have been able to stop this facade of a marriage.

She watched as the lionhawk disappeared from view. It would arrive at Asgar's castle in minutes, where it would take her hours on horse or carriage. Her magic was weak after being unused for so many years. Still, she could try to contact Cindy, but even if she did, would Cindy know how to answer? Heck, would Cindy recognize her voice or even realize that she was here?

She needed a spellstone. That would intensify the magic and help her until she regained full strength of her magic. Gathering up the skirt of the gown in a massive bunch of material, Alana ran back into Morna's castle. Her castle, she thought to herself. It was just as much my home as it is hers. Did leaving it so many years ago justify her being homeless? It didn't matter. She didn't want to live with Morna and that blundering fool Penrod, anyway.

Up the stairs she hobbled, trying valiantly to manage the bulky gown and still navigate. One of the servants tried to stop her, but she waved him off with her free hand and giggled when he flew against the stone wall and collapsed. Some of her magic still worked. In that, she was lucky.

Morna had taken up residence in her mother's old bedroom, or so she thought, but when she opened the door, she was surprised to see only Penrod's belongings. Shelves upon shelves were filled with toys and models. There was no sign of spellstones or any of the priceless treasures that were once her family's.

She ventured out into the hall, opening door after door, until finally she found something that intrigued her. Though the room seemed bare of any signs of life, it smelled, no wreaked, of magic.

This had to be it. Alana stepped into the room and turned around. The air was thick. It smelled like smoke from a burning, sweet tree. Unmistakably, a lot of magic was dispersed in this room. She began to rummage through the chests, but found nothing.

Morna was a great sorceress. They had been equals, but the years she spent with Howard had made her rusty. That gave her sister a great advantage. It was going to take Alana time to recuperate, and time was what she had little of.

Alana began to examine the room closely and nearly tripped over something. She fell forward, landing on the bed. Hoisting herself back to a standing position, she noticed a flickering in the corner of the room. The wall and the floor didn't meet.

An illusionary spell and false wall. Neatly done. Unless someone was staring at the corner they would never notice it. Now, she knew were the spellstones were kept, but how was she going to break the barrier? And this dress. It was driving her crazy.

Alana zapped herself into a pair of blue jeans and a sweatshirt. She chuckled to herself at how strange she would look to the Fortesans in this get up, but they were comfortable clothes. Much easier to get around in than a long dress. It was foolish of her to think she needed a gown. She had no desire to become an active part in the royal household

Alana crawled on the floor, feeling her way for an opening. All she needed was a tiny one, but larger than the one in the corner. After going over every inch of the illusory wall, she could find no other holes. The one in the corner would have to do.

Very carefully she slipped her right index finger in the space. She could feel the vibrations as she softly spoke an incantation. Her finger moved a bit and the crack grew a bit larger. This was going to work.

The combination of movement and magic began to tear a hole in the barrier. When it was large enough for Alana to fit into, she stepped inside.

It was like walking into another world, a very dark one at that. Horrible creatures were stuffed in jars. There must be hundreds of them, Alana thought. Spiders were everywhere, big yellow ones with nasty fur and sharp fangs. Mutations. There was a nest of them on one of the shelves and they were buzzing about making a clicking noise. It gave her the shivers. Disgusting and evil, but efficient guards. Morna had been dabbling in the dark arts. Had she the time, Alana would have destroyed it all, and taken her chances at incurring the wrath of her sister. It angered her that evil lurked in her house, the house her ancestors had built on a foundation of love and honor. Morna was a disgrace. But Cindy was in danger. She would have to deal with her sister later.

Now where could she be keeping the spellstones? Somewhere it would be safe and out of sight. The spiders. No one would dare get near them.

Alana grabbed a staff that was leaning on the opposite wall and used it to move the nest aside. Behind it was a cavity and the light that shone from it illuminated the whole room.

"Bingo!" Alana said and then covered her mouth. She looked around the room to make sure no one had heard her. If anyone had, no one came in, so she slipped the staff inside and jiggled it.

The clear ringing of crystal echoed in the chamber. It was the hum of spellstones echoing off each other. Maneuvering the staff, she was able to drag out a few stones. They sparkled even in the dark. Alana knocked them to the floor and bent down to pick them up.

A spellstone was more valuable than gold or diamonds to a magic user. Not only did they intensify the spell, but also the power rush that surged through their bodies was pleasant. It increased in equal measures to one's ability to use magic. The more powerful you were, the better you felt. Alana was ecstatic.

Not wasting a precious minute, Alana began to call for Cindy. She closed her eyes and concentrated, stirring the air with her fingers to make room for her message.

It's me, Cindy. It's Grandma. I'm here.

Her lips moved, the words scattered. Alana used her hands to compact them in the current and then, taking a deep breath, she blew hard. Eyes still closed, she envisioned the way to Asgar's. In the vast chambers of her mind, she could see the castle and the people milling about. Cindy was not there. She looked toward the castle and her thoughts opened the door.

Cindy. She was sitting on a bench. It didn't matter that she was with an elf or dwarf, for the spell was meant for her granddaughter. She directed the message and waited to see if she received it. When Cindy jumped up astonished, she knew she had been successful.

Alana began to speak again, but this time it was impossible to arrange the thoughts. She looked at the spellstones in her hand and they were dull. All used up.

As fast as she could, she began to fumble with the staff. So intent on getting a few more out, that she didn't notice the spider on the floor. Before Alana could scrape a few more out, the sharp fangs of the eight-legged monstrosity pierced the skin on her ankle.

The room began to spin. Alana's eyes bulged and froth foamed at her mouth. She tried to grab for the table to catch her balance, but she missed it and collapsed on the floor.

Alana awoke on the floor. Her head ached from hitting the stones hard and her hand...the pain was excruciating. She couldn't use it to balance herself as she struggled to get up. It took a few minutes to gain full consciousness and when her mind cleared she hurried to her feet.

The spider's bite wasn't visible in the swollen tissues that used to be her hand. It was all black and blue and tender. She could almost feel the poison move through her bloodstream. If she didn't do something quick, she would not only lose use of her hand but her whole arm as well.

On the table underneath the hive was a knife. Alana picked up the staff to move the blade to the other end and well out of the way of the spiders that were scurrying everywhere. Using her left hand, she cut a slit near the toe knuckles where it hurt the worst. A whitish, thick goo gushed out. It was one of the most difficult things she ever had to do, but she kept from screaming.

The foul odor coming from the wound was disgusting, but she had to draw blood to cleanse the sight from the poison. Though her right hand was shaking, she managed to squeeze the pus out. When finally it bled, she relaxed and sat on the edge of bed. She was dizzy.

What loathsome little creatures they were. It was so typical of her sister to choose spiders. A few were on the floor and Alana stomped on them. Then, tearing off a strip of the bedsheet, she bandaged the wound. She would have to be more careful, but she still needed to retrieve more stones.

This time, Alana made sure there were no spiders within harm's reach before sticking the staff back into the hole. It took three tries, but she managed to get a handful of the crystals. Two of them were large. They would have to do. Time was running out and she had no idea how long she had been unconscious.

She looked at the mess she had made and decided not to clean it up. Morna would know that someone had been in here even if she was able to put everything back in its place. Her sister was no dummy, she would know it was Alana as well. Oh well, she thought. It was just one more thing that would make Morna angry, no more than another drop in the ocean.

Alana closed the door behind her. With luck, she could be out of here and on her way before the couple returned. She wondered if Cindy had married Asgar and the thought made her physically sick. There was no annulment or divorce on Wildsidhe. Marriage was forever or until death' and killing a Fortesan was a crime against the country and punishable by death.

Before going outside, Alana went back to her old room and rummaged through her things, choosing only the bare necessities to take with her. She would need little, but she did need something to carry the spellstones in and grabbed a small, leather pouch. There was also the cameo brooch her mother had bequeathed to her and she took that too. Had there been time, she would have grabbed a few other tokens of her past, but there wasn't. Time was running out.

It was still light out when Alana ventured outside. Walking was out of the question. Spells of teleportation were difficult enough to perform as an accomplished mage and she was fifty years out of practice. Alana couldn't risk ending up in the middle of the ocean. So, that was out too.

There was another carriage parked by the drawbridge, but it was without horses. She could borrow it, harness the horses, and ride in comfort, but it would be so slow. Her only other choice was ride bareback. She hadn't done that in years. Fifty-two years to be exact. A long time to be out of touch with one so special as Champagne. Beautiful, majestic Champagne.

Alana pulled out the totem from her sweatshirt. Since arriving in Wildsidhe, it had never left her body. She had to stuff it in the pocket of her dress earlier, pinning it closed. Now it was safely tucked away under her shirt and held tight by the waistband of her pants.

Very carefully she set the wood carving on the grass, beneath the limbs of the old tree. Though the sun was setting and the evening breeze was refreshing, the shade would protect her dear friend's eyes. It had been fifty-two years since Champ had seen the light of day.

The spell was imbedded in her memory. It was as much a part of her as her arms and legs. This was her birthright. Well, it was Morna's too, but who's counting? Morna must not have missed it too much. Not once did she mention it to Alana.

With a spellstone clutched tightly in the palm of her hand, Alana whispered the words that would bring wood to life. She closed her eyes tightly, praying, hoping, commanding that Champ appear. When she opened them, Champagne was there.

The sound of his whiney was music to her ears. She took the few steps necessary to reach him and threw her arms around the neck of the magical beast.

CHAPTER 8

Champ whinnied. Alana looked at the majestic creature and stroked his neck. The unicorn nuzzled her hand softly at first.

"You haven't changed a bit, dear fellow. Still looking for some peppermint? Let me see... Have you been a good boy?"

Champ stomped on the ground twice and shook his head yes as if he understood. The golden, knotted horn bobbed up and down and glistened as it caught the fading rays of the setting sun.

Two nuggets appeared in the palm of Alana's hand and Champ nibbled at them gently. Alana continued stroking the unicorn, pressing her body close to feel his warmth.

"Ready for some exercise?" she asked "I have need of your swift gate and keen sense of direction."

Again Champ whinnied, this time lowering his head and curling his foreleg. Alana tried valiantly to throw her right leg over the unicorn's back but ended up falling on her bottom. She was way out of shape. Perhaps those aerobic classes would have done some good.

Grunting and groaning, Alana grasped the unicorn around the neck, her fingers entwined in the coarse, silvery-white mane. Twice she tried to hoist her leg up, the second time it rose no further than a foot off the ground. Champ snorted.

"Okay, so I'm not as nimble as I used to be. Have some patience. You're not as young as you look either.

Alana trying jumping this time. Both hands still grasped the mane and on the third hop, she gave it her all and ended up teetering on the unicorn's back before sliding down face first in the soft grass.

Champ nickered and shook his head as if to say no. His nostrils flared and his lips curled as if to smile.

"Well, are you going to do nothing? At least lay down. I'm in a hurry and every minute counts. My granddaughter's life depends on it."

Champ nudged her; his ears perked.

"A lot has happened since I called on you last, fellow. I'll fill you in later. Well over fifty years have passed even though to you it was just yesterday. But even though I'm not that young girl that you remember so well, I'm still the Alana that adores you. Please help an old lady."

Champ lowered himself to the ground, curling his forelegs beneath him. Alana didn't have to struggle to mount him and as soon as she was situated comfortably on his back, the unicorn rose to a standing position.

Alana leaned forward. "Take it slow at first. I need more magic before I can undo what time has done to these old bones, before we can ride with the wind. Follow the scent of human, like Howard. You remember him, don't you?"

The unicorn nodded and his mane swirled in the movement as he shook his head.

"Head south. When you pick up the scent, follow it. Now, hurry."

Alana patted Champ's neck softly and the unicorn took off. The sound of his hoofs galloping on the dried ground was music to Alana's ears. It didn't take long for her to get her back into her riding mode. Champs kept his rhythm even; his head steady. Alana pressed her knees softly into his side and soon she was sitting upright with the wind rippling through her hair and tingling at her cheeks. It felt good. She was truly home now and soon things would be even better than they were.

She had no aspirations to rule. Never did really. She was the one happy to just enjoy all that life had to offer. But things change. What she didn't want for herself, she wanted to be able to offer to her granddaughter. Perhaps Cindy would be the ruler Wildsidhe needed.

It was getting dark and the evening breeze had turned to chilling gusts. They whipped her exposed skin and her eyes burned and teared. Champ was racing down the dirt road. Alana had to once again lean forward. No matter how cold she felt, she had to hurry.

Alana refused to believe that all was lost. It wasn't supposed to be this way. Asgar would never be the type of husband Cindy deserved. He loved no one but himself. She has seen that when he courted her. That was why she turned his proposal down. What had seemed like the right thing to do then may have backfired on her.

There were only a few options left to her if the marriage had taken place. Accept it and keep Cindy from falling prey to Asgar's evil intentions or...

No one, not one single sane Fortesan in her life span or her ancestors had ever killed one of their own. The consequence laid out in the Treaty of Shadows was too severe. To trespass on that rule was to invite doom. Did she have the courage to take Asgar's life and condemn her own to the Shadows? Time would tell. Rules are like crackers she always said to the good doctor, made to be broken.

Alana had heard from Morna how Asgar had lost face by trying to stop the sacrifice to the Shadows. If she could stop this wedding, he'd lose even more face and maybe some political power.

For the first time in days, Cindy felt safe. She was grateful for Morna's supporting spell that allowed her to escape from Asgar's castle and her wedding, but it was Terri who she owed the real debt of gratitude to. It was her dear friend that kept Asgar from kidnapping her back. Terri was a true heroine.

Cindy smiled and allowed Terri her moment in the limelight. Terri was beaming from all the attention. She had saved the day and everyone, including her brother Wayne, was proud of her. Ben, also, was happily describing his great invention, the iron duster, that had run off Asgar. They were both heroes and rightfully so.

Asgar had left in a hurry, lionhawk and all. The sound of his screaming in defeat and pain was music to their ears. Magic versus ingenuity. If nothing else, it proved to them they had a chance. They weren't totally helpless.

Winklo the dwarf sat off in the corner where Nash, her elf boyfriend, was still sleeping soundly. He had missed most of the excitement. She leaned back against the wall, her tired eyes closing even though she tried to keep alert. They had helped Cindy escape. Unfortunately, elves were vulnerable to iron. Nash had gotten blisters from sitting near all the steel in the escape car.

"Are you okay?" asked Cindy.

"I'm just tired. It's been a rough couple of days and worrying about Nash doesn't help."

Cindy smiled and handed Winklo a tube. "Try this. It's an antibiotic cream."

"A what?"

"It's something we use on blisters. Helps it heal and keeps the wounds from getting infected. I can't promise you it will work, but it sure can't hurt. Just put some on your fingers and rub it gently on his face."

Winklo nodded and began squeezing the tube. "Nothing comes out."

"You have to take the cap off first. That little black thing at the top."

Winklo tried to pull on the cap. When it wouldn't budge, she put it between her teeth and started to tug on it. Cindy didn't even have a second to stop her. All of a sudden the cap broke off and the cream burst out covering Winklo's lips and chin.

"Blachhh," said Winklo, "This stuff tastes horrible."

A few of the kids who were watching began to laugh. Some of them even made some rude comments, calling Winklo stupid. Cindy could see the tears welling in her new friend's eyes. She was about to say something when Winklo waved her hand.

"You seem just as strange to me as Nash and I seem to you. Our customs are different, not better or worse. Here on Wildsidhe we use herbs and other sorts of vegetation to heal and cure, not metal-like tubes of exploding goo, but I trusted Cindy to do no harm. She has proven to be a good friend.

"You can laugh at me for my ignorance. It's something I wouldn't do, but I obviously have something you don't have, manners. We can leave if you want. Cindy offered your hospitality without checking with all of you. I know she meant well."

The laughter stopped. Most of the kids nodded while some looked down at their feet.

"I think I can speak for all of us when I say we're sorry. You are welcome here, to stay as long as you like and make a home with us. Any friend of Cindy's is a friend of ours," Wayne said.

The other kids chipped in with yes's and apologies. Brina even offered to show Winklo how to apply the salve. Cindy smiled at Wayne, silently thanking him for handling the situation in such a diplomatic way.

"It's getting late, guys, or should I say early. We've still a lot to do later today. The multi-purpose room is a disaster and needs to be cleaned. Let's all try to get some sleep," Wayne said walking over to the oil lamp.

When all had settled in, he extinguished all but one and headed to his blanket. The floor was hard but his mattress, as well as the others, was covered with glass. Cindy leaned against the wall not too far from Winklo and Nash. Justin laid down beside her, laying his head on her lap.

"You okay?" he whispered.

"Just a bit worried."

"About Asgar?"

"Yes. He will be back. I know it's not love that he feels for me. He's obsessed with power and somehow I'm just the means to procure it. This spell he has over me... I don't know what to do about it. In a sense, I'm useless, and in another, I'm a hindrance. It might be better for all of you if I just go ahead and marry him."

"Don't say that." Justin sat up. "You don't mean that do you?"

"Yes I do. What is the welfare of one person when it endangers all that you love? Don't think for a minute that I care two hoots for him. I hate him, but if means you'll be safe from him, we should consider it."

"No. Don't even bring that up. You're one of us. If things were reversed, would you feel that way? What if it were Terri he wanted?"

"You know what I mean, it's just that, well, I feel awful. I'm to blame for all of this."

Justin kissed Cindy on the cheek. "You beautiful, little troublemaker. Ya just can't help it if everybody falls in love with you."

Cindy pushed him away. "Oh you. Always turning everything into a joke."

"You gotta learn to laugh at things, Cindy. Life's too short to take it all so seriously. We got out of this mess and we'll get out of others. Now, why don't you get some sleep? Things always look better in the light of day."

"I guess you're right. There's no sense in worrying. I can't do anything about it right now."

"Exactly. Tomorrow we'll clean up and fortify the roof, bar the second floor windows, and take whatever precautions are necessary to turn our home into a safe place."

"Thanks, Justin. I feel better already."

Justin didn't answer. Cindy turned her head to find him sleeping. Many of the kids had simply fallen asleep where they were, not bothering to head back to the new sleeping area in the gym. She smiled to herself and nestled close to his body. When she was near him, she felt safe. He had come to her rescue. He was willing to fight the powerful Asgar for her. Justin didn't have to tell her that he loved her. His actions were proof.

Cindy was about to doze off when she heard the voice. It jolted her and she sat up abruptly. The room was silent except for the sounds of snoring and teeth grinding, noises that had become more pleasant than annoying for it meant she wasn't alone. Though it was dimly lit, she could tell that the voice didn't belong to anyone in this room.

Cindy, I'm coming.

She heard the words again. This time it echoed in her mind. It was more of a thought than an actual voice and very, very familiar. Cindy shivered. Asgar was after her and now this person was coming for her too. A woman. Morna?

Hang on, dumpling. Watch for me.

Cindy's heart began to race. The warm rush that encompassed her made her cry out loud, not thinking that she couldn't be heard.

"Grandma? Is that you?"

CHAPTER 9

Cindy jostled Justin, "Wake up, wake up. Grandma's coming."

"Whaaa?" Justin stirred and then threw the blanket over his head.

"Justin, I heard her. She's here. On Wildsidhe. Do you know what that means?"

"Are you sure? I didn't hear anything."

"Of course I am. I know the sound of her voice. She's speaking to me. In my head, but I know it's her."

"You sure it's not Morna?"

"Gut feeling. She'll know what to do. We're saved."

"Alana? She's here?"

"Not here, as in the building, but here on Wildsidhe. I hear her in my head, but I don't know how to respond. Do you think Nash will know?"

"He might. Let me ask him."

Justin started to shake Nash. He grumbled and groaned, swatting at his hand. "Let me sleep."

"Please wake up. We need you now. Cindy's hearing voices."

Nash bolted to a sitting position. "Voices eh? Any clue to who is talking to you?"

"It's my Grandma, Alana. She's coming. I want to tell her I'm okay."

"First things first," said Nash. "We have to be reasonably sure it's her. You say your grandmother left Wildsidhe a long time ago."

"Yes, but it is her, I just know it."

"Cindy, you're not in Penns wherever. Things aren't always what they seem to be here. Let me go outside and listen. My little green friends will fill me in."

"Your what? Who?" asked Justin.

Nash scrunched his nose. "Come with me."

Nash led the way outside with Winklo, who had just woken up, following right behind. Justin and Cindy were only one step behind. Outside, the air was still crisp and the stars, though less visible and dim, still twinkled. Soon the sun would rise, for the smell of morning was as strong as coffee brewing.

Justin whispered in Cindy's ear, "What's he doing?"

"Not sure, but Nash has power over plants and green things. He trained as a magic user and it was his spell over the tall grass that kept Asgar from finding us."

Justin shrugged. Nash knelt down on the damp lawn and tilted his head sideways. He looked as if he was listening to something. The blades of grass beneath his ear began to sway. It all seemed so strange as there was no breeze.

Winklo stepped back and stood next to Cindy. "He's talking to them. They'll tell him if something is heading this way."

"Give me a break," Justin said. "You mean to tell me he's having a conversation with plants?"

"Shhh," said Nash. "Let me finish."

Winklo put her index finger to her mouth, her head bobbing up and down. After a couple of minutes, Nash got up.

"There are two things, life forms heading this way. It's a bit too early for us to see them though. Four legs and one with two. One smells of beast and the other an animal of some sort. I wish I could tell you more. At any point they may change directions. I can check later, if you wish."

"Thank you. We may take you up on that." Cindy looked at Justin. "One of them is Grandma, I just know it."

Justin put his arm around Cindy. "It's impossible, hon. Alana is in a nursing home. Besides, how would she get here? The curse is just on us kids."

"She lived here once and made it to Sparta. If she could do that, she could conceivably make it back. Don't you believe me?"

"I think you want it so bad, you've convinced yourself."

Cindy shook her head. "No. Trust me. Please. When it's daylight, go to town and check around. We need some things anyway."

"It wouldn't hurt and you're right. Ben wants to look at some equipment and we do need more brooms and duct tape."

"Thanks Justin. I really mean it."

"I know you do. Just don't get too disappointed if we don't run into her. Okay?"

"It's a deal. And you, don't be too surprised if you do."

At first Justin wanted to go, but Wayne and Ben were the only two that really knew what they were looking for. Well, they had an idea of what they wanted, but needed some inspiration. Since neither one of them could really describe it, Justin backed down and agreed to stay and help the clean-up party.

The afternoon air had turned chilly. Weather on the Wildsidhe was as unpredictable as the creatures that stalked the land. Since Wayne had promised Ben some one-on-one time, they decided to walk. And truth be known, the last thing either boy wanted to do was clean. That was parent's work, but neither of them voiced their opinions. Here, in this new society they had formed, everyone was equal. Still, they hated pushing a broom more than they hated broccoli. The school grounds had been made into a small fortress, using scraps to fortify the steel fence that surrounded the property. The only way in or out was through the front gate. The kids on guard duty had to open the gate and close it behind them.

"You do know if we find what we're looking for, we'll have to bring a truck back?"

"I know," said Ben, "But if we drove now, well, we'd be forced to do housework. I hate doing chores."

"No more than I do. And even though it's cold, it's a nice day to walk. The hardware store isn't that far away. So, what was it you wanted to talk to me about alone?"

"Iris. I feel kinda bad about things."

"Oh, I wouldn't worry about it. Iris really does love you. It's just this brother and sister thing, you know, competition. Here, we have to work together just to get by. Things will smooth over between the two of you, heck, didn't she congratulate you on your invention? She really was proud of you."

"That's what I mean. See, Mom and Dad gave me something to give to her and well, I, she just made me so mad, I didn't. Now, I really do want her to have it and if I give it to her now, she'll get mad at me all over again. I don't know what to do."

Wayne shook his head. "That's a toughie, but the longer you wait, the harder it's going to be to explain."

"You're right. I just dread this."

Wayne patted Ben on the back. "If you want, I'll stick around when you tell her."

"Oh, great. Thanks. I really appreciate it."

"So, are you going to tell me what it is, or is it some big secret?

Ben was about to take the necklace from beneath his T-shirt when it started to rain. Wildsidhe was very unpredictable. It could be sunny one minute and storming the next. Wayne had thought ahead and opened the umbrella, but the shower turned into an all-out downpour. The two boys decided to turn back and take a car before either of them got drenched.

It was a hassle getting back through the gate. Because of the fear of Changelings taking their shape, they had to tell a password of all things, but it was easier than walking in the downpour.

Wayne zipped into the driver's seat of the first car he reached. Since there was little danger of any of the creatures that resided in the land stealing an iron car, the ones that they did have keys for, were left in glove compartments.

Ben shivered. The icy water had penetrated his shirt and made him cold and uncomfortable. Wayne suggested they run upstairs and change, but Ben didn't want to get talked into staying and cleaning up, so he said he was fine.

Though Wayne wasn't old enough to drive back in Sparta, he knew enough about driving from backing his father's car in and out of the garage. Besides, who was here to give him a ticket?

Ben was no expert on handling a car and Wayne was glad that he didn't comment on his driving skills. Justin would have teased him on the way he turned corners and how slow he went. Even though the two cousins were the best of friends, Wayne still felt uncomfortable about Justin knowing more than he did. He wasn't used to it. He was a jock who was also a brain. Plus, he was a year older. Even though there were no other cars on the road, Wayne was a bit cautious. There were plenty of telephone poles and mailboxes that were ready to jump in his way.

Wayne was so intent on staying in the lane that it was Ben who noticed the shadow of a figure ducking behind the oak tree at the corner.

"Did you see that?" he asked.

"I saw something move. Maybe I'd better check it out."

Wayne jolted the car to a halt and began to back up, swerving every which way. "If it wasn't so close to the school, I wouldn't be so concerned, but after last night's fight with Asgar, we better play it safe. Good thing I brought my bow and arrow."

"And I didn't forget the slingshot you gave me, even though I'm not a great shot," added Ben.

"Something tells me I'm going to regret this. I have this sick feeling in my stomach."

When they reached the tree where Ben said he saw the shadow, Wayne pulled over to the curb over shooting it by a good eight inches. The rain had made the ground muddy and the tires began to spin when he tried to jockey the car backwards.

"Good going. Now we're stuck."

"Sorry," Wayne said, "but I was too busy staring through the rear-view mirror. We don't get too many visitors here and the ones that do bless us with their company, we can do without."

"You're not kidding. What are we going to do?"

"I'm going out to see what's going on. You're going to stay here."

Ben was relieved, but protested a bit to make it look as if he wasn't a coward. It wasn't so much that he was afraid, but he did realize his shortcomings. He had awful aim and in this weather, the rain and the humidity were sure to fog his glasses up. Without his glasses he couldn't see a thing.

"I'll watch out the window. Holler if you need me."

Wayne nodded and stepped out of the car, slamming the door shut. Ben locked it after taking care of the passenger side first.

It was hard to see through the misty window. Even though he had left it open a crack, it still clouded up. Ben had no choice but to unwind it most of the way down.

Just a few feet away he could make out the figure of Wayne. Since it would be impossible to wield a bow and an umbrella, he had left it in the car. He tucked a tire iron in his belt. Ben watched as Wayne edged to the tree. From his vantage-point he could see very little. If it hadn't been for Wayne's red T-shirt, he might not have been able to see anything.

Ben began to worry. What if Wayne were attacked? Would he know it? Would he be able to help? Just then he spotted a shape darting from behind the tree trunk. It started to make a run for the car. Ben screamed.

Wayne turned. He too had gotten sight of the creature making a getaway.

"Lock the door and shut the windows," yelled Wayne.

He was a second too late. The creature was already tugging on the door handle. Ben screamed. Whatever it was, it looked exactly like Wayne.

CHAPTER 10

Wayne ran to the car when he heard Ben scream. All he saw was the back of the changeling. He didn't even see his head as the nasty thing was poking it inside the window.

Afraid that Ben was hurt and that the creature would turn and attack him he struck it with the tire iron before checking on his little friend's welfare.

The changeling reeled from the blow. Wayne had pulled him off the car and smacked him in the face with the tire iron, before he had a chance to shape shift. It was heavy and when it went almost limp in his hands, Wayne let go and dropped him to the ground. The changeling was already starting to stir. Sluggishly, it tried to attack him again. Wayne smashed him in the head again. The changeling grabbed Wayne's shirt and tore a piece off. Its fingers ended in claws which slashed Wayne's arm. A tiny trickle of blood ran down his arm. Wayne hit it again, then once more for good measure. The changeling finally fell to the ground unconscious. It wasn't like hitting a person. The thing wasn't even bleeding. If Wayne hadn't taken it by surprise, it would be him on the ground, and he would be bleeding. Heavily.

"Ben? Are you okay," he shouted, as Ben pulled up the lock.

Wayne opened the door to see Ben staggering to sit up. "I'm fine," he answered weakly. "It just scared me."

"Why in heaven's name did you roll your window down? I told you to stay in the car and to keep it closed and locked."

"I wanted to warn you. It ran right past you and you didn't see a thing."

Wayne smiled. "I appreciate your concern, but next time when I tell you something, you do it. Okay?"

Ben nodded. "What are we going to do with it? And it looks just like you. How can that be?"

"Me?" Wayne questioned. He turned the limp form of the changeling on his back and gasped. The face staring back at him was his own. "Well, I'll be...If I weren't me, I'd be fooled too.

"What are we going to do with it? Should we leave it out here? I think it's hurt, but it's still breathing. I can see its chest move."

"No way," Wayne said. "If we leave it out here, it could turn into a bird or something and fly right over the gate. Then it could get inside the school and attack us somehow. I can't allow that. A Changing Lord killed Todd."

Ben realized what the safest solution would be and it horrified him. "Are you going to kill it?"

"No. That would make us monsters too. We'll take him prisoner. There's a reason he's disguised as me. He must have known we were going out. I want to know what it's doing here and how it knows so much. Forewarned is forearmed. There's a good chance Asgar or Morna put it up to this. Would you mind opening the lid? I'm going to lay it in the trunk."

"Do we have to? Do you think it's safe?"

"I'll duct tape its hands together and lay it on its stomach. That way, if it awakens, it can't harm us." Ben got out of the car and helped Wayne drag the changeling into the trunk. The creature stirred, making them jump, but it didn't gain consciousness. Wayne hit it again for good measure. He wasn't violent by nature, but one of these creatures had almost killed him, his sister Terri, and his cousin Justin, plus a few others. As he said, it had killed Todd. He wasn't taking any chances. If the thing had managed to change shape, it would have been like the first time all over again. Or maybe not. The first time, they had been lulled into leaving their weapons behind. None of them would ever make that mistake again and maybe that would even the odds against the shape shifter. This one seemed weaker in human form.

"Man, it stinks," said Ben holding his nose, slamming the trunk.

"It sure does. I wonder why? I'll have to remember to ask it. The more we find out about these changelings, the better off we'll be. When we get back to the parking lot, you run in and get help. Make sure they all bring tire irons."

Ben nodded and waited for Wayne to take the wheel. After jockeying the car back and forth, he managed to get moving and he did a U-turn. Though the ride was short, the stench was awful even inside the car and both of them gagged and choked the entire way. The guards on gate duty opened as soon as verified that they knew the day's password. Wayne had initiated the system because of the risk of changelings pretending to be one of them. He smiled, thinking that even if he had been replaced, the changeling wouldn't have gotten in. He would have done his job, keeping everyone safe.

The pair drove up to one of the side doors. As soon as Wayne turned off the engine, they rushed out of the car.

"I'd keep the windows open to air it out, but then the seats will all get wet. I hope the smell doesn't linger."

"You and me both," said Ben as he took off for the building. "Be back in a jiff."

A couple minutes later Ben returned with Justin and Ron and three tire irons. The four boys pulled the changeling out of the car by its legs, careful not to let it drop to the concrete. Each one took an appendage and they waddled their way back into the school. Justin and Ron couldn't get over how much the creature looked like Wayne, even down to the red T-shirt. Justin had quizzed Ben to make sure they had the right one tied up.

As they made their way up the steps slowly, for Justin and Ben had to walk backwards, the creature began to stir. The boys tightened their grip and the thing wailed in pain.

Justin snarled. "What a sissy. We're not hurting you. You don't know the meaning of pain, yet."

The creature started to shimmer. Wayne dropped his limb and started hitting the changeling with the tire iron again.

"You try and change, and all four of us start pounding and we won't stop until you aren't moving," Wayne said. He didn't like having to resort to violence, but there were no cops here to turn him over to, no jail to put him in. Letting him go could get one of them killed. If Wayne hadn't been taken in by the other changeling, Todd might still be alive. He may not have liked the guy, but he was supposed to have protected him and he failed. He wouldn't fail again.

The Wayne-like being hissed.

"You sure are nasty, Wayne," said Ron. "And what sharp teeth you have."

The boys laughed. "Yeah, and you stink too."

The changeling spat at them. "You don't smell all that nice to me either."

"Shut up," Justin said. "You've got a lot of explaining to do."

"Make me."

Justin let go with one hand, then hit him in the head with a tire iron, stunning the creature. He too remembered one of them almost killing the lot of them.

"Okay. Talk again and you'll be eating your words soon. I'll ram them down your throat. Now shut up or I'll shut you up. Let's take him to one of the empty classrooms. No use in alarming everyone here."

Everyone agreed. Justin and Ben dropped the changeling's legs and they opened the door. Ron grabbed a steel chair and they sat the thing on it, tying its ankles to the metal bars.

"Now, who are you and why are you here?" Wayne said.

The creature gurgled. "I'm hurt. Leave me alone."

Wayne looked sheepish. Justin kept talking, knowing that they had to keep this thing scared.

"You haven't begun to hurt. Talk or we'll…"

Just then, Terri rolled in her wheelchair. "What's going on?"

She didn't need an answer. It took only a second for her to see the two Wayne's and access the situation. "Where'd you find it?"

"We'll tell you later," answered Justin. "Can you get one of the iron dusters? And lock the door when you get back. I don't want anyone else to know what is going on, especially Cindy. She's too hyped up and upset as it is."

"No problemo. Be back in a jiff."

Terri returned an instant later. "These little babies work real well. You are one smart kid, kiddo." Terri looked at Ben and smiled.

Ben returned it and went to stand next to Terri. He took the can and aimed it at the creature. "Answer him or I spray you with this," he said, bravely. They explained what the iron duster did, using the propellant from an air horn to blow iron dust out.

"As long as I'm in human form, iron won't hurt me," said the creature.

Ben looked at Wayne. That was news to him, but he was still new here.

"That's true, but how long can you stay human? I bet to heal, you have to revert. How much punishment can you take before you have to change? All you have to do is give us some answers and you won't get hurt."

The changeling tried to bite Wayne. Reacting on instinct, Wayne hit his double, causing the creature to yelp out in pain. The baritone voice that up to now sounded exactly like Wayne's, changed to a low, guttural rasp as the changeling cried out in agony.

"I need to change, but you said if I shifted, you'd start beating me," it said.

"If you don't try anything funny, we won't have any reason to hurt you," Justin said.

It took its natural form, a gray humanoid with no hair, a big head and saucer eyes. It had four fingers on each hand. Ben, who had never seen one, gasped. Now the iron in the steel chair was burning his legs. Ben pointed the duster at it.

"Get that thing away from me and I'll talk. Morna isn't worth losing my life over."

"Ahhhhhh," Wayne said, "Now we're getting somewhere. Morna put you up to this."

The changeling nodded.

"Ben, lower your arm, but keep it close. If this creature gives us any more trouble, spray some of it in its eyes. Iron can cause their Wildsidher skin to blister, and in the eyes, it could cause blindness."

"No," screamed the changeling. "I'll talk. Just keep it away from me."

"Then do it, now, and you better make it good."

The changeling shook. Wayne could see it squirm and shiver, trying hard to break the bonds that held it captive. Terri was in back of it.

"It's hands are starting to shimmer. It may be trying to shift out of the tape," Terri said.

"Don't make me use this," said Ben, in a tone so harsh he hardly believed it was him talking. The changeling believed him, because it stopped.

"You said you'd talk. We're listening, but I don't hear anything," Justin said.

"Morna put me up to it. I owed her a favor. Nothing personal. Now let me go."

"That wasn't much of an explanation. Keep talking."

Ben stared at Wayne, his mouth wide open. "Watch it, Wayne," he said. "Whatever that thing is, it has sharp, pointy teeth."

"I'll be careful. Don't worry. Besides, it has more to be concerned about than me. If it bites me, we'll spray its eyes for sure. I don't think it wants to be blind."

The creature snarled. "You all are idiots. Morna wanted me to spy on you. She didn't tell me why and I didn't ask. I owed her a favor."

"What did she want to know?"

"Anything, everything."

"Wrong answer," Wayne said. "Ben…Ben…"

"Give me a break," the changeling gurgled. "I told you all I know. Morna wanted to know what was going on. Something about this Cindy girl being captured by Asgar. Also, she's looking for her sister. Wanted to know if she was with you. Stuff like that. She thought if I changed myself into this Wayne, no one would question me. And that's it."

"Morna's sister? Tell me more about that," demanded Justin. "Who is Morna's sister and why would she be with us."

"I don't know why. Morna doesn't give me explanations. All I know is her name is Alana."

Justin glanced around the room. "Cindy might be right. She said she heard her Grandma calling. Did you see this woman, or a picture?"

"Not really. There's a portrait of her in the castle, but she was young and pretty then. Morna says she's old and wrinkly now."

"And Morna, she said for sure her sister was here in Wildsidhe?"

"Are you stupid? I just told you that. Yes, she's here. Morna said she stole some things."

"What did she steal?" asked Wayne.

"I don't know and I didn't ask. You don't ask the Fortesan Queen such questions."

"We're not getting the right answers. Perhaps you need some more convincing."

The changeling tried to scoot its chair back. "I've told you everything. I can't tell you what I don't know. Morna sent me here to spy on you and to find out if some old lady was here. That's it. I owed her a favor and that's the only reason I'm here. Believe me or not, that's the truth."

"Well guys," asked Justin, "Should we let it go?"

Terri chuckled. "Yeah, but he owes us a favor now."

"We're even now. I've told you everything I know. No favors. That's what got me in trouble in the first place."

Ben waved the can and the changeling sputtered.

"We don't take kindly to spies. I'm not letting you off that easy. I want you to find out why Morna's so interested in us."

"How am I supposed to do that? No one but High Fortesans mix with High Fortesans. I can't disguise myself as a High Fortesan. Their magic would see right through it. Just let me go and I promise to never come back."

"I don't think he knows any more, Justin," Terri said. "Just let it go. It gives me the shivers. It looks just like the one that killed Todd."

"Why don't you go through his … its pockets?" asked Ben.

"Good idea. I should've thought of it myself. Ben would you mind? I'm afraid if I get my hands on it, I'd be tempted to hurt it."

Ben felt good about his suggestion and handed the spray-can to Terri. He slipped his hand in the creature's pockets. His fingers felt something soft and he pulled it out. It was a black, felt pouch and he loosened the leather drawstring.

Turning it upside down, he emptied the contents in the palm of his hand. Out poured various sized crystals. There were so many that some spilled onto the ground.

"Diamonds!" cried Ben.

"Those aren't diamonds, but they sure look like the crystal we found, only smaller," Terri said. It had been a birthday gift to Cindy.

"Give them back to me," screeched the changeling.

"I don't think you're in any position to tell me what to do. What are these crystals?"

"Not going to tell you, no way. They're mine."

"It sure isn't very bright," Terri said waving the can around in the air.

"You filthy, little, five-fingers. They're magic containers and no use to the likes of you. Morna already told me you're incapable of magic. Now, give them back."

"Don't," said Ben. "They may be worthless to us, but obviously of use to Wildsidhers. Perhaps we could use them in the future, to trade for things we need."

"I think you've got something there, Ben. We'll let you go changeling, but we're going to keep this. That should teach you not to mess with us in the future."

"Please, give them back," the changeling's voice was no longer raspy. It sounded more like a child's. "It's all I own."

"I'll make you a deal…you go find out what Morna's up to, and why she wants to know what's going on here. When you return with the information, we'll give it back."

The changeling hissed. "Keep it. Not gonna go near that evil queen again. When I return to her without information, she won't think twice about killing me."

"You've enough information to tell her. Her sister isn't here and we have plenty of iron to keep our school safe. As for Asgar, Cindy is alive and well and doing fine. Terri give me the iron spray," Wayne said. "If you do anything funny, we'll bury you here in our garden. I bet you'd make great fertilizer. We are going to untie you from the chair. Then we are going to tie this rope around you and give the other end to Terri."

"Why?"

"She's going to fly you out of here," Wayne said.

"Fly?"

"Yep, but strictly no-frill for you," Terri said.

Wayne and the rest walked the changeling outside. Terri wrapped the rope several times around her armrest and took to the sky. With effort, she lifted the changeling up into the air and over the fence. She let go of the rope and the changeling fell to the ground.

The changeling stood, its hands shimmered, and the rope and duct tape fell to the ground. Terri landed back on the school grounds.

Snarling and baring his teeth, he turned his back and hobbled away. Wayne tossed a few crystals at him over the fence.

"Wait. Don't say we weren't fair, oh, and don't come back unless you have something useful to tell us."

The changeling quickly gathered up the few loose stones and took off running. Terri, Ben, Ron, Justin, and Wayne did a high five and chuckled.

"I bet it's the last we see of him," said Ben.

Terri shook her head. "It'll be back. These crystals must be pretty useful and powerful to magic users and there are over a hundred of them. I just wish I knew why Morna is so interested in what's going on here."

"Do you think it was telling us the truth?"

"I do. It's just a gut feeling, but it was pretty scared and those blisters looked plenty painful. And why would he lie about Alana being here? That's all very interesting."

"Even more interesting is that Morna is worried about her joining up with us. You know Asgar was looking for someone before he took the town. Do you think it could have been Alana he wanted? There's no way he could have known about Cindy, is there?" asked Wayne.

"Maybe, but I don't want to ask Cindy. She's really upset about all this. Last night she was talking about leaving. I think we should keep this secret from her for a while," Justin said. "Do you think that elf would know?"

Cindy stepped into the room followed by Winklo and Nash. Justin and the others looked surprised. They hadn't noticed her presence and when they did, it was easy to see she was angry. Both hands were on her hips and her usual smile wasn't evident. In its place was frown.

In a soft tone of voice, Justin managed a, "Hi, Cindy."

"Don't Cindy me. You're up to something. I want to know what secrets you're keeping from me and what you want to ask Nash."

CHAPTER 11

Alana guided the unicorn south along the worn path. It had been a long time since she had been here and she could tell that little had changed. The two worlds were so different, yet so remarkably alike. Domination. Whether it be humans or Fortesans, they lived for the acquisition of power. Morna had it, Asgar wanted it, and it rightly belonged to Alana. Had she remained in Wildsidhe, she could have been queen.

At one time, when she was very young, she wanted that. Morna and she would play at it, take turns being ruler and practicing punishment on their insect subjects. Queen Bee. Those memories were part of her past and there they would remain. She wanted no part in the struggle. All she wanted was to get to Cindy and prepare her for life here.

There were so many things she needed to teach her. How to use magic, who to trust, what life forms were useful and which ones to avoid. The pressing question was Asgar. Were they married? Had her magic been up to par, she could have snooped the ceremony, but even the simplest spells took their toll. It would be weeks before she would regain most of her abilities.

Her hand throbbed as she patted Champ's rump. "Hurry fellow," she whispered in his ears. "Time's a wastin'. We've slept much too long."

Champ snorted and bobbed his head. Alana clung to the thick mane as the steed picked up speed. It had been years since she had ridden and her bottom was sore. He was all that she missed.

The sun was almost directly overhead when she reached the school building. Alana had to steady herself to keep from falling off.

"We're here Champ. Whoa boy."

Alana tugged on the mane and the unicorn came to a halt. He was breathing heavily and she could feel his chest heaving as she slipped off his back. There were no signs of life outside the building and from where she was standing, she couldn't see any movement through the windows, but they were there.

"Follow me, Champ," Alana said as she began to walk down the street that led to the front gate. The unicorn stepped next to her and whinnied. She placed a soft kiss on his nuzzle and continued down to the fortified gate of the school.

"Wait here, fellow. I shouldn't be gone long. I'll get us both some water in a minute."

Alana tried the gate, but it was chained closed. At least the kids were sensible enough to secure the school. They had even set up watch towers around the fence line, but the one by the gate seemed to be empty.

"Hello?" she said. A pair of heads popped up in the tower. Apparently the guards had been making out while on duty.

"Who are you? Get away from that door or I'll fire."

Alana stared at the face of a young boy. He was holding an aerosol-can with a peculiar attachment on the nozzle. The girl next to him held a bow and arrow. She knew what the bow could do, but she couldn't read the container without her glasses and wondered what she was being threatened with. Bug spray?

"I'm Alana Freeman, Cindy's grandmother. Can you go get her?"

"Yeah, yeah, sure, sure. What would Cindy's grandmother be doing here? Adults didn't make it to the Wildsidhe, only kids."

"Just go get her. I promise to wait here."

The boy, Gary Holt, steadied his hand. "You're another one of them changelings. Your kind killed my brother. You must be pretty stupid to try the same thing twice in the same day. Wayne just sent one of you packing. I advise you to join it."

Alana shook her head. "I can see you've had it rough here and have met some of the more untrustworthy creatures, but really, I am her grandmother. Just call for her. Let her decide if I am real or not. I could cast a magic spell on you. See the unicorn?"

Gary looked at the old woman and then her hands. "A Fortesan then, one of Asgar's buddies. Only with normal fingers."

"A Fortesan, yes, but like you, I've no love for the man. Now get Cindy. I'm losing patience. I've refrained from turning you into a frog, but you're sorely tempting me."

"Come one step closer, lady, and I'm going to spray you. This can is full of iron powder. There's enough in this can to blister your whole body."

"You idiot. You're not worth wasting another minute on. Cindy! Cindy!" Alana shouted as loud as she could. "Cindy, it's Grandma. Hurry."

Gary leaned over the edge of the tower, his hand shaking as held the can outward. "You don't hear me, do you old lady? You must be as deaf as you are stupid."

"Wait!" Cindy screamed, running out of the building. "I know her. It's my grandmother."

Cindy shoved and pulled, trying to unlock the chains and open the gate. Gary and the girl, Renee Desilver, climbed down to stop her, but Wayne ran out and waved them off.

"Baby doll," Alana cried. "You're okay."

Cindy and Alana were grappling with the chains, doing their best to loosen them.

"Don't. She could be a changeling."

"She's no changeling, trust me, Gary. Don't you think I wouldn't know my own grandmother?"

"Wayne? They tricked us once. Don't let them trick us again," said Gary.

"It's okay. We've kind of been expecting her," Wayne said.

"Thanks for letting us guards know about it," griped Gary. Wayne turned red, realizing he should have said something.

"Why? Would you have stopped playing kissy face long enough to look out for me?" said Alana.

"You guys were supposed to be on watch," Wayne said, angry now.

"Watch? I had to shout to get them to notice me. And that was with Champ clomping down the street," said Alana, pointing behind her.

"Is that a real unicorn?" Cindy said.

"Yep," said Alana.

"You two are in big trouble," Wayne said. Alana turned her attention back to her granddaughter. It took another minute to get the gate open. Alana grabbed for Cindy and enveloped her in tight hug. "Oh my sweet, little girl. I've missed you so much."

Cindy was in tears and softly sobbing her words. "Oh Grandma, it's been awful. So much has gone on. I'm so glad you're here. Come on inside and get comfortable. There's so many things I want to know."

"There, there. Things will be all right now. Grandma's here and she's never going to leave you again."

The sound of footsteps on the stairway didn't disturb the homecoming. Neither one of them looked up to see who was there.

"It's not a changeling," said Nash. "Her aura is too powerful for a changeling. A changeling can't mimic that, not even a Changeling Lord. She's a Fortesan. A short one."

"Alana?" Justin said. "You're …"

Alana looked up. "Justin. Come here. Let me give you a hug. You too, Wayne. My handsome boys. Come give me a big welcome. Where's Terri?"

The two boys rushed into her arms. "Terri's not far. It's so good to see you. Cindy said she heard your voice, but I didn't believe her."

"You need to trust her, Justin. She has strong magic and as soon as I can teach her to use it, she will become a powerful source. Now, if you don't mind, I need some water for Champ and a chance to rest up. It's been a long ride."

"Champ?" asked Justin.

"My unicorn. Come see. He's a darlin' and someday, Cindy, he'll be yours."

Everyone but Nash followed Alana outside. He ran to the barrels where they stored rain and river water to fill a bucket. He got back to find half the kids surrounding the majestic creature.

"His name is Champagne, but I call him Champ for short. I bet you can't tell he's my favorite."

"Your favorite?" asked Justin. "There are more?"

"I command all the unicorns as they're my totem. Like Asgar has his lionhawks and Morna has the darkcats. There are thirteen totems. As soon as Champ's had his fill of water, I'll show you what I mean. Thank you, little elf for your kindness."

"My name is Nash and I'm at your service, M'lady. My mom used to speak of you many years ago."

"I hope only nice things," said Alana.

"Of course. She said you were the best of the lot, for a Fortesan. Mom didn't think much of the High Council and their kin, but she did say you were the only one with sense. Leaving this place and all."

Alana chuckled. "I like your honesty, Nash. Thanks."

Nash beamed and the kids oohed and ahhed as Champ drank from the pail. Alana stood closest to the unicorn, stroking his back and allowing the kids one by one to pet him also. Only Cindy stood off to the side.

"He speaks, doesn't he?"

Alana smiled. "Only to kin, hon. He knows who you are without me saying a word. Now come here and let me make this formal."

Cindy smiled and everyone stepped back as she approached the magical creature. Champ nuzzled her as she ran her fingers through his coarse mane. "He is so beautiful," she said. "I never dreamt unicorns really existed."

Cindy walked in front and touched the golden horn. It was hard and warm as she ran her palm up to the tip. "Amazing," she muttered.

Alana just smiled. "I felt the same way too, when Grandmama introduced me to him. He's been in our family since time began. It's our legacy."

"A legacy of unicorns, how beautiful," Terri said, landing her wheel chair beside the group. "I'm so jealous. I assume only you and Alana can ride him."

"With our permission and at our command, you can also. Later, when we have some time, all of you can have a turn. But for now, he needs to rest and I do too. There's so much to catch up on. Stand back, everyone. Champ, you ready?"

Champ whinnied. Alana closed her eyes and mumbled a few a words. The air in front of them sang softly as the unicorn turned into a vapor and swirled into the air. It hovered above them for a minute, picking up speed until it spun into a white tornado. The funnel touched the ground, cutting a path in the grass and both ends disappeared into each other forming a wooden figurine.

The children gasped. Cindy was speechless. "May I?" she asked.

"Please do, child," said Alana.

Cindy bent down and picked up the totem. It was a perfect miniature of Champ. Even the horn had the same markings. The wood was warm. She could feel a very slight vibration. "It's alive," she said.

"Of course it is. You are looking at one of the most powerful forms of magic we've got. Just like you have your stories of creation, from religious viewpoints to scientific theories, we have our own explanations. These totems date back to the beginning of life. When we have more time, I'll tell you. For now, just enjoy."

Cindy handed the totem to Alana, but she winked. "You keep it for a bit. I've had it all my life."

Cindy thanked her grandmother and showed her the way to the gymnasium. The others followed. Alana looked at all the mattresses scattered about the floor and shook her head. "You sleep here?"

"It's safer to sleep in one room, with no windows. That way, we don't lose anyone," Justin said.

"I suppose you're right. I've never considered how scary this world could be to an outsider."

"Let me go get another mattress and you can rest on Cindy's or mine in the meantime."

Justin pointed to the bedding right by the door. Cindy led Alana to hers and Alana grunted and groaned as she lowered herself to the floor.

"I've gotten old and out of shape. I used to ride for hours. Now, every bone in my body is on strike. Would you mind if I rested a bit? An hour, maybe two. Then we can catch each other up with the news."

"Sure. Get some sleep. Dinner will be ready by then and we can talk after you've eaten."

Cindy kissed her grandmother and covered her with Justin's blanket as well as her own. Alana was already asleep when she whispered in her ear, "Sleep well. I love you."

Justin returned and leaned the mattress against the wall. With Alana sound asleep, he didn't want to disturb her by moving things around. Cindy motioned for him to move and he followed her to the corner where they had moved the furniture from the teacher's lounge. They made themselves comfortable on the couch and Cindy snuggled in close to Justin.

"Nash was right on," Justin said. "He heard the four legged creature and here comes Alana on the unicorn."

"And what about me? You didn't believe me when I told you I heard her calling."

"I'm sorry, Cindy. I never gave any real thought to magic, except for the great Houdini and a few card tricks. Guess now's as good a time to start as any. I already believe there are if there are dragons, changelings, elves, and dwarves."

"Spiders," yelled Cindy.

"I believe in spiders. Ich," Justin said. "I don't like them at all."

Cindy stood up, pointing and shrieking. "No, no. Over there by Grandma. There are spiders everywhere. Look."

CHAPTER 12

Morna stomped around the guestroom, alternating between picking things up and throwing them down. Her worktable had been tampered with and some of her spell stones had been taken. Spiders were everywhere, humming and buzzing around.

"Some protection you were. Well at least she didn't find the big ones. I should have known Alana would have snooped. That will teach me."

"Who are you talking to, dear? I don't see anyone." Penrod opened the door wider and peeked in.

"No one. You don't see anyone because I'm alone."

Penrod already regretted starting this conversation. "I'll just see you later."

"Go, you aren't of any help. If you hadn't made me go to this farce of a wedding, none of this would have happened. It's all your fault."

"Yes, sweetie. I'm sorry."

Morna screamed. Her voice was so loud that the mirror hanging above the bed shattered. Penrod hurried out and shut the door behind him as he left. No sooner than the door was shut then he heard a loud crash. The door vibrated from the direct hit. He sighed. There was no talking to Morna when she was in a snit. It would be hours, maybe days, before she was civil again.

"That man makes me so mad. If it weren't punishable by death, I'd kill him." Morna sat down on the bed and flicked a spider off. "Alana, why? I had so hoped we could have been friends. That all the years of separation had dimmed the harsh feelings we had for each other. I so wanted to have a friend. It's lonely being queen, so very lonely."

Morna started to cry. The crown was hers but there was no fun in it. Too much responsibility. All work and very little play. It was harder keeping it than acquiring it, but she had to stop Asgar. He wanted it to exploit the inhabitants.

When Alana showed up on the front lawn, she was so happy to see her though she never would have admitted it. All those many years of verbal warfare and devious pranks lurked in the back of her mind. Yet, earlier in the day, they goofed around and teased each other. For a short while she thought there was hope.

Well, the competition is back on. Alana may not want the crown for herself, but she had a granddaughter now. She would fight for it for her sake. Morna had no children. The years with Penrod were barren. There was no heir from her womb. If it came to a vote, if Alana were to push it, the High

Council may take into consideration Alana's offspring. Morna couldn't take that chance. Who was Alana to think she could desert her people for so many years and just come back? She had no right to rule and this Cindy, if Asgar were to succeed and marry her, well, she'd be so lost under his spell., She'd be just as useless as Penrod.

Morna was tired from thinking. She lay down in the bed, pointed her finger at the mess and instantly the force-field knit together. The pillow squished under her head and she rolled on her side. A short nap would do her good. Perhaps after resting she would feel a better and a bit more optimistic.

The knock on her door awakened her just as she slipped into sleep. "Go away, I'm busy," she mumbled.

"Please, M'Lady, it's Sabo. He has news for you that can't wait, or so he says."

"Make him comfortable and tell him I'll be down shortly."

Morna waited for the servant's acknowledgment and slipped out of bed. No rest for the wicked, she thought, and then laughed at her own joke. The room looked as it did before her sister destroyed it. The barrier hid the mess. She would get to it later. Sabo might have news worth hearing.

The changeling was pacing when she entered the foyer. He had taken his own form in an attempt to be recognizable. Morna forced a smile and bid the creature hello. He stopped and bowed low when the queen entered the room.

"Did you not wish any refreshments, or was my hostess remiss in offering some to you?"

"Oh no, your royal majesty, Queen Morna, the gracious. I'm just in a hurry to get home and not hungry."

"Then let's make this short. What did you find out?"

Morna hated changelings, but they were useful. They made the best spies and usually worked relatively cheap, but they were such suck-ups and liars. Sabo hated her as much as she hated him. The politeness was just a cloak of civility. If nothing else, it spoke of his attempt at good manners.

"The one you were looking for, the silver-haired lady, she is with the kids."

Now Morna was the one pacing. I knew it. Couldn't trust her then and can't now. Drat, she thought. That spoils plan A.

Sabo glanced at the door and sighed softly when he saw it was unlocked. When Morna was upset it was best to make a fast getaway. She had a tendency to flash-freeze changelings and Sabo didn't like being stuck in one shape, even if was for a few hours.

"You're sure, then?"

"The kids found me. Tried to get information out of me, but I resisted. I told them nothing. She wasn't there then. I mean the old lady. Cindy was there and there was no golden braid on her that I could see. Also there was a green elf. Other than that, nothing. Except that they tortured and threatened me. They stole all but three spellstones. Luckily, I escaped with my life.

"Those humans are cruel and cunning, but I was one step ahead of them. Fast I am. They followed me, but I outwitted them all. Found a hiding place behind some bushes and waited to see what would happen. It was cold and the branches pricked my delicate skin, but for you, oh mistress, I would have weathered the fiercest twister to bring to you this important news."

"Yeah, yeah, you'd die for me if need be. I've heard it all before. Just go on." Troc, the Changeling Lord, was one of the few shifters with the backbone not to taint his reports with false praise and flattery. He was also one of the few with the power to rival a Fortesan, although not one of the High Council.

"True. Verily. Well, as I was saying, I was concealed amongst the thorny brambles when all of a sudden, out of nowhere, gallops this unicorn. He was a beautiful beast. Been years since I've seen one. Thought they were all extinct. It didn't see me nor did its rider, this silver-haired woman that matched your description. I watched her enter the school."

"My totem. Champagne. That contemptible excuse for a Fortesan. She's had it all these years. I suspected it, but now I have proof. How selfish she is. Alana had no use for unicorns on earth, nor could she summon enough magic to use them if she did need them. She stole the totem. My totem. I've had to make do with Penrod's darkcats."

The ornate vase sitting on the embroidered, lace doily shattered. Morna turned and the porcelain figurines on the mantle above the fireplace burst into a hundred, flying pieces. Sabo shuddered and inched closer to the door.

"Forgive me if I've upset you, oh powerful one, but I'm only the messenger and sorry, I am, to be the bringer of news that upsets you."

"Of course it's not your fault, but you don't know this evil woman the way I do. Oh. Why am I telling you this? Your kind cares little about politics and fair play. I'm done with you." Morna waved her hand twice. "If there's nothing else, you may leave."

"Nothing to tell, but there is this issue of payment. Your promise to make this worth my while."

Morna rolled her eyes and groaned. "Yes, I did promise you a reward." With a wave of her hand and crackling, burst of light, a handful of spellstones magically appeared in her hand. She held them out for Sabo to see and winked into existence a suede pouch. One by one the crystals poured from her fingers into the little bag and after closing it, she tossed it to Sabo.

He bowed low, thanking her over and over again, while slowly making his way to the door. "And what about the ones that were stolen?"

"Don't press your luck. I've been more than generous."

Morna glared and the changeling rushed out the door, not even closing it behind him. It was funny and Morna had to laugh. She laughed all the way to the door and all the way back to her room. Once she was alone, she threw herself on her bed and began to pound the pillow until she could no longer gather the strength to hit it again.

He stared at the figure sleeping on the bed. There was no doubt it was Morna, but the swelling of the tissues around his eyes made everything blurry. The blisters on his face oozed pus, and the few that had scabbed, itched.

His tongue felt thick and his throat burned. Talking took a lot of effort to do and he spoke with a gurgle. "Wake up Morna, we have a problem."

Morna rubbed her eyes and had to look twice at the man hovering above her. Though he was badly hurt, she knew him immediately.

"Asgar, oh my heavens. What happened to you?"

Morna sat up abruptly and stared at the once handsome prince leaning against her dresser. His reflection in the mirror revealed his wounds covered his backside as well, for his tunic clung to his body.

"They have a weapon. The human kids. It's devastating. I had to stand under a waterfall for what seemed like forever to wash off the tiny particles of iron that stuck to my skin. I feel as bad as I look. It took all of my strength to come here."

"It must be important for you to just appear in my bedchambers. I will overlook this indiscretion this time. Please sit and tell me what's wrong."

"You already know that Cindy escaped before the tying bonds that would have secured our future. She was to be my wife."

"Obviously, she didn't wish to marry you. Perhaps it's for the best. You really weren't in love with her."

"What has love got to do with it? You don't love Penrod. It's about power and I don't expect you to care. I know you're not stupid. If my plans had worked your throne would have been up for grabs."

"Maybe. You think too highly of yourself. The people may not like me personally, but there are no gripes about my reign. I see to it that they are well taken care of. You, on the other hand..."

"Stop. I didn't come here to argue with you."

"Then why are you here?"

"I think we can help each other out."

"I don't need anything from you."

"I wouldn't be so sure about that. Alana is back."

"We both know this. So?"

Asgar sat on the high-backed velvet cushioned chair and folded his leg. His black, knee-high leather boots were covered in mud. He looked as if he hadn't slept. "Don't play stupid. Let's drop the animosity and look at this situation like the adults we are. Alana may not be a threat to you, but her granddaughter, that's another nest of spiders. The people here find security in the line of succession and you are barren. Or perhaps it is Penrod's fault, but it doesn't matter. You have no heir."

Morna bit her lip. Smart he was. She needed to give him more credit; she had underestimated his grasp of the situation. "Go on, you have my attention."

"I have a plan that will get Alana out of the way. Without her, Cindy is helpless. She hasn't a clue how things are run here, nor does she know anyone on the high council. With Alana gone she poses no threat to you at all."

"Ah, but if you succeed in marrying her that all changes."

"True, but let's take it slow. First we have to get rid of Alana, permanently."

"Are you saying what I think you are? Are you proposing we kill her?"

"Absolutely not. Do you take me for a changeling? If I'm even suspected as her murderer, it would ruin my only chance to rule."

"I don't understand. You seem to be forgetting the Treaty of Shadows. Any Fortesan who kills another is claimed by the Shadows. If one of the High Council kills another member, the shadows can reclaim part or all of the Wildsidhe. Thanks to your actions at the sacrifice to the Shadows, we have already violated the treaty. I will not give the Shadows any more excuses to plague my people."

"I'm not an idiot. I'm not suggesting either of us do the deed. For that I need changelings. I've a few that I've recruited, but I need more to muster a counter attack. It's too dangerous for us to move in on the children now, but if we send them on ahead to rid us of those weapons and Alana, we stand a chance."

"These changelings aren't too bright, but they're not stupid either. They are as susceptible to iron also."

"Morna, you already know most of them will do anything for spellstones, including selling their offspring. Besides, as humans, iron will not harm them and they can stay human for a day at a time. If we promise to make it worth their while, they will do it."

"And where do we get these riches? You don't expect me to use the royal treasury? That belongs to the people."

"Just show them the vault. They don't have to know we've no intention of paying up. Most of them won't live long enough to tell of our deception and if a few do, well, there's no law against killing them. Maelstrom's appetite does get a bit much to control."

"So, you're saying, we send these ignorant changelings in to kill my sister? Then what?"

"We're back to square one. Alana is out of the way." Asgar smiled. "It's so simple."

"What's in it for you? What difference would it make who was ruling when you made your play for the throne?"

"With Alana out of the way, I can get my bride back. Things go back to where they were. You against me."

Morna's eyes lit up. With Alana out of the way, Cindy wouldn't be a threat. She had a fair chance beating Asgar, but she would fail if she had to fight them both. "Agreed."

Morna reached her hand out to shake on the pact. Asgar's hands were hot to the touch and covered in blisters. Touching him was repugnant, but it wasn't a contract unless they shook on it.

"May the best man win," said Asgar standing up.

"You mean, woman," Morna replied, squeezing his hand until he winced.

CHAPTER 13

They weren't easy to kill even with the wooden heels of a nearby pair of cowboy boots. Alana was out of it. The kids had to drag her away. Cindy had seen the open wound on her ankle and was attempting to bandage it when another fuzzy spider crawled out of it. She screamed so loud that Nash and Winklo, came running.

"OO, OO, OO. Nasty buzzers. They burrow under the skin and lay eggs. Hard to kill," said Winklo.

"What can we do? They're coming from Grandma's hand. I can't wake her."

Winklo looked at Nash. "If you can fetch some poleberries and blant leaves I can make a poultice."

"What?" asked Cindy.

"My Winky is a shaman. She knows everything about herbs and brews. Learned it from her mother. It's the only nice thing I can say about that woman. I did tell you about them trying to keep us apart, didn't I?" Nash began to ramble. "She didn't approve of me cause elves and dwarves..."

"Nash will you stop your incessant chatter and go get me those plants? Yes, you told Cindy and I'm sure she remembers and if she doesn't... you can tell her again, later. I need to take care of this nest before any more of these disgusting spiders hatch. And while you're out there get me some allo stalks."

"Yes, dear. Whatever you say, sweetie."

Nash squinted his eyes and curled his nose before disappearing out of the room. Cindy shook her head, stifling a chuckle.

"Things never change," said Winklo. "You love a person in spite of their faults. It used to be, when he ran off at the mouth, I'd get angry."

"And now?"

"I'm used to it. We've made this compromise, even though it sounds like I'm testy and he gets a bit snotty. I stop him in midstream if it's inappropriate and we're in a rush and he gets things done in a timely matter. Otherwise, I let him go on and on until the listener has had enough and then they can tell him so."

"I'm glad it works for you. I really don't mean to laugh either, but you sound like an old married couple."

"We are in a way. Been together for ages. As soon as we can get someone to marry us, we will."

"Can Grandma do it? She's a Fortesan."

"Why, yes she can. Do you think she would?"

"Of course. As soon as she wakes up I'll ask. Is she going to be okay?"

"Oh yeah. As soon as I make this dressing and administer it, she'll be as good as new. Right now, this poison that's flooding her bloodstream..."

"Poison?"

"Well it's more like a sleeping, numbing venom. It puts the person in a trance while the eggs hatch. Once they emerge the sore heals, but it can take days. But don't you worry. This stuff I make will kill the eggs in minutes. Like Nash said, my mom was the best medicine woman in the area. I learned it all from her."

Justin and the others had quit stomping on the crawlers and started to listen to Winklo as she talked about some of the things she was capable of doing.

"Winklo," Justin said, "Do you think you could train one of us? Set up some sort of little infirmary where we can store some of these potions? We can't expect you to do it all and at some time or another you won't be at hand to take care of things."

"That's a wonderful idea," Cindy said. "If Winklo wouldn't mind."

The dwarf beamed. "I'm glad to be able to help out. Nash and I appreciate you giving us a home here. We're more than willing to pay off the debt."

"It's not an obligation. Don't feel that you have to, but we sure would appreciate it."

"My pleasure. Nash can help with the gardening and planting of the herbs and vegetation. We'll need to stock our shelves. He does have a way with plants."

"Fantastic," Justin said. "As soon as we finish securing the building it will be a top priority. We just need to clear more space in the garden."

"I can help with that too," said Nash returning with a handful of leaves and branches. He handed them to Winklo along with a bucket and a cup of water.

The kids watched as Winklo set about mashing the prickly poleberries and mixing them with a few drops of water. After adding the pulp from the thick, yellow, blant leaves, the paste turned a murky brown. Winklo used her hand to apply the salve to the open wound on Alana's ankle. Even though the woman was unconscious, she made a face, crinkling her nose and scrunching her shut eyes.

"Does it hurt?" asked Cindy.

"It burns a bit, but don't worry, she'll be fine."

Alana woke up to the staring crowd of children hovering over her. Winklo winked as if to say, see, I know what I'm doing.

"What's going on here? Haven't you kids seen an old lady sleep before?"

"Oh, I forgot to tell you, the patient doesn't know what happened."

"You lost me. What's going on here?" asked Alana.

Winklo told her about the hive spiders and Alana shuddered. The sore on her ankle had already started to scab over and the swelling even had gone down. "Thank you so much, Winklo."

"It was my pleasure as well as an honor to serve you, M'Lady Alana." Winklo bowed, as did Nash.

"Oh, stop with that. Been gone too long to be treated like a royal Fortesan. Makes me uncomfortable. Just call me Alana, or goddess if you prefer."

Everyone laughed at the joke, especially Cindy who was glad to see the animation come back to her grandmother. Back in Sparta, she seemed to be slipping. Enough that she was concerned for her well-being, but here, she was her old self.

"Grandma, I was wondering if you'd be willing to perform the marriage ceremony for Winklo and Nash?"

"Me? I've never done one. Not sure it would even be legal."

"Oh but M'Lady, I mean Alana, you are a High Fortesan. All High Fortesans can preside over a marriage. As for the ceremony, we don't want much, but if you would prefer not to, don't worry about it." Winklo half-smiled, trying not to look disappointed.

"I'd be honored. Just say when."

"Tonight?" asked Nash.

"No, no," cried Cindy. "We need to get Winklo a dress and make some foods. This is a special occasion and we don't have too many like that here. I want this to be a dream wedding."

"But, you really don't need to go to a lot of trouble. Nash and I are simple folk."

Terri and Iris agreed with Cindy. There had never been a wedding here. Even Wayne and Justin agreed. "We owe you two so much. Please let us do it up right. We can get this school locked up in a day or two and then we can have it here. Cindy can help Winklo with a dress. We have a lot of houses we can rummage through. I'm sure we can find a pretty gown for Winklo to wear."

Winklo and Nash looked at each other and nodded. "It would be nice to wear something pretty," said Winklo.

"You are beautiful to me no matter what you have on, sweetie," said Nash and he kissed the dwarf.

Everyone clapped. "Let's say we get moving on the cleanup. The sooner we get done, the sooner they can become husband and wife," Justin said. "In the eyes of the kingdom."

Though everyone hated the thought of all the work that lay ahead of them, just thinking of the wedding made the work seem easier and time passed quickly. By evening, the floors had been swept of glass and most of the broken windows had been boarded up. Wayne and Ron had gone into town and picked up some barbwire fencing for the roof. They had started to put it up, but needed more hands and decided to wait until morning to do it.

Ben and Carmen worked on modifying more leaf blowers. The science room was filled with odds and ends of piping and nuts and bolts. Boxes of plastic gloves and facemasks were fitted with each hand-held weapon. Carmen had some really good ideas and with the help of the Bearclaw brothers, they designed some leather holsters for the air canister shooters.

Winklo began to transform the nurse's office into a doctor's office, as most of their medical supplies were already stored in there. With Nash's help they scoured the rooms for containers and hit the jackpot in a basement storage room. The room had a nasty odor to it and when they followed their noses, it led them to these huge, metal, box-like doors. Nash had to back off as the iron in them made him tingle, so poor Winklo had to dispose of all the containers of spoiled food.

It was dark when they returned to their mattresses to sleep. Winklo bid Nash a good night, kissing him softly on his cheek before heading to her own mattress. Cindy moved her belongings closer to her grandmother and curled up to sleep. The sound of Alana's breathing was comforting. Having her near made Cindy feel safe.

It was in the wee hours of the morning when Cindy awakened. The one oil lamp left burning shed an eerie glow on the polished, gym floor. Sounds of snoring and teeth gnashing told her all were asleep. It was a sound that one got used to for it meant all was well. Normally, she slept sound, but for some reason it had woken her up.

Cindy tried to go back to sleep, but she felt uneasy. Something bothered her and she couldn't place it. She sat up and looked around the room, squinting while her eyes tried to focus in the dim light. Once she made out the shadows, she walked to the door and peered into the hallway. From her position she could hear the rattling of doors and was about to dismiss it as the wind, when she thought she heard whispers. Carmen was on guard duty tonight. At night, the guards stayed inside the school. Was Carmen talking to someone? And if there was trouble, why didn't Carmen call for help? What was going on?

Her heart pounded furiously as she strained to hear. The mind can play tricks late at night and even the most common of noises can stir one's imagination. Cindy tried to keep calm. She moved back a step and tried to conceal herself as much as possible. The whispers continued and now she heard footsteps.

Very fast, she made her way through the maze of mattresses. "Justin," she said shaking him, "Someone's broken in. Wake up. Hurry."

Justin shot into a sitting position. "You sure? I'm sure Carmen would have alerted us to trouble."

"Not if something has happened to her. I'm going to wake Grandma."

Alana let out a snort and shuffled out of the blankets that she was cocooned in. "Shhhh," she said. "Stay here. Let me handle this."

Cindy followed her to the doorway and Alana shooed her away. "Are you deaf, child? Get away from the door."

Cindy took a couple steps back, not looking and bumped into Justin and Wayne. Startled, she was about to scream, but Justin had covered her mouth. "Get behind us and stay calm. Go get yourself a weapon."

Cindy did as she was told and grabbed an air can of powdered iron. Though she had tried her best to keep silent, the other kids were stirring and many had already awakened. Not knowing what was going on, the children began to whisper amongst themselves. Cindy failed at quieting them down, until all of a sudden a crackle of light flashed through the room.

The sight was so astounding that it hushed everyone up. Cindy's eyes darted to the doorway where she saw her grandmother moving her fingers in midair as if she was playing the piano. Again, lightning flickered through the room. It illuminated the hallway and from where she was standing, even she could see the figures that had rushed in and grabbed Alana.

It had happened so fast that Justin and Wayne didn't have a chance to use the spray. Now, with Alana as a hostage, they didn't dare. It was Ron and Miko who had enough sense to light more oil lamps. Wayne, Justin, and Cindy stood there frozen. It was horrible enough to see Alana struggling to break free. What was even worse was seeing her terrorist. As soon as the flames quit flickering it became obvious who their attackers were.

Cindy screamed.

CHAPTER 14

Morna closed her velvet cloak, clasping the material around the collar as she stood on the school grounds. She had had three of her darkcats smash the chain holding the front gate shut. Shalimar nuzzled her free hand and instinctively she began to scratch behind the great cat's ear.

"All's well that ends well, my pretty. Be patient. It's almost playtime."

The wind was chilling and her cape fluttered and flapped around her legs. Had she not been so nervous she'd have been annoyed. Alana was her sister. Blood, kinship, her own. She felt guilty. All her life she had looked up to Alana, wanting so bad to be her friend, but it was impossible. The resentment that escalated through the years and fueled by Grandmama's cruel comparisons made it impossible. Morna hated being second best.

All those years after Alana's desertion, she had finally come into her own. She was thought of as a good and fair ruler. Though she would never win any popularity contests for her personality, nor would anyone say they liked Morna as a friend, she was a very capable queen. Morna loved her people as a whole but individually, that was a different story.

If any one of her subjects ever found out she was a part of this plot, she would lose her crown. She lived her life in a fishbowl and was responsible for her actions. It was almost impossible to keep things a secret. The only thing she had going in her favor was that Asgar shared the same risk. He would no more tell this tale than Morna would.

She couldn't see Asgar from where she was standing but knew he was there. He and that awful bird. He had as much at stake as she did so she knew he was close by. They both were waiting for their cue. Anytime now she would be summoned. Then she heard the scream. All was going well. Morna smiled.

Cindy stared into the face of the assailant. It was Justin's double. Beside him were Wayne, John, Chuck, and two Carmens. Cindy guessed the real Carmen was the one tied and gagged. No wonder she didn't sound the alert. She thought Wayne, John, and Chuck were the real thing. They had broken in through a second floor window, that hadn't been covered over with steel yet.

The doubles were dressed in the same clothing the real people had worn the day before. Had her true friends not been with her in the room, there would've been no way they could have told the difference.

"Let her go," screamed Cindy.

"Or we'll spray you with iron powder," added John.

Justin the changeling laughed. "Go ahead. It will hurt her more than it will me. Iron doesn't affect us in human form."

Justin looked at Cindy in a knowing way. He shook his head and Cindy had to stifle the tears that were welling inside her.

"Why?" she asked. "Who put you up to this?"

Morna sashayed into the room followed by the darkcat, Shalimar. The Wayne changeling had unlocked the front door. The kids backed away and even the changelings stepped backwards.

"Need you ask? Why, Asgar of course. You totally humiliated him, Cindy. Did you think he would take this lying down? He's a man that's used to getting what he wants and he wants you."

"What do you want, Morna? You helped me get away from him before. What changed? What's in this for you?"

"The safety and well-being of all of you. I am the queen and I look after all my subjects. With my help you can defeat Asgar."

"Like you tried to help Bobby? And what do you expect in return?"

"I'm hurt that you should think like that." Morna reached down and stroked the cat. "Where I come from, we exchange favors. That way everyone gets something. It's only fair."

"Now we're talking. What did you have in mind?"

"Nothing at the moment. I'm not concerned with my needs at the moment. It's you kids I care about and of course, my dear sister."

"You don't care a thing about her or anyone else. All you care about is you. Why it wouldn't surprise me if I found out that you were a part of this. How else would you know when to come in?"

Justin had to hold onto Cindy to keep her from rushing Morna. He had never seen her so mad. "Calm down. Don't let the anger blind you."

"That's good advice, Justin," said Morna.

"I didn't ask for your opinion and answer her question. How did you know this was going on?"

Morna glared at him. "I know everything that goes on in this kingdom. I have spies everywhere. You kids are lucky that I keep a close watch, otherwise you'd be on your own. I didn't have to come here. Actually, it's to my advantage for Alana to be disposed of. But she is my sister and I care about her. I've come to help. So why shouldn't I make a bit in the deal?"

"You know we won't deal with the unknown. If you want something, then ask for it, if not, then leave and we'll handle this on our own," Justin said.

Morna straightened her posture and strolled down the empty space separating the changelings from the kids. "There is one little thing I want. One itsy, bitsy, teeny, weeny little thing. A promise."

"Get to the point, Morna," shouted Justin.

"Cindy, give up your rights to the throne. Sign this little document here and Alana goes free." Morna procured a scroll out of thin air and flipped it open with a flick of her wrist.

"It's for your own benefit. Not only will Alana go free, but it will also release Asgar's hold on you. If you've no claim on the throne, he has no reason to marry you."

Cindy looked at Justin and then at her grandmother. Alana was desperately trying to say something. She could hear the muffled cries even though Justin the changeling's hand clamped tighter around her grandmother's mouth.

"Alana doesn't want you to do that," Justin said. "Say no."

Cindy looked at him and then at everyone else in the room. "Maybe it's for the best. Morna's right. Asgar will give up on me if I relinquish my rights of succession. We'd all be safe. I've never wanted to rule. I don't even want to be here. I'm going to sign it, Grandma. Forgive me, but your safety is the most important thing in the world."

Morna smiled. "You are smart, as well as beautiful. But of course this would be so, as you're family."

She handed Cindy the parchment and Cindy walked over to the oil lamp to read. It was pretty much what Morna said it was. She was forfeiting all rights and privileges to rule Wildsidhe, and that included her offspring and all other generations from now until forever.

"Do I sign in blood?"

"Ink will do child. You've read too many fairy tales."

Cindy was about to touch quill to paper when Asgar burst through the door.

"You're a liar, Morna, and you'll burn in the Shadowlands for deceiving me."

Morna turned to face the intruder. "I have no idea what you're talking about. How dare you threaten my sister and her family? It is you who will reap what you sow. Harming a Fortesan is a punishable crime. Especially your queen."

Asgar's eyes were filled with a fire. "It's you who are turning everything around. My changelings are to incapacitate her, not hurt her. As soon as I have my bride we'll be gone. The deal is off. You're on your own. Cindy, come to me."

As the two Fortesans struck verbal blows, Justin struggled to hustle

Cindy as far away from Asgar as he could get her. Back in Asgar's presence, the spell of the Evals powder was working again. Cindy fought him every step of the way until they were out of Asgar's sight. "Stay here and don't move. You won't be any help if you're trying to go with Asgar."

Cindy nodded and sat down on a chair. "I just feel so helpless."

Justin was gone before he had heard Cindy's comment. He had no idea what was going on, but knew enough not to believe either one of the High Fortesans.

"Let's just make this a peaceful visit. Cindy comes with me, Alana is set free, and Morna and her cats go home. Simple. No one gets hurt."

"Cindy isn't going anywhere and both of you and your goons are going to leave peacefully. Get out, now, and leave us alone," Justin said.

"Brave and stupid," said Asgar shaking his head. "Let's go and take the old woman with you. I had so hoped this could have been accomplished with little fuss, but you've made your choice. Now I get Alana and Cindy."

The changelings, who had been standing quietly took their silent cue and rushed into the crowd of children. It became impossible to distinguish them from the real kids, except for the ones who were rushing toward Cindy.

Terri took off in her wheelchair and zipped to Cindy, arriving moments before the changelings. She hurried Cindy on her lap and the two took off, hovering as close to the ceiling as they could get.

"Thanks Terri," Cindy said.

"Don't thank me yet. It's not over by a long shot. Asgar won't be easy to beat. Trust me, I've fought him. Just watch. If things start looking bad, we can make a mad dash for the door."

Things did look bad. There was utter confusion. No one knew who was who. Wayne and Justin exchanged a knowing glance and the two of them rushed their doubles in an attempt to free Alana. Morna caught sight of what was going on and released Shalimar. The huge cat leapt in the air and landed between them. Both of the boys marveled at the animal's agility. The jump had to be more than twenty feet.

Shalimar snarled and bared her white, sharp fangs. Her whiskers twitched and eyes seemed to be challenging them.

"Aim down," yelled Justin and Wayne nodded.

The powdered iron sprayed out forcefully, covering the cat's face and getting in her eyes. Shalimar howled in pain and shook her head back forth, pawing at her eyes. Morna screamed. It was if she felt the pain herself.

Morna ran to her kitty's side, prying open the shut lids of her pet. The cat fought her efforts and clawed her by accident leaving a bloody gash on Morna's arm.

"You idiots! You'll pay for this."

Morna stood up and began to mumble some words, but in the few moments they had after wounding the cat, both Wayne and Justin had been able to free to Alana. Instead of facing the two boys, Morna ended up eye to eye with her sister.

"Don't go there, sister," said Alana. "Don't make this a blood match. You do care about losing the crown and if you harm me, I'll see that everyone on the council finds out. I, on the other hand, have nothing to lose, so don't press your odds."

Morna dropped her hands and glared. "I had no intentions of harming you. In fact, the only reason I came here at all was to offer assistance. I had no idea Asgar was going to go after you also."

"Pish tosh. You know what everyone is up too, you nosy old hag."

"Look who's calling whom, old," snapped Morna.

Wayne and Justin rushed into the crowd using the distraction to make their move, but they had to be careful. They were limited to fighting their doubles just to be on the safe side. From where they stood, there was no way to tell the difference between a changeling and a human.

Outside, the loud cries from Maelstrom pierced the skies. The bird was much too big to get inside, but he was out there waiting to join in the attack, should anyone try to escape. Asgar in the meantime was trying to pull Terri down with a magical net. Terri was fast and capable of dodging it, but Wayne could tell from her facial expression that she was tiring.

"She's not going to be able to do this much longer. We have to do something," Wayne said.

The two boys rushed at Asgar, but they bounced off him. The light that surrounded him protected him from harm's way. They could do little but watch helplessly. Asgar succeeded in netting the chair and he lowered it to the floor. Before they could do anything, Cindy was in the danger zone. His love spell kicked in and she ran into his awaiting arms.

Asgar held her closely in his arms. He turned and smiled. "Thanks everyone. You can all go home now."

The changelings stopped fighting and made a mad dash for the door. There was nothing anyone could do. Justin didn't want to spray Asgar with the powder as long as Cindy was in his arms. They started to follow him but the changelings stood guard at the steps and prevented them from passing.

"Get Alana," screamed Ron. "She'll know what to do."

Ron and Chuck yelled as loudly as they could. Alana, who had lost sight of what was going on, spun around and ran for the door. "We'll discuss this later, Morna. I don't know what the two of you had planned, but it won't take long to find out."

Alana ran to her mattress and pulled out her totem. "Let's get moving.

We have to stop Asgar before he gets to that bird."

As soon as the changelings saw Alana running down the hall, they scattered. Justin and the others followed, shoving the few that still stood in their way down the steps. As soon as they reached the outside of the building Alana waved them off.

The totem, in hand, began to glow. Instantly, Champ appeared followed by another unicorn. They seemed to appear out of thin air. After a few seconds there were six more beautiful, majestic creatures.

Alana scrambled on the back of Champ and ordered the other kids to follow. They didn't have to be told twice. Justin and Wayne mounted first, followed by Ron, Carmen, and the Bearclaw brothers.

"Let's get Asgar before he takes flight. The only thing we have in our favor is the bird needs a lot of empty space to land and it seems to remember how you blasted it the last time it came too close to the windows. Head for the intersection of Grand and Brewer. It's the closest," yelled Alana as the unicorn began to set his pace. Everyone riding a unicorn followed. The other kids, including Terri who was exhausted from staying aloft so long, stood guard by the door.

"Get him, Champ," whispered Alana as she leaned down. "We must save Cindy at any cost."

From a distance they could hear the rush of wind as the huge bird flew over them. Alana could see Asgar running, holding onto Cindy's hand, and pulling her along. They were so far ahead of her that she could barely make out their shapes. Only the blur of colors from their clothing was recognizable.

The unicorns were fast, but the lionhawk was faster. The great creature landed just where Alana had figured it would and though they were close behind, it looked as if they weren't going to make it in time. She watched helpless as her darling granddaughter climbed upon the lionhawk's back.

Alana sat upright on Champ, digging her knees in for balance, holding onto the huge spellstone that Cindy had given her. With it tightly clutched in her fist, she began to mumble a few words. All of a sudden a huge mass of swirling, crackling, blue energy appeared before her.

The blue tornado began to suck up everything on the block, pulling up bushes and flowers in its path. The faster it moved, the more it began to grow. Sputtering and flickering bolts of energy spew forth from the twister like arms and legs as it whirled its way down the street. Everyone stopped in their tracks as the cyclone tore off nearby rooftops. All around windows shattered. The dangerous shards fell like snow. Asgar looked up in horror and so did Cindy. There was no time to get out of its way.

CHAPTER 15

It was the most amazing thing. Cindy, as well as the others, would remember the events of the next few seconds all their life. In fact, no one, not even Asgar, in the retelling of the story, could dispute the courage and bravery displayed by one they thought so selfish and evil, Morna.

From out of nowhere, Morna appeared. Her tall frame seemed so tiny when compared to the twister, but there she was standing unarmed, defiantly facing the whirlwind. When asked later how she managed to get there so fast, Morna also couldn't recall how she did it.

The twister was out of control. It was certain death for Asgar and Cindy. Morna didn't stop to think of the consequences, there wasn't time, she said later. All she said was that her kin was in danger and she had to help. She mumbled some words of a spell, and out of nowhere, appeared between the menace and Cindy.

The high, velocity wind of the cyclone encompassed the queen; the light radiating from it was blinding. After gobbling her up, it dissipated, but not before exploding into a barrage of burning branches of electricity.

Rooftops caught fire; the surrounding trees split in half. Deafening thunder roared so loudly that for hours afterward, the kids could still hear the ringing in their ears. Morna seemed to be engulfed by the windy flames. Cindy screamed. Asgar ran and the lionhawk took flight. When a pillar of smoke was all that was left, the kids finally stirred. The first thing they caught sight of was Morna's pale, unconscious body.

"Is she dead?" asked Justin riding towards the motionless body.

He dismounted and so did the others who were riding unicorns. All the kids started to form a circle. Even some of the changelings stared and watched at a distance.

"I've never seen anything like it. She was so very brave."

"Don't bury me yet, humans," said Morna struggling to sit up. "I'm all right, I think. Is Asgar gone?"

"That coward took off as soon as he saw it coming," Wayne said. "Him and his chicken of a bird."

"Can anyone tell me what went on?" asked Justin. "What was that thing Alana created?"

"Grandma!" cried Cindy looking all around her. "I don't see her anywhere. Did that thing get her?"

"Help me up, kids," said Morna. "We'll find her, if there's something left to find."

It didn't take long. Champ whinnied and they followed the sound. Off to the side of one of the houses, shaded by a leafless tree, was Alana. Champ was lying on the ground beside her, a bit of fabric from her sweatshirt caught in his teeth. Somehow he managed to drag his mistress to the soft bed of grass. He fought off a trio of lionhawks before collapsing himself. Both of them looked badly burned.

Cindy ran to her. She dropped to her knees, afraid to lift the blistering head of her beloved grandmother. Instead, she bent over and whispered softly, choking on the words and praying for an answer. "Grandma, are you okay?"

Alana made a few attempts to open her eyes before succeeding. When she finally did, her voice was raspy and gurgly. "Thank heavens, child, you're all right. That's all that matters." Alana looked up and stared into the tearing eyes of her sister. "Morna, you saved her at the risk of losing your own life. I wish I could repay you."

Morna smiled. "You will, just as soon as you're better. You know I always collect on a favor."

"Oh how I wish I could. All these years I've spent thinking you hated me. Wasted. Now, at the end, I know you to be the sister that I've always wished for. If only there was more time."

"Don't talk like that. The burns will heal. We have poultices to take care of that."

Alana tried to speak again, but this time she could barely get the words out. "It's not the charred skin, it's my heart. I can't move my arms and legs. Too many years spent in a frail human body. It can't handle the strain of using so much magic. The pain..." Alana winced. "The electrical charge from that thing, I couldn't control it. We were too close. It hurt Champ so much. He wouldn't let those lionhawks hurt me, but now he's dying too."

"It can't be. Morna is alright. You're a Fortesan too. You can't die now. Not now." Cindy began to cry. "Isn't there some magic, anything that can save you?"

"Dry those tears, little darlin'. Grandma's lived and loved more than most. You should be so lucky to live the wonderful life that I've led. When I took a frail human body, I gave up my chance at a long, long life, so I made sure I had quality. I just hate the thought that I'll never see you wed with children of your own."

Cindy was crying hysterically. "Do something, Morna. Anything. Don't let her die. Just name the favor and I'll do it."

Morna stooped beside Cindy and put her arm around her. "I would do it gladly, with no payment. I love her, too. Over the years we've had our differences, but I've always held the flame of hope that we would be close friends as well as sisters someday. If my death could save her, I'd die for her. I've already proven that."

"Now stop it the two of you. If I start crying now, I'll never have the strength to make a last request and I must. For Cindy's sake."

Alana closed her eyes and started to drift. She looked pale and her breaths were shallow.

"Grandma? Grandma?" Cindy sobbed.

"I'm here, child. Hold my hand. Morna, promise me you'll do what I ask. As a Fortesan you're obligated to carry out a fellow Fortesan's deathwish, but I won't call on your sense of duty. As my sister, I beg of you to do this one last thing for me."

"Anything, Alana. Just name it and it shall be done."

"Take a piece of his horn from Champ and grind it into powder. Use it to free Cindy of Asgar's spell. And when all is said and done, give him a proper resting place. I owe him that. He served me well and was a good friend."

"Alana, I can take the unicorn powder and heal you with it. There would be more than enough to deal with Asgar's spell later. I'd forgotten how powerful unicorn magic is. It could make you better."

Alana choked and jerked. "No. That might work if I still had my Fortesan body or even a young human one. Now, even if it did work, I'd be crippled, both physically and magically. I don't want to live like that. I saw too many husks that used to be people in that nursing home. This way, I'll at least see my Howard again. Let me die in peace, knowing that Cindy will be able to live her life as she chooses. Promise me you'll do this, Morna. Promise me now."

"Of course I promise. I love you, Alana. I will carry this out immediately."

Alana gurgled. Each word became harder to hear, until finally all she was capable of doing was to whisper, "I love you both."

They were her last words. Alana took one last breath and closed her eyes. Her head fell sideways and her body went limp.

"Oh no. Grandma, don't die. Please don't leave me. I love you. I need you."

"She's dead, child," whispered Morna. The queen drew Cindy into her arms and hugged her tight. All around them the kids assembled, most of them crying too. No one knew what to say or to do.

"She was a wonderful woman, Cindy. I'm so sorry for you… and for me. I had so hoped we could become friends. I've waited all these years for her to come back to me and now she's gone. I never realized how much I loved her, until now."

Cindy sniffled and stood up. She looked at Morna through a blur of tear stained eyes. "Love? What do you know about love? Love is unselfish. Love means doing things for others without there being anything in it for you. If you hadn't been helping Asgar, none of this would have happened. You may have learned something by all this, but it's too late. Alana is gone and it's all your fault, Morna. Someday you will live to regret this. Though she didn't die by your hands, she is dead because of you and I hold you responsible. I'll never forgive you."

Morna overlooked the scathing words from her niece. She knew that they were spoken out of anger and half-truths. Perhaps keeping her promise would help to mend things between them. She was, after all, her aunt.

Later that evening, accompanied by Penrod, they arrived at the school building. Wayne opened the gate and let them in and led the way to the room where Alana was stretched on a table. Winklo was almost finished preparing the body for her funeral. When she saw Morna, she moved away.

Cindy looked up, watching them enter and said nothing. Justin stood beside her, his arm around her tightly. "Hello, Morna," he said.

It was Penrod who spoke. He stretched out his arm, introducing himself and conveyed his condolences. "Morna has something for you, Cindy."

"I don't want anything. Not from her," Cindy said.

"Please, allow her to fulfill your grandmother's last wishes. Do it for Alana, else she died in vain."

Cindy nodded. Justin stepped back. Everyone stopped to watch was going to happen. Morna stepped over to Cindy, pulling out a small, golden horn that she had tucked under her cloak.

"This is the gift of the unicorn. Not just any unicorn, though all are special. This belonged to Champ, her life-long friend and companion. Even in his last moments, he dragged his Mistress to safety and gave his life to protect her. The love he had for her makes this even more powerful. It will free you of Asgar's hold on you."

Morna tilted the horn over Cindy's head and the shimmering dust sprinkled over her in a golden shower. The particles glittered, bathing Cindy in light and she shivered and tingled as the particles touched her skin.

Cindy felt euphoric. For those few moments she felt free from all the pain and sorrow that had encompassed her. Every inch of her body quivered and those around her saw her take on a glow.

When the dust evaporated, Morna returned to Penrod's side. "You are safe from Asgar now. The healing properties of the unicorn will last a while. Enjoy Champ's gift."

"Thank you, Morna," Justin said.

"You're welcome. It's the very least I can do. I hope we can make peace. Cindy, will you forgive me?" She handed her the remains of the horn.

Cindy looked at the queen. "Only for her sake and only because she forgave you also. If she could find it in heart to love you in her dying moments, it's the least I can do. Thank you, Morna."

"No, thank you, Cindy. I'd like to make it all up to you if I can. Will you allow me to take her to hallowed ground and give her a proper Fortesan funeral?"

Cindy shook her head. "She belongs with us now. We will give her a fitting ceremony. You are more than welcome to attend. Tomorrow, at noon."

"We shall be there," said Morna.

Morna turned to leave, but Penrod was missing. In the gym, the Bearclaw brothers and Bobby Shelly were playing a basketball game against Bobby's twin sister Tina, Ron, and his sister Miko. Penrod had wandered in, and asked if he could play. Apparently, Chuck had offered to play him when he had met them during their rescue of Bobby. They agreed. He was on the Bearclaw team, while Carmen went on the Wang sibling's team to even out the sides. Penrod had the height advantage by about ten inches and once Chuck showed him how to slam dunk, it took Morna almost an hour to get him to leave.

Meanwhile, Cindy and Justin had stayed with Alana's body. "I'd like to be alone with her, if I may," she said as tears, once again, began to well in her eyes.

They left her alone, even though Winklo was not quite finished with the preparations. Justin stood outside the door. He too was crying, but did his best to keep from showing it. A great woman had died today trying to protect them. She would be missed.

CHAPTER 16

Nash headed out early in the morning accompanied by Wayne, Terri, Carmen, and Chuck. Cindy had wanted Alana buried near the garden, as she wanted her close, but other than take up valuable space there was no vacant area nearby that wasn't forested.

"What do we do?" asked Wayne. "There isn't enough time to cut down these trees."

"Allow me," said Nash. "It's time I earned my keep."

The kids stood back and watched as Nash performed his magic. Nash spoke with the trees and they listened. It was an amazing sight to see the trees hoist their roots from the ground and shuffle off into the distance. Wayne and the others were totally speechless. Nash just smiled.

"Where do you want them?" he asked.

"Over there," pointed Terri. "Could they form a semi-circle? Alana could rest in the shelter of their branches."

"Easy," said Nash as he commanded the birch trees to move. One by one the roots dug their way back in the soil. The branches entwined themselves and it looked as if they were holding hands. It was spectacular as they wove their limbs in and out, knitting a blanket of shelter that would mark the final resting-place of a great woman.

"Cindy will be so pleased. Thank you so much. Do you think, later, we could clear another area for planting?"

"You bet," said Nash. "As much as you need and I can help with the planting and their growth. Vegetation is my business. I was the chief gardener of the Enchanted Gardens of Curn. Held that position through four elections."

"We've never ventured far from the school," Terri said, "Maybe someday you can take us there. We'd love to see it."

"That would be great. I'd love to."

"I guess we better head back and tell the others we're ready. I can stay and dig a grave," Wayne said.

"A grave? What's that?" asked Nash.

"We bury our loved ones in the earth. Ashes to ashes, dust to dust. It's our custom."

"No, no, no," said Nash. "Can't do that here. People would grow."

"Grow? Into what?" asked Carmen.

"Don't know and don't want to know."

"Then what do we do?"

"There are many options. I'll build her a wooden altar. We set the body on it. It's high enough off the ground to keep the creatures away. Wildsidhe will claim her body. It's hard to explain, and it only happens for High Fortesans. You'll just have to see it."

"I'm not sure Cindy will like it," Carmen said.

"Don't worry about that. I'm sure once she understands she'll be okay with it," said Chuck. "Native Americans used to have similar customs. My grandfather told me about them. I'm sure it will be very beautiful."

"It will be," said Nash. "I promise."

And it was. The sun was shining brightly and the sky was of the deepest turquoise. White fluffy clouds, like cotton candy tufts, floated in the warm, gentle breeze. All the children had gathered around the wooden staked altar that Nash had built. It stood eight feet off the ground and it took wooden ladders and four people to hoist Alana's body to the blanketed bed atop that Nash had prepared.

Morna arrived with Penrod. They said their hellos and stood off to the side, a bit of a distance away from the kids. Lissy and her friends hovered nearby. Everyone made their greetings and then just stood there. None of the children had a clue what to do.

Nash whispered in Justin's ear. "Everyone needs to go to the foot of the altar and make their good-byes. It's the custom. I can start if you like."

Justin nodded and Winklo and Nash went up together. Justin followed and one by the others bid the great woman good-bye. Even the pixies, who weren't acquainted with Alana, wished her a safe journey. When all the kids but Cindy had said their piece, Morna took her place.

"We had so little time, sister, to bury the past. Still, I stand here grateful for those last few moments we did share. I was wrong in plotting against you, but I never planned to do you harm. Perhaps that is my punishment for being too competitive. I've lost the chance to enjoy a friendship with you. To make up for all the years we fought."

Morna began to cry. "May your journey be a safe one. All of Wildsidhe will mourn your loss. Forever and a day will I hold the memory and the love we shared and keep them safe within my heart."

Morna stood there sobbing, clinging to the wooden posts. She had tried to bring Asgar to trial for his hand in the slaying of a High Fortesan, but it looked like he would get off on two technicalities. One, over fifty years ago Alana had used her powers to make herself human and she had not changed herself back. Technically, she was human, not a Fortesan. He also argued that the lionhawks had slain her *after* he had left the scene, so they were no longer acting on his orders. Asgar claimed they were merely defending themselves against the unicorn and Alana was unlucky enough to get in the way. No one truly believed him, but Morna had not been able to prove he was lying either.

Penrod had to pry her hands loose to escort her away from the altar. She buried her head in his shoulder and the king held his queen tight.

Morna didn't even turn to watch as Cindy made her way up to say her good-bye.

She spoke softly as she stood facing the shrine. Tears streamed down her face and the anguish she felt choked her as the words came tumbling out.

"Wherever it is that you are going, may your voyage be peaceful. I hope that I can honor you by being the type of person you'd have been proud of. Every moment of our time here together will be cherished. I love you, Grandma, and I will miss you most of all."

Cindy stood there speechless. She was crying so hard that Justin had to pull her into his arms. Her head rested on his chest and he comforted her the best he could, wiping her tears with his fingers. He too was crying softly. All of the kids were.

They stood there quiet, surrounded by the eerie silence. Even the wind ceased to blow. No insects buzzed; no clouds moved. It was if the land had stopped in its tracks.

"Why don't we head back to the school? It might even be a nice gesture inviting Morna," Justin said. "Terri is going to try to convince her or Penrod to marry Nash and Winklo. If that's okay with you…"

Cindy pulled back and nodded. "Go ahead. I just want to stay a bit longer. I need some time to be alone."

Justin nodded. He kissed Cindy sweetly on the cheek and left to ask Morna if she wanted to join them back in the gym. Morna gratefully declined. She too wanted some time to reflect and left with Penrod. Morna had to literally pull him away, as the Bearclaws had invited him to play another game of basketball. He had agreed to perform the wedding in a few days' time.

The others followed Justin after he motioned for them all to leave.

Cindy stood at the foot of the altar, moving backwards just far enough to see the body of her grandmother lying on the soft blankets. It was so hard facing the facts that she would never be able to talk to her again. None of it seemed real.

She fingered the silver unicorn hanging around her neck and remembered the day her Grandma had created it for her. It seemed like eons ago.

Tears began to stream her face once again, burning the tender skin of her raw cheeks. She wondered if she would ever stop crying, when she heard a whisper. Cindy sniffled and looked around. No one was around.

She shrugged it off and decided that it was probably a good time to go back. Her friends were there and she needed to feel the warmth of their presence. As she turned in the opposite direction to head home she heard the sound again. This time, as she stared at the altar, things looked different.

It was aglow. A rainbow of colors arched over the body of Alana. The radiant light kept expanding and soon Cindy herself was encompassed in it. That's when she thought she saw Alana move. Even rubbing her eyes didn't change the vision. Her grandmother was standing by one of the posts.

Cindy started to run to the image. Alana looked so lovely, she was at least fifty years younger and looked exactly like the bride in the wedding portrait on her mother's dresser. Alana took her in her arms and though Cindy couldn't feel a body, she felt the warmth.

"I'll always be with you, little one. Not in body, but in soul. Now dry those tears and get on with your life. Justin's a fine boy and someday he'll make a good husband. Just be happy. It's not so bad here. Make the most of it. You'll have a chance to return to Sparta someday, but maybe by then you won't want to. You have roots here too. But, whatever you do, live life to the fullest. Enjoy all that it has to offer and never, ever forget that I'm with you always.

"I want you to have this. In all the hubbub of the past day, both Morna and you have forgotten the totem. I want you to have it. Guard it well. It is my legacy to you. And now I must go. It is time. I love you."

Alana disappeared and with her went the rainbow. The wind began to blow once more and the clouds started to turn gray. Cindy stood there staring in disbelief for a few minutes before heading back. Every few steps she would stop to glance at the altar to see if her Grandma would return. When she was far enough away she noticed the body had disappeared. Cindy sighed.

Alana was with her. She could feel her presence everywhere, from the cooling breeze that whipped through her hair to the sweet songs the birds were chirping. She was clutching tight the figurine of a unicorn. It had changed a bit from when she had seen it last. There was still a unicorn, but it looked different. Its horn had a unique twist.

She would call on the magical creature as soon as things settled down. He or she would be hers. The thought of having her own unicorn for a friend brought a smile to her face. It would be a new beginning and it would need a name. Grandma had called it her legacy and she would name it that. Legacy. It was her parting gift, a legacy of unicorns.

THE UNDERCOVER DRAGON

BOOK 5

Tony DiGerolamo

CHAPTER 1

Special Agent Robert Ficarro was surprised that his theater experience came in so handy for the cover up. Orchestrating an operation of this magnitude reminded him of the last, hurried hours of his production of *Much Ado About Nothing"* during his senior year in college. Yes, this was no mere theater of operations, but theater in its most raw and earnest form. He would convince thousands of people, the entire population of Sparta, Pennsylvania, that a gas pipe explosion – a silent gas pipe explosion – had engulfed just one small section of the town and vaporized three hundred children as well.

The buildings did not disappear, they exploded and burned away. The mysterious subject, Asgar, was not some otherworldly being, but an arsonist who perished in the explosion. Children did not continue to disappear due to the original incident, but rather, disappeared for completely unrelated reasons. And, finally, the 18 year-old, Ken Holt, who was recently released from FBI custody, did not return from this "other world." He had suffered head trauma and delusions as a result of being injured in the explosion.

Probably the best thing Robert had going for him was that the parents of the missing children now wanted to believe the gas pipe story. This truly was the tragedy of the disappearance of the children of Sparta. After months of having the entire town quarantined from the rest of the world, after weeks of interrogation by strange men in black suits from Washington, after countless sleepless nights trying to rectify the bizarre events in Sparta using their own personal experience, most of the exhausted parents now yearned for a sensible explanation. Any sensible explanation would give them closure and allow some semblance of normalcy to return to their lives.

The memorial was the lynch pin to Ficarro's entire plan. With the entire town paying homage to the missing children this way, they could at least get on with their lives. And if that didn't work, Ficarro's only other alternative was Plan B. His boss's plan. The risky plan.

Plan B was a long shot and Ficarro had fought his superiors against it. Plan B was originally Plan A, but Ficarro's well-practiced, even-tempered voice had convinced the boss otherwise. The FBI would calm the parents, cover up the incident, and then work on the solution in secret. Plan B would be set on the back burner, never to be enacted thanks to Ficarro's brilliant work. And even if they never rescued the 300 kids, Ficarro could still walk out of Sparta saying, "At least we put a lid on it."

The first part of the memorial went off flawlessly. Four dozen yellow road blockers lined the suburban street leading to the barren spot at the edge of town. The buses began arriving at 3pm, delivering the emotionally drained citizens of Sparta to a cordoned off area surrounded by 200 agents in black suits. Additionally, Ficarro had provided a sort of buffet consisting of pitchers of ice water, single cut roses, and pamphlets listing the missing children and their accomplishments. He hoped, quite correctly, the pamphlets would occupy the attention of the mourners for most of the ceremony.

Two of the seniors from the high school, Peter Grant and Tanesha DeSilver, would lay a wreath on the barren spot, there would be a prayer led by a local pastor, and then one by one the mourners would file past the wreath and get on a bus. Ficarro knew a speech would only rile up the town and there were far too many missing children to choose who or when or what the speeches would be about. Ficarro even provided two "reporters" (actually two of his men) who would pretend to cover the event with TV cameras. Yes, this is all perfectly normal. Just another disaster for the evening news and it's best you go home and try to put it out of your brain.

That had been Ficarro's plan all along. Over-sentimentalize it. Over-empathize. Over-console the townspeople. Push them ever further into wanting to forget the whole event. As the memorial started, Agent Debra Glass, Ficarro's right hand, coordinated the last few buses, then joined Ficarro at their pre-arranged "grassy knoll."

"The last bus is here," she reported flatly. "It's going to work, Robert," Debra said in a way that Ficarro knew meant, "Stop being nervous, it's fine."

"Give it two minutes, then it's show time," Ficarro instructed. "How's the reception hall?"

"Good, good," reported Debra. "Plenty of turkey sandwiches. Should make the most of them logy enough for bed before nine."

"I'm ready for bed right now," Ficarro sighed in exasperation. "How's the perimeter?"

"Rob," Debra said, her voice betraying annoyance. "Everyone's here and the fence is ten feet high with barbed wire."

Ficarro felt his stomach churning and popped another antacid. For a change, he felt it work almost immediately. As Grant and DeSilver lifted the wreath, one of Ficarro's men began playing soft church music. The volume was perfect. Families cried and hugged one another. Some, too distraught, got back on one of the buses. Ficarro's whole body relaxed. It was working. It was really working and he might even be able to start one bus on its way early.

"Thank God," Ficarro muttered to Debra. "With any luck, we could be back in D.C. and out of this Mayberry before Thursday."

Then, it happened. Grant and DeSilver crossed the threshold of the barren land, the land which had once held the rest of Sparta, several houses, a strip mall, and a school. The land which Ficarro had carefully scattered with debris to make it appear to have been a gas pipe explosion. The land which had been quarantined for months and that Ficarro had tried desperately to pass off as "normal."

But this wasn't normal land. Grant and DeSilver were suddenly encased in a shimmering blue light. Ficarro could just make out Grant saying, "What the...?" and DeSilver looking back at her mother, then poof! A cry of alarm and despair rippled across the citizenry of Sparta, Pennsylvania, even before the wreath hit the ground.

Ficarro's stomach churned so hard, he thought the stomach acid would start shooting out of the back of his spine. It was perfect and now it had all blown up in his face. Once again, he'd have over 2000 angry people on his hands and no explanation to give them. Once again, he'd have to call his superiors and try to explain, yet another bizarre event that occurred in Sparta, Pennsylvania. And, worst of all...

It was time for Plan B.

CHAPTER 2

Jamal Nichols hated high school with the sort of casual rage normally reserved for Christmas carolers and telephone solicitors. It wasn't enough that John Hancock High School was staffed with a slow, half-witted teaching staff that created such innovative programs as "Fire Prevention Poster Week" followed by "Fire Prevention Essay Week." Jamal also had to deal with the student body, who found the first week a challenge.

Apathetic and wandering, the senior class of John Hancock never seemed to tire of inane pep rallies for their basketball team (which had more losses than any other in Philadelphia), fighting in the cafeteria and, of course, the old joke of stealing the "H-A-N" on the sign in front of the school. It was the fighting that had brought Jamal. He was here to investigate as a special attachment to the Drug Enforcement Agency, or DEA.

Normally, the DEA never used agents as young as Jamal, but he was an exception as he had sued to be emancipated as an adult at 14. Graduating high school at 15 and college at 17, Jamal was working toward being the youngest field agent ever to graduate from Quantico and join the FBI. With his clean shaven head and precisely trimmed goatee, Jamal's athletic build would also let him pass for an adult, if need be. Everything Jamal did was done with the control and precision of the Tang Soo Karate he was so fond of practicing. Although Jamal felt he would be of more use infiltrating one of the L.A. drug gangs, his superiors had sent him to this inner city school to investigate the fighting at John Hancock and the rumors of an infiltration by the B-Dogs street gang.

Although there had been a shooting and a gang presence two years prior, since then, school officials had installed metal detectors and security guards. A crackdown on student violence had worked on almost every part of the school except the cafeteria. The administration had had to cut the budget to hire security guards, so the cafeteria aids were grossly understaffed. Aids wouldn't stop fights, so much as wrangle them and keep them from spreading.

Jamal's superiors had outfitted him with gang colors. Jamal ditched them immediately. This would be a dead giveaway to the students. Instead, he dressed in slightly above-average street clothes, all name brand, $400 sneakers and, of course, a genuine Rolex watch he bought during his trip to Germany.

Procedure dictated that Jamal locate and identify gang members, then infiltrate their group. Again, this was a dead giveaway. Jamal attended the school for two weeks and did nothing. He wasn't anti-social, but mostly kept to himself. But everywhere he went, he wore that Rolex watch.

By the end of the first day, he had two offers for dates. By the end of the week, he had an underclassman by the name of Huey opening and closing his locker for him. By the end of the second week, the entire school was convinced he was a player, definitely a drug dealer, and possibly connected to the mob. The imagined rep eventually earned him an introduction.

"Mr. Dime –" Jamal had been given a new identity when he went undercover. "I'm Tyree Allen," greeted the well-dressed student with bemused arrogance. "You can call me Tread. This is Abdul and Mr. Tillman."

The threesome had approached Jamal and Huey at Jamal's locker. Huey bristled nervously. Tread had on a suit, hat, and carried an expensive cane. Abdul and Tillman were obviously his muscle.

"W'sup, dog?" said Abdul, as if it was a threat.

Tillman greeted Huey roughly, pushing his hair out of place and knocking his baseball cap to the floor.

With a tap of his cane, Tread stopped the duo from going any further. Huey looked back and forth between Jamal and Tread nervously. Jamal looked back at Tread, bored.

"Rumor has it that you are a business man, like myself. Here at John Hancock, I am the sultan of all business transactions, legal and otherwise," smiled Tread. "Perhaps we can do business together."

"C'mon, yo!" added Abdul aggressively.

"I don't know what you're talkin' about," Jamal replied calmly. "I'm just here to go to class and get good grades."

Tread picked up Jamal's hand and examined his Rolex.

"Well, your grades must be outstandin'."

Abdul and Tillman laughed. Jamal pulled his hand away and gestured for Huey to follow him. "C'mon, Huey," he added. Jamal had tried his best to steer Huey clear of criminal activity, but he could only do so much under the circumstances.

"Mr. Dime," insisted Tread, his impatience showing. "Philadelphia is a dangerous city. Man needs to protect himself. You protect yourself, Mr. Dime? You protect the little brother, here?"

Jamal turned back and bristled. He came face to face with Tread.

"What do you want?" asked Jamal cautiously.

"To do business with you," Tread said innocently.

"You holdin' weight?"

"How heavy you wanna be?"

"Very heavy. I do a lot of business."

"Meet me on the block with two large and you'll be fat and all that."

After school, Jamal couldn't create a convincing story to keep Huey out of the line of fire, so he posted him two blocks away at a Mickey Dee's to keep look out. Of course, one block ahead of him, was a van full of the DEA's finest, including Jamal's supervisor and mentor, Lt. Myra Bells. Myra sat in the van communicating with Jamal via a head set he wore, which was disguised as a Bluetooth headset. An additional mike was made of a thin mesh and was sewn in the fabric of Jamal's shirt. Myra had an addiction to vending machine cinnamon buns, the wrappers of which littered her space in the van.

"You ready to bust these knuckleheads?" Myra asked, as Jamal exited through the gym.

"Yeah," mumbled Jamal, just audible enough for the mike. "But I think we're missing something. Should I hold off?"

"Too late, they spotted you. Maybe a few days in a cell and Mr. Tread will become chatty."

"The Block," as it was known to the students, was a row of abandoned store fronts, a block away from the high school. It was the usual scene of hijinks, graffiti, smoking, drugs, and whatever else wouldn't fly in the school. Jamal made his prearranged hand signal to Huey, then they shuffled over to Tread and his boys, who were standing in a store vestibule that was full of trash.

"You got your money, G?" demanded Abdul.

Jamal flashed a wad of hundred dollar bills.

"Show me what you got," Jamal instructed.

"What I got is state-of-the-art. Plastic guns. Can't no metal detectors sense these. We've been carryin' all day," bragged Tread.

"Plastic?" said Jamal in disbelief.

With his guys blocking the view of passersby, Tread opened a briefcase containing several pistols. Jamal examined one. They were far too light for guns. When Jamal opened the chamber, he found it was full of tiny yellow pellets.

"These are BB guns," Jamal said in disbelief.

"Are you kidding me?" he heard Myra say over the headset.

"Yo, straight up. These look like the real thing, know-what-I'm-sayin'? All you gotta do is flash it. And since no one else gets guns past the metal detector, we can rule the school. You set us up, we'll do the work."

Tread's bodyguards nodded anxiously. Jamal stifled a laugh.

"So let me get this straight," said Jamal, dropping any pretense. "You guys don't sell drugs and all the guns you got are these?"

"Drugs?" Tread said a bit bewildered, as Myra's van rolled up. "All the real gangstas moved up to Philadelphia Regional High last year. But with you and us joinin' forces, we gonna blow up. That's why we want to roll with you."

"Roll with me? You mean, you want to..."

"Join your posse, Mr. Dime. Just give us a chance," said Tread earnestly.

When Myra and the rest of the cops jumped out of the van, Jamal almost felt sorry for the three wanna-be criminals. Mr. Tillman surrendered immediately, while Abdul broke down and cried. Tread was a little more resistant, too stunned by the arrest to do anything else but plead, "Please! Please don't tell my moms! Please!"

"I don't believe this," said Jamal to Myra, a few minutes later. "How's this gonna look on a report?"

Myra offered him half of cinnamon bun, but he waved it away. "Look at it this way," consoled Myra, through the dough and frosting. "We found the one inner city school in America that apparently doesn't have a drug problem. Believe it or not, that's the best news any of us can hope for, Jamal."

"What's that?"

"That one day, we won't be needed anymore."

Huey, who had bolted at the first sign of the police, now wandered back, stunned that his hero was one of them.

"Hey," suggested Myra. "Why don't you do the honors of telling Principal Ricki his school is safe from the 'B-B gang.' I'm going to talk to HQ about getting you enrolled in Philadelphia Regional."

"Yes, ma'am."

Jamal turned, walked over to Huey and put his arm on his shoulder.

"You're one of them? You're 5-O?" asked Huey, disappointed. "I knew a real gangsta wouldn't make me do my homework."

"Hey, you listen here," instructed Jamal, surprised at how much he suddenly sounded like his father. "You see what happened to those knuckleheads? They didn't do their homework. I did my homework and I graduated at 15. Finished college six months ago."

"How old are you?"

"I'll be eighteen in two weeks. In a few months, I start my training at the FBI Academy in Quantico. Next year, I'm buying a new car. By the time I qualify to become a field agent, I should have my own house. Get married in ten years, have two kids. By age 42, I'll have enough for a pension. I'll start my own security business. Retire to Jamaica at 50."

"Damn, Jamal! You mapped out your whole life!"

"I got a plan, my brother, and you need to get one too."

"I don't know if I can plan that far. How about I just graduate first?"

"Deal."

The twosome entered the hall in front of Principal Ricki's office. There was a long silence, as Huey thought and then said, "Can FBI agents afford Lamborghini's?"

Blam!

The report of the assault rifle thundered down the hall, rattling the ancient student lockers. Jamal immediately pushed Huey to the floor and protected him. Just inside the principal's office, Jamal spotted Wilfred Lomes, aiming the gun at a distraught Principal Ricki. Wilfred was an honor student that was in Jamal's algebra class.

"See what you made me do?!" ranted Wilfred.

"Huey," whispered Jamal intently. "Go back outside and find the heavy set woman I was talking to. Tell her what's happening and then stay outside."

"What are you going to do?"

"I'm just going to talk to him, now go."

Reluctantly, Huey ran out the front door with the rest of the students that happened to be in the area. Jamal could hear Principal Ricki pleading inside.

"Wilfred!It's Bobby Dime!" called Jamal, using his undercover name.

"Who?!"

"Bobby from algebra!"

Just then, Myra and the rest of the team took a position just outside the school. Jamal gestured for them to stay back.

"Get out of here, Bobby," said Wilfred, choking back some tears. "I like you, man, don't make me hurt you!"

Myra was gesturing for Jamal to move towards her, but he waved her away.

"I'm coming around the corner, Wil. I just want to talk, okay?"

"No!"

"C'mon, man. I let you copy that question off me on Friday's test. You owe me that, at least."

Wilfred shifted uneasily, then relented.

"Walk around with your hands up!"

Jamal peered around the corner slowly. Ricki's secretary was hiding under her desk and Principal Ricki lay at the doorway to his office, holding his shoulder painfully. Wilfred aimed the assault rifle towards Jamal.

"Wil, what's going on?"

"What going on?" ranted Wilfred. "What's going on is, I am second in the senior class at John Hancock!"

"You're a smart guy. I always said..."

"No! No! Didn't you hear?! Second?! Second! At one of the lowest rated schools in the East! Second, behind that bitch Violet!"

Violet Keefe was ranked at the top of the class. She was pretty competitive and made no secret that she would grind her enemies in the dust with her whopping GPA. Even Jamal would've like to see her fail, but this? Madness. Wilfred's parents had pushed him hard to be the best, but they had pushed too hard. The fear that Wilfred might not get into an Ivy League school had sent Wilfred's father ranting and raving.

Despondent, Wilfred sulked in the basement, accidentally uncovering his father's assault rifle, which his father had carelessly left in an unlocked army footlocker. Using his "second rate" intelligence, Wilfred found the ammo, then went upstairs to confront his parents. Fortunately, his father had left with his mother trailing behind, trying to talk sense. That's when Wilfred decided to go to school, to set things "right." He followed one of the janitors in a back door to avoid the metal detector.

Jamal made eye contact with Wilfred, but he could see he was extremely agitated.

"This punk!" accused Wilfred, pointing at Ricki. "He ranked me lower! All because of gym?! Are you kidding me?! Now what am I supposed to do?!"

"Wil, I know where you're coming from..."

"Oh-oh-oh!" mocked Wilfred, threateningly. "You know, you know! You know what it's like to have your whole family depending on you to get into a good college?!"

"I know the pressures," replied Jamal sympathetic. "I know what it's like to sacrifice your life to the books. I know the feeling when you're taking an exam. You can't just pass..."

"You have to get a perfect score every time!" added Wilfred.

"Yeah, and we're not perfect!" responded Jamal.

"We're not computers!"

"My folks had a life, when do I get mine?!"

"Yeah! I-I-I can't live for them no more!"

"You're right, Wilfred, you can't. So give me, the gun."

Wilfred looked down at the rifle, as if seeing it for the first time. He dropped it on the floor in realization and horror. Then dropped to his knees, crying despondently. Jamal walked in carefully and moved the assault rifle away. Myra and the rest of the team rushed in to take care of business. Myra stopped. She and Jamal watched as they cuffed Wilfred and led him away.

"Little too close to home?" asked Myra carefully.

"Yeah," nodded Jamal. "Way too close."

Jamal handed Myra the gun and walked out in frustration. Hours later, Myra found Jamal pacing frantically beside one of the police cars. TV crews, ambulances, spectators, and police cars sat in a jumbled mess one half block away, just in front of the school.

"Yo," greeted Myra. "You're gonna wear a hole in the street."

"Do you believe this?!" gestured Jamal, towards the media circus.

"It happens. One of the parents called the news station. So what?"

"I don't want another news report about how bad the schools are. I wanted to… I thought… I just thought, that, I'd be different somehow. That I'd be a smarter cop and be able to make a difference."

Myra smiled, amused at his arrogance.

"You did, you saved Ricki, his secretary, and Wilfred."

"Yes, but that was an accident. We planned to bust drug dealers and they're not even… I couldn't plan for what Wilfred did."

"No one could. Don't blame yourself."

"Maybe the FBI's a mistake…"

"Jamal," Myra said, putting her arm on his shoulder. "You can't let this one thing rattle you. You're gonna make a difference in something, someday. Just give it some time."

Jamal smiled despite himself.

"It's a long life," assured Myra. "Try and live it one day at a time."

Just then, a couple in black business suits approached.

"Jamal Nichols?" asked the woman.

"Yes," replied Myra protectively.

"Special Agent Debra Glass, FBI," said Debra flashing her ID badge. "We need your help, Mr. Nichols. And we don't have a lot of time. Would you mind coming with us, sir?"

"What's this about?"

"I'm afraid you'll have to be debriefed on the way," explained Debra solemnly, then looking at Myra. "It's a matter of national security."

"What?" said Myra in disbelief. "Uh-uh, no way. You have to…"

"We've already cleared the paperwork with your superiors, lieutenant. I assure you, Jamal will be working with the best."

"Are you okay with this?" Myra asked Jamal.

"Yeah," Jamal said a little uneasy. "I guess I should be careful what I wish for."

"Well, in that case, here," said Myra, opening her coat. "I was going to wait to give you this, but, seein' as the country needs you and all – I got you this cellphone and it comes with all the latest apps."

"Thanks, boss," smiled Jamal.

The twosome hugged warmly. A nondescript black car rolled up. Debra and the other agent opened a door.

"Don't forget to call me after you save the world," added Myra, as Jamal got into the car. "I need some excitement. I don't have cable."

CHAPTER 3

"Mr. Nichols, what I'm about to show you is classified. You are not to discuss it with anyone, except for authorized personnel. Do you understand what that means?" Debra asked him, a little condescendingly.

"Yes, ma'am. I'm familiar with FBI protocols. Will I be reporting directly to you or is someone else the lead?" Jamal asked like a seasoned pro.

"Agent Robert Ficarro is the lead. We'll meet him on site," she replied, impressed by his response. "Are you sure you're 17?"

"Positive, ma'am. If you want, you can watch me get turned down for a beer."

She smiled knowingly. "A sense of humor," she noted. "Robert's gonna hate you."

The other agent, who was driving, laughed with Debra. She pulled out a thick file full of reports and photos.

"Ever hear of Sparta, Pennsylvania?"

"No."

She handed him several pictures of the town.

"It's a little backwater town, maybe two hours from here. The only thing remarkable about Sparta was that there was absolutely nothing remarkable about it, until several months ago."

More pictures. This time it was a police sketch of a man with piercing eyes, thin features and long blond hair. A second picture looked like it had come from a security camera. He was wearing a suit and dark sunglasses.

"This is our perp. He goes by the name of Asgar and we're not sure if it's a first, last name, or both. We don't know how he did it, but we believe he's responsible for the disappearance of half the town and 300 of its children."

Debra handed him two other photographs. The first was an old aerial photo of the town, which was dated 3 years prior. The second, which was dated 6 months ago, was another aerial photo. The town looked exactly the same, except for a gaping hole about ½ mile wide.

"A bomb?" asked Jamal, confused.

"Our cover story is that it was a gas pipe explosion, but we suspect that the kids are very much alive. They and the town were transported somehow."

"Transported? How can one man transport part of a town and 300 people?"

"Look closely at the photograph of Asgar. Look at his hands."

Jamal moved the security photo closer to his face. Asgar was entering what looked like a convenience store. His right hand was pushing the door handle and he could see that Asgar's fingers were about 2 inches longer than normal, with an extra joint where it shouldn't have been.

"Asgar may not be human," added Debra.

Jamal laughed and listened for the other agent's guffaws. They didn't come. She was serious.

"We don't know who or what Asgar is, but we do know this. He's prepared to do anything to achieve his goals. Including murder."

The car stopped at a helipad just outside the city. Jamal was ushered into a waiting helicopter with Debra. The chopper wasted no time in taking off. Debra noticed the teen shift his weight uneasily in his chair.

"First time in a chopper?" she asked.

"Yeah," smiled Jamal. "They take off pretty fast."

Debra sensed he was a little uneasy with flying, but didn't press the issue. In a few minutes, they were back into the debriefing.

"See on the map? The center of this hole is the Sparta school. We believe Asgar was targeting a particular student, Cindy Rowan Hartman."

The picture of Cindy was from the night before the disappearance. Her smile was as bright and eager as you'd expect a 15 year-old and her eyes had an intelligence that came across the photo. Jamal noticed a unicorn pendant around her neck.

"Why her? The parents?"

"The grandmother, Alana Freeman."

Debra handed him a family photo of Howard and Alana Freeman on vacation in Florida.

"The husband, Howard, died some months before Asgar arrived. They put Alana in a nursing home because they claimed she had been hallucinating. She claimed she knew where the kids were and had to get out to help her granddaughter. No one took her seriously."

"She's an old woman… Just lost her husband…"

"But wait, it gets better. The area you see on the map? The only people to disappear were between the ages of 11-18. Two days ago, we held a memorial service for the parents. When two of the seniors stepped across – Poof. Right in front of us. We had agents examining that area for weeks and didn't lose one."

"Is it like…magic?" Jamal said, incredulous.

"I think it is magic. How else do you explain only the kids getting transported? The kids and Alana Freeman. Another grandmother helped her escape the home. She was in a car chase with local police. Got out near the area. Her footprints went right into the area and then…"

"Right, poof."

Jamal looked at the photos again. Alana wore the same unicorn pendant that her granddaughter had.

"You want to send me over?" asked Jamal knowingly.

"Thus the rush. This is strictly volunteer, Jamal. I'm not going to blow sunshine up your butt, but the chances of you returning are slim. Only two of the students returned."

"How?"

"Asgar's some kind of ruler, on the other side. When the kids reach 18, he has to offer them a chance to escape. Some mystic escape clause in his spell. This is a picture of Ken Holt. He says the kids were alive when he left and Asgar won't let them leave until his demands are met, if at all. He hasn't said much beyond that, but we're hoping you might be able to talk to him."

"What about the other one?"

Debra grimaced, realizing how poorly she had chosen her words.

"I'm afraid he'll be no help to you. The other student, Todd Wilson, is dead. Ken carried his body back when he returned."

CHAPTER 4

Ficarro had set up his HQ in the Sparta Post Office. Incoming and outgoing mail was screened by a team of six agents, to keep word of the incident from leaving town. A trailer full of surveillance equipment had been set up behind the building, next to a makeshift helipad. The chopper dropped off Jamal and Debra and immediately departed. Ficarro wanted the illusion of normalcy to be kept as much as possible and helicopters just didn't jibe with small town America. A second base camp had been set up one mile outside of town. It was made up of an army of black SUV's, agents, equipment, and two choppers. If things got out of hand in Sparta, Ficarro's muscle was only a phone call away.

Ficarro's desk was a mess and he looked as if he'd hadn't slept in days. When Debra and Jamal entered, he barely looked up from his paperwork.

"Is this him?" Ficarro asked immediately. He then did a double take as he looked at Jamal. "Are they kidding me? I've got suits older than him!"

"Mr. Nichols," Debra introduced. "Special Agent Robert Ficarro."

"Mister Nichols?" noted Ficarro.

"Sir, I realize that I'm young, but I have been working undercover as a special agent for the DEA for six months and..."

Ficarro lifted a piece of paper from the mess and read from it.

"Five months, two weeks," he corrected. "Police academy training, DEA training, BS in Law Enforcement Studies... Kid, I've got agents with five times the experience here that can barely tie their shoes. I'm gonna be honest. I don't want you here and I certainly don't want to send a teenager into this mess."

"But, sir..."

"Save it, we're on the clock," he looked at Debra. "Has he been debriefed?"

"Mostly."

"Well, do it again and let him talk to the Holt kid," Ficarro instructed. "Your mission is to get in, find out the status of the kids, gather information on this Asgar, and get back. Just recon, no heroics. And I want a full report on what the Holt kid said before we blast you off to Camelot. Now move."

Jamal and Debra marched out of the office almost as quickly as they had arrived.

"Is he always like this?" asked Jamal, a little overwhelmed.

"Nah," smiled Debra. "He's pretty low key today. Probably only on his second pot of coffee. We don't have much time. After you re-read all the mission specs, we'll get you enrolled in the school as a transfer. Your cover story is that you and your parents were due to arrive in Sparta the day of the quarantine. You've just been let out and have no idea what's going on."

"Isn't that a little thin?" asked Jamal.

"It's the best we can do under the circumstances. Ken Holt was in our custody since he reappeared last week. We interrogated him, but he's taken the death of Todd Wilson pretty hard. They were best friends. We put him back in the makeshift high school for the kids left behind. You have two days to become Ken Holt's new best friend."

The Sparta Middle and High Schools had been recreated at the elementary school. Of course, it mostly contained classes for kids ten and under. Anyone over that age was a senior and had been away on the senior trip when the incident happened when Asgar arrived. Normal seniors would be picking out colleges at this point in the year. Unfortunately, with the FBI's crackdown on keeping everyone in town, college applications for all Sparta residents had either been "temporarily lost" or had gone unanswered. Ficarro was already making arrangements for some of the kids to take college level courses in town.

"This is total bull," Scott Fidell complained to Jamal on his first day in class. "All this junk happens in town and now my entrance into the Air Force Academy is magically delayed? What's up with that?"

"I tell you what's screwed up," added Gary Owenthal in the seat behind. "No prom. You know how long me and my girl were plannin' that night and now they won't let us have one?"

"Pfft," scoffed Scott. "You mean the night your girl was plannin' for you. She's got you on the shortest leash in the pound, Gar."

"Yo, shut up, at least I wasn't goin' with my cousin," retorted Gary.

"She is not my cousin. My dad is very distantly related to her mom and that's it. I would've been goin' with that chick, Marianne."

"Yo, that's just nasty."

"Man, I don't get this whole FBI thing," feigned Jamal, trying to refocus the conversation. "There's gotta be somebody in town that knows what's goin' on."

"What good would that do?" asked Gary. "They won't let anybody out of town. I heard one of the local cops tried to make a break for it and they even caught him. The only one to get out was Andrew Shelly and his two kids."

"Yeah, that's the rumor, but the FBI guys say he and his kids were quarantined for the measles."

"Yeah, right," scoffed Gary. "That was six months ago. Where are they now? Measles don't last that long."

Jamal began to realize why Ficarro was so tense. He'd been feeding the people of Sparta a line of bull for months. Now even the kids didn't believe it.

"There is one way out. Follow Peter and Tanesha," said Scott carefully.

"You're crazy," said Jamal. "After what you told me happened? They're dead!"

"Not dead," correct Scott. "Transported. To some kind of government lab. The problem is, they weren't ready. I'll be ready. I talked to Holt."

Bingo, thought Jamal.

"Who's Holt?"

"You talked to that freak?" scoffed Gary.

"He's no freak, dude. He was there. He saw it. Government experiments. All that stuff. They say Todd Wilson's dead, but it was just his clone," insisted Scott.

"Why do you call him a freak?" asked Jamal.

"Check him out," mumbled Gary just as Ken walked into the room.

Ken Holt clanked into the room. Clanked, because from head to toe, Ken had pieces of metal stuck through his clothes, hair and skin. Jamal was reminded of the punk kids he saw while visiting his cousin in New York last summer. One had a denim jacket that was covered entirely in safety pins, but Holt's outfit was a little over-the-top. The items included nails, pieces of cans and metal that had been worked with a hammer. His boots were steel-tipped. Pierced nose, chin and ears, he was wearing studded leather pants and a jacket. It was almost like he was covered in armor. Ken noticed Jamal staring at him. Jamal looked away, but he'd been caught.

"Yo, Ken," said one of rowdier kids. "Where's the Lion and the Scarecrow?"

A laughed ripped through the classroom, but Ken was stone. The bell rang. The class started. And for a few hours, Sparta settled into its normal monotony.

For the rest of the day, Jamal looked for an opportunity to strike up a conversation, but Ken avoided everyone. During English, Jamal managed to get a seat close to him and asked him to pass him a sheet of paper. Ken passed it without a word.

Frustrated, Jamal decided to follow Ken home at a distance to see if he could create an opportunity to talk. Halfway back to the Holts, Jamal ran out of places to hide. If Ken turned around, he'd see Jamal trailing him. But, with any luck, he was so wrapped up in his own world he wouldn't turn around. Just as Ken was turning a street corner, one of the neighborhood dogs abruptly started barking at Jamal.

Distracted, Jamal looked away for a second and when he looked back, Ken was gone. He cursed to himself and ran to the corner. Nothing. The street was empty. Jamal looked around and then, suddenly, Holt was standing in front of him with a knife.

"Why are you following me?" he demanded.

"Take it easy! Take it easy! My family just moved here. I don't know my way around," Jamal said coolly.

"You're lying," insisted Ken. "The government won't let anyone in here."

"We've been in quarantine for weeks. I don't know what's going on. I thought you could tell me."

"You're lying! They said Andrew Shelly's kids were in quarantine and I know they're not!"

"Look, why don't you put down that knife..."

"Then tell me the truth!" snapped Ken desperately.

Jamal looked Ken over. He seemed like an earnest and genuine person caught in a bizarre and desperate situation. He took a chance on him.

"Okay, I don't live here."

"I knew it!" said Ken satisfactorily, sheathing his knife and storming away.

"I'm with the FBI. They're sending me over."

Ken stopped in his tracks and turned around.

"To the Wildsidhe? You're going voluntarily? It's suicide," said Ken in amazement.

"I guess it is, if I don't have the right information."

Ken dropped a piece of metal at Jamal's feet.

"Pick it up."

"Why?"

"Do it!"

Jamal picked up the piece of metal. It appeared to be iron.

"Iron's your best friend on the Wildsidhe, never forget that. All the monsters are vulnerable to it. All except shape changers, when they look like humans," said Holt moving close. "Are you a shape changer?"

"Uh, no," said Jamal, trying not to laugh. "Is there any way I can prove that?"

"Yeah, answer my three questions as quick as possible. Their telepathy doesn't work very fast," explained Ken.

"They're telepathic?"

"I think so," said Ken, but he was wrong. Changelings were just very perceptive. "Where were you born?"

"Camden, New Jersey."

"Name the Three Stooges."

"Moe, Larry, and Curly. For a bonus, Shemp and Curly Joe."

"What's the price of a chicken sandwich at Chunk-a-Chicken?"

"How am I supposed to know that?"

"You're not. Who changed the game of B-ball?"

"Michael Jordan. That's four questions."

"Shape changers' can speak English and know basic things, but I figure, they don't live here, so they can't handle a lot of quick specific questions."

Ken eyed Jamal suspiciously, then, seemingly satisfied, started walking again.

"Follow me," he instructed.

Jamal followed Ken to the Holt house. Ken's mother popped her head out as they crossed the front yard.

"Hi, Ken," she beamed. "Who's your friend? Is he staying for dinner?"

"He's not staying, Mom. I'll be in the basement for a while," Ken said flatly.

"Hi," greeted Jamal, a little uncomfortable with Ken's standoffishness.

Ken escorted Jamal to a cellar door in the backyard.

"Mom's been pretty wrecked worrying about my brother and all."

"At least she's still got you," noted Jamal.

"Yeah," he replied flatly. "For what that's worth."

Ken unlocked the outside door of the cellar, then pressed a hidden latch. When he opened the door, there was a crossbow on a small mount on the other side.

"Hey!" said Jamal.

"It's okay, I disarmed it. Get inside."

A little reluctantly, Jamal followed inside. Ken locked the metal door behind them.

"First thing," instructed Ken. "Trust no one on this side. You and I now have a secret code word. When we meet again after you come back from the Wildsidhe, you look me straight in the eye and say... What's something you'll remember?"

"B-B guns," said Jamal knowingly. "You say Tread and I'll know it's you."

"Tread, got it. Like I said, all the monsters have a weakness for iron. Make sure you carry it at all times. Always make your weapons out of it. Steel works too because of the iron. The more powerful the monster, the greater the weakness."

"When you say monsters..."

"Dragons, giants, Fortesans... Anything magic."

"Fortesans?"

"They're kind of like tall faeries. Just listen to me, okay?" said Ken, too exasperated to go into detail.

"You're tellin' me, they're real? In this Wildsidhe. Vampires too?"

"That's only in movies," corrected Ken impatiently. "See this map? This is the part of town that got transported. Make your way towards the school. When you get across, make sure you talk to Justin. Tell him we spoke. You're still going to have to prove you're not a shape changer, but that might speed things up."

"What can you tell me about Asgar?"

"Only that he's responsible for this whole mess. Don't trust him ever. He's a megalomaniac, dude. Like Hitler with a magic wand."

"Do you have any idea why he did this?"

"Only that it has something to do with Cindy and the fact she has magic power. I think she's some kind of princess or something."

Ken walked over to a loose brick in the basement and removed it from the wall. Behind it was a small depression, an envelope, and a pouch.

"This pouch has iron shavings, could come in handy. This letter is for my brother, Gary. He's kind of a chunky kid, looks like me, only younger. Make sure he's all right, okay?"

"Sure, thanks for your help."

"No problem. Now, if you or Scott need any more help..."

"Scott? You mean he's really planning on crossing over?"

"Yeah, I figured you two must be together. He's got a thing for Marianne Blossum, don't ask me why. Although she got real foxy once we got to the Wildsidhe."

Satisfied, Jamal rushed back to Ficarro's makeshift office. He quickly knocked and burst in. Debra and Ficarro were arguing as he approached.

"I'm telling you he's ready!" argued Debra.

"Bull! He's not going!" insisted Ficarro.

"I'm sorry to interrupt," began Jamal.

"What are you doing here?!" Ficarro snapped.

"My cover's blown, but it's okay," Jamal explained.

"Oh, it's all okay," muttered Ficarro mockingly.

"I talked to Ken Holt. He told me iron is the weakness of the monsters and a few other things. But we have bigger problems..."

"We do, but you don't," corrected Ficarro.

"Jamal, I'm sorry," said Debra sheepishly. "They changed their minds."

"I just got here!" snapped Jamal, then composing himself. "I just debriefed Ken Holt."

"And I look forward to the report," added Ficarro smugly. "But I don't want you anywhere near the transport point. There's a new plan to send an entire squad of armed, ROTC recruits."

"I don't think you want to do that," said Jamal carefully. "This guy, Asgar... He's some kind of tyrant over there. If he gets a hold of guns...“

"It's not your problem," smiled Ficarro. "Agent Glass will get you back to Philadelphia. Thank you, Mr. Nichols."

"But I don't think...“

"Thank you."

Outside in the parking lot, Debra apologized profusely, while Jamal tried to convince her to go back inside to talk to Ficarro. Deep down, they both knew what the end result would be. Jamal would go home and return to the DEA and his perfectly planned career.

"I'm sorry, Jamal. Sometimes it happens," apologized Debra.

"Yeah, well. It's probably for the best," agreed Jamal. "To be honest, I still don't believe all this. There has to be a logical explanation, but... Well, it's not my problem anymore. You've got units looking for Scott Fidell?"

"Yeah. Agents are picking him up now. C'mon," smiled Debra. "I'll buy you dinner. On Robert's tab. We'll get you out of here before dark."

Just then, Scott came squealing around the corner driving a purple glittery dune buggy with a pile of gear in the back seat. Two agents pursued on foot, while a third attempted to chase him in a car.

"Oh, no," said Jamal. "I'm on him."

When agents had arrived at Scott's house, he spotted them from a second story window, while packing his gear for the crossover. As soon as he saw the car, he grabbed as much of his equipment as he could carry, threw it into the back of his brother's old dune buggy and took off through the backyard just as they knocked on the door. Only Scott's mother noted his hasty departure and told the agents as they entered. Debra immediately got into her car, but Jamal bolted across the street. Avoiding the agents and the cars, Scott crashed through the hedges which surrounded the square in the middle of town. Jamal ran at the dune buggy on an angle. While the agents shouted orders for Scott to stop, Jamal kept quiet. When Scott turned to cross the street behind the agents' car, he leaped onto the back of the dune buggy.

"Who is that?!" demanded Scott.

"Stop the car!" ordered Jamal.

"Jamal? All right, man! Take me to the other side!"

Cop cars and agent cars were now blocking off the streets leading to the barren area, but Scott cut through a row of backyards to avoid them. Jamal had to duck to avoid a clothesline as they passed under.

"Scott! This isn't the way! Let the FBI handle it!"

"Yeah, right!" he scoffed. "And wait for them to take me?! No way! C'mon, dude. You and me, we can blow the lid of this entire conspiracy!"

"Scott!" implored Jamal. "I'm working with the FBI. I'm one of them."

As proof, Jamal held up the temporary FBI ID Debra had issued him earlier. Scott was so stunned, he didn't realize he was right on top of the barren land. Jamal hollered, but it was too late. The dune buggy smashed into a fence support. Instinctive, Jamal tried to hold onto the dune buggy, but the impact was too great. All he succeeded in doing was flying head over heels onto the barren ground. He disappeared in a glow, same as the two seniors. Debra, who had just stopped about 100 feet down from the dune buggy, got out of her car just in time to see. A group of six agents, armed to the teeth and wearing flak jackets, looked to her for orders, while two others apprehended Scott. She buried her head in her hands.

"Robert's gonna kill me."

CHAPTER 5

Encased in a blue, shimmering light, for a second, Jamal thought he saw a river of a million shimmering colors which he was flying over, or more exactly, falling over. Then, normal returned, and the inertia of the dune buggy impact was gone. He was startled to realize he was standing on the sidewalk and nearly fell down. Jamal noticed a plastic shopping bag about ten feet away. It had printing on the side. Junk from inside it littered the sidewalk around him, as if someone had just thrown it there.

Jamal noticed he was standing at a clock tower. The street and sidewalk was pock marked with scorch marks, scratches and foot-shaped pot holes almost two meters across. Weeds and other vegetation had begun to grown through the cracks and around the foundations of the buildings. In the great distance, he could see unfamiliar forests and mountains. The terrain was somehow more vibrant and alive than anything he had seen on his travels around the U.S. or Europe. This was the missing section of Sparta and Jamal was standing at almost ground zero.

Down the street, he spotted Sparta's supermarket. A front window had been smashed and broken shopping carts lay scattered in the parking lot in front. In the distance, the main road that ran through town ended abruptly at trees and rocks. One of the houses at the edge had only gotten transported halfway and its living room and second floor had been ravaged by the elements for weeks. It was as if a giant had ripped apart the "Sparta Town Play Set" and placed it in the middle of the woods. With nothing else to do, he picked up the bag to look inside, when, from the other side of the clock tower, he heard a scuffling sound.

Using the stealth methods of Tang Soo Karate, Jamal backed up and quickly climbed up the beveled surface of the clock tower, preparing for an attack. Instead, a muscular teen carrying a crossbow and wearing homemade armor similar to Holt's, rounded the corner.

"Don't shoot," Jamal said gingerly.

The teen whirled around and Jamal could clearly see from his eyes that he had every intention of shooting, if need be.

"Don't move," said the teen. "What are you doing up there? Garbage picking?"

"Well, I heard this is a bad neighborhood," quipped Jamal. "Why don't you put that thing away and let me come down?"

"You can come down, slowly," instructed the teen suspiciously. "Don't give me a reason to shoot you."

Jamal slid down as cautiously as possible.

"I'm not a shape changer. You can give me the test. I talked to Ken Holt before I crossed over, he told me to ask for Justin."

"You'll meet Justin soon enough. Right now, you deal with me. You're not part of Sparta, who are you?"

"Jamal Nichols. I'm a special attachment with the DEA and FBI," said Jamal flashing his credentials. "I'm here to save you."

"Really?" laughed the teen, cautiously examining the wallet. "Where's your gun, 007?"

"Ah, yeah, well," said Jamal embarrassed. "Things didn't go as planned. You know Scott Fidell?"

"Oh, sure. He used to beat up kids for their lunch money. He's an idiot."

"Well, it was his fault."

"Did he get into trouble?"

"Probably got arrested."

"Cool. I'm John Bearclaw. Why don't you..."

Just then, John tensed up and Jamal could've sworn he heard someone passing gas.

"That wasn't me," assured Jamal.

"Duck!" shouted John.

Jamal hit the pavement and rolled, as John fired his crossbow. A little, evil looking, ear of corn with a mouthful of teeth leaped out of the vegetation growing at the base of the clock tower, propelling itself on a burst of gas. The crossbow bolt struck it dead center and pinned it against the building. Jamal stared, his mouth agape.

"Huskers," explained John while reloading his crossbow quickly. "They're like the plant version of piranhas, totally mindless. We have to move."

Jamal scrambled after John, just as a wave of three dozens, evil looking corn stalks, climbed out of the trees and sewers, stumbling forward on passing gas.

"What do they want?" asked Jamal as they ran.

"Nothing much," replied John wryly. "Just to kill you, eat you, and gnaw your bones, not to mention throw garbage around. And I thought Venus flytraps were creepy."

A particularly ambitious Husker had hidden in a mailbox up the street. Unfortunately, for the Husker, the surrounding iron in the box slowed its reflexes as it climbed out, dumping mail on the street. John nailed it, sending several undelivered letters, which got caught on the Husker, into the air. John snatched one as they ran by.

"Uh, oh. I hope the Motts thought to pay their phone bill again. This is from March," said John matter-of-factly. "Hey that reminds me, how did the Final Four turn out?"

Jamal glanced back. Huskers now poured into the street from every direction, jumping through low window panes and gurgling like the rude little monstrosities they were.

"Um, John, not that I don't want to answer your questions, but," said Jamal a little worried. "Are we gonna die?"

"Huh? Oh, the Huskers? Nah, they're easy. According to Nash…"

"Who's Nash?"

"An elf with magic powers over most plants. He can't do much with these bad boys, but he knows about them. Every year they migrate south, eating bugs or slow and unfortunate animals. Yesterday, Justin went after them with a monster truck. What a mess. We'll be fine after we turn on Grand Avenue."

The Huskers, despite their small stature and mindless nature, seemed determined to catch up to John and Jamal. By the time the twosome turned on Grand, the tide of little rude corncobs was closing. John ran to the center of the street, stopped and turned around. Jamal, hesitated but did the same.

"What are you doing?!"

"Sorry, we need to test. Get ready to run if they don't work."

"If what doesn't work?!"

The Huskers continued to close in.

"Wait for it," said John in anticipation. "So, how about the Stanley Cup?"

"I don't really follow sports," replied Jamal, preparing to flee. "Should we run just in case?"

"Now!"

On his word, several teens stood up on the buildings on either side of the street. Under John's supervision, they had constructed two new ballistae and catapults that would, when properly fired, rain down several dozen arrows at once. The one on the right side of the street worked perfectly, raining death down upon the evil Huskers. The second misfired, shooting the arrows into the roof right in front of the teens. The Huskers fled in panic. John, who seemed to barely take notice, started scolding the teens on the left building.

"No, no, no! I told you that was too much tension!"

"Sorry, John," apologized Ron, one of the teens.

The largest Husker, who was in the lead, rolled itself over, bleeding green everywhere. He nibbled on John's foot pathetically. Annoyed, John stomped the Husker to mush. It made one last little rude noise. The entire street now reeked of something that smelled not unlike Brussels sprouts.

"Little punks," muttered John. "Did I tell you the Huskers ate the last bag of cocktail weenies we somehow missed in the Supermarket? They were rotten! But they pretended to enjoy them! I think it was just to spite me. I love those things."

"Uh, yeah, listen John, maybe you should take me to see Justin," suggested Jamal.

"Oh, yeah," John suddenly remembered as the other teens approached. "Hey guys, this is Jamal. He's here to save us."

Laughter ripped through the group. They looked over Jamal, who was still holding an armful of items from the plastic bag, as if he had just finished a shopping spree at a yard sale.

"No way, John," said one of the teens in disbelief. "They must know what happens if you cross the threshold. He's gotta be a shape changer."

"He's too pathetic to be a shape changer," added another teen.

"Hey, c'mon. Ken sent me," insisted Jamal, feeling the tide turning against him.

When Jamal turned around, he noticed John had taken a step back from him and held his crossbow on him.

"We'll test him," assured John grimly. "Until then, everybody stay awake."

John gestured for Jamal to start walking and the group headed back to the school. Jamal immediately noticed that the fence around it had been reinforced with small guard towers on the corners and two additional ones on either side of the gate. John stopped Jamal from entering.

"You're gonna have to wait here until Justin and Wayne decide to let you in," explained John, taking Jamal's I.D. badge.

"Oh and I forgot to tell you. Peter and Tanesha told us about the government crackdown and everything. Most people are pretty upset about it."

John went inside and two of the heavily armed teens shut the gate.

"What do I do if the Huskers come back?" asked Jamal.

"You're a secret agent," smiled John. "I'm sure you'll figure out something."

Jamal waited, taking inventory of the items in the bag he had picked up and forgotten to put back down during all the excitement. It appeared to be an adult's shopping that got left behind when the town disappeared. One of the Huskers had probably uncovered it somewhere. Inside was a brown bag with three cheese sandwiches that still looked edible, thanks to the science of preservatives. There were also six chocolate bars, two road flares, a map of Pennsylvania, a disposable camera, a pair of sunglasses, an orange plastic beach bucket, a package of plant food, a blank CD-ROM, a hunter's vest, and a book on government conspiracies. He put on the hunter's vest, putting some of the more useful items in its pockets.

He thought about how he had gotten here and shook his head.

"Scott," said Jamal. "You are an idiot."

CHAPTER 6

About an hour later, John returned with a group. Jamal recognized Cindy from her photograph and he surmised the teen in the center with the air of authority was Justin. One of the girls rolled up in a wheelchair. She had a small crossbow mounted to the arm. Jamal figured it was something new. He heard someone mention that it wasn't fair that they hadn't found enough for all of them. Everyone was dressed in the same homemade armor and clothes, except for Peter and Tanesha, who still had the clothes they wore during the memorial. At first, Jamal thought it looked ridiculous, now he began to wonder when he would get his own.

"Jamal Nichols?" addressed Justin. "My name is Justin Burns. I'm in charge. Why are you here?"

Jamal sighed in exasperation, getting tired of being laughed at. He decided to take a more professional approach.

"I'm a special agent of the DEA working in conjunction with the FBI. My mission is to assess your condition and that of the rest of the 300 missing children, obtain reconnaissance on their captor Asgar and return to Sparta to formulate a rescue plan."

"Personally, I don't trust anyone that works for the government," said the Native American John, as if announcing it to the crowd. "They tend to take things that aren't theirs."

"Yeah, he looks real dangerous, John," said the girl in the wheelchair as sarcastically as she could manage. "And I doubt he's here to put us on a reservation."

"Terri," chided John. "You're too trusting."

"Oh, like a shape changer would know about the FBI," she scoffed back.

"If they knew about Principal Greene they would know about the FBI," Wayne said. "We don't know what they know. You can't trust anyone here. This isn't America. I'm in charge of security. I have to be sure about this before we risk it."

"That's for sure."

"Please," Justin said bristling. "We'll test him and then we'll know. End of story."

"I have a good feeling about him," added Cindy thoughtfully. "He's got an aura of a warrior, Jus'. Like you."

"I do have a degree in law enforcement," added Jamal smugly. "I think I know a little bit about security."

"Things are different over here. You don't work, you don't eat."

"I'm not here to eat, I'm..."

"Fine," Justin said quickly tossing Jamal's badge back. "Then you can sleep outside."

"Sorry," added Wayne.

"Whoa-whoa-whoa," said Jamal, trying to stop the kids from returning to the school. "I need your help. Please. I'm not against work, I'll work if you want."

Justin stopped and the others followed suit.

"You have to spend 30 hours in an iron locker. The Changelings can't hold their shape that long. Once they shift back to their nature form, the iron in the locker will incapacitate them," Wayne instructed.

"Fine, sure, whatever."

Justin nodded and the rest of the teens knew exactly what to do. The guards at the gate opened it, while four of Wayne's guards surrounded Jamal. He was a little worried one of them would accidentally shoot him, but they seemed proficient enough with the bows. He was led inside the school auditorium and placed inside the locker.

"I'm sorry, but there will be no further contact with you. We can't risk a Changeling escaping with any information on us. If you are who you say you are, I hope you won't be too uncomfortable. And if you're not, enjoy your last meal," explained Justin flatly.

A black curtain from the auditorium served as a covering for the sports equipment locker. Jamal tried his best to get comfortable on the gym mat at the bottom.

The next day, Jamal spent meditating. He went over the day's events in his head constructing different scenarios on how he would react if put in the same situation next time. Just as the self-evaluation grew tiresome, the auditorium curtain was torn away and light flooded the cracks. Justin, Wayne and the others surrounded the cage.

"Mr. Fuzzykins says he's been in there 30 and a half hours," Cindy said looking at the cartoon character on her watch.

Justin eyed her with a half smile.

"Only you could say Mr. Fuzzykins and expect people to take you seriously," Justin said.

"Then you should've given me something else for our anniversary," she said mockingly.

"Okay, let him out," sighed Justin in exasperation. "Someone tell the Goblin Eaters they can have the stage back."

"You have goblin eaters?" asked Jamal.

"That's Gary, Renee, and Conrad's band," explained Wayne, opening the door.

"You have a band?"

"Yeah, a bunch actually. They're real ticked you made them miss rehearsal. We're having a dance next Saturday and the Goblin Eaters are playing."

Justin headed off with Cindy, and a group of teens that had collected around him awaiting instructions or asking questions. Justin fielded them like a head of state. Jamal tried to run after him, but Wayne held him back.

"He's real busy, now," explained Wayne. "Try and catch him on Sunday, he's usually more relaxed."

"Wait, Justin!" called Jamal.

Wayne threw up his hands knowingly.

"Wayne will teach you the rules," assured Justin. "I've got a million things to do."

"But my mission..."

"You're not going anywhere until your eighteenth birthday, my friend. And that's only if you do a major favor for Asgar."

"Then bake me a cake, boss, because it's 12 days from now."

Justin stopped, waved away the entourage and walked back.

"What? You're kidding," he said a little surprised.

"That's why they sent me," explained Jamal, now taking the high ground. "According to Ken, Asgar has to give me a quest, right? I assess your condition, do Asgar's quest and pop back to give the FBI the information."

"Sounds like a plan," agreed Wayne.

"We could finally get a message home," added Cindy in anticipation.

"Speaking of which, I have a letter for Gary Holt from his brother Ken," said Jamal, patting the inside of his pocket.

A bunch of people started to talk at once.

"Everyone just calm down," insisted Justin. "Twelve days is not enough time to train someone to survive here, much less deal with Asgar."

Using his Tang Soo Karate, Jamal quickly pushed Wayne to the side, grabbed Justin's crossbow, tumbled between the legs of a guard, and fired the bolt dead center into a sandbag, which dangled from the rafters. Jamal handed the crossbow, butt first, back to Wayne.

"I think this one pulls to the left a little," noted Jamal.

"Wow, he really is a secret agent," Cindy said, impressed.

"Got everything, but my license to kill," smiled Jamal.

"Okay," relented Justin. "You can fight, but don't let your skill make you arrogant. The rules are different over here and if you forget that, you're dead."

Just then Gary, Renee, and Conrad entered carrying their instruments. Renee's bass drum had the words "Goblin Eaters" painted in sloppy Day-Glo paint. Her hair was dyed in bright green dreadlocks. Conrad had dyed his hair black and had styled it in a purposeful randomness. Gary, who Jamal recognized as Ken's younger brother, had tiny little blonde spikes all over his head. The threesome wore a lot of metal, but more in the punk fashion Jamal had seen in New York.

"Did you guys get rid of him yet or what?" said Gary impatiently.

"He's not a Changeling, so we didn't get rid of him," explained Wayne.

"Whatever," said Gary growing perturbed. "Can you get off the stage now? We already missed one rehearsal."

"Yeah, yeah, yeah," dismissed Wayne. "C'mon, Jamal, they need all the practice they can get."

"I heard that!" added Conrad. "Maybe if we could have some juice for the amps, we could practice for real."

"Wait," said Jamal, pulling the letter from his pocket. "Gary, your brother asked me to give this to you."

"You've seen Ken? Is he alright?" asked Gary, taking the letter.

Jamal hesitated a moment before answering. "He's good, all things considered."

"Thanks," said Gary. Jamal nodded and left with Wayne.

Wayne took Jamal on a tour of the school. At night, the gym was being used as sleeping quarters. During the day it was used for weapons training. The nurse's office was being used by a short little woman to make and bottle of some sort of goop.

"That's Winklo," introduced Wayne. "She's a dwarf."

Jamal went to say something, but Wayne gestured for him not to.

"Never interrupt her when she's working on making medicines. Gets real testy."

Behind the school, what was once a soccer field was now a well-tended garden of corn, tomatoes, beans, and other vegetables. There was another larger field of crops outside the school fence line. The roof to the sports equipment shed had been removed and replaced with the Plexiglas sneeze guards and dividers from the cafeteria. This created a makeshift greenhouse, which housed several small fruit trees. A young Hispanic girl was directing the action of a dozen kids who were weeding, planting or harvesting, depending on the crop. She occasionally would defer or nod to a short man who was standing just inside a small grove of berry bushes.

"This is probably where you'll be working until Justin decides your skills are better suited elsewhere," explained Wayne routinely.

"How gracious of him," muttered Jamal under his breath.

"Hmmm?"

"Nothing, nothing. Who's the green guy?"

"That's Nash the Elf. He and Winklo got married here by a king no less. Their families didn't approve of them even dating, so that's part of why they're here. Nash is like a wizard. He's got pretty cool plant powers."

"John mentioned him. Conrad said something about having no juice. You guys find a generator in town?"

"A few, but gas is limited. Sometimes we use the cars, but we need them to defend ourselves against the larger threats. You'd be surprised how quickly a darkcat and most monsters will run from a '96 sedan. Why do you ask?"

"How'd you like enough juice to run everything in the town again?"

CHAPTER 7

Jamal's father had wanted him to be a hydro-electrical engineer, like himself. And while it was true, Jamal had a knack for understanding the inner workings of everything from modern dams to simple Colonial-era saw mills, the classes just didn't interest Jamal. The twosome fought bitterly during the year that Jamal was applying for college.

Mr. Nichols had argued strongly for Jamal to apply to a college which had both a law enforcement and engineering degree program. Jamal knew his father feared that he might squander his intelligence and advanced education on $30,000-a-year policeman's salary. But to Jamal, it wasn't squandering, it was answering a higher calling to help people. And it was his father's success that had, ironically, afforded him the luxury of choosing something else.

And now, it was that irony that came full circle. After a couple of days of getting acclimated to the school and the kids, Jamal approached Justin with his plans for a water mill and generator. Justin worried that if the electricity was reinstated in the town, the kids he had worked so hard to train would let down their guard and they would be caught unprepared when Asgar eventually figured out how to cut the power.

Jamal, with Wayne's help, argued that with the town lit up at night, most of the natural predators would avoid the area. Batteries could be recharged and they could all make regular use of the hand radios. With short distance communication, they could make strides to expand the safe zone beyond the school and eventually recapture the town. This last bit of possibility appealed to Justin greatly, since he was anxious to finally go on the offensive against Asgar and the inhospitable world he had thrust upon them. Besides, the water mill would just be another element Asgar would have to contend with if he attacked and they could always fall back on their oil lamps and swords.

Jamal, Wayne, and a small contingent of the kids hiked to a waterfall, located about 200 yards from the edge of the town. Nash, the elf, came along to use his flora magic to clear the spot for the mill.

Gary Holt was one of the contingent. Since he crossed over, he hadn't shown too much emotion, but after he had read his brother's letter, he burst into tears. Jamal didn't see him for about a day, but when he returned he looked fit and ready for duty. Gary had secretly decided to be Jamal's personal guardian angel. Jamal secretly wondered what Ken would say if he knew how much weight his brother had lost.

Tina Shelly, another fairly recent crossover, volunteered for the hike in hopes of talking to Jamal. Tina's favorite pop music group was the "Heart Throb Boys", an all-male pop band that only 11 year-old girls could like. And anyone with information on their status, especially the lead singer, Brad, had to be questioned by Tina. Jamal had gotten the advanced word on Tina's fragile state of mind with regards to the band. And, like Peter and Tanesha, he didn't have the heart to tell her that the group had disbanded a few weeks after her crossover.

"Well, I'm sure they have at least one or two songs in the top 100," assured Jamal. "Their new songs are pretty popular."

"Could you hum one?" asked Tina excitedly. "Even just a little. I know how Brad works his riffs."

"Um, I really don't listen to music much," said Jamal, sadly.

"Oh, that's just what Peter and Tanesha said," muttered Tina in frustration.

Tina's armor was covered with tiny hearts and "HTB's," which was her own hand painted version of the Heart Throb Boys logo. Jamal had finally gotten his own suit of armor too. Bolstered by football padding, Chuck Bearclaw, John's older brother, had pounded him a new breast plate and other pieces of protection from a steel cubical wall in the vice principal's office. Jamal made an additional improvement by gluing fabric to the joints so the armor wouldn't clank. This allowed him to move silently while wearing the armor and using his martial arts training.

"I gotta get Chuck to do that to everyone's armor," thought Wayne aloud as they reached the waterfall.

"Okay, Nash," instructed Jamal. "This looks like a good spot. Can you clear about 100 square feet?"

"Sure," said Nash pleasantly. "But I can't just clear the area, I have to ask the plants and trees to move."

"Sorry," apologized Jamal. "I'm not that familiar with elf customs."

"We like plants," he added cheerfully. "Personally, I was the chief gardener of the Enchanted Gardens of Curn. Held that position through four elections."

"That's... great," said Jamal. The elf nodded.

Nash walked away from the group and began weaving his spell. The expression on his face changed a few times, as if he was conducting a conversation. The bark of the side of the tree twisted itself into a face and began to speak.

"Who disturbs me?" demanded the tree. "Me and my seed kin have lived by this stream for over 800 seasons! I don't see why we should leave!"

"He wants to talk to you," Nash said, a little embarrassed. Certain trees had gained the ability to talk, but they were few and far between.

"I'm the one that is asking you to move," admitted Jamal. "If you wouldn't mind it, we really need to...\"

"Mind?! Of course, I mind!" said the indignant oak. "Wouldn't you mind it if someone asked you to leave your home?!"

"I suppose you have a point," conceded Jamal.

"I think I speak for all the plants, when I say that moving is out of the question!" added the tree. "You humanoids trample my grass brothers under foot like they're not even there! You steal the fruit of my bark brothers! And murder the flowers for your decoration!"

"But we're trying to survive out here against Asgar the Fortesan," offered Wayne. "Don't you want to help us?"

"Help you what?" balk the tree. "Start a war that would burn my bark and trample my roots? The petty concerns of humanoids are naught to my kind. You will all be gone in a blink of eye."

"You know, those are all good points," said Jamal, trying to calm the raving plant. "Give me a second to confer with my friends here. Do you mind?"

"Take all the time you want. I am not as impatient as you humanoids," taunted the tree.

"Do all the trees have this attitude?" Jamal whispered to Nash.

"Not usually," the elf confided. "Most oaks are pretty friendly. Now, if you want to talk to the conifers, they can be downright nasty."

"Well, this tree is downright militant. What the heck am I supposed to say?" asked Jamal.

"I've got an axe," offered Wayne. "Maybe we could prune him down to size."

"Could we replant him?" asked Tina Shelly.

"His roots go down very deep," assured Nash. "The tree would have to move willingly."

"Maybe we can trade him something," suggested Gary. "What do trees like?"

Jamal remembered the plant food from the junk in the shopping bag. The package was still in his hunters vest. Jamal took it out and opened it.

"Perhaps we can trade," offered Jamal.

"Trade?!" the tree retorted, insulted. "I have the sun, the water and the earth. What do I need with..." Sniff! Sniff! "What is that?"

"It's Super Grow Plant Food," explained Jamal. "Have some."

Jamal placed a tiny bit in the mouth of the oak tree. "Put it on my roots, boy," spat the tree. The roots bit down and munched up the plant food as if it was eating a piece of candy.

"Mmmm!" said the oak. "My roots have never know such flavor! Give me this Super Grow!"

"Nah-uh," warned Jamal. "Not unless you and your buddies move."

"Fine, fine," assured the tree. "We shall move. Sorry for my rudeness before. It's been a very dry summer."

Jamal fed the tree the rest of the Super Grow Plant Food and the face on the tree faded away. Nash wove a second spell. Then, amazingly, the oak tree at the edge of the water pulled up its roots and shambled away, as did the rest of the plants in the area. As Jamal and the others watched, they were even more amazed to find a tiny, stone building at the base of the waterfall.

"What's that?" Jamal asked Wayne.

"Heck if I know," Wayne said. "I didn't know anyone else lived in this area before us."

"It looks like a tomb," said Gary. "Wonder if it has a curse or mummies or anything."

The stone structure had been buried for centuries and there was no sign of its occupant. The outer door had been smashed open by a rockslide ages ago, so the kids gained entry easily. The only contents were the stone slab in the center of the room. A tunnel lead deeper into the hillside to an inner door of some kind. Some kids wanted to explore, but Wayne vetoed the idea as too dangerous.

"This is perfect," said Jamal. "We cut a hole on the waterfall side for the wheel, place the generator on the slab and run a cable back to the school."

"Yeah, but the monsters will smash it up," said John.

"We'll make most of it out of steel and surround the tomb with the extra fencing we found in the hardware store. We'll bury the cable and it should be safe. Plus, Nash can drape the plants back over the tomb and the generator. The dumber monsters won't find it and maybe the smarter ones will be nervous about the tomb," Justin said.

"Perhaps we should be nervous too," said Gary.

"Nash, is there any reason to be nervous?" asked Justin.

"The tomb is a mystery to me, so I can't say," said Nash.

"But we still have to watch it," reminded Wayne. "I can't leave two of my guys out here, they'll get eaten."

"With the electricity running, we can set up a video camera monitor. In fact, we can set them all over town as an early warning system. I'm sure the school had an AV room, right?" said Jamal.

"Are you sure this is your first week in the Wildsidhe?" asked Gary knowingly.

"Positive," replied Jamal. "I still miss deodorant. Boy, do I miss deodorant."

Over the next week, Jamal supervised the construction of the generator mill, while taking instructions on the rules of magic and Fortesans from Cindy. The mill's wheel was constructed from the wheel of an old lawn mowing tractor.

The tire was removed and scoops were added to the rim every ten inches all the way around. To fasten the axle to the generator, Jamal had to teach some welding, with some equipment they had at the hardware store.

"Couldn't we just have pounded the axle into the generator?" asked John. Jamal removed his welding helmet and turned down the torch.

"But then you would've smashed the generator to pieces," Jamal politely countered.

Jamal knew that balancing the wheel so that the water could achieve the fastest spin, would take days, if not weeks. Maybe longer. And the logistics of monitoring the mill and keeping it safe had to be worked into the already top heavy schedule of the kids. However, the kids were fast learners and by the end of the week, he felt confident enough that they would not only get the mill up and running, but would no doubt make many improvements.

That Saturday, the kids had the party to end all parties. With the prospect of the generator mill in the not too distant future, Justin allowed the generator to be used for a portion of the party. With the Goblin Eaters playing at top volume, thanks to working amps, and plenty of music in between, not even the darkcats dared approach the cacophony of sound and teenage hormones. Brina Wilson's current boyfriend got into a fist fight with one of Wayne's guards after he caught them making out in the janitor's closet on the second floor. Fortunately, cooler heads prevailed and Terri managed to break it up before Justin found out and stopped the party.

At one point, the band did a jam session and made the mistake of allowing Lissy and the other pixies to sing at the microphone. The pixies found the amplification of their own singing voices absolutely addicting and began fighting for time at the mic. The Bearclaw brothers stage dove into the table holding Jamal's birthday cake. This sparked a cake fight to the right of the stage. On stage, Gary Holt had gotten so carried away with the music, he wanted to break his guitar. He instead, opted to tear down the "Sparta M.S. & H.S. Auditorium" sign and stamp it to pieces at the end of his solo.

Winklo and Nash quickly grew tired of the entire enterprise and retired to the classroom furthest from the auditorium to spend a quiet evening alone. Even Justin managed to loosen up and let Jamal supervise security for a few hours, while he and Wayne took a much needed break.

The chaos was very refreshing to Jamal. To him it meant that the kids were still human and that despite the hardships, deep down, they were just kids at heart. Everything seemed to be going smoothly, until Jamal got called to the front gate. He instructed one of Wayne's guard to alert Wayne if he didn't return in ten minutes.

When Jamal got outside, he immediately felt that something was wrong. By the gate, Conrad Grant, one of Wayne's guards, was cradling an injured teen. An arrow stuck out of his shoulder. Jamal instantly ran to his aide.

"How'd this happen? Where are the other guards?" he asked quickly.

"Called away," said Jerry Parker. Jamal could see the wounded kid, who also looked like Jerry. "I sent them away."

Jamal realized that there was a changeling in their midst. Earlier, Jerry had attended the party, but left dejected after getting dumped by his girlfriend of 3 weeks, Jodie Jordon. Too embarrassed to stay at the party, he took the place of one of Wayne's guards who was anxious to go.

After a few hours of guard duty and feeling sorry for himself, Jerry had to go to the bathroom. But rather than following procedure and going inside, he snuck out the front gate and went behind a tree. The changeling then ambushed him and dragged him back to the front gate. In the confusion, the other guards didn't realize it was Jerry Parker dragging Jerry Parker. He shouted that for them to go get help from inside. They got Jamal.

Before Jamal could reach for his crossbow, the changeling shoved the injured Jerry at him and morphed into Jamal.

The evil Jamal quickly attacked, punching him in the face and chest. Jamal dropped the crossbow and staggered back. The twosome then locked arms, each trying to push the other one away.

"Asgar sent me to give you a message, Agent Nichols," smiled the Changeling. "He'll be here tomorrow at 6 am to give you your quest. He suggests that you be ready. That is, if you're still alive by tomorrow."

"Tell Asgar, I'll be ready," gritted Jamal.

"I will," smiled the Changeling knowingly. "I promise you. I will."

The twosome exchanged several well-placed blows, each giving as good as they got.

"I shall have to remember this. Martial arts, I believe you call it," smiled the Changeling. "It's quite the thinking man's fighting style."

As the blood trickled out of Jamal's left nostril, he realized that he didn't think he could protect himself and the others. He chanced a look at the wounded kid.

"Yes, I'll have to kill him, but don't worry. He'll welcome it. He's a miserable little sod. Crying over a female. Pathetic!" the Changeling taunted.

A few more punches and Jamal crumpled into a heap. It was almost too easy. The Changeling picked up his crossbow.

"And now you're thinking about begging for your life!" the Changeling announced. "Don't bother. That won't distract me. Distract? Wait a minute, you're trying to..."

The Changeling turned around, but it was too late. The injured Jerry had managed to pick up his bow. From the ground, he shot the creature in the shoulder. It immediately reverted back to its normal state, a grey, hairless, big eyed humanoid. Jamal picked up one of the mini-iron dusters and blasted the Changeling. The creature screamed in pain as the iron burned into his flesh. The creature turned and fled.

"I wasn't crying," insisted Jerry, winded from the effort.

"Nice shot," added Jamal. "How'd you know it wasn't me?"

"Lucky guess. And I figured you wouldn't be mouthing off about how you'd kill me."

CHAPTER 8

Winklo was able to remove the arrow from Jerry. He would be laid up for a couple of weeks, but he would live.

Jamal spent the next few hours packing his equipment and tending to his injuries. In a hasty meeting, it was decided that it would be better if Jamal took a dirt bike, rather than one of the cars on his quest. Gas was running low and Justin figured that he could better navigate the narrow animal paths on two wheels rather than four.

The next morning, Jamal promptly dressed, meditated, did some warm up exercises and then had breakfast. He purposely hid his armor beneath regular street clothes. He wanted to appear as unchanged as possible to Asgar. At 6 AM, Jamal was still eating his breakfast calmly.

"Shouldn't you get going?" asked John, a little anxious.

"He's making Asgar wait," Justin noted. "It gives him the illusion of being in control."

"Exactly," smiled Jamal gesturing with his fork. "And no matter what you do, don't admit we hurt his Changeling messenger. The thing's probably in hiding, afraid of what Asgar will do to him. He'll know we did something and not admitting it will drive him crazy."

"How do you know Asgar so well without ever meeting him?" asked Wayne.

"Psychological profile," explained Jamal. "Asgar wants to be king. Why? To be in complete control. To dominate. Resist his domination by fighting him and you make him angry. However, if I'm right and the Changeling went underground rather than face Asgar, we undermine his control by making one of his servants disappear..."

"And you drive him crazy," finished Justin.

"Exactly and the crazier we make him, the easier it will be for you to exploit his weaknesses."

"What if he doesn't have a weakness?" asked Wayne.

"He's got one," assured Jamal confidently. "Everyone does."

Just then, there was a muffled explosion from outside the school cafeteria. Immediately, Ron popped his head through the window.

"You guys better get Jamal out here," said Ron. "Asgar's messenger is here and he's big and mad."

"It's time," Justin said.

Jamal gestured for him to wait one second and finished his orange juice.

"Ah!" grinned Jamal in satisfaction. "Tell Carlos he makes a mean breakfast."

Having already said his good byes the night before, Jamal marched towards the gate with the confidence of a Tang Soo master. Stomping around the front of the gate was Blurg, a giant. He had a bearskin loincloth and a tree for a club. Around his waist was a dirty hemp rope and the skulls of several humanoid creatures.

"Bring out the Jamal!" demanded Blurg. "Asgar waits! No Jamal? Me smash!"

Jamal walked outside the gate and the guards snapped it shut behind him.

"You come with me!" roared Blurg. "You no come, Blurg will..."

"Shut up," snapped Jamal. "Take me to see Asgar, now!"

Blurg was unaccustomed to taking orders from anyone other than a Fortesan or a bigger giant. Jamal's attitude caught him off guard. He couldn't not bring Jamal to Asgar, since that is what he was ordered to do, yet he hesitated in listening to Jamal.

"Are you deaf?!" repeated Jamal infuriated. "Take me to Asgar immediately, you fool!"

"Uh, y-yes," stammered Blurg. "This way."

Jamal followed Blurg to the empty Flagship Diner in town. Inside, Asgar stood outside in a suit and sunglasses, looking much the same way he did in the security photos. He relaxed, quietly stirring a steaming beverage in a mug.

"Jamal Nichols?" greeted Asgar as if he could be anyone else. He walked into the dinner. Jamal followed.

"Yes."

"Blurg," Asgar said, shouting out the door. The giant obviously couldn't fit in the small building. "Go, knock down a tree or something."

"Yes, master!" Blurg replied enthusiastically, thankful to have a task worthy of his brain power.

"Asgar of Wildsidhe?" greeted Jamal.

"Yes," replied Asgar, expecting a handshake.

Jamal took his hand and twisted it behind him.

"You're under arrest for the kidnapping of the children of Sparta, Pennsylvania, transporting minors over state lines, assault, depraved indifference, several counts of contributing to the delinquency of a minor..."

Asgar laughed heartily, probably harder than he had in years.

"My goodness, you're so forceful!" Asgar said amused. "I wonder if you could get those cuffs on me?"

With a quick turn and a flip, Asgar spun around and threw Jamal over the diner counter. He crashed into a shelf of plates and landed in a heap on the floor. Jamal hadn't anticipated his strength.

"Well, aren't you a funny little man?" laughed the Fortesan in fascination. "That was really a bold move you just pulled. If you were out to kill me, I think you would've actually hurt me. You know, I wish just one of my generals had that kind of initiative."

"Resisting arrest," added Jamal to the list, getting up slowly.

Asgar walked to the counter and sat down. Next to him was some kind of pie, which had been moldering under a cake dish for months. It currently had some sort of purple mushroom growing out of it.

"Serving Wench!" called Asgar to no one. "Can you bring my friend and me fresh pie? This one seems a bit stale. Oh, nevermind."

With a wave of his hand, Asgar sent porcelain coffee cups flying into Jamal. One hit him in the head with such force, it actually shattered and he shielded himself with his arms.

"Pull!" added Asgar.

After a few hits, Jamal managed to pick up a tray and blocked the last two cups.

"Are we ready to talk in a civilized manner, Mr. Nichols? Or shall I see what sort of cutlery this establishment has?"

"Stainless steel. It'd hurt you more than me. We can talk if you're ready to turn yourself in," said Jamal calmly. "I can't promise much leniency. Your crimes are pretty severe."

"Mmm, no, not today," admitted the Fortesan playfully. "Although, officer, I would like to file a missing persons report on my messenger. The one that came to you last night? Looked exactly like you?"

"Who?" asked Jamal knowingly.

The Fortesan bristled, then relaxed.

"Perhaps you forget where you are. This isn't the United States. It's not even Earth. In this world, I make and break the laws. And that includes the laws of physics.

"You work for me now, Mr. Nichols, and it can either be a pleasant experience or an agonizing one."

"I don't work for you," corrected Jamal.

"Maybe not yet…"

"Stop it," Jamal ordered Asgar. "You have a quest for me or not?"

With a wave Asgar conjured an illusion of a TV monitor.

"Your mission is to bring me the Grimstone Scepter!"

The monitor switched to a shot of the scepter. It appeared to be a red jewel about the size of a baseball atop a rod about 2 feet long.

"It's a gem about four inches across, red and mounted on a two foot rod of precious metal. However, the rod is really just for show. If you can't find it, I'll just take it out of your severance pay when you leave."

"How do I find this Grimstone?"

"Ooo, that's a sticky one, Agent Nichols."

The monitor showed a large mountain dotted with caves.

"Ankor, a Fortesan King, the only king who was not a High Fortesan, had his High Council create it. It made an almost magicless Low Fortesan, an upstart who just happened to marry the only available female of the royal bloodline, the most powerful king in our history. He disappeared in these caves a millennia ago. Half the caves are full of dragons, which are just a complete bother. And, the other half, are full of dwarves, with their clever little tricks and traps."

A small panel opened. It contained a medallion. On one side was the image of a dragon's claw and on the other side was a hammer.

"This medallion will allow you to appear and smell like a dragon or dwarf. With it, you can slip in, get the scepter, and slip out before anyone knows you've been there."

Jamal took the medallion.

"I just don't have the heart to send my soldiers up there. Could take us years and I don't even know if the scepter is even there. And, like I said, my generals aren't that bright."

Asgar realized that Jamal was looking around the room.

With a wave, the twosome were now standing in an interrogation room. Asgar was back in his suit and Jamal was sitting in the suspect's chair.

"So," continued Asgar routinely. "You retrieve the scepter and you can return to tell your FBI that the children are still alive because I allow it and that you know nothing more about their captor other than that he is very powerful, very intelligent, and devastatingly handsome."

"Not according to Cindy," said Jamal carefully.

"What do you know of it…child?"

"Oh, I'm no child in that department. Just seems a little odd that a rich and powerful guy like you can't get a date."

Asgar forced a chuckle despite himself.

"I like you, Jamal Nichols," admitted the Fortesan. "You remind me of myself."

"I'm nothing like you," assured Jamal.

"Oh, don't be too sure," grinned Asgar. "We're both men of action. Men of destiny. We want to change things and make a difference. A big difference in the world."

This struck a curious chord with Jamal, although he tried not to show it. Fortunately, the Fortesan, immersed in his own ego, was too busy imagining the glorious future that lied ahead.

"You and I," he said knowingly, "we've got plans."

With a wave, the twosome were standing in one of Asgar's palatial estates. The villa stood upon a rise overlooking much of the ornate Fortesan Kingdom. Impossibly thin spires reached skyward for hundreds of feet, tapering into majestic, misshapen cones resembling custard ice cream made of gold. The buildings of the Fortesan city resembled a mixture of Rome in its its glory and a Salvador Dali painting gone awry. A huge amphitheater made of green marble, was surrounded by hundreds of little buildings of different bright colors. And the streets of the city overflowed with tiny little dots of Fortesans. Hundreds of them, going about their day-to-day business.

Asgar was suddenly standing next to Jamal dressed in his regal clothes and holding two goblets.

"Drink with me, human," offered the Fortesan.

Jamal looked at him knowingly.

"Ah, yes, well I suppose Cindy would've mentioned Evals powder too. I didn't really expect you to fall for it. Ah, well. More for me."

Asgar sipped from both goblets.

"What's this, your summer home?" asked Jamal.

"This hovel? Bah, I wouldn't let my servants live here. I wanted to show you something. Come here."

Asgar led Jamal to a balcony at the back of the estate. He opened the intricately ornate glass and gold lame doors. Below was a courtyard that seemed to stretch for miles. Practicing in the courtyard were hundreds, perhaps thousands of Fortesan soldiers.

"Behold, the Army of Asgar," said the Fortesan proudly. "I designed the uniforms myself. What do you think? Too busy?"

The Fortesan soldiers were dressed in ornate, chrome-like armor with purple trim. Their groups moved not unlike the Greek Phalanx, which Jamal had read about in college. Additionally, there were several teams practicing with siege weapons like battering rams and catapults.

In the skies above, an elite squadron of riders rode lionhawks, horse-sized predators that Cindy had described to Jamal days ago. Against even Ficarro's SWAT team, the entire enterprise was a joke. But in this world, Asgar's army was state-of-the-art and potentially devastating to any kingdom that would resist him.

"What's it for exactly?" asked Jamal, unimpressed.

"To conquer. To rule. Oh, to think about all the time I wasted on

Cindy and court politics! This solution's so much simpler. Once I have the Grimstone I'll imprison the High Council and force King Penrod to do my bidding. That will teach them to shun me after the mistake I made with the Shadow sacrifice business. Then I can concentrate on finding a wife of an appropriate bloodline at my leisure. How do you like that, Morna?"

Jamal looked at him curiously.

"The queen, my sister-in-law. She's married to my idiot brother, Penrod."

"Why not just kill your enemies? Ambitious politicians on Earth do it all the time."

"Unlike leaders on Earth, I am restrained by more than mere morality thanks to the Treaty of Shadows. A High Fortesan who kills another Fortesan is claimed by the Shadows, a fate worse than death. If a member of the High Council killed another member, the Shadows could lay claim to the entire Wildsidhe. I will eventually triumph against Penrod, Morna, and those other fools, but not even I could hope to fight the Shadows," explained Asgar.

"And what about the kids?"

"Hmm," said Asgar, bothered. "I suppose I could kill them or let them go. Then again, why should I do either? Why give up an advantage when you have it? Why give up anything?"

"They're just children."

"Oh, boo-hoo," said the annoyed Fortesan. "Of course, if you were to decide to stay and become my general. Perhaps, I'd have no further use for them."

Jamal laughed and shook his head.

"Now, why would I want to stay here?"

"You'd be a hero. Isn't that what you want?"

Asgar gestured the headlines.

"Jamal Nichols saves 300 children on his first mission. You couldn't top that. There'd be no point in staying in the FBI."

"Great. So I stay here and be your lackey?"

"Not my lackey, my general!" offered the Fortesan excitedly. "You would command an army! And, once the kingdom was securely mine, you could spend your days on an estate twice the size of Philadelphia!"

Jamal looked at the Fortesan. He had to give him credit. Asgar had raised manipulating people to an art form. It was tempting. Save the kids, but at what cost?

With a wave of his hand, the Fortesan was back at the abandoned diner. The twosome walked out the front door onto the street. Jamal realized that it had all been an illusion.

"First, you have to deliver the scepter. If you get killed this is all pretty moot."

"I'll bring you your scepter. You can go now," taunted Jamal.

"Oh, may I?" laughed the Fortesan. "Oh, and one more thing."

"What?"

"Duck."

With a wave the Fortesan disappeared. Asgar himself had been only an illusion. Jamal became aware of something falling towards him. He dove away just in time to avoid a tree crashing down on the sidewalk. Blurg poked his head up from behind a second tree.

"I done it, master! I done it!" said the giant proudly. "Master?"

"He said to go home and smash trees there," replied Jamal.

"Thank you, master! Thank you!"

CHAPTER 9

When Jamal returned to the school, cheers rang up and there was a spontaneous lunch feast that nearly rivaled Saturday's dance. There were rumors, started mostly by Gary, that Jamal had actually scared Asgar away and had slain the giant all by himself. Justin, who knew the truth, only mildly corrected Gary. The kids' morale had been low since the death of Alana and Jamal's arrival had given everyone new hope.

After another brief farewell, Jamal took the dirt bike and tore out of the school. He crested a hill and popped a wheelie, giving one last wave to his fans, like a cowboy on white horse. Jamal hadn't mentioned Asgar's offer to them. He wondered if that meant he was actually considering it.

Justin and the kids had given him a map, a copy of a hand drawn one that originally belonged to Winklo. It plotted most of the Fortesan Kingdom and showed what they had determined was probably the mountain. Asgar didn't seem to be in a hurry to get this quest done. Jamal surmised that Asgar probably didn't expect the quest could be finished and that if he could finish it, his value to Asgar would end the moment he handed the Grimstone over.

For three days, Jamal followed the rivers up stream toward the mountain of dragons and dwarves. During his trip he saw sunflowers the size of radar dishes, mushrooms the size of mini-vans, mythical creatures he had only seen in role playing games source books come to life, and pristine, untouched wilderness with a vibrancy and life all its own.

About noon on the fourth day, Jamal reached a mountainous area and a wooden bridge which crossed a gorge about 80 feet deep. At the beginning of the bridge on the opposite side was a small sign facing away from him. Stepping off the dirt bike, Jamal began to walk it across the 50 foot span. About half way across, a tiny little man with a dirty red rag on his head, strutted out confidently. Jamal stopped.

"Yer on my bridge, my handsome troll," the little man smiled, his mouth full of crooked teeth. "Walk even a smidge and pay the toll."

"Oh, I'm sorry," Jamal said gingerly. "I didn't realize. I'll just find another way across."

As Jamal prepared to return the other way, several dozen little men, also with little red hats, clamored from beneath the bridge to block Jamal's way. Some crossed their arms in contempt, while others held homemade swords and clubs threateningly. The tallest one was no bigger than a teddy bear. The crowd of men spoke, separately, but their intonation was consistent as if they were speaking as one.

"The troll won't pay?!"

"He's ugly and cheats us."

"And he's more than halfway!"

"He thinks he can beat us!"

Jamal thought carefully for a moment, then spoke. "I'm not trying to cheat you and I'm not a troll. Had I known this was your bridge, I would've surely paid the toll."

"You speak Red Cap!" said the lone Red Cap on the other side. "You're words then are true! But you haven't the toll, then what will you do?"

"Could you be precise?" Jamal said, finding the exchange amusing. "What is your price?"

"Our prices do vary."

"For those who would cross."

"When exchanges grow wary."

"Off the bridge we would toss."

"Then stomachs we fill."

"With the meat of the dead."

"We gnaw at the bones."

"And chew on the head."

"It's horse flesh most often."

"Or sometimes of other."

"We once ate a dwarf."

"And let pass his brother."

"But you do speak Red Cap," countered the lone Red Cap curiously. "But you have no horse. If you did, you could toss it and continue your course."

For a second, Jamal had thought the Red Caps had intended to eat him, but all they really wanted was a free meal. He peeked over the edge of the bridge and noted several skulls that vaguely resembled horse-like animals. Doing a mental calculation in his head, Jamal concluded his supplies wouldn't be enough to placate the Red Caps, even if he could spare them. However, they did seem to be impressed with his rhyming.

"I know a new toll," suggested Jamal, "my stymied Red Cap. In my world, when we rhyme, we call it a rap."

For the next 30 minutes or so, Jamal regaled the Red Caps with the explicit lyrics of the street. Historically, Jamal didn't buy much music, but one of his cousins was a roadie for a Philadelphia rapper named Voodoo G. Over the years, his cousin had sent him dozens of free CD's and tapes. Voodoo G. wasn't much of a success, but his raps were annoyingly repetitive and easy to remember. This seemed to satisfy the Red Caps, who were already repeating his rhymes and bobbing to the beat of the delivery.

"You've impressed us much," smiled the lead Red Cap. "Your speech makes us dance! Will you return this way on your journeys perchance?"

"I am uncertain, it's a mountain I seek," replied Jamal. "Could you tell from my map, if I give you a peek?"

With the Red Caps complicated phrasing, it took a few minutes, but soon, Jamal realized that the mountain he thought held dragons and dwarves was wrong. As a matter of fact, the Red Caps directed him back the way he had come and then to a small fork in the road he had ignored a day before. This information would save him days, possibly weeks of travel.

Two days later, Jamal was back on the right path. He had made camp between two boulders and an ancient oak. Just as the sun came up, he was awakened by a rustling sound. He immediately got to his feet and looked around. After skulking around the perimeter of the camp, he found nothing and began to prepare breakfast. Just as he opened his pack, he spotted a gorgeous Fortesan woman standing between two gigantic black cats.

"Queen Morna, I assume," greeted Jamal. "Have you come to make me a counter offer?"

"Perhaps," she replied, skirting the issue. "You seem like a strong man. Sure of himself. Not like those other *children*."

"I also don't like to have my time wasted. I'm on a quest." Justin had spoken of a truce after Alana's, her sister and Cindy's grandmother's, death. Morna hadn't made a move on him or threatened the kids. Maybe the truce was still in effect. Maybe not.

"Ah, yes, King Ankor's Grimstone Scepter," Morna said satisfactorily.

Jamal was mildly impressed. It seemed that despite the lack of technology in this world of fantasy, like anywhere else, news traveled fast.

"It's very powerful, the Grimstone. It belonged to our greatest king. With it, he saved the Wildsidhe," added Morna. "You and your friends don't stand much of a chance against Asgar now, but with the Grimstone, his power could even rival mine. Can't have that, can we?"

One of the cats next to Morna seemed to be looking at something behind Jamal and the second cat bristled restlessly.

"Look, all I want to do is get the kids home safe," explained Jamal. "If you could make that happen, I'll give you the scepter."

"That would make sense," Morna said, putting a finger to her lip and looking intrigued. "Unfortunately, if I could send those meddlesome brats away, I would've done it long ago. Only the Fortesan who cast that major a spell can undo it. No, I think it's better than I manipulate them. But you, you don't look like the type to be manipulated. Your aura is strong. You're very capable."

At this point, Morna was looking deep into Jamal's eyes, hoping to keep him distracted. Jamal prepared himself.

"I think it would just be easier for you to…"

For a split second, Morna's eyes looked at the tree above and behind Jamal.

"Die!" she finished.

At that moment, a third cat leaped from the tree above, but Jamal had already grabbed the fork that was inside his pack. The humungous feline howled in pain, as Jamal's fork pierced its eye. Tumbling out of its way, Jamal whirled around and threw the pouch of iron dust towards Morna and the other two cats. They reeled just long enough for him to leap onto the dirt bike and speed away.

She leapt atop the back of the nearest one, cursing and screaming orders. Jamal sped away as fast as he could, but the terrain wasn't cleared for his kind of travel. Everywhere he turned, he had to smash through branches and turn away from rocks.

Unfortunately, Morna and her cats knew the woods and were quickly gaining lost ground. This was the one scenario Jamal had not accounted for. In all the previous encounters, Morna had offered the kids an alternative and even help against Asgar. Jamal figured she must've just run out of ideas or pegged him as being more trouble than he was worth.

"Does Asgar take me for that big of a fool?" she ranted bitterly. "Surrender yourself to me and you might yet live!"

"If I were you, I'd be getting ready for a fight!"

Just then, the dirt bike crested a hill. Jamal had no choice and followed the bike into the gorge. With split second timing, he twisted sideways, stopped the wheels in midair and crashed onto the ledge on the other side. Morna and her cats stopped on the other side, furtively looking for a way across.

"A fight from you?! Bah! You are nothing! Your world is nothing! Less than an insect!"

"But Asgar's no insect! He's got an army ready to move against you!"

Morna looked around frantically for a quick way across the gorge. She clearly wasn't taking Jamal's information seriously. She raised her long hands and a ball of magic energy began to form. Jamal looked down. There was a series of ledges, leading to a small hill below. Balancing the bike on one wheel, as he had seen on TV, he hopped the bike off the ledge, just before Morna's magic bolt exploded it to pebbles. He bounced his way down to the bottom on the back wheel, landed in a cloud of dust and took off, but already Morna had figured out how to get down the gorge on the opposite side.

Jamal got a good distance ahead of the cats, then up and out of the gorge. He sped another 500 feet or so and found himself at the edge of a cliff, overlooking a raging river about 80 feet below. He vaguely remembered a large river on the map Winklo had given them.

"Asgar raise an army against me?!" ranted Morna as she closed in. "He wouldn't dare raise his hand against another of the High Council! He'd violate the Treaty of Shadows."

"He's going to bully the king!" Jamal shouted back. The rest of his visit with Asgar had been an illusion. Maybe the army was as well. "If he can't have the crown, he'll control it and you!"

This last bit of info made Morna hesitate. Jamal tried to take advantage of the moment to gain more ground.

"Bah!" she dismissed. "Without the Grimstone, he would lose too much! And without you, he'll get nothing!"

Jamal figured if he backed the bike up about fifty feet, he could get up to speed and be able to land in the middle of the river and hopefully, the deepest part. After turning around and going about 30 feet, one of the cats peeked out of the underbrush and took a swipe at him. He spun out, shooting gravel into the angry feline's face. The dirt bike buzzed for the last time as Jamal shot out over the river and let the bike fall away. Morna arrived just in time to watch Jamal hit the water and the dirt bike crash and explode on the rocks below.

"These humans are mad, Asgar," muttered Morna to herself. "They shall be the death of us all."

Somewhere downstream, Jamal managed to drag himself out of the raging waters. Without a map or compass, he was now completely lost. And, without his provisions, he was likely to starve in the unfriendly wilderness. Fortunately, as he stumbled away from the river, he came across a road. He followed it for a few hours and then he heard voices of people and the sound of a wagon and a mule-like beast. Jamal reached in his pocket, found the medallion, and put it on. He felt a tingling sensation, but didn't otherwise feel different. The wagon cleared the trees and stopped. The driver and his passenger were both dwarves.

"Ho, friend," greeted the driver warmly. "Tis a cold day for a swim."

"Yes, friend," Jamal greeted back. "My fishing boat was wrecked on the rocks. I nearly drowned and now I'm lost."

"A fisherman, ye be, eh?" said the dwarf, impressed. "My brother and I have never met a dwarven fisherman, but it's a large world, I suppose. Climb aboard. The Fortesan village of Glenmarsh is not far from here. What do they call you, fisherman dwarf?"

"They call me Ishmael," replied Jamal.

"Well, Friend Ishmael, I am Granf and this is my brother, Shart. We are of the Silver Hammer Clan. Which clan are ye?"

"The, uh, Cracked Bell Clan," replied Jamal, suddenly thinking of the Liberty Bell. "It's pretty far from here, you probably haven't heard of us."

"Tis true," said Granf. "But we don't follow other clans much."

The dwarven brothers reminded Jamal of Winklo, only even friendlier. Although Jamal couldn't see what he looked like as a dwarf, he assumed the medallion had worked because the dwarfs seemed to accept him so readily. The only snag was when he climbed into the wagon. Shart gave Granf a confused look, as the wagon shifted more than he expected from the weight. But, in general, the brothers were pretty easy going and they were just as happy to have someone new to talk to during the boring ride to Glenmarsh.

Granf was the older of the two dwarves and his beard was black with streaks of gray. The gray wavered down the length of the facial hair like veins of ore in a rock. His clothes were loose fitting and made from leather and his hair was long and a little bit unkempt. Shart was a lot more uptight in personality and appearance. His clothes were immaculate and he wore a small helmet that was highly polished. His hair and beard were meticulously trimmed and a bronze ring held the braid of his beard in place.

"So, what will ye do now that ye boat is gone?" asked Shart.

"I have family in the caves near here. The ones where the dragons live. Do you know them?" asked Jamal casually.

"Oh, aye, that's where our clan lives. We'll take ye there if ye like," Granf smiled happily. "Perhaps we're related. Do ye know..."

"I'm not good with names," interrupted Jamal carefully, trying to stave off a long session of answering "No."

Granf let it go. He had secretly toyed with the idea of becoming a cave fisherman years ago, but his wife had laughed at him. With Jamal around, he figured, he finally had enough ammo for a major career change.

"I'd appreciate the ride. I'll work for my part," offered Jamal.

"Good," agreed Shart.

"Nah, wouldn't hear of it," corrected Granf. "You're our guest! A guest shouldn't work."

Shart cast a bewildered glance back at his brother. Surely he wasn't thinking of letting the stranger ride for free? Jamal also learned that the dwarves called each other "friend" much like he used the term "brother" back home. Fitting in as a dwarf was going to be a lot easier than he had thought.

Glenmarsh was a village of about 500 souls, mostly Low Fortesans, meaning those without much magic power. The largest minority was dwarf. There were a few other races there as well, including pixies, elves, and even a few Jamal didn't recognize. The Hammer Brothers got rooms at an inn run by dwarves. Since Jamal didn't have any money, the innkeeper let him bunk in the stable hayloft for free.

Jamal quickly discovered that while dwarves were generally gruff and untalkative to most people, when amongst their own kind you couldn't shut them up. Granf and Shart insisted that Jamal meet everyone in the bar. Most of the dwarves were like Granf and Shart, merchants or mining representatives, here to trade goods before returning to the mines. Apparently, none of the dwarves had ever fished and they all insisted Jamal regale them with tales of the open sea, or at least, the open river.

Finally, just as Jamal had managed to excuse himself for the evening and head for the loft, Granf came running after him.

"C'mon Granf," said Jamal, exhausted. "I got up early today."

"Yes, I know, but they're having a night auction tonight!"

"But, I... Okay, what is it?"

"It's an invitation only auction of the bizarre and the unusual!" smiled Granf in anticipation. "Perhaps we can find you a new dwarven boat!"

Jamal started to think of some excuse, but Granf was determined to get Jamal in his debt. Before Jamal could reply, Granf grabbed him by the arm and pulled him towards the secret night auction. It turned out that the secret night auction wasn't much of a secret. The dwarves that had packed the inn earlier, now moved their drinks into the basement.

"What's the big secret?" asked Jamal.

"The Fortesans can't bid," assured Granf. "They don't even know we're having this! That's the secret part."

"Would they care?" asked Jamal, trying to keep his eyes open.

"Of course! Look at this merchandise!"

The "merchandise" consisted mostly of junk – a dwarven face carved from quartz with the nose chipped off, a Fortesan drinking stein made from pewter that was partially melted, an obscene painting of a group of pixie women, a bottle of whisky made from fermented skunk innards and on and on. Each item was presented as if it was a Van Gough painting being auctioned at Christy's. Just as Jamal began to doze off, the dwarven auctioneer held something aloft that caught his eye.

"Behold!" said the auctioneer dramatically. "From the faraway lands of Penn Sylvania! A Sylvan mouse!"

The auctioneer held up a plastic computer mouse, its cord cut and frayed at the end where the connector would be. There was only one place that could've come from.

"Bid on that," Jamal instructed Granf.

"Doesn't look much like a mouse to me," scoffed the dwarf, a little drunk.

"I need to know where that came from, bid on that."

"Excuse me, Friend Ishmael," Shart interrupted, trying to keep his inebriated brother from wasting money. "Our hospitality only goes so far."

Jamal reach into his pocket. He still had change that he had put in his pocket weeks ago for parking around Philadelphia.

"Are these any good here?" Jamal asked the brothers.

"Silver?" said Granf. "Of course!"

"One silver coin!" bid Jamal.

"Two silver!" came a drunken bid from across the room.

"Seven!"

A hush fell over the room. The dwarves murmured amongst themselves. Who was this crazy fisherman dwarf?

"If you had money, why didn't you pay us?" whispered Shart.

"Actually," Jamal announced to the room. "I have some unusual items for your auction that I found during my travels. I'd be willing to trade if you can tell me where you found that mouse."

"Doesn't even look like a mouse," repeated Granf.

"All right, friend, Ishmael. What have you?"

"Behold!" presented Jamal taking a road map from his hunter's vest. "A map of the mystical land, Penn Sylvania!"

The crowd made an impressed noise. Jamal held up the blank CD-ROM.

"Behold! A disc of gold!"

"Oooo," said the crowd, impressed.

Jamal held up the book on government conspiracies.

"And finally, a book of forbidden knowledge!"

"Ooooo!" said the crowd.

The dwarves now applauded and then went into their pouches to find money. Jamal approached the auctioneer.

"Where did you get it?"

"A young woman sold it to me today. She said she was from Penn Sylvania. She had Sylvan features, you can always tell."

"Was she a Fortesan?"

"I suppose, but it was the strangest thing. Her hands appeared to be missing a joint. She was anxious to trade, I didn't question her further."

"What was her name? Where is she staying?"

"She said her name was Joanna. I don't know where she was staying. Her clothes were strange. Bright blue, but worn from excessive use."

During Jamal's stay at the school, he had gone over the whereabouts of missing kids. Most had chosen to stay in the school, but a few had taken off, unaware of the world that they had been thrust into. Jamal remembered one of the missing names was Joanna Wilkins, a junior. She had left with two other boys in a 4-wheel-drive.

"Thank you," said Jamal, giving the auctioneer two quarters.

"Next item up for bids!" said the auctioneer. "The strange coins of… Liberty!"

Jamal hurried his way across the room, back upstairs and out the door. The Hammer brothers followed him.

"Ishmael! Why did ye not share this treasure?" demanded Shart.

"Here, Shart," said Jamal handing him the rest of the quarters. "It's very important that I find Joanna, do you understand?"

"But it's late and the auction…" whined Granf.

"You have been keeping me up all night with eating and drinking and wacky auctions," insisted Jamal, a little peeved. "This girl is in danger and you want to go to sleep?"

"I will help," said Shart, hopeful of more reward in the future.

"Fine," Granf agreed, tossing the rest of his ale into the street.

The threesome went from door to door waking everyone in town. After separating from the Hammer Brothers, Jamal removed his necklace. Keeping his hands in his vest pockets, he passed himself off as a Fortesan and traced Joanna's movements for the past couple of weeks.

Joanna had arrived in town, alone and on foot. Although the dwarves were friendly to her, they would not hire her at the dwarven inn because they feared the Fortesans would be angry that a Fortesan would work for a dwarf. The Fortesans eventually hired her at several places, but Joanna, like most American teenagers, wasn't used to the kind of back-breaking labor a medieval type village would offer her. Her hands also repulsed most of her Fortesan employers and for the last week, she had gotten most of her meals by begging.

Eventually, Jamal tracked her movements to an abandoned farm house. One look at the footprints outside in the mud and Jamal immediately recognized sneaker treads. Carefully, he opened the farm house door.

Inside he found Joanna, hovering over the flickering flames of a fireplace. She held a sharp dagger to her wrist. Joanna was half Philippine and half Afro-American and her exotic good looks shone through the wear and tear on her face. She was still wearing tattered jeans and a bomber jacket, just like the first day she arrived here.

Unlike most of the kids, however, she hadn't adapted to the new surroundings and now she was about to give up hope. Standing over her, was a shadowy figure of a woman. Jamal opened the door and said the only thing he could think of.

"Nobody move! FBI!"

"Oh, thank God!" cried Joanna, immediately.

She dropped the dagger and ran for Jamal. The shadowy figure, however, morphed away and instantly reformed between the two. Jamal could see that the shadowy figure was actually made from a shadow. The various tones of gray formed a stunningly good-looking cheerleader in a Sparta high school uniform.

"Who are you?" demanded the shadow angrily. "You're interrupting."

"I-I changed my mind, Marianne," said Joanna desperately. "I don't want to be a shadow!"

"I don't believe this!" sighed Marianne in contempt. "You wanna be human in this place? Like him?"

Jamal suddenly remembered Justin telling him about Marianne Blossum and how she was taken in by Queen Morna. The kids had assumed Morna killed her. Being killed might have been kind compared to the thing of power and evil Marianne had been turned into.

"Look, Marianne, come back with me. Maybe there's some way we could change you back," offered Jamal.

"Change back?" said Marianne incredulous. "Look at me!"

Marianne proceeded to morph into various outfits. They were all designer and all looked fabulous on her.

"Imagine a perfect body, like mine," she laughed as she morphed. "Now imagine that it never gets old and never dies. Beauty eternal and power unlimited."

"You don't want to change back?" said Jamal, a little unnerved.

"Duh! And I was about to bring Joanna in on it before you barged in here!"

"Joanna, my name's Jamal Nichols..."

"Stop talking to her! She's mine!"

Jamal felt the cold grip of Marianne's icy grasp and she hurled him across the room.

"You see how men are!" Marianne insisted to Joanna. "You want to go back to that?!"

"I'm afraid," said Joanna crying. "Let's wait until tomorrow."

"No!" insisted Marianne, her eyes now turning black. "Kill yourself now or I'll do it for you!"

"No!" cried Joanna.

Marianne grabbed Joanna by the wrist and caused the dagger to fly up into the air and into her free hand. Jamal fumbled in the pockets of his hunter's vest and came up with a road flare as Marianne prepared to strike. The magnesium lit up the farm house almost as bright as day and Marianne's shadow form almost burst apart. Screeching in pain, the world's most evil cheerleader took on her true form – that of a grossly, misshapen, shadow of her former soul. The foul thing retreated into the night with a whimper. Joanna broke down in tears and hugged Jamal thankfully.

After Joanna pulled herself together, Jamal explained the basics of the situation. It was important that the Hammer Brothers still believe he was a dwarf. He put the medallion back on.

"How do I look?" asked Jamal.

Joanna laughed despite herself.

"Kind of like Gary Coleman with a beard," she teased.

Eventually, the twosome found the Hammer Brothers arguing with a Fortesan farmer about waking his chickens. Jamal told them Joanna was a Fortesan who had been separated from her caravan when it was attacked by giants. Joanna made a point of keeping her hands in her pockets in front of the dwarves. This seemed to be enough explanation for the brothers and the group agreed to meet late tomorrow and head for the mountain. Back at the hayloft, Jamal and Joanna laid down in the hay and quickly fell into an exhausted sleep.

CHAPTER 10

The next day, Jamal was dragged to the dwarven equivalent of brunch, which lasted two hours and included such rich food Jamal thought he would have to roll back to the hay loft. He brought Joanna some food. She ate hungrily while telling her story.

When the town had initially crossed over, most of the kids didn't believe they were in any real danger. With very little supplies, Joanna got into one of the 4-wheel-drives with her boyfriend Robert and his friend Mike. Unfortunately, after driving for a day, they quickly became lost in the wilderness. The 4-wheel-drive eventually ran out of gas three days away from the town.

Mike and Robert convinced Joanna to stay in the car while they went for help, but after two days, they hadn't returned. Hungry and alone, Joanna spent the next few days wandering the wilderness. Eventually, she was taken in by a group of Fortesan fur trappers. She cooked and cleaned for them for a few weeks, until they showed her the way to town. For the next few months, she wandered from village to village, looking for Robert and Mike or any sign of the other kids.

"It's so strange," she said later, resting in the hay. "It's like our whole world doesn't exist here. I'd given up hope, but thank God, now we can go home."

"Ah," said Jamal thoughtfully. "We're not ready to go home yet."

"We're not? Why? You said you were from the FBI."

"We'll get home, we'll get home," assured Jamal. "It's still a little more complicated than just going. Once I get the Grimstone Scepter, I'll go back and we'll formulate a rescue plan."

"How can you rescue us if you leave and can't come back? What if you can't come back?!"

"Joanna," said Jamal holding her hand. "You have to have faith. In me and in yourself. If you can't, you're beaten before we ever start. Getting rescued is all part of the plan."

"The plan?" laughed Joanna incredulously. "Is that all you're about? Plan this, plan that?"

"I like to be organized," countered Jamal. "The way I figure it, if you don't have a plan, how can you organize your life?"

"Life isn't just about keeping yourself in control."

"Hey, no offense," Jamal said bristling. "But if you had given some thought about leaving the town, you might not have needed to be rescued."

"Okay, so that didn't work out like I expected it, but... it's not like I'm planning my whole life out. Things happen. You can't anticipate it all."

"Yeah and you can't let it get you depressed and despondent."

"Okay," admitted Joanna. "I lost it back there. But, Jamal, you have to be a little flexible in life. If not for yourself, for those around you. We're only human. And we might not ever get back."

Joanna started crying again and Jamal shifted positions. The cellphone Myra had given him, fell out of the pocket.

"Wait a minute. Couldn't you call for help?" asked Joanna.

"Nah, there aren't any phone towers here. I'd never be able to hear anything. Besides, I already tried."

"But wait, your phone has the feature for radios. My dad's in construction and has one just like it. You should be able to call someone if they have a walkie talkie."

"One of the kids, Ben Mazel, has a short-wave radio," remembered Jamal. "Every day at about 4:05pm he tries to see if anyone can hear him on the other side."

"That should work."

"Okay then. When we get to a high point, I'll turn it on and give it a try."

The next day, the Hammer Brothers, after a little convincing, agreed to take both Joanna and Jamal to the caves. Joanna, of course, could not actually enter the caves since she wasn't a dwarf. When the group arrived three days later, Jamal and the dwarves provided her with provisions and a small cave nearby would act as her shelter.

Jamal tried calling on the radio of his cell phone, but to no avail. He left the cellphone with Joanna hoping that she would have better luck.

"If I'm not out of there in six days, you try and make it back to the school," instructed Jamal. He also gave Joanna the other road flare. "You can make it, you've just got to believe."

"Okay," said Joanna, terrified. She kissed him on the cheek. "Good luck."

Jamal got back in the wagon with the Hammer Brothers. Shart looked at him, impressed.

"Kissed by a Fortesan. Ye lead an interesting life, friend Ishmael," commented Shart.

"Sometimes, it gets a little too interesting," admitted Jamal.

The wagon entered the cave and now the only light the travelers would have would be the oil lantern which hung near Granf and bounced along. The beast pulling the wagon slowed its pace, but the brothers assured Jamal the animal knew the trip blindfolded.

The trip ended at the dwarven village of Stonehelm. Essentially, it was a large cave dotted with a few wooden structures and many small caves on the side. The entire area was dimly lit by glowing fungi, which stretched for hundreds of feet. The dank air made Jamal feel a little claustrophobic, but the dwarves seem to thrive on it.

"Have you ever had homemade, purple mushroom stew, Ishmael?" asked Granf.

Jamal rolled his eyes. The dwarves put mushrooms in just about everything that they ate.

"Can't say that I have, friend, Granf, but I'm sure your wife has a great recipe," sighed Jamal.

"That she does, friend, Ishmael," added Shart, rubbing his hands together in anticipation.

Jamal didn't really have anything against mushrooms when he started this mission. He could take them or leave them. However, after Granf's wife served him mushroom stew, mushroom muffins, grilled mushroom fillets, mushroom bread, mushroom salad, and mushroom pudding, he vowed that if he ever got back to civilization, he'd never eat a mushroom again.

"Mushroom tart?" offered Granf's wife, sometime after dinner.

"No, thank you," Jamal said quickly. "Really, I couldn't eat another bite."

Granf came back from tucking in his four children and lit a pipe.

"You're welcome to stay as long as you like," offered Granf.

"I can't, friend Granf, I must find my relatives and begin to raise money to buy a boat again."

"Take me with ye," said Granf suddenly. "I have the sea in my blood! I know it! I want to be a fisherman like ye."

Jamal thought for a moment. The poor guy was so earnest.

"You'd miss your family," assured Jamal. "With fishing, sometimes you're away for months at a time. And I've been away for years."

"Really?" said Granf disappointed.

"You've got to go where the fish are. You might have to leave this area all together."

Jamal had sensed that Granf was a bit of a homebody. This revelation finally brought him down to Earth. Jamal, however, didn't want to leave him without hope.

"You could always fish for sport," suggested Jamal.

"Sport?" said Granf curiously.

"Yes, like a hobby. Like whittling wood or something."

Granf's eyes lit up. There was a way.

"Will ye show me how to make a fishing rod?" asked Granf.

"I promise," assured Jamal. "But first, I need to look at the records."

"Records?"

"The births and deaths of the people of the clan. Your history."

"Oh, history," said the dwarf, understanding. "For that, you must talk to our clan elders. That will be difficult."

"Why?"

"They are very busy. They hear our disputes and settle our differences. They make decisions that affect the entire clan and how we will move against the dragons."

"You're moving against the dragons?"

"We must. For every shaft we mine, they create another hungry brood of loathsome reptiles."

"There must be one way that they will see me."

"Well," thought Granf. "It would be easy if you could play Bones."

"You mean...dice?"

"No, I mean, Bones. Like this."

Granf took several dice-like objects from his pocket, shook them up, and threw them on the mantle. They appeared to be carved from bones.

"Teach me and I'll make you a fishing rod."

Bones turned out to be the dwarven equivalent of craps and the village elders, being too feeble for any major activity, spent their off time gambling heavily. For his part, Jamal made Granf a fishing rod as best as he knew how. The rod was a of piece wood from the wagon, the line was spun from an old shirt, and the hook was made from a piece of wire Jamal pulled off his still hidden armor.

"Where did ye get that metal?" asked Granf curiously.

"Shh, don't tell anyone. I'm wearing metal armor."

"Ye fool! No wonder ye foot is so heavy!"

The next day, the Hammer Brothers took Jamal to the House of Elders. Here, the ancient dwarves of the Silver Hammer Clan sat in modest comfort, hearing the squabbles of their brethren and laying down their wisdom. Most of the disputes involved arguments over mining rights or petty thefts. Hours later, after most of the other dwarves had left, the Head Elder, Kalaff, aimed a wary eye toward Jamal and the Hammer Brothers.

"What dispute have ye?" he asked.

"No, dispute, friend Kalaff," said Granf humbly. "Friend Ishmael has come far to visit. He wishes to drink from your fountain of wisdom."

"And play Bones," added Shart.

"And play Bones, friend Kalaff."

"We have enough players," Kalaff said gruffly. "Go back to whatever it is that you do, Ishmael."

"But I am a fisherman without a boat, friend Kalaff."

A murmur ran through the group of elders. Jamal had surmised correctly that they had never heard of a dwarven fisherman either.

"Such activity is reserved for Fortesans. Dwarves do not fish," assured Kalaff.

"Then how do you explain this?" offered Jamal.

Jamal held up the fishing rod. The elders seemed to be impressed.

"Your occupation interests us," said Kalaff. "We will answer your questions, if you will show us how to fish."

Jamal was beginning to believe that he was single-handedly creating the sport fishing industry on the Wildsidhe, at least for dwarves, anyway. After another tedious discussion about fishing, Jamal posed his question.

"Where can I find the Grimstone Scepter?"

Kalaff looked at Granf bewildered. "You said he was looking for his family."

"I-I thought he was, Elder," assured the flustered dwarf.

"I seek the Grimstone Scepter, where is it?" repeated Jamal.

"Friend Ishmael, you ask too much. The scepter is Fortesan magic and its influences are evil and corrupt!"

"I must find it. Lives depend upon it," assured Jamal.

"His mouth is full of lies!" accused Shart. "We should cast him out!"

"No," Kalaff said. "I promised to answer his question and I am as good as my word. The Grimstone Scepter is located in a Fortesan catacomb ten miles from here. It is not part of dwarven territory. It is rumored to be the resting place of King Ankor the great."

All the dwarves bowed their heads respectfully, which threw Jamal. The dwarves seemed to despise the Fortesans. Why was Ankor so special? Morna had said he saved the Wildsidhe.

Before he could ponder more, the ancient dwarf leaned in close, his face illuminated by the glow of a torch light.

"Ye must be brave to face dragons," the elder dwarf revealed. "Are ye brave?"

CHAPTER 11

The Hammer Brothers were sharply divided about what to do about Jamal. Shart wanted to cast him out, but Granf was willing to hear Jamal's explanation.

"Friend Ishmael," said Granf, back at his home. "Ye may speak freely. Will ye not share ye true intentions."

"He lies!" insisted Shart.

"Close the door," said Jamal. "What I'm about to show you, must not be revealed to the other dwarves and especially not to the Fortesans."

Jamal removed his medallion. The dwarves looked up at him, wide-eyed.

"I am Jamal Nichols, a human," explained Jamal. "Asgar holds 300 of my kind in your world. He has promised to return me to my world if I give him the Grimstone Scepter."

"Ye can't!" insisted Granf.

"If I don't, he will tear apart these mountains looking for it. My people have an army to fight him, but they can't get here if I don't return home."

"Ye are brave to fight the Royal Fortesans, but if ye give him the Grimstone Scepter, ye make him even more powerful. Have ye considered this?" asked Shart.

"If I don't, I'm stuck here, like Joanna. She's counting on me to get home."

"What difference does it make?" Granf said to Shart. "If Asgar has one Grimstone Scepter or a hundred... He is a Fortesan and he will always rule us. But this one, he may escape his clutches."

"Will you take me with you?" asked Shart. "I should like to see your world. This Penn Sylvania."

"If I can. Who knows? Maybe one day, we'll all go fishing."

Supplied with provisions of dried mushrooms, a map, some torches and a pack, Granf and Shart guided Jamal to the edge of the Dwarven Territory. The dwarves had several large traps in place to guard entrances. If the dragons attacked, they would surely loose quite a bit of fight when razor sharp boulders came raining down upon them.

"This is as far as we can go, friend Jamal," said Granf. "Beyond this point is the unknown. We wish ye well on ye quest."

"Tis suicide," muttered Shart. "Stay with us."

"Don't worry, guys. I've got it covered."

And with that, Jamal flipped over the medallion. Shart immediately fled, then came running back to drag his stunned brother along. Jamal looked down into a puddle. He did indeed look like a dragon and his illusionary metallic scales glistened in the torchlight.

After a few hundred yards, Jamal came across the rotting carcass of a real dragon. Its head had been crushed by a large, square boulder. The moldering ropes around the rock meant that it was a dwarven trap. The dragon's hide did not rot, but insects, especially large beetles of every shape, bored in and out of its eyes and mouth. While Jamal stared gaping in fascination, he heard a clicking sound. He looked up just in time to see three giant beetles, one the size of a garbage can, climb over the carcass. Jamal fled as the beetles pursued.

He turned down what he thought was the passage he had just left and found himself cornered. Just as he turned to fight the beetles, a blast of fire came from a side cave. An orange dragon, about the size of a mini-bus, roasted the beetles. The insects flipped over and expired.

"Thank you," said Jamal.

"Oh, not at all, Shiny. These are my favorite kind!" replied the dragon, popping one of the beetles in her mouth and crunching down.

"I'm Vawna. Brood of four... Well, actually five, if you count Sebastian back there."

"He was your brother? I'm sorry."

"Sorry? For what? You didn't do it. It was those icky dwarves! Eww! If they didn't taste so much like mushrooms, I'd eat me a whole broodful! Sebastian was an idiot anyways. Typical male, always trying to mate or get treasure. Kind of pathetic really. Speaks to his insecurity. How about you, Shiny? What's your brood?"

"I'm Jamal. Brood of five," smiled Jamal, inwardly picturing his brothers and sisters as his brood.

Vawna appeared to be impressed. Apparently, dragons of a larger brood held more clout.

"Jamal?" she said curiously. "That's a funny name. Is it Sepian?"

"I'm not sure. What's Vawna from?"

"Oh, I'm named after my mother's brood mother," Vawna said annoyed. "They're always on me to be like her and... You sure you don't want a beetle?"

"Positive."

The dragon popped the other two into her mouth and continued to talk. Occasionally, Jamal caught a glimpse of the insect's innards being smashed to bits.

"Old Vawna was a real terror back in the day. Towards the end, they say she would only eat Fortesans who were pure of thought! Well, she's dead now. Probably starved to death!"

Vawna wasn't what Jamal expected in a dragon at all. Talking to her was almost like talking to Tina Shelly, minus the constant references to the Heart Throb Boys. Vawna swallowed the last of the beetles and looked around.

"Okay, this is boring. Let's go."

And with that, the dragon tore down the nearest cave. Jamal followed as best he could, but Vawna would use her wings to glide over gaps in the cave. Jamal, even though he looked like a dragon, couldn't fly like one and had to climb over rocks and depressions in the cave floor.

"Slow down!" called Jamal.

Vawna's laugh echoed through the cave. She thought it was hilarious that he couldn't keep up. After an hour of Vawna teasing him and flying back and taking off again, Jamal was just about out of steam. Then he heard a crash. A few minutes later he caught up to Vawna, pinned beneath a small boulder. She struggled in vain to free one of her wings that got pinned beneath. Jamal could clearly see another pile of boulders ready to fall on top of her.

"Vawna don't move!" ordered Jamal.

"But it hurts!" she whined.

"You haven't set off the rest of the trap, if you keep moving, you'll be completely buried."

Reluctantly, but still whimpering, Vawna stopped moving. Jamal looked around. He had learned that the dwarves were sticklers about their traps and he knew there had to be a lever to reset it. It was part of the Dwarven Code of Construction. After feeling around in the dark for a minute, he found the switch and the boulder lifted. Vawna didn't wait for it to get back in place and instead pulled herself out, setting off the trap again. This time, it just missed her. Jamal ran out of the way of the remaining boulders.

"Hey!" Jamal objected. "Are you trying to get me killed?! I told you not to move! Which part of that didn't you understand?"

"But it hurt!" whined Vawna. "You were taking too long anyway and you didn't catch me. What's wrong with you? Are you slow or something?"

"A Fortesan zapped me with some kind of spell. I haven't recovered enough to fly yet. I can't mate for a while either."

"Oh, no wonder you weren't chasing me!" said Vawna realizing. "Tch, that's a shame, I could really use a mate right now. Oh, well. Race you!"

Vawna zoomed out of the cave.

"I can't race you!" called Jamal jogging after her.

Vawna zoomed back.

"Oh, right. Sorry. You look thirsty. You look tired. You want to come back to the nest? There's water there. You can drink. You can ride on my back if you want."

"Okay. Thanks," said Jamal, trying to keep up with her frazzled thoughts. Jamal climbed aboard.

"Wow, you're really light," noted Vawna. "Is that part of the spell?"

"Yep."

"Hmm. Whatever."

Vawna rocketed down the tunnels, the way you might expect a teenager to fly when he or she first got her flying license. She never thought very far ahead, moved very fast, and would occasionally get distracted by objects on her journey.

"Ooo, waterfall," she said suddenly at top speed.

Jamal grabbed her by the neck and pulled her away from an oncoming stalagmite. She tipped to one side and sailed by it effortlessly.

"Gosh, don't be such an egg," said the dragon, annoyed. "I can fly these caves with my eyes closed."

"Please don't," begged Jamal.

Finally, the cave she was zooming down opened up into the largest, inside space Jamal had ever seen. The cavern stretched for miles in every direction and shafts of light poured in from the sunlight above. In this cavern, you almost got the sense the entire mountain was hollow. And, everywhere he looked, Jamal saw dragons of every shape, size, color, and age.

Perched on the lowest ledges were dragons Vawna's age. The male dragons locked horns and wrestled with each other, while the females flitted about watching in anticipation. On the mid-level, young hatchlings were learning to fly and hover at the behest of proud mothers, while males skulked in their caves counting their treasure. On the higher levels, nests of new eggs were carefully guarded by both male and female alike, while at the top most levels, ancient dragons slept on piles of treasure, yet undreamed by even the most greedy of dwarf.

Two other female dragons, one pink and one bright yellow, glided up to meet Vawna and kept speed with her through the cavern.

"Hi, Vawna," they said cattily.

"Who's your new fly mate?" asked the pink one, while the orange laughed.

"This is Jamal," Vawna blushed. "He's hurt, I'm just giving him a ride."

"Sure, Vawna. Riiight," giggled the duo, as they glided away.

"Tch, oh!" said Vawna, trying to sound casual. "Just ignore them. My sisters can be like, incredibly jealous. You were thirsty right?"

"Well..."

Before Jamal could continue to respond, Vawna dove head first into the lake of crystal clear water in the center of the cave. Jamal scrambled to the shore quickly. He had no idea how the water would affect his disguise. One of the baby dragons, colored bright blue and carrying a beetle on a stick, eyed him suspiciously.

"You're weird," said the blue dragon.

A larger, female dragon took her son by the claw.

"But, Mommy, that dragon's weird!" insisted the little dragon.

"Timothy, I told you to either stay in the cave or no more beetles."

"But mom!"

An ancient, partially blind dragon, his scales almost completely gray, shambled up to the water hole and took a drink. Jamal figured he'd better take a drink while he could.

"I fought Saint George to a standstill, ya know," claimed the ancient dragon. "Broke his lance right here. I still have a piece in me."

"Wow, that's very impressive," Jamal said, trying to be polite.

Across the lake, Jamal noticed a group of dragons having a discussion around a large fire. Vawna suddenly surfaced, splashing Jamal and the old dragon.

"Oh!" said the old dragon, surprised. "You children have no respect anymore! In my day, you didn't swim where you drank!"

"Hey, this guy fought..."

"Saint George, I know. Drakk tells that to everybody. Nobody even knows who Saint George is. You want to swim? You want to eat? Are you sure you still can't mate?"

"Um, positive. What's going on over there?"

"Oh," said Vawna as bored as possible. "Dragon Council. You don't want to go there."

"The Dragon Council's very important!" insisted Drakk. "I'm on my way now, just as soon as I have a little nap."

And like that, Drakk was out like a light and snoring away the day.

"What's the Dragon Council do?" asked Jamal.

"They decide stuff and vote and talk and talk and talk," Vawna sighed in exasperation. "Do you really want to go over there?"

"Just for a few minutes?" asked Jamal gingerly.

Vawna rolled her eyes in annoyance and Jamal was reminded of his first girlfriend, Janice. She was 14 when he was 15 and she couldn't keep a thought in her head for more than five seconds either.

"Tch, fine."

The Dragon Council consisted of about three dozen dragons, most at their peak and most of them male. The lead dragon was Hannibal and he talked about waging a campaign against the dwarves. Even with their traps, Jamal didn't think the dwarves would stand a chance. Then he looked at the other dragons and realized why things had become such a stalemate.

Most of the dragons in attendance weren't even paying attention. They were either too apathetic to care or, like Vawna, were too consumed with their own urges and desires to set them aside even a second for the good of the group.

"Want to go exploring?" Jamal said to Vawna suddenly, hoping to turn her reckless energy to his advantage.

"Nah, I'm tired," she yawned. "Let's sleep for a while."

This prospect worried Jamal for a few reasons. The first was, he had often read that dragons slept for days and even years. The second was, of course, that he was not a dragon and there was a good chance Vawna would discover that being so close to him. She flew him to a surprisingly high ledge and from the noises he heard in the surrounding caves, Jamal surmised that this was the dragon equivalent of "Make Out Point".

"C'mere Jamal," Vawna cooed. "Let me kiss it and make it better."

"Wow," thought Jamal to himself. "She is just like Janice."

"What's wrong? Don't you like me? You don't like me," Vawna said. "Did you want a beetle? I could've given you one."

"No, it's not that. I told you. The spell," explained Jamal gingerly.

"You're always talking about that stupid spell!" snapped the dragon. "I'm sick of it. You can just sleep here by yourself and I don't care!"

And with that, head strong dragon zoomed away.

"I never thought I'd meet anyone that would make me miss Janice," Jamal thought to himself.

Without anywhere else to go, Jamal decided to sack out for the evening. Vawna's nest was a bed of bright green moss and discarded beetle husks. After getting comfortable, Jamal thought it best to make sure all the husks were actually husks and not sleeping beetles. He then sacked out for the night.

That night, Jamal dreamed of the Fortesan Kingdom in ruin. The beautiful spires had been smashed, its buildings were rubble and the countryside had been set ablaze. Everywhere he looked lay the broken bodies of soldiers, Fortesan, dwarf, elf, and the kids. Atop one of the hills, a dark rider on a horse. He was heavily armored with a purple cape, a sword, and the Grimstone Scepter.

CHAPTER 12

As Jamal peered in closer, the rider lifted his helmet visor. Beneath it was his own face.

It was difficult to tell how long he slept, but Jamal felt rested when he awoke. He looked out of the cave. Vawna had perched him on a ledge hundreds of feet above the other caves. It would take him at least a day to climb down and he would probably attract the attention of every dragon in the cave. He thought about asking one of the other dragons nearby, but it was clear that they were engaged in an activity you should never interrupt if you want to get on the good side of anyone.

Just when he had decided to attempt the climb, Vawna's sisters zoomed up to the ledge.

"Hi, Jamal," they giggled.

"Where's Vawna?" asked the yellow one.

"She's a little upset with me because I wouldn't mate."

The dragon girls giggled.

"No, it's not like that, I'm hurt. A Fortesan put a spell on me," assured Jamal.

"Well, you've put a spell on me!" giggled the pink one.

"You know, I would really appreciate it if one of you could give me a ride to the ground."

The girls hesitated, then moved forward. Suddenly, an orange blur shot up between them. It was Vawna. She growled at her sisters and they fled. She turned back toward Jamal.

"I don't like you anymore," she insisted. "You're lame. You'll probably starve up here. I won't bring you food."

Jamal thought for a minute. Whenever Janice was mad at him, he'd buy her chocolate. Jamal remembered he still had a candy bar in his vest.

"Do you like chocolate?" Jamal smiled, opening the package.

"Where did you get that?" asked Vawna, very interested. "I've never smelled that. That smells good. What is that?"

"It's chocolate. You want a piece? I'll give you a piece if you give me a ride," said Jamal, trying to ape her thought process. "Then we could go exploring. I like exploring. Here."

Jamal broke off a little square and the dragon picked it up with her prehensile tongue. At first her eyes bugged out a little, then she smiled dreamily and made "Mmm! Mmm!" sounds that echoed all over the caves. She flitted about in utter ecstasy and finally flew into Jamal's arms and kissed him.

"You must be some kind of wizard!" she exclaimed. "I must have more chocolate! More! More! More!"

"I have more, but, uh, too much will make you sick. Only one piece a day."

"I like you Jamal. I'm thirsty. Did you say exploring? Let's get a drink and explore! Drink first though!"

And with that, he was back in Vawna's good graces. After a quick drink by the lake, Jamal convinced her to go exploring. Vawna scooped him up and zoomed down the nearest cave, blowing past a henpecked dragon male carrying debris for his wife's nest.

"Vawna," said Jamal, trying not to lose his lunch on the flight. "Do you know where the Fortesan catacombs are?"

"Sure I do! I don't go there. No one does. It's icky. Ooo, look at that crystal! Let's lick it!"

Vawna perched near a crystalline stalagmite and began to lick it. Jamal reluctantly played along. The crystal was disgustingly salty. He wretched a little bit and Vawna took the moment to lick his face.

"Are you feeling better yet?" she asked. "Because if you are and you want to mate, we can. How long does that spell last?"

"Vawna, can I ask you something? It's very personal and I want you to listen."

"Okay," smiled the dragon, wrongly anticipating that he wanted to mate. "Do you like me?"

"Yes. I like you. I know I said I didn't, but I was mad before. I like you, Jamal, do you like me?"

"Yes."

The dragon crept a little closer to him. Jamal tried to keep his distance. "Would you like me even if I was old?"

"But you're not old! Drakk is old."

"But what if I was old," Jamal explained carefully. "Would you still like me?"

"I guess. But you're not old," corrected the dragon.

"What if I was different?"

"You mean, a different color?"

"No, what if I wasn't a dragon."

"You're not a dragon?!"

Jamal removed the medallion, Vawna reeled back in surprise. Then, a look of total relief came across her face.

"Oh, no wonder!" she laughed. "No wonder you wouldn't mate! I thought it was me! But it was you! No wonder! What are you? Are you a wizard? I thought you were a wizard."

"I'm sort of a wizard, I guess. We're still friends, right?"

"Sure. Okay. Friends," agreed the dragon. "Friends get chocolate, right?"

"Every day," assured Jamal. "But I really need your help, Vawna. Can you take me to the Fortesan catacombs? I need to find something."

"Eww. Are you sure you want to go there? It's icky. No one goes."

"Why?"

"Bad magic."

"Well, my friends really need this item that's in the catacombs and they're the ones that have most of the chocolate."

Vawna's face changed expression and just like that, her mind changed as well.

"Okay, whatever, let's go."

The young dragon scooped him up and zoomed down several caves. Eventually, they reached a foreboding-looking tomb entrance. It looked even more dark and dank than the rest of the cavern and that was an accomplishment considering its location. Two thick stone doors were the entrance of the tomb, flanked by the statues of two Fortesan warriors.

One of the doors was ajar and the lower half of a skeleton poked out. Jamal lit up a torch and peered in. The skeleton had been beheaded by a blade trap just inside the door. Jamal tried to take the skeleton's sword, but it crumbled in his hand.

"I'd better go inside alone."

"No, I'll go. I'll protect you," insisted Vawna shoving the other door open. "Dragons are good protectors. Watch."

The other door opened and a second blade swung across, beheading Jamal's torch. He fumbled in his pack and a minute later ignited another one. Vawna had an embarrassed expression on her face.

"I'm sorry."

"You can come, but you have to do exactly what I say."

"But..."

"Exactly. Or no more chocolate."

"Okay."

Carefully, the twosome made their way inside. There was a long hallway, flanked with ancient suits of Fortesan armor. The floor was tiled in marble and the tiles formed a checkerboard pattern. About every ten feet or so, there was a square block of checkerboard surrounded by a border. Most of the ten foot squares were covered in mold and water. After passing six squares, they reached one that was perfectly clean.

"Steady me," Jamal instructed Vawna.

She grabbed him by the back of his armor. Jamal stamped on the next square. It immediately opened up to a pit, about 20 feet deep. Below was a floor of spikes and a second skeleton, impaled. Vawna pulled Jamal away from the edge.

"Can we go now?" she asked.

"Not yet. We have to find the Grimstone Scepter."

"Is that it?" asked Vawna pointing to a suite of armor.

"No."

"Is that it?" she asked, pointing to a sword.

"No."

"Is that it?"

"No!"

"Is that..."

"Look, do you even know what a Grimstone Scepter looks like?"

"No."

"Then will you please stop asking me?!"

Jamal skirted around the pit trap, while Vawna stepped right over it. The corridor then ended in a T-shaped intersection. To the left was another passage and to the right was the facade of another passage and a third skeleton impaled on a row of spikes.

"It's a good thing these guys went through first."

Vawna started to move towards the right. Jamal pulled her back towards the left. The left side passage had a set of stairs that led to a small platform. Atop the platform was a statue sitting on a throne and holding a dusty scepter. It must have been in Ankor's image. Cindy had told him what at happened at her grandmother's funeral. Alana's body had vanished in a rainbow light, but apparently that only happened with High Fortesans. This king was supposed to have been a Low Fortesan, so Jamal had no idea if his body could be around here or it the statue was somehow him, transformed into stone by a spell gone bad. Nash had also said that many Wildsidhers used tombs because they couldn't bury bodies in the ground. Nash claimed it was because people would grow. It sounded impossible, but since arriving on the Wildsidhe Jamal's view of reality had widened a bit. It was better not to think about it.

"Can you lift me up there?"

Vawna grabbed Jamal by the collar again and hefted him to the throne.

"Don't set me down," he instructed. "I'll grab it from here."

Carefully, Jamal took hold of the dusty scepter. The rod appeared to be made of wood, painted like platinum. The gem fell off the top and smashed into a million pieces on the floor. Jamal examined the pieces, they appeared to be glass.

"Was that it?" asked Vawna.

"Someone wanted us to think that was it, but it was actually a fake. The real one must be hidden somewhere."

"Well, if I were gonna hide it. I'd hide it in the pit. That's the toughest place to reach."

Jamal looked at her.

"What?"

"That's actually a good idea."

The twosome returned to the pit. While Vawna held Jamal by the ankles, he felt around the sides of the pit for a secret passage. Using the end of the hilt of the sword from Ankor's statue, Jamal disturbed a beetle the size of a Frisbee. He skewered it and threw it up in the air behind him.

"Lunch, coming up!"

Vawna caught it and swallowed it in a gulp. Finally, there was an audible click and a small passage opened. It look just wide enough from Jamal to crawl inside. Vawna lowered him inside and Jamal took the torch.

"Vawna," instructed Jamal carefully. "You're gonna stay right here and not get distracted right?"

"Oh, I promise, Jamal. No distractions. I'll stay right here. I'll nap if I have to."

"No! No, naps. Just watch for me, okay?"

"Okay."

With torch in hand, Jamal crawled down a dank and slimy stone passage for about thirty feet. It opened into the tomb of the Fortesan King. But as Jamal looked, he realized it wasn't for the king. There was a statue that was most definitely a woman. Maybe Ankor's queen? Both this and the one of the king looked so lifelike, he almost expected them to move.

The statue rested atop an ornate slab. The room was about ten feet around, oval with a weird green light that seemed to come from the walls of the room. Jamal examined the slab and the statue carefully. The Grimstone Scepter was clutched tightly against her chest. There appeared to be no other switches or traps and the skeleton itself did not appear to be a trap.

"All right," Jamal said to himself. "There'd be no reason to trap this room because no one could find it right? So what am I paranoid about?"

And with that, Jamal slid the Grimstone Scepter out of the statue's hand. He dusted off the cobwebs and the gem glowed eerily. It appeared to be the real deal. Jamal looked around, the passage didn't close, the ceiling didn't start to lower, and there appeared to be no giant boulder to squish him. He shrugged and started back down the passage.

At the top of the pit, Vawna heard footsteps, but she screwed up all the concentration she could muster and refused to look. As Jamal knelt down to crawl back down the passage he heard a creaking sound. The statues of the Fortesan warriors were looking at him with glowing red eyes.

"Ankor's…scepter…" one hissed.

Jamal's eyes went wide and he scrambled down the passage as fast as he could.

"Vawna!"

Up top, the dragon refused to get distracted by at least six separate sets of foot stomps. Out of the corner of her eye, one of the suits of armor moved. It appeared to have a skeleton inside.

"Scepter…scepter…" hissed the Fortesan statues, as they crawled down the passage after Jamal.

Jamal stuck his head out of the pit just in time to see six skeletons in Fortesan armor lifting their swords to strike Vawna.

"Vawna, look out!"

"What? Where?! Eww!"

On "What" Vawna turned her head to the left and her tail to the right. This maneuver knocked over two of the skeletons. She still didn't really see them and turned the opposite direction on "Where," which knocked down two more. By this time, she had an inkling that she was surrounded and jumped to the other side of the pit on "Eww." The two remaining Low Fortesan skeletons clobbered each other with their swords.

The entire enterprise took less than four seconds.

"Vawna! Pull me out!"

"Scepter…scepter…"

Vawna reached down and grabbed Jamal by the arm. The Fortesan warrior grabbed Jamal by the leg and the twosome were stuck in a tug of war. Below Jamal, the skeleton that had been impaled on the spikes began to move.

"Vawna!"

"You want me to breath on him?"

"No! You'll roast me! I'm not made of asbestos!"

"What's asbestos?"

"Just pull me up!"

Finally the dragon managed to pull Jamal out of the pit and the twosome stumbled backwards. Low Fortesan skeletons brandishing weapons and armor were popping up everywhere. Vawna backed them both into an alcove.

"This is scary!" she said, burying her head in Jamal's vest. "I want to go home. Let's leave. Do you have more chocolate?"

Cornered and with nowhere else to go, Jamal suddenly stood and pointed the Grimstone Scepter at the nearest skeleton. A red ball of energy blasted him to smithereens.

"Cool," commented Jamal.

He pointed to each of the skeletons. The Grimstone Scepter blasted each one as fast as he could point. Unfortunately, however, the blasts passed right through the skeletons and hit the sides of the tomb. Before Jamal realized it, the entire tomb was falling apart around them.

"C'mon Vawna! We have to leave now!"

"Scepter..." hissed the skull of the Fortesan Warrior as they fled. Jamal looked up to see the statue of Ankor and he swore he saw it turn its head.

Vawna scooped Jamal up and had him outside the tomb in a flash. The rumbling continued and the ancient tomb collapsed on top of itself, burying the ancient king, maybe forever.

"Are we done exploring?"

"Yes."

"Can we go home now?"

"Well, that depends. How would you like to go home with me?"

"Are there other dragons?"

"There are pixies, an elf, a dwarf, and a lot of humans like me."

"And they have the chocolate?"

"Yep."

"Okay. I'll go. Do you think they'll like me? Are any of them wizards? Can I keep my treasure there?"

"Um, yes. I think. What treasure?"

"That pretty scepter thingee in your hand."

"Oh, this. Well, tell you what. You can have the rod and I'll take the gem. Fair?"

"Well, the red does go better with my eyes..."

"Yeah, but I think the platinum on the rod really brings out the highlights on your scales."

"You think so? Really? Maybe I should get more. I'll get more if we find them. I hate gems anyways."

CHAPTER 13

Jamal donned the medallion again and Vawna was able to fly them back to the dragon cave. She bid farewell to her sisters. At first they were devastated, then they became completely distracted by a large male dragon and flitted away. The twosome made their way back to the dwarven caves, eventually arriving to the spot where Sebastian's dragon hide still lay.

"All right, here's the plan," Jamal explained to Vawna. "I'm going to put this medallion on you. It'll make you look and smell like a dwarf."

"Eww!"

"It's only temporary. I left my friend at the exit to the dwarven caves so we have to go back through," said Jamal. "Try not to draw attention to yourself, okay?"

"I can do that," assured Vawna.

"Now remember, just because you look like a dwarf, doesn't mean you're as small as a dwarf."

"Right. Small as a dwarf."

"No, not small as a dwarf. You only look that way."

"Okay, okay, okay," Vawna said impatiently.

Carefully, Jamal put the medallion over Vawna's head and stepped back. Immediately, she shimmered and now appeared to be a teenage, female dwarf with striking features. Jamal made a concerned face.

"What's wrong?" asked Vawna. "Am I ugly? Is there something in my teeth? Ooo, look at that fungus."

"Nothing, now hold still."

Jamal climbed back on Vawna's back and told her to look into a nearby puddle. Sure enough, the medallion made him look like a dwarf too. A dwarf that was piggyback riding on another. Occasionally, the magic flickered and Vawna's head returned to normal for a split second, or Jamal appeared in mid-air above the dwarf. They were apparently over taxing the medallion.

"Okay, let's make this fast."

"Right!"

Vawna zipped down the cave. For a second, Jamal thought she would blow past the two dwarven guards up ahead, but she stopped the appropriate distance and shambled forward. Fortunately, the two guards were pretty far apart and with Jamal's help, Vawna had easily avoided the traps. She appeared to be finally listening to him.

"Hello friends," Jamal greeted.

"I'm a dwarf!" added Vawna. "How do I smell? Do I smell right?"

The guards looked at each other, bewildered by the comments.

"Are ye okay, friend?" asked one of the guards.

"I've twisted my ankle, but my sister here is carrying me home," explained Jamal.

"If ye is too heavy, we can help," offered the second guard, smiling at Vawna. "One so beautiful, should not have to work so hard."

"Tee, hee, hee," giggled Vawna. "Oh, stop."

Vawna gave him a little playful shove, but she didn't realize her own strength and the guard flew up against the side of the cave.

"Ooo! I'm sorry! I hope I didn't hurt you! I'm really strong! I mean, for a dwarf I'm strong. I really am a dwarf, you know."

The first guard helped the second to his feet.

"We really have to go, sister. It's time for dinner. You don't want your mushrooms to get cold."

"I love mushrooms! I'm a dwarf!"

The twosome managed to cross much the dwarven city without much more fuss. Occasionally, a dwarf would stumbled into Vawna's real body, which was concealed by the medallion and extended beyond the image of the cute, teenage dwarf. And once, while trader was checking Vawna out through a bar room window, the medallion flickered and he saw Vawna's dragon form. He looked into his mug curiously, then dumped the remainder of his drink into the street. Finally, the twosome reached the exit cave.

"Okay, that's it. Once we're through there, we're home free," whispered Jamal.

"I'm hungry," whined Vawna. "Can I have some mushrooms?"

"You said you hated mushrooms."

"I did? I don't remember saying that. Did I say I hated all mushrooms or just certain ones?"

"All of them. You said... Wait! Stop!" hissed Jamal.

Standing at the entrance, arguing with a merchant, was Shart. He seemed to be bickering over the price of wooden poles with the supplier. Since Jamal had left, he and his brother had invested in fishing rods. Sport fishing was rapidly becoming more popular than Bones.

"We'll have to wait here a minute," Jamal explained. "If that dwarf sees me, we're stuck."

A dwarven housewife carrying a basket of mushrooms passed the duo. She eyed them strangely, but when met with Jamal's gaze, she put her head down and continued on her way. Jamal heard a crackling sound and the medallion began to flicker much more continuously and Shart showed no signs of leaving the area of the exit. Jamal leapt off of Vawna's back. The medallion stabilized and Vawna's image held fast.

"But they'll see you!" whispered Vawna.

"Better me than you, when I give you the signal, run for the exit," instructed Jamal.

"Friend Jamal!"

It was Granf.

"Hello, Granf. This is my friend, Vawna."

"Uh, yes, indeed. Hello, miss," greeted Granf. "You're only a little younger than my brother, Shart. Have you met?"

Shart was now making a scene and calling for the guards. His exchange with the merchant became more heated and showed no sign of cooling down. Jamal had crouched down behind a water barrel, but it was just a matter of minutes before he was seen.

"I don't think that would be a good idea," interrupted Jamal. "Vawna is another in disguise."

"Oh, really?" said Granf fascinated. "You wizards do lead the life! Tell me Vawna, did you see many of the foul wyrms beyond our caves?"

"Mmmm, worms. You're making me hungry," laughed Vawna. "I could go for a few giant night crawlers right now."

"No, no, friend Vawna, when I say foul wyrms, I mean the evil, scaly monstrosities that plague us. The dragons."

"You're talking about dragons?" asked Vawna, shocked and hurt.

"Yes, their foul breath, their misshapen claws, their ugly teeth!" Granf continued.

Vawna began to scrunch up her face in anger. Jamal looked back at Shart, then to Vawna and Granf and then, towards the street, where one of the dwarven guards, leading a security force of 12 dwarf soldiers, pointed Vawna out.

"Forget this," said Jamal.

And with that, Jamal leaped upon Vawna's back.

"Fly Vawna!"

"Dwarves fly?" she asked, momentarily distracted.

"Yes! Fly us out of here right now!"

And with that, Vawna zoomed over the dwarves and through the cave. Granf, the security force and the merchant watched in stunned silence, while Shart, who had just missed it, looked at them curiously.

"Brother, did you see the flying dwarf?" asked Granf looking after Vawna.

"No," Shart replied, looking at the others dwarves suspiciously. "*What sort of mushrooms have you all been eating?*"

Vawna and Jamal took off through the entrance cave, eventually spotting one of the sunlit caverns. The passage led to the top of the mountain and from his vantage point, Jamal could see for miles. He took the medallion off Vawna.

To his right, the Fortesan Kingdom stretched to the horizon, reaching into the misty tops of the mountains and as far as the crystal blue ocean. To his left, the clock tower of Sparta was just barely visible on the horizon. Jamal would have to talk to Justin about that. Perhaps the clock tower was giving too much of their position away. Vawna landed by the base of the mountain and Jamal went into the cave to find Joanna.

The cave contained the ashes of a campfire, which still felt warm to Jamal. The bed roll Joanna had purchased days before lay unmade on one side of the cave. On the other side of the cave, Joanna had scrounged some of the edible plants in the area. It all looked as if she had been here only minutes before. Suddenly, Jamal heard a scream. He ran back to Vawna.

"Vawna, look over there. Do you see another human? Like me only female?"

Vawna's keen eye sight could allow her to spot a field mouse from the distance of over two miles and she said so. Spotting Joanna through the trees was easy. She was surprised that Jamal couldn't see her.

"Yep. The darkcats are chasing her. Is this your home?"

"C'mon. Vawna. we have to save her!"

The dragon skirted the tree tops. Joanna had been discovered by the darkcats only a few minutes ago. They chased her up a tree, which hung precariously on a hillside. The only thing preventing the cats from getting to her, was that they were wary that the tree would fall with all of them. The four cats, however, were still leaning their weight on the base of the tree and eventually it would fall.

Vawna swooped down and scooped up Joanna. Jamal caught her. The dragon then roared, dispersing the darkcats into the woods.

"Hi, I'm Vawna. This is Jamal," Vawna introduced.

"I'm Joanna. Thanks for saving me," she smiled, then looked at Jamal. "Again."

"Anytime," Jamal smiled back.

"You should mate with him. I would, but I can't because I'm a dragon. If he was a dragon, I would. You should," added Vawna.

"I can't believe I'm saying this," Joanna said suspiciously. "But, what have you been telling this dragon?"

"Nothing, I swear," promised Jamal, a little defensive.

A few hours later, the threesome made it back to Sparta. After Jamal gave his password, they were greeted with the kind of welcome that made a celebration on New Year's pale by comparison. The kids were especially interested in Vawna, who loved the attention.

"You're pretty," said Tina Shelly to Vawna. "Can I have a ride? Do you breathe fire? What's it like to fly?"

"Thanks. Okay. Yes. It's great!" answered the dragon, happy to find someone that thought at her speed. "Let's be friends!"

"Okay!"

"Somehow, I knew they'd get along," said Jamal to Justin, while standing at the front gate. "So when does Asgar show up to get his prize?"

With the mention of his name the sky became dark with lionhawks. Asgar, riding Maelstrom, the largest lionhawk, swooped down with five more of the beasts just outside the gate. He was dressed in full armor and decided to retrieve the Grimstone Scepter personally.

Jamal looked to Justin, who nodded. He whispered to Wayne, "Get the iron dusters." Wayne nodded and ran off to get the only weapon they had that was able to hurt Asgar.

The gate was opened. Jamal and Justin walked out to meet Asgar.

"Ah, Mr. Nichols," the would-be tyrant grinned. "I see you have my scepter. Well, at least the important part anyways. Be a good chap and hand it over, hmm? I can get you started as my general today."

"General?" asked Justin.

"He offered me a job," admitted Jamal. "I'm afraid I'll have to turn you down, Asgar. I'm just not cut out to be a murdering psychopath."

"Fine," said the Fortesan impatiently hopping off his mount. "Give me the gem and I'll send you on your way then. There's a good fellow."

"What about the kids?"

"The kids, the kids, the kids! You're like one of Morna's parroting pixies! The quest was for you and you alone! Only you can cross back to Earth once you give me the Grimstone. Do you want to please your masters at the FBI or not?"

"Yeah, I do," said Jamal. He dropped the Grimstone on the ground and crushed it with his heel. A large burst of magic illuminated Jamal, crackling around him with an intense red light. The medallion he still carried somehow protected Jamal as the air around him became white hot and melted the soles of the sneakers he wore. With a final blinding burst, the Grimstone's magic burned itself out, leaving Jamal pale and shaken in its wake.

"What a ride," said Jamal, stumbling slightly, before becoming steady again.

"I've decided I'm going to take you back, in these handcuffs," promised

Jamal, holding up his handcuffs. "You're gonna do hard time for what you've done to these people."

"You insolent fool!" ranted the Fortesan. "You and these worms only live because I allow it! Perhaps I should allow it no further!"

Justin looked behind him, but Wayne hadn't made it out with the iron dusters yet. Things were about to get messy.

"You're making a lot of noise!" said Vawna, poking her head up from behind the school.

Tina had gone to show Vawna the garden. Asgar hadn't spotted the dragon from behind the building. The Fortesan reeled back in surprise and his lionhawks stirred restlessly.

"What? A dragon? In league with these peasants? It's insane!"

"I like them and I don't like you," Vawna said simply. "Go away. Lionhawks smell bad. You're a jerk."

And with that, Vawna punctuated her last statement with a roar. The lionhawks immediately fled and Asgar was caught in his own mount's reigns. The large lionhawk dragged his master into the sky, cursing and ranting all the way. The kids cheered.

"Well, it looks like I'm stuck here," Jamal said to Justin.

"We can always use the help," Justin said, shaking his hand.

"Don't worry," assured Wayne. "According to what Alana told us, he's gotta give you another quest in three years."

"Three years? Nah. I don't think I plan on staying that long. I'll find a way back without Asgar's help."

"Well, what's your plan?" asked Joanna.

"These days," said Jamal thoughtfully. "I'm keeping it flexible, Jo. Keeping it flexible."

A DAY ON THE WILDSIDHE

A WILDSIDHE CHRONICLES STORY

Deb Wunder, Diane Raetz & Patrick Thomas

Jared lay in a small heap, trying not to cry. *Why didn't I listen to them?* He gingerly tried to get his leg to move, but the angle it was at scared him. His father was going to kill him. He never dreamed the path this day would take when it started out.

Jared had woke grumpily as the sun rose. It was his father's rule that the entire family woke at first light. Bleary eyed, he looked into his mirror. He saw a twelve-year-old Fortesan, not yet a man, but older than a boy. Like many his age he was in a hurry to grow up.

"Why can't I begin studying magic? My father says I have to be at least thirteen, but why? I'm old for my age, everyone says so!" he had muttered to himself. "Its so boring here with the protective wards up. Father's wrong. There's no danger. He just wants to keep me caged inside the castle walls so I can't get into any trouble. I can't even go visit my horsehound, Elias. So what if there are problems at court? No one would dare bother the son of the Huntmaster. Unfortunately, no one pays attention to me either, except as Rael's son."

Jared stamped away from the mirror and his room. Jared began wandering around the castle aimlessly. Eventually his steps took him to his father's spell room. Jared turned the door handle, never expecting the room to be unlocked.

"Wow, Dad must be really upset to forget to lock this door. There must be bigger problems than I thought!" Jared knew that he should stay out of the room, but his curiosity got the better of him and he went in.

He was surrounded by all of this father's spell books and supplies. Most important of all, there were dozens of spell gems, stones that look like quartz and stored magical energy. An idea came to Jared. What if he was able to cast a spell that would break the castle warding? Then he could go to the stables and visit the horsehounds. Most important, if he were able to cast a spell and break the warding, his father would know he was old enough to work magic now. This year, not next year!

For a few hours, Jared poured over his father's spell books. Not one spell was right for his needs. There were love potions, talking animal spells, summoning spells and even a spell to turn a person purple. But not one spell that would allow him to break his father's warding. He devised a foolish plan. If he couldn't find the spell he wanted, he'd make one up.

Jared knew the theory of spell casting. It was a mix of skill and will. If the spell caster did not have control over a spell, wild magic came into play. Every Fortesan was told how dangerous that could be. Proving to his father that he was ready to study magic would be worth the risk.

Jared prowled around the room, looking for something to help him with his spell. His eyes lit upon the Gazing Mirror. His father used it to look out over the world. Sometimes, when his father wasn't busy, Jared would come with him to look at the Wildsidhe. Lately, he used it to keep tabs on the feuding between Queen Morna and Asgar. Asgar had plans to oust King Penrod, but Morna would never allow it. Rael had dared even suggest that Asgar would kill Penrod if he could. Jared knew he must be wrong. For a High Fortesan to kill another would break the Treaty of Shadows and allow the darkness to reclaim the Wildsidhe. Every living thing would die. No one would be that stupid.

In his quest for power, Asgar had kidnaped three hundred human children and part of the town of Sparta, Pennsylvania from Earth. One of the Spartans was even rumored to be part Fortesan. Ever since they arrived, the kids had been used and abused by both Morna and Asgar in the pair's quest for control. Amazingly, the humans had held their own against two of the most powerful members of the High Council. Even Rael had talked admiringly about the humans. Jared was dying to meet them; kids his own age living without parental control and surviving nicely. They had it so easy.

Thinking vaguely about the humans, Jared had looked into the Gazing Mirror. It was all foggy, not like when his father controlled the scrying. Jared had seen a faint image of a big fence and some strange looking brick building.

Jared recognized it as the human's home. He decided to concentrate on the fence, held a spell gem in both hands and chanted, "I want to go out, I want to go out!" all the while staring into the Gazing Mirror.

Jared's world quickly became foggy. It was hard to see. Jared had never experienced anything like it. A moment later, dizziness washed over him like a wave and he had the feeling that he was being picked up and hurled like a ball. A bright light flashed and the fog was gone. He wasn't in the spell room anymore.

Jared didn't know where he was. He was only sure of two things, that his leg hurt and that his father would be very angry. He would worry about that later. Right now, he had to figure out how to get home.

Dragging himself to his knees, he started inching his way in what he hoped was the right direction. Jared had been trained as a hunter and tracker since he could walk. Normally, that meant he could have found his way home from anywhere on the Wildsidhe, but the pain of a broken leg was something the young Fortesan had never before experienced, and it was overwhelming.

Briefly, he wondered whether his injuries would cause his parents to postpone his punishment until he was healed, then put that toward the back of his mind, too, and concentrated on making his way over the unfamiliar rough surface. He had never seen asphalt before. Then he passed out.

Wayne Burns looked at the patrol sternly. "I want you all to be very careful," he said somberly. "We don't know how long these hucksters are going to be around. So far, there seems to be less of them today, but they are out there and they're hungry."

"They're always hungry," Chuck Bearclaw said, shivering at the memory of the carnivorous plants that resembled corn on the cob.

"Which is why you have to be careful. Only check the perimeter of the school, no more than a block away from the fenceline. Stay together and don't take any risks. If there are more than a couple, come back right away. "

"Aye, aye boss," said John Bearclaw, Chuck's brother, while making a face at Wayne. "You've only said the same thing like three of four times now. Anything else you'd like to repeat, you know, like to keep our bows and arrows with us at all times? Or maybe not to let any changelings in? Come on Wayne, you know we know this stuff."

"John, shut up," Jane Blossum said. She had a crush on their security chief. "Wayne is responsible for our safety and we should listen to him." Jane added with a grin, "Even if he does tell us stuff we already know."

"Gee Jane, thanks for your support," said Wayne. Miko Wang and Chuck Bearclaw chuckled under their breath, but shut up after one glare from Wayne.

"Any time Wayne, any time," said Jane.

"Don't worry bro – I'll take care of them," Wayne's sister Terri said from her wheelchair. Wayne looked even more nervous than before.

"That's what I'm afraid of," he said.

Terri, Jane, Miko, and the Bearclaw brothers grabbed their bows and arrows. They passed outside the main gate and started out on patrol on their assigned rounds. The group was oddly dressed, each one of the kids, except Terri, had iron or steel on his or her clothing. Since iron was one of the best defenses against magical beasts and people, the kids always dressed in their "armor" while outside of the school.

The kids spilt up into pairs, the Bearclaws going one way and Miko and Jane the other. Terri went solo or maybe "so high" would be a better term. The other four watched with envy as the young girl with spina bifida lifted off the ground like a helium balloon with a jet pack. When they had first ended up on the Wildsidhe, Cindy Hartman had unwittingly cast a spell. Ever since, Terri and her wheelchair had been able to fly.

The girls and the Bearclaws went in opposite directions around the school compound.

Miko was an orderly, neat little girl, Her long, black hair was braided neatly over one shoulder and her clothing seemed less rumpled and cleaner than Jane. Without electricity, all the washing machines they had were useless and not everyone had taken to the more primitive laundry methods easily. Jane had a rougher time on the Wildsidhe than most.

In an ugly series of events, Jane's sister Marianne had betrayed the rest of the kids of Sparta and been carried off by Queen Morna on the back of a darkcat to be sacrificed to the Shadows. On his quest to earn his way home from Asgar, Jamal had met Marianne. She had become a shadow. None of them was sure exactly what that meant, only that it was bad. It would be some time before they learned just how bad.

After her sister's betrayal, the other kids had shied away from Jane for a while. Miko was a couple of years older but had proven to be a good friend. She carried a lot of influence as one of Wayne's security captains, not to mention the best of the Spartans with a sword. Miko had been instrumental in convincing the others not to shun Jane. They were now fast friends.

Jane got bored on patrol. It was mostly a bunch of walking around. She did a cartwheel.

"Wayne wouldn't like us to be doing gymnastics on duty." Miko's grin took the sting out of the barb.

"Yeah, but who'd tell?"

"Not me."

"Me neither."

They heard movement in the tall grasses ahead of them. The lawns had grown wild since there was no time or desire to mow the dozens of lawns. Miko froze, as Jane cautiously inched forward. They were both thinking darkcat or worse.

"Miko." Jane sounded relieved and worried at the same time. "I think you're gonna have to get Wayne or the Bearclaws. There's a kid here, and I think he's hurt."

"A kid? One of ours?"

"I don't think so." She turned back to the collapsed Fortesan. "What's your name? What are you doing out here? Are you okay?"

"I'm Jared and I'm not sure what I'm doing here. My leg hurts."

"Are you alone?" asked Miko.

"Unfortunately. My parents probably haven't noticed I'm gone yet."

"Parents?" the girls said in unison. Their parents were a world away. Jared definitely wasn't one of them.

Miko noticed the extra joint on Jared's fingers, and nudged Jane.

"You're a Fortesan, aren't you? Better tell the truth, too, or we'll let you rot here." Miko's voice was harsh, but life had hardened all of them. She only hoped he couldn't tell she was bluffing.

"I am. I was trying to do magic and ended up here." Jared explained everything that had happened.

"So, when your dad finds out, you're in deep trouble?"

"Yes. And he'll figure that out once he notices I'm not there, which should be soon."

"Miko, maybe you should get Terri. She could fly him to safety. I'll wait with Jared," said Jane.

"Wayne will never let us bring him inside the school," said Miko, who looked dubious at the whole idea.

"We can't leave him out here as huckster chow."

"Hucksters?" said Jared, his face turning pale.

"You have a better suggestion? Besides, you run faster," said Jane. Miko nodded and took off at her top speed.

Eventually she saw Terri hovering in the sky and managed to wave her down.

"Hey, Miko. What's wrong?"

"We need help."

Terri and her wheelchair froze in midair. "What kind of help? Is Jane okay?"

"She's fine. We found a kid who's hurt."

"Hurt how? One of ours?"

"I think his leg is broken, but he's definitely not one of ours. He's a Fortesan kid. Has that extra joint in his fingers. Jane's waiting with him."

"I can see more Hucksters in the distance, probably at least an hour away. We need to find shelter. I'll follow you. Is he big?" While Terri could take on passengers, she got more tired the more weight she carried. She had been practicing, but without knowing how heavy he was it was best to conserve her energy, so she landed.

"He was on the ground, but he looks tall. What about getting him past Wayne?"

"We'll deal with my brother later. Let's go."

"So, tell me more about horsehounds." Jane was interested but, more importantly, she wanted to keep Jared talking. It was clear that his broken leg hurt.

"I thought everyone knew what the totems looked like. Horsehounds are about as tall as a horse, which is about 14 hands high or so, and have doggish sorts of faces and builds, but on horse size legs, so that they can move really fast." Jane gigled at the thought of her mother's beagle, Petey, on a horse's legs. "They are also very brave, and..."

"Do you have one?" asked Jane.

"Well, Elias is a horsehound colt. He's not fully-grown yet, that takes years, but he will be my totem when my time comes. Elias is amazing. He's always been a good companion. I wish he was here. Then I could get home." Jared stopped for air. "No offense."

"None taken. He sounds neat. Where I come from, we just have dogs, cats, and the occasional fish or bird for pets."

"Totems aren't just pets."

"I know. I've seen darkcats, lionhawks, and unicorns."

"Unicorns? I thought that totem was lost, stolen by Alana when she ran off to Earth."

"Alana came back. She died helping us. She left the totem with her granddaughter, Cindy."

"I bet that made Queen Morna angry. The unicorn totem should have been her's when her sister left. The darkcat totem she uses is actually King

Penrod's. Is Cindy learning how to use it?"

Actually, Cindy had not been able to work it since Alana died, but Jared was still a stranger and that was information that could hurt the Spartans. Jane decided to change the subject.

"Morna's evil. She keeps trying to kill us." That had only stopped after her sister Alana's death. No one was sure how long the uneasy peace would last. "She sacrificed my sister to the Shadows."

"Marriane Blossum was your sister? I'm very sorry for you, but had Queen Morna not done that, every living thing on the Wildsidhe would be dead now. Including you. Your sister is considered a hero. Everyone on the Wildsidhe knows of her sacrifice."

"A hero? Really?"

Jared nodded. Knowing this helped Jane.

"What was Marianne like?" asked Jared.

Her sister's betrayal was still raw in Jane's memory, but she tried to be fair. "Well, Marianne might have been mean to me sometimes, but she never would let anyone else be. Older sisters are supposed to protect you, and she mostly did. Before everything happened, I thought she was the greatest. Now..."

Jane was interrupted by the arrival of Miko and Terri. After a brief conversation and introductions, they loaded Jared onto Terri's wheelchair.

"I'll take him back to the driveway outside the main gate. You two will have to hoof it."

Terri took off into the sky. Miko and Jane followed quickly on foot.

Jared was lain on a mattress which had been dragged outside the gate, while Terri went to find Wayne or Justin. Jane again sat with Jared.

"What will your friends do with me?"

"Well, Wayne will want to test you to make sure you aren't a changeling."

"If I were, I would have changed into something without a broken leg and gone home on my own."

"Yeah, but we have these rules so that no one gets hurt."

"That makes sense I guess."

At that moment, Wayne and Terri appeared. Wayne questioned Jared extensively and appeared satisfied.

"Jared, we have a problem here. We need to test you to make sure you aren't a shape-changer, but I'm afraid to do so because of your injury. By our rules, I can't let you into the compound unless I do. If I make an exception and someone gets hurt..." People had been hurt and one had even been killed since they got here. Wayne had sworn to never let that happen again. He would not make an exception. "However, if you are telling the truth, I can't leave you for the hucksters."

"Thank you." Jared seemed genuinely relieved. He had once witnessed the migrating hucksters pick the meat off a full-grown elk in a matter of minutes. The elk was still alive for most of it.

"Wayne, could you let him stay here in the yard? I'll stay with him, if you want."

"No can do, Jane. If he's a changeling, I'd be putting you in danger."

"But he's not."

"Jane, you don't know that."

"I do." Jane was adamant.

"How?" Wayne asked.

"I'm not sure. I just know that he's not a changeling."

"Do you realize the risk you'd be taking? The risk you'd be asking all of us to take?" asked Wayne.

"I do and I'd stake my life on it," said Jane.

"You might just be doing that and I won't allow it."

"Please, don't argue over me. I don't want to breach the security of your camp. My father has taught me the importance of such things."

"Could we get something iron and put it near him?" Jane was almost pleading.

"No! It could kill me," said Jared.

Terri lifted up into the air and looked into the distance. "Decide fast, bro. Hucksters are moving in fast."

Wayne believed Jared's story, but couldn't let him inside. Justin, their leader, was securing the other side of the school compound. It was his call.

"Okay, here's the deal. Get a SUV out of the parking lot and put Jared flat in the back. The hucksters have pretty much left the cars and vehicles alone. The iron and steel will make Jared feel sick, but none of it will have to touch him. He should be safe."

"I'll stay with him," said Jane.

"You'll get inside the school with everyone else," ordered Wayne.

"I'm not leaving him alone."

"And I'm not leaving you alone with someone who could be a changeling. Have you forgotten what Troc did to Todd?"

"But..."

"No buts Jane. No one else is going to die if I can help it. Either you go inside or I carry you in," said Wayne. Jane started to open her mouth.

"Don't argue with me. You won't win."

"Jane, go. I'll be fine," said Jared. "And thank you Wayne."

Jared's wild teleportation spell had screamed across the entire Wildsidhe with raw power. Here was power and a new spell to be had. Many High Fortesans heard the call. Three set out to answer it, each with reasons of their own.

The latest wave of the huckster migration trampled everything in its path. Even from inside the SUV, the aroma of blood from Jared's wounds drifted out, attracting the ravenous plants like so many tiny sharks. Dozens would swarm over the SUV, scream in pain from contact with the steel and jump off. Unfortunately, even more hucksters leapt up to take their place. They quickly realized they could stand on the glass without pain and focused their attack there.

From inside, the Spartans watched in horror.

"They're going to eat him!" screamed Jane.

Wayne looked, debated, and finally said, "No they're not." Wayne was covered in his homemade iron armor, as were most of the kids. "We're getting him out of there. We'll have to put him inside the fence line." The fence looked like it was made in a bizarre iron junkyard, reinforced until there was no open space or holes. The hucksters had never managed to get past it before.

"John, Chuck, Miko, you're with me. We'll get him out and Terri you airlift him over."

"Will do," said Terri. She couldn't lift any of the rescuers over the fence easily as their iron armor made her sick when she flew. It's also why she couldn't wear any.

"Once Terri has him, the rest of you get ready to pull us back over with ropes. Jane, you're in charge of that."

Wayne and the others climbed up onto the watchtower and climbed down. Quickly, using steel swords, they tried to sweep the hucksters away from the SUV. It was like holding back a stream of water with a net, but they did their best.

Wayne managed to get the hatchback open. "Cover me."

Miko moved in, slicing through huckster upon huckster, but they still kept coming. Wayne pulled Jared out. With the young Fortesan in his arms he leapt onto the hood and then the roof.

"Terri, now!" he screamed. His sister swooped in and Wayne dumped

Jared in her lap. Moments later, the pair were safe inside the fence line.

"Retreat!" ordered Wayne, as he brushed off a trio of hucksters that had managed to climb up his legs. Jane and others threw ropes down to the four person rescue party. Before they could tie the ends around their waists, Chuck noticed familiar shapes in the sky getting closer.

"Lionhawks!" he screamed.

Wayne cursed under his breath. They didn't need to deal with Asgar right now.

Miko looked in the other direction and the color drained from her face. "Morna and her darkcats are coming!"

Morna was waving her hands in front of her and gusts of wind were sweeping away any hucksters in her path.

Jane looked down the street and saw a bushy man on the back of a giant dog. Several other giant dogs followed. He held his hands out and fire flew from his fingertips like a flamethrower, incinerating any carnivorous plants that blocked his way.

"I think we have incoming horsehounds!" Jane said.

"Oh no," said Wayne. "Everybody over the wall."

It was too late for that. Asgar was already overhead and had his lionhawks beat their wings faster and faster. It blew away the hucksters, but also pinned Wayne, Miko, and the Bearclaws to the pavement.

"Don't leave on my account. So, just what had my dear little Cindy been up to?" Asgar asked from his lofty perch.

"It wasn't my grandneice, Asgar," said Queen Morna. "Kindly stop your beasts' incessant flapping."

"My pleasure, my Queen," said Asgar. The polite conversation barely hid a deep hatred each had for the other. "Regardless of which of these whelps cast the spell, whoever did it is coming with me."

The third Fortesan on horsehound arrived just then. "Asgar, you had best rethink that."

"Hello, Rael. I didn't realize you had an interest in these human children. I thought you had always maintained that they should be left alone. One major display of power and your beliefs fly away."

"Asgar, I am in no mood for your politics." Rael waved his hand and a circle of flame surrounded those on the ground, keeping the hucksters at bay.

"Really? What use does the Huntmaster have for a teleportation spell?" Asgar asked.

"None, but I have claims on the caster," said Rael. Meanwhile, the horsehounds and darkcats quietly growled at each other. After a screech from a lionhawk the beasts turned their efforts on the sky borne totems.

"You have a claim on a human?" asked Asgar.

"Only so far as they appear to be holding my son and I demand that they hand him over to me immediately or suffer the consequences," said Rael.

Wayne and the others had used the distraction to climb into the SUV. Used as a ram, a SUV would hurt totem or Fortesan if it came to that.

It didn't. Terri floated over the fence, Jared in her lap and landed in front of Rael. The Huntmaster leapt off his mount and embraced his son.

"Are you okay, boy? Have they hurt you?" asked Rael.

"My leg is broken, but that's my fault. Jane and her friends saved me from the hucksters," said Jared. He told his father everything that happened.

"We will deal with your disobedience when we get home, young one. Meanwhile, I brought a friend who was worried about you," said Rael.

A horsehound leapt out of the pack and began licking Jared's face."Elias!" The young Fortesan hugged the canine's neck.

"My apologies for jumping to conclusions. Saving my son puts me in your debt. Is there anything I can do for you?" Rael asked.

"Can you send us home?" Jane asked, from up on the watchtower.

Asger snickered. Morna's face remained impassive.

"Sadly, no. We know of no way to break this kind of spell. If there was, I believe the Queen would have sent you back to Earth long ago. The only way home is performing a task for Asgar when you reach eighteen. Is there anything else?" There was no consensus. "There is no rush. I am in your debt. Time will not lessen that."

"I'm sure that the Huntmaster is anxious to return home," Asgar said.

"I am in no hurry. I need to set my son's leg better and make him ready for travel. I will also stay until this threat to the Spartans is past," Rael said.

"There is no need," Asgar said.

"I think there is. You however, may leave," Rael said.

Asgar considered this silently. He had enough enemies in court. He did not need to pick a pointless fight. He simply pulled on his lionhawk's reigns and soared off into the sky.

"And you my Queen?" Rael asked.

"I merely came out of concern for the children," Morna said. She sounded sincere, but there was too much history for the kids not to have doubts. The Queen said her goodbyes, then she and her darkcats left.

With the other two Fortesans gone, Wayne and the others got out of the SUV. Introductions were made. The circle of fire was beginning to burn out.

"The hucksters will soon return. May we come in?" asked Rael.

It was beyond doubt that Rael was a High Fortesan. No changeling could have so easily gotten Asgar and Morna to leave. On the Wildsidhe they had too few friends or even allies. Wayne had the chance to change that now.

Wayne nodded and motioned for Jane to open the gate.

CAR TROUBLE
Book 6

Myle Cole

CHAPTER 1

Wayne Burns was particularly excited. With the responsibility of his position as head of security for the school compound, he had little time to spare for sports and a game of baseball was just what he needed. His brown, spiky hair positively shined in the warm afternoon sun; his usually serious face was smiling broadly.

Smiling, that is, right up until his sister Terri, her strong arms bulging above the arm-rests of her wheelchair, hit one out of the park for the opposing team, then the familiar seriousness returned in an instant.

"C'mon!" He called to Carlos Perez, who had just thrown out the pitch, "What are you trying to do to me!?" The thin farm boy shrugged his skinny shoulders, and looked genuinely ashamed. His sister Carmen, up next to bat, played the protector as usual and told Wayne to leave the kid alone.

"Ah, he's just being a spoil sport," called Terri, rolling her chair around the bases, taking her time and enjoying the effect it was having on her brother, Wayne. She could easily have used her enchanted chair to fly across the bases, but using the magic drained her strength, and she wanted to preserve her strength for even more homeruns.

Wayne smiled and doffed his cap to the opposing team's captain, his cousin Justin, under whose direction the school compound had been thriving for the past several months. Justin returned an exaggerated bow.

Lissy, her gossamer wings flapping animatedly, stretched herself up to her full ten inches and cheered wildly. The pixie was manning the scoreboard, made of piles of apples, since most of the number-bearing plates had been stolen by mischievous Pixies long before the music/farming treaty had been concluded. As it stood, the two piles were fairly even, with Justin's team ahead by two apples now that Terri had scored her latest homerun. Lissy munched contentedly on an apple from the basket beside the piles. Apples grew wild plentifully on the Wildsidhe as well as on earth.

"Just don't eat any of the ones keeping score!" Chuck Bearclaw called to her from the sidelines, but Lissy only pouted and threw an apple at him. Lissy's playful, childish nature masked a dedication and courage that all of the children were well acquainted with. They might laugh at Lissy, but they never took her for granted.

"All right, all right, let's get down to business," Carmen said, stepping up to the plate and tapping the bat against the side of her sneaker. Carlos looked nervous and doubtful about pitching against his sister, but Carmen cast him a reassuring glance as he wound up. Carlos, to his surprise, struck his sister out with three fastballs.

As the teams switched sides, with Wayne's crew coming up to bat, smiles and pats on the back were exchanged all around.

Cindy Hartman was up first. She postured awkwardly, unused to ball games.

"Batterbatterbattersuhwingbatter!" Justin hooted, his good-natured catcall barely concealing his genuine discomfort at having her on the opposing team. He'd put in Winklo to pitch and the heavily muscled dwarf threw a mean fastball. She meant well, but sometimes underestimated her own strength playing with human children, and had already knocked Wayne on his duff, dazed but unhurt, in the first inning.

"Careful now," whispered Carmen, squatting behind her in the catcher's position.

Cindy cocked the bat, looking more than a bit nervous at the dwarf's broad shoulders. She squinted her green eyes and held her hips back in an anticipatory twitch. Winklo took her nervousness as a compliment and hammed it up, faking at least two pitches, each one earning an exaggerated flinch from Cindy, who was terrified of suffering the same fate as Wayne.

"Come on, Winklo! Give her a break!" Justin shouted, which earned laughter from both sides.

"Don't worry about it, I've got her," Carmen replied, but Justin didn't look reassured at all.

Finally, Cindy settled down and a look of hard determination blossomed across her face. "It's okay Justin, I've got it." Justin had seen that look once before, as Cindy stood over her grandmother Alana's quiet form, issuing Asgar his final warning to leave before it was too late.

He knew better than to argue with that look.

Winklo got down to business too. She wound up and let fly. It turned out not to be such a bad pitch after all. It was still faster than most humans could throw, but it certainly wasn't going to knock Cindy over. She stepped into her swing, closed her eyes, and put her hips into the shot.

It would have been perfect, if Carmen hadn't sprung forward and shouted "OMIGOSH!" at the top of her lungs. Cindy, wound tight as a spring as it was, screamed and dropped the bat, sidestepping the ball, which settled easily into Carmen's mitt with a satisfying thud.

The laughter broke out again, even worse than last time. Winklo was laughing so hard, she had to sit down. Even Justin was hard pressed to counter his mirth with the genuine sympathy he felt. Cindy looked bewildered at first, then annoyed, and finally amused. Soon she added her laughter to Winklo's, happy to still be alive after all that had happened and to be in the company of friends.

Winklo remained the strongest arm on Wayne's team, and she held to the mound, striking out her husband Nash, whose thin Elven arms could extract little more than a tippy foul from her blazing fastballs. But Nash and Winklo had been together even before Cindy had first met them in Asgar's castle, and Nash knew his wife well enough not to fear her strength. She was strong, to be sure, but she wasn't about to hurt anyone.

Last up was Jamal Nichols, strutting as usual, wiggling his hips and pointing his bat at "the blue monster," a large pile of blue gym mats that had been dragged out to the outfield a couple of weeks before. It was used to designate the home run marker, and Justin had immediately renamed the mats for the green monster of his beloved Fenway Park.

"Bring it on now!" Jamal catcalled, taking a few practice swings with the bat. Winklo's eyes narrowed to slits. She was no fool. Jamal was one heck of a ball player, and she knew it. It was her turn to be timid, and she tossed a couple of wide curve balls that were clearly wide. Carmen actually had to reach to catch them, distracting Jamal the whole time, even going as far as to tug on the back of his belt loop. She tried faking a few hard pitches as she had with Cindy, but Jamal only set his eye and looked even fiercer than before, not falling for the ruse in the slightest.

"Settle down there, big guy!" Miko Wang yelled from her position at first base.

"Easy, there, he'll turn you in to the feds!" Carmen called back to her from her position behind the young FBI special agent. Jamal was grinning easily.

But Jamal was not to be easily put off, and after a change-up brought the count to 0 and 3, Winklo knew she had to throw one straight down the middle. Jamal knew it too, and hunkered down his shoulders for the big hit, his eyes on the blue monster sitting in the distance.

Winklo gave it everything she had, cocking back her shoulder, and reaching with her leg, she threw her whole body into one fearsome, arrow straight and dazzling pitch. The ball positively screamed from her hand, blazing a white, leather trail through the reluctant air, screaming its way across home plate, where Jamal met it with equal force.

Jamal likewise gave it his all, stepping into the swing with picture perfect grace, snapping his hips and letting his arms whip out the bat with terrific force and near perfect accuracy. The resounding crack could be heard by those kids working in the farthest reaches of the school compound, sorting supplies, cleaning, mending fences, and making certain their home was safe from whatever threats the Wildsidhe could throw at them.

And the ball went three feet, barely. The force of Winklo's pitch had totally overwhelmed his swing. The wooden bat practically reverberated in his stinging hands. For all his strength and energy, it had barely been a bunt.

As Jamal stood there in stunned silence, his hands hurting and his jaw open, Miko walked over, scooped up the ball and gently tagged him with it.

"Umm. You're out," she said sweetly.

This time, it took the children a couple of minutes to stop laughing and get on with the game. Winklo stood for a while on the mound, beaming with pride. She savored the moment for a few more seconds before she walked over, shook Jamal's hand, and got in line to bat.

In the ensuing silence, Justin suddenly realized that Lissy was singing "Jamal! Jamal! He's our man!" at the top of her tiny lungs from behind the scoreboard.

"He didn't even score!" he called out to her, but the Pixie ignored him and continued singing even louder than before.

"Don't you pay him any mind now, Lissy," Wayne shouted back, grinning even wider when Justin muttered under his breath, "She doesn't even know what side she's cheering for."

Wayne's grin broadened even further, and he had to cover his mouth to suppress a chuckle, as he realized that Justin's apple count had his team now only leading by one despite the fact that Winklo had struck his team out, and Lissy was munching contentedly on yet another apple.

Wayne put Carlos back on the mound, in spite of the home run he'd given up to Terri. He had a good arm and a better heart. He struck out Miko and walked Chuck, in spite of Chuck's brother John's best efforts to distract him, tugging on his long ponytail from his catcher's position behind him, and whispering jokes to him in their tribal language. Chuck was used to his brother's antics, however, and didn't so much as blink, though his smile was broad and quite evident.

But then Winklo came up to bat and that was that. Carlos was obviously frightened of what the powerful dwarf could do, in spite of Carmen's encouraging sideline coaching. Carlos tried to curve the ball, but it wound up as a slower slider and Winklo cracked it so hard that the bat nearly broke. It would definitely have been a home run if the zealous dwarf had angled the bat lower, but as it turned out, she didn't and the powerful hit turned into a line drive that thudded into the blue monster with such terrific force that it knocked the mats backward with a loud thud, leaving the ball stuck in them like a cannonball. The ball was nowhere to be seen, leaving everyone with some time to stand around wondering what to do next. Wayne walked over to Justin and they conferred quietly some distance away from the others while Lissy, cheering her little heart out for Winklo this time, searched the scattered mats for the missing ball.

Nash grinned like a fool, beaming with pride at his love.

When Wayne and Justin returned, they had elected to declare the hit a homerun, even if it had hit the monster, since it had effectively gone through it. It was agreed however, that Winklo would stay up at bat until she had hit a proper homerun. The decision was cheered by all, and sent Lissy into ecstatic fits of cheering, especially since she had located the ball, the cover knocked clean off, some distance beyond the mats.

There was some wincing on the part of Justin and Wayne, resource conscious as ever, as Chuck busied himself in the compound for a few minutes before returning with another ball, dropping off the old ball in the supply room so that the rubber could be reused. While the children had most of the town to rummage through in order to obtain what they needed from day to day, industry on the Wildsidhe was virtually nonexistent. There was a slim chance that each kid could be sent back to Sparta, Pennsylvania on their eighteenth birthday, provided they could complete whatever task the Fortesan Asgar demanded as the price of their passage home. Most of them would be stuck on the Wildsidhe for several years.

Winklo grinned so hard that it threatened to divide her broad face. Carlos cringed as she wielded the bat, brandishing it about her head like a sword. Both teams, and several spectators, grateful to be away from their daily tasks, cheered loudly. Lissy jumped about with delight.

Carlos was clearly intimidated, his shoulders hunched and his jaw set. But he also seemed determined, and steadied himself, blowing out his breath and squaring his shoulders. Winklo showed no mercy, looking him dead in the eyes and laughing mischievously.

"Take your time, Carlos!" Carmen shouted to her brother, and even Justin, though captaining the opposing team, shouted encouragement.

Carlos seemed to take heart. He did indeed take his time, pausing and thinking. When he finally did wind up to pitch again, he had clearly picked up something. He tried to pitch smarter instead of faster, turning his sliders into tricky change-ups and more than a little confusing screwballs. Winklo did get a lucky hit in, which of course rocketed the ball out of the park. It would have easily been a homer if it hadn't been foul, but that was all that she managed to squeeze out before Carlos struck her out to great acclaim from all the players, including the mighty Winklo herself.

As the teams retired once again, three more apples had been added to Justin's pile, which still seemed to not be too much larger than Wayne's. Lissy, now standing in the midst of a rather sizeable pile of discarded apple-cores, was looking a bit full. Pixies, despite their small size, were like hummingbirds back on Earth. They had to eat several times their body weight each day.

Chuck had brought in the extra run. As he trotted home, he paused only to make a face at his brother John. He was the strongest batter, second only to Wayne and having the best chance of evening up the score after Winklo's terrific roll.

In spite of her fantastic pitching in the previous inning, Winklo declined to throw out the ball this time. Her team was ahead, so she told Justin to give someone else a turn while she played the outfield. Nobody was eager to take up the job after Winklo's dazzling performance, but Justin eventually convinced the middle Desilver sister, Yeshika, to give it a try. The heavy girl looked fairly awkward on the pitching mound at first, but soon impressed everyone with her ability to throw change-ups almost naturally. They were that odd sort of off-speed change-ups that could be hit, but were hard to get more than a foul or a pop fly out of.

After Yeshika's off-speed pitching had caused both Wayne and Nash to foul out, Bobby Shelly called out, "Where'd you learn to pitch like that?" Yeshika simply shrugged her shoulders and smiled.

It was a different story with Carlos up at bat. Despite his skinny size, he met Yeshika's pitch with surprising force, sending it high and out into right field. Winklo, now an outfielder, scrambled for the ball. Despite her amazing strength, her muscular frame had short legs, and it proved impossible for her to hustle to the ball in time. It landed in the soft grass with a thud, and Carlos had made second base long before Winklo could get the ball back infield. Lissy cheered through a mouth full of apple.

With Carlos on second, and the weakness in Justin's team clearly exposed, everyone began hitting it high and right, and Winklo was soon huffing and puffing with the strain of trying to keep up with the numerous pop flies. After two runners had come home, Justin was beginning to get nervous.

That's when Cindy came up to bat again, eyeing Winklo like each hitter before her. The dwarf stood huffing and puffing in the outfield, praying for a break in the barrage of balls. Yeshika wound up and let fly another off-speed, and Cindy stepped into the swing, popping it high and right. With a sigh and a look of near total resignation, Winklo began to beat feet for the outfield, but it was clear that there was no way she could make it in time.

The ball arched high in the air, as if taking its time, savoring the labor of the slow moving dwarf beneath. Just as it reached its apex, it slammed into Terri's mitt with a satisfying sound.

Terri had flown her enchanted wheelchair high into the air to pick off the pop fly.

After the initial shock wore off, everyone burst out cheering. The loudest was Lissy, who was even willing to set down her apple, to better clap her tiny hands together.

Terri hovered for a moment and then did a quick double turn in the air, spinning the chair on its pivot points and making screeching noises from the corners of her mouth. Wayne stood dumbfounded, watching his sister defeat his team's seemingly sole chance to even up the score.

"Love ya, big bro!" Terri called down to him, beginning to huff from the effort of flying about in her chair, and blew a mocking kiss to gouts of fresh laughter from both sides. Even Wayne couldn't stifle a smile. He wasn't smiling after Terri's flying act had stymied another pop fly and what would have been a home run, cracked by an enthusiastic Bobby, he wasn't smiling at all.

"Come on!" he called to Justin, "This is ridiculous! She can't play in the air, for cryin' out loud! Some of those hits would have been out of the park! Who ever heard of playing mid-air? What kind of position is that?" Lissy placed her hands on her hips and added a resounding "Yeah!" glaring in Justin's direction.

Justin was laughing so hard he could barely respond. "Relax, cuz. You've heard of playing the field haven't you?" Wayne didn't appear to understand, let alone be amused by the question, so Justin softened his tone. "Aw, come on. You can't fault Terri for using her natural talents."

Wayne, ignoring that Lissy's fondness for apples had by now rendered the score almost wholly inaccurate, pursued the issue.

"That's crap. There's nothing natural about it, that wheelchair is magic!"

"Tough." replied Justin. "Leave it, dude. You're holding up the game." This sentiment, at least, was echoed by everyone, so Wayne had to reluctantly let the matter drop, grumbling all the while.

Terri continued her aerial antics, whooping at the top of her lungs and whirling about, exceeded only in volume by Lissy, ecstatic at witnessing a human experience the joy of flight that her kind had known all their lives.

There were a couple more base hits, but Wayne's team's doom was sealed. Terri caught another potential line drive by swooping in low and fast, the wind from the passing of her aluminum chair stirring the grass as she went.

With the inning finally over, Terri gratefully lowered her chair back onto the soft grass. The effort of the swooping had drained her and though she looked excited, she was clearly tired.

Wayne was still muttering to himself as sides were switched once again.

Wayne stuck with his old faithful pitcher, Carlos, who was at long last beginning to shed some of his natural timidity. The realization was beginning to dawn on him that he was a fairly competent pitcher. He stood the mound with growing ease and even began throwing out the ball to some of the infielders, trading jokes and smiles. Carmen nodded approvingly from the sidelines.

Justin was first up at bat this time, smiling deliberately towards first base, where Wayne was hunkered over, frowning as one in deep thought.

Carlos was more comfortable with Justin and decided to work him a little with simple fastballs. The first one came speeding across the plate, and Justin, swinging rather lamely, earned himself his first strike. Wayne clapped a bit too loudly at this, and Lissy, confused as ever as to who she was rooting for, cheered at the top of her lungs, now practically up to her knees in apple cores.

Justin smiled and readied for his second swing. Carlos made an elaborate and ridiculous hand signal to the catcher, and then threw the pitch. The ball came rocketing inwards, then broke suddenly for the plate, precisely as Justin stepped into his swing. The change-up earned him a second strike. Now Justin stopped smiling, cloaking himself in the concentration of one who is determined not to mess up the next swing. To Justin's great frustration, Wayne suddenly called a time out, probably to break his cousin's concentration. Justin planted his bat on the plate and slapped his hip. "What's going on? Let's play some ball here!" He was clearly annoyed at having his stride broken.

Wayne must have been aiming at exactly that, for the only other player he conferred with was Nash, who was playing second base. The two stood there chatting, and Nash's broad smile soon broke into laughter, as if Wayne had told him a good joke. After a few more moments, during which Justin could hardly keep himself from hopping up and down in frustration, Wayne returned to his position at first base, clapping and shouting and calling for Justin to bring it on. Justin crouched over, trying to settle back into his groove. Carlos, apparently as confused about what Wayne had talked about as everyone else, cocked back for the pitch.

Justin narrowed his eyes and leaned into it.

Carlos let fly and the ball raced toward Justin. It was no change-up this time, this was the speediest fastball the skinny kid had ever thrown. It sped across the plate in perfect level with Justin's flying bat. His aim was perfect, his swing dead on.

He closed his eyes, ready to savor what was certain to be an absolutely fabulous homerun, perhaps the best one of the entire game.

The bat sliced through the air. Justin surprised by the lack of solid contact. He had swung so hard that he spun himself around and off his feet. He wound up in a heap on home plate, the bat handle sticking straight up in the air like a memorial for confused ballplayers.

It was only the handle that was straight. The rest of it had been ensorcelled. The wood was flimsy and slipped out of the way as Justin had swung. The wood beneath the lacquer was still green in patches where the fibers had been brought to life by magic. Traces of its current still flowed through the veins in light, sparkling trails.

There was only one player on either team with the gift of power over natural, growing things.

"Nash!" Justin cried out, getting to his feet and dusting himself off. Nash, along with nearly everybody else, laughed so hard that Justin had to struggle to make himself heard over the din, but this he did admirably. "That is not cool! You can't do that!"

Wayne, doubling over with laughter, struggled to force words out. "Relax, cuz, you can't fault Nash for using his natural talents!" The laughter rang out in fresh peals. Justin's face turned pink as his words came back to haunt him.

When things had calmed down, Wayne and Justin conferred at the mound. They shook hands over the joke. Justin, glancing over Wayne's shoulder mumbled, "So what's the score?" They both went over to the apple pile to check.

The score, as the groaning Lissy clearly illustrated, one hand resting on her swollen tummy, was not entirely clear. While both captains knew surely that Justin's team was ahead, both apple piles were equally decimated and practically spilling over into one another.

The team captains chuckled and shrugged their shoulders. In the end they decided that the score hadn't really mattered all that much anyway, since the game had been so much fun.

"Tell you what," Wayne said. "We'll go to sudden-death overtime. Whoever scores the next homer, wins."

Justin agreed and they shook hands. They decided to alternate players on both sides to see who could crack the first one out of the park. Just to make things fair, there was nobody playing the field and Winklo got to pitch.

Miko was the first one up, with Justin clapping and carrying on for her. Giving Nash a gently scolding look which made the Elf blush a deep blue, she wisely chose an aluminum bat for her swing.

The pranks were not over yet. Jamal, prompted by Nash and Wayne, slipped his medallion over his neck, his own form shimmering as the illusion began to take hold. With the magic amulet, he could take on the shape of a dwarf or a dragon, depending on which face of the medallion was up. He had chosen the later. Jamal crept slowly up behind Miko. Winklo's smirk was already beginning to tip Miko off to the massive, scaly, form that was beginning to rear up behind her.

The joke was cut short, as the school's old air raid siren was sounded. The old siren was a throwback to the cold war fifties and had languished in the school basement until the children had taken it out, dusted it off, and hooked it up to an old car battery as part of Wayne's increasingly stringent security measures. Carmen had been instrumental in this, as she was in all matters involving the several dozen scattered cars that had long since proved to be the most effective weapons on the Wildsidhe. This was the first time it had been used, except for a couple of drills. This was no drill, or Justin and Wayne would have known about it. They all knew what it meant. An intruder had been sighted.

Wayne, pausing only briefly to lament the end of his game, dropped everything and began barking orders. "Battle stations!"

CHAPTER 2

Before long, the school compound gates were swarming with Wayne's crack security team. The gate itself, four towers, and the new wall that ran off from it, had been one of Wayne's better ideas, assembled as it was from the metal park bleachers, further protected by the original yard fencing. The whole construction was further patched at various intervals by whatever scraps of iron bearing metal that could be scrounged up until needed elsewhere: signs, car parts, bits of discarded machinery. The entire structure had an almost eerie Frankenstein appearance lent to it by its patchy construction. The bleachers functioned as a catwalk, giving the defenders a higher vantage point, and the entire metal contraption bent and shook with the weight of their running feet, raising a racket every bit as fearsome as the defenders themselves.

The impressive structure of the gate was further supported by the massive amount of iron present in both its fabric and in the additional bits of metal hung all over it. The presence of the iron assured the children a great deal of additional protection against most Wildsidhers, and those who could withstand it would at least be the weaker, less magical variety who would be easier to deal with.

The defenders bristled with iron weaponry, mostly sporting arrows nocked in plastic bows from the gym's supply room or compound bows and crossbows raided from the strip mall. A few track and field javelins supplemented the supply.

The top of the gate was crowded with defenders bristling with their makeshift weaponry. The kids were clad in homemade armor made from scavenged sporting equipment and sheet metal. The lot more closely resembled some kind of post-apocalyptic medieval army than the group of scared children that they actually were.

To say that the response to the threat, justified as it may have been by past experiences, was overkill, would be a vast understatement. Standing in the shadow of this fairly awesome display of armed determination was another rather unimpressive group. Short and stocky, the motley group of fifteen or so Wildsidhers stood at the entrance, shading their eyes from the warm afternoon sun. They were clearly ill at ease with their surroundings. A closer look at their small forms revealed them to be fairly massive with muscle, almost gnarled or ropy looking. Some had long beards braided and gathered about their waists with shining rings wrought from precious metals. one of two wore their faces clean-shaven. Still another had his beard short and neatly trimmed. Their garb was simple, tight fitting coats of leather adorned with yellow metals that glinted duly in the light.

The children, coming at a trot from their game, leapt up onto the bleacher catwalk to get a better vantage point. They recognized them as dwarves. Winklo was instantly ill at ease, for though she longed for the company of her own kind, she was tired of the derision constantly heaped upon her for her love of a forest-dwelling Elf. Lest Nash sense this and be dismayed, she trotted to his side at once and clasped his hand tightly. Nash, instantly understanding her gesture, gave a quick squeeze in return.

The dwarven party halted just short of the main gate, clearly awed by the impressive display of defense, both man and metal. They stood for a moment pondering what to do. Justin, Wayne and Miko had taken their positions at the very top of the main tower. From there, they surveyed the small and nervous looking band below.

Justin was still in a good mood from the game and the dwarves didn't seem to be much of a threat. Relieved that there was no real danger, he clapped Wayne gently on the back. "So, what do you think? Should we send Lissy out to talk with them?"

Wayne did not share Justin's casual assessment. Any Wildsidhers near the compound made him very nervous. He was responsible for the safety of three hundred kids and it was a duty he took seriously. When he screwed up, people got hurt. Wayne was determined not to screw up.

"Quit kidding around, Justin. They could be Changelings, or worse. We don't know what other surprises this place has hidden up its sleeve."

The dwarves remained at the foot of the gate in a tight knot, muttering amongst themselves, clearly trying to figure out what to do next and not entirely in agreement as to what that might be.

"Well, they don't look too dangerous to me," Justin said, his smile faltering only slightly. "I'm not sure absolutely everything on this side is determined to harm us, Wayne. I appreciate your worry, but let's at least find out what they want before we wind up driving them out of here."

Wayne nodded and gave a short grunt. He then looked up and called for Winklo. The dwarf's stubby legs made climbing the bleachers to Wayne's side a difficult task, but she was quickly there.

"Winklo, can you ask them what it is they want?"

Winklo shook her head. "Nothing against any of you, but I think that would do more harm than good. The Tunnel-Folk prize loyalty above all, and my betrayal of my people is probably near legend by now."

"That's ridiculous!" cried Justin. "You're following your heart. Loving Nash doesn't make you any less a dwarf yourself!"

Winklo only sighed and blew out her breath. "How do you humans say. . . you are preaching to the choir? I know this as well as any of you, but the Tunnel-Folk are as hard as the rock they hew, and their minds are as closed as the passages where they make their homes. Our memories are long and our ways far older than even your greatest of grandparents. While they love stories of love, fate or tragedy, first comes loyalty and the ways of their own."

Justin opened and closed his mouth several times and made as if to speak again, when Miko put her hand on his shoulder. "Leave it, Justin. She's right. None of us like it any more than you do, but if we're going to make it on the Wildsidhe at all, we're going to have to learn a little respect for the way of things here."

Wayne nodded in agreement. Justin's face hardened for a moment, as if he wanted to debate the issue further, but a quick glance at the sadness in Winklo's eyes shut him down.

"Whatever." He half-growled. "You handle it, Wayne."

"Fine." Wayne shrugged his shoulders, clearly relieved not to have to force the issue with Justin.

While the kids thronging the bleachers chattered and squawked like a bunch of crows, Miko alone seemed calm. Wayne was impressed by this and also by her clear understanding of Winklo's refusal to negotiate with the dwarven party.

"Miko, I want you to take Chuck, John, and Jamal and head down to the gate to talk to them," Wayne said.

Miko, who had been secretly hoping to be given that very assignment, instantly turned on her heel, but Wayne caught her arm and looked her forcefully in the eye.

"Arm yourselves first," he whispered.

A short while later, the gates slowly clinked open. A hush settled over the defenders, broken only by the tension of drawn bowstrings and taught arms ready for any sudden move. Miko, Jamal, and the Bearclaw brothers stepped through the gate, weapons ready. Miko, as always, carried a sword. Her father had competed in fencing and saber in college and he had trained his children, Miko and Ron, since they were able to walk. Miko was even more skilled than Ron and she was in charge of training the other kids.

Miko and the others surveyed the dwarven group cautiously. The dwarves appeared not to have weapons, though their great strength easily made their bare hands worthy of at least some caution. They made no hostile moves, in spite of the caution of the children approaching them. Miko gestured to her band to stop some fifteen feet away from the dwarves, who were beginning to mill nervously at the proximity of the armed humans.

There was an awkward silence that seemed to last an awfully long time, as both sides waited for the other to speak. Finally, Miko cleared her throat, but was so nervous she stumbled over her first words.

This caused a good bit of belly laughter from the dwarves, a laugh that the children had heard from Winklo before and that Jamal knew fairly intimately from his escapades among the dwarves in search of the Grimstone. It was a deep laugh, dark in tone, with a touch of rasp that made it satisfying somehow. Jamal grinned in spite of himself, as did Winklo perched up in the bleachers. Nobody could laugh like a dwarf.

When the laughter had subsided a bit, one of the larger dwarves, still a bit smaller than the fourteen-year-old Miko, stood forward. His blond beard was braided and tucked into his belt, the brass buckle of which was emblazoned with an image of tilting scales. It reminded Miko of the justice symbol used in her home back on Earth. The dwarf spread his arms and bowed slightly.

"We come in peace," he said, his voice deep and every bit as brass as the buckle about his waist. "If you will take your time and speak with us, we will understand you well enough." His language was comprehensible, but heavily accented and the children had to consider what he said for a short moment before deciphering it.

Jamal was trying to be helpful. He knew dwarves were much more formal with outsiders than they were among themselves. Remembering what little dwarven custom he had garnered during his infiltration of the tunnels, he raised his fist in a dwarven salute he had seen guards use – touching his chest first, then extending his hand palm open.

It had the opposite of the desired effect, and the dwarves only narrowed their eyes and huddled closer together, muttering suspiciously. Miko shot Jamal a glance, and from the bleachers, Wayne's eyes bored into his back. Jamal opened his mouth, then closed it and looked at his feet.

"Very well," said Miko, doing her best to pitch her high voice low and give it some authority. She didn't want to let these Wildsidhers know just how scared she was. "We are the people of Sparta, Pennsylvania and this is our home. I am Miko and I speak for our people. We are peaceful folk, but we have learned caution, because the Wildsidhe is a place that demands it. Why have you come here?"

The lead dwarf responded well to the formality of her tone, apparently used to this manner of discourse. He stepped forward and saluted, touched his hand to his nose and then held it open above his right shoulder. "The Wildsidhe does indeed call for care, but you have no need of it with us, for we come in peace. I am Haamer, Trademaster of the Braag tunnels. These are the Chaincounters," he gestured to the party behind him, "and we come to you on a mission not of war or even diplomacy, but of commerce. The Trade Gate to Braag is not far to the east of this place. Long have we watched you build your fortress and till your fields since first the Fortesan Asgar brought you here. We have watched your battles, we have seen your toil. We have watched you prosper and we are pleased. We propose an arrangement that we believe will be mutually beneficial to both our struggling peoples in these dark times." With this, Haamer bowed slightly and spread his arms wide.

Miko, for a brief moment, simply did not know what to do. What little contact the children had had with the Wildsidhers since their arrival had been mostly hostile. A trade proposal was the last thing any of them had expected. She stood for a brief moment, trying to figure out what to say and desperately hoping that she wasn't looking like a fool, or worse, a child. Finally, she stammered, "Wait here." Then she turned, motioned to the others and strode back through the gates, which were hurriedly dragged back open to permit her passage. The dwarves, looking dismayed, milled about uneasily but otherwise respected her request.

Back inside, she nearly started giggling from a combination of relief and shock. Justin and Wayne came trotting over, looking flushed and excited. "Well?" demanded Wayne. "What happened?"

"You're not going to believe this," said Miko, still stunned from the entire encounter. "It's a trade delegation. They think we're a mall."

Now it was Justin and Wayne's turn to stare. Only Winklo seemed unsurprised by the entire encounter.

"This is fitting," she said. "The Tunnel-Folk are a merchant people. We often trade for needed goods and this patch of your Earth that Asgar brought here contains a wealth of goods my people could never obtain elsewhere."

Justin and Wayne both paused, neither willing to make a decision on what to do next. Miko and her party stood by patiently. Finally, Justin mastered himself and said, "Well....we should....um......trade with them, I guess." He then smiled at his own lack of experience. "This is ridiculous. I've never had to do something like this before. How do you open up trade negotiations?"

Wayne shrugged his shoulders, smiling easily now that Justin had admitted his lack of experience. "I don't know. I guess we should ask them what they have to offer us."

"What could they possibly have to offer us?" Miko asked pensively. "Between Nash helping us grow crops and the Bearclaw's hunting parties, we're finally doing fine on food. For other things, we still have most of the transported portion of town to rummage through. Eventually, we'll use up most of the stuff, but I'd imagine that day is a long way off."

"I don't really know what they would have," Justin said. "Jamal, you were down there. What could the dwarves have that we would want?"

"It was a different clan, but I imagine they aren't too different. They love mushrooms. They put them in almost everything. They are skilled at rigging booby traps for the dragons because dwarves and dragons are in a constant turf war for control of the tunnels. They seem able to make just about anything from metal, not to mention they have incredible skill with stone, but most of it is in an iron-age context. Believe me when I tell you that they're not going to produce anything we can use to meet our most desperate needs at present." There was no need for Jamal to elaborate what those needs were, everyone present knew implicitly.

Fuel.

Whether it was power to run batteries or gasoline for cars, fuel of any kind, and the prospect of its eventually running out, was the constant fear that plagued the kids. The modern amenities powered by industrial-age fuels were the one thing that gave them an edge on the Wildsidhe, the one thing that enabled them to survive.

Winklo, looking grim and thoughtful, nodded her agreement. Her assent seemed to give Jamal renewed credibility in Justin and Wayne's eyes.

"But," Jamal continued, encouraged by the positive reception, "tangible goods are not the only things that can be traded. Knowledge is a commodity, as is manpower. Who knows what these Tunnel-Folk could teach us? From what little I've seen of the underground halls, they are superior engineers, and they look like hard workers and brave fighters too. Plus, they *know* the Wildsidhe—they know the culture, customs, people, plants, animals, traps, and pitfalls. We are still building the generator mill outside of town at the waterfall. We are getting some electricity from the few gas powered generators we have, but the more we use them, the less gas we have. Same with recharging the car batteries after we use them. I say forget things, let's ask them to send us people. Preferably people who can help us work, help us fight, build, and maybe teach us a thing or two. Maybe we can even finish the generator mill."

The pitch of Jamal's voice had been steadily rising throughout his little monologue, and he ended with an almost jubilant shout. The generator mill at the waterfall outside of town was his pet project. If they could get it working, they would have electricity again.

Justin smiled, impressed with his enthusiasm and his quick thinking. "Excellent idea, Jamal. Okay. Miko, go invite them in..."

"Whoa there!" Wayne cut him short. "I'm sorry, Justin, I know this is your gig, but there is no way I'm letting a pack of strangers into the compound, no matter how much they may have to offer us. Let's have them meet in town. And while I like Jamal's suggestion, I'm not letting anybody else into the compound unless we're double sure that we can trust them and that they aren't Changelings."

Justin considered Wayne's suggestion and nodded in agreement. "Okay. Wayne is right. Jamal, you had your meeting with Asgar in the old Flagship Diner?"

Jamal nodded.

"What condition is it in?"

Jamal paused in thought and then answered, "It's okay. Asgar smashed up a few plates and cups and it's dusty. There's certainly no food left in it, except a moldy pie. You guys did a good job early on with your foraging parties. But the booths and windows and stuff are still intact if that's what you're after."

Justin nodded. "Yeah. So you could meet there?"

Miko nodded back. "Shouldn't be a problem. It's not first class accommodations or anything, but it'll do in a pinch if we need something outside of the compound."

Jane Blossum had wandered over and was listening to the conversation. She had been playing on Justin's team. All of the children had been making an extra effort to include her in any leisure activities since she'd lost her sister, Marianne. As much as the children thought of Marianne as a traitor after she handed Bobby Shelly over to Queen Morna, they understood that it was hard on Jane. Perhaps the extra indulgence had made her forget herself slightly, for now she wrinkled her nose and said,

"That old place? You're going to turn your trade meeting into a misery date." Jane had taken some time to warm up to Winklo when the dwarf had first arrived in the compound, but she still wasn't a huge fan of native Wildsidhers overall.

Wayne shot her an alarmed glance and Justin frowned briefly at her before turning back to Miko and nodding his approval. "Take Jamal and the Bearclaw brothers with you and make sure you bring your weapons and stay on guard. I don't think there'll be a problem, but there's no sense in taking unnecessary risks."

Wayne signaled to Cindy. "Cindy, can you go grab one of those air horns from the supply locker?"

"There's only a few that Ben didn't convert into iron blasters," Cindy said. Ben Mazel had pulled a rabbit out of a hat with his idea to convert leaf blowers and air horns into iron sprayers. It was the only thing they had so far that could really hurt Asgar.

"The iron dusters will be as useless on the rest of the Tunnel-Folk as they are on me," said Winklo. Winklo tended to get a mild rash from iron, as opposed to Nash or Lissy, whom it could burn and hurt severely. Iron was more dangerous to Wildsidhers who had more magic and dwarves were pretty low on the list.

"We actually need the horn," Wayne said.

"I'll get it," Cindy said.

"Thanks, hon," Wayne said.

Cindy sprinted off, as Wayne ignored Justin's glare at his use of the familiar word with her. Wayne chuckled inwardly. She soon returned with a small canister of compressed air with a plastic horn fitted to the top, the kind used by crowds at sporting events. Wayne handed it to Miko.

"Take this," he said, "it's definitely loud enough for us to hear it from the Flagship and we'll know something's up. I'll have a squad on standby."

Miko turned the horn over in her hands, lightly tapping the green plastic trigger with her thumb to test it, and emitting a low pitched blat so loud that everyone in the vicinity jumped. They'd be able to hear it all right, Miko thought. They'd be able to hear it if she sounded it from the deepest dungeon of Morna's castle.

Miko looked up from the horn to Winklo, opened her mouth, and closed it without speaking several times. There was an uncomfortable silence and much shifting of feet, even Justin looked on at the dwarf expectantly.

Winklo finally cracked a smile and spoke up. "What are you waiting for? My personal blessing? A bit of dwarven wisdom? There is none. I tell you again my presence would do more harm than good. The Tunnel-Folk would not want me there and there is nothing I can do for you here."

Justin kicked at some loose gravel and murmured a barely audible, "I know, it's just. . . "

Winklo put a hand on his shoulder. "Justin, all of you. You are my people now. This is a good thing. After all," she said, smiling broadly and glancing over at Nash, "there is probably no other place on the entire Wildsidhe where we could be together in peace."

Nash grinned back and squeezed her hand.

"I, on the other hand, am going with you," Wayne said, breaking the dramatic ice formed by Winklo's proclamation. "It'll be noon soon anyway, and somebody needs to be out by the clock to welcome any newcomers." Wayne had made a habit of making sure he or someone else went out to the clock on town hall each day at the stroke of noon to welcome any newcomers arriving from the townside. It was part of Asgar's curse, that by virtue of reaching turning eleven, any kid that lived in Sparta when the spell was cast came over at noon on his or her birthday. It didn't matter where they were. The Shelly's had managed to outwit the FBI and get out of the part of Sparta that was still on Earth. It didn't do them any good. As the kids had no records of whose birthday fell on what day in what year, it was impossible to predict when new children would be coming over from townside, so they went out every day, so no kid had to face their exile alone.

"The town square is right next to the Flagship. Heck, you won't have to use the air horn to let me know if you need me."

"I just hope you don't have to cut these negotiations *short*… Get it?" Jane snorted out laughter, doing little to conceal her contempt for the dwarves' diminutive stature. Winklo only frowned a little, used to this sort of ribbing from all the children, and she always gave as good as she got.

Justin, however, was less amused. "That's fine, Jane. You can assist Miko in the negotiations. Miko, with all these guys having to stand guard, you're going to need someone to take notes, right? A secretary?"

Miko smiled assent. In actuality, she hadn't thought of that and it was an excellent idea. Jane was as well suited for that as anyone else.

"Good," Justin said, "Jane, go grab a pen and paper and meet Miko and the dwarven party at the Flagship. Bring another guard with you. Ask Carmen if she wants to go."

Now it was Jane's turn to open and close her mouth without speaking. She paused only a brief moment before racing off, calling Carmen's name.

Miko nodded, feeling much better about the entire arrangement once she knew she would have this sort of backup. She thanked Wayne and not really knowing what else to do, flashed Justin a quick salute that left him looking more than a little confused. With this, she turned on her heel and strode back out through the gates, with her armed escort in tow.

CHAPTER 3

The dwarves were exactly as she had left them, standing about uncertainly and muttering to one another. Seeing Miko's return, they stopped and turned expectantly.

Miko did her best to sound official, though it was hard to appear imposing when one was a slight girl of only fourteen and barely an inch taller than the largest dwarf in the party. Her tone was formal in her nervousness. "We have spoken with our… high, er, council and we have decided that we will meet with you to consider how best our two societies can benefit through a just barter of essential goods." She beamed inwardly, proud of how she had at least concluded the sentence, matching how the dwarves spoke.

Haamer stepped forward and saluted her. "On behalf of the Tunnel-Folk of Braag and in my capacity as Trademaster, I have full authority to negotiate such a treaty. Let us begin at once."

Miko bowed slightly, warming considerably to her task. "Okay," she said, "but instead of meeting in the compound, we have chosen another meeting place. Please come with us."

Jamal and the Bearclaws immediately set off in the direction of the Flagship, but stopped short as soon as they saw that the dwarves were suspicious of this maneuver.

They huddled together closely, bunching their huge fists. "Where are you taking us?" Haamer asked sternly. "We know nothing of this place."

Miko could see that the children had made an error in judgment in their choice to meet at the Flagship. The dwarves had been watching the compound for some time, but probably knew little of the town. Suspicious folk by nature, they believed they were being led into a trap. In spite of their great strength, they were weaponless, and the children armed to the teeth. For a brief moment, Miko saw it from their perspective, and scrambled mentally to come up with some way to set their minds at ease.

"Please understand, Lord Trademaster, an armed fortress is not a good place for important trade discussions. We would rather take you to one of the finer sights of our old Earthen home, a place where, in its day, our people regularly met for meetings." Miko winced as she waited for a response.

Haamer's composure lightened visibly, and after a rushed consultation with the Chaincounters, he turned back to Miko and said, "Very well. We will put our faith in you. Your manner is certainly proper. Lead us to this place."

Miko bowed deeply and said, "You honor me with you trust, Lord Trademaster, and I assure you this is the first step in a mutually profitable relationship between our peoples."

Jamal and the Bearclaw brothers continued to stare at her in amazement. This girl, who had been little more than a quiet wallflower the entire time they had known her Earthside was proving herself a natural diplomat. She had already proved she was the best with a sword, a lesson Jamal and the Bearclaw brothers had all found humbling.

They followed her with newfound respect, straightening up and playing the role of an honor guard without being told, influenced by Miko's shining example. Influenced to a point. Chuck and John couldn't resist whispering to each other and chuckling under their breath as they walked. It wasn't long before Miko knew why, for in spite of all the formality, Jamal couldn't resist trotting up alongside her and whispering in her ear.

"Lord Trademaster?" he hissed.

"Shut up," she whispered back. "I'm making this up as I go along. If you think you can do better, you come up with a title for him." The Bearclaws were still chuckling. "And go tie down those other jokers too."

Jamal stifled a giggle and dropped back into place, whispering to the Bearclaws, who got out their last giggles and finally put on straight faces.

The Flagship was only a five minute walk from the compound. The old diner stood at one of the main intersections near the school grounds and had been there as long as any of the children could remember. Back on Earth, it had subsisted mostly on juniors and seniors who got sick of cafeteria slop and spent their lunch money on inexpensive hamburgers and cheese fries. It was a typical downtown diner, done in a fifties motif, complete with cardboard cutouts of James Dean and Marilyn Monroe standing out front, bearing menus and welcoming smiles. A giant, deliberately lopsided neon sign, long since out of juice, was outside. In better times, it would have flashed "FLAGSHIP," in bright pink letters day and night. Now, much of the glass tubing had been pilfered either by Pixies or the children themselves for use in various projects.

The kids had been in a fight for survival since they arrived on the Wildsidhe. There hadn't been much of an opportunity to stop and appreciate their old haunts as anything more than a place to scrounge for supplies. Seeing the old diner pulled hard on their heartstrings, reminding them of another time when the world had, in spite of its problems, been safe and familiar, and they had been children instead of warriors and diplomats.

For the dwarves, the diner, and the entire town, was a sight to behold. They stood in awe of the place, talking in low whispers among themselves and glancing up at the huge sign in utter amazement. "Never have I seen such a structure," Haamer breathed. "I had always thought our people boasted the finest engineers in all the world, I had never before seen what the Townsiders could do."

Miko stifled a laugh. Of course he would think it fantastic. Stainless steel and neon weren't exactly common on the Wildsidhe.

One of the Chaincounters poked curiously at the cardboard James Dean. "This one is a giant. Are these Townside gods, or heroes?"

Chuck made as if he would answer, and probably sarcastically, but Miko silenced him with a glance. The truth was the best policy.

"They are adults," she answered. "We have none among us."

Haamer turned to her, clearly startled, "You mean that you are all children?"

Miko nodded, "We are. Most of us will live another sixty years at least, and back on Earth, wouldn't be recognized as legal adults for another four years or more."

The dwarves began to speak among themselves in their own tongue, and knowing exactly what they were thinking, she figured she'd better head it off at the pass. "I understand, my good Chaincounters, that you are concerned about the prospect of talking with children, but I tell you that children are all you have to talk with in this case. Children or not, we have beaten the terrors of this place, built a fortress right under your noses, and defeated even the mightiest of Fortesans, Asgar and Queen Morna herself."

She almost added that they had befriended a dragon, but remembered the animosity between the two races in time to bite her tongue.

"What full-grown dwarf can say that? I advise you to treat us with the same respect you showed me outside the gate."

She barely had time to be proud of her newfound formality when she heard Chuck whisper to John, "Where did she learn to talk like this?" The brothers both giggled under their breath, neither quite able to keep themselves totally straight-faced, but careful enough to avoid alerting the dwarves.

There was no way the dwarves could deny the truth of what she said. "You are a short-lived folk and have had little time to know the workings of the world," replied Haamer. "But you are right, and we will deal with you as equals."

"Of course," Miko replied graciously. "Let's go inside and get down to business."

The party headed inside, Miko and her escort walking tall with newfound pride.

As the upholstered interior of the door swung shut before them, Miko briefly wondered if Justin had made the right choice about sending them here. The interior of the Flagship was dustier than she had thought it would be and bore the musty smell of buildings long abandoned. A quick scan revealed no insects, but the baseboards revealed that at least a few families of whatever passed for rodents on the Wildsidhe had begun to avail themselves of the place. More than a few old items either missed or passed over by the foraging parties sat moldering in plain view and the dishware that Asgar had smashed in his meeting with Jamal still lay on the floor.

In retrospect, Miko thought that she should not have been surprised at the Chaincounter's reaction. They were Tunnel-Folk after all, used to dwelling years at a time in the dark and damp corridors hewn in the rock under the ground. They seemed quite at home and even squinted irritably when Miko had the Bearclaw brothers draw the blinds and let some light into the place. It startled a nest of some kind of dragonfly-like insect who had made a home in the malted milk machine. They burst up in small cloud, making a peeping sound like chirruping frogs at night, and then vanished in clouds of sparkling iridescent blue, glowing from their long abdomens.

Meanwhile, the dwarven delegation had seated themselves at a booth, not even bothering to wipe the considerable dust from the cracked red leather upholstery. Haamer looked around impatiently, eager to get down to business, but the Chaincounters remained curious as ever. One of them playing with the jukebox built into the wall, pushing the black plastic buttons endlessly. Another crawling under the table, confused by the Formica top and attempting to discern if it was wood or stone, or both. Still others were wandering about the place, staring at the construction of the stainless steel counters and gawking at those bits of glass and flatware that hadn't been scavenged as of yet.

Miko did her best to indulge their curiosity, answering all of the questions pelted at her. She found herself wishing she knew more about machining and construction, which was the primary interest of the Chaincounters.

"What is this red material?" one asked. "It feels soft, yet it is like the hide of no animal that I have ever seen."

"I think we call it vinyl," answered Miko, "but I'm not really sure, it could be some other kind of plastic."

"Plastic?" asked the dwarf.

Miko didn't even know how to begin to answer that one, and she feared they would never sit down to business, when finally Jane arrived with Carmen at her side, carrying a pad of paper and several pens and looking very put out indeed.

"Nice place you've got here," she said, coughing slightly and waving her hand in front of her face in a vain effort to clear the dust.

Miko, finally having an excuse to cut the exploring short and get the meeting started, had Jamal drag a few tables together to extend the booths range enough to accommodate them all.

It was Haamer who began the dialogue, standing and pounding his fist against his breast, while playing nervously with his braided beard. "We ask that the Stone Father bless these proceedings and help us to work with a fair hand."

It didn't take long for the children to realize that Haamer was opening the proceedings with a prayer. Doing their best to be respectful, they all muttered "amen" in perfect synchronicity, except Jane, who was writing as fast as she possibly could.

"Umm…thanks," said Miko, "and now let's get down to business. What have you got to offer we… Spartans?"

Haamer bowed slightly and turned to one of the Chaincounters, who handed him a small bundle of some kind of scaly hide. He spread it out on the table, and from it gleamed and glimmered thousands of stones and metals, so bright that it was all the children could do to keep from gasping out loud. There were many things the children recognized, silver, gold, iron, bronze, as well as diamonds, rubies, emeralds, topaz, and aquamarine. But even more spectacular were the things they had never seen. Here was a dull colored metal with a faint green and several things they could not identify. There was a multi-faceted gem that changed colors with every pass of the light. It was a spellstone, probably the most valuable of the bunch because of its ability to store and amplify magic.

Haamer smiled with evident pride. "In the working of metal and stone," he said, his tone taking on a decidedly mercantile tone, "the Braag are unsurpassed. We have veins of the finest minerals and ore running through all ends of our land, and what's more, the ability to work them into any shape your people could ever want. Think of it, weapons, armor, pots, tools, jewelry for your queens, we even have a means to thin stone so that it shuts out the outside world and still admits light. There is more."

Another Chaincounter spread out another bundle, this one stuffed with fat, brown mushrooms, and several long strips of equally brown dried meat. "The Trade Gate boasts a farm with great mushroom fields and several herds of Tro. It is all surplus crop and would be more than enough to feed your people should your own farms fail."

The children instinctively wrinkled their noses. The food looked decidedly brown and shriveled, and smelled every bit as musty and mildewed as the inside of the Flagship. Miko thought it was a good thing that they were not short on food. As for the metals and jewels, while they were certainly beautiful, she knew the children had little use for them. Cindy and Nash were the only ones among them that would find the spellstone valuable, and Cindy hadn't learned how to control her spells yet. As far as tools and useful metal items went, they had plenty, having most of the school and the town to rummage through. In spite of the indisputably excellent workmanship of the dwarves, modern, machined tools were going to be far superior to anything they could produce. Pretty stones were nice in easier times, but here on the Wildsidhe, they would do the children little good, especially in the communal atmosphere of the compound, where everything was shared and survival the only real goal.

"Lord Trademaster," Miko replied, "the craft of the Braag is indeed amazing, I have never seen better. However, I have been instructed by our high council to ask for a different item."

Hammer looked at her quizzically. "What would you have of us?"

Miko took a deep breath, hoping that the dwarf would not take offense. "Simply put, we would have you." Miko paused for a moment to gauge the dwarven reaction, but they regarded only with level interest, so she continued. "We wish the Braag to send us a delegation, wise men and women, warriors, engineers, laborers. The number can be fixed against whatever we offer in trade and the duration of their stay as well. These Tunnel-Folk must live among us, under the command of our leadership, and teach us the ways of the Wildsidhe, as well as in the craft of the Tunnel-Folk. They must help us fight and work as well. We also have a large construction project that could benefit from your help."

The dwarves stood in amazement, but no offense was apparent. If anything, they appeared pleasantly surprised by the request. Haamer turned to the Chaincounters and they spoke amongst themselves. Jane, grateful for a break, put down the pen and cracked her knuckles.

When at last they turned back, Haamer smiled broadly, showing teeth that would have made a horse jealous through the coarse hair of his braided moustache. "I must take your offer to the Grand Hall, but I am pleased with these terms. Hopefully we can forge a trade agreement that will someday become an alliance."

Miko grinned broadly at his reply, basking in her newfound skills as an ambassador.

"Now," Haamer continued, "what have you to offer in trade? Surely such a great price in the best of our people must be worth something equally great."

Now it was Miko's turn to be stunned. Even in her brief conversation with Wayne and Justin, they had completely neglected to consider what they could possibly have to offer the dwarves in return. A million possibilities swirled through her mind: machined tools, food from their farms, plastic products, electronics. The only problem was, most of the modern amenities were being horded by the kids because of their scarcity. Miko could not willingly offer them in trade, though they were what the dwarves would undoubtedly be most interested in.

It was here that John came to the rescue, tapping the sunglasses he perpetually wore. "Sun hurts your eyes, doesn't it?" he asked.

The dwarves looked up at him suddenly, the big Bearclaw boy had a way of blending into the background in spite of his size. "Indeed it does," replied one of the Chaincounters, still squinting in the sunlight that came filtering in through the windows.

"Try these," John said, pulling off his sunglasses and passing them to Haamer. "They ought to do the trick, and there's plenty where they came from."

Though the plastic arms stretched to contain the expanse of Haamer's broad face, the dwarf managed to wrestle the sunglasses on and strode about the room, clearly awestruck.

"Fantastic!" he exclaimed, and the glasses were immediately passed around the delegation.

Miko was thrilled inwardly because here was something the children could easily part with. She cursed herself for not thinking of it earlier. Winklo had been wearing sunglasses perpetually ever since she had come to live in the compound, her tunnel born eyes unused to the hard light of the surface.

"How many do you have?" asked Haamer, trying to snatch back the pair from one of the Chaincounters who was in danger of breaking one of the lenses.

Miko thought of the sunglasses store in the strip mall that had been transported over with the patch of town affected by the curse, especially its overloaded stockroom.

"Thousands," she replied.

There was a hurried muttering among the delegation. When it was through, Haamer turned back and nodded. "Excellent. With these we can enjoy the surface much more fully. This is an excellent commodity. I will take this pair as an initial offering with your proposal to the Grand Hall and return to you with their answer."

With that, the delegation rose and resumed their exploration of the diner. It was some time before the entire party managed to extricate themselves and step back outside to proceed back to the compound.

Miko walked proudly, greatly satisfied with the results of her, or any human's as far as she knew, first attempt at negotiation with a Wildsidhe race.

But she hadn't walked far before Haamer coughed nervously and tapped her on the shoulder. The entire delegation stopped and dwarves all stepped in closely, almost surrounding the children. Both Jamal and the Bearclaws perked up nervously, not wanting to offend the dwarves by appearing overly guarded, but nervous just the same.

Haamer's expression was suddenly stern, all mirth and good nature gone from it in a blink. "There is one other matter, I'm afraid."

Miko felt the color drain from her face. She told herself not to be silly, that she had made a stunning impression on the dwarven party, but she couldn't shake the feeling that something was terribly wrong.

"The metal carts you use, the ones that move on their own..." Haamer went on, standing still closer.

"Cars," replied Miko, taking half a step backwards. "They're called cars."

"Caars. Fine. Yes, well. I think it would greatly impress the Grand Hall if you would make a gift of one to us to take back as a token of your good faith in our forthcoming arrangement."

Miko felt her stomach turn somersaults. Since the kids were almost totally without magic, the few cars still running were the greatest military advantage that the children had on the Wildsidhe. With their speed, movement and iron content, few Wildsidhers could face them.

"I'm sorry," she stammered, her voice uncertain as it had been once she first had begun her attempts to negotiate with the dwarves. "We can't make a gift of the cars, they are much needed here."

Haamer looked very indignant. He raised his voice slightly. "This is intolerable! We come all this way to make an overture of friendship to you. Isolated and alone on the Wildsidhe, we offer you the most precious things we have to offer, and you rebuff our simple request for one simple gift!? One of no value?"

The Chaincounters pressed even closer, Miko could feel their breath on her face. "I'm sorry," she gasped, desperate to keep her success from washing away in this sudden, dark turn of events, "but the cars are hardly of no value."

"Fine!" Haamer thundered. "We shall pay you handsomely for them. He produced the bundle containing the gems and precious metals that he had shown her inside the diner and attempted to thrust it into her hands. "You may take it all!"

"No!" Miko cried. "They're not for sale!"

"Hey!" Wayne called out, stalking across the road, on his way back from the clock, empty-handed. There was no new addition to the Wildsidhe today. "What's going on here? Are you okay, Miko?"

Wayne was not a small guy. While Miko was not much larger than even Haamer, Wayne towered over even the biggest dwarf. He had a long iron bar, probably once having served as a cart axle, propped over his shoulder, and this he slid out and let it drag on the ground, making a raking sound that was unsettling to say the least.

Watching his approach, the dwarves began to back off. Jamal, Carmen and the Bearclaws stepped forward and clustered around Miko protectively. Miko began to get some confidence back with Wayne's arrival, and she puffed out her chest. "Yes, Wayne, I'm fine, but these dwarves are getting all hot because we don't want to give up one of the cars! I keep telling them that they're not for sale, but they're acting like I just insulted them!"

"Who is this?" asked Haamer indignantly, looking Wayne up and down. He hadn't met Wayne yet or even seen him before, and so, viewed the big boy as an intruder. Haamer used his irritation as a lever to regain his confidence, and the Chaincounters stepped in again, looking more annoyed than ever. "We were told that you spoke for the children," Haamer said, "and now you send this giant to threaten us?"

"Nobody is threatening anybody," Wayne said, clearly irritated but trying to soften his tone to calm the situation. "It looked to me like you were getting a little hot with Miko. What seems to be the problem here?" Miko appreciated his question in silence. He already knew what was going on, but was giving the dwarves a chance to tell their side of the story.

If the dwarves appreciated it, they didn't show it. Haamer stood forward, gesturing wildly, and spoke in a cool but angry tone. "We come from the Tunnels to set up trade with your people. We come in good faith and bring the most precious gifts that our people have to offer. Your people ask a great price from us in trade, our own people to come and help you gain a foothold on the Wildsidhe. In return, we ask for a simple token, a tiny nothing, and then you come clobbering around, waving your weapon and threatening us!"

Even the Bearclaws had stopped their customary joking around, and stood staring in amazement. "What are you talking about?" asked Carmen, her voice high and disbelieving, "Nobody is threatening you! We just don't want to give up a car!"

"This is ridiculous!" added Miko.

The Chaincounters responded with their own chorus of shouts and accusations. Pressing even closer and clucking like a pack of angry hens.

"Enough," Wayne said evenly, his deep voice carrying over all the shouting even though he was speaking fairly quietly. "I know exactly what's going on here. You're trying to intimidate us into giving you what you want."

He thought briefly of his encounter with the bully Todd, before he changed his ways and ended up sacrificing his life to save Wayne and several others. He remembered the countless other bullies he'd squared off with since his earliest days in school. There was only one way to deal with bullies, only one that worked, anyhow. "Well, it won't fly here. The cars are not for sale, or for trade, or given as gifts, and that's that. If you want to have good relations with us, you're simply going to have to treat us with respect. Threatening us won't get you anything but a fight, and I can assure you that while we don't want that, we'll give it to you if you ask for it." He shouldered his bar, and Miko's escort fanned out around her.

Wayne wasn't surprised at the results. He had seem the same look spread across the faces of bullies in the past. First shock and amazement that their prey was resisting, and later fear, as they realized that their bluff was being called and that if they truly wanted to get their way, they were going to have to ante up and put their money where their mouth was. Haamer's face, along with all the Chaincounters, went through this range of emotions together. It was so predictable that Wayne had to stifle a grin. The dwarves, red-faced and clearly terrified, looked ridiculous. Haamer reacted as a bully put in such a situation, with blustering rage that only served to make a bad situation worse.

"This is an outrage! How dare you threaten the Tunnel-Folk! The Braag are not mere children to be treated so! This negotiation is at an end! We will return to our people and tell them of your deliberate mistreatment of their representatives!" Haamer's face was quite red now, and even the Chaincounters were taken aback by his fury. They stepped back a bit to give him room to rant, debating what could best be done to calm him down.

"Besides," Haamer went on, in quite a fine rage by now, "we're not children like you! We're not only traders and merchants, but warriors as well! If we want one of your caars, we can simply take one!"

That did it. Wayne didn't like aggression and bullying, but he liked downright threats even less. His brow darkened and his mouth drew into a hard line that could only be taken as a frown of extreme anger. "Very well." He said, his voice low and dangerous. "If that's the way you want it."

He held out his hand to Miko, and without even having to be told, she handed him the plastic topped air horn that he had given to her earlier. The Chaincounters, not knowing if this was a weapon, a magic device, or just a mere gadget, stepped back in alarm, throwing up their arms in defense.

Wayne lifted the air horn and blew it in a single, long note, the dark, brassy sound hanging on the air for a few seconds so loudly that the entire group covered their ears and gritted their teeth. The Chaincounters, were clearly not used to such sudden and loud noises, and they practically cowered where they stood, checking their bodies for injuries.

"What magic is this?" one of them cried.

The single note of the air horn was answered by four coughing growls, that gradually rose in pitch, and in tone, until the children recognized them as the starting and revving of automobile engines. The dwarves clustered together in confusion, all of them trying to run in different directions, but succeeding only in bumping into one another and not going anywhere. The Bearclaws were laughing so hard that soon the rest of the children were smiling in spite of themselves.

Within moments, four cars had wheeled into view. One, an old hunk of junk with peeling yellow paint, drove in close and slammed on the brakes, leaving long, dark tire tracks. It kicked up a cloud of dust that only added to the confusion and dismay of the dwarves. The other three cars followed suit, each blocking a direction, north, south, east, and west, until the dwarves were completely surrounded. From behind the wheel of the yellow car, Carlos grinned hugely, waving alternately at the dwarves and at his sister.

The dwarves, finally gave up on running and stood back to back with one another, looking around in utter terror. There was a dreadful pause as both sides waited to see what the other would do. The silence was thick. When the dwarves at last could stand it no more, Haamer opened his mouth as if to speak, but his words turned into a grunt as he was pelted in the head with a small, and not quite ripe apple.

"Aiiieeee!" cried Terri, swooping about over their heads in her chair. Her lap was covered with an old sweatshirt that contained a large bunch of spotty looking crab apples, which she now hurled with abandon, each shot punctuated with a shriek.

If the dwarves hadn't looked silly running into each other as the cars surrounded them, they looked downright funny now, the running and bumping resumed, this time under a rain of half-rotten apples from the airborne Terri, shrieking and whooping at the top of her lungs.

Wayne, looking satisfied, stepped forward and crossed his arms in from of his chest. He half-wished Vawna was around. The dwarves would really have been terrified then, dragons and dwarves being natural enemies. Unfortunately, although Vawna visited, their dragon friend had opted not to live in town, at least for now. Even without the dragon, the kids had made a good showing. "Still want to take a car?" he asked softly. "Well, here they are. Go ahead and take one."

The dwarves finally stopped running as Terri landed, and tried to gather up what dignity they could. All the color was gone from Haamer's face. One of the other Chaincounters moved as if to fight, but Haamer held him back.

"No, we are Braag. We will not harm children, at least if it can be helped," Haamer whispered, looking more than a bit defeated. The dwarves were clearly both outnumbered and outgunned. Facing adults they would fight, even against these odds. "It might yet come to battle, but all other means must be exhausted first."

The other Chaincounters looked torn and relieved. The revving engines sounded like thunder to the dwarves.

"We won't take your Caars," Haamer said in a louder voice. "We apologize for the unfortunate misunderstanding. If you will call off your machines, your guards, and your…flying…" he gestured at Terri, smiling happily from her chair, "girl. We would go in peace."

Wayne nodded and Carlos backed the yellow car out of the way so that the dwarves could leave. "Go tell your boss or king or whoever you work for, that the next time the Tunnel-Folk send us a delegation, it had better have learned some manners. We're more than willing to be friendly here, but not if you mistreat us."

The dwarves only bowed silently and shuffled off with hunched shoulders. Wayne was not one to let his guard down and insisted that the children remain, cars, weapons and all, and watch until they were out of sight.

Wayne was silent and moody all the way back to the compound, not wanting to risk releasing the storm that was obviously gathering in his mind, everyone gave him plenty of room.

The Bearclaws, goofballs as ever, could not be stopped however, and they joked and high-fived one another as they headed back. "That was great! Did you see that? They were practically tripping over each other to get out of there! And Wheels (Chuck's nickname for Terri) when you showed up… with the apples…" Chuck was off in another fit of laughter, taking his brother and Terri with him. "They won't be coming around here anymore. That's for sure."

Carmen added, "I think the Wildsidhe has finally met its match."

"Yeah," snorted Jamal. "This place isn't so tough."

Miko was silent and brooding, just like Wayne. Her chin tucked against her chest and her hands in her pockets.

"Aw, come on Miko!" said John, trotting up to her and clapping her on the shoulder. "We're fine. It's over now. You did great! Heck, we all did! We showed them who was boss, they won't be back. Don't take it hard. It was just a little stand-off is all."

But his efforts to cheer her up fell short. "I don't know about that." Miko said, just as brooding as ever. "I think that was a little too easy. I've got a bad feeling about this."

The Bearclaws were about to continue to laugh this off when Wayne turned around and fixed them with a look that made them all stop in their tracks. "Miko's right. That *was* too easy. Way too easy. Don't you see what happened back there? Those dwarves didn't want to trade with us. That whole negotiation thing was just a cover for their real mission, to get one of the cars. Now, I can't think of why they'd want one right now, but I think if we have time to sit down and put our heads together, we could probably figure it out. But I'll tell you this, and I'm pretty sure of it. If they're willing to come all this way, and put up such an elaborate ruse, and even risk having a conflict with an enormous armed camp right outside one of their tunnels, then I'm pretty sure that they must really, *really* want one of those cars. And if they want it that badly, they're not going to give up easily. No sir, they're not going to give up easily at all."

The silence that followed Wayne's words was total. The children stood in shock as they considered the seriousness of the situation. Even the Bearclaws stopped their customary joking around.

"Now let's get back to the compound," Wayne said. "Once we're there, we need to figure out some additional security measures. Things are going to have to be tighter around here until we know just what we're up against."

CHAPTER 4

And tighter they were.

Back at the compound, Justin and Wayne sat high in the bleachers above the gate, as Wayne described at length the events of the day, the facts occasionally shored up by Miko, who sat with them, saying as little as possible.

Justin listened carefully to what they had to say, and then sat in silence, briefly. "You're right," he finally said, blowing out his breath in a long sigh. "I think this is serious. For the life of me, I can't figure out why they want a car. As a weapon, it isn't going to do them much good, seeing as they can't drive it, especially in their tunnels. I wonder if the iron content wouldn't prevent them from using it at all."

"I don't think so," Wayne said, "Winklo only gets a rash when she touches iron, and if that's the reaction that most dwarves have to it, then they don't have much to worry about. Besides, she's ridden in cars before. But I agree with you, I can't think of why they'd want a car so badly."

"Either way," continued Justin, "you're right to want to lock things down around here. What do you suggest?"

Wayne didn't hesitate at all. The whole walk back from the diner, the wheels in his head had been turning, and he had a good idea of what he wanted done. "First off, we need regular patrols around the compound, both on foot and bike. I want the guards in teams, not just pairs, and I want them armed and armored. Even at night."

Justin smiled awkwardly. "All right, I understand that you're worried here, man, but don't you think that's a bit extreme? The kids aren't going to like being on patrol all night." Up until this point, they had simply locked themselves in the school when darkness fell.

Wayne shook his head. "No, Justin. I'm serious here. We need those patrols. Both Morna and Asgar have attacked us at night. We need double the guards that we have during the day."

"I don't see how that's going to help. We already have everyone in the compound pulling regular guard duty as it is." Justin was picking his words carefully, he could see that his cousin was in one of his "paranoid" moods as he often got into when thinking about the safety of the compound. On the one hand, Justin felt it was a bit extreme. On the other, he was grateful to have such a careful person in charge of security.

"Well, until this threat is over, the patrols can back up the guards, but I still want to double the regular duty, twice as many people walking twice as many shifts." He looked at the disagreement registering across Justin's face. "Until this whole thing blows over at least."

"No way, Wayne. I'll meet you halfway. You can have the patrols, although that's not going to go over so well, but as for doubling the guard, I'm never going to be able to pull that off. There's too much else to get done."

Wayne looked as if he'd like to argue further, but Miko squeezed his shoulder and he didn't bother. "Fine, this'll work for now. I just hope we aren't letting our guard down too much. If those Tunnel-Folk have got something nasty in store for us, I'd like to catch it before it gets delivered."

"You've got to relax, cuz," Justin said. "I mean, I understand that we have to be on guard, but it's like you said, we scared the marbles out of those guys. They won't be coming back anytime soon. It's not as big a deal as you think."

Wayne stood up, shaking his head, hoping that Justin was right.

CHAPTER 5

It wasn't long before Wayne's "paranoia" began to pay off. The reports began to trickle in over the next few days.

Wayne, Winklo, and Nash, stood at the base of the flagpole out in front of the school, testing the shaft for iron content. Winklo had been rubbing her arm against the surface, trying to see if a rash developed. The one that did spring up was light and limited, so the children had been right on the verge of concluding that it was made of aluminum or something without much iron when one of the bicycle patrol rode up.

It was Jane, the note-taker from the negotiations. She sped up to the group on her bike and then slammed on the brakes so hard that her back wheel rose off the ground ever so slightly. She looked a bit panicked.

Wayne was instantly alert. "What's going on, Jane?"

Jane was so out of breath that it took her two or three times to get her words out. "We caught a whole bunch of dwarves trying to get through the fence."

Nash and Winklo stated forward, but were stopped by Wayne, who grabbed a hold of the handlebars and fixed Jane with a hard look. "What do you mean? How many? Did they get in? Is anybody hurt?"

Jane only shook her head and Wayne waited with obvious impatience for her to calm down enough to answer his questions. "I don't know how many exactly, but I'm sure we spotted three or four. They took off running when we showed up. There wasn't any fighting. Nobody got hurt on either side."

"Did they get in? How were they getting through the fence? How come the guards didn't stop them? Where were the guards?" Wayne's voice was rising now, and that only made it harder for Jane to get her bearings.

"No, they didn't get in. They were trying to tunnel under the fence, see how far it went down. You should have seen 'em, half of 'em had these awful rashes all over their faces and arms. I mean it was ugly and I bet it itched too, from the way they were scratching…"

"Yes, get on with it," Wayne said, losing his patience and shaking the bike a bit. "They didn't get inside, so where was the guard?"

"Oh, yeah. Well. I don't know. I mean, the boundary of the compound is pretty big, we can't cover all sides at once. That's why these patrols come in handy. They were just tunneling away, scratching at their arms and stuff, when we came along, and then we shouted 'hey!' and they just took off running, they didn't even bother to take their tools with them."

Wayne nodded. He'd been right after all. "Where are the tools, I want to have a look at them."

Jane shook her head. "They should still be by the fence. I came straight to you and Iris was buddied up with me. She went to go tell Justin."

"Good," Wayne said. "Maybe now he'll listen to me about doubling the guard. Well, take me to where they tried to get in."

It wasn't far from where they were standing. After about ten minutes, they stood at the side of the high boundary fence, surveying a large hole that had been dug in the ground. The dwarves had dug down pretty far but the fence had been laid with the help of a backhoe, and they would have had to dig down much farther if they'd wanted to get under it.

The tools were dropped where they'd been left, just a few feet out from the fence. There was a gate door not six feet down from the hole and Wayne quickly unlocked it, stepped through, and examined the tools. They seemed plain enough, a bronze-headed pick-axe, a shovel made of some greenish metal he could not identify, some trowels carved of hardwood. One thing was clear, the dwarves didn't possess any tools that could dig a hole with enough speed to be a real threat to their defenses, and once Wayne convinced Justin to double the guard, the dwarves would be under the gun the whole time they were digging. Wayne smiled to himself as he considered that he now finally had enough evidence to convince Justin.

Then, one of the tools drew his eye. It had looked like a shovel, and so he had passed it over as he searched around. But now, from the corner of his vision, it seemed to be quivering. He kneeled down for a closer look. It did indeed look like a shovel, but fastened to the end of the shaft was no metal head, it was rather, a small fury animal harnessed into a socket.

Wayne bent closer. The small shape was brown and furry, it looked a lot like a mole, save that it had six legs, and a pointed snout with large protruding teeth. It turned huge, fearful eyes in his direction and chattered nervously. He smiled at first, the creature was kind of cute its own way, but its nervous movements were somewhat eerie, even dangerous looking. Wayne tested the theory by poking a short stick at it. It barked furiously, a high chirping sound that he'd heard when his pet cat had wounded a chipmunk back Earthside, and lunged for the stick, its sharp teeth biting it in half as its spinning claws stripped it clean of bark in a matter of seconds.

"Whoa!" Wayne said, leaping back and dropping it.

"What's wrong? You all right?" Winklo called to him from the other side of the fence.

"Yeah, I'm fine. There's a. . . hang on a second."

He picked up the stick, careful to keep his hands away from the creature at the far end. Then gently, he thrust it into the hole.

The creature, who had been staring at him the entire time, let out a shriek as it came in contact with the ground. There was a buzzing sound as it scrabbled at the dirt and earth came flying out of the hole. It dug fast and furious, and in only thirty seconds had excavated six inches.

Wayne pulled it out of the hole, and immediately, the creature stopped digging. He blew a low whistle. Now *this* was a threat. It ate more than the Huskers that had attacked the town during their migration. One of these could dig a tunnel under that fence in under an hour.

Wayne reentered the compound and showed the creature to Winklo. The dwarf kept well clear of it. "A fury-mole. I should have known."

"Oh, it's so cute," said Nash, starting forward.

Winklo held him back with a sweep of her muscular arm. "You won't think it's so cute when it bites off your finger."

"So, you know this," Wayne said, looking at Winklo expectantly.

"Of course," said Winklo, "I don't know about the Braag, but we used them to bust through harder rock. Granite, Certa-Stone, that sort of thing. They do it to get minerals they need from the rock."

"They've got a lot of these?" Wayne asked, obviously anxious.

"Store-rooms full."

"Why not just have them eat through the fence?" Wayne asked. Winklo took the furry mole carrier and held it closer to the iron laced fence fortifications. It began to shriek in terror. The screams got louder the closer it got.

"Magic is the only thing that lets the furry moles digest their diet. Eating iron would kill them, painfully, from the inside out," said Winklo.

"Come with me." Wayne headed off in the direction of the school, Winklo in tow.

It wasn't long before they were running into other patrollers with similar reports. Gary Holt, never one for physical exercise, came puffing over on foot, red-faced and sweating, to tell Wayne that his patrol, made of his fellow Goblin Eater band members, had also spotted dwarves trying to find a way through the fence on the other side.

Wayne and the others found Justin talking to some other patrollers outside the main entrance to the school. They must have been giving him the same reports, because as Wayne approached, Justin raised his head and smiled good-naturedly. "Looks like you were right, Wayne. They seem pretty interested in getting inside."

"I told you, Justin. I hope you have the evidence you need to take me up on my suggestion and double the guard."

Justin initially avoided the subject. Asking Wayne what he'd seen, what he'd heard, if he could confirm any of the reports. They added up the patrols that had reported in and determined that there had been no less than seven attempts to get into the compound. As far as either of them knew, none of them had succeeded. Within a few minutes, a fairly large crowd had gathered.

"I'm telling you Justin, we got lucky here. Without proper manpower on the fence line, it's just a matter of time before they get in. If they're under the gun the whole time they're digging, then we're safe. But if we leave them enough time to dig in peace, or to figure a way to cut through the fence or whatever, then we're going to have a fight on our own turf here."

Justin looked a little frightened, or at least like he was taking the situation seriously, his usual joking manner was gone. He stood silently, running his hand through his hair. Wayne waited patiently, but it was Winklo who finally stood forward. "Justin, please take the advice of a dwarf in this matter. We are a stubborn folk, and are not going to let up easily. We are known to the elves as the People of The Rock, not only because of our love for stone, but because of our hard character. If these Tunnel-Folk have set their sights on a car, then they are not going to stop until they have a car, or you show them that getting a car is more trouble than it is worth. Listen to Wayne, double the guard."

Justin looked first at Winklo, then back at Wayne. "The kids are not going to like this. Double duty is going to put a strain on everyone, and it's going to take away from other jobs that are important."

"I know, Justin," Wayne said smiling, knowing that Justin was about to give in, "but I'm here to tell you, nothing is more important than our security here. If we lose that, all the farming, trading, building, and research in the world won't be able to help us. It's like we learned in auto-shop. Safety first."

Justin grinned at the last statement. "Okay. Double the shifts. Go ahead and get a line-up together and I'll make an announcement. This is going to suck, though."

Wayne smiled and clapped Justin on the shoulder. "I know, but you won't regret it. Thanks."

With that, Wayne trotted off to draw up the list. As he made his way to the supply room to grab a paper and pen, he heard the old air raid siren sound again, but in a short blast, signaling a town meeting. Justin was losing no time in making his announcement.

By the time he'd got back to the flagpole in front of the school, all those children not on essential duty were gathering around, looking confused and worried, not understanding why the sudden meeting had been called. Justin stood up on the raised base of the flagpole so that he could be seen by everyone.

"I'm going to make this short, because we all have work to do and I don't want to interrupt too long." His voice carried far and the command in it was impossible to miss. Even Wayne, who was much bigger than Justin, felt inspired by him. His cousin was a born leader.

"Everybody knows that we had a little visit from some dwarves yesterday," Justin went on. "Well, it didn't go so well."

"I'll say!" called out Chuck from somewhere in the crowd. This was met by a chorus of chuckles from the audience. Word of what had happened had already long since spread throughout the compound.

Justin smiled. "They got pretty rude and tried to rough up Miko and we had to run them off. We didn't want to do it but Miko and Jane and the others who were there will tell you that we did our best to be nice and to get things to go smoothly, but they didn't want it. In the end, it turns out they just wanted one of our cars, and now they're trying to steal one, or worse."

"Let's just give 'em one!" cried out a voice from the group.

"We can't do that," Wayne said. "They're the only real defense we have out here."

Justin nodded. "Wayne's right. Our fence line can ward off lionhawks and darkcats, but would it stop a speeding car? I don't want to find out the hard way. We can't afford to lose any of the cars, and worse than that, we can't afford to give in to bullies. How many of you here have been bullied before?" There was a hushed silence, nobody said a word, which was all the answer Justin needed. "Well, I have been bullied, and if there's one thing I learned, it's that if you ever want bullies to back off and leave you alone, you've got to stand up to them. We can't give these guys a car just because they push us around a little. Then they'll just come back looking for more.

"Since we ran them off, they've been trying to break through under the fence and into the compound. It's pretty serious and they've got really good digger animals, so we've got to do what we can to stop them. Now I know you're not going to like this, but we can't afford to have them getting in here, so I'm calling for double guard shifts until we're sure that this thing is over with."

This was met with a huge groan from the crowd and least one or two of the kids swore out loud.

"If that fence falls, there's nothing between us and the rest of the Wildsidhe. That includes Asgar and Morna. Wayne will be assigning the details," Justin went on after the complaints had died down. "I don't want anybody giving him any grief about it. This is serious here, and we're doing this to protect all of you." He raised his voice slightly with his last words and that silenced the crowd totally.

"Sorry to be a jerk here, but we have to do what we have to do. Wayne will be coming around to each of you to make selections for the guard duty."

Wayne sat down and began to plan furiously. When he finally went around to assign posts, he found that most of the children were annoyed, but understood what was required of them. The kids may not have liked it, but they knew Justin was right. The ones who were particularly difficult, he assigned with good buddies, who would make sure that they did their job. As it stood, the guard always patrolled in twos, with a buddy to provide back up or go for help if anything should happen.

Though it probably wasn't the best idea, Wayne couldn't bring himself to separate Chuck and John. The brothers insisted on walking night patrol, and on walking it together. With the moon high in the sky, the two brothers walked along silently, pacing the fence line and looking up at the stars. Though the Bearclaws were goofballs by nature, there was something about that night that kept them solemn and quiet. It was an atmosphere of contemplation, not of excitement.

Until they came to the hole in the fence. When they thought about it later, it wasn't actually that big, but at the time it had seemed enormous, big enough to let an army through. John swore under his breath and knelt to examine it. Neither of the boys were metal workers, but long hours spent tinkering around the compound or tailing Carmen on her latest project had taught them a thing or two.

"What did it?" Asked Chuck, the normal humor in his voice gone.

"Wire-cutters, or something like it. Look here, these are clean cuts. They cut the wire we used to attach the sheet metal, pulled them off, then they cut the chain link fence." John knelt and examined the edges, the cuts were indeed clean, and he hissed as he drew back his hand.

The Bearclaw brothers may not have been metalworkers, but they were most certainly trackers. They quickly began examining the ground for signs of who had done this. It wasn't long before they spotted two sets of small footprints leading off into the darkness.

"How long?" asked John, as his brother bent down to get a closer look.

"Not long at all, I'd say less than ten minutes. Looks like two of 'em. Man, Wayne is going to kill us."

He looked up, but John was already sprinting off in the direction of the parking lot behind the school. He paused just long enough to shout "come on!" over his shoulder before putting on another burst of speed. Chuck jumped to his feet and took off after him.

There was no need for either of them to follow the footprints closely, they knew where they were headed.

They dashed to the parking lot, and arrived at the edge of the paving out of breath and gasping. They made no effort to be silent, but it didn't matter, the two dwarves who had broken into one of the cars were far too busy to notice them.

The parking lot was crowded with vehicles, as every automobile that could be moved had been rounded up by the foraging parties, then driven or towed in where they could be protected by the fence. Several had been stripped for their steel panels, trunks and hood to reinforce the fence line.

The dwarves had been in a hurry, and had gone straight for the first car in the lot. Surprisingly, it was the yellow car that Carlos had driven when they'd first run off the trading party. They'd broken a window and were busying themselves with trying to get the thing started. They were cursing softly to themselves as they pushed on the steering wheel, yanked on the wiper controls, and even accidentally honked the horn, the sound of which made them jump so hard that one of them banged his head on the roof.

Chuck and John, after all their panicked running across the compound, quickly figured out that these two weren't going anywhere. The dwarves' hands were already swollen and red from the contact with the metal and they continually scratched and cursed.

Getting some of their old humor back, Chuck and John approached slowly, being careful not to make a sound. In a fit of frustration, one of the dwarves had finally gotten out of the car and gone around behind it, where he first kicked at the trunk, then tried to push on it. When that didn't work, he stood back and placed his hands on his hips, muttering under his breath.

John began to lose patience, "Come on, let's go break this party up."

"No, wait!" Chuck put his hand over his mouth and pointed with the other hand.

The dwarf, an "I got it!" look dawning on his face, had gotten down on his knees and started blowing into the tailpipe. His lips were already swelling up from contact with the iron, but he seemed to think he was on the right track.

"You're not going to start it that way." Chuck said out loud.

"Perhaps we can help?" asked John.

The two dwarves practically jumped out of their skins. The dwarf in the driver's seat hit his head on the roof yet again and the one behind the car started up and banged his head on the bottom of the bumper so hard that it nearly made the whole car jump.

Chuck and John broke down laughing. They were still laughing, when the dwarves took stock of the situation and took off on their stubby legs for the hole in the fence. Chuck was about to start after them when John stopped him. "Wait a minute, man, there could be more. We should go for help."

But by the time they returned to the fence with Wayne, the dwarves had gone. The Bearclaws related the entire story with the greatest effort, doing their best to keep from doubling over with laughter at each description of the dwarves bumbling efforts to start the car.

Wayne didn't even smile. "This is serious, you two. I was worried something like this would happen."

The Bearclaws did their best to sober up, but couldn't help but smirk and giggle under their breath as Wayne went on. "We've got a serious problem here. I don't know what they used to cut through that fence, but what matters here is that they did cut through the fence, and that means that they have a way in. How can we keep the entire fence watched all the time?"

"We could set up security cameras," suggested John.

"We've been over this. We don't have enough juice from a few generators to do it. If we had Jamal's generator mill up and running, maybe, but that's a long way off. The dwarves may have been able to help with that, but I doubt they'd do it now," Wayne said.

Chuck, still smiling, patted Wayne's shoulder. "Relax, man. Seriously, they couldn't have cut through the fence more than five minutes before we showed up. For the most part, we've got this place locked down tight, and even if they did get in, they wouldn't have more than a minute or two before the whole place came down on them. Look what happened here. Those two went running home to mommy to cry about how they got caught. I think that probably put a little good ol' fashioned scare in 'em. They'll think twice before they come back."

Wayne didn't look convinced. "That's what you two said after the first time we ran them off." His voice was dark and final.

The Bearclaws managed to stop laughing and patiently described in detail every aspect of the event. Wayne questioned them in depth. Wayne then nodded, satisfied, and they all went off to consult with Justin yet again, as to what should be done.

Justin looked tired of the whole thing, but did his best to be patient as Wayne went on about the threat this particular breach of security imposed. As the Bearclaw brothers described their story, he couldn't help but laugh along with them, especially when they related the part with the dwarven intruders banging their heads on the car.

"What can I say, Wayne?" Justin sounded worn-out, even if he was laughing, "You're right. But I don't see how we can possibly beef up security anymore then we already have. We've got foot and bike patrols, not to mention double duty guard shifts that are already making everybody grumble. I want to protect us here, but I'm not willing to do it at the cost of making every kid in this compound drop dead from walking patrols all day long. It doesn't look like there was any harm done here anyway."

"The problem is," Chuck broke in, "that these dwarves aren't really affected by iron like the rest of the Wildsidhers. I mean, they get a rash and all, but it's not a serious problem like it is for other creatures, and that has always been our biggest advantage out here. Without the benefit of iron, it's basically just us against them, and that means doing the normal things you do when you fight."

"What? What normal things?" asked Justin, looking alarmed. "You mean hurting them? Are you suggesting that we hurt these dwarves?"

"I don't know," answered Chuck, clearly upset with the idea himself, "I just think there may not be another way. Those dwarves are a lot shorter than adult humans, but they're not all that smaller than most of us, and they're a lot stronger too. And let's face it, we don't have any hard numbers, but I'll bet there are a lot more of them than there are of us. I just think that's something to think about."

John looked at Wayne, who had been standing silently by the entire time. "Well, Wayne? What do you think?"

Wayne was quiet for a long time. "Man, that is tough. I mean, Chuck has a really good point there. But on the other hand, I don't want to start a war here. I mean, let's think about this seriously. They are trying to steal from us, granted, but they aren't trying to kill us, and I think that maiming or killing them wouldn't be justified. Of course, if they change their tactics and actually start attacking the guards, we may have to change our tune. Our first priority has to be our safety."

After that, nobody felt much of an urge to talk at all.

CHAPTER 6

The next morning, the sun rose high and hot, and by the time Wayne was up and about his duties, those children who'd pulled the late night into early morning guard shift were already sweating and cursing the heat. Wayne thought it would be smart to check in with all of the guards and make sure they had what they needed. They were grumbling enough as it was and he wanted to be certain that they didn't start slacking off. But first, he had some business to attend to.

He headed out across the field where the baseball game had been played only a couple of days earlier. The remains of the blue monster were still scattered about where Winklo's homerun had rocketed through. At the far end of the field was a long line of blue plastic port-a-potties stood, bright and out of place against the broad, green background. One of the problems with the compound was, while they had a lot of children, some of who, like Carmen and Ben, were pretty mechanically sharp, they still couldn't get the plumbing to function properly. The portable toilets presented the only alternative to digging a latrine, which they had done in the beginning. Still, the smell was strong even at this distance, and the cleaning agent that was used to treat the sewage was in short supply, and thus had to be used in half-measures. The only duty that was more disliked than the new late night guard shifts, was the "potty patrol," those unlucky kids whose turn came up to drag the plastic toilets, mounted on small and barely adequate plastic wheels, outside the town to be dumped in freshly dug trenches. While "Potty patrol" was so unpopular that is was sometimes used as a punishment for bad behavior, everybody in the compound had to pull that detail sooner or later. If you were a troublemaker, you'd find yourself pulling it more often than most. The one consolation was that the swimming hole, where a lot of the children went to wash, was nearby and ready for a quick dip after hard work on a hot day.

Cindy was standing in the middle of the field. Wayne first had thought that she was headed out for the facilities or on "potty patrol" herself, but as he drew nearer he noticed that she wasn't moving and seemed upset. Cindy stood, holding in her hands a small white statue. She was running her hands over its smooth surface and chanting slowly under her breath. Sweat stood out on her forehead and Wayne saw that as it slid down her face it mingled with fresh tears coming from the corners of her eyes. The statue itself was so beautiful that Wayne forgot where he was heading, and even the obvious distress of Cindy and stared at it. It so smooth as to be absolutely frictionless, and so brightly white, it almost hurt his eyes to look at it. It showed a muscular, white-coated horse, looking strong and prominent, rearing up on its hind legs and pawing at the air, while its single spiraling horn cut a line through the sky. He realized it was her totem, the one Alana had given to her, just before she died from her lionhawk-inflicted wounds. Cindy was the only human among them who had any magic powers of her own. Or at least the only one they knew about.

"Wow," Wayne said, wincing as soon as the words came out, it probably wasn't what an upset girl wanted to hear. "It's beautiful."

"It doesn't matter," Cindy replied through her tears. "It doesn't matter how beautiful it is anymore. It doesn't work."

"What do you mean?" Wayne put his hands on his hips and stared at her now, his attention finally turned away from the magnificent statue.

"I can't get it to work," Cindy said. "I don't know if Morna cursed me, or if it's broken, or if my magic is fading, or what. I can't call the unicorns! I don't know. I wish my grandmother was here to help me."

On hearing this, Wayne dismissed thoughts of unicorns and magic. This he could help her with. Her gave her a sympathetic look and folded her in his arms, rocking her gently.

Cindy held the statue tightly and swayed with him, crying as if the tears would never stop. Wayne rocked her back and forth, trying desperately to think of something that would help her.

And then the ground rippled.

At first he didn't know if it was an aftershock of the magic Cindy had been trying to call, or simply a trick of his mind, given all the swaying he was doing, so at first he did nothing but straighten up. Before long, it happened again. The surface of the grass seemed to lift and fall gently, like a wave on the water coming in with the tide.

It was getting closer.

Cindy realized that something was wrong and stepped back from him. Wayne caught her arm and drew her out of the way of the moving mound.

"Is this your magic?" Wayne asked her, stepping back another pace. The ground was positively rolling now.

Cindy only shook her head. "I don't know what this is."

There was a tiny sound arising from the rolling mound now, it was moving very slowly, maybe only a few inches each minute, as if something was digging furiously under the earth, but what could dig so fast?

The sound continued, rising from a dull rumble to a higher chattering, which eventually cleared into almost understandable words. Words spoken by voices that Wayne recognized.

His fear vanished instantly. "Come on, Cindy!" He said, grabbing her wrist and leading her over to the potties as the mound trundled slowly on. Wayne was positively grinning. Seeing Wayne's expression, Cindy felt much less afraid, but her fear was replaced with confusion. "Wait a minute, Wayne," she said, tugging at his arm. "What's going on?"

"Don't worry about it," Wayne smiled back. "This is going to be cool."

Wayne positioned himself behind one of the potties and grabbing the handle, tilted it back. Cindy could hear the contents sloshing about inside, and the smell was almost unbearable, but Wayne, making some effort to be quiet now, directed her to do the same. With an 'I can't believe I'm doing this' look on her face, Cindy complied.

Wayne then rolled the potty out in front of the mound as it moved across the field, it had almost made it half way. Cindy did her best to keep up with him, but the potty was very heavy, and she just barely caught up and got hers into position as the mound was reaching their feet. Still, as slowly as it was moving, they had a minute or two to wait, during which Wayne stood tapping his foot and beaming at the ground, like a kid waiting for his favorite fireworks display.

At last the mound reached almost to their feet. The sound of talking and grunts of effort could be heard clearly from inside. Wayne tapped the ground with his foot, hard.

"We're here!" a voice said enthusiastically from below, and a furry mole digger burst through the top of the mound. Within a few moments, shovels had cleared most of the dirt, to reveal two sweaty and tired looking dwarves who had obviously been tunneling beneath the ground into the compound. They blinked into the sunlight looking surprised and confused. Wherever they had hoped to end up in their tunnel, this clearly wasn't it.

Wayne paused only long enough to smile at them and say, "I don't think so."

Cindy didn't need Wayne to tell her what to do, and the dwarves screamed in horror as the children tipped the potties forward and let the contents pour into the hole. In spite of the horrible stink, the pair laughed until their sides hurt. The dwarves, cursing and screaming, fled back down the hole they had come from.

Finally, the children recovered from their hysterics and began to wipe the tears from their eyes.

"Ug," Cindy said, "this stinks. Let's get these potties back and get the hole plugged up."

But Wayne, not surprisingly, had sobered up a great deal rather quickly, and was already thinking about what this meant. "Yeah, we better get this hole filled in, but I want you to run back to Justin and tell him to put the whole compound on alert. I don't think this was a random prank. After what happened last night, combined with this, I think we're about to have a pretty serious disagreement with these dwarves."

Cindy looked a bit more serious now. "Do you really think they're going to attack us?"

"I don't know," Wayne answered, dusting off his jeans, "but it's better to be safe than sorry."

Cindy nodded and they were both off like a shot.

There were no objections from Justin this time. He simply nodded with a dark look in his eyes as Wayne related the news. "Well, I guess you're right Wayne. Let's get this place locked down. We'll get the walls manned, and everybody armed up." He cursed under his breath. "I was hoping we could avoid something like this."

Wayne put his arm around Justin's shoulders. "We all were, Justin. You're doing the right thing here."

And so, for the second time that week, the wailing of the old air raid siren echoed through every corner of the compound, followed immediately by shouting and stomping as the children armed themselves and rushed to their posts.

Wayne watched the kids with satisfaction. He had trained them well, every boy and girl knew exactly where they needed to be and what they needed to be doing. Wayne watched as one boy rushed past, wearing an old hockey helmet, and shoulder pads, carrying a plastic bow with a quiver of iron tipped arrows. He quickly took up a position by the gate and got his bow strung and ready.

If I'm wrong about this attack, I've done a lot of harm, thought Wayne. The children were already nervous and on edge from the heightened security, and a false alarm like this would only serve to fray their nerves further and make Wayne look bad in front of everyone. But Wayne's nose for trouble is what got him the job of head of security in the first place. He had long since learned to trust that nose, and, over time the other children had come to trust it too. Wayne was determined to be worthy of that trust.

And this time, at least, he was. It wasn't long before the dwarves appeared in force, thundering over the hills and making for a line of fence that they deemed to be weakly defended.

The dwarven army was impressive. Haamer had informed the Braag of the age of their adversaries. Because of their sense of honor, none of the dwarves wished to slaughter children, but they needed a car to protect their clan. Most of the dwarves had chosen to enter battle weaponless, relying instead on their great strength to strike against their enemies and their dense muscles to protect them from harm. A few of them wore thick leather hides as armor, and some had helmets and breastplates fashioned from the same brass Wayne had seen on Haamer's buckle. There were a few weapons visible as well, mostly hammers and clubs, but even without these, the threat was fearsome indeed.

The dwarves advanced directly towards the fence line without stopping for a moment. Wayne could now see Haamer in their midst, mounted on a long white lizard, white reptile skin looking uncomfortable in the sun. Haamer was wearing the sunglasses the children had given him.

Wayne had always thought that battle was a thing of noise. That some great cry would go up from the Braag as they threw themselves at the compound, but there was only eerie silence as the dwarves moved quietly forward and the children stood in near panic at the thought of a pitched battle.

For a moment, Wayne was infected with the same panic, and stood with his mouth open.

But only for a moment.

In the next instant, Terri whooshed by overhead, doing an impression of Tarzan's call as loud as she could. Carmen had rigged up a kind of passenger seat behind the chair that held another person in much the same way as a mother's papoose held a baby. The extra weight would Terri tire more quickly, the same as a normal person would carrying a person on their back, but for now it was working fine. Carlos hung back there, a bag tucked underneath his arm, looking more than a little nervous and sick from both the height and the speed.

The dwarves paused in their advance to look up as Terri swooped in low. The effect of her sudden appearance on the battlefield snapped Wayne out of his paralysis. He began barking orders at once, concentrating the troops on the point of attack, telling one boy to look lively, another to run around to the other side of the compound to fetch more arrows. He also told him to bring back one out of every two guards stationed there to reinforce the section of fence the dwarves were attacking.

The compound's defense shaped up almost instantly, as the children were quick to take advantage of the pause in the dwarven advance.

The dwarves looked up in amazement at Terri, and there several shouts and hurled curses. A few of them threw hammers or rocks at her, but she was moving much too fast for them to hit with any real accuracy. Terri turned back to Carlos and nodded at him, and Carlos closing his eyes against the heights, reached into the bag and began to produce several balloons.

"What the heck is he doing?" Wayne asked of nobody in particular.

"Just watch," replied Carmen, trotting up beside him. "It's a little something he thought up."

Wayne watched in amazement as one by one, Carlos lobbed the balloons down among the enemy, they fell quickly, and Wayne guessed they were fairly heavy. When they landed, he could hear the dull thud of the report from where he stood. Huge clouds of red smoke rose where the balloons had landed, spreading out and blanketing the horde of dwarves, who began to yell.

"What is this?" Wayne asked Carmen, "Fruit punch mix?"

"Better," answered Carmen, grinning fiercely. "The red color is from rust. That's iron dust from old filed down junk. Think of it as dwarf itching powder."

And sure enough, Wayne could see the dwarves already scattering, itching furiously and shaking their fists at Terri's swooping chair. Wayne chuckled to himself but his merriment didn't last long. A mere rash wouldn't stop the attackers for long, and from what he could see from where he stood, Terri was tiring already. It was hard enough keeping her chair aloft, and with the added weight of Carlos dragged along, the strain was already beginning to show.

It wasn't long before Carlos had run out of balloons and Terri was clearly too tired to keep it up any longer. With a final raspberry in the general direction of the dwarven army, she turned her chair back toward the compound and landed near Wayne in a hail of cheers. The dwarves, still howling and wearing ugly rashes all over, regrouped and resumed their advance.

They're angry now, thought Wayne. *This could get ugly.*

Luckily, Carmen and Carlos' bag of tricks wasn't empty just yet. She'd dragged out the old automatic pitcher from the practice batting cages used by the baseball team. It had been mounted in one of the towers where it stood with a kind of dark metal menace that had forced many a child to resist laughing at the military adaptation of what was essentially a sporting good. Now, the kids put it good use and it hummed on its highest setting, cranking hard-faced baseball after baseball at speeds that even Winklo's arm would have envied, straight into the advancing army.

CRACK!

One of the dwarves was knocked off his feet with such a loud "oof!" that he could be heard above the clamor of the advancing army.

WHACK!

Another dwarf was knocked into the air and landed three feet away from his boots, rooted in the ground where he'd been standing just moments before. But as impressive as this display was, it wasn't truly slowing down the advance, and before long, the horde had reached the fence, howling and ready for a fight.

Now the children set themselves to the hard job of fighting them off. The dwarves couldn't reach them through the chain-link, so they set themselves to the difficult task of pulling it down, finding handholds where they could, they set their great strength against the fence. The fence had been fortified by the kids and without real construction experience, or motorized tools, the children had been unable to properly dig new post holes, not to mention that most of the fencing was scrap material anyway. Wayne joined the guards who were desperately swatting at the dwarven fingers, poking at their hands, desperately trying to get them to let go of the fence, while up above, those kids on the catwalk rained rocks down on them. But in spite of all their efforts, the barrier began to slowly give way.

Wayne watched some of the supporting posts dig furrows in the ground as the weight of the metal began to force them out of position. Rashes were springing up on the bare dwarven hands, but many of the warriors had gloves, and even those who didn't were angry and desperate enough to ignore the discomfort. Before long, the children were dividing their efforts between fighting off the dwarves and desperately trying to hold the fence up. Wayne watched as Miko hurled herself at the inside of the fence, shimmying up it and holding on for dear life. She looked almost funny, like a bug caught in a net. But the circumstances weren't funny at all. Miko was trying to lend her slim weight to the inside of the fence to keep the dwarves from pulling it down.

In spite of their first successes, the dwarves began to gain ground, and the children fought more desperately. Wayne watched in horror as two of the dwarves exploited a gap in the crumbling fence, grabbed one of the guards and dragged him kicking and screaming, out of the compound. The first prisoner of the conflict.

But not the last one.

There was something of an explosion from the gap the two dwarves had created, and Wayne could see a number of dwarves go flying through the air and several others knocked aside by what appeared to be a moving cloud of dust. The cloud moved with greater fury into the ranks of the advancing army, and it wasn't long before the dwarves were scattering before it. There was a brief pause as the cloud paused outside the fence and dust began to settle. The two armies stared in awe and took a welcome pause from the hard work of the fighting.

The dust began to settle and the cloud fell away to reveal a very angry Winklo. She was clutching an iron street sign post, the green paint worn away by her thick gardening gloves, that protected her sensitive hands from the contact. The end of the post was crowned, appropriately enough, by a large red octagon bearing the words "STOP" in large, imposing letters. The sign had earned a few dents that were not surprisingly shaped like dwarven heads.

She whirled the sign over her head threatening a number of dwarves who appeared to be at least considering making a comeback. Surveyed the pause in the battle that her entrance had caused and smiled, clearly pleased, enjoying the power she commanded. As a healer and a shaman, she had limited experience as a warrior. She found she liked it.

Haamer sat up in the saddle, determined not to let Winklo upstage the entire battle and frighten his troops. "Go home, traitor!" he cried out. "You're an elf lover! Do you think you can frighten the might of the Braag by knocking a few of us on our heads? Go home to your new family, go home to the child Spartans! Go home or it will be worse for you!"

The silence was complete, only the settling dust broke it.

Winklo folded her arms and stared at Haamer levelly. "I'm not here to take orders from a glorified shopkeeper. Especially one who comes in command of an army bent on nothing more than theft. You want me to go home, you can climb down from your pet and send me home." This last bit was punctuated by a brief *BANG!* as she smashed a dwarf who was trying to sneak up behind her. The would-be attacker's eyes crossed and he fell down in a heap.

"I'm not going anywhere until you return the captive you just took. And there'll be a whole lot more of this unless you give him back and quickly!"

Haamer was amazed. Here was one brave dwarf, outside the friendly gates where her friends could come to her aid, in the midst of an enemy army, making demands of him! He couldn't help but admire her incredible courage, but he could never let that admiration show to his own troops, who would have to fight her.

"Enough! You are a traitor to all Tunnel-Folk on the Wildsidhe! We will not bargain with you. Go home! Before I take you up on your offer and send you there myself!" He hefted his club to underline this last threat, but it looked lame after Winklo's amazing entrance.

It was Winklo's turn to look surprised. She stood in silence for a moment before saying, "Fine. Then I will take a hostage of my own." And with that, she reached behind her, picked up the dwarf she had just knocked out and threw him over her shoulder. Nobody even made an attempt to stop her as she carried him back inside the gap in the fence, which the children closed behind her and set about securing.

"When we get ours back, you'll get yours back," she shouted back through it.

Nobody moved as Winklo walked a few hundred feet further into the compound and then dropped her captive on the ground. She then knelt beside him and proceeded to being slapping him around the head, trying to bring him around. She was still a shaman and she would tend to the warrior she had wounded. Finally, she called out to Wayne to get her some cold water. Wayne, who wasn't used to taking orders from anybody except Justin, and even then only rarely, actually hurried to obey.

It was several minutes before both sides recovered from the shock of the whole scene to start fighting again. And it started with fresh fury. Haamer, embarrassed by the encounter with Winklo, rode his lizard right up to the base of the fence, screaming at his troops to fight harder, pull the fence from the ground.

Wayne, who had just returned from making sure that somebody got Winklo the water she'd asked for, had come running back to the fence, bringing what few children he could pull away from the far side of the compound in a hurry. The fence was not looking good. In several sections, it had come away totally, and only steadfast groups of children fighting for all they were worth were preventing the dwarves from coming in. Before long, Justin was at his side, wearing a football helmet and carrying a baseball bat. From the sweat and dirt streaking his face, Wayne could tell he'd been in the thick of the fighting, like the leader he was. "We don't have long," he said. His voice wasn't nervous, just matter of fact. Justin wasn't one to panic, but he also wasn't one to mince words or act positive in the hopes of lifting the spirits of those around him. It was this kind of simple honesty that kept everyone so loyal and content under his leadership.

"I know," Wayne said, waving at the gaps in the fence where the kids, fighting furiously, were being pushed back. "They outnumber us by at least three to one. We can't hold them for long, and once they break through one of those gaps, they'll run us over like a runaway truck."

"The Terri-dive-bombing thing was pretty cool though, huh?" asked Justin, managing to find the silver lining in even the worst situation.

Wayne smiled. "Yeah, but that was just a show, and it looks like we failed to scare 'em off. Now it's down to the hard fighting, and there just isn't enough of us. Is every single person we have in there?"

Justin nodded. "Yup. I called up everybody from the whole perimeter. If the dwarves were smart they'd just attack from another side."

"But they're not smart, thank God," Wayne said. "Unfortunately, they're strong and there's an awful lot of them."

Justin was quiet for a minute. "So what do we do now?"

Wayne thought about it. He looked for Carmen, the Bearclaw Brothers, Jamal, Ben Matzel, anybody who might have some last ditch miracle plan to save them. He couldn't spot any of them, his best guess was that they were hip deep in the fighting at the fence.

Where he should be.

Wayne finally said, "We pray for a miracle and then we fight." And then he headed back into the fray. Justin shrugged his shoulders and went with him.

The two stood shoulder to shoulder, jumping into the same gap that Winklo had gone through to claim her captive. The gap was thick with the bodies of dwarf warriors, they positively scrambled over one another to get at the children, stack up two and three high, standing on each other's shoulders. They were strong. As soon as Wayne and Justin stepped into the gap, another one of the children was grabbed and hauled screaming through the gap. Wayne shook his head, not wanting to even try to guess at the number of captives taken since the fighting had started.

The dwarves surged forward, kicking and punching, howling at the top of their lungs, they were so close that Wayne could feel their breath on his face. Justin wasted no time, wading into the mess and swinging his bat. He grinned, trying to take some pleasure in the grim work at hand.

"You're outta here!" he cried, as he cracked one dwarf across the nose with his bat, sending him sprawling outside the fence.

Wayne nodded with approval. "Hey, man! You cracked that one out of the park!"

Justin smiled and pointed with his bat as if they were back on the baseball field, and he was going to wail one right over the blue monster. "Batter up!" he cried, and stepped into a monster swing that sent another three dwarves head over heels flying out of the press.

Behind them, some ways back into the compound, Winklo stood over her captive with a cold bucket of water, chilled from the supplies kept in the cold storage of the school's basement, mostly old refrigerators buried in the coolest parts of the ground. The dwarf was already starting to come around, but he was still groggy and stunned. Stunned, that is, until Winklo threw the water in his face. Drenched and sputtering, he crawled to his feet, looking like a drowned lump and shivering.

"Wha... What'd you do that for?" he cried out like an angry child.

"Because," said Winklo, "I don't have time to stand around here all day while you take a nap. I need some answers, and I need them now."

The dwarf groaned and sank to his knees, running the spot on his head where he'd been struck by the sign. "Ug. It feels like the worst headache I've ever had in my life."

"It *is* the worst headache you've had in your life and you'll get worse unless you answer some questions for me." Winklo leaned in close, pushing the weakened dwarf back into a sitting position.

The captive squinted, a slow realization dawning across his face of where he was and his exact situation. "Forget it, elf-lover, I'm not telling you nothing." With this last he spit on the ground and looked at his lap. "Do your worst," he muttered.

Winklo knelt beside him, her jaw clenched and eyes blazing. "Now you listen to me, you fat-headed fool. Do you think these Spartans are going away anytime soon? No. There are more and more coming every day, who knows how long Asgar's curse will last? If you know the Fortesans like I do, then you'll know that curse will most likely stick, and stick for some time. Do you think the humans will stop coming? No, my friend, they will come, and they will come in a flood. Do you think the old ways can hold them off? You've already seen how strong they are, how smart, how *determined*. Sooner or later, you'll have to reckon with them, and that reckoning will not come from this stupid battle."

She had her captive's attention now. His look was no longer sullen, but intent, and he gazed into her eyes with fear and amazement. She gripped him by the shoulders and shook him.

"Now," she said, her voice rising, "we don't have a lot of time. In just a few minutes I'm going to have to get back in there and you can bet that I'm not just going to be banging heads this time. Tell me, *why*? Why are you doing all this? Why would the Braag want a car so badly that they'd be willing to risk all-out war to get it?"

The dwarf was silent for some time, and Winklo had begun to think that she was going to have to abandon him, when he suddenly looked up, shrugged his shoulders, and told her.

Back at the gap, things were going badly for the defenders. Though Wayne and Justin had been joined by the Bearclaw brothers, and the entire crew was having quite a difficult time of the baseball wargame that knocking these dwarves about had become. There were simply too many of them. For every dwarf they sent sprawling into the dust on the far side of the gap, three more took his place, spitting, swearing and throwing kicks and punches of enormous power.

For all their joking, John had already earned quite a bruise over one of his eyes and Wayne was limping where one of the dwarves had gotten a lucky kick through that had nearly sent him to his knees. The dwarves were steadily gaining ground, widening the gap as they threw more and more warriors into the task of pulling down the fence. With every inch it gave, Wayne had to commit another guard to closing the gap, which meant that person wasn't available to shore up the fence. The group fighting at the gap was already beginning to spread a little too thin, and here and there a dwarf scampered through the ranks, only to turn and throw himself on the children from behind. Wayne began ordering some of the children to hold in reserve to pick off these flankers, but with their numbers increasing every moment, it was becoming an increasingly difficult task. The line of children defending the gap had begun to bow inward under the constant driving pressure of the attacking dwarves, and more and more of the children were being knocked senseless by a punch or a hammer blow and thrown over the dwarven line to be taken prisoner. Their screams drifted back to the defenders, and to say that they weren't helping morale would be the greatest understatement.

Wayne watched the faces of the children fighting beside and around him. They didn't look confident at all, many looked downright terrified, putting up only a feeble resistance for fear that if they through themselves into the combat, they would be captured as well. More than a few were crying. A few broke and ran as Wayne watched.

We're going to lose this fight. The thought didn't bring as much despair as he had thought it might. He had no idea what the dwarves would do with the children. Enslave them? Sell them to the Fortesans? Kill them? He didn't know and, strangely enough, at this moment, he didn't care. The rhythm of the fighting had reached a level of comfort, the ache in his muscles and the samba of his swings had almost become a dancing prayer for his salvation. He swung the bat over his head and stepped into the throng, putting his hips into it. In the rhythm there was peace and hiding from the notion of loss, that all the children had worked for since Asgar had first cast his curse over their hometown. Wayne was about to collapse under the weight of a thousand cursing, angry dwarves, all squeezing against the gap, screaming threats and promising the children just what would happen when they got their hands on them.

So Wayne continued with the dance, and then, with a final gasp, what was left of the fence came tumbling in and the dwarves came dashing through.

The line gave completely, the children began to drop their weapons and run to save themselves. There was no chance for an ordered retreat, it became an instant rout. *Where can we run*? Thought Wayne. He wouldn't be bothered. There was simply no place in this beautiful, magical, hostile world in which they found themselves where the children could take refuge.

Better to stand and be taken or killed, at least it was more dignified than running like a frightened child.

Then he saw Jamal run away toward the parking lot and he shook his head. Jamal was the last person he'd ever thought he'd see run from a fight.

Wayne stood shoulder to shoulder with Justin, and they faced the oncoming army alone, suddenly not afraid at all, glowing images of the men they would someday become.

The storm of surging dwarves took them quickly and they barely had time to swing their respective clubs once before they were thrown to the ground, their weapons stomped from their hands.

Wayne tried to gaze through the hail of blows and tapping dwarf feet to get a glimpse of Justin, being roughly hauled to his feet and, Wayne assumed, taken prisoner. Justin was barely moving, his head lolled to one side, and Wayne assumed that he'd been knocked out. Wayne tried to fight to his feet, to get to Justin so he could help him, but rough hands held him down. Something struck him on the side of his head hard. Then it came again. His vision swam, he could make out a blurred shape sliding before him, but couldn't be sure if it was Justin or not. He cried out Justin's name, and stretched out his arm to reach for him, but the very movement brought on a wave of nausea.

So this is it, Wayne thought. *It's over. We've lost. I've lost. I'm either going to be killed or captured, or God knows what.*

Now the sadness of it overwhelmed him, and he put back his head and began to cry. The rough hands were still on him, but he was no longer being jostled around. The dwarves were probably in command of the compound, and so had no need to move, or worse, they were steadying him for a final blow.

The thought made Wayne cry all the more. He felt pathetic and useless, all his efforts at security, all his skill as a fighter, coming to this end, helpless like an infant in the arms of his captors. He felt embarrassed that the last thing anyone would see of him was sniveling and crying, but he supposed it didn't matter anymore anyway, and that set him off again, this time even worse.

Wayne heard a whispering amid the buzzing in his head, it was oddly peaceful, yet as full of danger as a gathering storm. *Am I dead already?* He thought, *is this the sound of heaven opening up to claim me?* But he dismissed the idea almost instantly, as he felt the gathering wind against his skin. The whispering sound was most certainly the whipping wind, which had picked up rather suddenly. Now Wayne felt his hopes soar as he realized that he was not dead. The reason the dwarves were not roughing him up anymore is because they were standing, amazed at the sudden hard wind that picked up, blowing so hard that both armies had to pay attention to keep their footing.

Wayne's head finally began to clear, and the first thing he saw was Justin, dazed but standing on his own, eyes wide in amazement at what was happening around him.

The wind had picked up to gale force, and was now whipping across the compound, howling as if in anger. The dwarves covered their heads and looked nervously towards the sky.

But that, as it turned out, was the wrong direction.

With a sound like a thousand pieces of cloth being ripped apart, the grass itself sprang out of the ground, shooting out like long, whipping snakes. The stronger weeds, the tufts of bush growing along the fence line all followed suit, stretching forward with astonishing speed, growing with all their might.

At first, Wayne jumped straight up in the air, as if his tiny leap could somehow save him from the angry plants, but it was quickly clear that the plants had different prey in mind. They twisted and whipped at the dwarves, tangling their feet, scratching at their eyes, grabbing them by the arms and pinning them to the ground. In most cases, the dwarves were more than strong enough to fight the plants, snapping blades of grass and thrashing bushes, but there were always more and they provided more than a sufficient distraction to allow the children to rally.

Wayne and Justin locked eyes across the few feet between them and grinned. Fighting plants could only mean one thing.

Nash.

Sure enough the elf was standing a few yards back from them, peeking from around the corner of the main stairway leading up into the school. The careful concentration on his small face was a clear indicator that he was behind the magic that had brought the plants to life. He held a handful of spellstones and it was clear he was draining his supply of stored magic energy for this spell.

Wayne's head was now fully cleared and he felt that, while bruised, he was well enough to keep up the fight. He also realized that Nash had given the children a rare opportunity, one that he intended to take full advantage of.

"Hit them!" Wayne cried, nodding to Justin and pointing at the same time.

Justin and Wayne had shared so much over the time since they had first arrived on the Wildsidhe, that they needed no special instruction. They leapt right back into the combat, swinging their recovered bats at the distracted dwarves, most of whom were far too busy with the plants to provide much resistance at all. He saw Lissy, alone of all the pixies, fighting alongside them, dive bombing dwarve's eyes, to distract them from attacking the kids.

As Wayne concentrated on pushing the dwarves out of the gap, he noticed in the distance two or three large trees rampaging among the dwarven army outside the fence. Haamer was nowhere to be seen.

The dwarven army suddenly froze, staring at the parking lot. Wayne turned and was amazed at what he saw. A dragon riding a motorcycle! It took him a moment to realize what had happened. Jamal hadn't run away. He was causing a distraction. He had used his medallion to call up his dragon illusion. He drove the motorcycle through the crowd and out the hole in the fence. It had the reaction he wanted. Many of the dwarves, seeing one of their lifelong enemies in their midst, forgot about the kids. In actions that were more instinct than thought, dozens who were not trapped by the snaking grass, turned to chase the dragon. Jamal sped the motorcycle down Grand Avenue, a horde of dwarves hot on his heels.

That ought to hold them for a while. Wayne thought, *and it will at least give us enough time to get cleaned up in here. I only wish we had some way to call Vawna. A real dragon would turn the odds in our favor.* Wayne made a mental note to figure out a way to do that if he survived.

The children quickly followed Nash and Jamal's lead. Most of the kids who had started to run recovered their dropped weapons and ran back to the battle. The braver children, who had been broken into pockets of resistance, but who had continued to fight on, now pushed wildly back at the dwarves fighting with renewed hope at the sight of the army coming back to life.

Wayne let out a shout of joy as the dwarves were pushed back through the fence and out into the land beyond. Nash's fighting plants harassed them at every step. The kids were heartened by the sight and fought wildly to throw the dwarves out beyond the gate.

Before long, it was the dwarves who were casting frightened glances over their shoulders, having little stomach for an army of children who came back from the brink of destruction with the aid of an army of fighting grasses and shrubs.

Wayne saw their fear and cried out, calling on the children to push harder. The kids responded, forcing their way forward. Terri, who had now had enough time to rest a bit, soared overhead once more, whooping at the top of her lungs, with Carlos' irritating iron powder bombs raising huge clouds of itching smoke among the dwarves. She disappeared into the distance.

A few moments later, a great cry went up among the dwarves as they glanced skyward at "Dragon" Jamal. Terri had picked him up and now he appeared to glide menacingly behind her flying chair. Seeing their great natural enemy joining the fray, the dwarves began to shake with fear.

Cindy, seeing a chance to add to the magical distraction, tried desperately to concentrate on her totem and bring forth the unicorn Legacy, but she had much the same luck she'd had with Wayne by the potties earlier. She cursed her inability to control her magic.

In the midst of the confusion and the renewed attack, many of the dwarves began to drop their weapons and flee. The children, amazed at the sudden turn of events, let out a hearty cheer, went shooting through the fence after them, taking the battle outside the compound for the first time.

The attack had not been bloodthirsty like it would have been with Asgar or Morna. If the Braag had simply changed their tactics to use deadly force, they could have won. At some level Wayne realized this and winced at this sudden surge, worrying that the kids might overextend themselves, and also not wanting to press the fight against an enemy who'd he rather have as allies. But he knew that the enthusiasm of his troops would not be contained and regardless of their tactics, the Braag did attack them first. They had to be taught not to mess with the Spartans, so Wayne didn't even bother to try to call out to them to get them to pull back. He did manage to send out several of them in cars. He couldn't earlier without opening the gates and there wasn't enough room to use them inside the fence line without risking running over as many kids as dwarves. Now they simply drove through the hole in the fence the battle had left to face the enemy army.

As it turned out, the dwarven morale was almost completely broken. A few groups of dwarves put up a bit of a fight outside the fence. However, at the sight of the cars speeding at them, most were turning tail and running, or throwing down their weapons in surrender. Still more were hesitating out of the range of battle, trying to decide what to do.

Even Wayne, his normally level head cast aside, was caught up in the joyful frenzy as the children chased the enemy. All of the despair, rage, and humiliation he had felt, captured and crying in the hands of the enemy, now melted away into relief and happiness as he saw victory emerge from an almost sure defeat in a matter of minutes.

"Hit 'em! Hit 'em!" he cried out again, leading the children in a charge to round up and finish off the rest of the dwarves once and for all. They would think twice before bothering the Spartans next time, that was for sure.

He began to scream, letting all of the anger and frustration of dealing with these dwarves flow out of him, and into brutal swings with the bat. The dwarves continued to run, some of them crying out in fear from the advancing children. Wayne was no longer thinking, just reacting.

Wayne felt a hand on his arm, holding him back, trying to keep him from fighting any more. Probably an enemy, he instantly thought, but the words in his ear were gentle, even soothing, though they were hard to hear over the buzz of rage in his head. He tried to shrug the hand off, ignore the voice, hold on to the wild joy he was feeling in the midst of the victory, but whoever it was wouldn't let him go. Slowly, gradually, he began to come to his senses. He turned, hearing the sounds of the battle drawing to a close take a background seat to the sound of the voice, which now he saw, belonged to Justin.

"It's okay, Wayne." Justin was saying. "Stand down, buddy. It's over, we've got them. We're calling it off."

"What?" asked Wayne. "Why call it off? We've got them! Let's win this once and for all! Let's make sure they never bother us again!"

Justin looked stern and shook his head. "No way, Wayne. This isn't about that. That's not what we're about. We'd be worse than them if we did that. There are lots of people hurt on both sides, but so far nobody's died. I want to keep it that way. They're beaten and they know it, that's enough for now."

Wayne could hear Justin's words, and deep down, knew that he was right, but some part of him struggled to hold on to that cloud of victory that he'd been riding on since he first realized that the battle would be won. He stood his ground, knowing enough not to argue, but not able to bring himself to agree either. His bloodthirst shamed him.

"Hey. Take it easy, cuz." Justin went on, "like I said, we got it. Besides, Winklo found some stuff out that kind of puts things in a new light. We need to talk to these guys now."

"You know what they were up to? Why they were willing to risk this war just for a stupid car?"

Justin nodded. "Come on, let's talk to Winklo."

Winklo, surprisingly enough, was grinning with scarcely concealed delight as Wayne and Justin approached her. Her captive looked completely defeated, and sat with his knees drawn up to his chin, held in place by Winklo's strong hand on the back of his head, his hair balled up in her fist.

"You're looking awfully chipper," Justin said.

Winklo only nodded, her smile growing wider by the second.

"Come on, Winklo," Wayne said, in no mood for games. "Are you going to stand there for the rest of the day grinning like a cat or are you going to tell us what's going on?"

Winklo's forehead wrinkled at Wayne's harsh tone, but she knew what they had all been through.

"Impatient, aren't we? Well don't worry about it. I've had a little chat with our friend here." She gave the captive a not so gentle nudge with her knee. "He's made it pretty clear why we were in this mess in the first place."

"Because the Braag are a bunch of thieves?" asked Wayne none too kindly, drawing an angry look from the captive, who thought better of saying anything when he considered the grip Winklo had on his head.

"Close, but, as you humans say, no cigar," Winklo answered. "The Braag want a car because of the Fortesans. You remember the great battle between Alana and Asgar when Nash and I first joined you here? Well, I don't think you fully appreciate how fast news travels on the Wildsidhe. It wasn't long before everybody who had an ear to the ground heard about what happened here.

"The dwarves have been under the thumb of the Fortesans for a lot longer than you have. We don't have strong magic like most of the other races here, and the Fortesans haven't exactly been slow to take advantage of that. Many different clans of Tunnel-Folk wind up paying "tolls" and "regional taxes" to them. In some years, these tolls have nearly wiped out the Braag food stores, and right before harsh winters where they would be needed. If what this guy is telling me is even half true, the Braag have already paid more than their fair share of metal work from their mines.

"When the word of the battle got to them, the legend of the cars was hot." Winklo smiled as she continued, "You should have heard this guy describing them! He made it sound as if they were living weapons! Of course, I guess that's how I thought of them too before I came to live with you and got used to the whole thing. Anyway, they figured that it was the cars that won that battle with Asgar and Morna, and that if they could get their hands on one, they could break the yoke once and for all. Not to mention the fact that it would help them clear squatting dragons out of their tunnels and generally tip the scales in their favor combat-wise. This has nothing to do with *us*, Justin, they don't have a bone to pick with us at all. They just want the cars to deal with the problems they've been facing since before you kids were even "a blip on the radar" as Carmen is so fond of saying."

Justin and Wayne stood in silence and Winklo looked at them expectantly. The only noise came from the captive, who sniffled plaintively.

Finally, Winklo let go of him and stepped forward, placing her hand on Justin's shoulder. "Justin, you have to see reason here. You wanted the Braag as allies to begin with, didn't you? Here's a chance to make that happen.

We've beaten them here already, look over your shoulder. You can see them running. You can run them off, win a great victory here, but unless you kill every last one of them, you have earned an enemy for life. The Braag will grow up telling their children of their three greatest enemies: the dragons, the Fortesans, and the children of Sparta. Or you can swallow your pride, and just *give* them a car. Help them to help themselves."

Wayne let out a disbelieving breath. Winklo responded to him instantly.

"Think about it. They're not trying to do anything more than you did when you first came here. Make their way as best they can. You have what they need to protect themselves. If you are serious about being allies, it's time to put your money where your mouth is. You have to help them, give them something worth their while."

Wayne only looked at his feet, but Justin seemed convinced. "Okay, Winklo, we'll give them a car. Do you think you can get a hold of Haamer in all this mess and talk to him?"

Winklo was already nodding, but Wayne cut in. "Are you crazy? After all they've done to us? After all their attempts to steal from us and push us around, and now we're going to just up and give them a car, after the battle we just fought?"

"Wayne," Justin said, his voice even and patient. "I know you're only thinking about the safety of the compound, but try to understand what we're doing here. Your thinking is the same kind we used to have in my gang in Boston. Destroy your enemies, no matter what the cost. Winklo is right. It's up to us to be bigger about this. We have to think long-term. What kind of relationship do we want to have with the Braag? Look, Wayne, we're going to be here a long time, and if it's all the same to you, I'd rather not be surrounded by enemies."

Justin's last words came out harder than he'd wanted, but Wayne saw that he and Winklo were right. "Okay," he said, nodding, but red-faced. "Let's go find Haamer."

Haamer turned out to be easy to find. His lizard steed had run off, but the old dwarf was leaning heavily against his broken saddle, obviously out of steam. He was still doing his best to rally his fleeing army. "Get back into it, lads!" he shouted at them, but the Braag were not listening. "You're going to let a bunch of infants beat you?"

Haamer had to move in between his shouting to keep from getting run over on more than one occasion, especially when the "dragon" Jamal, riding on Terri's wheelchair, flew by. Several of the kids in cars were busy chasing down dwarves. Justin was relieved to see Cindy at the wheel of one, as his girlfriend's well-being and safety had him worried to the point of distraction.

Haamer flinched as the children approached him, a look of despair dawning across his face as he finally realized that his superior army had, in fact, lost this contest.

Haamer looked so resigned, so defeated, that Wayne almost felt sorry for the dwarf in spite of all he had tried to do to them. Haamer looked up at the "dragon" Jamal flying away. Terri was heading behind the school to land. She was so exhausted she would probably sleep for an entire day. By dropping out of sight, she would allow Jamal to drop his dragon illusion, with the dwarves being none the wiser. "You even have dragons that do your bidding. I know we have lost. Go ahead," Haamer said, trying to appear dignified in spite of being incredibly tired. "Get it over with. Kill me, put me in chains, do your worst. I am a Chaincounter, and the Forge-father will watch over me."

Winklo looked positively sad. It was clearly painful for her to see another dwarf's pride laid so low.

"Don't sweat it," Justin said. "Nobody is going to kill you, nobody is going to slap chains on you. We're going to let what prisoners we've taken go. All we want is to call a truce."

Haamer, and the few Chaincounters standing around him, stood in silence, their mouths open, clearly unable to believe Justin's words.

"Enough," Haamer said, after an awkward pause. "Stop with your joking. We admit defeat, but allow us at least a little dignity. Stop playing around."

"Nobody is playing around," said Winklo. "You and your men are free to go, we're not taking any prisoners, nor is there going to be any punishment. We've decided in fact, to give you what you came for."

Now the Chaincounters appeared to be grappling with their doubt and actually embracing the impossible concept that the kids might actually be telling the truth. Haamer's enormous moustache curled momentarily in what might have been a brief smile. "You mean this?"

"We mean it," Wayne said, looking at his feet and kicking at the dust there. He felt a twinge of pain in his injured knee, but ignored it.

"We want the same deal we talked about the last time you came to negotiate. We still get a group of dwarves to help us get this compound and our generator mill set up right. We need workers, teachers, engineers, and we'll lease you a car, give you fuel, I'll even assign Carmen to teach you how to drive it."

"There is no special catch to all of this?" asked Haamer, finally beginning to believe.

"No, there is one catch," Wayne cut in, drawing an angry look from Justin, but he went ahead anyway. "You must swear, or get your chief or whoever else is in charge of the Braag to also swear, that you will never, ever again attack or attempt to steal from us. What's more, if anyone else ever attempts to do us harm, you will come to help us immediately with everything you've got."

Winklo sucked in her breath at this demand, and gave Wayne a sharp look, but Justin nodded calmly. They did need to make an alliance with these dwarves, but at the same time, they might as well make it a real alliance, with all of the military meaning that such a bond would hold.

"Will you do the same for the Braag?" asked Haamer.

Justin thought about it long and hard before he answered. "Yes."

Haamer looked defeated, but at the same time, he shrugged his shoulders. "Very well. There is no sense in trying to wrangle this issue any more. You can see that we seem to be at a disadvantage. What of your dragon allies? Will they abide by this treaty and not attack the Braag?"

"We only are friends with two dragons. I can only speak for the dragon Jamal, who helped us today. He will not bother you so long as you keep the treaty. I can't speak for the dragon Vawna, but I will ask Jamal to make the same request of Vawna. Is that enough?"

By this time, the rest of the children had gathered around what was obviously an important meeting. The Bearclaw brothers were, for the first time since this whole mess had started, sober and quiet.

"It should be," said Haamer. "Of course, it is not my decision to make, I am only the Trademaster, but I will certainly take it up with the Braag Lord." Justin looked at him hard. "Of course, Lord Raga has been known to defer to me in most of these matters. So I don't doubt that he will be reasonable in considering your demands."

"That's good," Justin said. "Because it doesn't take a genius to look around and see what the situation is here. We've got you, Haamer. We've got all the Braag I would think, but try to see what we're doing here. We're not interested in whooping you guys. We're interested in working together with you. We all have enemies and the Wildshide can be a scary place. I think if we work together, we can at least make it better for our two peoples." At this a soft murmur of agreement went up from the whole crowd and Haamer's face softened visibly.

"You may be children, but you are smarter than you look." Haamer said.

Much of the rest of the day was spent cleaning up. What prisoners had been taken were exchanged back to their respective armies and the torn ground mulled over and reseeded so plants could grow there. This was done at Nash's insistence, and while many of the children and dwarves alike failed to see the point, nobody wanted to risk angering the elf after his command performance during the height of the battle. The fragments of the mangled fence were recovered and the hard job of patching up the perimeter begun under Carmen's expert direction. The young girl immediately set about grabbing whatever scrap iron she could to shore up the fence. Of course, the dwarves bowed out of helping for this particular task as they weren't too fond of the rashes that would pop up all over their exposed skin when they did this kind of work. But they did do their part in supervising the reconstruction and lent their expertise in metalwork and engineering as they explained how to shore up the fence and make it even stronger than before.

The children were well into it by the time that Haamer returned with a rather stately looking dwarf, who could only have been the Lord of the Braag. Justin was surprised, he had expected an old and stately looking dwarf, like Haamer and some of the senior Chaincounters, but the Braag Lord Raga, was young and bright cheeked, clean shaven and taller by far than most of the dwarves around him. He smiled good-naturedly at Justin.

"Wow. This is quite a place you've got here," said Raga, his voice surprisingly high and very friendly.

Justin and the rest could only stand and stare, so surprised were they that this was the great leader behind their former enemies.

"Haamer has told me all about your deal and I think its fine. I'm really sorry about all the trouble we've caused, but you have to understand we were really under a lot of pressure. I promise you we'll make good on all the trouble we've caused and I look forward to having our two kingdoms work together."

Justin smiled and shook Raga's hand. Haamer scowled at this, one should bow before a Lord, but Raga only smiled wider and pumped Justin's hand vigorously.

"That's great, um. . . sire. But you need to understand that we're not a kingdom here, I sort of help out directing things here, but we make all of our decisions as a group."

Raga seemed uninterested. "Whatever. So, let's go see these Caars! I've been hearing all about them for quite some time now."

The Bearclaw brothers humorous mood returned almost instantly at this, and they began clamoring to be the ones to show their newfound friend how to drive. Justin laughed at their enthusiasm, but wound up assigning that task to Carmen, who really knew the most about cars and driving out of all of them.

"What about our demands, Lord Raga?" asked Wayne. "Are you going to send us the experts we asked for?"

Raga nodded impatiently. "Don't worry about all that. Haamer will take care of the details. You can trust the Braag to keep our word, and it's not like we have much of an army left to fight you off anymore!"

Justin figured that he had come this far in trusting the Braag, if the newfound alliance was going to stand on its own two feet at all, it might as well start now. "Okay," Justin said. "I'll send Miko to work out the details with Haamer." With this, he nodded to Miko, who had joined the throng of children clustering around to see the Braag Lord and sent her off to discuss the expertise that the Braag would send to help the children. Miko and Haamer got along quite well considering what had happened the last time negotiations had been attempted.

Before long, Wayne and Justin stood outside the old ball field, where they'd been playing a light-hearted game of baseball not so long ago, even though it felt like ages.

In the distance, Lord Raga was doing donuts in an old blue sports car, kicking up huge clouds of dust and whooping at the top of his lungs like a delighted child. Carmen sat in the passenger seat, smiling at his evident joy, but trying to keep him from crashing the car and killing both of them in the same gesture.

"Amazing, isn't it?" Justin asked.

Wayne nodded, still concerned.

"Wayne, let it go. I know it's hard, but the Wildsidhe is going to be our home for a long time now. It's about time we started making it a place that we can stand living in. With the Braag as allies, we'll be twice as secure as before, which was pretty damn safe, considering all of the fine work you've done."

Wayne smiled uncomfortably, but trying to do his best to adjust to what was apparently a new order.

"Instead of worrying about how to protect ourselves from them, Wayne, let's think about what we can teach them. This is a trading of knowledge after all, not just cars for jewels. Maybe we will get that generator mill up and running. Imagine what we can do with enough electricity."

Wayne thought about it for a moment, and then started down the hill.

"Where are you going?" asked Justin.

"I just thought of something I could teach them." He laughed, jogging towards where the children kept the cars.

"I can teach them to race."

Don't call him Baby Bear...

Babe B. Bear came home from school one day to find the notorious burglar Goldilocks had broken into his house. After he and his friend Rapunzel Hightower managed to track the thief down and capture her, suddenly everyone thinks he's a detective. So what's a bear to do? Open up the Babe B. Bear Detective Agency with his two best friends Rapunzel and Notso Badwolf.

When a mermaid on two legs walks into his treehouse office to hire them to find something she's lost, the three kids are thrown into a world of crime and magic. They have to track down the lost item, survive a confrontation with a witch, and convince a detective that they aren't faking a kidnapping.

A detective's work is never done.

www.talehaven.com

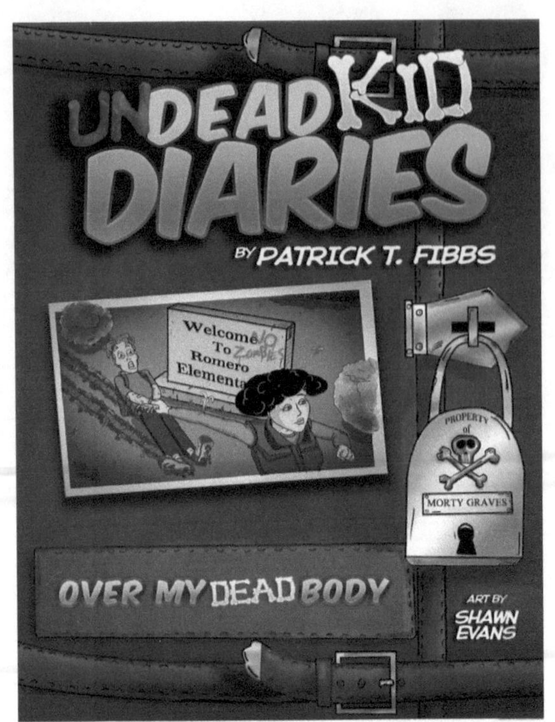

The zombie apocalypse is over...
Now even undead kids have to go to school

Morty Graves survived the apocalypse. Well, technically he didn't survive so much as get turned into a zombie. But when a vaccine stops the spread of the zombie virus, the world goes back to almost normal. Kid zombie kept their minds, unlike the adults. Morty's lawyer mother sued for him to have full human civil rights. Morty liked the idea in theory until he realized that meant he had to go back to school. Now Morty will have to deal with fitting in among live kids without being able to speak, an assistant principal who has it ou for him, a vicious bully, and kids who don't get his joke.

It's going to be a long school year.

www.talehaven.com

The Ughabooz are bored! What are five silly monsters supposed to do? Why jump on their friend Zed of course. And not even their Mummy or the Mad Doctor can get them to stop. What will happen to these cute monsters? Read on to find out!

www.talehaven.com